"The Beast in the Jungle," one of James' last tales, and possibly his best. That formidable figure whom James represented so truly and affectingly—the American Girl, independent, forthright, innocent—is the subject here of two tales, the classic "Daisy Miller," and "Pandora." Dr. Edel also includes four of James' shorter tales, "The Author of Beltraffio," "Owen Wingrave," "The Real Thing," and "The Two Faces."

This volume, then, offers the choicest of James' most popular fiction, and reveals him in his major moods and styles, the master of character and story. As Dr. Edel writes, "We deal essentially with a writer at once grave and melancholy, one in whom the tragic countenance lies just behind the comic—for whom existence is a large and ironic affair, compounded of human frailties and endless frustrations. In spite of this, there is in James a joy in the adventure of life...a relish for the unexpected, the subtle, the unusual in human situations; he is fascinated by idiosyncrasies of human character."

LEON EDEL is the biographer of Henry James, and the foremost authority on his life and works. In 1962, following the publication of the second and third volumes of his life of James, Dr. Edel was awarded both the Pulitzer Prize in biography and the National Book Award for non-fiction. The author and editor of numerous other books in the field of English and American literature, he is a Fellow of the American Academy of Arts and Sciences and secretary of the National Institute of Arts and Letters. Dr. Edel is Professor of English at New York University.

THE HENRY JAMES READER

THE
Henry James
READER

Selected with a Foreword and Headnotes by
LEON EDEL

CHARLES SCRIBNER'S SONS
New York

PS2112
E3
1965

Contents

FOREWORD   vii

Washington Square   1
The Aspern Papers   165
The Turn of the Screw   255
The Beast in the Jungle   357

THE AMERICAN GIRL
    Daisy Miller   403
    Pandora   462

FOUR TALES
    The Author of Beltraffio   511
    Owen Wingrave   555
    The Real Thing   588
    The Two Faces   613

Foreword

THIS book contains the best-loved stories of Henry James— those which most endeared him to his readers during his lifetime and since his death fifty years ago. Some, like *Washington Square,* "The Aspern Papers" and "The Turn of the Screw," have been translated into all the media of our day—the stage, the screen, television—and the latter story has also been made into an opera. Other stories here included have been reprinted many times. If it is asked why I am reprinting them again, my answer is that a James "Reader" cannot do better than offer the established favorites, the time-tested works by which we know a classic: offer them, indeed, not only to those who may want to reread them or to have them in a single volume, but to make them available to a new generation which asks itself, "Where, in Henry James, does one start?" The choice is not easy. James wrote twenty novels and one hundred and twelve tales. It has always seemed to me he is best encountered in the freshness of his early style, in a work such as *Washington Square;* and I always urge that the masterpiece "The Aspern Papers" be read next. After that, it seems to me, one can proceed to the more complicated tales, for by then one has begun to grasp the leisurely kind of storytelling which James practiced and the curiously formal and personal way in which he expressed himself.

A single volume can offer but a small part of a writer who had such abundance in him—yet what is here belongs to all that was most characteristic and various in James. The long-standing battles of the critics over him can here be set aside. It little concerns us, for instance, whether his late work is better than his early work; it is possible for some readers to enjoy both, while others prefer the early lucidities and simplicities to the later highly mannered style. By the same token we need not concern ourselves with the battles about the James "cult." Such battles indicate simply that James has always been a figure of controversy. We know that it takes a large man with a highly individual style and an original mind to become the subject of recurring battles of the books. A mediocrity never inspires critical passions. The best answer to those who have argued "the question of Henry James," or to those who seem to feel that the James "revival"

has passed its high-water mark, has been given by the new generations. James continues to be read, and to be accepted for what he
offered to the world.

We can perhaps approach him negatively by enumerating what he
did not offer. In his work we find very little violence and not much
action. His people are cultivated and well-mannered; they face
certain intense quandaries of a highly personal kind, and the story is
nearly always concerned with how they seek to resolve these quandaries. There is talk of marriage, but marriages usually do not take
place; or, when they do, they seem always to run into difficulties.
James's tales belong to an old society and are governed by old laws
and old conventions. These may seem quaint and outmoded now,
but no more so than in the novels of Trollope or Jane Austen. A
modern reader might wonder, for instance, why there should be so
much fuss over Daisy Miller's "dating" an Italian in Rome. This is
one way of discovering how far our manners and morals have
changed since the Victorian era. Many of James's stories are fairy
tales, placed by him in a real, a palpable, world. His people are
transported to Europe and to "high life" by happy accidents, often
through the generosity of rich relatives or of wealthy patrons. To-
day a painter like Roderick Hudson, the hero of James's first important novel, would go to Rome on a foundation fellowship rather
than through the good offices of a friend; but his story might still
take the same turn. James's American schoolteachers would probably have little difficulty now in getting to Europe on a Fulbright;
yet their dilemma in that foreign society would not be completely
changed—there would still be the displacement from one civiliza-
tion to another, there would still be the encounter of two different
points of view. Americans are still critical of Europe; and we know
how the Europeans feel about Americans. Customs may have
changed; automobiles have replaced James's carriages; yet the life,
the situations, the problems, in some of these early stories, remain
as vivid and as dramatic as they were a century ago.

One could make a long list of things omitted by Henry James. But
the critics who have done this are using a kind of perverse logic
which seems to argue that there are certain subjects every novelist
must include. Dreiser's omissions are no less striking than James's;
and one of the reasons we speak of a Dickens novel, or a Conrad
novel, is that each novelist creates his own particular and personal

kind of story. A great many things are present in the James novel which such critics overlook. There is in James's fiction a profound understanding of the psychology of human relations. He sees into human motives; he knows what really makes the daughter resist the father in *Washington Square*, and in that stately house he can create a vivid drama of the clash of ego with ego. The father is right in protecting his daughter against her suitor; but his being right does not alter his clumsiness, and his failure to understand the girl's feelings. We are shown two opposing wills, in a kind of love-hate, the eternal battle between fathers and children, which Balzac showed in *Eugénie Grandet* or Turgenev in his immortal novel. James is not only a great psychologist; he is a fierce moralist. He dresses before us—as in "The Turn of the Screw"—a sense of evil as a terrible extra-human force, capable of withering young life and of bringing a terror-inspiring destructive element into the broad light of common day.

It is this capacity for transfiguring the ordinary, for arraying before us the quieter and deeper passions, for making us aware of loneliness in great cities, or the dangers to privacy that may reside in an old, run-down, out-of-the-way palace in Venice, that gives to James's stories their particular originality and power. They unfold slowly; he is never in a hurry; the descriptive detail is rich, and rendered with high humor and shrewd observation. We deal essentially with a writer at once grave and melancholy, one in whom the tragic countenance lies just behind the comic—for whom existence is a large and ironic affair, compounded of human frailties and endless frustrations. In spite of this, there is in James a joy in the adventure of life. Existence may be grim, but somehow he grits his teeth and pushes on; and when he has faced the hard and the real, he can laugh and say also that life can be very amusing, a voyage filled with surprises. For all his melancholy, he has a relish for the unexpected, the subtle, the unusual in human situations; he is fascinated by idiosyncrasies of human character.

This is the heart of Henry James. He is a figure wholly literary; and in his work, literature and life come together, for James believed that the writer, drawing upon life in his imaginings, also draws upon the great fund of imagination created by man through the centuries. He understands, as few writers did before him, what happens when two or more persons face each other in a room—what strange ambiguous chemistry is brought into play; how one person makes another uncomfortable or anxious; how a little remark may disturb or amuse. What is the essence of "The Turn of the Screw"—if we cast aside for a moment the ghostly element—if it is not the relationship between an anxious, fluttered young woman and two children? She tells us of her anxieties and makes us aware of the struggle of the children to cope with them. Read as a document of interpersonal relations, that story takes on a terrible dimension of horror. The reader begins to ask himself who, in reality, is haunting whom? The governess is haunted—of that there can be no question. But what does she do to the children in her charge?

This is the particular and subtle element in Henry James—the "ambiguous" side of him that has had an insistent claim upon the attention of our century. His plots are often fantastic, for he ultimately shed the Balzacian realism he had sought to emulate. He knew that he could allow his imagination free play as long as he created an "air of reality." Like Balzac, he cared little whether there were coincidences or if plausibility suffered; his sense of place, his way of creating an atmosphere and of mystifying the reader, imparted life even to the most contrived pieces. That is why "The Beast in the Jungle" has been so remarkable a fable for our century—the story of two persons in a shadowy metropolis, two silhouettes held together—by what? They move in a world that seems fog-bound and unreal. What is real is the terror of the man, the dissociation of his experience, his blindness to the woman's hope that some day he will understand her devotion to him. The imagery is that of deep jungle; the dangerous path; the beasts that lurk in the morass of a life. When the beast springs, and the man must face his egotism, we participate in the reality of his terror; we see even more than the protagonist has seen. We have arrived at the moment within the impenetrable darkness when there is blinding illumination. A great and tragic irony is brought into awareness; it speaks for the decay of life, the waste of the years, the sense of time unlived.

From this it can be seen that James is a special and unusual case in the history of the novel. He was a novelist who emerged from an America but half-formed, who travelled abroad in search of fellow novelists, partly to mitigate the loneliness of his artist's quest, and partly because he felt that his craft needed the nourishment of older civilizations. His quest was for beauty, for creation, for style. He wanted to see life, a certain part of it, and he had the faculty for seeing into it. James moved through well-travelled cities, and remained largely an observant, civilized, sentient, unengaged artist—a man satisfied with small surfaces, but eager to explore them in depth. Possessing a limited audience, he yet accomplished what most American writers failed to do; he lived by his pen and by his style. He did this by writing constantly in a "professional" way—disdaining no opportunity to contribute to the journals of his time. He commanded his price; and he sometimes produced three or four books in a year. His writing is of high quality; even those stories which he contrived for any given magazine are touched by art. Like all fertile artists he could not always work at the pitch of perfection; he often had to be satisfied with the "pot-boiler." Yet some of his most deliberate pot-boilers end up as masterpieces—"The Turn of the Screw" was one of these. Where America's list of geniuses is small, James remains as the example of the healthy, vigorous artist who went out to meet the world in his role as man of letters; he did not shrink from it, like Hawthorne or Faulkner, and he functioned not only as a writer of imaginative literature, but as a critic and as a literary journalist. He was the most "literary" of our writers—and he wrote for fifty years.

He was born in New York in 1843 and was taken abroad in his childhood by an erratic and restless father. His elder brother was William James, later to become America's first psychologist and the philosopher of pragmatism. Henry James grew up in a New York in which Washington Square was "uptown," and in a United States that had begun to shape itself within the industrial revolution. Educated by tutors and governesses, he spent a few months at the Harvard Law School, but turned from the law at nineteen and began to write. He was published from the start. By his middle twenties he was spoken of as one of the best storytellers in America. By thirty he was in Paris with Turgenev, Flaubert, Zola, Maupassant and Daudet. He was famous by thirty-five, and he made his home in England for forty years, rarely returning to the United States—only twice in the 1880's and twice between 1900 and 1914.

"Daisy Miller," published in 1878, caught the fancy of both American and English readers and established his fame. In his first phase, that is between the time of his year in Paris (1875–76) and his American visit of 1882, he wrote a series of novels and tales about Americans abroad, *Roderick Hudson*, *The American* and *The Portrait of a Lady*; in shorter works like *The Europeans* and "An International Episode" he reversed his "international" formula and brought Europeans to America. He was a conscientious student of comparative manners and national idiosyncrasies. In this period he cultivated clarity of style, and he showed a highly developed genius for comedy and satire. His middle phase, from 1882 to 1889, saw the writing of three long novels, *The Bostonians*, *The Princess Casamassima* and *The Tragic Muse*, in which he abandoned international manners for naturalistic study of cities and the life within them. He focused on reformers and on the quest for freedom of individuals of high sensitivity—artist types—called upon to cope with "the world" and materialistic and philistine society.

Between 1890 and 1895 James wrote only short stories in order to be free to write plays. While he had a high sense of drama (as dramatizations of his works since his death have demonstrated), he was hopelessly at a loss in the competitive conditions of the actual theatre. His best play, *Guy Domville*, was booed in 1895 and James returned to the novel. In fast succession, between 1895 and 1900, he produced a series of experimental novels in which he embodied some of his scenic experience—*The Spoils of Poynton*, *The Other House*, *What Maisie Knew*, *The Awkward Age* and *The Sacred Fount*. Then, in the first years of our century, he wrote the three large novels of his late phase—*The Ambassadors*, *The Wings of the Dove* and *The Golden Bowl*. These are regarded by modern critics as his greatest contribution to the art of fiction. They are unique in their creation of characters and scenes which attempt to explore human motivation and perception, and they have provoked a large body of explicative critical works. Complex in design and written in an elaborate idiosyncratic style, they contrast markedly with the lighter "readable" works of his earlier years.

In 1904 and 1905 James toured the United States and for the only time in his life delivered lectures in various cities. During this period he arranged for the publication of the selective New York Edition of his novels and tales by Charles Scribner's Sons, a monumental collection in twenty-four volumes for which he revised and systematically arranged what he judged to be his best work. For this edition he wrote also a series of critical and autobiographical prefaces. The edition remains today at the very center of any study of the novelist.

Henry James received many honors and had many friends. In addition to moving with ease among the Edwardians, he had his intimate circle of American expatriates, whose principal figure was Edith Wharton. She proved a close and loyal friend during his last years. He lived from 1898 to the outbreak of the war in his country home, Lamb House, in Rye, Sussex, and from 1912 on, during the winters, in a London flat in Cheyne Walk. With the coming of the war, he threw in his lot with Britain and in 1915, six months before his death, he became a British subject. The king reciprocated by bestowing on him the rare Order of Merit, conferred a few weeks before he died. Death came on February 28, 1916.

His works stand as wise and witty studies of the confrontation of the Old World and the New. He conceived and created for fiction the myth of the American in Europe. This was his largest subject, as may be seen from the stories given here. He had other subjects within this frame: the self-made American girl, the nature of art, the plasticity of childhood, the cruelty of society, the power of jealousy, the invasion of privacy, the blindness of egotism. He was America's foremost representative in the great era of the novel in the nineteenth century; and he is rightly ranked with the figures of that period. One sees him in the line of George Eliot, on the one hand, and Thackeray and Trollope on the other; but he also anticipates Joyce and Kafka in his exploration of the subjective side of man. In his technical virtuosity he paved the way for many of the innovations in the twentieth-century novel. That is why his name is invoked so often today. Even those critics who will not allow his greatness, bow before the strength and richness of his prose, the vigor of his insights, the largeness of his verbal imagination. He has endured because he said memorable things—and because he told memorable stories.

LEON EDEL

NOTE: The text of *Washington Square* is that of the original edition, published in 1880 in New York. The remaining stories in this volume follow the text of the "Definitive Edition"—the *New York Edition of the Novels and Tales* published by Charles Scribner's Sons.

Washington Square

Washington Square was written by Henry James in his thirty-seventh year, early in 1880; it was serialized in the *Cornhill Magazine* in England and in *Harper's* in the United States, with illustrations by George du Maurier. The novel was based on an anecdote told him by the actress Fanny Kemble: her brother had jilted an heiress when he discovered that her father would disinherit the girl if she married him. This James transferred to one of the great houses in the New York of his childhood, in the Square, which he describes so affectionately in the opening pages of the book. In writing the story James had the real-life situation in mind; but he was thinking also of Balzac's Eugénie Grandet, the girl in the provinces who had great wealth and fell in love with a cousin from the city and found the courage to resist but not conquer her powerful father. In both James's tale and that of his predecessor, the young women are plain and even dull. They love in a direct and innocent way: their tragedy is that the men they love are unworthy of them.

This is a quiet, almost static story. One could say that nothing happens in it save for the few brief days of happiness experienced by the heroine. Yet in that great house in Washington Square, intense moments of feeling occur; and these moments, when dramatized, made of *The Heiress* a singularly delicate and subtle play, one of the most successful of our century. The book is a perfect piece of psychological realism, with its four personages—the father, the daughter, the lover and the sentimental aunt; it is a human drama worked out to an inevitable end. James himself judged the book in his later years as a rather uncomplicated piece of work, quite minor when set beside his larger novels. He rejected it from the "definitive edition" of his works which Scribners published in 1907–1909. But his readers did not share his opinion, and it stands now as an American classic.

L. E.

DURING a portion of the first half of the present century, and more particularly during the latter part of it, there flourished and practised in the city of New York a physician who enjoyed perhaps an exceptional share of the consideration which, in the United States, has always been bestowed upon distinguished members of the medical profession. This profession in America has constantly been held in honor, and more successfully than elsewhere has put forward a claim to the epithet of "liberal." In a country in which, to play a social part, you must either earn your income or make believe that you earn it, the healing art has appeared in a high degree to combine two recognized sources of credit. It belongs to the realm of the practical, which in the United States is a great recommendation; and it is touched by the light of science—a merit appreciated in a community in which the love of knowledge has not always been accompanied by leisure and opportunity.

It was an element in Doctor Sloper's reputation that his learning and his skill were very evenly balanced; he was what you might call a scholarly doctor, and yet there was nothing abstract in his remedies—he always ordered you to take something. Though he was felt to be extremely thorough, he was not uncomfortably theoretic; and if he sometimes explained matters rather more minutely than might seem of use to the patient, he never went so far (like some practitioners one had heard of) as to trust to the explanation alone, but always left behind him an inscrutable prescription. There were some doctors that left the prescription without offering any explanation at all; and he did not belong to that class either, which was after all the most vulgar. It will be seen that I am describing a clever man; and this is really the reason why Doctor Sloper had become a local celebrity.

At the time at which we are chiefly concerned with him he was some fifty years of age, and his popularity was at its height. He was very witty, and he passed in the best society of New York for a man of the world—which, indeed, he was, in a very sufficient degree. I hasten to add, to anticipate possible misconception, that he was not the least of a charlatan. He was a thoroughly honest man—honest in a degree of which he had perhaps lacked the opportunity to give the complete measure; and, putting aside the great good-nature of the circle in which he practised, which was rather fond of boasting that it possessed the "brightest" doctor in the country, he daily justified his claim to the talents attributed to him by the popular voice. He was an observer, even a philosopher, and to be bright was so natural to him, and (as the popular voice said) came so easily, that he never aimed at mere effect, and had none of the little tricks and pretensions of second-rate reputations. It must be confessed that fortune had favored him, and that he had found the path to prosperity very soft to his tread. He had married, at the age of twenty-seven, for love, a very charming girl, Miss Catherine Harrington, of New York, who, in addition to her charms, had brought him a solid dowry. Mrs. Sloper was amiable, graceful, accomplished, elegant, and in 1820 she had been one of the pretty girls of the small but promising capital which clustered about the Battery and overlooked the Bay, and of which the uppermost boundary was indicated by the grassy waysides of Canal Street. Even at the age of twenty-seven Austin Sloper had made his mark sufficiently to mitigate the anomaly of his having been chosen among a dozen suitors by a young woman of high fashion, who had ten thousand dollars of income and the most charming eyes in the island of Manhattan. These eyes, and some of their accompaniments, were for about five years a source of extreme satisfaction to the young physician, who was both a devoted and a very happy husband.

The fact of his having married a rich woman made no difference in the line he had traced for himself, and he cultivated his profession with as definite a purpose as if he still had no other resources than his fraction of the modest patrimony which, on his father's death, he had shared with his brothers and sisters. This purpose had not been preponderantly to make money—it had been rather to learn something and to do something. To learn something interesting, and to do something useful—this was, roughly speaking, the programme he had sketched, and of which the accident of his wife having an income appeared to him in no degree to modify the validity. He was fond of his practice, and of exercising a skill of which he was agreeably conscious, and it was so patent a truth that if he were not a doctor there was nothing else he could be, that a doctor he persisted in being, in the best possible conditions. Of course his easy domestic situation saved him a good deal of drudgery, and his wife's affiliation to the "best people" brought him a good many of those patients whose symptoms are, if not more interesting in themselves than those of the lower orders, at least more consistently displayed. He desired experience, and in the course of twenty years he got a great deal. It must be added that it came to him in some forms which, whatever might have been their intrinsic value, made it the reverse of welcome. His first child, a little boy of extraordinary promise, as the Doctor, who was not addicted to easy enthusiasm, firmly believed, died at three years of age, in spite of everything that the mother's tenderness and the father's science could invent to save him. Two years later Mrs. Sloper gave birth to a second infant—an infant of a sex which rendered the poor child, to the Doctor's sense, an inadequate substitute for his lamented first-born, of whom he had promised himself to make an admirable man. The little girl was a disappointment; but this was not the worst. A week after her birth the young mother, who, as the phrase is, had been doing well, suddenly betrayed alarming symptoms, and before another week had elapsed Austin Sloper was a widower.

For a man whose trade was to keep people alive he had certainly done poorly in his own family; and a bright doctor who within three years loses his wife and his little boy should perhaps be prepared to see either his skill or his affection impugned. Our friend, however, escaped criticism; that is, he escaped all criticism but his own, which was much the most competent and most formidable. He walked under the weight of this very private censure for the rest of his days, and bore forever the scars of a castigation to which the strongest hand he knew had treated him on the night that followed his wife's death. The world, which, as I have said, appreciated him, pitied him too much to be ironical; his misfortune made him more interesting, and even helped him to be the fashion. It was observed that even medical families cannot escape the more insidious forms of disease, and that, after all, Doctor Sloper had lost other patients besides the two I have mentioned; which constituted an honorable precedent. His little girl remained to him; and though she was not what he had desired, he proposed to himself to make the best of her. He had on hand a stock of unexpended authority, by which the child, in its early years, profited largely. She had been named, as a matter of course, after her poor mother, and even in her most diminutive babyhood the Doctor never called her anything but Catherine. She grew up a very robust and healthy child, and her father, as he looked at her, often said to himself that, such as she was, he at least need have no fear of losing her. I say "such as she was," because to tell the truth— But this is a truth of which I will defer the telling.

2

WHEN the child was about ten years old, he invited his sister, Mrs. Penniman, to come and stay with him. The Miss Slopers had been but two in number, and both of them had married early in life. The younger, Mrs. Almond by name, was the wife of a prosperous merchant and the mother of a blooming family. She bloomed herself, indeed, and was a comely, comfortable, reasonable woman, and a favorite with her clever brother, who, in the matter of women, even when they were nearly related to him, was a man of distinct preferences. He preferred Mrs. Almond to his sister Lavinia, who had married a poor clergyman, of a sickly constitution and a flowery style of eloquence, and then, at the age of thirty-three, had been left a widow—without children, without fortune—with nothing but the memory of Mr. Penniman's flowers of speech, a certain vague aroma of which hovered about her own conversation. Nevertheless, he had offered her a home under his own roof, which Lavinia accepted with the alacrity of a woman who had spent the ten years of her married life in the town of Poughkeepsie. The Doctor had not proposed to Mrs. Penniman to come and live with him indefinitely; he had suggested that she should make an asylum of his house while she looked about for unfurnished lodgings. It is uncertain whether Mrs. Penniman ever instituted a search for unfurnished lodgings, but it is beyond dispute that she never found them. She settled herself with her brother and never went away, and, when Catherine was twenty years old, her Aunt Lavinia was still one of the most striking features of her immediate *entourage*. Mrs. Penniman's own account of the matter was that she had remained to take charge of her niece's education. She had given this account, at least, to every one but the Doctor, who never asked for explanations which he could entertain himself any day with inventing. Mrs. Penniman, moreover, though she had a good deal of a certain sort of artificial assurance, shrunk, for indefinable reasons, from presenting herself to her brother as a fountain of instruction. She had not a high sense of humor, but she had enough to prevent her from making this mistake; and her brother, on his side, had enough to excuse her, in her situation, for laying him under contribution during a considerable part of a lifetime. He therefore assented tacitly to the proposition which Mrs. Penniman had tacitly laid down, that it was of importance that the poor motherless girl should have a brilliant woman near her. His assent could only be tacit, for he had never been dazzled by his sister's intellectual lustre. Save when he fell in love with Catherine Harrington, he had never been dazzled, indeed, by any feminine characteristics whatever; and though he was to a certain extent what is called a ladies' doctor, his private opinion of the more complicated sex was not exalted. He regarded its complications as more curious than edifying, and he had an idea of the beauty of *reason,* which was, on the whole, meagrely gratified by what he observed in his female patients. His wife had been a reasonable woman, but she was a bright exception; among several things that he was sure of, this was perhaps the principal. Such a conviction, of course, did little either to mitigate or to abbreviate his widowhood; and it set a limit to his recognition, at the best, of Catherine's possibilities and of Mrs. Penniman's ministrations. He nevertheless, at the end of six months, accepted his sister's permanent presence as an accomplished fact, and as Catherine grew older, perceived that there were in effect good reasons why she should have a companion of her own imperfect sex. He was extremely polite to Lavinia, scrupulously, formally polite; and she had never seen him in anger but once in her life, when he lost his temper in a theological discussion with her late husband. With her he never discussed theology, nor, indeed, discussed anything; he contented himself with making known, very distinctly, in the form of a lucid ultimatum, his wishes with regard to Catherine.

Once, when the girl was about twelve years old, he had said to her—

"Try and make a clever woman of her, Lavinia; I should like her to be a clever woman."

Mrs. Penniman, at this, looked thoughtful a moment. "My dear Austin," she then inquired, "do you think it is better to be clever than to be good?"

"Good for what?" asked the Doctor. "You are good for nothing unless you are clever."

From this assertion Mrs. Penniman saw no reason to dissent; she possibly reflected that her own great use in the world was owing to her aptitude for many things.

"Of course I wish Catherine to be good," the Doctor said next day; "but she won't be any the less virtuous for not being a fool. I am not afraid of her being wicked; she will never have the salt of malice in her character. She is 'as good as good bread,' as the French say; but six years hence I don't want to have to compare her to good bread-and-butter."

"Are you afraid she will be insipid? My dear brother, it is I who supply the butter; so you needn't fear!" said Mrs. Penniman, who had taken in hand the child's "accomplishments," overlooking her at the piano, where Catherine displayed a certain talent, and going with her to the dancing-class, where it must be confessed that she made but a modest figure.

Mrs. Penniman was a tall, thin, fair, rather faded woman, with a perfectly amiable disposition, a high standard of gentility, a taste for light literature, and a certain foolish indirectness and obliquity of character. She was romantic; she was sentimental; she had a passion for little secrets and mysteries—a very innocent passion, for her secrets had hitherto always been as unpractical as addled eggs. She was not absolutely veracious; but this defect was of no great consequence, for she had never had anything to conceal. She would have liked to have a lover, and to correspond with him under an assumed name, in letters left at a shop. I am bound to say that her imagination never carried the intimacy further than this. Mrs. Penniman had never had a lover, but her brother, who was very shrewd, understood her turn of mind. "When Catherine is about seventeen," he said to himself, "Lavinia will try and persuade her that some young man with a mustache is in love with her. It will be quite untrue; no young man, with a mustache or without, will ever be in love with Catherine. But Lavinia will take it up, and talk to her about it; perhaps, even, if her taste for clandestine operations doesn't prevail with her, she will talk to me about it. Catherine won't see it, and won't believe it, fortunately for her peace of mind; poor Catherine isn't romantic."

She was a healthy, well-grown child, without a trace of her

mother's beauty. She was not ugly; she had simply a plain, dull, gentle countenance. The most that had ever been said for her was that she had a "nice" face; and, though she was an heiress, no one had ever thought of regarding her as a belle. Her father's opinion of her moral purity was abundantly justified; she was excellently, imperturbably good; affectionate, docile, obedient, and much addicted to speaking the truth. In her younger years she was a good deal of a romp, and, though it is an awkward confession to make about one's heroine, I must add that she was something of a glutton. She never, that I know of, stole raisins out of the pantry; but she devoted her pocket-money to the purchase of cream-cakes. As regards this, however, a critical attitude would be inconsistent with a candid reference to the early annals of any biographer. Catherine was decidedly not clever; she was not quick with her book, nor, indeed, with anything else. She was not abnormally deficient, and she mustered learning enough to acquit herself respectably in conversation with her contemporaries—among whom it must be avowed, however, that she occupied a secondary place. It is well known that in New York it is possible for a young girl to occupy a primary one. Catherine, who was extremely modest, had no desire to shine, and on most social occasions, as they are called, you would have found her lurking in the background. She was extremely fond of her father, and very much afraid of him; she thought him the cleverest and handsomest and most celebrated of men. The poor girl found her account so completely in the exercise of her affections that the little tremor of fear that mixed itself with her filial passion gave the thing an extra relish rather than blunted its edge. Her deepest desire was to please him, and her conception of happiness was to know that she had succeeded in pleasing him. She had never succeeded beyond a certain point. Though, on the whole, he was very kind to her, she was perfectly aware of this, and to go beyond the point in question seemed to her really something to live for. What she could not know, of course, was that she disappointed him, though on three or four occasions the Doctor had been almost frank about it. She grew up peacefully and prosperously; but at the age of eighteen Mrs. Penniman had not made a clever woman of her. Doctor Sloper would have liked to be proud of his daughter; but there was nothing to be proud of in poor Catherine. There was nothing, of course, to be ashamed of; but this was not enough for the Doctor, who was a proud man, and would have enjoyed being able to think of his daughter as an unusual girl. There would have been a fitness in her being pretty and graceful, intelligent and distinguished—for her mother had been the most charming woman of her little day—and as regards her father, of course he knew his own value. He had moments of irritation at having produced a commonplace child, and he even went so far at times as to take a certain satisfaction in the thought that his wife had not lived to find her out. He was naturally slow in making this discovery himself, and it was not till Catherine had become a young lady grown that he regarded the matter as settled. He gave her the benefit of a great many doubts; he was in no haste to conclude. Mrs. Penniman frequently assured him that his daughter had a delightful nature; but he knew how to interpret this assurance. It meant, to his sense, that Catherine was not wise enough to discover that her aunt was a goose—a limitation of mind that could not fail to be agreeable to Mrs. Penniman. Both she and her brother, however, exaggerated the young girl's limitations; for Catherine, though she was very fond of her aunt, and conscious of the gratitude she owed her, regarded her without a particle of that gentle dread which gave its stamp to her admiration of her father. To her mind there was nothing of the infinite about Mrs. Penniman; Catherine saw her all at once, as it were, and was not dazzled by the apparition; whereas her father's great faculties seemed, as they stretched away, to lose themselves in a sort of luminous vagueness, which indicated, not that they stopped, but that Catherine's own mind ceased to follow them.

It must not be supposed that Doctor Sloper visited his disappointment upon the poor girl, or ever let her suspect that she had played him a trick. On the contrary, for fear of being unjust to her, he did his duty with exemplary zeal, and recognized that she was a faithful and affectionate child. Besides, he was a philosopher: he smoked a good many cigars over his disappointment, and in the fulness of time he got used to it. He satisfied himself that he had expected nothing, though, indeed, with a certain oddity of reasoning. "I expect nothing," he said to himself; "so that, if she gives me a surprise, it will be all clear gain. If she doesn't, it will be no loss." This was about the time Catherine had reached her eighteenth year; so that it will be seen her father had not been precipitate. At this time she seemed not only incapable of giving surprises; it was almost a question whether she could have received one—she was so quiet and irresponsive. People who expressed themselves roughly called her stolid. But she was irresponsive because she was shy, uncomfortably, painfully shy. This was not always understood, and she sometimes produced an impression of insensibility. In reality, she was the softest creature in the world.

✥ 3 ✥

As A CHILD she had promised to be tall; but when she was sixteen she ceased to grow, and her stature, like most other points in her composition, was not unusual. She was strong, however, and properly made, and, fortunately, her health was excellent. It has been noted that the Doctor was a philosopher, but I would not have answered for his philosophy if the poor girl had proved a sickly and suffering person. Her appearance of health constituted her principal claim to beauty; and her clear, fresh complexion, in which white and red were very equally distributed, was, indeed, an excellent thing to see. Her eye was small and quiet, her features were rather thick, her tresses brown and smooth. A dull, plain girl she was called by rigorous critics—a quiet, ladylike girl, by those of the more imaginative sort; but by neither class was she very elaborately discussed. When it had been duly impressed upon her that she was a young lady—it was a good while before she could believe it—she suddenly developed a lively taste for dress: a lively taste is quite the expression to use. I feel as if I ought to write it very small, her judgment in this matter was by no means infallible; it was liable to confusions and embarrassments. Her great indulgence of it was really the desire of a rather inarticulate nature to manifest itself; she sought to be eloquent in her garments, and to make up for her diffidence of speech by a fine frankness of costume. But if she expressed herself in her clothes, it is certain that people were not to blame for not thinking her a witty person. It must be added that, though she had the expectation of a fortune—Doctor Sloper for a long time had been making twenty thousand dollars a year by his profession, and laying aside the half of it—the amount of money at her disposal was not greater than the allowance made to many poorer girls. In those days,

in New York, there were still a few altar-fires flickering in the temple
of Republican simplicity, and Doctor Sloper would have been glad
to see his daughter present herself, with a classic grace, as a priestess
of this mild faith. It made him fairly grimace, in private, to think
that a child of his should be both ugly and overdressed. For himself,
he was fond of the good things of life, and he made a considerable
use of them; but he had a dread of vulgarity, and even a theory that
it was increasing in the society that surrounded him. Moreover, the
standard of luxury in the United States thirty years ago was carried
by no means so high as at present, and Catherine's clever father took
the old-fashioned view of the education of young persons. He had no
particular theory on the subject; it had scarcely as yet become a
necessity of self-defence to have a collection of theories. It simply
appeared to him proper and reasonable that a well-bred young
woman should not carry half her fortune on her back. Catherine's
back was a broad one, and would have carried a good deal; but to the
weight of the paternal displeasure she never ventured to expose it,
and our heroine was twenty years old before she treated herself, for
evening wear, to a red satin gown trimmed with gold fringe; though
this was an article which, for many years, she had coveted in secret. It
made her look, when she sported it, like a woman of thirty; but
oddly enough, in spite of her taste for fine clothes, she had not a
grain of coquetry, and her anxiety when she put them on was as to
whether they, and not she, would look well. It is a point on which
history has not been explicit, but the assumption is warrantable; it
was in the royal raiment just mentioned that she presented herself at
a little entertainment given by her aunt, Mrs. Almond. The girl was
at this time in her twenty-first year, and Mrs. Almond's party was the
beginning of something very important.

Some three or four years before this, Doctor Sloper had moved his
household gods up town, as they say in New York. He had been
living ever since his marriage in an edifice of red brick, with granite
copings and an enormous fan-light over the door, standing in a street
within five minutes' walk of the City Hall, which saw its best days
(from the social point of view) about 1820. After this, the tide of
fashion began to set steadily northward, as, indeed, in New York,
thanks to the narrow channel in which it flows, it is obliged to do,
and the great hum of traffic rolled farther to the right and left of
Broadway. By the time the Doctor changed his residence, the mur-

mur of trade had become a mighty uproar, which was music in the
ears of all good citizens interested in the commercial development, as
they delighted to call it, of their fortunate isle. Doctor Sloper's
interest in this phenomenon was only indirect—though, seeing that,
as the years went on, half his patients came to be overworked men of
business, it might have been more immediate—and when most of his
neighbors' dwellings (also ornamented with granite copings and
large fan-lights) had been converted into offices, warehouses, and
shipping agencies, and otherwise applied to the base uses of commerce, he determined to look out for a quieter home. The ideal of
quiet and of genteel retirement, in 1835, was found in Washington
Square, where the Doctor built himself a handsome, modern, wide-
fronted house, with a big balcony before the drawing-room windows,
and a flight of white marble steps ascending to a portal which was
also faced with white marble. This structure, and many of its neighbors, which it exactly resembled, were supposed, forty years ago, to
embody the last results of architectural science, and they remain to
this day very solid and honorable dwellings. In front of them was the
Square, containing a considerable quantity of inexpensive vegetation, enclosed by a wooden paling, which increased its rural and
accessible appearance; and round the corner was the more august
precinct of the Fifth Avenue, taking its origin at this point with a
spacious and confident air which already marked it for high des-
tinies. I know not whether it is owing to the tenderness of early
associations, but this portion of New York appears to many persons
the most delectable. It has a kind of established repose which is not
of frequent occurrence in other quarters of the long, shrill city; it has
a riper, richer, more honorable look than any of the upper ramifica-
tions of the great longitudinal thoroughfare—the look of having had
something of a social history. It was here, as you might have been
informed on good authority, that you had come into a world which
appeared to offer a variety of sources of interest; it was here that your
grandmother lived, in venerable solitude, and dispensed a hospitality which commended itself alike to the infant imagination and the
infant palate; it was here that you took your first walks abroad,
following the nursery-maid with unequal step, and sniffing up the
strange odor of the ailanthus-trees which at that time formed the
principal umbrage of the Square, and diffused an aroma that you
were not yet critical enough to dislike as it deserved; it was here,

finally, that your first school, kept by a broad-bosomed, broad-based old lady with a ferule, who was always having tea in a blue cup, with a saucer that didn't match, enlarged the circle both of your observations and your sensations. It was here, at any rate, that my heroine spent many years of her life; which is my excuse for this topographical parenthesis.

Mrs. Almond lived much farther up town, in an embryonic street, with a high number—a region where the extension of the city began to assume a theoretic air, where poplars grew beside the pavement (when there was one), and mingled their shade with the steep roofs of desultory Dutch houses, and where pigs and chickens disported themselves in the gutter. These elements of rural picturesqueness have now wholly departed from New York street scenery; but they were to be found within the memory of middle-aged persons in quarters which now would blush to be reminded of them. Catherine had a great many cousins, and with her Aunt Almond's children, who ended by being nine in number, she lived on terms of considerable intimacy. When she was younger they had been rather afraid of her; she was believed, as the phrase is, to be highly educated, and a person who lived in the intimacy of their Aunt Penniman had something of reflected grandeur. Mrs. Penniman, among the little Almonds, was an object of more admiration than sympathy. Her manners were strange and formidable, and her mourning robes—she dressed in black for twenty years after her husband's death, and then suddenly appeared, one morning, with pink roses in her cap—were complicated in odd, unexpected places with buckles, bugles, and pins, which discouraged familiarity. She took children too hard, both for good and for evil, and had an oppressive air of expecting subtle things of them; so that going to see her was a good deal like being taken to church and made to sit in a front pew. It was discovered after awhile, however, that Aunt Penniman was but an accident in Catherine's existence, and not a part of its essence, and that when the girl came to spend a Saturday with her cousins, she was available for "follow-my-master," and even for leap-frog. On this basis an understanding was easily arrived at, and for several years Catherine fraternized with her young kinsmen. I say young kinsmen, because seven of the little Almonds were boys, and Catherine had a preference for those games which are most conveniently played in trousers. By degrees, however, the little Almonds' trousers began to lengthen, and the wearers to disperse and settle themselves in life. The elder children were older than Catherine, and the boys were sent to college or placed in counting-rooms. Of the girls, one married very punctually, and the other as punctually became engaged. It was to celebrate this latter event that Mrs. Almond gave the little party I have mentioned. Her daughter was to marry a stout young stock-broker, a boy of twenty: it was thought a very good thing.

✺ 4 ✺

MRS. PENNIMAN, with more buckles and bangles than ever, came, of course, to the entertainment, accompanied by her niece; the Doctor, too, had promised to look in later in the evening. There was to be a good deal of dancing, and before it had gone very far Marian Almond came up to Catherine, in company with a tall young man. She introduced the young man as a person who had a great desire to make our heroine's acquaintance, and as a cousin of Arthur Townsend, her own intended.

Marian Almond was a pretty little person of seventeen, with a very small figure and a very big sash, to the elegance of whose manners matrimony had nothing to add. She already had all the airs of a hostess, receiving the company, shaking her fan, saying that with so many people to attend to she should have no time to dance. She made a long speech about Mr. Townsend's cousin, to whom she administered a tap with her fan before turning away to other cares. Catherine had not understood all that she said; her attention was given to enjoying Marian's ease of manner and flow of ideas, and to looking at the young man, who was remarkably handsome. She had succeeded, however, as she often failed to do when people were presented to her, in catching his name, which appeared to be the same as that of Marian's little stock-broker. Catherine was always agitated by an introduction; it seemed a difficult moment, and she wondered that some people—her new acquaintance at this moment, for instance—should mind it so little. She wondered what she ought to say, and what would be the consequences of her saying nothing.

The consequences at present were very agreeable. Mr. Townsend, leaving her no time for embarrassment, began to talk to her with an easy smile, as if he had known her for a year.

"What a delightful party! What a charming house! What an interesting family! What a pretty girl your cousin is!"

These observations, in themselves of no great profundity, Mr. Townsend seemed to offer for what they were worth, and as a contribution to an acquaintance. He looked straight into Catherine's eyes. She answered nothing; she only listened, and looked at him; and he, as if he expected no particular reply, went on to say many other things in the same comfortable and natural manner. Catherine, though she felt tongue-tied, was conscious of no embarrassment; it seemed proper that he should talk, and that she should simply look at him. What made it natural was that he was so handsome, or, rather, as she phrased it to herself, so beautiful. The music had been silent for awhile, but it suddenly began again; and then he asked her, with a deeper, intenser smile, if she would do him the honor of dancing with him. Even to this inquiry she gave no audible assent; she simply let him put his arm round her waist—as she did so, it occurred to her more vividly than it had ever done before that this was a singular place for a gentleman's arm to be—and in a moment he was guiding her round the room in the harmonious rotation of the polka. When they paused, she felt that she was red; and then, for some moments, she stopped looking at him. She fanned herself, and looked at the flowers that were painted on her fan. He asked her if she would begin again, and she hesitated to answer, still looking at the flowers.

"Does it make you dizzy?" he asked, in a tone of great kindness.

Then Catherine looked up at him; he was certainly beautiful, and not at all red. "Yes," she said; she hardly knew why, for dancing had never made her dizzy.

"Ah, well, in that case," said Mr. Townsend, "we will sit still and talk. I will find a good place to sit."

He found a good place—a charming place; a little sofa that seemed meant only for two persons. The rooms by this time were very full; the dancers increased in number, and people stood close in front of them, turning their backs, so that Catherine and her companion seemed secluded and unobserved. "We will talk," the young man had said; but he still did all the talking. Catherine leaned back in her place, with her eyes fixed upon him, smiling, and thinking him very clever. He had features like young men in pictures; Catherine had never seen such features—so delicate, so chiselled and finished—among the young New Yorkers whom she passed in the streets and met at dancing-parties. He was tall and slim, but he looked extremely strong. Catherine thought he looked like a statue. But a statue would not talk like that, and, above all, would not have eyes of so rare a color. He had never been at Mrs. Almond's before; he felt very much like a stranger; and it was very kind of Catherine to take pity on him. He was Arthur Townsend's cousin—not very near; several times removed—and Arthur had brought him to present him to the family. In fact, he was a great stranger in New York. It was his native place; but he had not been there for many years. He had been knocking about the world, and living in queer corners; he had only come back a month or two before. New York was very pleasant, only he felt lonely.

"You see, people forget you," he said, smiling at Catherine with his delightful gaze, while he leaned forward obliquely, turning toward her, with his elbows on his knees.

It seemed to Catherine that no one who had once seen him would ever forget him; but though she made this reflection she kept it to herself, almost as you would keep something precious.

They sat there for some time. He was very amusing. He asked her about the people that were near them; he tried to guess who some of them were, and he made the most laughable mistakes. He criticised them very freely, in a positive, off-hand way. Catherine had never heard any one—especially any young man—talk just like that. It was the way a young man might talk in a novel; or, better still, in a play, on the stage, close before the foot-lights, looking at the audience, and with every one looking at him, so that you wondered at his presence of mind. And yet Mr. Townsend was not like an actor; he seemed so sincere, so natural. This was very interesting; but in the midst of it Marian Almond came pushing through the crowd, with a little ironical cry, when she found these young people still together, which made every one turn round, and cost Catherine a conscious blush. Marian broke up their talk, and told Mr. Townsend—whom she treated as if she were already married, and he had become her cousin—to run away to her mother, who had been wishing for the last half-hour to introduce him to Mr. Almond.

"We shall meet again," he said to Catherine as he left her, and Catherine thought it a very original speech.

Her cousin took her by the arm, and made her walk about. "I needn't ask you what you think of Morris," the young girl exclaimed.

"Is that his name?"

"I don't ask you what you think of his name, but what you think of himself," said Marian.

"Oh, nothing particular," Catherine answered, dissembling for the first time in her life.

"I have half a mind to tell him that!" cried Marian. "It will do him good; he's so terribly conceited."

"Conceited?" said Catherine, staring.

"So Arthur says, and Arthur knows about him."

"Oh, don't tell him!" Catherine murmured, imploringly.

"Don't tell him he's conceited! I have told him so a dozen times."

At this profession of audacity Catherine looked down at her little companion in amazement. She supposed it was because Marian was going to be married that she took so much on herself; but she wondered too, whether, when she herself should become engaged, such exploits would be expected of her.

Half an hour later she saw her Aunt Penniman sitting in the embrasure of a window, with her head a little on one side, and her gold eye-glass raised to her eyes, which were wandering about the room. In front of her was a gentleman, bending forward a little, with his back turned to Catherine. She knew his back immediately, though she had never seen it; for when he left her, at Marian's instigation, he had retreated in the best order, without turning round. Morris Townsend—the name had already become very familiar to her, as if some one had been repeating it in her ear for the last half-hour—Morris Townsend was giving his impressions of the company to her aunt, as he had done to herself; he was saying clever things, and Mrs. Penniman was smiling, as if she approved of them. As soon as Catherine had perceived this she moved away; she would not have liked him to turn round and see her. But it gave her pleasure—the whole thing. That he should talk with Mrs. Penniman, with whom she lived and whom she saw and talked with every day—that seemed to keep him near her, and to make him even easier to contemplate than if she herself had been the object of his civilities; and that Aunt Lavinia should like him, should not be shocked or startled by what he said, this also appeared to the girl a personal gain; for Aunt Lavinia's standard was extremely high, planted as it was over the grave of her late husband, in which, as she had convinced every one, the very genius of conversation was buried. One of the Almond boys, as Catherine called them, invited our heroine to dance a quadrille, and for a quarter of an hour her feet at least were occupied. This time she was not dizzy; her head was very clear. Just when the dance was over, she found herself in the crowd face to face with her father. Doctor Sloper had usually a little smile, never a very big one, and with this little smile playing in his clear eyes and on his neatly-shaved lips, he looked at his daughter's crimson gown.

"Is it possible that this magnificent person is my child?" he said.

You would have surprised him if you had told him so; but it is a literal fact that he almost never addressed his daughter save in the ironical form. Whenever he addressed her he gave her pleasure; but she had to cut her pleasure out of the piece, as it were. There were portions left over, light remnants and snippets of irony, which she never knew what to do with, which seemed too delicate for her own use; and yet Catherine, lamenting the limitations of her understanding, felt that they were too valuable to waste, and had a belief that if they passed over her head they yet contributed to the general sum of human wisdom.

"I am not magnificent," she said, mildly, wishing that she had put on another dress.

"You are sumptuous, opulent, expensive," her father rejoined. "You look as if you had eighty thousand a year."

"Well, so long as I haven't—" said Catherine, illogically. Her conception of her prospective wealth was as yet very indefinite.

"So long as you haven't you shouldn't look as if you had. Have you enjoyed your party?"

Catherine hesitated a moment; and then, looking away, "I am rather tired," she murmured. I have said that this entertainment was the beginning of something important for Catherine. For the second time in her life she made an indirect answer; and the beginning of a period of dissimulation is certainly a significant date. Catherine was not so easily tired as that.

Nevertheless, in the carriage, as they drove home, she was as quiet as if fatigue had been her portion. Doctor Sloper's manner of addressing his sister Lavinia had a good deal of resemblance to the tone he had adopted toward Catherine.

"Who was the young man that was making love to you?" he presently asked.

"Oh, my good brother!" murmured Mrs. Penniman, in deprecation.

"He seemed uncommonly tender. Whenever I looked at you for half an hour, he had the most devoted air."

"The devotion was not to me," said Mrs. Penniman. "It was to Catherine; he talked to me of her."

Catherine had been listening with all her ears. "Oh, Aunt Penniman!" she exclaimed, faintly.

"He is very handsome; he is very clever; he expressed himself with a great deal—a great deal of felicity," her aunt went on.

"He is in love with this regal creature, then?" the Doctor inquired, humorously.

"Oh, father!" cried the girl, still more faintly, devoutly thankful the carriage was dark.

"I don't know that; but he admired her dress."

Catherine did not say to herself in the dark, "My dress only?" Mrs. Penniman's announcement struck her by its richness, not by its meagreness.

"You see," said her father, "he thinks you have eighty thousand a year."

"I don't believe he thinks of that," said Mrs. Penniman; "he is too refined."

"He must be tremendously refined not to think of that!"

"Well, he is!" Catherine exclaimed, before she knew it.

"I thought you had gone to sleep," her father answered. "The hour has come!" he added to himself. "Lavinia is going to get up a romance for Catherine. It's a shame to play such tricks on the girl. What is the gentleman's name?" he went on, aloud.

"I didn't catch it, and I didn't like to ask him. He asked to be introduced to me," said Mrs. Penniman, with a certain grandeur; "but you know how indistinctly Jefferson speaks." Jefferson was Mr. Almond. "Catherine, dear, what was the gentleman's name?"

For a minute, if it had not been for the rumbling of the carriage, you might have heard a pin drop.

"I don't know, Aunt Lavinia," said Catherine, very softly. And, with all his irony, her father believed her.

❦ 5 ❦

HE LEARNED what he had asked some three or four days later, after Morris Townsend, with his cousin, had called in Washington Square. Mrs. Penniman did not tell her brother, on the drive home, that she had intimated to this agreeable young man, whose name she did not know, that, with her niece, she should be very glad to see him; but she was greatly pleased, and even a little flattered, when, late on a Sunday afternoon, the two gentlemen made their appearance. His coming with Arthur Townsend made it more natural and easy; the latter young man was on the point of becoming connected with the family, and Mrs. Penniman had remarked to Catherine that, as he was going to marry Marian, it would be polite in him to call. These events came to pass late in the autumn, and Catherine and her aunt had been sitting together in the closing dusk, by the fire-light, in the high back-parlor.

Arthur Townsend fell to Catherine's portion, while his companion placed himself on the sofa beside Mrs. Penniman. Catherine had hitherto not been a harsh critic; she was easy to please—she liked to talk with young men. But Marian's betrothed, this evening, made her feel vaguely fastidious; he sat looking at the fire and rubbing his knees with his hands. As for Catherine, she scarcely even pretended to keep up the conversation; her attention had fixed itself on the other side of the room; she was listening to what went on between the other Mr. Townsend and her aunt. Every now and then he looked over at Catherine herself and smiled, as if to show that what he said was for her benefit too. Catherine would have liked to change her place, to go and sit near them, where she might see and hear him better. But she was afraid of seeming bold—of looking eager; and, besides, it would not have been polite to Marian's little suitor. She wondered why the other gentleman had picked out her aunt—how he came to have so much to say to Mrs. Penniman, to whom, usually, young men were not especially devoted. She was not at all jealous of Aunt Lavinia, but she was a little envious, and, above all, she wondered; for Morris Townsend was an object on which she found that her imagination could exercise itself indefinitely. His cousin had been describing a house that he had taken in view of his union with Marian, and the domestic conveniences he meant to introduce into it; how Marian wanted a larger one, and Mrs. Almond recommended a smaller one, and how he himself was convinced that he had got the neatest house in New York.

"It doesn't matter," he said; "it's only for three or four years. At the end of three or four years we'll move. That's the way to live in New York—to move every three or four years. Then you always get the last thing. It's because the city's growing so quick—you've got to keep up with it. It's going straight up town—that's where New York's going. If I wasn't afraid Marian would be lonely, I'd go up there—right up to the top—and wait for it. Only have to wait ten years—they'll all come up after you. But Marian says she wants some neighbors—she doesn't want to be a pioneer. She says that if she's got to be the first settler she had better go out to Minnesota. I guess we'll move up little by little; when we get tired of one street we'll go higher. So you see we'll always have a new house; it's a great advantage to have a new house; you get all the latest improvements. They invent everything all over again about every five years, and it's a great thing to keep up with the new things. I always try and keep up with the new things of every kind. Don't you think that's a good motto for a young couple—to keep 'going higher?' What's the name of that piece of poetry—what do they call it?—*Excelsior!*"

Catherine bestowed on her junior visitor only just enough attention to feel that this was not the way Mr. Morris Townsend had talked the other night, or that he was talking now to her fortunate aunt. But suddenly his aspiring kinsman became more interesting. He seemed to have become conscious that she was affected by his companion's presence, and he thought it proper to explain it.

"My cousin asked me to bring him, or I shouldn't have taken the liberty. He seemed to want very much to come; you know he's awfully sociable. I told him I wanted to ask you first, but he said Mrs. Penniman had invited him. He isn't particular what he says when he wants to come somewhere. But Mrs. Penniman seems to think it's all right."

"We are very glad to see him," said Catherine. And she wished to talk more about him, but she hardly knew what to say. "I never saw him before," she went on, presently.

Arthur Townsend stared.

"Why, he told me he talked with you for over half an hour the other night."

"I mean before the other night. That was the first time."

"Oh, he has been away from New York—he has been all round the world. He doesn't know many people here, but he's very sociable, and he wants to know every one."

"Every one?" said Catherine.

"Well, I mean all the good ones. All the pretty young ladies—like Mrs. Penniman!" And Arthur Townsend gave a private laugh.

"My aunt likes him very much," said Catherine.

"Most people like him—he's so brilliant."

"He's more like a foreigner," Catherine suggested.

"Well, I never knew a foreigner," said young Townsend, in a tone which seemed to indicate that his ignorance had been optional.

"Neither have I," Catherine confessed, with more humility. "They say they are generally brilliant," she added, vaguely.

"Well, the people of this city are clever enough for me. I know some of them that think they are too clever for me; but they ain't."

"I suppose you can't be too clever," said Catherine, still with humility.

"I don't know. I know some people that call my cousin too clever."

Catherine listened to this statement with extreme interest, and a feeling that if Morris Townsend had a fault it would naturally be that one. But she did not commit herself, and in a moment she asked, "Now that he has come back, will he stay here always?"

"Ah!" said Arthur, "if he can get something to do."

"Something to do?"

"Some place or other; some business."

"Hasn't he got any?" said Catherine, who had never heard of a young man—of the upper class—in this situation.

"No; he's looking round. But he can't find anything."

"I am very sorry," Catherine permitted herself to observe.

"Oh, he doesn't mind," said young Townsend. "He takes it easy—he isn't in a hurry. He is very particular."

Catherine thought he naturally would be, and gave herself up for some moments to the contemplation of this idea, in several of its bearings.

"Won't his father take him into his business—his office?" she at last inquired.

"He hasn't got any father—he has only got a sister. Your sister can't help you much."

It seemed to Catherine that if she were his sister she would disprove this axiom. "Is she—is she pleasant?" she asked in a moment.

"I don't know—I believe she's very respectable," said young Townsend. And then he looked across to his cousin and began to laugh. "I say, we are talking about you," he added.

Morris Townsend paused in his conversation with Mrs. Penniman, and stared, with a little smile. Then he got up, as if he were going.

"As far as you are concerned, I can't return the compliment," he said to Catherine's companion. "But as regards Miss Sloper, it's another affair."

Catherine thought this little speech wonderfully well turned; but she was embarrassed by it, and she also got up. Morris Townsend stood looking at her and smiling; he put out his hand for farewell. He was going, without having said anything to her; but even on these terms she was glad to have seen him.

"I will tell her what you have said—when you go!" said Mrs. Penniman, with a little significant laugh.

Catherine blushed, for she felt almost as if they were making sport of her. What in the world could this beautiful young man have said? He looked at her still, in spite of her blush, but very kindly and respectfully.

"I have had no talk with you," he said, "and that was what I came for. But it will be a good reason for coming another time; a little pretext—if I am obliged to give one. I am not afraid of what your aunt will say when I go."

With this the two young men took their departure; after which Catherine, with her blush still lingering, directed a serious and interrogative eye to Mrs. Penniman. She was incapable of elaborate artifice, and she resorted to no jocular device—to no affectation of the belief that she had been maligned—to learn what she desired.

"What did you say you would tell me?" she asked.

Mrs. Penniman came up to her, smiling and nodding a little, looked at her all over, and gave a twist to the knot of ribbon in her neck. "It's a great secret, my dear child; but he is coming a-courting!"

Catherine was serious still. "Is that what he told you?"

"He didn't say so exactly; but he left me to guess it. I'm a good guesser."

"Do you mean a-courting me?"

"Not me, certainly, miss; though I must say he is a hundred times more polite to a person who has no longer extreme youth to recommend her than most of the young men. He is thinking of some one else." And Mrs. Penniman gave her niece a delicate little kiss. "You must be very gracious to him."

Catherine stared—she was bewildered. "I don't understand you," she said; "he doesn't know me."

"Oh yes, he does; more than you think. I have told him all about you."

"Oh, Aunt Penniman!" murmured Catherine, as if this had been a breach of trust. "He is a perfect stranger—we don't know him." There was infinite modesty in the poor girl's "we."

Aunt Penniman, however, took no account of it; she spoke even with a touch of acrimony. "My dear Catherine, you know very well that you admire him."

"Oh, Aunt Penniman!" Catherine could only murmur again. It might very well be that she admired him—though this did not seem to her a thing to talk about. But that this brilliant stranger—this sudden apparition, who had barely heard the sound of her voice—took that sort of interest in her that was expressed by the romantic phrase of which Mrs. Penniman had just made use—this could only be a figment of the restless brain of Aunt Lavinia, whom every one knew to be a woman of powerful imagination.

✼ 6 ✼

Mrs. Penniman even took for granted at times that other people had as much imagination as herself; so that when, half an hour later, her brother came in, she addressed him quite on this principle.

"He has just been here, Austin; it's such a pity you missed him."

"Whom in the world have I missed?" asked the Doctor.

"Mr. Morris Townsend; he has made us such a delightful visit."

"And who in the world is Mr. Morris Townsend?"

"Aunt Penniman means the gentleman—the gentleman whose name I couldn't remember," said Catherine.

"The gentleman at Elizabeth's party who was so struck with Catherine," Mrs. Penniman added.

"Oh, his name is Morris Townsend, is it? And did he come here to propose to you?"

"Oh, father!" murmured the girl for an answer, turning away to the window, where the dusk had deepened to darkness.

"I hope he won't do that without your permission," said Mrs. Penniman, very graciously.

"After all, my dear, he seems to have yours," her brother answered.

Lavinia simpered, as if this might not be quite enough, and Catherine, with her forehead touching the window-panes, listened to this exchange of epigrams as reservedly as if they had not each been a pin-prick in her own destiny.

"The next time he comes," the Doctor added, "you had better call me. He might like to see me."

Morris Townsend came again some five days afterward; but Doctor Sloper was not called, as he was absent from home at the time. Catherine was with her aunt when the young man's name was brought in, and Mrs. Penniman, effacing and protesting, made a great point of her niece's going into the drawing-room alone.

"This time it's for you—for you only," she said. "Before, when he talked to me, it was only preliminary—it was to gain my confidence. Literally, my dear, I should not have the *courage* to show myself to-day."

And this was perfectly true. Mrs. Penniman was not a brave woman, and Morris Townsend had struck her as a young man of great force of character, and of remarkable powers of satire—a keen, resolute, brilliant nature, with which one must exercise a great deal of tact. She said to herself that he was "imperious," and she liked the word and the idea. She was not the least jealous of her niece, and she had been perfectly happy with Mr. Penniman, but in the bottom of her heart she permitted herself the observation, "That's the sort of husband I should have had!" He was certainly much more imperious—she ended by calling it imperial—than Mr. Penniman.

So Catherine saw Mr. Townsend alone, and her aunt did not come in even at the end of the visit. The visit was a long one; he sat there, in the front parlor, in the biggest arm-chair, for more than an hour. He seemed more at home this time—more familiar; lounging a little in the chair, slapping a cushion that was near him with his stick, and looking round the room a good deal, and at the objects it contained, as well as at Catherine; whom, however, he also contemplated freely. There was a smile of respectful devotion in his handsome eyes which seemed to Catherine almost solemnly beautiful; it made her think of a young knight in a poem. His talk, however, was not particularly knightly; it was light and easy and friendly; it took a practical turn, and he asked a number of questions about herself—what were her tastes—if she liked this and that—what were her habits. He said to her, with his charming smile, "Tell me about yourself; give me a little sketch." Catherine had very little to tell, and she had no talent for sketching; but before he went she had confided to him that she had a secret passion for the theatre, which had been but scantily gratified, and a taste for operatic music—that of Bellini and Donizetti, in especial (it must be remembered, in extenuation of this primitive young woman, that she held these opinions in an age of general darkness) —which she rarely had an occasion to hear, except on the hand-organ. She confessed that she was not particularly fond of literature. Morris Townsend agreed with her that books were tiresome things; only, as he said, you had to read a good many before you found it out. He had been to places that people had written books about, and they were not a bit like the descriptions. To see for yourself—that was the great thing; he always tried to see for himself. He had seen all the principal actors—he had been to all the best theatres in London and Paris. But the actors were always like the authors—they always exaggerated. He liked everything to be natural. Suddenly he stopped, looking at Catherine with his smile.

"That's what I like you for; you are so natural. Excuse me," he added; "you see I am natural myself."

And before she had time to think whether she excused him or not—which afterward, at leisure, she became conscious that she did—he began to talk about music, and to say that it was his greatest pleasure in life. He had heard all the great singers in Paris and London—Pasta and Rubini and Lablache—and when you had done that, you could say that you knew what singing was.

"I sing a little myself," he said; "some day I will show you. Not to-day, but some other time."

And then he got up to go. He had omitted, by accident, to say that he would sing to her if she would play to him. He thought of this after he got into the street; but he might have spared his compunction, for Catherine had not noticed the lapse. She was thinking only that "some other time" had a delightful sound; it seemed to spread itself over the future.

This was all the more reason, however, though she was ashamed and uncomfortable, why she should tell her father that Mr. Morris Townsend had called again. She announced the fact abruptly, almost violently, as soon as the Doctor came into the house; and having done so—it was her duty—she took measures to leave the room. But she could not leave it fast enough; her father stopped her just as she reached the door.

"Well, my dear, did he propose to you to-day?" the Doctor asked.

This was just what she had been afraid he would say; and yet she had no answer ready. Of course she would have liked to take it as a joke—as her father must have meant it; and yet she would have liked also, in denying it, to be a little positive, a little sharp, so that he would perhaps not ask the question again. She didn't like it—it made her unhappy. But Catherine could never be sharp; and for a moment she only stood, with her hand on the door-knob, looking at her satiric parent, and giving a little laugh.

"Decidedly," said the Doctor to himself, "my daughter is not brilliant!"

But he had no sooner made this reflection than Catherine found something; she had decided, on the whole, to take the thing as a joke.

"Perhaps he will do it the next time," she exclaimed, with a repetition of her laugh; and she quickly got out of the room.

The Doctor stood staring; he wondered whether his daughter were serious. Catherine went straight to her own room, and by the time she reached it she bethought herself that there was something else—something better—she might have said. She almost wished, now, that her father would ask his question again, so that she might reply, "Oh yes, Mr. Morris Townsend proposed to me, and I refused him."

The Doctor, however, began to put his questions elsewhere; it naturally having occurred to him that he ought to inform himself properly about this handsome young man, who had formed the habit of running in and out of his house. He addressed himself to the elder of his sisters, Mrs. Almond—not going to her for the purpose; there was no such hurry as that; but having made a note of the matter for the first opportunity. The Doctor was never eager, never impatient or nervous; but he made notes of everything, and he regularly consulted his notes. Among them the information he obtained from Mrs. Almond about Morris Townsend took its place.

"Lavinia has already been to ask me," she said. "Lavinia is most excited; I don't understand it. It's not, after all, Lavinia that the young man is supposed to have designs upon. She is very peculiar."

"Ah, my dear," the Doctor replied, "she has not lived with me these twelve years without my finding it out."

"She has got such an artificial mind," said Mrs. Almond, who always enjoyed an opportunity to discuss Lavinia's peculiarities with her brother. "She didn't want me to tell you that she had asked me about Mr. Townsend; but I told her I would. She always wants to conceal everything."

"And yet at moments no one blurts things out with such crudity. She is like a revolving lighthouse—pitch darkness alternating with a dazzling brilliancy! But what did you tell her?" the Doctor asked.

"What I tell you—that I know very little of him."

"Lavinia must have been disappointed at that," said the Doctor; "she would prefer him to have been guilty of some romantic crime. However, we must make the best of people. They tell me our gentleman is the cousin of the little boy to whom you are about to intrust the future of your little girl."

"Arthur is not a little boy; he is a very old man; you and I will never be so old! He is a distant relation of Lavinia's *protégé*. The name is the same, but I am given to understand that there are Townsends and Townsends. So Arthur's mother tells me; she talked about 'branches'—younger branches, elder branches, inferior branches—as if it were a royal house. Arthur, it appears, is of the reigning line, but poor Lavinia's young man is not. Beyond this,

Arthur's mother knows very little about him; she has only a vague story that he has been 'wild.' But I know his sister a little, and she is a very nice woman. Her name is Mrs. Montgomery; she is a widow, with a little property and five children. She lives in the Second Avenue."

"What does Mrs. Montgomery say about him?"

"That he has talents by which he might distinguish himself."

"Only he is lazy, eh?"

"She doesn't say so."

"That's family pride," said the Doctor. "What is his profession?"

"He hasn't got any; he is looking for something. I believe he was once in the Navy."

"Once? What is his age?"

"I suppose he is upward of thirty. He must have gone into the Navy very young. I think Arthur told me that he inherited a small property—which was perhaps the cause of his leaving the Navy—and that he spent it all in a few years. He travelled all over the world, lived abroad, amused himself. I believe it was a kind of system, a theory he had. He has lately come back to America with the intention, as he tells Arthur, of beginning life in earnest."

"Is he in earnest about Catherine, then?"

"I don't see why you should be incredulous," said Mrs. Almond. "It seems to me that you have never done Catherine justice. You must remember that she has the prospect of thirty thousand a year."

The Doctor looked at his sister a moment, and then, with the lightest touch of bitterness, "You at least appreciate her," he said.

Mrs. Almond blushed.

"I don't mean that is her only merit; I simply mean that it is a great one. A great many young men think so; and you appear to me never to have been properly aware of that. You have always had a little way of alluding to her as an unmarriageable girl."

"My allusions are as kind as yours, Elizabeth," said the Doctor, frankly. "How many suitors has Catherine had, with all her expectations—how much attention has she ever received? Catherine is not unmarriageable, but she is absolutely unattractive. What other reason is there for Lavinia being so charmed with the idea that there is a lover in the house? There has never been one before, and Lavinia, with her sensitive, sympathetic nature, is not used to the idea. It affects her imagination. I must do the young men of New York the justice to say that they strike me as very disinterested. They prefer pretty girls—lively girls—girls like your own. Catherine is neither pretty nor lively."

"Catherine does very well; she has a style of her own—which is more than my poor Marian has, who has no style at all," said Mrs. Almond. "The reason Catherine has received so little attention, is that she seems to all the young men to be older than themselves. She is so large, and she dresses so richly. They are rather afraid of her, I think; she looks as if she had been married already, and you know they don't like married women. And if our young men appear disinterested," the Doctor's wiser sister went on, "it is because they marry, as a general thing, so young—before twenty-five, at the age of innocence and sincerity—before the age of calculation. If they only waited a little, Catherine would fare better."

"As a calculation? Thank you very much," said the Doctor.

"Wait till some intelligent man of forty comes along, and he will be delighted with Catherine," Mrs. Almond continued.

"Mr. Townsend is not old enough, then? His motives may be pure."

"It is very possible that his motives are pure; I should be very sorry to take the contrary for granted. Lavinia is sure of it; and, as he is a very prepossessing youth, you might give him the benefit of the doubt."

Doctor Sloper reflected a moment.

"What are his present means of subsistence?"

"I have no idea. He lives, as I say, with his sister."

"A widow, with five children? Do you mean he lives *upon* her?"

Mrs. Almond got up, and with a certain impatience, "Had you not better ask Mrs. Montgomery herself?" she inquired.

"Perhaps I may come to that," said the Doctor. "Did you say the Second Avenue?" He made a note of the Second Avenue.

❧ 7 ❧

HE WAS, however, by no means so much in earnest as this might seem to indicate; and, indeed, he was more than anything else amused with the whole situation. He was not in the least in a state of tension or of vigilance with regard to Catherine's prospects; he was even on his guard against the ridicule that might attach itself to the spectacle of a house thrown into agitation by its daughter and heiress receiving attentions unprecedented in its annals. More than this, he went so far as to promise himself some entertainment from the little drama—if drama it was—of which Mrs. Penniman desired to represent the ingenious Mr. Townsend as the hero. He had no intention, as yet, of regulating the *dénouement*. He was perfectly willing, as Elizabeth had suggested, to give the young man the benefit of every doubt. There was no great danger in it; for Catherine, at the age of twenty-two, was, after all, a rather mature blossom, such as could be plucked from the stem only by a vigorous jerk. The fact that Morris Townsend was poor, was not of necessity against him; the Doctor had never made up his mind that his daughter should marry a rich man. The fortune she would inherit struck him as a very sufficient provision for two reasonable persons, and if a penniless swain who could give a good account of himself should enter the lists, he should be judged quite upon his personal merits. There were other things besides. The Doctor thought it very vulgar to be precipitate in accusing people of mercenary motives, inasmuch as his door had as yet not been in the least besieged by fortune-hunters; and, lastly, he was very curious to see whether Catherine might really be loved for her moral worth. He smiled as he reflected that poor Mr. Townsend had been only twice to the house, and he said to Mrs. Penniman that the next time he should come she must ask him to dinner.

He came very soon again, and Mrs. Penniman had of course great pleasure in executing this mission. Morris Townsend accepted her invitation with equal good grace, and the dinner took place a few days later. The Doctor had said to himself, justly enough, that they must not have the young man alone; this would partake too much of the nature of encouragement. So two or three other persons were invited; but Morris Townsend, though he was by no means the ostensible, was the real occasion of the feast. There is every reason to suppose that he desired to make a good impression; and if he fell short of this result, it was not for want of a good deal of intelligent effort. The Doctor talked to him very little during dinner; but he observed him attentively, and after the ladies had gone out he pushed him the wine and asked him several questions. Morris was not a young man who needed to be pressed, and he found quite enough encouragement in the superior quality of the claret. The

Doctor's wine was admirable, and it may be communicated to the reader that while he sipped it Morris reflected that a cellarful of good liquor—there was evidently a cellarful here—would be a most attractive idiosyncrasy in a father-in-law. The Doctor was struck with his appreciative guest; he saw that he was not a commonplace young man. "He has ability," said Catherine's father, "decided ability; he has a very good head if he chooses to use it. And he is uncommonly well turned out; quite the sort of figure that pleases the ladies; but I don't think I like him." The Doctor, however, kept his reflections to himself, and talked to his visitors about foreign lands, concerning which Morris offered him more information than he was ready, as he mentally phrased it, to swallow. Doctor Sloper had travelled but little, and he took the liberty of not believing everything that his talkative guest narrated. He prided himself on being something of a physiognomist; and while the young man, chatting with easy assurance, puffed his cigar and filled his glass again, the Doctor sat with his eyes quietly fixed on his bright, expressive face. "He has the assurance of the devil himself!" said Morris's host; "I don't think I ever saw such assurance. And his powers of invention are most remarkable. He is very knowing; they were not so knowing as that in my time. And a good head, did I say? I should think so—after a bottle of Madeira, and a bottle and a half of claret!"

After dinner Morris Townsend went and stood before Catherine, who was standing before the fire in her red satin dress.

"He doesn't like me—he doesn't like me at all," said the young man.

"Who doesn't like you?" asked Catherine.

"Your father; extraordinary man!"

"I don't see how you know," said Catherine, blushing.

"I feel; I am very quick to feel."

"Perhaps you are mistaken."

"Ah, well! you ask him, and you will see."

"I would rather not ask him, if there is any danger of his saying what you think."

Morris looked at her with an air of mock melancholy.

"It wouldn't give you any pleasure to contradict him?"

"I never contradict him," said Catherine.

"Will you hear me abused without opening your lips in my defence?"

"My father won't abuse you. He doesn't know you enough."

Morris Townsend gave a loud laugh, and Catherine began to blush again.

"I shall never mention you," she said, to take refuge from her confusion.

"That is very well; but it is not quite what I should have liked you to say. I should have liked you to say, 'If my father doesn't think well of you, what does it matter?' "

"Ah, but it would matter; I couldn't say that!" the girl exclaimed.

He looked at her for a moment, smiling a little; and the Doctor, if he had been watching him just then, would have seen a gleam of fine impatience in the sociable softness of his eye. But there was no impatience in his rejoinder—none, at least, save what was expressed in a little appealing sigh. "Ah, well! then I must not give up the hope of bringing him round."

He expressed it more frankly to Mrs. Penniman later in the evening. But before that he sang two or three songs at Catherine's timid request; not that he flattered himself that this would help to bring her father round. He had a sweet, light tenor voice, and, when he had finished, every one made some exclamation—every one, that is, save Catherine, who remained intensely silent. Mrs. Penniman declared that his manner of singing was "most artistic," and Doctor Sloper said it was "very taking—very taking, indeed"; speaking loudly and distinctly, but with a certain dryness.

"He doesn't like me—he doesn't like me at all," said Morris Townsend, addressing the aunt in the same manner as he had done the niece. "He thinks I am all wrong."

Unlike her niece, Mrs. Penniman asked for no explanation. She only smiled very sweetly, as if she understood everything; and, unlike Catherine too, she made no attempt to contradict him. "Pray, what does it matter?" she murmured, softly.

"Ah, you say the right thing!" said Morris, greatly to the gratification of Mrs. Penniman, who prided herself on always saying the right thing.

The Doctor, the next time he saw his sister Elizabeth, let her know that he had made the acquaintance of Lavinia's *protégé*.

"Physically," he said, "he's uncommonly well set up. As an anatomist, it is really a pleasure to me to see such a beautiful *s*tructure; although, if people were all like him, I suppose there would be very little need for doctors."

"Don't you see anything in people but their bones?" Mrs. Almond rejoined. "What do you think of him as a father?"

"As a father? Thank Heaven, I am not his father!"

"No; but you are Catherine's. Lavinia tells me she is in love."

"She must get over it. He is not a gentleman."

"Ah, take care! Remember that he is a branch of the Townsends."

"He is not what I call a gentleman; he has not the soul of one. He is extremely insinuating; but it's a vulgar nature. I saw through it in a minute. He is altogether too familiar;—I hate familiarity. He is a plausible coxcomb."

"Ah, well," said Mrs. Almond, "if you make up your mind so easily, it's a great advantage."

"I don't make up my mind easily. What I tell you is the result of thirty years of observation; and in order to be able to form that judgment in a single evening, I have had to spend a lifetime in study."

"Very possibly you are right. But the thing is for Catherine to see it."

"I will present her with a pair of spectacles!" said the Doctor.

❧ 8 ☙

IF IT were true that she was in love, she was certainly very quiet about it; but the Doctor was of course prepared to admit that her quietness might mean volumes. She had told Morris Townsend that she would not mention him to her father, and she saw no reason to retract this vow of discretion. It was no more than decently civil, of course, that, after having dined in Washington Square, Morris should call there again; and it was no more than natural that, having been kindly received on this occasion, he should continue to present himself. He had had plenty of leisure on his hands; and thirty years ago, in New York, a young man of leisure had reason to be thankful for aids to self-oblivion. Catherine said nothing to her father about these visits, though they had rapidly become the most important, the most absorbing thing in her life. The girl was very happy. She knew not as yet what would come of it; but the present had suddenly grown rich and solemn. If she had been told she was in love, she would have been a good deal surprised; for she had an idea that love was an eager and exacting passion, and her own heart was filled in these days with the impulse of self-effacement and sacrifice. Whenever Morris Townsend had left the house, her imagination projected itself, with all its strength, into the idea of his soon coming back; but if she had been told at such a moment that he would not return for a year, or even that he would never return, she would not have complained or rebelled, but would have humbly accepted the decree, and sought for consolation in thinking over the times she had already seen him, the words he had spoken, the sound of his voice, of his tread, the expression of his face. Love demands certain things as a right; but Catherine had no sense of her rights; she had only a consciousness of immense and unexpected favors. Her very gratitude for these things had hushed itself; for it seemed to her that there would be something of impudence in making a festival of her secret. Her father suspected Morris Townsend's visits, and noted her reserve. She seemed to beg pardon for it; she looked at him constantly in silence, as if she meant to say that she said nothing because she was afraid of irritating him. But the poor girl's dumb eloquence irritated him more than anything else would have done, and he caught himself murmuring more than once that it was a grievous pity his only child was a simpleton. His murmurs, however, were inaudible; and for awhile he said nothing to any one. He would have liked to know exactly how often young Townsend came; but he had determined to ask no questions of the girl herself—to say nothing more to her that would show that he watched her. The Doctor had a great idea of being largely just: he wished to leave his daughter her liberty, and interfere only when the danger should be proved. It was not in his manner to obtain information by indirect methods, and it never even occurred to him to question the servants. As for Lavinia, he hated to talk to her about the matter; she annoyed him with her mock romanticism. But he had to come to this. Mrs. Penniman's convictions as regards the relations of her niece and the clever young visitor, who saved appearances by coming ostensibly for both the ladies—Mrs. Penniman's convictions had passed into a riper and richer phase. There was to be no crudity in Mrs. Penniman's treatment of the situation; she had become as uncommunicative as Catherine herself. She was tasting of the sweets of concealment; she had taken up the line of mystery. "She would be enchanted to be able to prove to herself that she is persecuted," said the Doctor; and when at last he questioned her, he was sure she would contrive to extract from his words a pretext for this belief.

"Be so good as to let me know what is going on in the house," he said to her, in a tone which, under the circumstances, he himself deemed genial.

"Going on, Austin?" Mrs. Penniman exclaimed. "Why, I am sure I don't know. I believe that last night the old gray cat had kittens."

"At her age?" said the Doctor. "The idea is startling—almost shocking. Be so good as to see that they are all drowned. But what else has happened?"

"Ah, the dear little kittens!" cried Mrs. Penniman. "I wouldn't have them drowned for the world!"

Her brother puffed his cigar a few moments in silence. "Your sympathy with kittens, Lavinia," he presently resumed, "arises from a feline element in your own character."

"Cats are very graceful, and very clean," said Mrs. Penniman, smiling.

"And very stealthy. You are the embodiment both of grace and of neatness; but you are wanting in frankness."

"You certainly are not, dear brother."

"I don't pretend to be graceful, though I try to be neat. Why haven't you let me know that Mr. Morris Townsend is coming to the house four times a week?"

Mrs. Penniman lifted her eyebrows. "Four times a week!"

"Three times, then, or five times, if you prefer it. I am away all day, and I see nothing. But when such things happen, you should let me know."

Mrs. Penniman, with her eyebrows still raised, reflected intently. "Dear Austin," she said at last, "I am incapable of betraying a confidence. I would rather suffer anything."

"Never fear; you shall not suffer. To whose confidence is it you allude? Has Catherine made you take a vow of eternal secrecy?"

"By no means. Catherine has not told me as much as she might. She has not been very trustful."

"It is the young man, then, who has made you his confidante? Allow me to say that it is extremely indiscreet of you to form secret alliances with young men; you don't know where they may lead you."

"I don't know what you mean by an alliance," said Mrs. Penniman. "I take a great interest in Mr. Townsend; I won't conceal that. But that's all."

"Under the circumstances, that is quite enough. What is the source of your interest in Mr. Townsend?"

"Why," said Mrs. Penniman, musing, and then breaking into her smile, "that he is so interesting!"

The Doctor felt that he had need of his patience. "And what makes him interesting?—his good looks?"

"His misfortunes, Austin."

"Ah, he has had misfortunes? That, of course, is always interesting. Are you at liberty to mention a few of Mr. Townsend's?"

"I don't know that he would like it," said Mrs. Penniman. "He has told me a great deal about himself—he has told me, in fact, his whole history. But I don't think I ought to repeat those things. He would tell them to you, I am sure, if he thought you would listen to him kindly. With kindness you may do anything with him."

The Doctor gave a laugh. "I shall request him very kindly, then, to leave Catherine alone."

"Ah!" said Mrs. Penniman, shaking her forefinger at her brother, with her little finger turned out, "Catherine has probably said something to him kinder than that!"

"Said that she loved him?—do you mean that?"

Mrs. Penniman fixed her eyes on the floor. "As I tell you, Austin, she doesn't confide in me."

"You have an opinion, I suppose, all the same. It is that I ask you for; though I don't conceal from you that I shall not regard it as conclusive."

Mrs. Penniman's gaze continued to rest on the carpet; but at last she lifted it, and then her brother thought it very expressive. "I think Catherine is very happy; that is all I can say."

"Townsend is trying to marry her—is that what you mean?"

"He is greatly interested in her."

"He finds her such an attractive girl?"

"Catherine has a lovely nature, Austin," said Mrs. Penniman, "and Mr. Townsend has had the intelligence to discover that."

"With a little help from you, I suppose. My dear Lavinia," cried the Doctor, "you are an admirable aunt!"

"So Mr. Townsend says," observed Lavinia, smiling.

"Do you think he is sincere?" asked her brother.

"In saying that?"

"No; that's of course. But in his admiration for Catherine?"

"Deeply sincere. He has said to me the most appreciative, the most charming things about her. He would say them to you, if he were sure you would listen to him—gently."

"I doubt whether I can undertake it. He appears to require a great deal of gentleness."

"He is a sympathetic, sensitive nature," said Mrs. Penniman.

Her brother puffed his cigar again in silence. "These delicate qualities have survived his vicissitudes, eh? All this while you haven't told me about his misfortunes."

"It is a long story," said Mrs. Penniman, "and I regard it as a sacred trust. But I suppose there is no objection to my saying that he has been wild—he frankly confesses that. But he has paid for it."

"That's what has impoverished him, eh?"

"I don't mean simply in money. He is very much alone in the world."

"Do you mean that he has behaved so badly that his friends have given him up?"

"He has had false friends, who have deceived and betrayed him."

"He seems to have some good ones too. He has a devoted sister, and half a dozen nephews and nieces."

Mrs. Penniman was silent a minute. "The nephews and nieces are children, and the sister is not a very attractive person."

"I hope he doesn't abuse her to you," said the Doctor; "for I am told he lives upon her."

"Lives upon her?"

"Lives with her, and does nothing for himself; it is about the same thing."

"He is looking for a position most earnestly," said Mrs. Penniman. "He hopes every day to find one."

"Precisely. He is looking for it here—over there in the front parlor. The position of husband of a weak-minded woman with a large fortune would suit him to perfection!"

Mrs. Penniman was truly amiable, but she now gave signs of

temper. She rose with much animation, and stood for a moment looking at her brother. "My dear Austin," she remarked, "if you regard Catherine as a weak-minded woman you are particularly mistaken!" And with this she moved majestically away.

❧ 9 ❧

IT WAS a regular custom with the family in Washington Square to go and spend Sunday evening at Mrs. Almond's. On the Sunday after the conversation I have just narrated this custom was not intermitted; and on this occasion, toward the middle of the evening, Doctor Sloper found reason to withdraw to the library with his brother-in-law, to talk over a matter of business. He was absent some twenty minutes, and when he came back into the circle, which was enlivened by the presence of several friends of the family, he saw that Morris Townsend had come in, and had lost as little time as possible in seating himself on a small sofa beside Catherine. In the large room, where several different groups had been formed, and the hum of voices and of laughter was loud, these two young persons might confabulate, as the Doctor phrased it to himself, without attracting attention. He saw in a moment, however, that his daughter was painfully conscious of his own observation. She sat motionless, with her eyes bent down, staring at her open fan, deeply flushed, shrinking together as if to minimize the indiscretion of which she confessed herself guilty.

The Doctor almost pitied her. Poor Catherine was not defiant; she had no genius for bravado, and as she felt that her father viewed her companion's attentions with an unsympathizing eye, there was nothing but discomfort for her in the accident of seeming to challenge him. The Doctor felt, indeed, so sorry for her that he turned away, to spare her the sense of being watched; and he was so intelligent a man that, in his thoughts, he rendered a sort of poetic justice to her situation.

"It must be deucedly pleasant for a plain, inanimate girl like that to have a beautiful young fellow come and sit down beside her, and whisper to her that he is her slave—if that is what this one whispers.

No wonder she likes it, and that she thinks me a cruel tyrant; which of course she does, though she is afraid—she hasn't the animation necessary—to admit it to herself. Poor old Catherine!" mused the Doctor; "I verily believe she is capable of defending me when Townsend abuses me!"

And the force of this reflection, for the moment, was such in making him feel the natural opposition between his point of view and that of an infatuated child, that he said to himself that he was perhaps after all taking things too hard, and crying out before he was hurt. He must not condemn Morris Townsend unheard. He had a great aversion to taking things too hard; he thought that half the discomfort and many of the disappointments of life come from it; and for an instant he asked himself whether, possibly, he did not appear ridiculous to this intelligent young man, whose private perception of incongruities he suspected of being keen. At the end of a quarter of an hour Catherine had got rid of him, and Townsend was now standing before the fireplace in conversation with Mrs. Almond.

"We will try him again," said the Doctor. And he crossed the room and joined his sister and her companion, making her a sign that she should leave the young man to him. She presently did so, while Morris looked at him, smiling, without a sign of evasiveness in his affable eye.

"He's amazingly conceited!" thought the Doctor; and then he said, aloud, "I am told you are looking out for a position."

"Oh, a position is more than I should presume to call it," Morris Townsend answered. "That sounds so fine. I would like some quiet work—something to turn an honest penny."

"What sort of thing should you prefer?"

"Do you mean what am I fit for? Very little, I am afraid. I have nothing but my good right arm, as they say in the melodramas."

"You are too modest," said the Doctor. "In addition to your good right arm you have your subtle brain. I know nothing of you but what I see; but I see by your physiognomy that you are extremely intelligent."

"Ah," Townsend murmured. "I don't know what to answer when you say that. You advise me, then, not to despair?"

And he looked at his interlocutor as if the question might have a double meaning. The Doctor caught the look and weighed it a moment before he replied. "I should be very sorry to admit that a robust and well-disposed young man need ever despair. If he doesn't succeed in one thing, he can try another. Only, I should add, he should choose his line with discretion."

"Ah, yes, with discretion," Morris Townsend repeated, sympathetically. "Well, I have been indiscreet, formerly; but I think I have got over it. I am very steady now." And he stood a moment, looking down at his remarkably neat shoes. Then at last, "Were you kindly intending to propose something to my advantage?" he inquired, looking up and smiling.

"D—n his impudence!" the Doctor exclaimed, privately. But in a moment he reflected that he himself had, after all, touched first upon this delicate point, and that his words might have been construed as an offer of assistance. "I have no particular proposal to make," he presently said; "but it occurred to me to let you know that I have you in my mind. Sometimes one hears of opportunities. For instance, should you object to leaving New York—to going to a distance?"

"I am afraid I shouldn't be able to manage that. I must seek my fortune here or nowhere. You see," added Morris Townsend, "I have ties—I have responsibilities here. I have a sister, a widow, from whom I have been separated for a long time, and to whom I am almost everything. I shouldn't like to say to her that I must leave her. She rather depends upon me, you see."

"Ah, that's very proper; family feeling is very proper," said Doctor Sloper. "I often think there is not enough of it in our city. I think I have heard of your sister."

"It is possible, but I rather doubt it; she lives so very quietly."

"As quietly, you mean," the Doctor went on, with a short laugh, "as a lady may do who has several young children."

"Ah, my little nephews and nieces—that's the very point! I am helping to bring them up," said Morris Townsend. "I am a kind of amateur tutor; I give them lessons."

"That's very proper, as I say; but it is hardly a career."

"It won't make my fortune," the young man confessed.

"You must not be too much bent on a fortune," said the Doctor. "But I assure you I will keep you in mind; I won't lose sight of you."

"If my situation becomes desperate I shall perhaps take the liberty of reminding you," Morris rejoined, raising his voice a little, with a brighter smile, as his interlocutor turned away.

Before he left the house the Doctor had a few words with Mrs. Almond.

"I should like to see his sister," he said. "What do you call her—Mrs. Montgomery? I should like to have a little talk with her."

"I will try and manage it," Mrs. Almond responded. "I will take the first opportunity of inviting her, and you shall come and meet her; unless, indeed," Mrs. Almond added, "she first takes it into her head to be sick and to send for you."

"Ah no, not that; she must have trouble enough without that. But it would have its advantages, for then I should see the children. I should like very much to see the children."

"You are very thorough. Do you want to catechise them about their uncle?"

"Precisely. Their uncle tells me he has charge of their education, that he saves their mother the expense of school-bills. I should like to ask them a few questions in the commoner branches."

"He certainly has not the cut of a school-master," Mrs. Almond said to herself a short time afterward, as she saw Morris Townsend in a corner bending over her niece, who was seated.

And there was, indeed, nothing in the young man's discourse at this moment that savored of the pedagogue.

"Will you meet me somewhere to-morrow or next day?" he said, in a low tone, to Catherine.

"Meet you?" she asked, lifting her frightened eyes.

"I have something particular to say to you—very particular."

"Can't you come to the house? Can't you say it there?"

Townsend shook his head gloomily. "I can't enter your doors again."

"Oh, Mr. Townsend!" murmured Catherine. She trembled as she wondered what had happened—whether her father had forbidden it.

"I can't, in self-respect," said the young man. "Your father has insulted me."

"Insulted you?"

"He has taunted me with my poverty."

"Oh, you are mistaken—you misunderstood him!" Catherine spoke with energy, getting up from her chair.

"Perhaps I am too proud—too sensitive. But would you have me otherwise?" he asked, tenderly.

"Where my father is concerned, you must not be sure. He is full of goodness," said Catherine.

"He laughed at me for having no position. I took it quietly; but only because he belongs to you."

"I don't know," said Catherine—"I don't know what he thinks. I am sure he means to be kind. You must not be too proud."

"I will be proud only of you," Morris answered. "Will you meet me in the Square in the afternoon?"

A great blush on Catherine's part had been the answer to the declaration I have just quoted. She turned away, heedless of his question.

"Will you meet me?" he repeated. "It is very quiet there—no one need see us—toward dusk."

"It is you who are unkind, it is you who laugh, when you say such things as that."

"My dear girl!" the young man murmured.

"You know how little there is in me to be proud of. I am ugly and stupid."

Morris greeted this remark with an ardent murmur, in which she recognized nothing articulate but an assurance that she was his own dearest.

But she went on. "I am not even—I am not even—" And she paused a moment.

"You are not what?"

"I am not even brave."

"Ah, then, if you are afraid, what shall we do?"

She hesitated awhile; then at last—"You must come to the house," she said; "I am not afraid of that."

"I would rather it were in the Square," the young man urged. "You know how empty it is, often. No one will see us."

"I don't care who sees us. But leave me now."

He left her resignedly; he had got what he wanted. Fortunately he was ignorant that half an hour later, going home with her father, and feeling him near, the poor girl, in spite of her sudden declaration of courage, began to tremble again. Her father said nothing; but she had an idea his eyes were fixed upon her in the darkness. Mrs. Penniman also was silent; Morris Townsend had told her that her niece preferred, unromantically, an interview in a chintz-covered parlor to a sentimental tryst beside a fountain sheeted with dead leaves, and she was lost in wonderment at the oddity—almost the perversity—of the choice.

✣ 10 ✣

CATHERINE received the young man the next day on the ground she had chosen—amidst the chaste upholstery of a New York drawing-room furnished in the fashion of fifty years ago. Morris had swallowed his pride, and made the effort necessary to cross the threshold of her too derisive parent—an act of magnanimity which could not fail to render him doubly interesting.

"We must settle something—we must take a line," he declared, passing his hand through his hair and giving a glance at the long, narrow mirror which adorned the space between the two windows, and which had at its base a little gilded bracket covered by a thin slab of white marble, supporting in its turn a backgammon-board folded together in the shape of two volumes—two shining folios inscribed, in greenish-gilt letters, *History of England*. If Morris had been pleased to decribe the master of the house as a heartless scoffer, it is because he thought him too much on his guard, and this was the easiest way to express his own dissatisfaction—a dissatisfaction which he had made a point of concealing from the Doctor. It will probably seem to the reader, however, that the Doctor's vigilance was by no means excessive, and that these two young people had an open field. Their intimacy was now considerable, and it may appear that, for a shrinking and retiring person, our heroine had been liberal of her favors. The young man, within a few days, had made her listen to things for which she had not supposed that she was prepared; having a lively foreboding of difficulties, he proceeded to gain as much ground as possible in the present. He remembered that fortune favors the brave, and even if he had forgotten it, Mrs.

Penniman would have remembered it for him. Mrs. Penniman delighted of all things in a drama, and she flattered herself that a drama would now be enacted. Combining as she did the zeal of the prompter with the impatience of the spectator, she had long since done her utmost to pull up the curtain. She, too, expected to figure in the performance—to be the confidante, the Chorus, to speak the epilogue. It may even be said that there were times when she lost sight altogether of the modest heroine of the play in the contemplation of certain great scenes which would naturally occur between the hero and herself.

What Morris had told Catherine at last was simply that he loved her, or rather adored her. Virtually, he had made known as much already—his visits had been a series of eloquent intimations of it. But now he had affirmed it in lover's vows, and, as a memorable sign of it, he had passed his arm round the girl's waist and taken a kiss. This happy certitude had come sooner than Catherine expected, and she had regarded it, very naturally, as a priceless treasure. It may even be doubted whether she had ever definitely expected to possess it; she had not been waiting for it, and she had never said to herself that at a given moment it must come. As I have tried to explain, she was not eager and exacting; she took what was given her from day to day; and if the delightful custom of her lover's visits, which yielded her a happiness in which confidence and timidity were strangely blended, had suddenly come to an end, she would not only not have spoken of herself as one of the forsaken, but she would not have thought of herself as one of the disappointed. After Morris had kissed her, the last time he was with her, as a ripe assurance of his devotion, she begged him to go away, to leave her alone, to let her think. Morris went away, taking another kiss first. But Catherine's meditations had lacked a certain coherence. She felt his kisses on her lips and on her cheeks for a long time afterward; the sensation was rather an obstacle than an aid to reflection. She would have liked to see her situation all clearly before her, to make up her mind what she should do if, as she feared, her father should tell her that he disapproved of Morris Townsend. But all that she could see with any vividness was that it was terribly strange that any one should disapprove of him; that there must in that case be some mistake, some mystery, which in a little while would be set at rest. She put off deciding and choosing; before the vision of a conflict with her father she dropped her eyes and sat motionless, holding her breath and waiting. It made her heart beat; it was intensely painful. When Morris kissed her and said these things—that also made her heart beat; but this was worse, and it frightened her. Nevertheless, to-day, when the young man spoke of settling something, taking a line, she felt that it was the truth, and she answered very simply and without hesitating.

"We must do our duty," she said; "we must speak to my father. I will do it to-night; you must do it to-morrow."

"It is very good of you to do it first," Morris answered. "The young man—the happy lover—generally does that. But just as you please."

It pleased Catherine to think that she should be brave for his sake, and in her satisfaction she even gave a little smile. "Women have more tact," she said; "they ought to do it first. They are more conciliating; they can persuade better."

"You will need all your powers of persuasion. But, after all," Morris added, "you are irresistible."

"Please don't speak that way—and promise me this: To-morrow, when you talk with father, you will be very gentle and respectful."

"As much so as possible," Morris promised. "It won't be much use, but I shall try. I certainly would rather have you easily than have to fight for you."

"Don't talk about fighting; we shall not fight."

"Ah, we must be prepared," Morris rejoined; "you especially, because for you it must come hardest. Do you know the first thing your father will say to you?"

"No, Morris; please tell me."

"He will tell you I am mercenary."

"Mercenary!"

"It's a big word, but it means a low thing. It means that I am after your money."

"Oh!" murmured Catherine, softly.

The exclamation was so deprecating and touching that Morris indulged in another little demonstration of affection. "But he will be sure to say it," he added.

"It will be easy to be prepared for that," Catherine said. "I shall simply say that he is mistaken—that other men may be that way, but that you are not."

"You must make a great point of that, for it will be his own great point."

Catherine looked at her lover a minute, and then she said, "I shall persuade him. But I am glad we shall be rich," she added.

Morris turned away, looking into the crown of his hat. "No it's a misfortune," he said at last. "It is from that our difficulty will come."

"Well, if it is the worst misfortune, we are not so unhappy. Many people would not think it so bad. I will persuade him, and after that we shall be very glad we have money."

Morris Townsend listened to this robust logic in silence. "I will leave my defence to you; it's a charge that a man has to stoop to defend himself from."

Catherine on her side was silent for awhile; she was looking at him while he looked, with a good deal of fixedness, out of the window. "Morris," she said, abruptly, "are you very sure you love me?"

He turned round, and in a moment he was bending over her. "My own dearest, can you doubt it?"

"I have only known it five days," she said; "but now it seems to me as if I could never do without it."

"You will never be called upon to try." And he gave a little tender, reassuring laugh. Then, in a moment, he added, "There is something you must tell me, too." She had closed her eyes after the last words she uttered, and kept them closed; and at this she nodded her head, without opening them. "You must tell me," he went on, "that if your father is dead against me, if he absolutely forbids our marriage, you will still be faithful."

Catherine opened her eyes, gazing at him, and she could give no better promise than what he read there.

"You will cleave to me?" said Morris. "You know you are your own mistress—you are of age."

"Ah, Morris!" she murmured, for all answer; or rather not for all, for she put her hand into his own. He kept it awhile, and presently he kissed her again. This is all that need be recorded of their conversation; but Mrs. Penniman, if she had been present, would probably have admitted that it was as well it had not taken place beside the fountain in Washington Square.

✤ 11 ✤

CATHERINE listened for her father when he came in that evening, and she heard him go to his study. She sat quiet, though her heart was beating fast, for nearly half an hour; then she went and knocked at his door—a ceremony without which she never crossed the threshold of his apartment. On entering it now, she found him in his chair beside the fire, entertaining himself with a cigar and the evening paper.

"I have something to say to you," she began very gently; and she sat down in the first place that offered.

"I shall be very happy to hear it, my dear," said her father. He waited—waited, looking at her—while she stared, in a long silence, at the fire. He was curious and impatient, for he was sure she was going to speak of Morris Townsend; but he let her take her own time, for he was determined to be very mild.

"I am engaged to be married!" Catherine announced at last, still staring at the fire.

The Doctor was startled; the accomplished fact was more than he had expected; but he betrayed no surprise. "You do right to tell me," he simply said. "And who is the happy mortal whom you have honored with your choice?"

"Mr. Morris Townsend." And as she pronounced her lover's name Catherine looked at him. What she saw was her father's still gray eye and his clear-cut definite smile. She contemplated these objects for a moment, and then she looked aback at the fire; it was much warmer.

"When was this arrangement made?" the Doctor asked.

"This afternoon—two hours ago."

"Was Mr. Townsend here?"

"Yes, father; in the front-parlor." She was very glad that she was not obliged to tell him that the ceremony of their betrothal had taken place out there under the bare ailanthus-trees.

"Is it serious?" said the Doctor.

"Very serious, father."

Her father was silent a moment. "Mr. Townsend ought to have told me."

"He means to tell you to-morrow."

"After I know all about it from you? He ought to have told me before. Does he think I didn't care, because I left you so much liberty?"

"Oh no," said Catherine; "he knew you would care. And we have been so much obliged to you for—for the liberty."

The Doctor gave a short laugh. "You might have made a better use of it, Catherine."

"Please don't say that, father!" the girl urged, softly, fixing her dull and gentle eyes upon him.

He puffed his cigar awhile, meditatively. "You have gone very fast," he said, at last.

"Yes," Catherine answered, simply; "I think we have."

Her father glanced at her an instant, removing his eyes from the fire. "I don't wonder Mr. Townsend likes you; you are so simple and so good."

"I don't know why it is; but he *does* like me. I am sure of that."

"And you are very fond of Mr. Townsend?"

"I like him very much, of course, or I shouldn't consent to marry him."

"But you have known him a very short time, my dear."

"Oh," said Catherine, with some eagerness, "it doesn't take long to like a person—when once you begin."

"You must have begun very quickly. Was it the first time you saw him—that night at your aunt's party?"

"I don't know, father," the girl answered. "I can't tell you about that."

"Of course; that's your own affair. You will have observed that I have acted on that principle. I have not interfered; I have left you your liberty; I have remembered that you are no longer a little girl—that you have arrived at years of discretion."

"I feel very old—and very wise," said Catherine, smiling faintly.

"I am afraid that before long you will feel older and wiser yet. I don't like your engagement."

"Ah!" Catherine exclaimed, softly, getting up from her chair.

"No, my dear. I am sorry to give you pain; but I don't like it. You should have consulted me before you settled it. I have been too easy with you, and I feel as if you had taken advantage of my indulgence. Most decidedly you should have spoken to me first."

Catherine hesitated a moment, and then—"It was because I was afraid you wouldn't like it," she confessed.

"Ah, there it is! You had a bad conscience."

"No, I have not a bad conscience, father!" the girl cried out, with considerable energy. "Please don't accuse me of anything so dreadful!" These words, in fact, represented to her imagination something very terrible indeed, something base and cruel, which she associated with malefactors and prisoners. "It was because I was afraid—afraid—" she went on.

"If you were afraid, it was because you had been foolish."

"I was afraid you didn't like Mr. Townsend."

"You were quite right. I don't like him."

"Dear father, you don't know him," said Catherine, in a voice so timidly argumentative that it might have touched him.

"Very true; I don't know him intimately. But I know him enough; I have my impression of him. You don't know him either."

She stood before the fire with her hands lightly clasped in front of her; and her father, leaning back in his chair and looking up at her, made this remark with a placidity that might have been irritating.

I doubt, however, whether Catherine was irritated, though she broke into a vehement protest. "I don't know him?" she cried. "Why, I know him—better than I have ever known any one!"

"You know a part of him—what he has chosen to show you. But you don't know the rest."

"The rest? What is the rest?"

"Whatever it may be, there is sure to be plenty of it."

"I know what you mean," said Catherine, remembering how Morris had forewarned her. "You mean that he is mercenary."

Her father looked up at her still, with his cold, quiet, reasonable eye. "If I meant it, my dear, I should say it! But there is an error I wish particularly to avoid—that of rendering Mr. Townsend more interesting to you by saying hard things about him."

"I won't think them hard if they are true," said Catherine.

"If you don't, you will be a remarkably sensible young woman!"

"They will be your reasons, at any rate, and you will want me to hear your reasons."

The Doctor smiled a little. "Very true. You have a perfect right to ask for them." And he puffed his cigar a few moments. "Very well, then; without accusing Mr. Townsend of being in love only with your fortune—and with the fortune that you justly expect—I will say that there is every reason to suppose that these good things have entered into his calculation more largely than a tender solicitude for your happiness strictly requires. There is, of course, nothing impossible in an intelligent young man entertaining a disinterested affection for you. You are an honest, amiable girl, and an intelligent young man might easily find it out. But the principal thing that we know about this young man—who is, indeed, very intelligent—leads us to suppose that, however much he may value your personal merits, he values your money more. The principal thing we know about him is that he has led a life of dissipation, and has spent a fortune of his own in doing so. That is enough for me, my dear. I wish you to marry a young man with other antecedents—a young man who could give positive guarantees. If Morris Townsend has spent his own fortune in amusing himself, there is every reason to believe that he would spend yours."

The Doctor delivered himself of these remarks slowly, deliberately, with occasional pauses and prolongations of accent, which made no great allowance for poor Catherine's suspense as to his conclusion. She sat down at last, with her head bent and her eyes still fixed upon him; and strangely enough—I hardly know how to tell it —even while she felt that what he said went so terribly against her, she admitted his neatness and nobleness of expression. There was something hopeless and oppressive in having to argue with her father; but she too, on her side, must try to be clear. He was so quiet; he was not at all angry; and she, too, must be quiet. But her very effort to be quiet made her tremble.

"That is not the principal thing we know about him," she said; and there was a touch of her tremor in her voice. "There are other things—many other things. He has very high abilities—he wants so much to do something. He is kind, and generous, and true," said poor Catherine, who had not suspected hitherto the resources of her eloquence. "And his fortune—his fortune that he spent—was very small."

"All the more reason he shouldn't have spent it," cried the Doctor, getting up with a laugh. Then, as Catherine, who had also risen to her feet again, stood there in her rather angular earnestness, wishing so much and expressing so little, he drew her toward him, and kissed her. "You won't think me cruel?" he said, holding her a moment.

This question was not reassuring; it seemed to Catherine, on the contrary, to suggest possibilities which made her feel sick. But she answered coherently enough, "No, dear father; because if you knew how I feel—and you must know, you know everything—you would be so kind, so gentle."

"Yes, I think I know how you feel," the Doctor said. "I will be very kind—be sure of that. And I will see Mr. Townsend to-morrow. Meanwhile, and for the present, be so good as to mention to no one that you are engaged."

12

ON THE morrow, in the afternoon, he stayed at home, awaiting Mr. Townsend's call—a proceeding by which it appeared to him (justly perhaps, for he was a very busy man) that he paid Catherine's suitor great honor, and gave both these young people so much the less to complain of. Morris presented himself with a countenance sufficiently serene—he appeared to have forgotten the "insult" for which he had solicited Catherine's sympathy two evenings before—and Doctor Sloper lost no time in letting him know that he had been prepared for his visit.

"Catherine told me yesterday what has been going on between you," he said. "You must allow me to say that it would have been becoming of you to give me notice of your intentions before they had gone so far."

"I should have done so," Morris answered, "if you had not had so much the appearance of leaving your daughter at liberty. She seems to be quite her own mistress."

"Literally, she is. But she has not emancipated herself morally quite so far, I trust, as to choose a husband without consulting me. I have left her at liberty, but I have not been in the least indifferent. The truth is, that your little affair has come to a head with a rapidity that surprises me. It was only the other day that Catherine made your acquaintance."

"It was not long ago, certainly," said Morris, with great gravity. "I admit that we have not been slow to—to arrive at an understanding. But that was very natural, from the moment we were sure of ourselves—and of each other. My interest in Miss Sloper began the first time I saw her."

"Did it not by chance precede your first meeting?" the Doctor asked.

Morris looked at him an instant. "I certainly had already heard that she was a charming girl."

"A charming girl—that's what you think of her?"

"Assuredly. Otherwise I should not be sitting here."

The Doctor meditated a moment. "My dear young man," he said at last, "you must be very susceptible. As Catherine's father I have, I trust, a just and tender appreciation of her many good qualities; but I don't mind telling you that I have never thought of her as a charming girl, and never suspected any one else to do so."

Morris Townsend received this statement with a smile that was not wholly devoid of deference. "I don't know what I might think of her if I were her father. I can't put myself in that place. I speak from my own point of view."

"You speak very well," said the Doctor; "but that is not all that is necessary. I told Catherine yesterday that I disapproved of her engagement."

"She let me know as much, and I was very sorry to hear it. I am greatly disappointed." And Morris sat in silence awhile, looking at the floor.

"Did you really expect I would say I was delighted, and throw my daughter into your arms?"

"Oh no; I had an idea you didn't like me."

"What gave you the idea?"

"The fact that I am poor."

"That has a harsh sound," said the Doctor, "but it is about the truth—speaking of you strictly as a son-in-law. Your absence of means, of a profession, of visible resources or prospects, places you in a category from which it would be imprudent for me to select a husband for my daughter, who is a weak young woman with a large fortune. In any other capacity I am perfectly prepared to like you. As a son-in-law, I abominate you."

Morris Townsend listened respectfully. "I don't think Miss Sloper is a weak woman," he presently said.

"Of course you must defend her—it's the least you can do. But I have known my child twenty years, and you have known her six weeks. Even if she were not weak, however, you would still be a penniless man."

"Ah, yes; that is *my* weakness! And therefore, you mean, I am mercenary—I only want your daughter's money."

"I don't say that. I am not obliged to say it; and to say it, save under stress of compulsion, would be very bad taste. I say simply that you belong to the wrong category."

"But your daughter doesn't marry a category," Townsend urged, with his handsome smile. "She marries an individual—an individual whom she is so good as to say she loves."

"An individual who offers so little in return."

"Is it possible to offer more than the most tender affection and a life-long devotion?" the young man demanded.

"It depends how we take it. It is possible to offer a few other things besides, and not only is it possible, but it is the custom. A life-long devotion is measured after the fact; and meanwhile it is usual in these cases to give a few material securities. What are yours? A very handsome face and figure, and a very good manner. They are excellent as far as they go, but they don't go far enough."

"There is one thing you should add to them," said Morris—"the word of a gentleman."

"The word of a gentleman that you will always love Catherine? You must be a fine gentleman to be sure of that."

"The word of a gentleman that I am not mercenary; that my affection for Miss Sloper is as pure and disinterested a sentiment as was ever lodged in a human breast. I care no more for her fortune than for the ashes in that grate."

"I take note—I take note," said the Doctor. "But, having done so, I turn to our category again. Even with that solemn vow on your lips, you take your place in it. There is nothing against you but an accident, if you will; but, with my thirty years' medical practice, I have seen that accidents may have far-reaching consequences."

Morris smoothed his hat—it was already remarkably glossy—and continued to display a self-control which, as the Doctor was obliged to admit, was extremely creditable to him. But his disappointment was evidently keen.

"Is there nothing I can do to make you believe in me?"

"If there were, I should be sorry to suggest it, for—don't you see?—I don't want to believe in you," said the Doctor, smiling.

"I would go and dig in the fields."

"That would be foolish."

"I will take the first work that offers to-morrow."

"Do so by all means—but for your own sake, not for mine."

"I see; you think I am an idler!" Morris exclaimed, a little too much in the tone of a man who has made a discovery. But he saw his error immediately, and blushed.

"It doesn't matter what I think, when once I have told you I don't think of you as a son-in-law."

But Morris persisted: "You think I would squander her money?"

The Doctor smiled. "It doesn't matter, as I say; but I plead guilty to that."

"That's because I spent my own, I suppose," said Morris. "I frankly confess that. I have been wild; I have been foolish. I will tell you every crazy thing I ever did, if you like. There were some great follies among the number—I have never concealed that. But I have sown my wild-oats. Isn't there some proverb about a reformed rake? I was not a rake, but I assure you I have reformed. It is better to have amused one's self for awhile and have done with it. Your daughter would never care for a milksop; and I will take the liberty of saying that you would like one quite as little. Besides, between my money and hers there is a great difference. I spent my own; it was because it was my own that I spent it. And I made no debts; when it was gone I stopped. I don't owe a penny in the world."

"Allow me to inquire what you are living on now—though I admit," the Doctor added, "that the question, on my part, is inconsistent."

"I am living on the remnants of my property," said Morris Townsend.

"Thank you," the Doctor gravely replied.

Yes, certainly, Morris's self-control was laudable. "Even admitting I attach an undue importance to Miss Sloper's fortune," he went on, "would not that be in itself an assurance that I would take good care of it?"

"That you should take too much care would be quite as bad as that you should take too little. Catherine might suffer as much by your economy as by your extravagance."

"I think you are very unjust!" The young man made this declaration decently, civilly, without violence.

"It is your privilege to think so, and I surrender my reputation to you! I certainly don't flatter myself, I gratify you."

"Don't you care a little to gratify your daughter? Do you enjoy the idea of making her miserable?"

"I am perfectly resigned to her thinking me a tyrant for a twelve-month."

"For a twelve-month!" exclaimed Morris, with a laugh.

"For a lifetime, then. She may as well be miserable in that way as in the other."

Here at last Morris lost his temper. "Ah, you are not polite, sir!" he cried.

"You push me to it—you argue too much."

"I have a great deal at stake."

"Well, whatever it is," said the Doctor, "you have lost it."

"Are you sure of that?" asked Morris; "are you sure your daughter will give me up?"

"I mean, of course, you have lost it as far as I am concerned. As for Catherine's giving you up—no, I am not sure of it. But as I shall strongly recommend it, as I have a great fund of respect and affection in my daughter's mind to draw upon, and as she has the sentiment of duty developed in a very high degree, I think it extremely possible."

Morris Townsend began to smooth his hat again. "I, too, have a fund of affection to draw upon," he observed, at last.

The Doctor at this point showed his own first symptoms of irritation. "Do you mean to defy me?"

"Call it what you please, sir. I mean not to give your daughter up."

The Doctor shook his head. "I haven't the least fear of your pining away your life. You are made to enjoy it."

Morris gave a laugh. "Your opposition to my marriage is all the more cruel, then. Do you intend to forbid your daughter to see me again?"

"She is past the age at which people are forbidden, and I am not a father in an old-fashioned novel. But I shall strongly urge her to break with you."

"I don't think she will," said Morris Townsend.

"Perhaps not; but I shall have done what I could."

"She has gone too far—" Morris went on.

"To retreat? Then let her stop where she is."

"Too far to stop, I mean."

The Doctor looked at him a moment; Morris had his hand on the door. "There is a great deal of impertinence in your saying it."

"I will say no more, sir," Morris answered; and, making his bow, he left the room.

13

IT MAY be thought the Doctor was too positive, and Mrs. Almond intimated as much. But, as he said, he had his impression; it seemed to him sufficient, and he had no wish to modify it. He had passed his life in estimating people (it was part of the medical trade), and in nineteen cases out of twenty he was right.

"Perhaps Mr. Townsend is the twentieth case," said Mrs. Almond.

"Perhaps he is, though he doesn't look to me at all like a twentieth case. But I will give him the benefit of the doubt, and, to make sure, I will go and talk with Mrs. Montgomery. She will almost certainly tell me I have done right; but it is just possible that she will prove to me that I have made the greatest mistake of my life. If she does, I will beg Mr. Townsend's pardon. You needn't invite her to meet me, as you kindly proposed; I will write her a frank letter, telling her how matters stand, and asking leave to come and see her."

"I am afraid the frankness will be chiefly on your part. The poor little woman will stand up for her brother, whatever he may be."

"Whatever he may be! I doubt that. People are not always so fond of their brothers."

"Ah," said Mrs. Almond, "when it's a question of thirty thousand a year coming into a family—"

"If she stands up for him on account of the money, she will be a humbug. If she is a humbug, I shall see it. If I see it, I won't waste time with her."

"She is not a humbug—she is an exemplary woman. She will not wish to play her brother a trick simply because he is selfish."

"If she is worth talking to, she will sooner play him a trick than that he should play Catherine one. Has she seen Catherine, by-the-way—does she know her?"

"Not to my knowledge. Mr. Townsend can have had no particular interest in bringing them together."

"If she is an exemplary woman, no. But we shall see to what extent she answers your description."

"I shall be curious to hear her description of you," said Mrs. Almond with a laugh. "And, meanwhile, how is Catherine taking it?"

"As she takes everything—as a matter of course."

"Doesn't she make a noise? Hasn't she made a scene?"

"She is not scenic."

"I thought a lovelorn maiden was always scenic."

"A ridiculous widow is more so. Lavinia has made me a speech; she thinks me very arbitrary."

"She has a talent for being in the wrong," said Mrs. Almond. "But I am very sorry for Catherine, all the same."

"So am I. But she will get over it."

"You believe she will give him up?"

"I count upon it. She has had such an admiration for her father."

"Oh, we know all about that. But it only makes me pity her the more. It makes her dilemma the more painful, and the effort of choosing between you and her lover almost impossible."

"If she can't choose, all the better."

"Yes; but he will stand there entreating her to choose, and Lavinia will pull on that side."

"I am glad she is not on my side; she is capable of ruining an excellent cause. The day Lavinia gets into your boat it capsizes. But she had better be careful," said the Doctor. "I will have no treason in my house."

"I suspect she will be careful; for she is at bottom very much afraid of you."

"They are both afraid of me, harmless as I am," the Doctor answered. "And it is on that that I build—on the salutary terror I inspire."

14

HE WROTE his frank letter to Mrs. Montgomery, who punctually answered it, mentioning an hour at which he might present himself in the Second Avenue. She lived in a neat little house of red brick, which had been freshly painted, with the edges of the bricks very sharply marked out in white. It has now disappeared, with its companions, to make room for a row of structures more majestic. There were green shutters upon the windows without slats, but pierced with little holes, arranged in groups; and before the house was a diminutive "yard," ornamented with a bush of mysterious character, and surrounded by a low wooden paling, painted in the same green as the shutters. The place looked like a magnified baby-house, and might have been taken down from a shelf in a toy-shop. Doctor Sloper, when he went to call, said to himself, as he glanced at the objects I have enumerated, that Mrs. Montgomery was evidently a thrifty and self-respecting little person—the modest proportions of her dwelling seemed to indicate that she was of small stature—who took a virtuous satisfaction in keeping herself tidy, and had resolved that, since she might not be splendid, she would at least be immaculate. She received him in a little parlor, which was precisely the parlor he had expected: a small unspeckled bower, ornamented with a desultory foliage of tissue-paper, and with clusters of glass drops, amidst which—to carry out the analogy—the temperature of the leafy season was maintained by means of a cast-iron stove, emitting a dry blue flame, and smelling strongly of varnish. The walls were embellished with engravings swathed in pink gauze, and the tables ornamented with volumes of extracts from the poets, usually bound in black cloth stamped with florid designs in jaundiced gilt. The Doctor had time to take cognizance of these details; for Mrs. Montgomery, whose conduct he pronounced under the circumstances inexcusable, kept him waiting some ten minutes before she appeared. At last, however, she rustled in, smoothing down a stiff poplin dress, with a little frightened flush in a gracefully rounded cheek.

She was a small, plump, fair woman, with a bright, clear eye, and an extraordinary air of neatness and briskness. But these qualities were evidently combined with an unaffected humility, and the Doctor gave her his esteem as soon as he had looked at her. A brave little person, with lively perceptions, and yet a disbelief in her own talent for social, as distinguished from practical, affairs—this was his rapid mental *résumé* of Mrs. Montgomery; who, as he saw, was flattered by what she regarded as the honor of his visit. Mrs. Montgomery, in her little red house in the Second Avenue, was a person for whom Dr. Sloper was one of the great men—one of the fine gentlemen of New York; and while she fixed her agitated eyes upon him, while she clasped her mittened hands together in her glossy poplin lap, she had the appearance of saying to herself that he quite answered her idea of what a distinguished guest would naturally be. She apologized for being late; but he interrupted her.

"It doesn't matter," he said; "for while I sat here I had time to think over what I wish to say to you, and to make up my mind how to begin."

"Oh, do begin!" murmured Mrs. Montgomery.

"It is not so easy," said the Doctor, smiling. "You will have gathered from my letter that I wish to ask you a few questions, and you may not find it very comfortable to answer them."

"Yes; I have thought what I should say. It is not very easy."

"But you must understand my situation—my state of mind. Your brother wishes to marry my daughter, and I wish to find out what sort of a young man he is. A good way to do so seemed to be to come and ask you, which I have proceeded to do."

Mrs. Montgomery evidently took the situation very seriously; she was in a state of extreme moral concentration. She kept her pretty eyes, which were illumined by a sort of brilliant modesty, attached to his own countenance, and evidently paid the most earnest attention to each of his words. Her expression indicated that she thought his idea of coming to see her a very superior conception, but that she was really afraid to have opinions on strange subjects.

"I am extremely glad to see you," she said, in a tone which seemed to admit, at the same time, that this had nothing to do with the question.

The Doctor took advantage of this admission. "I didn't come to see you for your pleasure; I came to make you say disagreeable things—and you can't like that. What sort of a gentleman is your brother?"

Mrs. Montgomery's illuminated gaze grew vague, and began to wander. She smiled a little, and for some time made no answer, so that the Doctor at last became impatient. And her answer, when it came, was not satisfactory. "It is difficult to talk about one's brother."

"Not when one is fond of him, and when one has plenty of good to say."

"Yes, even then, when a good deal depends on it," said Mrs. Montgomery.

"Nothing depends on it for you."

"I mean for—for—" and she hesitated.

"For your brother himself. I see."

"I mean for Miss Sloper," said Mrs. Montgomery.

The Doctor liked this; it had the accent of sincerity. "Exactly; that's the point. If my poor girl should marry your brother, everything—as regards her happiness—would depend on his being a good fellow. She is the best creature in the world, and she could never do him a grain of injury. He, on the other hand, if he should not be all that we desire, might make her very miserable. That is why I want you to throw some light upon his character, you know. Of course, you are not bound to do it. My daughter, whom you have never seen, is nothing to you; and I, possibly, am only an indiscreet and impertinent old man. It is perfectly open to you to tell me that my visit is in very bad taste, and that I had better go about my business. But I don't think you will do this; because I think we shall interest you—my poor girl and I. I am sure that if you were to see Catherine she would interest you very much. I don't mean because she is interesting in the usual sense of the word, but because you would feel sorry for her. She is so soft, so simple-minded, she would be such an easy victim! A bad husband would have remarkable facilities for making her miserable; for she would have neither the intelligence nor the resolution to get the better of him, and yet she would have an exaggerated power of suffering. I see," added the Doctor, with his most insinuating, his most professional laugh, "you are already interested."

"I have been interested from the moment he told me he was engaged," said Mrs. Montgomery.

"Ah! he says that—he calls it an engagement?"

"Oh, he has told me you didn't like it."

"Did he tell you that I don't like *him?*"

"Yes, he told me that too. I said I couldn't help it," added Mrs. Montgomery.

"Of course you can't. But what you can do is to tell me I am right—to give me an attestation, as it were." And the Doctor accompanied this remark with another professional smile.

Mrs. Montgomery, however, smiled not at all; it was obvious that she could not take the humorous view of his appeal. "That is a good deal to ask," she said, at last.

"There can be no doubt of that; and I must, in conscience, remind you of the advantages a young man marrying my daughter would enjoy. She has an income of ten thousand dollars in her own right, left her by her mother; if she marries a husband I approve, she will come into almost twice as much more at my death."

Mrs. Montgomery listened in great earnestness to this splendid financial statement; she had never heard thousands of dollars so familiarly talked about. She flushed a little with excitement. "Your daughter will be immensely rich," she said, softly.

"Precisely—that's the bother of it."

"And if Morris should marry her, he—he—" And she hesitated, timidly.

"He would be master of all that money? By no means. He would be master of the ten thousand a year that she has from her mother; but I should leave every penny of my own fortune, earned in the laborious exercise of my profession, to my nephews and nieces."

Mrs. Montgomery dropped her eyes at this, and sat for some time gazing at the straw matting which covered her floor.

"I suppose it seems to you," said the Doctor, laughing, "that in so doing I should play your brother a very shabby trick."

"Not at all. That is too much money to get possession of so easily by marrying. I don't think it would be right."

"It's right to get all one can. But in this case your brother wouldn't be able. If Catherine marries without my consent, she doesn't get a penny from my own pocket."

"Is that certain?" asked Mrs. Montgomery, looking up.

"As certain as that I sit here."

"Even if she should pine away?"

"Even if she should pine to a shadow, which isn't probable."

"Does Morris know this?"

"I shall be most happy to inform him," the Doctor exclaimed.

Mrs. Montgomery resumed her meditations; and her visitor, who was prepared to give time to the affair, asked himself whether, in spite of her little conscientious air, she was not playing into her brother's hands. At the same time he was half ashamed of the ordeal to which he had subjected her, and was touched by the gentleness with which she bore it. "If she were a humbug," he said, "she would get angry, unless she be very deep indeed. It is not probable that she is as deep as that."

"What makes you dislike Morris so much?" she presently asked, emerging from her reflections.

"I don't dislike him in the least as a friend, as a companion. He seems to me a charming fellow, and I think he would be excellent company. I dislike him exclusively as a son-in-law. If the only office of a son-in-law were to dine at the paternal table, I should set a high value upon your brother: he dines capitally. But that is a small part of his function, which, in general, is to be a protector and care-taker of my child, who is singularly ill-adapted to take care of herself. It is there that he doesn't satisfy me. I confess I have nothing but my impression to go by; but I am in the habit of trusting my impression. Of course you are at liberty to contradict it flat. He strikes me as selfish and shallow."

Mrs. Montgomery's eyes expanded a little, and the Doctor fancied he saw the light of admiration in them. "I wonder you have discovered he is selfish," she exclaimed.

"Do you think he hides it so well?"

"Very well indeed," said Mrs. Montgomery. "And I think we are all rather selfish," she added, quickly.

"I think so too; but I have seen people hide it better than he. You see I am helped by a habit I have of dividing people into classes, into types. I may easily be mistaken about your brother as an individual, but his type is written on his whole person."

"He is very good-looking," said Mrs. Montgomery.

The Doctor eyed her a moment. "You women are all the same! But the type to which your brother belongs was made to be the ruin of you, and you were made to be its handmaids and victims. The sign of the type in question is the determination—sometimes terrible in its quiet intensity—to accept nothing of life but its pleasures, and to secure these pleasures chiefly by the aid of your complaisant sex.

Young men of this class never do anything for themselves that they can get other people to do for them, and it is the infatuation, the devotion, the superstition of others that keeps them going. These others, in ninety-nine cases out of a hundred, are women. What our young friends chiefly insist upon is that some one else shall suffer for them; and women do that sort of thing, as you must know, wonderfully well." The Doctor paused a moment, and then he added, abruptly, "You have suffered immensely for your brother!"

This exclamation was abrupt, as I say, but it was also perfectly calculated. The Doctor had been rather disappointed at not finding his compact and comfortable little hostess surrounded in a more visible degree by the ravages of Morris Townsend's immorality; but he had said to himself that this was not because the young man had spared her, but because she had contrived to plaster up her wounds. They were aching there behind the varnished stove, the festooned engravings, beneath her own neat little poplin bosom; and if he could only touch the tender spot, she would make a movement that would betray her. The words I have just quoted were an attempt to put his finger suddenly upon the place, and they had some of the success that he looked for. The tears sprung for a moment to Mrs. Montgomery's eyes, and she indulged in a proud little jerk of the head.

"I don't know how you have found that out!" she exclaimed.

"By a philosophic trick—by what they call induction. You know you have always your option of contradicting me. But kindly answer me a question: Don't you give your brother money? I think you ought to answer that."

"Yes, I have given him money," said Mrs. Montgomery.

"And you have not had much to give him?"

She was silent a moment. "If you ask me for a confession of poverty, that is easily made. I am very poor."

"One would never suppose it from your—your charming house," said the Doctor. "I learned from my sister that your income was moderate, and your family numerous."

"I have five children," Mrs. Montgomery observed; "but I am happy to say that I can bring them up decently."

"Of course you can—accomplished and devoted as you are. But your brother has counted them over, I suppose?"

"Counted them over?"

"He knows there are five, I mean. He tells me it is he that brings them up."

Mrs. Montgomery stared a moment, and then quickly— "Oh yes; he teaches them—Spanish."

The Doctor laughed out. "That must take a great deal off your hands! Your brother also knows, of course, that you have very little money?"

"I have often told him so," Mrs. Montgomery exclaimed, more unreservedly than she had yet spoken. She was apparently taking some comfort in the Doctor's clairvoyance.

"Which means that you have often occasion to, and that he often sponges on you. Excuse the crudity of my language; I simply express a fact. I don't ask you how much of your money he has had, it is none of my business. I have ascertained what I suspected—what I wished." And the Doctor got up, gently smoothing his hat. "Your brother lives on you," he said, as he stood there.

Mrs. Montgomery quickly rose from her chair, following her visitor's movements with a look of fascination. But then, with a certain inconsequence—"I have never complained of him," she said.

"You needn't protest—you have not betrayed him. But I advise you not to give him any more money."

"Don't you see it is in my interest that he should marry a rich person?" she asked. "If, as you say, he lives on me, I can only wish to get rid of him; and to put obstacles in the way of his marrying is to increase my own difficulties."

"I wish very much you would come to me with your difficulties," said the Doctor. "Certainly, if I throw him back on your hands, the least I can do is to help you to bear the burden. If you will allow me to say so, then, I shall take the liberty of placing in your hands, for the present, a certain fund for your brother's support."

Mrs. Montgomery stared; she evidently thought he was jesting; but she presently saw that he was not, and the complication of her feelings became painful. "It seems to me that I ought to be very much offended with you," she murmured.

"Because I have offered you money? That's a superstition," said the Doctor. "You must let me come and see you again, and we will talk about these things. I suppose that some of your children are girls?"

"I have two little girls," said Mrs. Montgomery.

"Well, when they grow up, and begin to think of taking husbands, you will see how anxious you will be about the moral character of these husbands. Then you will understand this visit of mine."

"Ah, you are not to believe that Morris's moral character is bad."

The Doctor looked at her a little, with folded arms. "There is something I should greatly like, as a moral satisfaction. I should like to hear you say, 'He is abominably selfish.'"

The words came out with the grave distinctness of his voice, and they seemed for an instant to create, to poor Mrs. Montgomery's troubled vision, a material image. She gazed at it an instant, and then she turned away. "You distress me, sir!" she exclaimed. "He is, after all, my brother; and his talents, his talents—" On these last words her voice quavered, and before he knew it she had burst into tears.

"His talents are first-rate," said the Doctor. "We must find the proper field for them." And he assured her most respectfully of his regret at having so greatly discomposed her. "It's all for my poor Catherine," he went on. "You must know her, and you will see."

Mrs. Montgomery brushed away her tears, and blushed at having shed them. "I should like to know your daughter," she answered; and then, in an instant—"Don't let her marry him!"

Doctor Sloper went away with the words gently humming in his ears—"Don't let her marry him!" They gave him the moral satisfaction of which he had just spoken, and their value was the greater that they had evidently cost a pang to poor little Mrs. Montgomery's family pride.

❧ 15 ❧

HE HAD been puzzled by the way that Catherine carried herself; her attitude at this sentimental crisis seemed to him unnaturally passive. She had not spoken to him again after that scene in the library, the day before his interview with Morris; and a week had elapsed without making any change in her manner. There was nothing in it that appealed for pity, and he was even a little disappointed at her not giving him an opportunity to make up for his harshness by some manifestation of liberality which should operate as a compensation. He thought a little of offering to take her for a tour in Europe; but he was determined to do this only in case she should seem mutely to reproach him. He had an idea that she would display a talent for mute reproaches, and he was surprised at not finding himself exposed to these silent batteries. She said nothing, either tacitly or explicitly, and as she was never very talkative, there was now no especial eloquence in her reserve. And poor Catherine was not sulky—a style of behavior for which she had too little histrionic talent—she was simply very patient. Of course she was thinking over her situation, and she was apparently doing so in a deliberate and unimpassioned manner, with a view of making the best of it.

"She will do as I have bidden her," said the Doctor; and he made the further reflection that his daughter was not a woman of a great spirit.

I know not whether he had hoped for a little more resistance for the sake of a little more entertainment; but he said to himself, as he had said before, that though it might have its momentary alarms, paternity was, after all, not an exciting vocation.

Catherine meanwhile had made a discovery of a very difficult sort; it had become vivid to her that there was a great excitement in trying to be a good daughter. She had an entirely new feeling, which may be described as a state of expectant suspense about her own actions. She watched herself as she would have watched another person, and wondered what she would do. It was as if this other person, who was both herself and not herself, had suddenly sprung into being, inspiring her with a natural curiosity as to the performance of untested functions.

"I am glad I have such a good daughter," said her father, kissing her, after the lapse of several days.

"I am trying to be good," she answered, turning away, with a conscience not altogether clear.

"If there is anything you would like to say to me, you know you must not hesitate. You needn't feel obliged to be so quiet. I shouldn't care that Mr. Townsend should be a frequent topic of conversation, but whenever you have anything particular to say about him I shall be very glad to hear it."

"Thank you," said Catherine; "I have nothing particular at present."

He never asked her whether she had seen Morris again, because he was sure that if this had been the case she would tell him. She had, in fact, not seen him; she had only written him a long letter. The letter, at least, was long for her; and, it may be added, that it was long for Morris; it consisted of five pages, in a remarkably neat and handsome hand. Catherine's handwriting was beautiful, and she was even a little proud of it: she was extremely fond of copying, and possessed volumes of extracts which testified to this accomplishment; volumes which she had exhibited one day to her lover, when the bliss of feeling that she was important in his eyes was exceptionally keen. She told Morris, in writing, that her father had expressed the wish that she should not see him again, and that she begged he would not come to the house until she should have "made up her mind." Morris replied with a passionate epistle, in which he asked to what, in Heaven's name, she wished to make up her mind. Had not her mind been made up two weeks before, and could it be possible that she entertained the idea of throwing him off? Did she mean to break down at the very beginning of their ordeal, after all the promises of fidelity she had both given and extracted? And he gave an account of his own interview with her father—an account not identical at all points with that offered in these pages. "He was terribly violent," Morris wrote, "but you know my self-control. I have need of it all when I remember that I have it in my power to break in upon your cruel captivity." Catherine sent him, in answer to this, a note of three lines. "I am in great trouble; do not doubt of my affection, but let me wait a little and think." The idea of a struggle with her father, of setting up her will against his own, was heavy on her soul, and it kept her quiet, as a great physical weight keeps us motionless. It never entered into her mind to throw her lover off; but from the first she tried to assure herself that there would be a peaceful way out of their difficulty. The assurance was vague, for it contained no element of positive conviction that her father would change his mind. She only had an idea that if she should be very good, the situation would in some mysterious manner improve. To be good she must be patient, outwardly submissive, abstain from judging her father too harshly, and from committing any act of open defiance. He was perhaps right, after all, to think as he did; by which Catherine meant not in the least that his judgment of Morris's motives in seeking to marry her was perhaps a just one, but that it was probably natural and proper that conscientious parents should be suspicious and even unjust. There were probably people in the world as bad as her father supposed Morris to be, and if there were the slightest chance of Morris being one of these sinister persons, the Doctor was right in taking it into account. Of course he could not know what she knew—how the purest love and truth were seated in the young man's eyes; but Heaven, in its time, might appoint a way of bringing him to such knowledge. Catherine expected a good deal of Heaven, and referred to the skies the initiative, as the French say, in dealing with her dilemma. She could not imagine herself imparting any kind of knowledge to her father; there was something superior even in his injustice, and absolute in his mistakes. But she could at least be good, and if she were only good enough, Heaven would invent some way of reconciling all things—the dignity of her father's errors and the sweetness of her own confidence, the strict performance of her filial duties, and the enjoyment of Morris Townsend's affection.

Poor Catherine would have been glad to regard Mrs. Penniman as an illuminating agent, a part which this lady herself, indeed, was but imperfectly prepared to play. Mrs. Penniman took too much satisfaction in the sentimental shadows of this little drama to have, for the moment, any great interest in dissipating them. She wished the plot to thicken, and the advice that she gave her niece tended, in her own imagination, to produce this result. It was rather incoherent counsel, and from one day to another it contradicted itself; but it was pervaded by an earnest desire that Catherine should do something striking. "You must *act,* my dear; in your situation the great thing is to act," said Mrs. Penniman, who found her niece altogether beneath her opportunities. Mrs. Penniman's real hope was that the girl would make a secret marriage, at which she would officiate as bride's-woman or duenna. She had a vision of this ceremony being performed in some subterranean chapel; subterranean chapels in New York were not frequent, but Mrs. Penniman's imagination was not chilled by trifles; and of the guilty couple—she liked to think of poor Catherine and her suitor as the guilty couple—being shuffled away in a fast-whirling vehicle to some obscure lodging in the suburbs, where she would pay them (in a thick veil) clandestine visits; where

they would endure a period of romantic privation; and when ultimately, after she should have been their earthly providence, their in-
tercessor, their advocate, and their medium of communication with
the world, they would be reconciled to her brother in an artistic
tableau, in which she herself should be somehow the central figure.
She hesitated as yet to recommend this course to Catherine, but she
attempted to draw an attractive picture of it to Morris Townsend.
She was in daily communication with the young man, whom she kept
informed by letters of the state of affairs in Washington Square. As
he had been banished, as she said, from the house, she no longer saw
him; but she ended by writing to him that she longed for an
interview. This interview could take place only on neutral ground,
and she bethought herself greatly before selecting a place of meeting.
She had an inclination for Greenwood Cemetery, but she gave it up
as too distant; she could not absent herself for so long, as she said,
without exciting suspicion. Then she thought of the Battery, but
that was rather cold and windy, besides one's being exposed to
intrusion from the Irish emigrants who at this point alight, with
large appetites, in the New World; and at last she fixed upon an
oyster saloon in the Seventh Avenue, kept by a Negro—an establishment of which she knew nothing save that she had noticed it in
passing. She made an appointment with Morris Townsend to meet
him there, and she went to the tryst at dusk, enveloped in an
impenetrable veil. He kept her waiting for half an hour—he had
almost the whole width of the city to traverse—but she liked to wait,
it seemed, to intensify the situation. She ordered a cup of tea, which
proved excessively bad, and this gave her a sense that she was
suffering in a romantic cause. When Morris at last arrived, they sat
together for half an hour in the duskiest corner of the back shop; and
it is hardly too much to say that this was the happiest half-hour that
Mrs. Penniman had known for years. The situation was really thrilling, and it scarcely seemed to her a false note when her companion
asked for an oyster stew, and proceeded to consume it before her
eyes. Morris, indeed, needed all the satisfaction that stewed oysters
could give him; for it may be intimated to the reader that he
regarded Mrs. Penniman in the light of a fifth wheel to his coach. He
was in a state of irritation natural to a gentleman of fine parts who
had been snubbed in a benevolent attempt to confer a distinction
upon a young woman of inferior characteristics, and the insinuating
sympathy of this somewhat desiccated matron appeared to offer him

no practical relief. He thought her a humbug, and he judged of humbugs with a good deal of confidence. He had listened and made himself agreeable to her at first, in order to get a footing in Washington Square; and at present he needed all his self-command to be decently civil. It would have gratified him to tell her that she was a fantastic old woman, and that he would like to put her into an omnibus and send her home. We know, however, that Morris possessed the virtue of self-control, and he had moreover the constant habit of seeking to be agreeable; so that, although Mrs. Penniman's demeanor only exasperated his already unquiet nerves, he listened to her with a sombre deference in which she found much to admire.

❧ 16 ❧

THEY had of course immediately spoken of Catherine. "Did she send me a message, or—or anything?" Morris asked. He appeared to think that she might have sent him a trinket or a lock of her hair.

Mrs. Penniman was slightly embarrassed, for she had not told her niece of her intended expedition. "Not exactly a message," she said; "I didn't ask her for one, because I was afraid to—to excite her."

"I am afraid she is not very excitable." And Morris gave a smile of some bitterness.

"She is better than that—she is steadfast, she is true."

"Do you think she will hold fast, then?"

"To the death!"

"Oh, I hope it won't come to that," said Morris.

"We must be prepared for the worst, and that is what I wish to speak to you about."

"What do you call the worst?"

"Well," said Mrs. Penniman, "my brother's hard, intellectual nature."

"Oh, the devil!"

"He is impervious to pity," Mrs. Penniman added, by way of explanation.

"Do you mean that he won't come round?"

"He will never be vanquished by argument. I have studied him. He will be vanquished only by the accomplished fact."

"The accomplished fact?"

"He will come round afterward," said Mrs. Penniman, with extreme significance. "He cares for nothing but facts—he must be met by facts."

"Well," rejoined Morris, "it is a fact that I wish to marry his daughter. I met him with that the other day, but he was not at all vanquished."

Mrs. Penniman was silent a little, and her smile beneath the shadow of her capacious bonnet, on the edge of which her black veil was arranged curtainwise, fixed itself upon Morris's face with a still more tender brilliancy. "Marry Catherine first, and meet him afterward!" she exclaimed.

"Do you recommend that?" asked the young man, frowning heavily.

She was a little frightened, but she went on with considerable boldness. "That is the way I see it: a private marriage—a private marriage." She repeated the phrase because she liked it.

"Do you mean that I should carry Catherine off! What do they call it—elope with her?"

"It is not a crime when you are driven to it," said Mrs. Penniman. "My husband, as I have told you, was a distinguished clergyman—one of the most eloquent men of his day. He once married a young couple that had fled from the house of the young lady's father; he was so interested in their story. He had no hesitation, and everything came out beautifully. The father was afterward reconciled, and thought everything of the young man. Mr. Penniman married them in the evening, about seven o'clock. The church was so dark you could scarcely see, and Mr. Penniman was intensely agitated—he was so sympathetic. I don't believe he could have done it again."

"Unfortunately, Catherine and I have not Mr. Penniman to marry us," said Morris.

"No, but you have me!" rejoined Mrs. Penniman, expressively. "I can't perform the ceremony, but I can help you; I can watch!"

"The woman's an idiot!" thought Morris; but he was obliged to say something different. It was not, however, materially more civil. "Was it in order to tell me this that you requested I would meet you here?"

Mrs. Penniman had been conscious of a certain vagueness in her errand, and of not being able to offer him any very tangible reward for his long walk. "I thought perhaps you would like to see one who is so near to Catherine," she observed, with considerable majesty; "and also," she added, "that you would value an opportunity of sending her something."

Morris extended his empty hands with a melancholy smile. "I am greatly obliged to you, but I have nothing to send."

"Haven't you a *word?*" asked his companion, with her suggestive smile coming back.

Morris frowned again. "Tell her to hold fast," he said, rather curtly.

"That is a good word—a noble word: it will make her happy for many days. She is very touching, very brave," Mrs. Penniman went on, arranging her mantle and preparing to depart. While she was so engaged she had an inspiration; she found the phrase that she could boldly offer as a vindication of the step she had taken. "If you marry Catherine at all risks," she said, "you will give my brother a proof of your being what he pretends to doubt."

"What he pretends to doubt?"

"Don't you know what that is?" Mrs. Penniman said, almost playfully.

"It does not concern me to know," said Morris grandly.

"Of course it makes you angry."

"I despise it," Morris declared.

"Ah, you know what it is, then?" said Mrs. Penniman, shaking her finger at him. "He pretends that you like—you like the money."

Morris hesitated a moment; and then, as if he spoke advisedly, "I *do* like the money!"

"Ah, but not—but not as he means it. You don't like it more than Catherine?"

He leaned his elbows on the table and buried his head in his hands. "You torture me!" he murmured. And, indeed, this was almost the effect of the poor lady's too importunate interest in his situation.

But she insisted in making her point. "If you marry her in spite of him, he will take for granted that you expect nothing of him, and are prepared to do without it; and so he will see that you are disinterested."

Morris raised his head a little, following this argument. "And what shall I gain by that?"

"Why, that he will see that he has been wrong in thinking that you wished to get his money."

"And seeing that I wish he would go to the deuce with it, he will leave it to a hospital. Is that what you mean?" asked Morris.

"No, I don't mean that; though that would be very grand," Mrs. Penniman quickly added. "I mean that, having done you such an injustice, he will think it his duty, at the end, to make some amends."

Morris shook his head, though it must be confessed he was a little struck with this idea. "Do you think he is so sentimental?"

"He is not sentimental," said Mrs. Penniman; "but, to be perfectly fair to him, I think he has, in his own narrow way, a certain sense of duty."

There passed through Morris Townsend's mind a rapid wonder as to what he might, even under a remote contingency, be indebted to from the action of this principle in Doctor Sloper's breast, and the inquiry exhausted itself in his sense of the ludicrous. "Your brother has no duties to me," he said presently, "and I none to him."

"Ah, but he has duties to Catherine."

"Yes; but you see, on that principle Catherine has duties to him as well."

Mrs. Penniman got up with a melancholy sigh, as if she thought him very unimaginative. "She has always performed them faithfully; and now do you think she has no duties to *you?*" Mrs. Penniman always, even in conversation, italicized her personal pronouns.

"It would sound harsh to say so. I am so grateful for her love," Morris added.

"I will tell her you said that. And now, remember that if you need me I am there." And Mrs. Penniman, who could think of nothing more to say, nodded vaguely in the direction of Washington Square.

Morris looked some moments at the sanded floor of the shop; he seemed to be disposed to linger a moment. At last, looking up with a certain abruptness, "It is your belief that if she marries me he will cut her off?" he asked.

Mrs. Penniman stared a little, and smiled. "Why, I have explained to you what I think would happen—that in the end it would be the best thing to do."

"You mean that, whatever she does, in the long-run she will get the money?"

"It doesn't depend upon her, but upon you. Venture to appear as disinterested as you are," said Mrs. Penniman, ingeniously. Morris dropped his eyes on the sanded floor again, pondering this, and she pursued: "Mr. Penniman and I had nothing, and we were very happy. Catherine, moreover, has her mother's fortune, which, at the time my sister-in-law married, was considered a very handsome one."

"Oh, don't speak of that!" said Morris; and indeed it was quite superfluous, for he had contemplated the fact in all its lights.

"Austin married a wife with money—why shouldn't you?"

"Ah! but your brother was a doctor," Morris objected.

"Well, all young men can't be doctors."

"I should think it an extremely loathsome profession," said Morris, with an air of intellectual independence; then, in a moment, he went on rather inconsequently, "Do you suppose there is a will already made in Catherine's favor?"

"I suppose so—even doctors must die; and perhaps a little in mine," Mrs. Penniman frankly added.

"And you believe he would certainly change it—as regards Catherine?"

"Yes; and then change it back again."

"Ah, but one can't depend on that," said Morris.

"Do you want to *depend* on it?" Mrs. Penniman asked.

Morris blushed a little. "Well, I am certainly afraid of being the cause of an injury to Catherine."

"Ah! you must not be afraid. Be afraid of nothing, and everything will go well."

And then Mrs. Penniman paid for her cup of tea, and Morris paid for his oyster stew, and they went out together into the dimly-lighted wilderness of the Seventh Avenue. The dusk had closed in completely, and the street lamps were separated by wide intervals of a pavement in which cavities and fissures played a disproportionate part. An omnibus, emblazoned with strange pictures, went tumbling over the dislocated cobble-stones.

"How will you go home?" Morris asked, following this vehicle with an interested eye. Mrs. Penniman had taken his arm.

She hesitated a moment. "I think this manner would be pleasant," she said; and she continued to let him feel the value of his support.

So he walked with her through the devious ways of the west side of the town, and through the bustle of gathering nightfall in populous streets, to the quiet precinct of Washington Square. They lingered a moment at the foot of Doctor Sloper's white marble steps, above which a spotless white door, adorned with a glittering silver plate, seemed to figure for Morris the closed portal of happiness; and then Mrs. Penniman's companion rested a melancholy eye upon a lighted window in the upper part of the house.

"That is my room—my dear little room!" Mrs. Penniman remarked.

Morris started. "Then I needn't come walking round the Square to gaze at it."

"That's as you please. But Catherine's is behind; two noble windows on the second floor. I think you can see them from the other street."

"I don't want to see them, ma'am." And Morris turned his back to the house.

"I will tell her you have been *here*, at any rate," said Mrs. Penniman, pointing to the spot where they stood; "and I will give her your message—that she is to hold fast."

"Oh yes; of course. You know I write her all that."

"It seems to say more when it is spoken. And remember, if you need me, that I am *there*," and Mrs. Penniman glanced at the third floor.

On this they separated, and Morris, left to himself, stood looking at the house a moment; after which he turned away, and took a gloomy walk round the Square, on the opposite side, close to the wooden fence. Then he came back, and paused for a minute in front of Doctor Sloper's dwelling. His eyes travelled over it; they even rested on the ruddy windows of Mrs. Penniman's apartment. He thought it a devilish comfortable house.

✤ 17 ✤

MRS. PENNIMAN told Catherine that evening—the two ladies were sitting in the back-parlor—that she had had an interview with Morris Townsend; and on receiving this news the girl started with a sense of pain. She felt angry for the moment; it was almost the first time she had ever felt angry. It seemed to her that her aunt was meddlesome; and from this came a vague apprehension that she would spoil something.

"I don't see why you should have seen him. I don't think it was right," Catherine said.

"I was so sorry for him—it seemed to me some one ought to see him."

"No one but I," said Catherine, who felt as if she were making the most presumptuous speech of her life, and yet at the same time had an instinct that she was right in doing so.

"But you wouldn't, my dear," Aunt Lavinia rejoined; "and I didn't know what might have become of him."

"I have not seen him because my father has forbidden it," Catherine said, very simply.

There was a simplicity in this, indeed, which fairly vexed Mrs. Penniman. "If your father forbade you to go to sleep, I suppose you would keep awake!" she commented.

Catherine looked at her. "I don't understand you. You seem to me very strange."

"Well, my dear, you will understand me some day!" And Mrs. Penniman, who was reading the evening paper, which she perused daily from the first line to the last, resumed her occupation. She wrapped herself in silence; she was determined Catherine should ask her for an account of her interview with Morris. But Catherine was silent for so long that she almost lost patience; and she was on the point of remarking to her that she was very heartless, when the girl at last spoke.

"What did he say?" she asked.

"He said he is ready to marry you any day, in spite of everything."

Catherine made no answer to this, and Mrs. Penniman almost lost patience again; owing to which she at last volunteered the information that Morris looked very handsome, but terribly haggard.

"Did he seem sad?" asked her niece.

"He was dark under the eyes," said Mrs. Penniman. "So different from when I first saw him; though I am not sure that if I had seen him in this condition the first time, I should not have been even more struck with him. There is something brilliant in his very misery."

This was, to Catherine's sense, a vivid picture, and though she disapproved, she felt herself gazing at it. "Where did you see him?" she asked, presently.

"In—in the Bowery; at a confectioner's," said Mrs. Penniman, who had a general idea that she ought to dissemble a little.

"Whereabouts is the place?" Catherine inquired, after another pause.

"Do you wish to go there, my dear?" said her aunt.

"Oh no." And Catherine got up from her seat and went to the fire, where she stood looking awhile at the glowing coals.

"Why are you so dry, Catherine?" Mrs. Penniman said at last.

"So dry?"

"So cold—so irresponsive."

The girl turned very quickly. "Did *he* say that?"

Mrs. Penniman hesitated a moment. "I will tell you what he said. He said he feared only one thing—that you would be afraid."

"Afraid of what?"

"Afraid of your father."

Catherine turned back to the fire again, and then, after a pause, she said, "I *am* afraid of my father."

Mrs. Penniman got quickly up from her chair and approached her niece. "Do you mean to give him up, then?"

Catherine for some time never moved; she kept her eyes on the coals. At last she raised her head and looked at her aunt. "Why do you push me so?" she asked.

"I don't push you. When have I spoken to you before?"

"It seems to me that you have spoken to me several times."

"I am afraid it is necessary, then, Catherine," said Mrs. Penniman, with a good deal of solemnity. "I am afraid you don't feel the importance"—she paused a little; Catherine was looking at her—"the importance of not disappointing that gallant young heart!" And Mrs. Penniman went back to her chair by the lamp, and, with a little jerk, picked up the evening paper again.

Catherine stood there before the fire, with her hands behind her, looking at her aunt, to whom it seemed that the girl had never had just this dark fixedness in her gaze. "I don't think you understand or that you know me," she said.

"If I don't, it is not wonderful; you trust me so little."

Catherine made no attempt to deny this charge, and for some time more nothing was said. But Mrs. Penniman's imagination was restless, and the evening paper failed on this occasion to enchain it.

"If you succumb to the dread of your father's wrath," she said, "I don't know what will become of us."

"Did *he* tell you to say these things to me?"

"He told me to use my influence."

"You must be mistaken," said Catherine. "He trusts me."

"I hope he may never repent of it!" And Mrs. Penniman gave a little sharp slap to her newspaper. She knew not what to make of her niece, who had suddenly become stern and contradictious.

This tendency on Catherine's part was presently even more apparent. "You had much better not make any more appointments with Mr. Townsend," she said. "I don't think it is right."

Mrs. Penniman rose with considerable majesty. "My poor child, are you jealous of me?" she inquired.

"Oh, Aunt Lavinia!" murmured Catherine, blushing.

"I don't think it is your place to teach me what is right."

On this point Catherine made no concession. "It can't be right to deceive."

"I certainly have not deceived *you!*"

"Yes; but I promised my father—"

"I have no doubt you promised your father. But I have promised him nothing."

Catherine had to admit this, and she did so in silence. "I don't believe Mr. Townsend himself likes it," she said, at last.

"Doesn't like meeting me?"

"Not in secret."

"It was not in secret; the place was full of people."

"But it was a secret place—away off in the Bowery."

Mrs. Penniman flinched a little. "Gentlemen enjoy such things," she remarked, presently. "I know what gentlemen like."

"My father wouldn't like it, if he knew."

"Pray, do you propose to inform him?" Mrs. Penniman inquired.

"No, Aunt Lavinia. But please don't do it again."

"If I do it again you will inform him—is that what you mean? I do not share your dread of my brother; I have always known how to defend my own position. But I shall certainly never again take any step on your behalf; you are much too thankless. I knew you were not a spontaneous nature, but I believed you were firm, and I told your father that he would find you so. I am disappointed, but your father will not be." And with this Mrs. Penniman offered her niece a brief good-night, and withdrew to her own apartment.

❖ 18 ❖

CATHERINE sat alone by the parlor fire—sat there for more than an hour, lost in her meditations. Her aunt seemed to her aggressive and foolish; and to see it so clearly—to judge Mrs. Penniman so positively—made her feel old and grave. She did not resent the imputation of weakness; it made no impression on her, for she had not the sense of weakness, and she was not hurt at not being appreciated. She had an immense respect for her father, and she felt that to displease him would be a misdemeanor analogous to an act of profanity in a great temple: but her purpose had slowly ripened, and she believed that her prayers had purified it of its violence. The evening advanced, and the lamp burnt dim without her noticing it; her eyes were fixed upon her terrible plan. She knew her father was in his study—that he had been there all the evening; from time to time she expected to hear him move. She thought he would perhaps come, as he sometimes came, into the parlor. At last the clock struck eleven, and the house was wrapped in silence; the servants had gone to bed. Catherine got up and went slowly to the door of the library, where she waited a moment, motionless. Then she knocked, and then she waited again. Her father had answered her, but she had not the courage to turn the latch. What she had said to her aunt was true enough—she was afraid of him; and in saying that she had no sense of weakness, she meant that she was not afraid of herself. She heard him move within, and he came and opened the door for her.

"What is the matter?" asked the Doctor. "You are standing there like a ghost!"

She went into the room, but it was some time before she contrived to say what she had come to say. Her father, who was in his dressing-gown and slippers, had been busy at his writing-table, and after looking at her for some moments, and waiting for her to speak, he went and seated himself at his papers again. His back was turned to her—she began to hear the scratching of his pen. She remained near the door, with her heart thumping beneath her bodice; and she was very glad that his back was turned, for it seemed to her that she could more easily address herself to this portion of his person than to his face. At last she began, watching it while she spoke:

"You told me that if I should have anything more to say about Mr. Townsend you would be glad to listen to it."

"Exactly, my dear," said the Doctor, not turning round, but stopping his pen.

Catherine wished it would go on, but she herself continued: "I thought I would tell you that I have not seen him again, but that I should like to do so."

"To bid him good-bye?" asked the Doctor.

The girl hesitated a moment. "He is not going away."

The Doctor wheeled slowly round in his chair, with a smile that seemed to accuse her of an epigram; but extremes meet, and Catherine had not intended one. "It is not to bid him good-bye, then?" her father said.

"No, father, not that; at least not forever. I have not seen him again, but I should like to see him," Catherine repeated.

The Doctor slowly rubbed his underlip with the feather of his quill.

"Have you written to him?"

"Yes, four times."

"You have not dismissed him, then. Once would have done that."

"No," said Catherine; "I have asked him—asked him to wait."

Her father sat looking at her, and she was afraid he was going to break out into wrath, his eyes were so fine and cold.

"You are a dear, faithful child," he said, at last. "Come here to your father." And he got up, holding out his hands toward her.

The words were a surprise, and they gave her an exquisite joy. She went to him, and he put his arm round her tenderly, soothingly; and then he kissed her. After this he said,

"Do you wish to make me very happy?"

"I should like to—but I am afraid I can't," Catherine answered.

"You can if you will. It all depends on your will."

"Is it to give him up?" said Catherine.

"Yes, it is to give him up."

And he held her still, with the same tenderness, looking into her face and resting his eyes on her averted eyes. There was a long silence; she wished he would release her.

"You are happier than I, father," she said, at last.

"I have no doubt you are unhappy just now. But it is better to be unhappy for three months and get over it, than for many years and never get over it."

"Yes, if that were so," said Catherine.

"It would be so; I am sure of that." She answered nothing, and he went on: "Have you no faith in my wisdom, in my tenderness, in my solicitude for your future?"

"Oh, father!" murmured the girl.

"Don't you suppose that I know something of men—their vices, their follies, their falsities?"

She detached herself, and turned upon him. "He is not vicious—he is not false!"

Her father kept looking at her with his sharp, pure eye. "You make nothing of my judgment, then?"

"I can't believe that!"

"I don't ask you to believe it, but to take it on trust."

Catherine was far from saying to herself that this was an ingenious sophism; but she met the appeal none the less squarely. "What has he done—what do you know?"

"He has never done anything—he is a selfish idler."

"Oh, father, don't abuse him!" she exclaimed, pleadingly.

"I don't mean to abuse him; it would be a great mistake. You may do as you choose," he added, turning away.

"I may see him again?"

"Just as you choose."

"Will you forgive me?"

"By no means."

"It will only be for once."

"I don't know what you mean by once. You must either give him up or continue the acquaintance."

"I wish to explain—to tell him to wait."

"To wait for what?"

"Till you know him better—till you consent."

"Don't tell him any such nonsense as that. I know him well enough, and I shall never consent."

"But we can wait a long time," said poor Catherine, in a tone which was meant to express the humblest conciliation, but which had upon her father's nerves the effect of an iteration not characterized by tact.

The Doctor answered, however, quietly enough: "Of course; you can wait till I die, if you like."

Catherine gave a cry of natural horror.

"Your engagement will have one delightful effect upon you; it will make you extremely impatient for that event."

Catherine stood staring, and the Doctor enjoyed the point he had made. It came to Catherine with the force—or rather with the vague impressiveness—of a logical axiom which it was not in her province to controvert; and yet, though it was a scientific truth, she felt wholly unable to accept it.

"I would rather not marry, if that were true," she said.

"Give me a proof of it, then; for it is beyond a question that by engaging yourself to Morris Townsend you simply wait for my death."

She turned away, feeling sick and faint; and the Doctor went on: "And if you wait for it with impatience, judge, if you please, what *his* eagerness will be."

Catherine turned it over—her father's words had such an authority for her that her very thoughts were capable of obeying him. There was a dreadful ugliness in it, which seemed to glare at her through the interposing medium of her own feebler reason. Suddenly, however, she had an inspiration—she almost knew it to be an inspiration.

"If I don't marry before your death, I will not after," she said.

To her father, it must be admitted, this seemed only another epigram; and as obstinacy, in unaccomplished minds, does not usually select such a mode of expression, he was the more surprised at this wanton play of a fixed idea.

"Do you mean that for an impertinence?" he inquired; an inquiry of which, as he made it, he quite perceived the grossness.

"An impertinence? Oh, father, what terrible things you say!"

"If you don't wait for my death, you might as well marry immediately; there is nothing else to wait for."

For some time Catherine made no answer; but finally she said,

"I think Morris—little by little—might persuade you."

"I shall never let him speak to me again. I dislike him too much."

Catherine gave a long, low sigh; she tried to stifle it, for she had made up her mind that it was wrong to make a parade of her trouble, and to endeavor to act upon her father by the meretricious aid of emotion. Indeed, she even though it wrong—in the sense of being inconsiderate—to attempt to act upon his feelings at all; her part was to effect some gentle, gradual change in his intellectual perception of poor Morris's character. But the means of effecting such a change were at present shrouded in mystery, and she felt miserably helpless and hopeless. She had exhausted all arguments, all replies. Her father might have pitied her, and in fact he did so; but he was sure he was right.

"There is one thing you can tell Mr. Townsend when you see him again," he said, "that if you marry without my consent, I don't leave you a farthing of money. That will interest him more than anything else you can tell him."

"That would be very right," Catherine answered. "I ought not in that case to have a farthing of your money."

"My dear child," the Doctor observed, laughing, "your simplicity is touching. Make that remark, in that tone, and with that expression of countenance, to Mr. Townsend, and take a note of his answer. It won't be polite—it will express irritation; and I shall be glad of that, as it will put me in the right; unless, indeed—which is perfectly possible—you should like him the better for being rude to you."

"He will never be rude to me," said Catherine, gently.

"Tell him what I say, all the same."

She looked at her father, and her quiet eyes filled with tears.

"I think I will see him, then," she murmured, in her timid voice.

"Exactly as you choose." And he went to the door and opened it for her to go out. The movement gave her a terrible sense of his turning her off.

"It will be only once, for the present," she added, lingering a moment.

"Exactly as you choose," he repeated, standing there with his hand on the door. "I have told you what I think. If you see him, you will be an ungrateful, cruel child; you will have given your old father the greatest pain of his life."

This was more than the poor girl could bear; her tears overflowed, and she moved toward her grimly consistent parent with a pitiful cry. Her hands were raised in supplication, but he sternly evaded this appeal. Instead of letting her sob out her misery on his shoulder, he simply took her by the arm and directed her course across the threshold, closing the door gently but firmly behind her. After he had done so, he remained listening. For a long time there was no sound; he knew that she was standing outside. He was sorry for her, as I have said; but he was so sure he was right. At last he heard her move away, and then her footstep creaked faintly upon the stairs.

The Doctor took several turns round his study, with his hands in his pockets, and a thin sparkle, possibly of irritation, but partly also of something like humor, in his eye. "By Jove," he said to himself, "I believe she will stick—I believe she will stick!" And this idea of Catherine "sticking" appeared to have a comical side, and to offer a prospect of entertainment. He determined, as he said to himself, to see it out.

✢ 19 ✢

IT WAS for reasons connected with this determination that on the morrow he sought a few words of private conversation with Mrs. Penniman. He sent for her to the library, and he there informed her that he hoped very much that, as regarded this affair of Catherine's, she would mind her p's and q's.

"I don't know what you mean by such an expression," said his sister. "You speak as if I were learning the alphabet."

"The alphabet of common-sense is something you will never learn," the Doctor permitted himself to respond.

"Have you called me here to insult me?" Mrs. Penniman inquired.

"Not at all. Simply to advise you. You have taken up young Townsend; that's your own affair. I have nothing to do with your sentiments, your fancies, your affections, your delusions; but what I request of you is that you will keep these things to yourself. I have explained my views to Catherine; she understands them perfectly, and anything that she does further in the way of encouraging Mr.

Townsend's attentions will be in deliberate opposition to my wishes. Anything that you should do in the way of giving her aid and comfort will be—permit me the expression—distinctly treasonable. You know high-treason is a capital offence: take care how you incur the penalty."

Mrs. Penniman threw back her head, with a certain expansion of the eye which she occasionally practiced. "It seems to me that you talk like a great autocrat."

"I talk like my daughter's father."

"Not like your sister's brother," cried Lavinia.

"My dear Lavinia," said the Doctor. "I sometimes wonder whether I *am* your brother, we are so extremely different. In spite of differences, however, we can, at a pinch, understand each other; and that is the essential thing just now. Walk straight with regard to Mr. Townsend; that's all I ask. It is highly probable you have been corresponding with him for the last three weeks—perhaps even seeing him. I don't ask you—you needn't tell me." He had a moral conviction that she would contrive to tell a fib about the matter, which it would disgust him to listen to. "Whatever you have done, stop doing it; that's all I wish."

"Don't you wish also by chance to murder your child?" Mrs. Penniman inquired.

"On the contrary, I wish to make her live and be happy."

"You will kill her: she passed a dreadful night."

"She won't die of one dreadful night, nor of a dozen. Remember that I am a distinguished physician."

Mrs. Penniman hesitated a moment; then she risked her retort. "Your being a distinguished physician has not prevented you from already losing *two members* of your family."

She had risked it, but her brother gave her such a terribly incisive look—a look so like a surgeon's lancet—that she was frightened at her courage. And he answered her, in words that corresponded to the look, "It may not prevent me, either, from losing the society of still another."

Mrs. Penniman took herself off with whatever air of depreciated merit was at her command, and repaired to Catherine's room, where the poor girl was closeted. She knew all about her dreadful night, for the two had met again, the evening before, after Catherine left her father. Mrs. Penniman was on the landing of the second floor when her niece came upstairs; it was not remarkable that a person of so much subtlety should have discovered that Catherine had been shut up with the Doctor. It was still less remarkable that she should have felt an extreme curiosity to learn the result of this interview, and that this sentiment, combined with her great amiability and generosity, should have prompted her to regret the sharp words lately exchanged between her niece and herself. As the unhappy girl came into sight in the dusky corridor, she made a lively demonstration of sympathy. Catherine's bursting heart was equally oblivious; she only knew that her aunt was taking her into her arms. Mrs. Penniman drew her into Catherine's own room, and the two women sat there together far into the small hours, the younger one with her head on the other's lap, sobbing, and sobbing at first in a soundless, stifled manner, and then at last perfectly still. It gratified Mrs. Penniman to be able to feel conscientiously that this scene virtually removed the interdict which Catherine had placed upon her indulging in further communion with Morris Townsend. She was not gratified, however, when, in coming back to her niece's room before breakfast, she found that Catherine had risen and was preparing herself for this meal.

"You should not go to breakfast," she said; "you are not well enough, after your fearful night."

"Yes, I am very well, and I am only afraid of being late."

"I can't understand you," Mrs. Penniman cried. "You should stay in bed for three days."

"Oh, I could never do that," said Catherine, to whom this idea presented no attractions.

Mrs. Penniman was in despair; and she noted, with extreme annoyance, that the trace of the night's tears had completely vanished from Catherine's eyes. She had a most impracticable physique. "What effect do you expect to have upon your father," her aunt demanded, "if you come plumping down, without a vestige of any sort of feeling, as if nothing in the world had happened?"

"He would not like me to lie in bed," said Catherine, simply.

"All the more reason for your doing it. How else do you expect to move him?"

Catherine thought a little. "I don't know how; but not in that way. I wish to be just as usual." And she finished dressing—and, according to her aunt's expression, went plumping down into the paternal presence. She was really too modest for consistent pathos.

And yet it was perfectly true that she had had a dreadful night. Even after Mrs. Penniman left her she had had no sleep; she lay staring at the uncomforting gloom, with her eyes and ears filled with the movement with which her father had turned her out of his room, and of the words in which he had told her that she was a heartless daughter. Her heart was breaking; she had heart enough for that. At moments it seemed to her that she believed him, and that to do what she was doing a girl must indeed be bad. She *was* bad; but she couldn't help it. She would try to appear good, even if her heart were perverted; and from time to time she had a fancy that she might accomplish something by ingenious concessions to form, though she should persist in caring for Morris. Catherine's ingenuities were indefinite, and we are not called upon to expose their hollowness. The best of them, perhaps, showed itself in that freshness of aspect which was so discouraging to Mrs. Penniman, who was amazed at the absence of haggardness in a young woman who for a whole night had lain quivering beneath a father's curse. Poor Catherine was conscious of her freshness; it gave her a feeling about the future which rather added to the weight upon her mind. It seemed a proof that she was strong and solid and dense, and would live to a great age—longer than might be generally convenient; and this idea was pressing, for it appeared to saddle her with a pretension the more, just when the cultivation of any pretension was inconsistent with her doing right. She wrote that day to Morris Townsend, requesting him to come and see her on the morrow, using very few words, and explaining nothing. She would explain everything face to face.

❧ 20 ❧

ON THE morrow, in the afternoon, she heard his voice at the door, and his step in the hall. She received him in the big, bright front-parlor, and she instructed the servant that, if any one should call, she was particularly engaged. She was not afraid of her father's coming in, for at that hour he was always driving about town. When Morris stood there before her, the first thing that she was conscious of was that he was even more beautiful to look at than fond recollection had painted him; the next was that he had pressed her in his arms.

When she was free again it appeared to her that she had now indeed thrown herself into the gulf of defiance, and even, for an instant, that she had been married to him.

He told her that she had been very cruel, and had made him very unhappy; and Catherine felt acutely the difficulty of her destiny, which forced her to give pain in such opposite quarters. But she wished that, instead of reproaches, however tender, he would give her help; he was certainly wise enough and clever enough to invent some issue from their troubles. She expressed this belief, and Morris received the assurance as if he thought it natural; but he interrogated at first—as was natural too—rather than committed himself to marking out a course.

"You should not have made me wait so long," he said. "I don't know how I have been living; every hour seemed like years. You should have decided sooner."

"Decided?" Catherine asked.

"Decided whether you would keep me or give me up."

"Oh, Morris," she cried, with a long, tender murmur, "I never thought of giving you up!"

"What, then, were you waiting for?" The young man was ardently logical.

"I thought my father might—might—" and she hesitated.

"Might see how unhappy you were?"

"Oh no. But that he might look at it differently."

"And now you have sent for me to tell me that at last he does so. Is that it?"

This hypothetical optimism gave the poor girl a pang. "No, Morris," she said, solemnly, "he looks at it still in the same way."

"Then why have you sent for me?"

"Because I wanted to see you," cried Catherine, piteously.

"That's an excellent reason, surely. But did you want to look at me only? Have you nothing to tell me?"

His beautiful persuasive eyes were fixed upon her face, and she wondered what answer would be noble enough to make to such a gaze as that. For a moment her own eyes took it in, and then—"I *did* want to look at you," she said, gently. But after this speech, most inconsistently, she hid her face.

Morris watched her for a moment attentively. "Will you marry me to-morrow?" he asked, suddenly.

"To-morrow?"

"Next week, then—any time within a month?"

"Isn't it better to wait?" said Catherine.

"To wait for what?"

She hardly knew for what; but this tremendous leap alarmed her. "Till we have thought about it a little more."

He shook his head sadly and reproachfully. "I thought you had been thinking about it these three weeks. Do you want to turn it over in your mind for five years? You have given me more than time enough. My poor girl," he added, in a moment, "you are not sincere."

Catherine colored from brow to chin, and her eyes filled with tears. "Oh, how can you say that?" she murmured.

"Why, you must take me or leave me," said Morris, very reasonably. "You can't please your father and me both; you must choose between us."

"I have chosen you," she said, passionately.

"Then marry me next week!"

She stood gazing at him. "Isn't there any other way?"

"None that I know of for arriving at the same result. If there is, I should be happy to hear of it."

Catherine could think of nothing of the kind, and Morris's luminosity seemed almost pitiless. The only thing she could think of was that her father might, after all, come round; and she articulated, with an awkward sense of her helplessness in doing so, a wish that this miracle might happen.

"Do you think it is in the least degree likely?" Morris asked.

"It would be, if he could only know you."

"He can know me if he will. What is to prevent it?"

"His ideas, his reasons," said Catherine. "They are so—so terribly strong." She trembled with the recollection of them yet.

"Strong!" cried Morris. "I would rather you should think them weak."

"Oh, nothing about my father is weak," said the girl.

Morris turned away, walking to the window, where he stood looking out. "You are terribly afraid of him," he remarked at last.

She felt no impulse to deny it, because she had no shame in it; for, if it was no honor to herself, at least it was an honor to him. "I suppose I must be," she said, simply.

"Then you don't love me—not as I love you. If you fear your father more than you love me, then your love is not what I hoped it was."

"Ah, my friend!" she said, going to him.

"Do *I* fear anything?" he demanded, turning round on her. "For your sake what am I not ready to face?"

"You are noble—you are brave!" she answered, stopping short at a distance that was almost respectful.

"Small good it does me, if you are so timid."

"I don't think I am—*really*," said Catherine.

"I don't know what you mean by 'really.' It is really enough to make us miserable."

"I should be strong enough to wait—to wait a long time."

"And suppose after a long time your father should hate me worse than ever?"

"He wouldn't—he couldn't."

"He would be touched by my fidelity; is that what you mean? If he is so easily touched, then why should you be afraid of him?"

This was much to the point, and Catherine was struck by it. "I will try not to be," she said. And she stood there submissively, the image, in advance, of a dutiful and responsible wife. This image could not fail to recommend itself to Morris Townsend, and he continued to give proof of the high estimation in which he held her. It could only have been at the prompting of such a sentiment that he presently mentioned to her that the course recommended by Mrs. Penniman was an immediate union, regardless of consequences.

"Yes, Aunt Penniman would like that," Catherine said, simply, and yet with a certain shrewdness. It must, however, have been in pure simplicity, and from motives quite untouched by sarcasm, that a few moments after she went on to say to Morris that her father had given her a message for him. It was quite on her conscience to deliver this message, and had the mission been ten times more painful, she would have as scrupulously performed it. "He told me to tell you—to tell you very distinctly, and directly from himself—that if I marry without his consent, I shall not inherit a penny of his fortune. He made a great point of this. He seemed to think—he seemed to think—"

Morris flushed, as any young man of spirit might have flushed at an imputation of baseness. "What did he seem to think?"

"That it would make a difference."

"It *will* make a difference—in many things. We shall be of many thousands of dollars the poorer; and that is a great difference. But it will make none in my affection."

"We shall not want the money," said Catherine; "for you know I have a good deal myself."

"Yes, my dear girl, I know you have something. And he can't touch that."

"He would never," said Catherine. "My mother left it to me."

Morris was silent awhile. "He was very positive about this, was he?" he asked at last. "He thought such a message would annoy me terribly, and make me throw off the mask, eh?"

"I don't know what he thought," said Catherine, sadly.

"Please tell him that I care for his message as much as for that!" and Morris snapped his fingers sonorously.

"I don't think I could tell him that."

"Do you know you sometimes disappoint me," said Morris.

"I should think I might. I disappoint every one—father and Aunt Penniman."

"Well, it doesn't matter with me, because I am fonder of you than they are."

"Yes, Morris," said the girl, with her imagination—what there was of it—swimming in this happy truth, which seemed, after all, invidious to no one.

"Is it your belief that he will stick to it—stick to it forever—to this idea of disinheriting you?—that your goodness and patience will never wear out his cruelty?"

"The trouble is that if I marry you he will think I am not good. He will think that a proof."

"Ah, then he will never forgive you!"

This idea, sharply expressed by Morris's handsome lips, renewed for a moment to the poor girl's temporarily pacified conscience all its dreadful vividness. "Oh, you must love me very much!" she cried.

"There is no doubt of that, my dear," her lover rejoined. "You don't like that word 'disinherited,' " he added, in a moment.

"It isn't the money; it is that he should—that he should feel so."

"I suppose it seems to you a kind of curse?" said Morris. "It must be very dismal. But don't you think," he went on, presently, "that if you were to try to be very clever, and to set rightly about it, you might in the end conjure it away? Don't you think," he continued further, in a tone of sympathetic speculation, "that a really clever woman, in your place, might bring him round at last? Don't you think—"

Here, suddenly, Morris was interrupted; these ingenious inquiries had not reached Catherine's ears. The terrible word "disinheritance," with all its impressive moral reprobation, was still ringing there—seemed, indeed, to gather force as it lingered. The mortal chill of her situation struck more deeply into her childlike heart, and she was overwhelmed by a feeling of loneliness and danger. But her refuge was there, close to her, and she put out her hands to grasp it. "Ah, Morris," she said, with a shudder, "I will marry you as soon as you please!" and she surrendered herself, leaning her head on his shoulder.

"My dear good girl!" he exclaimed, looking down at his prize. And then he looked up again, rather vaguely, with parted lips and lifted eyebrows.

❧ 21 ❧

DOCTOR SLOPER very soon imparted his conviction to Mrs. Almond in the same terms in which he had announced it to himself. "She's going to stick, by Jove! she's going to stick."

"Do you mean that she is going to marry him?" Mrs. Almond inquired.

"I don't know that; but she is not going to break down. She is going to drag out the engagement, in the hope of making me relent."

"And shall you not relent?"

"Shall a geometrical proposition relent? I am not so superficial."

"Doesn't geometry treat of surfaces?" asked Mrs. Almond, who, as we know, was clever, smiling.

"Yes, but it treats of them profoundly. Catherine and her young man are my surfaces; I have taken their measure."

"You speak as if it surprised you."

"It is immense; there will be a great deal to observe."

"You are shockingly cold-blooded!" said Mrs. Almond.

"I need to be, with all this hot blood about me. Young Townsend, indeed, is cool; I must allow him that merit."

"I can't judge him," Mrs. Almond answered; "but I am not at all surprised at Catherine."

"I confess I am a little; she must have been so deucedly divided and bothered."

"Say it amuses you outright. I don't see why it should be such a joke that your daughter adores you."

"It is the point where the adoration stops that I find it interesting to fix."

"It stops where the other sentiment begins."

"Not at all; that would be simple enough. The two things are extremely mixed up, and the mixture is extremely odd. It will produce some third element, and that's what I'm waiting to see. I wait with suspense—with positive excitement; and that is a sort of emotion that I didn't suppose Catherine would ever provide for me. I am really very much obliged to her."

"She will cling," said Mrs. Almond; "she will certainly cling."

"Yes, as I say, she will stick."

"Cling is prettier. That's what those very simple natures always do, and nothing could be simpler than Catherine. She doesn't take many impressions; but when she takes one, she keeps it. She is like a copper kettle that receives a dent: you may polish up the kettle, but you can't efface the mark."

"We must try and polish up Catherine," said the Doctor. "I will take her to Europe!"

"She won't forget him in Europe."

"He will forget her, then."

Mrs. Almond looked grave. "Should you really like that?"

"Extremely," said the Doctor.

Mrs. Penniman, meanwhile, lost little time in putting herself again in communication with Morris Townsend. She requested him to favor her with another interview, but she did not on this occasion select an oyster saloon as the scene of their meeting. She proposed that he should join her at the door of a certain church after service on Sunday afternoon; and she was careful not to appoint the place of worship which she usually visited, and where, as she said, the congregation would have spied upon her. She picked out a less elegant resort, and on issuing from its portal at the hour she had fixed she saw the young man standing apart. She offered him no recognition until she had crossed the street, and he had followed her to some distance. Here, with a smile, "excuse my apparent want of cordiality," she said. "You know what to believe about that. Prudence before everything." And on his asking her in what direction they should walk, "Where we shall be least observed," she murmured.

Morris was not in high good-humor, and his response to this speech was not particularly gallant. "I don't flatter myself we shall be much observed anywhere." Then he turned recklessly toward the centre of the town. "I hope you have come to tell me that he has knocked under," he went on.

"I am afraid I am not altogether a harbinger of good; and yet, too, I am to a certain extent a messenger of peace. I have been thinking a great deal, Mr. Townsend," said Mrs. Penniman.

"You think too much."

"I suppose I do; but I can't help it, my mind is so terribly active. When I give myself, I give myself. I pay the penalty in my headaches, my famous headaches—a perfect circlet of pain! But I carry it as a queen carries her crown. Would you believe that I have one now? I wouldn't, however, have missed our rendezvous for anything. I have something very important to tell you."

"Well, let's have it," said Morris.

"I was perhaps a little headlong the other day in advising you to marry immediately. I have been thinking it over, and now I see it just a little differently."

"You seem to have a great many different ways of seeing the same object."

"Their number is infinite!" said Mrs. Penniman, in a tone which seemed to suggest that this convenient faculty was one of her brightest attributes.

"I recommend you to take one way, and stick to it," Morris replied.

"Ah, but it isn't easy to choose. My imagination is never quiet, never satisfied. It makes me a bad adviser, perhaps, but it makes me a capital friend."

"A capital friend who gives bad advice!" said Morris.

"Not intentionally—and who hurries off, at every risk, to make the most humble excuses."

"Well, what do you advise me now?"

"To be very patient; to watch and wait."

"And is that bad advice or good?"

"That is not for me to say," Mrs. Penniman rejoined, with some dignity. "I only claim it is sincere."

"And will you come to me next week and recommend something different and equally sincere?"

"I may come to you next week, and tell you that I am in the streets."

"In the streets?"

"I have had a terrible scene with my brother, and he threatens, if anything happens, to turn me out of the house. You know I am a poor woman."

Morris had a speculative idea that she had a little property; but he naturally did not press this.

"I should be very sorry to see you suffer martyrdom for me," he said. "But you make your brother out a regular Turk."

Mrs. Penniman hesitated a little.

"I certainly do not regard Austin as an orthodox Christian."

"And am I to wait till he is converted?"

"Wait at any rate till he is less violent. Bide your time, Mr. Townsend; remember the prize is great."

Morris walked along some time in silence, tapping the railings and gate-posts very sharply with his stick.

"You certainly are devilish inconsistent!" he broke out at last. "I have already got Catherine to consent to a private marriage."

Mrs. Penniman was indeed inconsistent, for at this news she gave a little jump of gratification.

"Oh, when and where?" she cried. And then she stopped short.

Morris was a little vague about this.

"That isn't fixed; but she consents. It's deuced awkward now to back out."

Mrs. Penniman, as I say, had stopped short; and she stood there with her eyes fixed brilliantly on her companion.

"Mr. Townsend," she proceeded, "shall I tell you something? Catherine loves you so much that you may do anything."

This declaration was slightly ambiguous, and Morris opened his eyes.

"I am happy to hear it. But what do you mean by 'anything'?"

"You may postpone—you may change about; she won't think the worse of you."

Morris stood there still, with his raised eyebrows; then he said, simply and rather dryly, "Ah!" After this he remarked to Mrs. Penniman that if she walked so slowly she would attract notice, and he succeeded, after a fashion, in hurrying her back to the domicile of which her tenure had become so insecure.

❧ 22 ❧

HE HAD slightly misrepresented the matter in saying that Catherine had consented to take the great step. We left her just now declaring that she would burn her ships behind her; but Morris, after having elicited this declaration, had become conscious of good reasons for not taking it up. He avoided, gracefully enough, fixing a day, though he left her under the impression that he had his eye on one. Catherine may have had her difficulties; but those of her circumspect suitor are also worthy of consideration. The prize was certainly great; but it was only to be won by striking the happy mean between precipitancy and caution. It would be all very well to take one's jump and trust to Providence; Providence was more especially on the side of clever people, and clever people were known by an indisposition to risk their bones.

The ultimate reward of a union with a young woman who was both unattractive and impoverished ought to be connected with immediate disadvantages by some very palpable chain. Between the fear of losing Catherine and her possible fortune altogether, and the fear of taking her too soon and finding this possible fortune as void of actuality as a collection of emptied bottles, it was not comfortable for Morris Townsend to choose—a fact that should be remembered by readers disposed to judge harshly of a young man who may have struck them as making but an indifferently successful use of fine natural parts. He had not forgotten that in any event Catherine had her own ten thousand a year; he had devoted an abundance of meditation to this circumstance. But with his fine parts he rated himself high, and he had a perfectly definite appreciation of his value, which seemed to him inadequately represented by the sum I have mentioned. At the same time he reminded himself that this sum was considerable, that everything is relative, and that if a modest income is less desirable than a large one, the complete absence of revenue is nowhere accounted an advantage.

These reflections gave him plenty of occupation, and made it necessary that he should trim his sail. Doctor Sloper's opposition was the unknown quantity in the problem he had to work out. The natural way to work it out was by marrying Catherine; but in mathematics there are many short cuts, and Morris was not without a hope that he should yet discover one. When Catherine took him at his word, and consented to renounce the attempt to mollify her father, he drew back skilfully enough, as I have said, and kept the wedding-day still an open question. Her faith in his sincerity was so complete that she was incapable of suspecting that he was playing with her; her trouble just now was of another kind. The poor girl had an admirable sense of honor, and from the moment she had brought herself to the point of violating her father's wish, it seemed to her that she had no right to enjoy his protection. It was on her conscience that she ought to live under his roof only so long as she conformed to his wisdom. There was a great deal of glory in such a position, but poor Catherine felt that she had forfeited her claim to it. She had cast her lot with a young man against whom he had solemnly warned her, and broken the contract under which he provided her with a happy home. She could not give up the young man, so she must leave the home; and the sooner the object of her preference offered her another, the sooner her situation would lose its awkward twist. This was close reasoning; but it was commingled with an infinite amount of merely instinctive penitence. Catherine's days, at this time, were dismal, and the weight of some of her hours was almost more than she could bear. Her father never looked at her, never spoke to her. He knew perfectly what he was about, and this was part of a plan. She looked at him as much as she dared (for she was afraid of seeming to offer herself to his observation), and she pitied him for the sorrow she had brought upon him. She held up her head and busied her hands, and went about her daily occupations; and when the state of things in Washington Square seemed intolerable, she closed her eyes and indulged herself with an intellectual vision of the man for whose sake she had broken a sacred law.

Mrs. Penniman, of the three persons in Washington Square, had much the most of the manner that belongs to a great crisis. If Catherine was quiet, she was quietly quiet, as I may say, and her pathetic effects, which there was no one to notice, were entirely unstudied and unintended. If the Doctor was stiff and dry, and absolutely indifferent to the presence of his companions, it was so lightly, neatly, easily done, that you would have had to know him well to discover that, on the whole, he rather enjoyed having to be so disagreeable. But Mrs. Penniman was elaborately reserved and significantly silent; there was a richer rustle in the very deliberate movements to which she confined herself, and when she occasionally spoke, in connection with some very trivial event, she had the air of meaning something deeper than what she said. Between Catherine and her father nothing had passed since the evening she went to speak to him in his study. She had something to say to him—it seemed to her she ought to say it—but she kept it back for fear of irritating him. He also had something to say to her; but he was determined not to speak first. He was interested, as we know, in seeing how, if she were left to herself, she would "stick." At last she told him she had seen Morris Townsend again, and that their relations remained quite the same.

"I think we shall marry—before very long. And probably, meanwhile, I shall see him rather often; about once a week—not more."

The Doctor looked at her coldly from head to foot, as if she had been a stranger. It was the first time his eyes had rested on her for a week, which was fortunate, if that was to be their expression. "Why not three times a day?" he asked. "What prevents you meeting as often as you choose?"

She turned away a moment; there were tears in her eyes. Then she said, "It is better once a week."

"I don't see how it is better. It is as bad as it can be. If you flatter yourself that I care for little modifications of that sort, you are very much mistaken. It is as wrong of you to see him once a week as it would be to see him all day long. Not that it matters to me, however."

Catherine tried to follow these words, but they seemed to lead toward a vague horror from which she recoiled. "I think we shall marry pretty soon," she repeated, at last.

Her father gave her his dreadful look again, as if she were some one else. "Why do you tell me that? It's no concern of mine."

"Oh, father," she broke out, "don't you care, even if you do feel so?"

"Not a button. Once you marry, it's quite the same to me when, or where, or why you do it; and if you think to compound for your folly by hoisting your fly in this way, you may spare yourself the trouble."

With this he turned away. But the next day he spoke to her of his own accord, and his manner was somewhat changed. "Shall you be married within the next four or five months?" he asked.

"I don't know, father," said Catherine. "It is not very easy for us to make up our minds."

"Put it off, then, for six months, and in the meantime I will take you to Europe. I should like you very much to go."

It gave her such delight, after his words of the day before, to hear that he should "like" her to do something, and that he still had in his heart any of the tenderness of preference, that she gave a little exclamation of joy. But then she became conscious that Morris was not included in this proposal, and that—as regards really going—she would greatly prefer to remain at home with him. But she blushed none the less more comfortably than she had done of late. "It would be delightful to go to Europe," she remarked, with a sense that the idea was not original, and that her tone was not all it might be.

"Very well, then, we will go. Pack up your clothes."

"I had better tell Mr. Townsend," said Catherine.

Her father fixed his cold eyes upon her. "If you mean that you had better ask his leave, all that remains to me is to hope he will give it."

The girl was sharply touched by the pathetic ring of the words; it was the most calculated, the most dramatic little speech the Doctor had ever uttered. She felt that it was a great thing for her, under the circumstances, to have this fine opportunity of showing him her respect; and yet there was something else that she felt as well, and that she presently expressed. "I sometimes think that if I do what you dislike so much, I ought not to stay with you."

"To stay with me?"

"If I live with you, I ought to obey you."

"If that's your theory, it's certainly mine," said the Doctor, with a dry laugh.

"But if I don't obey you, I ought not to live with you—to enjoy your kindness and protection."

This striking argument gave the Doctor a sudden sense of having underestimated his daughter; it seemed even more than worthy of a young woman who had revealed the quality of unaggressive obstinacy. But it displeased him—displeased him deeply, and he signified as much. "That idea is in very bad taste," he said. "Did you get it from Mr. Townsend?"

"Oh no, it's my own," said Catherine, eagerly.

"Keep it to yourself, then," her father answered, more than ever determined she should go to Europe.

❧ 23 ❧

If Morris Townsend was not to be included in this journey, no more was Mrs. Penniman, who would have been thankful for an invitation, but who (to do her justice) bore her disappointment in a perfectly lady-like manner. "I should enjoy seeing the works of Raphael and the ruins—the ruins of the Pantheon," she said to Mrs. Almond; "but, on the other hand, I shall not be sorry to be alone and at peace for the next few months in Washington Square. I want rest; I have been through so much in the last four months." Mrs. Almond thought it rather cruel that her brother should not take poor Lavinia abroad; but she easily understood that, if the purpose of his expedition was to make Catherine forget her lover, it was not in his interest to give his daughter this young man's best friend as a companion. "If Lavinia had not been so foolish, she might visit the ruins of the Pantheon," she said to herself; and she continued to regret her sister's folly, even though the latter assured her that she had often heard the relics in question most satisfactorily described by Mr. Penniman. Mrs. Penniman was perfectly aware that her brother's motive in undertaking a foreign tour was to lay a trap for Catherine's constancy; and she imparted this conviction very frankly to her niece.

"He thinks it will make you forget Morris," she said (she always called the young man "Morris" now) : "out of sight, out of mind, you know. He thinks that all the things you will see over there will drive him out of your thoughts."

Catherine looked greatly alarmed. "If he thinks that, I ought to tell him beforehand."

Mrs. Penniman shook her head. "Tell him afterward, my dear—after he has had all the trouble and expense. That's the way to serve him." And she added, in a softer key, that it must be delightful to think of those who love us among the ruins of the Pantheon.

Her father's displeasure had cost the girl, as we know, a great deal of deep-welling sorrow—sorrow of the purest and most generous kind, without a touch of resentment or rancor; but for the first time, after he had dismissed with such contemptuous brevity her apology for being a charge upon him, there was a spark of anger in her grief. She had felt his contempt; it had scorched her; that speech about her bad taste had made her ears burn for three days. During this period she was less considerate; she had an idea—a rather vague one, but it was agreeable to her sense of injury—that now she was absolved from penance, and might do what she chose. She chose to write to Morris Townsend to meet her in the Square and take her to walk about the town. If she were going to Europe out of respect to her father, she might at least give herself this satisfaction. She felt in every way at present more free and more resolute; there was a force that urged her. Now at last, completely and unreservedly, her passion possessed her.

Morris met her at last, and they took a long walk. She told him immediately what had happened; that her father wished to take her away—it would be for six months—to Europe; she would do absolutely what Morris should think best. She hoped inexpressibly that he would think it best she should stay at home. It was some time before he said what he thought; he asked, as they walked along, a great many questions. There was one that especially struck her; it seemed so incongruous.

"Should you like to see all those celebrated things over there?"

"Oh no, Morris!" said Catherine, quite deprecatingly.

"Gracious Heaven, what a dull woman!" Morris exclaimed to himself.

"He thinks I will forget you," said Catherine; "that all these things will drive you out of my mind."

"Well, my dear, perhaps they will."

"Please don't say that," Catherine answered, gently, as they walked along. "Poor father will be disappointed."

Morris gave a little laugh. "Yes, I verily believe that your poor father will be disappointed. But you will have seen Europe," he added, humorously. "What a take-in!"

"I don't care for seeing Europe," Catherine said.

"You ought to care, my dear; and it may mollify your father."

Catherine, conscious of her obstinacy, expected little of this, and could not rid herself of the idea that in going abroad and yet remaining firm, she should play her father a trick. "Don't you think it would be a kind of deception?" she asked.

"Doesn't he want to deceive you?" cried Morris. "It will serve him right. I really think you had better go."

"And not be married for so long?"

"Be married when you come back. You can buy your wedding-clothes in Paris." And then Morris, with great kindness of tone, explained his view of the matter. It would be a good thing that she should go; it would put them completely in the right. It would show they were reasonable, and willing to wait. Once they were so sure of each other, they could afford to wait—what had they to fear? If there was a particle of chance that her father would be favorably affected by her going, that ought to settle it; for, after all, Morris was very unwilling to be the cause of her being disinherited. It was not for himself, it was for her and for her children. He was willing to wait for her; it would be hard, but he could do it. And over there, among beautiful scenes and noble monuments, perhaps the old gentleman would be softened; such things were supposed to exert a humanizing influence. He might be touched by her gentleness, her patience, her willingness to make any sacrifice but *that* one; and if she should appeal to him some day, in some celebrated spot—in Italy, say, in the evening; in Venice, in a gondola, by moonlight—if she should be a little clever about it, and touch the right chord, perhaps he would fold her in his arms, and tell her that he forgave her. Catherine was immensely struck with this conception of the affair, which seemed eminently worthy of her lover's brilliant intellect, though she viewed it askance in so far as it depended upon her own powers of execution. The idea of being "clever" in a gondola by moonlight appeared to her to involve elements of which her grasp was not active. But it was settled between them that she should tell her father that she was ready to follow him obediently anywhere, making the mental reservation that she loved Morris Townsend more than ever.

She informed the Doctor she was ready to embark, and he made rapid arrangements for this event. Catherine had many farewells to make, but with only two of them are we actively concerned. Mrs. Penniman took a discriminating view of her niece's journey; it seemed to her very proper that Mr. Townsend's destined bride should wish to embellish her mind by a foreign tour.

"You leave him in good hands," she said, pressing her lips to Catherine's forehead. (She was very fond of kissing people's foreheads; it was an involuntary expression of sympathy with the intellectual part.) "I shall see him often; I shall feel like one of the vestals of old tending the sacred flame."

"You behave beautifully about not going with us," Catherine answered, not presuming to examine this analogy.

"It is my pride that keeps me up," said Mrs. Penniman, tapping the body of her dress, which always gave forth a sort of metallic ring.

Catherine's parting with her lover was short, and few words were exchanged.

"Shall I find you just the same when I come back?" she asked; though the question was not the fruit of scepticism.

"The same—only more so," said Morris, smiling.

It does not enter into our scheme to narrate in detail Doctor Sloper's proceedings in the Eastern hemisphere. He made the grand tour of Europe, travelled in considerable splendor, and (as was to have been expected in a man of his high cultivation) found so much in art and antiquity to interest him, that he remained abroad, not for six months, but for twelve. Mrs. Penniman, in Washington Square, accommodated herself to his absence. She enjoyed her uncontested dominion in the empty house, and flattered herself that she made it more attractive to their friends than when her brother was at home. To Morris Townsend, at least, it would have appeared that she made it singularly attractive. He was altogether her most frequent visitor, and Mrs. Penniman was very fond of asking him to tea. He had his chair—a very easy one—at the fireside in the back parlor (when the great mahogany sliding doors, with silver knobs and hinges, which divided this apartment from its more formal neighbor, were closed), and he used to smoke cigars in the Doctor's study, where he often spent an hour in turning over the curious collections of its absent proprietor. He thought Mrs. Penniman a goose, as we know; but he was no goose himself, and, as a young man of luxurious tastes and scanty resources, he found the house a perfect castle of indolence. It became for him a club with a single member. Mrs. Penniman saw much less of her sister than while the Doctor was at home; for Mrs. Almond had felt moved to tell her that she disapproved of her relations with Mr. Townsend. She had no business to be so friendly to a young man of whom their brother thought so meanly, and Mrs. Almond was surprised at her levity in foisting a most deplorable engagement upon Catherine.

"Deplorable!" cried Lavinia. "He will make her a lovely husband."

"I don't believe in lovely husbands," said Mrs. Almond; "I only believe in good ones. If he marries her, and she comes into Austin's money, they may get on. He will be an idle, amiable, selfish, and, doubtless, tolerably good-natured fellow. But if she doesn't get the money, and he finds himself tied to her, Heaven have mercy on her! He will have none. He will hate her for his disappointment, and take his revenge; he will be pitiless and cruel. Woe betide poor Catherine! I recommend you to talk a little with his sister; it's a pity Catherine can't marry *her!*"

Mrs. Penniman had no appetite whatever for conversation with Mrs. Montgomery, whose acquaintance she made no trouble to cultivate; and the effect of this alarming forecast of her niece's destiny was to make her think it indeed a thousand pities that Mr. Townsend's generous nature should be embittered. Bright enjoyment was his natural element, and how could he be comfortable if there should prove to be nothing to enjoy? It became a fixed idea with Mrs. Penniman that he should yet enjoy her brother's fortune, on which she had acuteness enough to perceive that her own claim was small.

"If he doesn't leave it to Catherine, it certainly won't be to leave it to me," she said.

24

The Doctor, during the first six months he was abroad, never spoke to his daughter of their little difference, partly on system, and partly because he had a great many other things to think about. It was idle to attempt to ascertain the state of her affections without direct inquiry, because if she had not had an expressive manner among the familiar influences of home, she failed to gather animation from the mountains of Switzerland or the monuments of Italy. She was always her father's docile and reasonable associate—going through their sight-seeing in deferential silence, never complaining of fatigue, always ready to start at the hour he had appointed overnight, making no foolish criticisms, and indulging in no refinements of appreciation. "She is about as intelligent as the bundle of shawls," the Doctor said, her main superiority being that, while the bundle of shawls sometimes got lost, or tumbled out of the carriage, Catherine was always at her post, and had a firm and ample seat. But her father had expected this, and he was not constrained to set down her intellectual limitations as a tourist to sentimental depression; she had completely divested herself of the characteristics of a victim, and during the whole time that they were abroad she never uttered an audible sigh. He supposed she was in correspondence with Morris Townsend, but he held his peace about it, for he never saw the young man's letters, and Catherine's own missives were always given to the courier to post. She heard from her lover with considerable regularity, but his letters came enclosed in Mrs. Penniman's; so that, whenever the Doctor handed her a packet addressed in his sister's hand, he was an involuntary instrument of the passion he condemned. Catherine made this reflection, and six months earlier she would have felt bound to give him warning; but now she deemed herself absolved. There was a sore spot in her heart that his own words had made when once she spoke to him as she thought honor prompted; she would try and please him as far as she could, but she would never speak that way again. She read her lover's letters in secret.

One day, at the end of the summer, the two travellers found

themselves in a lonely valley of the Alps. They were crossing one of the passes, and on the long ascent they had got out of the carriage and had wandered much in advance. After awhile the Doctor descried a foot-path which, leading through a transverse valley, would bring them out, as he justly supposed, at a much higher point of the ascent. They followed this devious way, and finally lost the path; the valley proved very wild and rough, and their walk became rather a scramble. They were good walkers, however, and they took their adventure easily; from time to time they stopped, that Catherine might rest; and then she sat upon a stone and looked about her at the hard-featured rocks and the glowing sky. It was late in the afternoon, in the last of August; night was coming on, and as they had reached a great elevation, the air was cold and sharp. In the west there was a great suffusion of colored light, which made the sides of the little valley look only the more rugged and dusky. During one of their pauses her father left her and wandered away to some high place, at a distance, to get a view. He was out of sight; she sat there alone in the stillness, which was just touched by the vague murmur somewhere of a mountain brook. She thought of Morris Townsend, and the place was so desolate and lonely that he seemed very far away. Her father remained absent a long time; she began to wonder what had become of him. But at last he reappeared, coming toward her in the clear twilight, and she got up to go on. He made no motion to proceed, however, but came close to her, as if he had something to say. He stopped in front of her, and stood looking at her with eyes that had kept the light of the flushing snow-summits on which they had just been fixed. Then, abruptly, in a low tone, he asked her an unexpected question,

"Have you given him up?"

The question was unexpected, but Catherine was only superficially unprepared.

"No, father," she answered.

He looked at her again for some moments without speaking.

"Does he write to you?" he asked.

"Yes, about twice a month."

The Doctor looked up and down the valley, swinging his stick; then he said to her, in the same low tone,

"I am very angry."

She wondered what he meant—whether he wished to frighten her.

If he did, the place was well chosen: this hard, melancholy dell, abandoned by the summer light, made her feel her loneliness. She looked around her, and her heart grew cold; for a moment her fear was great. But she could think of nothing to say, save to murmur, gently, "I am sorry."

"You try my patience," her father went on, "and you ought to know what I am. I am not a very good man. Though I am very smooth externally, at bottom I am very passionate; and I assure you I can be very hard."

She could not think why he told her these things. Had he brought her there on purpose, and was it part of a plan? What was the plan? Catherine asked herself. Was it to startle her suddenly into a retraction—to take an advantage of her by dread? Dread of what? The place was ugly and lonely, but the place could do her no harm. There was a kind of still intensity about her father which made him dangerous, but Catherine hardly went so far as to say to herself that it might be part of his plan to fasten his hand—the neat, fine, supple hand of a distinguished physician—in her throat. Nevertheless, she receded a step. "I am sure you can be anything you please," she said; and it was her simple belief.

"I am very angry," he replied, more sharply.

"Why has it taken you so suddenly?"

"It has not taken me suddenly. I have been raging inwardly for the last six months. But just now this seemed a good place to flare out. It's so quiet, and we are alone."

"Yes, it's very quiet," said Catherine, vaguely looking about her. "Won't you come back to the carriage?"

"In a moment. Do you mean that in all this time you have not yielded an inch?"

"I would if I could, father; but I can't."

The Doctor looked round him too. "Should you like to be left in such a place as this, to starve?"

"What do you mean?" cried the girl.

"That will be your fate—that's how he will leave you."

He would not touch her, but he had touched Morris. The warmth came back to her heart. "That is not true, father," she broke out, "and you ought not to say it. It is not right, and it's not true."

He shook his head slowly. "No, it's not right, because you won't believe it. But it *is* true. Come back to the carriage."

He turned away, and she followed him; he went faster, and was presently much in advance. But from time to time he stopped, without turning round, to let her keep up with him, and she made her way forward with difficulty, her heart beating with the excitement of having for the first time spoken to him in violence. By this time it had grown almost dark, and she ended by losing sight of him. But she kept her course, and after a little, the valley making a sudden turn, she gained the road, where the carriage stood waiting. In it sat her father, rigid and silent; in silence, too, she took her place beside him.

It seemed to her, later, in looking back upon all this, that for days afterward not a word had been exchanged between them. The scene had been a strange one, but it had not permanently affected her feeling toward her father, for it was natural, after all, that he should occasionally make a scene of some kind, and he had let her alone for six months. The strangest part of it was that he had said he was not a good man; Catherine wondered a good deal what he had meant by that. The statement failed to appeal to her credence, and it was not grateful to any resentment that she entertained. Even in the utmost bitterness that she might feel, it would give her no satisfaction to think him less complete. Such a saying as that was a part of his great subtlety—men so clever as he might say anything and mean anything; and as to his being hard, that surely, in a man, was a virtue.

He let her alone for six months more—six months during which she accommodated herself without a protest to the extension of their tour. But he spoke again at the end of this time: it was at the very last, the night before they embarked for New York, in the hotel at Liverpool. They had been dining together in a great, dim, musty sitting-room; and then the cloth had been removed, and the Doctor walked slowly up and down. Catherine at last took her candle to go to bed, but her father motioned her to stay.

"What do you mean to do when you get home?" he asked, while she stood there with her candle in her hand.

"Do you mean about Mr. Townsend?"

"About Mr. Townsend."

"We shall probably marry."

The Doctor took several turns again while she waited. "Do you hear from him as much as ever?"

"Yes, twice a month," said Catherine, promptly.

"And does he always talk about marriage?"

"Oh yes; that is, he talks about other things too, but he always says something about that."

"I am glad to hear he varies his subjects; his letters might otherwise be monotonous."

"He writes beautifully," said Catherine, who was very glad of a chance to say it.

"They always write beautifully. However, in a given case that doesn't diminish the merit. So, as soon as you arrive, you are going off with him?"

This seemed a rather gross way of putting it, and something that there was of dignity in Catherine resented it. "I cannot tell you till we arrive," she said.

"That's reasonable enough," her father answered. "That's all I ask of you—that you *do* tell me, that you give me definite notice. When a poor man is to lose his only child, he likes to have an inkling of it beforehand."

"Oh father! you will not lose me," Catherine said, spilling her candle wax.

"Three days before will do," he went on, "if you are in a position to be positive then. He ought to be very thankful to me, do you know. I have done a mighty good thing for him in taking you abroad; your value is twice as great, with all the knowledge and taste that you have acquired. A year ago, you were perhaps a little limited—a little rustic; but now you have seen everything, and appreciated everything, and you will be a most entertaining companion. We have fattened the sheep for him before he kills it." Catherine turned away, and stood staring at the blank door. "Go to bed," said her father; "and as we don't go abroad till noon, you may sleep late. We shall probably have a most uncomfortable voyage."

❧ 25 ❧

THE voyage was indeed uncomfortable, and Catherine, on arriving in New York, had not the compensation of "going off," in her father's phrase, with Morris Townsend. She saw him, however, the day after she landed; and in the meantime he formed a natural subject of conversation between our heroine and her aunt Lavinia, with whom, the night she disembarked, the girl was closeted for a long time before either lady retired to rest.

"I have seen a great deal of him," said Mrs. Penniman. "He is not very easy to know. I suppose you think you know him; but you don't, my dear. You will some day; but it will only be after you have lived with him. I may almost say *I* have lived with him," Mrs. Penniman proceeded, while Catherine stared. "I think I know him now; I have had such remarkable opportunities. You will have the same—or, rather, you will have better"; and Aunt Lavinia smiled. "Then you will see what I mean. It's a wonderful character, full of passion and energy, and just as true."

Catherine listened with a mixture of interest and apprehension. Aunt Lavinia was intensely sympathetic, and Catherine, for the past year, while she wandered through foreign galleries and churches, and rolled over the smoothness of posting roads, nursing the thoughts that never passed her lips, had often longed for the company of some intelligent person of her own sex. To tell her story to some kind woman—at moments it seemed to her that this would give her comfort, and she had more than once been on the point of taking the landlady, or the nice young person from the dressmaker's, into her confidence. If a woman had been near her, she would on certain occasions have treated such a companion to a fit of weeping; and she had an apprehension that, on her return, this would form her response to Aunt Lavinia's first embrace. In fact, however, the two ladies had met, in Washington Square, without tears; and when they found themselves alone together a certain dryness fell upon the girl's emotion. It came over her with a greater force that Mrs. Penniman had enjoyed a whole year of her lover's society, and it was not a pleasure to her to hear her aunt explain and interpret the young man, speaking of him as if her own knowledge of him were supreme. It was not that Catherine was jealous; but her sense of Mrs. Penniman's innocent falsity, which had lain dormant, began to haunt her again, and she was glad that she was safely at home. With this, however, it was a blessing to be able to talk of Morris, to sound his name, to be with a person who was not unjust to him.

"You have been very kind to him," said Catherine. "He has written me that, often. I shall never forget that, Aunt Lavinia."

"I have done what I could; it has been very little. To let him come and talk to me, and give him his cup of tea—that was all. Your aunt Almond thought it was too much, and used to scold me terribly; but she promised me, at least, not to betray me."

"To betray you?"

"Not to tell your father. He used to sit in your father's study," said Mrs. Penniman, with a little laugh.

Catherine was silent a moment. This idea was disagreeable to her, and she was reminded again, with pain, of her aunt's secretive habits. Morris, the reader may be informed, had had the tact not to tell her that he sat in her father's study. He had known her but for a few months, and her aunt had known her for fifteen years; and yet he would not have made the mistake of thinking that Catherine would see the joke of the thing. "I am sorry you made him go into father's room," she said, after awhile.

"I didn't send him; he went himself. He liked to look at the books, and at all those things in the glass cases. He knows all about them; he knows all about everything."

Catherine was silent again; then, "I wish he had found some employment," she said.

"He has found some employment. It's beautiful news, and he told me to tell you as soon as you arrive. He has gone into partnership with a commission merchant. It was all settled, quite suddenly, a week ago."

This seemed to Catherine indeed beautiful news; it had a fine prosperous air. "Oh, I'm so glad!" she said; and now, for a moment, she was disposed to throw herself on Aunt Lavinia's neck.

"It's much better than being under some one; and he has never been used to that," Mrs. Penniman went on. "He is just as good as his partner—they are perfectly equal. You see how right he was to wait. I should like to know what your father can say now! They have got an office in Duane Street, and little printed cards; he brought me one to show me. I have got it in my room, and you shall see it to-morrow. That's what he said to me the last time he was here—'You see how right I was to wait.' He has got other people under him instead of being a subordinate. He could never be a subordinate; I have often told him I could never think of him in that way."

Catherine assented to this proposition, and was very happy to know that Morris was his own master; but she was deprived of the satisfaction of thinking that she might communicate this news in triumph to her father. Her father would care equally little whether Morris were established in business or transported for life. Her trunks had been brought into her room, and further reference to her lover was for a short time suspended, while she opened them and displayed to her aunt some of the spoils of foreign travel. These were rich and abundant; and Catherine had brought home a present to every one—to every one save Morris, to whom she had brought simply her undiverted heart. To Mrs. Penniman she had been lavishly generous, and Aunt Lavinia spent half an hour in unfolding and folding again, with little ejaculations of gratitude and taste. She marched about for some time in a splendid cashmere shawl, which Catherine had begged her to accept, settling it on her shoulders, and twisting down her head to see how low the point descended behind.

"I shall regard it only as a loan," she said. "I will leave it to you again when I die; or, rather," she added, kissing her niece again, "I will leave it to your first-born little girl." And draped in her shawl, she stood there smiling.

"You had better wait till she comes," said Catherine.

"I don't like the way you say that," Mrs. Penniman rejoined, in a moment. "Catherine, are you changed?"

"No; I am the same."

"You have not swerved a line?"

"I am exactly the same," Catherine repeated, wishing her aunt were a little less sympathetic.

"Well, I am glad"; and Mrs. Penniman surveyed her cashmere in the glass. Then, "How is your father?" she asked, in a moment, with her eyes on her niece. "Your letters were so meagre—I could never tell."

"Father is very well."

"Ah, you know what I mean," said Mrs. Penniman, with a dignity to which the cashmere gave a richer effect. "Is he still implacable?"

"Oh, yes!"

"Quite unchanged?"

"He is, if possible, more firm."

Mrs. Penniman took off her great shawl, and slowly folded it up. "That is very bad. You had no success with your little project?"

"What little project?"

"Morris told me all about it. The idea of turning the tables on him, in Europe; of watching him, when he was agreeably impressed by some celebrated sight—he pretends to be so artistic, you know—and then just pleading with him and bringing him round."

"I never tried it. It was Morris's idea; but if he had been with us in Europe, he would have seen that father was never impressed in that way. He *is* artistic—tremendously artistic; but the more celebrated places we visited, and the more he admired them, the less use it would have been to plead with him. They seemed only to make him more determined—more terrible," said poor Catherine. "I shall never bring him round, and I expect nothing now."

"Well, I must say," Mrs. Penniman answered, "I never supposed you were going to give it up."

"I have given it up. I don't care now."

"You have grown very brave," said Mrs. Penniman, with a short laugh. "I didn't advise you to sacrifice your property."

"Yes, I am braver than I was. You asked me if I had changed; I have changed in that way. Oh," the girl went on, "I have changed very much. And it isn't my property. If *he* doesn't care for it, why should I?"

Mrs. Penniman hesitated. "Perhaps he does care for it."

"He cares for it for my sake, because he doesn't want to injure me. But he will know—he knows already—how little he need be afraid about that. Besides," said Catherine, "I have got plenty of money of my own. We shall be very well off; and now hasn't he got his business? I am delighted about that business." She went on talking, showing a good deal of excitement as she proceeded. Her aunt had never seen her with just this manner, and Mrs. Penniman, observing her, set it down to foreign travel, which had made her more positive, more mature. She thought also that Catherine had improved in appearance; she looked rather handsome. Mrs. Penniman wondered whether Morris Townsend would be struck with that. While she was engaged in this speculation, Catherine broke out, with a certain sharpness, "Why are you so contradictory, Aunt Penniman? You seem to think one thing at one time, and another at another. A year ago, before I went away, you wished me not to mind about displeasing father, and now you seem to recommend me to take another line. You change about so."

This attack was unexpected, for Mrs. Penniman was not used, in any discussion, to seeing the war carried into her own country—possibly because the enemy generally had doubts of finding subsistence there. To her own consciousness, the flowery fields of her reason had rarely been ravaged by a hostile force. It was perhaps on this account that in defending them she was majestic rather than agile.

"I don't know what you accuse me of, save of being too deeply interested in your happiness. It is the first time I have been told I am capricious. That fault is not what I am usually reproached with."

"You were angry last year that I wouldn't marry immediately, and now you talk about my winning my father over. You told me it would serve him right if he should take me to Europe for nothing. Well, he has taken me for nothing, and you ought to be satisfied. Nothing is changed—nothing but my feeling about father. I don't mind nearly so much now. I have been as good as I could, but he doesn't care. Now I don't care either. I don't know whether I have grown bad; perhaps I have. But I don't care for that. I have come home to be married—that's all I know. That ought to please you, unless you have taken up some new idea; you are so strange. You may do as you please, but you must never speak to me again about pleading with father. I shall never plead with him for anything; that is all over. He has put me off. I am come home to be married."

This was a more authoritative speech than she had ever heard on her niece's lips, and Mrs. Penniman was proportionately startled. She was, indeed, a little awestruck, and the force of the girl's emotion and resolution left her nothing to reply. She was easily frightened, and she always carried off her discomfiture by a concession—a concession which was often accompanied, as in the present case, by a little nervous laugh.

26

IF she had disturbed her niece's temper—she began from this moment forward to talk a good deal about Catherine's temper, an article which up to that time had never been mentioned in connection with our heroine—Catherine had opportunity on the morrow to recover her serenity. Mrs. Penniman had given her a message from Morris Townsend to the effect that he would come and welcome her home on the day after her arrival. He came in the afternoon; but, as may be imagined, he was not on this occasion made free of Doctor Sloper's study. He had been coming and going, for the past year, so comfortably and irresponsibly, that he had a certain sense of being wronged by finding himself reminded that he must now limit his horizon to the front parlor, which was Catherine's particular province.

"I am very glad you have come back," he said; "it makes me very happy to see you again." And he looked at her, smiling, from head to foot, though it did not appear afterward that he agreed with Mrs. Penniman (who, woman-like, went into more details) in thinking her embellished.

To Catherine he appeared resplendent; it was some time before she could believe again that this beautiful young man was her own exclusive property. They had a great deal of characteristic lovers' talk—a soft exchange of inquiries and assurances. In these matters Morris had an excellent grace, which flung a picturesque interest even over the account of his début in the commission business—a subject as to which his companion earnestly questioned him. From time to time he got up from the sofa where they sat together, and walked about the room; after which he came back, smiling and passing his hand through his hair. He was unquiet, as was natural in a young man who has just been reunited to a long-absent mistress, and Catherine made the reflection that she had never seen him so excited. It gave her pleasure, somehow, to note this fact. He asked her questions about her travels, to some of which she was unable to reply, for she had forgotten the names of places and the order of her father's journey. But for the moment she was so happy, so lifted up by the belief that her troubles at last were over, that she forgot to be ashamed of her meagre answers. It seemed to her now that she could marry him without the remnant of a scruple, or a single tremor save those that belonged to joy. Without waiting for him to ask, she told him that her father had come back in exactly the same state of mind—that he had not yielded an inch.

"We must not expect it now," she said, "and we must do without it."

Morris sat looking and smiling. "My poor, dear girl!" he exclaimed.

"You mustn't pity me," said Catherine. "I don't mind it now; I am used to it."

Morris continued to smile, and then he got up and walked about again. "You had better let me try him."

"Try to bring him over? You would only make him worse," Catherine answered, resolutely.

"You say that because I managed it so badly before. But I should manage it differently now. I am much wiser; I have had a year to think of it. I have more tact."

"Is that what you have been thinking of for a year?"

"Much of the time. You see, the idea sticks in my crop. I don't like to be beaten."

"How are you beaten if we marry?"

"Of course I am not beaten on the main issue; but I am, don't you see? on all the rest of it—on the question of my reputation, of my relations with your father, of my relations with my own children, if we should have any."

"We shall have enough for our children; we shall have enough for everything. Don't you expect to succeed in business?"

"Brilliantly, and we shall certainly be very comfortable. But it isn't of the mere material comfort I speak; it is of the moral comfort," said Morris—"of the intellectual satisfaction."

"I have great moral comfort now," Catherine declared, very simply.

"Of course you have. But with me it is different. I have staked my pride on proving to your father that he is wrong, and now that I am at the head of a flourishing business, I can deal with him as an equal. I have a capital plan—do let me go at him!"

He stood before her with his bright face, his jaunty air, his hands in his pockets; and she got up, with her eyes resting on his own. "Please don't, Morris; please don't," she said; and there was a certain mild, sad firmness in her tone which he heard for the first time. "We must ask no favors of him—we must ask nothing more. He won't relent, and nothing good will come of it. I know it now—I have a very good reason."

"And pray what is your reason?"

She hesitated to bring it out, but at last it came. "He is not very fond of me."

"Oh, bother!" cried Morris, angrily.

"I wouldn't say such a thing without being sure. I saw it, I felt it, in England, just before he came away. He talked to me one night—the last night—and then it came over me. You can tell when a person feels that way. I wouldn't accuse him if he hadn't made me feel that way. I don't accuse him; I just tell you that that's how it is. He can't help it; we can't govern our affections. Do I govern mine? Mightn't he say that to me? It's because he is so fond of my mother, whom we lost so long ago. She was beautiful, and very, very brilliant; he is always thinking of her. I am not at all like her; Aunt Penniman has told me that. Of course it isn't my fault; but neither is it his fault. All I mean is, it's true; and it's a stronger reason for his never being reconciled than simply his dislike for you."

" 'Simply?' " cried Morris, with a laugh. "I am much obliged for that."

"I don't mind about his disliking you now; I mind everything less. I feel differently; I feel separated from my father."

"Upon my word," said Morris, "you are a queer family."

"Don't say that—don't say anything unkind," the girl entreated. "You must be very kind to me now, because, Morris, because"—and she hesitated a moment—"because I have done a great deal for you."

"Oh, I know that, my dear."

She had spoken up to this moment without vehemence or outward sign of emotion, gently, reasoningly, only trying to explain. But her emotion had been ineffectually smothered, and it betrayed itself at last in the trembling of her voice. "It is a great thing to be separated like that from your father, when you have worshipped him before. It has made me very unhappy; or it would have made me so if I didn't love you. You can tell when a person speaks to you as if—as if—"

"As if what?"

"As if they despised you!" said Catherine, passionately. "He spoke that way the night before we sailed. It wasn't much, but it was enough, and I thought of it on the voyage all the time. Then I made up my mind. I will never ask him for anything again, or expect anything from him. It would not be natural now. We must be very happy together, and we must not seem to depend upon his forgiveness. And, Morris, Morris, you must never despise me!"

This was an easy promise to make, and Morris made it with fine effect. But for the moment he undertook nothing more onerous.

✵ 27 ✵

THE DOCTOR, of course, on his return, had a good deal of talk with his sisters. He was at no great pains to narrate his travels or to communicate his impressions of distant lands to Mrs. Penniman, upon whom he contented himself with bestowing a memento of his enviable experience in the shape of a velvet gown. But he conversed with her at some length about matters nearer home, and lost no time in assuring her that he was still an inflexible father.

"I have no doubt you have seen a great deal of Mr. Townsend, and done your best to console him for Catherine's absence," he said. "I don't ask you, and you needn't deny it. I wouldn't put the question to you for the world, and expose you to the inconvenience of having to—a—excogitate an answer. No one has betrayed you, and there has been no spy upon your proceedings. Elizabeth has told no tales, and has never mentioned you except to praise your good looks and good spirits. The thing is simply an inference of my own—an induction, as the philosophers say. It seems to me likely that you would have offered an asylum to an interesting sufferer. Mr. Townsend has been a good deal in the house; there is something in the house that tells me so. We doctors, you know, end by acquiring fine perceptions, and it is impressed upon my sensorium that he has sat in these chairs, in a very easy attitude, and warmed himself at that fire. I don't grudge him the comfort of it; it is the only one he will ever enjoy at my expense. It seems likely, indeed, that I shall be able to economize at his own. I don't know what you may have said to him, or what you may say hereafter; but I should like you to know that if you have encouraged him to believe that he will gain anything by hanging on, or that I have budged a hair-breadth from the position I took up a year ago, you have played him a trick for which he may exact reparation. I'm not sure that he may not bring a suit against you. Of course you have done it conscientiously; you have made yourself believe that I can be tired out. This is the most baseless hallucination that ever visited the brain of a genial optimist. I am not in the least tired; I am as fresh as when I started; I am good for fifty years yet. Catherine appears not to have budged an inch either; she is equally fresh; so we are about where we were before. This, however, you know as well as I. What I wish is simply to give you notice of my own state of mind. Take it to heart, dear Lavinia. Beware of the just resentment of a deluded fortune-hunter!"

"I can't say I expected it," said Mrs. Penniman. "And I had a sort of foolish hope that you would come home without that odious ironical tone with which you treat the most sacred subjects."

"Don't undervalue irony; it is often of great use. It is not, however, always necessary, and I will show you how gracefully I can lay it aside. I should like to know whether you think Morris Townsend will hang on?"

"I will answer you with your own weapons," said Mrs. Penniman. "You had better wait and see."

"Do you call such a speech as that one of my own weapons? I never said anything so rough."

"He will hang on long enough to make you very uncomfortable, then."

"My dear Lavinia," exclaimed the Doctor, "do you call that irony? I call it pugilism."

Mrs. Penniman, however, in spite of her pugilism, was a good deal frightened, and she took counsel of her fears. Her brother meanwhile took counsel, with many reservations, of Mrs. Almond, to whom he was no less generous than to Lavinia, and a good deal more communicative.

"I suppose she has had him there all the while," he said. "I must look into the state of my wine. You needn't mind telling me now; I have already said all I mean to say to her on the subject."

"I believe he was in the house a good deal," Mrs. Almond answered. "But you must admit that your leaving Lavinia quite alone was a great change for her, and that it was natural she should want some society."

"I do admit that, and that is why I shall make no row about the wine; I shall set it down as compensation to Lavinia. She is capable of telling me that she drank it all herself. Think of the inconceivable bad taste, in the circumstances, of that fellow making free with the house—or coming there at all! If that doesn't describe him, he is indescribable."

"His plan is to get what he can. Lavinia will have supported him for a year," said Mrs. Almond. "It's so much gained."

"She will have to support him for the rest of his life, then," cried the Doctor; "but without wine, as they say at the *tables d'hôte.*"

"Catherine tells me he has set up a business, and is making a great deal of money."

The Doctor stared. "She has not told me that—and Lavinia didn't deign. Ah!" he cried, "Catherine has given me up. Not that it matters, for all that the business amounts to."

"She has not given up Mr. Townsend," said Mrs. Almond; "I saw that in the first half-minute. She has come home exactly the same."

"Exactly the same; not a grain more intelligent. She didn't notice a stick or a stone all the while we were away—not a picture nor a view, not a statue nor a cathedral."

"How could she notice? She had other things to think of; they are never for an instant out of her mind. She touches me very much."

"She would touch me if she didn't irritate me. That's the effect she has upon me now. I have tried everything upon her; I really have been quite merciless. But it is of no use whatever; she is absolutely *glued.* I have passed, in consequence, into the exasperated stage. At first I had a good deal of a certain genial curiosity about it; I wanted to see if she really would stick. But, good Lord, one's curiosity is satisfied! I see she is capable of it, and now she can let go."

"She will never let go," said Mrs. Almond.

"Take care, or you will exasperate me too. If she doesn't let go, she will be shaken off—sent tumbling into the dust. That's a nice position for my daughter. She can't see that if you are going to be pushed, you had better jump. And then she will complain of her bruises."

"She will never complain," said Mrs. Almond.

"That I shall object to even more. But the deuce will be that I can't prevent anything."

"If she is to have a fall," said Mrs. Almond, with a gentle laugh, "we must spread as many carpets as we can." And she carried out this idea by showing a great deal of motherly kindness to the girl.

Mrs. Penniman immediately wrote to Morris Townsend. The intimacy between these two was by this time consummate, but I must content myself with noting but a few of its features. Mrs. Penniman's own share in it was a singular sentiment, which might have been misinterpreted, but which in itself was not discreditable to the poor lady. It was a romantic interest in this attractive and unfortunate young man, and yet it was not such an interest as Catherine might have been jealous of. Mrs. Penniman had not a particle of jealousy of her niece. For herself, she felt as if she were Morris's mother or sister—a mother or sister of an emotional temperament—and she had an absorbing desire to make him comfortable and happy. She had striven to do so during the year that her brother left her an open field, and her efforts had been attended with the success that has been pointed out. She had never had a child of her own, and Catherine, whom she had done her best to invest with the impor-tance that would naturally belong to a youthful Penniman, had only partly rewarded her zeal. Catherine, as an object of affection and solicitude, had never had that picturesque charm which (as it seemed to her) would have been a natural attribute of her own progeny. Even the maternal passion in Mrs. Penniman would have been romantic and factitious, and Catherine was not constituted to inspire a romantic passion. Mrs. Penniman was as fond of her as ever, but she had grown to feel that with Catherine she lacked opportunity. Sentimentally speaking, therefore, she had (though she had not disinherited her niece) adopted Morris Townsend, who gave her opportunity in abundance. She would have been very happy to have a handsome and tyrannical son, and would have taken an extreme interest in his love affairs. This was the light in which she had come to regard Morris, who had conciliated her at first, and made his impression by his delicate and calculated deference—a sort of exhibition to which Mrs. Penniman was particularly sensitive. He had largely abated his deference afterward, for he economized his resources, but the impression was made, and the young man's very brutality came to have a sort of filial value. If Mrs. Penniman had had a son, she would probably have been afraid of him, and at this stage of our narrative she was certainly afraid of Morris Townsend. This was one of the results of his domestication in Washington Square. He took his ease with her—as, for that matter, he would certainly have done with his own mother.

28

THE letter was a word of warning; it informed him that the Doctor had come home more impracticable than ever. She might have reflected that Catherine would supply him with all the information he needed on this point; but we know that Mrs. Penniman's reflections were rarely just; and, moreover, she felt that it was not for her to depend on what Catherine might do. She was to do her duty, quite irrespective of Catherine. I have said that her young friend took his ease with her, and it is an illustration of the fact that he made no answer to her letter. He took note of it amply; but he lighted his cigar with it, and he waited, in tranquil confidence that he should receive another. "His state of mind really freezes my blood," Mrs. Penniman had written, alluding to her brother; and it would have seemed that upon this statement she could hardly improve. Nevertheless, she wrote again, expressing herself with the aid of a different figure. "His hatred of you burns with a lurid flame—the flame that never dies," she wrote. "But it doesn't light up the darkness of your future. If my affection could do so, all the years of your life would be an eternal sunshine. I can extract nothing from C.; she is so terribly secretive, like her father. She seems to expect to be married very soon, and has evidently made preparations in Europe—quantities of clothing, ten pairs of shoes, etc. My dear friend, you cannot set up in married life simply with a few pairs of shoes, can you? Tell me what you think of this. I am intensely anxious to see you, I have so much to say. I miss you dreadfully; the house seems so empty without you. What is the news down town? Is the business extending?—that dear little business: I think it's so brave of you! Couldn't I come to your office?—just for three minutes? I might pass for a customer—is that what you call them? I might come in to buy something—some shares or some railroad things. *Tell me what you think of this plan.* I would carry a little reticule, like a woman of the people."

In spite of the suggestion about the reticule, Morris appeared to think poorly of the plan, for he gave Mrs. Penniman no encouragement whatever to visit his office, which he had already represented to her as a place peculiarly and unnaturally difficult to find. But as she persisted in desiring an interview—up to the last, after months of intimate colloquy, she called these meetings "interviews"—he agreed that they should take a walk together, and was even kind enough to leave his office for this purpose during the hours at which business might have been supposed to be liveliest. It was no surprise to him, when they met at a street corner, in a region of empty lots and undeveloped pavements (Mrs. Penniman being

attired as much as possible like a "woman of the people"), to find
that, in spite of her urgency, what she chiefly had to convey to him
was the assurance of her sympathy. Of such assurances, however, he
had already a voluminous collection, and it would not have been
worth his while to forsake a fruitful avocation merely to hear Mrs.
Penniman say, for the thousandth time, that she had made his cause
her own. Morris had something of his own to say. It was not an easy
thing to bring out, and while he turned it over, the difficulty made
him acrimonious.

"Oh yes, I know perfectly that he combines the properties of a
lump of ice and a red-hot coal," he observed. "Catherine has made it
thoroughly clear, and you have told me so till I am sick of it. You
needn't tell me again; I am perfectly satisfied. He will never give us a
penny; I regard that as mathematically proved."

Mrs. Penniman at this point had an inspiration.

"Couldn't you bring a lawsuit against him?" She wondered that
this simple expedient had never occurred to her before.

"I will bring a lawsuit against *you*," said Morris, "if you ask me
any more such aggravating questions. A man should know when he
is beaten," he added, in a moment. "I must give her up!"

Mrs. Penniman received this declaration in silence, though it
made her heart beat a little. It found her by no means unprepared,
for she had accustomed herself to the thought that, if Morris should
decidedly not be able to get her brother's money, it would not do for
him to marry Catherine without it. "It would not do," was a vague
way of putting the thing; but Mrs. Penniman's natural affection
completed the idea, which, though it had not as yet been so crudely
expressed between them as in the form that Morris had just given it,
had nevertheless been implied so often, in certain easy intervals of
talk, as he sat stretching his legs in the Doctor's well-stuffed arm-
chairs, that she had grown first to regard it with an emotion which
she flattered herself was philosophic, and then to have a secret
tenderness for it. The fact that she kept her tenderness secret proves,
of course, that she was ashamed of it; but she managed to blink her
shame by reminding herself that she was, after all, the official protector of her niece's marriage. Her logic would scarcely have passed
muster with the Doctor. In the first place, Morris *must* get the
money, and she would help him to it. In the second, it was plain it
would never come to him, and it would be a grievous pity he should

marry without it—a young man who might so easily find something better. After her brother had delivered himself, on his return from Europe, of that incisive little address that has been quoted, Morris's cause seemed so hopeless that Mrs. Penniman fixed her attention exclusively upon the latter branch of her argument. If Morris had been her son, she would certainly have sacrificed Catherine to a superior conception of his future; and to be ready to do so, as the case stood, was therefore even a finer degree of devotion. Nevertheless, it checked her breath a little to have the sacrificial knife, as it were, suddenly thrust into her hand.

Morris walked along a moment, and then he repeated, harshly, "I must give her up!"

"I think I understand you," said Mrs. Penniman, gently.

"I certainly say it distinctly enough—brutally and vulgarly enough."

He was ashamed of himself, and his shame was uncomfortable; and as he was extremely intolerant of discomfort, he felt vicious and cruel. He wanted to abuse somebody, and he began, cautiously—for he was always cautious—with himself.

"Couldn't you take her down a little?" he asked.

"Take her down?"

"Prepare her—try and ease me off."

Mrs. Penniman stopped, looking at him very solemnly.

"My poor Morris, do you know how much she loves you?"

"No, I don't. I don't want to know. I have always tried to keep from knowing. It would be too painful."

"She will suffer much," said Mrs. Penniman.

"You must console her. If you are as good a friend to me as you pretend to be, you will manage it."

Mrs. Penniman shook her head sadly.

"You talk of my 'pretending' to like you; but I can't pretend to hate you. I can only tell her I think very highly of you; and how will that console her for losing you?"

"The Doctor will help you. He will be delighted at the thing being broken off; and as he is a knowing fellow, he will invent something to comfort her."

"He will invent a new torture," cried Mrs. Penniman. "Heaven deliver her from her father's comfort! It will consist of his crowing over her, and saying, 'I always told you so!'"

Morris colored a most uncomfortable red.

"If you don't console her any better than you console me, you certainly won't be of much use. It's a damned disagreeable necessity; I feel it extremely, and you ought to make it easy for me."

"I will be your friend for life," Mrs. Penniman declared.

"Be my friend *now!*" and Morris walked on.

She went with him; she was almost trembling.

"Should you like me to tell her?" she asked.

"You mustn't tell her, but you can—you can—" And he hesitated, trying to think what Mrs. Penniman could do. "You can explain to her why it is. It's because I can't bring myself to step in between her and her father—to give him the pretext he grasps at so eagerly (it's a hideous sight!) for depriving her of her rights."

Mrs. Penniman felt with remarkable promptitude the charm of this formula.

"That's so like you," she said; "it's so finely felt."

Morris gave his stick an angry swing.

"Oh damnation!" he exclaimed, perversely.

Mrs. Penniman, however, was not discouraged.

"It may turn out better than you think. Catherine is, after all, so very peculiar." And she thought she might take it upon herself to assure him that, whatever happened, the girl would be very quiet—she wouldn't make a noise. They extended their walk, and while they proceeded Mrs. Penniman took upon herself other things besides, and ended by having assumed a considerable burden; Morris being ready enough, as may be imagined, to put everything off upon her. But he was not for a single instant the dupe of her blundering alacrity; he knew that of what she promised she was competent to perform but an insignificant fraction, and the more she professed her willingness to serve him, the greater fool he thought her.

"What will you do if you don't marry her?" she ventured to inquire in the course of this conversation.

"Something brilliant," said Morris. "Shouldn't you like me to do something brilliant?"

The idea gave Mrs. Penniman exceeding pleasure.

"I shall feel sadly taken in if you don't."

"I shall have to, to make up for this. This isn't at all brilliant, you know."

Mrs. Penniman mused a little, as if there might be some way of making out that it was; but she had to give up the attempt, and, to carry off the awkwardness of failure, she risked a new inquiry.

"Do you mean—do you mean another marriage?"

Morris greeted this question with a reflection which was hardly the less impudent from being inaudible. "Surely women are more crude than men!" And then he answered, audibly,

"Never in the world!"

Mrs. Penniman felt disappointed and snubbed, and she relieved herself in a little vaguely sarcastic cry. He was certainly perverse.

"I give her up, not for another woman, but for a wider career," Morris announced.

This was very grand; but still Mrs. Penniman, who felt that she had exposed herself, was faintly rancorous.

"Do you mean never to come to see her again?" she asked, with some sharpness.

"Oh no, I shall come again; but what is the use of dragging it out? I have been four times since she came back, and it's terribly awkward work. I can't keep it up indefinitely; she oughtn't to expect that, you know. A woman should never keep a man dangling," he added, finely.

"Ah, but you must have your last parting!" urged his companion, in whose imagination the idea of last partings occupied a place inferior in dignity only to that of first meetings.

⚘ 29 ⚘

HE CAME again, without managing the last parting; and again and again, without finding that Mrs. Penniman had as yet done much to pave the path of retreat with flowers. It was devilish awkward, as he said, and he felt a lively animosity for Catherine's aunt, who, as he had now quite formed the habit of saying to himself, had dragged him into the mess, and was bound in common charity to get him out of it. Mrs. Penniman, to tell the truth, had, in the seclusion of her own apartment—and, I may add, amid the suggestiveness of Catherine's, which wore in those days the appearance of that of a young lady laying out her *trousseau*—Mrs. Penniman had measured her responsibilities, and taken fright at their magnitude. The task of preparing Catherine and easing off Morris presented difficulties which increased in the execution, and even led the impulsive Lavinia to ask herself whether the modification of the young man's original project had been conceived in a happy spirit. A brilliant future, a wider career, a conscience exempt from the reproach of interference between a young lady and her natural rights—these excellent things might be too troublesomely purchased. From Catherine herself Mrs. Penniman received no assistance whatever; the poor girl was apparently without suspicion of her danger. She looked at her lover with eyes of undiminished trust, and though she had less confidence in her aunt than in a young man with whom she had exchanged so many tender vows, she gave her no handle for explaining or confessing. Mrs. Penniman, faltering and wavering, declared Catherine was very stupid, put off the great scene, as she would have called it, from day to day, and wandered about, very uncomfortably, with her unexploded bomb in her hands. Morris's own scenes were very small ones just now; but even these were beyond his strength. He made his visits as brief as possible, and, while he sat with his mistress, found terribly little to talk about. She was waiting for him, in vulgar parlance, to name the day; and so long as he was unprepared to be explicit on this point, it seemed a mockery to pretend to talk about matters more abstract. She had no airs and no arts; she never attempted to disguise her expectancy. She was waiting on his good pleasure, and would wait modestly and patiently; his hanging back at this supreme time might appear strange, but of course he must have a good reason for it. Catherine would have made a wife of the gentle, old-fashioned pattern—regarding reasons as favors and windfalls, but no more expecting one every day than she would have expected a bouquet of camellias. During the period of her engagement, however, a young lady even of the most slender pretensions counts upon more bouquets than at other times; and there was a want of perfume in the air at this moment which at last excited the girl's alarm.

"Are you sick?" she asked of Morris. "You seem so restless, and you look pale."

"I am not at all well," said Morris; and it occurred to him that, if he could only make her pity him enough, he might get off.

"I am afraid you are overworked; you oughtn't to work so much."

"I must do that." And then he added, with a sort of calculated brutality, "I don't want to owe you everything."

"Ah, how can you say that?"

"I am too proud," said Morris.

"Yes—you are too proud."

"Well, you must take me as I am," he went on; "you can never change me."

"I don't want to change you," she said gently; "I will take you as you are." And she stood looking at him.

"You know people talk tremendously about a man's marrying a rich girl," Morris remarked. "It's excessively disagreeable."

"But I am not rich," said Catherine.

"You are rich enough to make me talked about."

"Of course you are talked about. It's an honor."

"It's an honor I could easily dispense with."

She was on the point of asking him whether it was not a compensation for this annoyance that the poor girl who had the misfortune to bring it upon him loved him so dearly and believed in him so truly; but she hesitated, thinking that this would perhaps seem an exacting speech, and while she hesitated, he suddenly left her.

The next time he came, however, she brought it out, and she told him again that he was too proud. He repeated that he couldn't change, and this time she felt the impulse to say that with a little effort he might change.

Sometimes he thought that if he could only make a quarrel with her it might help him; but the question was how to quarrel with a young woman who had such treasures of concession. "I suppose you think the effort is all on your side," he broke out. "Don't you believe that I have my own effort to make?"

"It's all yours now," she said; "my effort is finished and done with."

"Well, mine is not."

"We must bear things together," said Catherine. "That's what we ought to do."

Morris attempted a natural smile. "There are some things which we can't very well bear together—for instance, separation."

"Why do you speak of separation?"

"Ah! you don't like it; I knew you wouldn't."

"Where are you going, Morris?" she suddenly asked.

He fixed his eye on her a moment, and for a part of that moment she was afraid of it. "Will you promise not to make a scene?"

"A scene!—do I make scenes?"

"All women do!" said Morris, with the tone of large experience.

"I don't. Where are you going?"

"If I should say I was going away on business, should you think it very strange?"

She wondered a moment, gazing at him. "Yes—no. Not if you will take me with you."

"Take you with me—on business?"

"What is your business? Your business is to be with me."

"I don't earn my living with you," said Morris. "Or, rather," he cried, with a sudden inspiration, "that's just what I do—or what the world says I do!"

This ought perhaps to have been a great stroke, but it miscarried. "Where are you going?" Catherine simply repeated.

"To New Orleans—about buying some cotton."

"I am perfectly willing to go to New Orleans," Catherine said.

"Do you suppose I would take you to a nest of yellow-fever?" cried Morris. "Do you suppose I would expose you at such a time as this?"

"If there is yellow-fever, why should you go? Morris, you must not go."

"It is to make six thousand dollars," said Morris. "Do you grudge me that satisfaction?"

"We have no need of six thousand dollars. You think too much about money."

"You can afford to say that. This is a great chance; we heard of it last night." And he explained to her in what the chance consisted; and told her a long story, going over more than once several of the details, about the remarkable stroke of business which he and his partner had planned between them.

But Catherine's imagination, for reasons best known to herself, absolutely refused to be fired. "If you can go to New Orleans, I can go," she said. "Why shouldn't you catch yellow-fever quite as easily as I? I am every bit as strong as you, and not in the least afraid of any fever. When we were in Europe we were in very unhealthy places; my father used to make me take some pills. I never caught anything, and I never was nervous. What will be the use of six thousand dollars if you die of a fever? When persons are going to be married they oughtn't to think so much about business. You shouldn't think about cotton; you should think about me. You can go to New Orleans some other time—there will always be plenty of cotton. It isn't the moment to choose: we have waited too long already." She spoke more forcibly and volubly than he had ever heard her, and she held his arm in her two hands.

"You said you wouldn't make a scene," cried Morris. "I call this a scene."

"It's you that are making it. I have never asked you anything before. We have waited too long already." And it was a comfort to her to think that she had hitherto asked so little; it seemed to make her right to insist the greater now.

Morris bethought himself a little. "Very well, then; we won't talk about it any more. I will transact my business by letter." And he began to smooth his hat, as if to take leave.

"You won't go?" and she stood looking up at him.

He could not give up his idea of provoking a quarrel; it was so much the simplest way. He bent his eyes on her upturned face with the darkest frown he could achieve. "You are not discreet; you mustn't bully me."

But, as usual, she conceded everything. "No, I am not discreet; I know I am too pressing. But isn't it natural? It is only for a moment."

"In a moment you may do a great deal of harm. Try and be calmer the next time I come."

"When will you come?"

"Do you want to make conditions?" Morris asked. "I will come next Saturday."

"Come to-morrow," Catherine begged; "I want you to come to-morrow. I will be very quiet," she added; and her agitation had by this time become so great that the assurance was not unbecoming. A sudden fear had come over her; it was like the solid conjunction of a dozen disembodied doubts, and her imagination, at a single bound, had traversed an enormous distance. All her being, for the moment, was centred in the wish to keep him in the room.

Morris bent his head and kissed her forehead. "When you are quiet, you are perfection," he said; "but when you are violent, you are not in character."

It was Catherine's wish that there should be no violence about her save the beating of her heart, which she could not help; and she went on, as gently as possible, "Will you promise to come to-morrow?"

"I said Saturday!" Morris answered, smiling. He tried a frown at one moment, a smile at another; he was at his wit's end.

"Yes, Saturday too," she answered, trying to smile. "But to-morrow first." He was going to the door, and she went with him quickly. She leaned her shoulder against it; it seemed to her that she would do anything to keep him.

"If I am prevented from coming to-morrow, you will say I have deceived you," he said.

"How can you be prevented? You can come if you will."

"I am a busy man—I am not a dangler!" cried Morris, sternly.

His voice was so hard and unnatural that, with a helpless look at him, she turned away; and then he quickly laid his hand on the door-knob. He felt as if he were absolutely running away from her. But in an instant she was close to him again, and murmuring in a tone none the less penetrating for being low, "Morris, you are going to leave me."

"Yes, for a little while."

"For how long?"

"Till you are reasonable again."

"I shall never be reasonable, in that way." And she tried to keep him longer; it was almost a struggle. "Think of what I have done!" she broke out. "Morris, I have given up everything."

"You shall have everything back."

"You wouldn't say that if you didn't mean something. What is it?—what has happened?—what have I done?—what has changed you?"

"I will write to you—that is better," Morris stammered.

"Ah, you won't come back!" she cried, bursting into tears.

"Dear Catherine," he said, "don't believe that. I promise you that you shall see me again." And he managed to get away, and to close the door behind him.

❦ 30 ❦

IT WAS almost the last outbreak of passion of her life; at least, she never indulged in another that the world knew anything about. But this one was long and terrible; she flung herself on the sofa and gave herself up to her grief. She hardly knew what had happened; ostensibly she had only had a difference with her lover, as other girls had had before, and the thing was not only not a rupture, but she was under no obligation to regard it even as a menace. Nevertheless, she felt a wound, even if he had not dealt it; it seemed to her that a mask had suddenly fallen from his face. He had wished to get away from her; he had been angry and cruel, and said strange things, with strange looks. She was smothered and stunned; she buried her head in the cushions, sobbing and talking to herself. But at last she raised herself, with the fear that either her father or Mrs. Penniman would come in; and then she sat there, staring before her, while the room grew darker. She said to herself that perhaps he would come back to tell her he had not meant what he said; and she listened for his ring at the door, trying to believe that this was probable. A long time passed, but Morris remained absent; the shadows gathered; the evening settled down on the meagre elegance of the light, clear-colored room; the fire went out. When it had grown dark, Catherine went to the window and looked out; she stood there for half an hour, on the mere chance that he would come up the steps. At last she turned away, for she saw her father come in. He had seen her at the window looking out, and he stopped a moment at the bottom of the white steps, and gravely, with an air of exaggerated courtesy, lifted his hat to her. The gesture was so incongruous to the condition she was in, this stately tribute of respect to a poor girl despised and forsaken was so out of place, that the thing gave her a kind of horror, and she hurried away to her room. It seemed to her that she had given Morris up.

She had to show herself half an hour later, and she was sustained at table by the immensity of her desire that her father should not perceive that anything had happened. This was a great help to her afterward, and it served her (though never as much as she supposed) from the first. On this occasion Doctor Sloper was rather talkative. He told a great many stories about a wonderful poodle that he had seen at the house of an old lady whom he visited professionally. Catherine not only tried to appear to listen to the anecdotes of the poodle, but she endeavored to interest herself in them, so as not to think of her scene with Morris. That perhaps was an hallucination; he was mistaken, she was jealous; people didn't change like that from one day to another. Then she knew that she had had doubts before—strange suspicions, that were at once vague and acute—and that he had been different ever since her return from Europe: whereupon she tried again to listen to her father, who told a story so remarkably well. Afterward she went straight to her own room; it was beyond her strength to undertake to spend the evening with her aunt. All the evening, alone, she questioned herself. Her trouble was terrible; but was it a thing of her imagination, engendered by an extravagant sensibility, or did it represent a clear-cut reality, and had the worst that was possible actually come to pass? Mrs. Penniman, with a degree of tact that was as unusual as it was commendable, took the line of leaving her alone. The truth is, that her suspicions having been aroused, she indulged a desire, natural to a timid person, that the explosion should be localized. So long as the air still vibrated she kept out of the way.

She passed and repassed Catherine's door several times in the course of the evening, as if she expected to hear a plaintive moan behind it. But the room remained perfectly still; and accordingly, the last thing before retiring to her own couch, she applied for admittance. Catherine was sitting up, and had a book that she pretended to be reading. She had no wish to go to bed, for she had no expectation of sleeping. After Mrs. Penniman had left her she sat up half the night, and she offered her visitor no inducement to remain. Her aunt came stealing in very gently, and approached her with great solemnity.

"I am afraid you are in trouble, my dear. Can I do anything to help you?"

"I am not in any trouble whatever, and do not need any help," said Catherine, fibbing roundly, and proving thereby that not only our faults, but our most involuntary misfortunes, tend to corrupt our morals.

"Has nothing happened to you?"

"Nothing whatever."

"Are you very sure, dear?"

"Perfectly sure."

"And can I really do nothing for you?"

"Nothing, aunt, but kindly leave me alone," said Catherine.

Mrs. Penniman, though she had been afraid of too warm a welcome before, was now disappointed at so cold a one; and in relating afterward, as she did to many persons, and with considerable variations of detail, the history of the termination of her niece's engagement, she was usually careful to mention that the young lady, on a certain occasion, had "hustled" her out of the room. It was characteristic of Mrs. Penniman that she related this fact, not in the least out of malignity to Catherine, whom she very sufficiently pitied, but simply from a natural disposition to embellish any subject that she touched.

Catherine, as I have said, sat up half the night, as if she still expected to hear Morris Townsend ring at the door. On the morrow this expectation was less unreasonable; but it was not gratified by the reappearance of the young man. Neither had he written; there was not a word of explanation or reassurance. Fortunately for Catherine, she could take refuge from her excitement, which had now become intense, in her determination that her father should see nothing of it. How well she deceived her father we shall have occasion to learn; but her innocent arts were of little avail before a person of the rare perspicacity of Mrs. Penniman. This lady easily saw that she was agitated, and if there was any agitation going forward, Mrs. Penniman was not a person to forfeit her natural share in it. She returned to the charge the next evening, and requested her niece to confide in her—to unburden her heart. Perhaps she should be able to explain certain things that now seemed dark, and that she knew more about than Catherine supposed. If Catherine had been frigid the night before, today she was haughty.

"You are completely mistaken, and I have not the least idea what you mean. I don't know what you are trying to fasten on me, and I have never had less need of any one's explanations in my life."

In this way the girl delivered herself, and from hour to hour kept her aunt at bay. From hour to hour Mrs. Penniman's curiosity grew. She would have given her little finger to know what Morris had said and done, what tone he had taken, what pretext he had found. She wrote to him, naturally, to request an interview; but she received, as naturally, no answer to her petition. Morris was not in a writing mood; for Catherine had addressed him two short notes which met with no acknowledgment. These notes were so brief that I may give them entire. "Won't you give me some sign that you didn't mean to be so cruel as you seemed on Tuesday?"—that was the first; the other was a little longer. "If I was unreasonable or suspicious on Tuesday—if I annoyed you or troubled you in any way—I beg your forgiveness, and I promise never again to be so foolish. I am punished enough, and I don't understand. Dear Morris, you are killing me!" These notes were despatched on the Friday and Saturday; but Saturday and Sunday passed without bringing the poor girl the satisfaction she desired. Her punishment accumulated; she continued to bear it, however, with a good deal of superficial fortitude. On Saturday morning, the Doctor, who had been watching in silence, spoke to his sister Lavinia.

"The thing has happened—the scoundrel has backed out!"

"Never!" cried Mrs. Penniman, who had bethought herself what she should say to Catherine, but was not provided with a line of defence against her brother, so that indignant negation was the only weapon in her hands.

"He has begged for a reprieve, then, if you like that better!"

"It seems to make you very happy that your daughter's affections have been trifled with."

"It does," said the Doctor; "for I had foretold it! It's a great pleasure to be in the right."

"Your pleasures make one shudder!" his sister exclaimed.

Catherine went rigidly through her usual occupations; that is, up to the point of going with her aunt to church on Sunday morning. She generally went to afternoon service as well; but on this occasion her courage faltered, and she begged of Mrs. Penniman to go without her.

"I am sure you have a secret," said Mrs. Penniman, with great significance, looking at her rather grimly.

"If I have, I shall keep it!" Catherine answered, turning away.

Mrs. Penniman started for church; but before she had arrived, she stopped and turned back, and before twenty minutes had elapsed she re-entered the house, looked into the empty parlors, and then went upstairs and knocked at Catherine's door. She got no answer; Catherine was not in her room, and Mrs. Penniman presently ascertained that she was not in the house. "She has gone to him! she has fled!" Lavinia cried, clasping her hands with admiration and envy. But she soon perceived that Catherine had taken nothing with her—all her personal property in her room was intact—and then she jumped at the hypothesis that the girl had gone forth, not in tenderness, but in resentment. "She has followed him to his own door! she has burst upon him in his own apartment!" It was in these terms that Mrs. Penniman depicted to herself her niece's errand, which, viewed in this light, gratified her sense of the picturesque only a shade less strongly than the idea of a clandestine marriage. To visit one's lover, with tears and reproaches, at his own residence, was an image so agreeable to Mrs. Penniman's mind that she felt a sort of æsthetic disappointment at its lacking, in this case, the harmonious accompaniments of darkness and storm. A quiet Sunday afternoon appeared an inadequate setting for it; and, indeed, Mrs. Penniman was quite out of humor with the conditions of the time, which passed very slowly as she sat in the front parlor, in her bonnet and her cashmere shawl, awaiting Catherine's return.

This event at last took place. She saw her—at the window—mount the steps, and she went to await her in the hall, where she pounced upon her as soon as she had entered the house, and drew her into the parlor, closing the door with solemnity. Catherine was flushed, and her eye was bright. Mrs. Penniman hardly knew what to think.

"May I venture to ask where you have been?" she demanded.

"I have been to take a walk," said Catherine. "I thought you had gone to church."

"I did go to church; but the service was shorter than usual. And pray where did you walk?"

"I don't know!" said Catherine.

"Your ignorance is most extraordinary! Dear Catherine, you can trust me."

"What am I to trust you with?"

"With your secret—your sorrow."

"I have no sorrow!" said Catherine, fiercely.

"My poor child," Mrs. Penniman insisted, "you can't deceive me. I know everything. I have been requested to—a—to converse with you."

"I don't want to converse!"

"It will relieve you. Don't you know Shakespeare's lines?—'The grief that does not speak!' My dear girl, it is better as it is!"

"What is better?" Catherine asked.

She was really too perverse. A certain amount of perversity was to be allowed for in a young lady whose lover had thrown her over; but not such an amount as would prove inconvenient to his apologists. "That you should be reasonable," said Mrs. Penniman, with some sternness; "that you should take counsel of worldly prudence, and submit to practical considerations; that you should agree to—a—separate."

Catherine had been ice up to this moment, but at this word she flamed up. "Separate? What do you know about our separating?"

Mrs. Penniman shook her head with a sadness in which there was almost a sense of injury. "Your pride is my pride, and your suscepti-bilities are mine. I see your side perfectly, but I also—" and she smiled with melancholy suggestiveness—"I also see the situation as a whole!"

This suggestiveness was lost upon Catherine, who repeated her violent inquiry. "Why do you talk about separation; what do you know about it?"

"We must study resignation," said Mrs. Penniman, hesitating, but sententious at a venture.

"Resignation to what?"

"To a change of—of our plans."

"My plans have not changed!" said Catherine, with a little laugh.

"Ah, but Mr. Townsend's have," her aunt answered, very gently.

"What do you mean?"

There was an imperious brevity in the tone of this inquiry, against which Mrs. Penniman felt bound to protest; the information with which she had undertaken to supply her niece was after all a favor. She had tried sharpness, and she had tried sternness; but neither would do; she was shocked at the girl's obstinacy. "Ah well," she said, "if he hasn't told you! . . ." and she turned away.

Catherine watched her a moment in silence; then she hurried after her, stopping her before she reached the door. "Told me what? What do you mean? What are you hinting at and threatening me with?"

"Isn't it broken off?" asked Mrs. Penniman.

"My engagement? Not in the least!"

"I beg your pardon in that case. I have spoken too soon!"

"Too soon? Soon or late," Catherine broke out, "you speak fool-ishly and cruelly!"

"What has happened between you then?" asked her aunt, struck by the sincerity of this cry; "for something certainly has hap-pened."

"Nothing has happened but that I love him more and more!"

Mrs. Penniman was silent an instant. "I suppose that's the reason you went to see him this afternoon."

Catherine flushed as if she had been struck. "Yes, I did go to see him! But that's my own business."

"Very well, then; we won't talk about it." And Mrs. Penniman moved toward the door again; but she was stopped by a sudden imploring cry from the girl.

"Aunt Lavinia, *where* has he gone?"

"Ah, you admit then that he has gone away! Didn't they know at his house?"

"They said he had left town. I asked no more questions; I was ashamed," said Catherine, simply enough.

"You needn't have taken so compromising a step if you had had a little more confidence in me," Mrs. Penniman observed, with a good deal of grandeur.

"Is it to New Orleans?" Catherine went on, irrelevantly.

It was the first time Mrs. Penniman had heard of New Orleans in this connection; but she was averse to letting Catherine know that she was in the dark. She attempted to strike an illumination from the instructions she had received from Morris. "My dear Catherine," she said, "when a separation has been agreed upon, the farther he goes away the better."

"Agreed upon? Has he agreed upon it with you?" A consummate sense of her aunt's meddlesome folly had come over her during the last five minutes, and she was sickened at the thought that Mrs. Penniman had been let loose, as it were, upon her happiness.

"He certainly has sometimes advised with me," said Mrs. Penni-man.

"Is it you, then, that has changed him and made him so unnatu-ral?" Catherine cried. "Is it you that have worked on him and taken him from me? He doesn't belong to you, and I don't see how you have anything to do with what is between us! Is it you that have made this plot, and told him to leave me? How could you be so wicked, so cruel? What have I ever done to you? Why can't you leave me alone? I was afraid you would spoil everything: for you *do* spoil everything you touch! I was afraid of you all the time we were abroad; I had no rest when I thought that you were always talking to him." Catherine went on with growing vehemence, pouring out, in her bitterness and in the clairvoyance of her passion (which suddenly, jumping all processes, made her judge her aunt finally and without appeal), the uneasiness which had lain for so many months upon her heart.

Mrs. Penniman was scared and bewildered; she saw no prospect of introducing her little account of the purity of Morris's motives. "You are a most ungrateful girl!" she cried. "Do you scold me for talking with him? I'm sure we never talked of anything but you!"

"Yes; and that was the way you worried him; you made him tired of my very name! I wish you had never spoken of me to him; I never asked your help!"

"I am sure if it hadn't been for me he would never have come to the house, and you would never have known that he thought of you," Mrs. Penniman rejoined, with a good deal of justice.

"I wish he never had come to the house, and that I never had known it! That's better than this," said poor Catherine.

"You are a very ungrateful girl," Aunt Lavinia repeated.

Catherine's outbreak of anger and the sense of wrong gave her, while they lasted, the satisfaction that comes from all assertion of force; they hurried her along, and there is always a sort of pleasure in cleaving the air. But at bottom she hated to be violent, and she was conscious of no aptitude for organized resentment. She calmed herself with a great effort, but with great rapidity, and walked about the room a few moments, trying to say to herself that her aunt had meant everything for the best. She did not succeed in saying it with much conviction, but after a little she was able to speak quietly enough.

"I am not ungrateful, but I am very unhappy. It's hard to be grateful for that," she said. "Will you please tell me where he is?"

"I haven't the least idea; I am not in secret correspondence with him!" And Mrs. Penniman wished, indeed, that she were, so that she might let him know how Catherine abused her, after all she had done.

"Was it a plan of his, then, to break off—?" By this time Catherine had become completely quiet.

Mrs. Penniman began again to have a glimpse of her chance for explaining. "He shrunk—he shrunk," she said; "he lacked courage, but it was the courage to injure you! He couldn't bear to bring down on you your father's curse."

Catherine listened to this with her eyes fixed upon her aunt, and continued to gaze at her for some time afterward. "Did he tell you to say that?"

"He told me to say many things—all so delicate, so discriminating; and he told me to tell you he hoped you wouldn't despise him."

"I don't," said Catherine; and then she added, "And will he stay away forever?"

"Oh, forever is a long time. Your father, perhaps, won't live forever."

"Perhaps not."

"I am sure you appreciate—you understand—even though your heart bleeds," said Mrs. Penniman. "You doubtless think him too scrupulous. So do I, but I respect his scruples. What he asks of you is that you should do the same."

Catherine was still gazing at her aunt, but she spoke at last as if she had not heard or not understood her. "It has been a regular plan, then. He has broken it off deliberately; he has given me up."

"For the present, dear Catherine; he has put it off, only."

"He has left me alone," Catherine went on.

"Haven't you *me?*" asked Mrs. Penniman, with some solemnity.

Catherine shook her head slowly. "I don't believe it!" and she left the room.

❧ 31 ❧

THOUGH she had forced herself to be calm, she preferred practising this virtue in private, and she forbore to show herself at tea—a repast which, on Sundays, at six o'clock, took the place of dinner. Doctor Sloper and his sister sat face to face, but Mrs. Penniman never met her brother's eye. Late in the evening she went with him, but without Catherine, to their sister Almond's, where, between the two ladies, Catherine's unhappy situation was discussed with a frankness that was conditioned by a good deal of mysterious reticence on Mrs. Penniman's part.

"I am delighted he is not to marry her," said Mrs. Almond, "but he ought to be horsewhipped all the same."

Mrs. Penniman, who was shocked at her sister's coarseness, replied that he had been actuated by the noblest of motives—the desire not to impoverish Catherine.

"I am very happy that Catherine is not to be impoverished—but I hope he may never have a penny too much! And what does the poor girl say to *you?*" Mrs. Almond asked.

"She says I have a genius for consolation," said Mrs. Penniman.

This was the account of the matter that she gave to her sister, and it was perhaps with the consciousness of genius that, on her return that evening to Washington Square, she again presented herself for admittance at Catherine's door. Catherine came and opened it; she was apparently very quiet.

"I only want to give you a little word of advice," she said. "If your father asks you, say that everything is going on."

Catherine stood there, with her hand on the knob, looking at her aunt, but not asking her to come in. "Do you think he will ask me?"

"I am sure he will. He asked me just now, on our way home from your aunt Elizabeth's. I explained the whole thing to your aunt Elizabeth. I said to your father I knew nothing about it."

"Do you think he will ask me, when he sees—when he sees—?" But here Catherine stopped.

"The more he sees, the more disagreeable he will be," said her aunt.

"He shall see as little as possible!" Catherine declared.

"Tell him you are to be married."

"So I am," said Catherine, softly; and she closed the door upon her aunt.

She could not have said this two days later—for instance, on Tuesday, when she at last received a letter from Morris Townsend. It was an epistle of considerable length, measuring five large square pages, and written at Philadelphia. It was an explanatory document, and it explained a great many things, chief among which were the considerations that had led the writer to take advantage of an urgent "professional" absence to try and banish from his mind the image of one whose path he had crossed only to scatter it with ruins. He ventured to expect but partial success in this attempt, but he could promise her that, whatever his failure, he would never again interpose between her generous heart and her brilliant prospects and filial duties. He closed with an intimation that his professional pursuits might compel him to travel for some months, and with the hope that when they should each have accommodated themselves to what was sternly involved in their respective positions—even should this result not be reached for years—they should meet as friends, as fellow sufferers, as innocent but philosophic victims of a great social law. That her life should be peaceful and happy was the dearest wish of him who ventured still to subscribe himself her most obedient servant. The letter was beautifully written, and Catherine, who kept it for many years after this, was able, when her sense of the bitterness of its meaning and the hollowness of its tone had grown less acute, to admire its grace of expression. At present, for a long time after she received it, all she had to help her was the determination, daily more rigid, to make no appeal to the compassion of her father.

He suffered a week to elapse, and then one day, in the morning, at an hour at which she rarely saw him, he strolled into the back-parlor. He had watched his time, and he found her alone. She was sitting with some work, and he came and stood in front of her. He was going out; he had on his hat, and was drawing on his gloves.

"It doesn't seem to me that you are treating me just now with all the consideration I deserve," he said in a moment.

"I don't know what I have done," Catherine answered, with her eyes on her work.

"You have apparently quite banished from your mind the request I made you at Liverpool before we sailed—the request that you would notify me in advance before leaving my house."

"I have not left your house," said Catherine.

"But you intend to leave it, and, by what you gave me to understand, your departure must be impending. In fact, though you are still here in body, you are already absent in spirit. Your mind has taken up its residence with your prospective husband, and you might quite as well be lodged under the conjugal roof for all the benefit we get from your society."

"I will try and be more cheerful," said Catherine.

"You certainly ought to be cheerful; you ask a great deal if you are not. To the pleasure of marrying a charming young man you add that of having your own way; you strike me as a very lucky young lady!"

Catherine got up; she was suffocating. But she folded her work deliberately and correctly, bending her burning face upon it. Her father stood where he had planted himself; she hoped he would go, but he smoothed and buttoned his gloves, and then he rested his hands upon his hips.

"It would be a convenience to me to know when I may expect to have an empty house," he went on. "When you go, your aunt marches."

She looked at him at last, with a long, silent gaze, which, in spite of her pride and her resolution, uttered part of the appeal she had tried not to make. Her father's cold gray eye sounded her own, and he insisted on his point.

"Is it to-morrow? Is it next week, or the week after?"

"I shall not go away!" said Catherine.

The Doctor raised his eyebrows. "Has he backed out?"

"I have broken off my engagement."

"Broken it off?"

"I have asked him to leave New York, and he has gone away for a long time."

The Doctor was both puzzled and disappointed, but he solved his perplexity by saying to himself that his daughter simply misrepresented—justifiably, if one would, but nevertheless, misrepresented—the facts; and he eased off his disappointment, which was that of a man losing a chance for a little triumph that he had rather counted on, by a few words that he uttered aloud.

"How does he take his dismissal?"

"I don't know!" said Catherine, less ingeniously than she had hitherto spoken.

"You mean you don't care? You are rather cruel, after encouraging him and playing with him for so long!"

The Doctor had his revenge, after all.

32

OUR STORY has hitherto moved with very short steps, but as it approaches its termination it must take a long stride. As time went on, it might have appeared to the Doctor that his daughter's account of her rupture with Morris Townsend, mere bravado as he had deemed it, was in some degree justified by the sequel. Morris remained as rigidly and unremittingly absent as if he had died of a broken heart, and Catherine had apparently buried the memory of this fruitless episode as deep as if it had terminated by her own choice. We know that she had been deeply and incurably wounded, but the Doctor had no means of knowing it. He was certainly curious about it, and would have given a good deal to discover the exact truth; but it was his punishment that he never knew—his punishment, I mean, for the abuse of sarcasm in his relations with his daughter. There was a good deal of effective sarcasm in her keeping him in the dark, and the rest of the world conspired with her, in this sense, to be sarcastic. Mrs. Penniman told him nothing, partly because he never questioned her—he made too light of Mrs. Penniman for that—and partly because she flattered herself that a tormenting reserve, and a serene profession of ignorance, would avenge her for his theory that she had meddled in the matter. He went two or three times to see Mrs. Montgomery, but Mrs. Montgomery had nothing to impart. She simply knew that her brother's engagement was broken off; and now that Miss Sloper was out of danger, she preferred not to bear witness in any way against Morris. She had done so before— however unwillingly—because she was sorry for Miss Sloper; but she was not sorry for Miss Sloper now—not at all sorry. Morris had told her nothing about his relations with Miss Sloper at the time, and he had told her nothing since. He was always away, and he very seldom wrote to her; she believed he had gone to California. Mrs. Almond had, in her sister's phrase, "taken up" Catherine violently since the recent catastrophe; but, though the girl was very grateful to her for her kindness, she revealed no secrets, and the good lady could give the Doctor no satisfaction. Even, however, had she been able to narrate to him the private history of his daughter's unhappy love affair, it would have given her a certain comfort to leave him in ignorance; for Mrs. Almond was at this time not altogether in sympathy with her brother. She had guessed for herself that Catherine had been cruelly jilted—she knew nothing from Mrs. Penniman, for Mrs. Penniman had not ventured to lay the famous explanation of Morris's motives before Mrs. Almond, though she had thought it good enough for Catherine—and she pronounced her brother too consistently indifferent to what the poor creature must have suffered and must still be suffering. Doctor Sloper had his theory, and he rarely altered his theories. The marriage would have been an abominable one, and the girl had had a blessed escape. She was not to be pitied for that, and to pretend to condole with her would have been to make concessions to the idea that she had ever had a right to think of Morris.

"I put my foot on this idea from the first, and I keep it there now," said the Doctor. "I don't see anything cruel in that; one can't keep it there too long." To this Mrs. Almond more than once replied that, if Catherine had got rid of her incongruous lover, she deserved the credit of it, and that to bring herself to her father's enlightened view of the matter must have cost her an effort that he was bound to appreciate.

"I am by no means sure she has got rid of him," the Doctor said. "There is not the smallest probability that, after having been as obstinate as a mule for two years, she suddenly became amenable to reason. It is infinitely more probable that he got rid of her."

"All the more reason you should be gentle with her."

"I *am* gentle with her. But I can't do the pathetic; I can't pump up tears, to look graceful, over the most fortunate thing that ever happened to her."

"You have no sympathy," said Mrs. Almond; "that was never your strong point. You have only to look at her to see that, right or wrong, and whether the rupture came from herself or from him, her poor little heart is grievously bruised."

"Handling bruises, and even dropping tears on them, doesn't make them any better! My business is to see she gets no more knocks, and that I shall carefully attend to. But I don't at all recognize your description of Catherine. She doesn't strike me in the least as a young woman going about in search of a moral poultice. In fact, she seems to me much better than while the fellow was hanging about. She is perfectly comfortable and blooming; she eats and sleeps, takes her usual exercise, and overloads herself, as usual, with finery. She is always knitting some purse or embroidering some handkerchief, and it seems to me she turns these articles out about as fast as ever. She hasn't much to say; but when had she anything to say? She had her little dance, and now she is sitting down to rest. I suspect that, on the whole, she enjoys it."

"She enjoys it as people enjoy getting rid of a leg that has been crushed. The state of mind after amputation is doubtless one of comparative repose."

"If your leg is a metaphor for young Townsend, I can assure you he has never been crushed. Crushed? Not he! He is alive and perfectly intact; and that's why I am not satisfied."

"Should you have liked to kill him?" asked Mrs. Almond.

"Yes, very much. I think it is quite possible that it is all a blind."

"A blind?"

"An arrangement between them. *Il fait le mort,* as they say in France; but he is looking out of the corner of his eye. You can depend upon it, he has not burnt his ships; he has kept one to come back in. When I am dead, he will set sail again, and then she will marry him."

"It is interesting to know that you accuse your only daughter of being the vilest of hypocrites," said Mrs. Almond.

"I don't see what difference her being my only daughter makes. It is better to accuse one than a dozen. But I don't accuse any one. There is not the smallest hypocrisy about Catherine, and I deny that she even pretends to be miserable."

The Doctor's idea that the thing was a "blind" had its intermissions and revivals; but it may be said, on the whole, to have increased as he grew older; together with his impressions of Catherine's blooming and comfortable condition. Naturally, if he had not found grounds for viewing her as a lovelorn maiden during the year or two that followed her great trouble, he found none at a time when she had completely recovered her self-possession. He was obliged to recognize the fact that, if the two young people were waiting for him to get out of the way, they were at least waiting very patiently. He had heard from time to time that Morris was in New York; but he never remained there long, and, to the best of the Doctor's belief, had no communication with Catherine. He was sure they never met, and he had reason to suspect that Morris never wrote to her. After the letter that has been mentioned, she heard from him twice again, at considerable intervals; but on none of these occasions did she write herself. On the other hand, as the Doctor observed, she averted herself rigidly from the idea of marrying other people. Her opportunities for doing so were not numerous, but they occurred often enough to test her disposition. She refused a widower, a man with a genial temperament, a handsome fortune, and three little girls (he had heard that she was very fond of children, and he pointed to his own with some confidence) ; and she turned a deaf ear to the solicitations of a clever young lawyer, who, with the prospect of a great practice, and the reputation of a most agreeable man, had had the shrewdness, when he came to look about him for a wife, to believe that she would suit him better than several younger and prettier girls. Mr. Macalister, the widower, had desired to make a marriage of reason, and had chosen Catherine for what he supposed to be her latent matronly qualities; but John Ludlow, who was a year the girl's junior, and spoken of always as a young man who might have his "pick," was seriously in love with her. Catherine, however, would never look at him; she made it plain to him that she thought he came to see her too often. He afterward consoled himself, and married a very different person, little Miss Sturtevant, whose attractions were obvious to the dullest comprehension. Catherine, at the time of these events, had left her thirtieth year well behind her, and had quite taken her place as an old maid. Her father would have preferred she should marry, and he once told her that he hoped she would not be too fastidious. "I should like to see you an honest man's wife before I die," he said. This was after John Ludlow had been compelled to give it up, though the Doctor had advised him to persevere. The Doctor exercised no further pressure, and had the credit of not "worrying" at all over his daughter's singleness; in fact, he worried rather more than appeared, and there were considerable periods during which he felt sure that Morris Townsend was hidden behind some door. "If he is not, why doesn't she marry?" he asked himself. "Limited as her intelligence may be, she must understand perfectly well that she is made to do the usual thing." Catherine, however, became an admirable old maid. She formed habits, regulated her days upon a system of her own, interested herself in charitable institutions, asylums, hospitals, and aid societies; and went generally, with an even and noiseless step, about the rigid business of her life. This life had, however, a secret history as well as a public one—if I may talk of the public history of a mature and diffident spinster for whom publicity had always a combination of terrors. From her own point of view the great facts of her career were that Morris Townsend had trifled with her affection, and that her father had broken its spring. Nothing could ever alter these facts; they were always there, like her name, her age, her plain face. Nothing could ever undo the wrong or cure the pain that Morris had inflicted on her, and nothing could ever make her feel toward her father as she felt in her younger years. There was something dead in her life, and her duty was to try and fill the void. Catherine recognized this duty to the utmost; she had a great disapproval of brooding and moping. She had, of course, no faculty for quenching memory in dissipation; but she mingled freely in the usual gaieties of the town, and she became at last an inevitable figure at all respectable entertainments. She was greatly liked, and as time went on she grew to be a sort of kindly maiden-aunt to the younger portion of society. Young girls were apt to confide to her their love affairs (which they never did to Mrs. Penniman), and young men to be fond of her without knowing why. She developed a few harmless eccentricities; her habits, once formed, were rather stiffly maintained; her opinions, on all moral and social matters, were extremely conservative; and before she was forty she was regarded as an old-fashioned person, and an authority on customs that had passed away. Mrs. Penniman, in comparison, was quite a girlish figure; she grew younger as she advanced in life. She lost none of her relish for beauty and mystery, but she had little opportunity to exercise it. With Catherine's later wooers she failed to establish relations as intimate as those which had given her so many interesting hours in the society of Morris Townsend. These gentlemen had an indefinable mistrust of her good offices, and they never talked to her about Catherine's charms. Her ringlets, her buckles and bangles glistened more brightly with each succeeding year, and she remained quite the same officious and imaginative Mrs. Penniman, and the odd mixture of impetuosity and circumspection, that we have hitherto known. As regards one point, however, her circumspection prevailed, and she must be given due credit for it. For upward of seventeen years she never mentioned Morris Townsend's name to her niece. Catherine was grateful to her, but this consistent silence, so little in accord with her aunt's character, gave her a certain alarm, and she could never wholly rid herself of a suspicion that Mrs. Penniman sometimes had news of him.

❧ 33 ❧

LITTLE by little Doctor Sloper had retired from his profession; he visited only those patients in whose symptoms he recognized a certain originality. He went again to Europe, and remained two years; Catherine went with him, and on this occasion Mrs. Penniman was of the party. Europe apparently had few surprises for Mrs. Penniman, who frequently remarked, in the most romantic sites, "You know I am very familiar with all this." It should be added that such remarks were usually not addressed to her brother, or yet to her niece, but to fellow tourists who happened to be at hand, or even to the cicerone or the goat-herd in the foreground.

One day, after his return from Europe, the Doctor said something to his daughter that made her start—it seemed to come from so far out of the past.

"I should like you to promise me something before I die."

"Why do you talk about your dying?" she asked.

"Because I am sixty-eight years old."

"I hope you will live a long time," said Catherine.

"I hope I shall! But some day I shall take a bad cold, and then it will not matter much what any one hopes. That will be the manner of my exit, and when it takes place, remember I told you so. Promise me not to marry Morris Townsend after I am gone."

This was what made Catherine start, as I have said; but her start was a silent one, and for some moments she said nothing. "Why do you speak of him?" she asked at last.

"You challenge everything I say. I speak of him because he's a topic, like any other. He's to be seen, like any one else, and he is still looking for a wife—having had one and got rid of her, I don't know by what means. He has lately been in New York, and at your cousin Marian's house; your aunt Elizabeth saw him there."

"They neither of them told me," said Catherine.

"That's their merit; it's not yours. He has grown fat and bald, and he has not made his fortune. But I can't trust those facts alone to steel your heart against him, and that's why I ask you to promise."

"Fat and bald"; these words presented a strange image to Catherine's mind, out of which the memory of the most beautiful young man in the world had never faded. "I don't think you understand," she said. "I very seldom think of Mr. Townsend."

"It will be very easy for you to go on, then. Promise me, after my death, to do the same."

Again, for some moments, Catherine was silent; her father's request deeply amazed her; it opened an old wound, and made it ache afresh. "I don't think I can promise that," she answered.

"It would be a great satisfaction," said her father.

"You don't understand. I can't promise that."

The Doctor was silent a minute. "I ask you for a particular reason. I am altering my will."

This reason failed to strike Catherine; and indeed she scarcely understood it. All her feelings were merged in the sense that he was trying to treat her as he had treated her years before. She had suffered from it then; and now all her experience, all her acquired tranquillity and rigidity protested. She had been so humble in her youth that she could now afford to have a little pride, and there was something in this request, and in her father's thinking himself so free to make it, that seemed an injury to her dignity. Poor Catherine's dignity was not aggressive; it never sat in state; but if you pushed far enough you could find it. Her father had pushed very far.

"I can't promise," she simply repeated.

"You are very obstinate," said the Doctor.

"I don't think you understand."

"Please explain, then."

"I can't explain," said Catherine; "and I can't promise."

"Upon my word," her father exclaimed, "I had no idea how obstinate you are!"

She knew herself that she was obstinate, and it gave her a certain joy. She was now a middle-aged woman.

About a year after this, the accident that the Doctor had spoken of occurred: he took a violent cold. Driving out to Bloomingdale one April day to see a patient of unsound mind, who was confined in a private asylum for the insane, and whose family greatly desired a medical opinion from an eminent source, he was caught in a spring shower, and being in a buggy, without a hood, he found himself soaked to the skin. He came home with an ominous chill, and on the morrow he was seriously ill. "It is congestion of the lungs," he said to Catherine; "I shall need very good nursing. It will make no difference, for I shall not recover; but I wish everything to be done, to the smallest detail, as if I should. I hate an ill-conducted sick-room, and you will be so good as to nurse me, on the hypothesis that I shall get well." He told her which of his fellow physicians to send for, and gave her a multitude of minute directions; it was quite on the optimistic hypothesis that she nursed him. But he had never been wrong in his life, and he was not wrong now. He was touching his seventieth year, and though he had a very well-tempered constitution, his hold upon life had lost its firmness. He died after three weeks' illness, during which Mrs. Penniman, as well as his daughter, had been assiduous at his bedside.

On his will being opened, after a decent interval, it was found to consist of two portions. The first of these dated from ten years back, and consisted of a series of dispositions by which he left the great mass of his property to his daughter, with becoming legacies to his two sisters. The second was a codicil of recent origin, maintaining the annuities to Mrs. Penniman and Mrs. Almond, but reducing Catherine's share to a fifth of what he had first bequeathed her. "She is amply provided for from her mother's side," the document ran, "never having spent more than a fraction of her income from this source; so that her fortune is already more than sufficient to attract those unscrupulous adventurers whom she has given me reason to believe that she persists in regarding as an interesting class." The large remainder of his property, therefore, Doctor Sloper had divided into seven unequal parts, which he left, as endowments, to as many different hospitals and schools of medicine in various cities of the Union.

To Mrs. Penniman it seemed monstrous that a man should play such tricks with other people's money; for after his death, of course, as she said, it was other people's. "Of course, you will immediately break the will," she remarked to Catherine.

"Oh no," Catherine answered, "I like it very much. Only I wish it had been expressed a little differently!"

❧ 34 ❧

IT WAS her habit to remain in town very late in the summer; she preferred the house in Washington Square to any other habitation whatever, and it was under protest that she used to go to the seaside for the month of August. At the sea she spent her month at an hotel. The year that her father died she intermitted this custom altogether, not thinking it consistent with deep mourning; and the year after that she put off her departure till so late that the middle of August found her still in the heated solitude of Washington Square. Mrs. Penniman, who was fond of a change, was usually eager for a visit to the country; but this year she appeared quite content with such rural impressions as she could gather at the parlor-window from the ailanthus-trees behind the wooden paling. The peculiar fragrance of this vegetation used to diffuse itself in the evening air, and Mrs. Penniman, on the warm nights of July, often sat at the open window and inhaled it. This was a happy moment for Mrs. Penniman; after the death of her brother she felt more free to obey her impulses. A vague oppression had disappeared from her life, and she enjoyed a sense of freedom of which she had not been conscious since the memorable time, so long ago, when the Doctor went abroad with Catherine and left her at home to entertain Morris Townsend. The year that had elapsed since her brother's death reminded her of that happy time, because, although Catherine, in growing older, had become a person to be reckoned with, yet her society was a very different thing, as Mrs. Penniman said, from that of a tank of cold water. The elder lady hardly knew what use to make of this larger margin of her life; she sat and looked at it very much as she had often sat, with her poised needle in her hand, before her tapestry-frame. She had a confident hope, however, that her rich impulses, her talent for embroidery, would still find their application, and this confidence was justified before many months had elapsed.

Catherine continued to live in her father's house, in spite of its being represented to her that a maiden lady of quiet habits might find a more convenient abode in one of the smaller dwellings, with brown stone fronts, which had at this time begun to adorn the transverse thoroughfares in the upper part of the town. She liked the earlier structure—it had begun by this time to be called an "old" house—and proposed to herself to end her days in it. If it was too large for a pair of unpretending gentlewomen, this was better than the opposite fault; for Catherine had no desire to find herself in closer quarters with her aunt. She expected to spend the rest of her life in Washington Square, and to enjoy Mrs. Penniman's society for the whole of this period; as she had a conviction that, long as she might live, her aunt would live at least as long, and always retain her brilliancy and activity. Mrs. Penniman suggested to her the idea of a rich vitality.

On one of those warm evenings in July of which mention has been made, the two ladies sat together at an open window, looking out on the quiet Square. It was too hot for lighted lamps, for reading, or for work; it might have appeared too hot even for conversation, Mrs. Penniman having long been speechless. She sat forward in the window, half on the balcony, humming a little song. Catherine was within the room, in a low rocking-chair, dressed in white, and slowly using a large palmetto fan. It was in this way, at this season, that the aunt and niece, after they had had tea, habitually spent their evenings.

"Catherine," said Mrs. Penniman at last, "I am going to say something that will surprise you."

"Pray do," Catherine answered; "I like surprises. And it is so quiet now."

"Well, then, I have seen Morris Townsend."

If Catherine was surprised, she checked the expression of it; she gave neither a start nor an exclamation. She remained, indeed, for some moments intensely still, and this may very well have been a symptom of emotion. "I hope he was well," she said at last.

"I don't know; he is a great deal changed. He would like very much to see you."

"I would rather not see him," said Catherine quickly.

"I was afraid you would say that. But you don't seem surprised!"

"I am—very much."

"I met him at Marian's," said Mrs. Penniman. "He goes to Marian's, and they are so afraid you will meet him there. It's my belief that that's why he goes. He wants so much to see you." Catherine made no response to this, and Mrs. Penniman went on. "I didn't know him at first, he is so remarkably changed; but he knew me in a minute. He says I am not in the least changed. You know how polite he always was. He was coming away when I came, and we walked a little distance together. He is still very handsome, only of course he looks older, and he is not so—so animated as he used to be. There was a touch of sadness about him; but there was a touch of sadness about him before, especially when he went away. I am afraid he has not been very successful—that he has never got thoroughly established. I don't suppose he is sufficiently plodding, and that, after all, is what succeeds in this world." Mrs. Penniman had not mentioned Morris Townsend's name to her niece for upwards of the fifth of a century; but now that she had broken the spell, she seemed to wish to make up for lost time, as if there had been a sort of exhilaration in hearing herself talk of him. She proceeded, however, with considerable caution, pausing occasionally to let Catherine give some sign. Catherine gave no other sign than to stop the rocking of her chair and the swaying of her fan; she sat motionless and silent. "It was on Tuesday last," said Mrs. Penniman, "and I have been hesitating ever since about telling you. I didn't know how you might like it. At last I thought that it was so long ago that you would probably not have any particular feeling. I saw him again after meeting him at Marian's. I met him in the street, and he went a few steps with me. The first thing he said was about you; he asked ever so many questions. Marian didn't want me to speak to you; she didn't want you to know that they receive him. I told him I was sure that after all these years you couldn't have any feeling about that; you couldn't grudge him the hospitality of his own cousin's house. I said you would be bitter indeed if you did that. Marian has the most extraordinary ideas about what happened between you; she seems to think he behaved in some very unusual manner. I took the liberty of reminding her of the real facts, and placing the story in its true light. *He* has no bitterness, Catherine, I can assure you; and he might be excused for it, for things have not gone well with him. He has been all over the world, and tried to establish himself everywhere; but his evil star was against him. It is most interesting to hear him talk of his evil star. Everything failed; everything but his—you know, you remember—his proud, high spirit. I believe he married some lady somewhere in Europe. You know they marry in such a peculiar matter-of-course way in Europe; a marriage of reason they call it. She died soon afterward; as he said to me, she only flitted across his life.

He has not been in New York for ten years; he came back a few days ago. The first thing he did was to ask me about you. He had heard you had never married; he seemed very much interested about that. He said you had been the real romance of his life."

Catherine had suffered her companion to proceed from point to point, and pause to pause, without interrupting her; she fixed her eyes on the ground and listened. But the last phrase I have quoted was followed by a pause of peculiar significance, and then, at last, Catherine spoke. It will be observed that before doing so she had received a good deal of information about Morris Townsend. "Please say no more; please don't follow up that subject."

"Doesn't it interest you?" asked Mrs. Penniman, with a certain timorous archness.

"It pains me," said Catherine.

"I was afraid you would say that. But don't you think you could get used to it? He wants so much to see you."

"Please don't, Aunt Lavinia," said Catherine, getting up from her seat. She moved quickly away, and went to the other window, which stood open to the balcony; and here, in the embrasure, concealed from her aunt by the white curtains, she remained a long time, looking out into the warm darkness. She had had a great shock; it was as if the gulf of the past had suddenly opened, and a spectral figure had risen out of it. There were some things she believed she had got over, some feelings that she had thought of as dead; but apparently there was a certain vitality in them still. Mrs. Penniman had made them stir themselves. It was but a momentary agitation, Catherine said to herself; it would presently pass away. She was trembling, and her heart was beating so that she could feel it; but this also would subside. Then suddenly, while she waited for a return of her calmness, she burst into tears. But her tears flowed very silently, so that Mrs. Penniman had no observation of them. It was perhaps, however, because Mrs. Penniman suspected them that she said no more that evening about Morris Townsend.

❦ 35 ❦

HER refreshed attention to this gentleman had not those limits of which Catherine desired, for herself, to be conscious; it lasted long enough to enable her to wait another week before speaking of him again. It was under the same circumstances that she once more attacked the subject. She had been sitting with her niece in the evening; only on this occasion, as the night was not so warm, the lamp had been lighted, and Catherine had placed herself near it with a morsel of fancy-work. Mrs. Penniman went and sat alone for half an hour on the balcony; then she came in, moving vaguely about the room. At last she sunk into a seat near Catherine, with clasped hands, and a little look of excitement.

"Shall you be angry if I speak to you again about *him?*" she asked.

Catherine looked up at her quietly. "Who is *he?*"

"He whom you once loved."

"I shall not be angry, but I shall not like it."

"He sent you a message," said Mrs. Penniman. "I promised him to deliver it, and I must keep my promise."

In all these years Catherine had had time to forget how little she had to thank her aunt for in the season of her misery; she had long ago forgiven Mrs. Penniman for taking too much upon herself. But for a moment this attitude of interposition and disinterestedness, this carrying of messages and redeeming of promises, brought back the sense that her companion was a dangerous woman. She had said she would not be angry; but for an instant she felt sore. "I don't care what you do with your promise!" she answered.

Mrs. Penniman, however, with her high conception of the sanctity of pledges, carried her point. "I have gone too far to retreat," she said, though precisely what this meant she was not at pains to explain. "Mr. Townsend wishes most particularly to see you, Catherine; he believes that if you knew how much, and why, he wishes it, you would consent to do so."

"There can be no reason," said Catherine; "no good reason."

"His happiness depends upon it. Is not that a good reason?" asked Mrs. Penniman, impressively.

"Not for me. My happiness does not."

"I think you will be happier after you have seen him. He is going away again—going to resume his wanderings. It is a very lonely, restless, joyless life. Before he goes he wishes to speak to you; it is a fixed idea with him—he is always thinking of it. He has something very important to say to you. He believes that you never understood him—that you never judged him rightly, and the belief has always weighed upon him terribly. He wishes to justify himself; he believes that in a very few words he could do so. He wishes to meet you as a friend."

Catherine listened to this wonderful speech without pausing in her work; she had now had several days to accustom herself to think of Morris Townsend again as an actuality. When it was over she said simply, "Please say to Mr. Townsend that I wish he would leave me alone."

She had hardly spoken when a sharp, firm ring at the door vibrated through the summer night. Catherine looked up at the clock; it marked a quarter past nine—a very late hour for visitors, especially in the empty condition of the town. Mrs. Penniman at the same moment gave a little start, and then Catherine's eyes turned quickly to her aunt. They met Mrs. Penniman's, and sounded them for a moment sharply. Mrs. Penniman was blushing; her look was a conscious one; it seemed to confess something. Catherine guessed its meaning, and rose quickly from her chair.

"Aunt Penniman," she said, in a tone that scared her companion, "have you taken *the liberty* . . . ?"

"My dearest Catherine," stammered Mrs. Penniman, "just wait till you see him!"

Catherine had frightened her aunt, but she was also frightened herself; she was on the point of rushing to give orders to the servant, who was passing to the door, to admit no one; but the fear of meeting her visitor checked her.

"Mr. Morris Townsend."

This was what she heard, vaguely but recognizably, articulated by the domestic, while she hesitated. She had her back turned to the door of the parlor, and for some moments she kept it turned, feeling that he had come in. He had not spoken, however, and at last she faced about. Then she saw a gentleman standing in the middle of the room, from which her aunt had discreetly retired.

She would never have known him. He was forty-five years old, and his figure was not that of the straight, slim young man she remembered. But it was a very fine presence, and a fair and lustrous beard, spreading itself upon a well-presented chest, contributed to its effect. After a moment Catherine recognized the upper half of the face, which, though her visitor's clustering locks had grown thin, was still remarkably handsome. He stood in a deeply deferential attitude, with his eyes on her face. "I have ventured—I have ventured"; he said, and then he paused, looking about him, as if he expected her to ask him to sit down. It was the old voice; but it had not the old charm. Catherine, for a minute, was conscious of a distinct determination not to invite him to take a seat. Why had he come? It was wrong for him to come. Morris was embarrassed, but Catherine gave him no help. It was not that she was glad of his embarrassment; on the contrary, it excited all her own liabilities of this kind, and gave her great pain. But how could she welcome him when she felt so vividly that he ought not to have come? "I wanted so much—I was determined," Morris went on. But he stopped again; it was not easy. Catherine still said nothing, and he may well have recalled with apprehension her ancient faculty of silence. She continued to look at him, however, and as she did so she made the strangest observation. It seemed to be he, and yet not he; it was the man who had been everything, and yet this person was nothing. How long ago it was—how old she had grown—how much she had lived! She had lived on something that was connected with *him,* and she had consumed it in doing so. This person did not look unhappy. He was fair and well-preserved, perfectly dressed, mature and complete. As Catherine looked at him, the story of his life defined itself in his eyes; he had made himself comfortable, and he had never been caught. But even while her perception opened itself to this, she had no desire to catch him; his presence was painful to her, and she only wished he would go.

"Will you not sit down?" he asked.

"I think we had better not," said Catherine.

"I offend you by coming?" He was very grave; he spoke in a tone of the richest respect.

"I don't think you ought to have come."

"Did not Mrs. Penniman tell you—did she not give you my message?"

"She told me something, but I did not understand."

"I wish you would let *me* tell you—let me speak for myself."

"I don't think it is necessary," said Catherine.

"Not for you, perhaps, but for me. It would be a great satisfaction—and I have not many." He seemed to be coming nearer; Catherine turned away. "Can we not be friends again?" he asked.

"We are not enemies," said Catherine. "I have none but friendly feelings to you."

"Ah, I wonder whether you know the happiness it gives me to hear you say that!" Catherine uttered no intimation that she measured the influence of her words; and he presently went on, "You have not changed—the years have passed happily for you."

"They have passed very quietly," said Catherine.

"They have left no marks; you are admirably young." This time he succeeded in coming nearer—he was close to her; she saw his glossy perfumed beard, and his eyes above it looking strange and hard. It was very different from his old—from his young—face. If she had first seen him this way she would not have liked him. It seemed to her that he was smiling, or trying to smile. "Catherine," he said, lowering his voice, "I have never ceased to think of you."

"Please don't say these things," she answered.

"Do you hate me?"

"Oh no," said Catherine.

Something in her tone discouraged him, but in a moment he recovered himself. "Have you still some kindness for me, then?"

"I don't know why you have come here to ask me such things!" Catherine exclaimed.

"Because for many years it has been the desire of my life that we should be friends again."

"That is impossible."

"Why so? Not if you will allow it."

"I will not allow it," said Catherine.

He looked at her again in silence. "I see; my presence troubles you and pains you. I will go away; but you must give me leave to come again."

"Please don't come again," she said.

"Never?—never?"

She made a great effort; she wished to say something that would make it impossible he should ever again cross her threshold. "It is wrong of you. There is no propriety in it—no reason for it."

"Ah, dearest lady, you do me injustice!" cried Morris Townsend. "We have only waited, and now we are free."

"You treated me badly," said Catherine.

"Not if you think of it rightly. You had your quiet life with your father—which was just what I could not make up my mind to rob you of."

"Yes; I had that."

Morris felt it to be a considerable damage to his cause that he could not add that she had had something more besides; for it is needless to say that he had learned the contents of Doctor Sloper's will. He was, nevertheless, not at a loss. "There are worse fates than that!" he exclaimed, with expression; and he might have been supposed to refer to his own unprotected situation. Then he added, with a deeper tenderness, "Catherine, have you never forgiven me?"

"I forgave you years ago, but it is useless for us to attempt to be friends."

"Not if we forget the past. We have still a future, thank God!"

"I can't forget—I don't forget," said Catherine. "You treated me too badly. I felt it very much; I felt it for years." And then she went on, with her wish to show him that he must not come to her this way, "I can't begin again—I can't take it up. Everything is dead and buried. It was too serious; it made a great change in my life. I never expected to see you here."

"Ah, you are angry!" cried Morris, who wished immensely that he could extort some flash of passion from her calmness. In that case he might hope.

"No, I am not angry. Anger does not last that way for years. But there are other things. Impressions last, when they have been strong. But I can't talk."

Morris stood stroking his beard, with a clouded eye. "Why have you never married?" he asked, abruptly. "You have had opportunities."

"I didn't wish to marry."

"Yes, you are rich, you are free; you had nothing to gain."

"I had nothing to gain," said Catherine.

Morris looked vaguely round him, and gave a deep sigh. "Well, I was in hopes that we might still have been friends."

"I meant to tell you, by my aunt, in answer to your message—if you had waited for an answer—that it was unnecessary for you to come in that hope."

"Good-bye, then," said Morris. "Excuse my indiscretion."

He bowed, and she turned away—standing there, averted, with her eyes on the ground, for some moments after she had heard him close the door of the room.

In the hall he found Mrs. Penniman, fluttered and eager; she appeared to have been hovering there under the irreconcilable promptings of her curiosity and her dignity.

"That was a precious plan of yours!" said Morris, clapping on his hat.

"Is she so hard?" asked Mrs. Penniman.

"She doesn't care a button for me—with her confounded little dry manner."

"Was it very dry?" pursued Mrs. Penniman, with solicitude.

Morris took no notice of her question; he stood musing an instant, with his hat on. "But why the deuce, then, would she never marry?"

"Yes—why indeed?" sighed Mrs. Penniman. And then, as if from a sense of the inadequacy of this explanation, "But you will not despair—you will come back?"

"Come back? Damnation!" And Morris Townsend strode out of the house, leaving Mrs. Penniman staring.

Catherine, meanwhile, in the parlor, picking up her morsel of fancy-work, had seated herself with it again—for life, as it were.

The Aspern Papers

Some of the world's greatest stories have been set in Venice. One thinks of *Othello* and *The Merchant of Venice;* and later of *Volpone* and *Venice Preserved,* but one thinks also of Thomas Mann's *Death in Venice:* and with these and other master works one must group Henry James's ironic comedy of "The Aspern Papers." In the modern world Venice is as much a symbol of decay and death as it is of the vivid pulsing life of its people. These elements are combined by Henry James in this tale. Told by an unnamed storyteller—who characterizes himself in the telling—it is a light fantasy of the quest for the love letters of a long dead poet, the survival of his aged mistress in a mouldering old Venetian palace, and the cat-and-mouse game between the acquisitive "publishing scoundrel" and the ancient lady seeking to protect her private life.

Out of these ingredients James spins his tale, a kind of moral detective story that stands motionless through the hot Venetian spring days; and then suddenly the narrator is trapped in his own contrivance. One thinks particularly of that old Levantine, Volpone, caught in his supersubtle Venetian trap. James's tale winds up to a tight climax and uncoils into a brilliant second climax, like one of the "well-made" plays of the last century. The visitor in Venice today can trace all the comings and goings of the story and even find Juliana's palace on the Rio Marin, near the railway station, with its rare garden and its air of another time. James set himself the task of trying to evoke in his tale "the poetry of the thing outlived and lost and gone." For readers who have a feeling for the "sense of the past," this story provides this poetry, an atmosphere and an enchantment. The story is told with a rhythmic and measured tread—one of the great short narratives of the Western world.

L. E.

❄ 1 ❄

I HAD taken Mrs. Prest into my confidence; without her in truth I should have made but little advance, for the fruitful idea in the whole business dropped from her friendly lips. It was she who found the short cut and loosed the Gordian knot. It is not supposed easy for women to rise to the large free view of anything, anything to be done; but they sometimes throw off a bold conception—such as a man wouldn't have risen to—with singular serenity. "Simply make them take you in on the footing of a lodger"—I don't think that unaided I should have risen to that. I was beating about the bush, trying to be ingenious, wondering by what combination of arts I might become an acquaintance, when she offered this happy suggestion that the way to become an acquaintance was first to become an intimate. Her actual knowledge of the Misses Bordereau was scarcely larger than mine, and indeed I had brought with me from England some definite facts that were new to her. Their name had been mixed up ages before with one of the greatest names of the century, and they now lived obscurely in Venice, lived on very small means, unvisited, unapproachable, in a sequestered and dilapidated old palace: this was the substance of my friend's impression of them. She herself had been established in Venice some fifteen years and had done a great deal of good there; but the circle of her benevolence had never embraced the two shy, mysterious and, as was somehow supposed, scarcely respectable Americans—they were believed to have lost in their long exile all national quality, besides being as their name implied of some remoter French affiliation—who asked no favours and desired no attention. In the early years of her residence she had made an attempt to see them, but this had been successful only as regards the little one, as Mrs. Prest called the niece; though in fact I afterwards found her the bigger of the two in inches. She had heard Miss Bordereau was ill and had a suspicion she was in want, and had gone to the house to offer aid, so that if there were suffering, American suffering in particular, she shouldn't have it on her conscience. The "little one" had received her in the great cold tarnished Venetian sala, the central hall of the house, paved with marble and roofed with dim cross-beams, and hadn't even asked her to sit down. This was not encouraging for me, who wished to sit so fast, and I remarked as much to Mrs. Prest. She replied however with profundity "Ah, but there's all the difference: I went to confer a favour and you'll go to ask one. If they're proud you'll be on the right side." And she offered to show me their house to begin with—to row me thither in her gondola. I let her know I had already been to look at it half a dozen times; but I accepted her invitation, for it charmed me to hover about the place. I had made my way to it the day after my arrival in Venice—it had been described to me in advance by the friend in England to whom I owed definite information as to their possession of the papers—laying siege to it with my eyes while I considered my plan of campaign. Jeffrey Aspern had never been in it that I knew of, but some note of his voice seemed to abide there by a roundabout implication and in a "dying fall."

Mrs. Prest knew nothing about the papers, but was interested in my curiosity, as always in the joys and sorrows of her friends. As we went, however, in her gondola, gliding there under the sociable hood with the bright Venetian picture framed on either side by the moveable window, I saw how my eagerness amused her and that she found my interest in my possible spoil a fine case of monomania. "One would think you expected from it the answer to the riddle of the universe," she said; and I denied the impeachment only by replying that if I had to choose between that precious solution and a bundle of Jeffrey Aspern's letters I knew indeed which would appear to me the greater boon. She pretended to make light of his genius and I took no pains to defend him. One doesn't defend one's god: one's god is in himself a defence. Besides, to-day, after his long comparative obscuration, he hangs high in the heaven of our literature for all the world to see; he's a part of the light by which we walk. The most I said was that he was no doubt not a woman's poet; to which she rejoined aptly enough that he had been at least Miss Bordereau's. The strange thing had been for me to discover in England that she was still alive: it was as if I had been told Mrs. Siddons was, or Queen Caroline, or the famous Lady Hamilton, for it seemed to me that she belonged to a generation as extinct. "Why she must be tremendously old—at least a hundred," I had said; but on coming to consider dates I saw it not strictly involved that she should have far exceeded the common span. None the less she was of venerable age and her relations with Jeffrey Aspern had occurred in her early womanhood. "That's her excuse," said Mrs. Prest half-sententiously and yet also somewhat as if she were ashamed of making a speech so little in the real tone of Venice. As if a woman needed an excuse for having loved the divine poet! He had been not only one of the most brilliant minds of his day—and in those years, when the century was young, there were, as every one knows, many—but one of the most genial men and one of the handsomest.

The niece, according to Mrs. Prest, was of minor antiquity, and the conjecture was risked that she was only a grand-niece. This was possible; I had nothing but my share in the very limited knowledge of my English fellow worshipper John Cumnor, who had never seen the couple. The world, as I say, had recognised Jeffrey Aspern, but Cumnor and I had recognised him most. The multitude to-day flocked to his temple, but of that temple he and I regarded ourselves as the appointed ministers. We held, justly, as I think, that we had done more for his memory than any one else, and had done it simply by opening lights into his life. He had nothing to fear from us because he had nothing to fear from the truth, which alone at such a distance of time we could be interested in establishing. His early death had been the only dark spot, as it were, on his fame, unless the papers in Miss Bordereau's hands should perversely bring out others. There had been an impression about 1825 that he had "treated her badly," just as there had been an impression that he had "served," as the London populace says, several other ladies in the same masterful way. Each of these cases Cumnor and I had been able to investigate, and we had never failed to acquit him conscientiously of any grossness. I judged him perhaps more indulgently than my friend; certainly, at any rate, it appeared to me that no man could have walked straighter in the given circumstances. These had been almost always difficult and dangerous. Half the women of his time, to speak liberally, had flung themselves at his head, and while the fury raged—the more that it was very catching—accidents, some of them grave, had not failed to occur. He was not a woman's poet, as I had said to Mrs. Prest, in the modern phase of his reputation; but the situation had been different when the man's own voice was mingled with his song. That voice, by every testimony, was one of the most charming ever heard. "Orpheus and the Mænads!" had been of course my foreseen judgement when first I turned over his correspondence. Almost all the Mænads were unreasonable and many of them unbearable; it struck me that he had been kinder and more considerate than in his place—if I could imagine myself in any such box—I should have found the trick of.

It was certainly strange beyond all strangeness, and I shall not take up space with attempting to explain it, that whereas among all these other relations and in these other directions of research we had to deal with phantoms and dust, the mere echoes of echoes, the one living source of information that had lingered on into our time had been unheeded by us. Every one of Aspern's contemporaries had, according to our belief, passed away; we had not been able to look into a single pair of eyes into which his had looked or to feel a transmitted contact in any aged hand that his had touched. Most dead of all did poor Miss Bordereau appear, and yet she alone had survived. We exhausted in the course of months our wonder that we had not found her out sooner, and the substance of our explanation was that she had kept so quiet. The poor lady on the whole had had reason for doing so. But it was a revelation to us that self-effacement on such a scale had been possible in the latter half of the nineteenth century—the age of newspapers and telegrams and photographs and interviewers. She had taken no great trouble for it either—hadn't hidden herself away in an undiscoverable hole, had boldly settled down in a city of exhibition. The one apparent secret of her safety had been that Venice contained so many much greater curiosities. And then accident had somehow favoured her, as was shown for example in the fact that Mrs. Prest had never happened to name her to me, though I had spent three weeks in Venice—under her nose, as it were—five years before. My friend indeed had not named her much to any one; she appeared almost to have forgotten the fact of her continuance. Of course Mrs. Prest hadn't the nerves of an editor. It was meanwhile no explanation of the old woman's having eluded us to say that she lived abroad, for our researches had again and again taken us—not only by correspondence but by personal enquiry—to France, to Germany, to Italy, in which countries, not counting his important stay in England, so many of the too few years of Aspern's career had been spent. We were glad to think at least that in all our promulgations—some people now consider I believe that we have overdone them—we had only touched in passing and in the most discreet manner on Miss Bordereau's connexion. Oddly enough, even if we had had the material—and we had often wondered what could have become of it—this would have been the most difficult episode to handle.

The gondola stopped, the old palace was there; it was a house of the class which in Venice carries even in extreme dilapidation the dignified name. "How charming! It's grey and pink!" my companion exclaimed; and that is the most comprehensive description of it. It was not particularly old, only two or three centuries; and it had an air not so much of decay as of quiet discouragement, as if it had rather missed its career. But its wide front, with a stone balcony from end to end of the *piano nobile* or most important floor, was architectural enough, with the aid of various pilasters and arches; and the stucco with which in the intervals it had long ago been endued was rosy in the April afternoon. It overlooked a clean melancholy rather lonely canal, which had a narrow *riva* or convenient footway on either side. "I don't know why—there are no brick gables," said Mrs. Prest, "but this corner has seemed to me before more Dutch than Italian, more like Amsterdam than like Venice. It's eccentrically neat, for reasons of its own; and though you may pass on foot scarcely any one ever thinks of doing so. It's as negative—considering *where* it is—as a Protestant Sunday. Perhaps the people are afraid of the Misses Bordereau. I dare say they have the reputation of witches."

I forget what answer I made to this—I was given up to two other reflexions. The first of these was that if the old lady lived in such a big and imposing house she couldn't be in any sort of misery and therefore wouldn't be tempted by a chance to let a couple of rooms. I expressed this fear to Mrs. Prest, who gave me a very straight answer. "If she didn't live in a big house how could it be a question of her having rooms to spare? If she were not amply lodged you'd lack ground to approach her. Besides, a big house here, and especially in this *quartier perdu*, proves nothing at all: it's perfectly consistent with a state of penury. Dilapidated old palazzi, if you'll go out of the way for them, are to be had for five shillings a year. And as for the people who live in them—no, until you've explored Venice socially as much as I have, you can form no idea of their domestic desolation. They live on nothing, for they've nothing to live on." The other idea that had come into my head was connected with a high blank wall which appeared to confine an expanse of ground on one side of the house. Blank I call it, but it was figured over with the patches that please a painter, repaired breaches, crumblings of plaster, extrusions of brick that had turned pink with time; while a few thin trees, with the poles of certain rickety trellises, were visible over the top. The place was a garden and apparently attached to the house. I suddenly felt that so attached it gave me my pretext.

I sat looking out on all this with Mrs. Prest (it was covered with the golden glow of Venice) from the shade of our *felze*, and she asked me if I would go in then, while she waited for me, or come back another time. At first I couldn't decide—it was doubtless very weak of me. I wanted still to think I *might* get a footing, and was afraid to meet failure, for it would leave me, as I remarked to my companion, without another arrow for my bow. "Why not another?" she enquired as I sat there hesitating and thinking it over; and she wished to know why even now and before taking the trouble of becoming an inmate—which might be wretchedly uncomfortable after all, even if it succeeded—I hadn't the resource of simply offering them a sum of money down. In that way I might get what I wanted without bad nights.

"Dearest lady," I exclaimed, "excuse the impatience of my tone when I suggest that you must have forgotten the very fact—surely I communicated it to you—which threw me on your ingenuity. The old woman won't have her relics and tokens so much as spoken of; they're personal, delicate, intimate, and she hasn't the feelings of the day, God bless her! If I should sound that note first I should certainly spoil the game. I can arrive at my spoils only by putting her off her guard, and I can put her off her guard only by ingratiating diplomatic arts. Hypocrisy, duplicity are my only chance. I'm sorry for it, but there's no baseness I wouldn't commit for Jeffrey Aspern's sake. First I must take tea with her—then tackle the main job." And I told over what had happened to John Cumnor on his respectfully writing to her. No notice whatever had been taken of his first letter, and the second had been answered very sharply, in six lines, by the niece. "Miss Bordereau requested her to say that she couldn't imagine what he meant by troubling them. They had none of Mr. Aspern's 'literary remains,' and if they *had* had wouldn't have dreamed of showing them to any one on any account whatever. She couldn't imagine what he was talking about and begged he would let her alone." I certainly didn't want to be met that way.

"Well," said Mrs. Prest after a moment and all provokingly,

"perhaps they really haven't anything. If they deny it flat how are you sure?"

"John Cumnor's sure, and it would take me long to tell you how his conviction, or his very strong presumption—strong enough to stand against the old lady's not unnatural fib—has built itself up. Besides, he makes much of the internal evidence of the niece's letter."

"The internal evidence?"

"Her calling him 'Mr. Aspern.'"

"I don't see what that proves."

"It proves familiarity, and familiarity implies the possession of mementoes, of tangible objects. I can't tell you how that 'Mr.' affects me—how it bridges over the gulf of time and brings our hero near to me—nor what an edge it gives to my desire to see Juliana. You don't say 'Mr.' Shakespeare."

"Would I, any more, if I had a box full of his letters?"

"Yes, if he had been your lover and some one wanted them." And I added that John Cumnor was so convinced, and so all the more convinced by Miss Bordereau's tone, that he would have come himself to Venice on the undertaking were it not for the obstacle of his having, for any confidence, to disprove his identity with the person who had written to them, which the old ladies would be sure to suspect in spite of dissimulation and a change of name. If they were to ask him point-blank if he were not their snubbed correspondent it would be too awkward for him to lie; whereas I was fortunately not tied in that way. I was a fresh hand—I could protest without lying.

"But you'll have to take a false name," said Mrs. Prest. "Juliana lives out of the world as much as it is possible to live, but she has none the less probably heard of Mr. Aspern's editors. She perhaps possesses what you've published."

"I've thought of that," I returned; and I drew out of my pocketbook a visting-card neatly engraved with a well-chosen *nom de guerre.*

"You're very extravagant—it adds to your immorality. You might have done it in pencil or ink," said my companion.

"This looks more genuine."

"Certainly you've the courage of your curiosity. But it will be awkward about your letters; they won't come to you in that mask."

"My banker will take them in and I shall go every day to get them. It will give me a little walk."

"Shall you depend all on that?" asked Mrs. Prest. "Aren't you coming to see me?"

"Oh you'll have left Venice for the hot months long before there are any results. I'm prepared to roast all summer—as well as through the long hereafter perhaps you'll say! Meanwhile John Cumnor will bombard me with letters addressed, in my feigned name, to the care of the padrona."

"She'll recognise his hand," my companion suggested.

"On the envelope he can disguise it."

"Well, you're a precious pair! Doesn't it occur to you that even if you're able to say you're not Mr. Cumnor in person they may still suspect you of being his emissary?"

"Certainly, and I see only one way to parry that."

"And what may that be?"

I hesitated a moment. "To make love to the niece."

"Ah," cried my friend, "wait till you see her!"

❧ 2 ❧

"I MUST work the garden—I must work the garden," I said to myself five minutes later and while I waited, upstairs, in the long, dusky sala, where the bare scagliola floor gleamed vaguely in a chink of the closed shutters. The place was impressive, yet looked somehow cold and cautious. Mrs. Prest had floated away, giving me a rendezvous at the end of half an hour by some neighbouring water-steps; and I had been let into the house, after pulling the rusty bell-wire, by a small red-headed and white-faced maid-servant, who was very young and not ugly and wore clicking pattens and a shawl in the fashion of a hood. She had not contented herself with opening the door from above by the usual arrangement of a creaking pulley, though she had looked down at me first from an upper window, dropping the cautious challenge which in Italy precedes the act of admission. I was irritated as a general thing by this survival of mediæval manners, though as so fond, if yet so special, an antiquarian I suppose I ought to have liked it; but, with my resolve to be genial from the threshold at any price, I took my false card out of my pocket and held it up to her, smiling as if it were a magic token. It had the effect of one indeed, for it brought her, as I say, all the way down. I begged her to hand it to her mistress, having first written on it in Italian the words: "Could you very kindly see a gentleman, a travelling American, for a moment?" The little maid wasn't hostile—even that was perhaps something gained. She coloured, she smiled and looked both frightened and pleased. I could see that my arrival was a great affair, that visits in such a house were rare and that she was a person who would have liked a bustling place. When she pushed forward the heavy door behind me I felt my foot in the citadel and promised myself ever so firmly to keep it there. She pattered across the damp stony lower hall and I followed her up the high staircase—stonier still, as it seemed—without an invitation. I think she had meant I should wait for her below, but such was not my idea, and I took up my station in the sala. She flitted, at the far end of it, into impenetrable regions, and I looked at the place with my heart beating as I had known it to do in dentists' parlours. It had a gloomy grandeur, but owed its character almost all to its noble shape and to the fine architectural doors, as high as those of grand frontages, which, leading into the various rooms, repeated themselves on either side at intervals. They were surmounted with old faded painted escutcheons, and here and there in the spaces between them hung brown pictures, which I noted as speciously bad, in battered and tarnished frames that were yet more desirable than the canvases themselves. With the exception of several straw-bottomed chairs that kept their backs to the wall the grand obscure vista contained little else to minister to effect. It was evidently never used save as a passage, and scantly even as that. I may add that by the time the door through which the maid-servant had escaped opened again my eyes had grown used to the want of light.

I hadn't meanwhile meant by my private ejaculation that I must myself cultivate the soil of the tangled enclosure which lay beneath the windows, but the lady who came toward me from the distance over the hard shining floor might have supposed as much from the way in which, as I went rapidly to meet her, I exclaimed, taking care to speak Italian: "The garden, the garden—do me the pleasure to tell me if it's yours!"

She stopped short, looking at me with wonder; and then, "Nothing here is mine," she answered in English, coldly and sadly.

"Oh you're English; how delightful!" I ingenuously cried. "But surely the garden belongs to the house?"

"Yes, but the house doesn't belong to me." She was a long lean pale person, habited apparently in a dull-coloured dressing-gown, and she spoke very simply and mildly. She didn't ask me to sit down, any more than years before—if she were the niece—she had asked Mrs. Prest, and we stood face to face in the empty pompous hall.

"Well then, would you kindly tell me to whom I must address myself? I'm afraid you'll think me horribly intrusive, but you know I *must* have a garden—upon my honour I must!"

Her face was not young, but it was candid; it was not fresh, but it was clear. She had large eyes which were not bright, and a great deal of hair which was not "dressed," and long fine hands which were—possibly—not clean. She clasped these members almost convulsively as, with a confused alarmed look, she broke out: "Oh don't take it away from us; we like it ourselves!"

"You have the use of it then?"

"Oh yes. If it wasn't for that—!" And she gave a wan vague smile.

"Isn't it a luxury, precisely? That's why, intending to be in Venice some weeks, possibly all summer, and having some literary work, some reading and writing to do, so that I must be quiet and yet if possible a great deal in the open air—that's why I've felt a garden to be really indispensable. I appeal to your own experience," I went on with as sociable a smile as I could risk. "Now can't I look at yours?"

"I don't know, I don't understand," the poor woman murmured, planted there and letting her weak wonder deal—helplessly enough, as I felt—with my strangeness.

"I mean only from one of those windows—such grand ones as you have here—if you'll let me open the shutters." And I walked toward the back of the house. When I had advanced halfway I stopped and waited as in the belief she would accompany me. I had been of necessity quite abrupt, but I strove at the same time to give her the impression of extreme courtesy. "I've looked at furnished rooms all over the place, and it seems impossible to find any with a garden attached. Naturally in a place like Venice gardens are rare. It's absurd if you like, for a man, but I can't live without flowers."

"There are none to speak of down there." She came nearer, as if, though she mistrusted me, I had drawn her by an invisible thread. I went on again, and she continued as she followed me: "We've a few, but they're very common. It costs too much to cultivate them; one has to have a man."

"Why shouldn't I be the man?" I asked. "I'll work without wages; or rather I'll put in a gardener. You shall have the sweetest flowers in Venice."

She protested against this with a small quaver of sound that might have been at the same time a gush of rapture for my free sketch. Then she gasped: "We don't know you—we don't know you."

"You know me as much as I know you; or rather much more, because you know my name. And if you're English I'm almost a countryman."

"We're not English," said my companion, watching me in practical submission while I threw open the shutters of one of the divisions of the wide high window.

"You speak the language so beautifully: might I ask what you are?" Seen from above the garden was in truth shabby, yet I felt at a glance that it had great capabilities. She made no rejoinder, she was so lost in her blankness and gentleness, and I exclaimed: "You don't mean to say you're also by chance American?"

"I don't know. We used to be."

"Used to be? Surely you haven't changed?"

"It's so many years ago. We don't seem to be anything now."

"So many years that you've been living here? Well, I don't wonder at that; it's a grand old house. I suppose you all use the garden," I went on, "but I assure you I shouldn't be in your way. I'd be very quiet and stay quite in one corner."

"We all use it?" she repeated after me vaguely, not coming close to the window but looking at my shoes. She appeared to think me capable of throwing her out.

"I mean all your family—as many as you are."

"There's only one other than me. She's very old. She never goes down."

I feel again my thrill at this close identification of Juliana; in spite of which, however, I kept my head. "Only one other in all this great house!" I feigned to be not only amazed but almost scandalised. "Dear lady, you must have space then to spare!"

"To spare?" she repeated—almost as for the rich unwonted joy to her of spoken words.

"Why you surely don't live (two quiet women—I see *you* are

quiet, at any rate) in fifty rooms!" Then with a burst of hope and cheer I put the question straight. "Couldn't you for a good rent *let* me two or three? That would set me up!"

I had now struck the note that translated my purpose, and I needn't reproduce the whole of the tune I played. I ended by making my entertainer believe me an undesigning person, though of course I didn't even attempt to persuade her I was not an eccentric one. I repeated that I had studies to pursue; that I wanted quiet; that I delighted in a garden and had vainly sought one up and down the city; that I would undertake that before another month was over the dear old house should be smothered in flowers. I think it was the flowers that won my suit, for I afterwards found that Miss Tina—for such the name of this high tremulous spinster proved somewhat incongruously to be—had an insatiable appetite for them. When I speak of my suit as won I mean that before I left her she had promised me she would refer the question to her aunt. I invited information as to who her aunt might be and she answered "Why Miss Bordereau!" with an air of surprise, as if I might have been expected to know. There were contradictions like this in Miss Tina which, as I observed later, contributed to make her rather pleasingly incalculable and interesting. It was the study of the two ladies to live so that the world shouldn't talk of them or touch them, and yet they had never altogether accepted the idea that it didn't hear of them. In Miss Tina at any rate a grateful susceptibility to human contact had not died out, and contact of a limited order there would be if I should come to live in the house.

"We've never done anything of the sort; we've never had a lodger or any kind of inmate." So much as this she made a point of saying to me. "We're very poor, we live very badly—almost on nothing. The rooms are very bare—those you might take; they've nothing at all in them. I don't know how you'd sleep, how you'd eat."

"With your permission I could easily put in a bed and a few tables and chairs. *C'est la moindre des choses* and the affair of an hour or two. I know a little man from whom I can hire for a trifle what I should so briefly want, what I should use; my gondolier can bring the things round in his boat. Of course in this great house you must have a second kitchen, and my servant, who's a wonderfully handy fellow"—this personage was an evocation of the moment—"can easily cook me a chop there. My tastes and habits are of the simplest:

I live on flowers!" And then I ventured to add that if they were very poor it was all the more reason they should let their rooms. They were bad economists—I had never heard of such a waste of material.

I saw in a moment my good lady had never before been spoken to in any such fashion—with a humorous firmness that didn't exclude sympathy, that was quite founded on it. She might easily have told me that my sympathy was impertinent, but this by good fortune didn't occur to her. I left her with the understanding that she would submit the question to her aunt and that I might come back the next day for their decision.

"The aunt will refuse; she'll think the whole proceeding very *louche!*" Mrs. Prest declared shortly after this, when I had resumed my place in her gondola. She had put the idea into my head and now—so little are women to be counted on—she appeared to take a despondent view of it. Her pessimism provoked me and I pretended to have the best hopes; I went so far as to boast of a distinct prevision of success. Upon this Mrs. Prest broke out: "Oh I see what's in your head! You fancy you've made such an impression in five minutes that she's dying for you to come and can be depended on to bring the old one round. If you do get in you'll count it as a triumph."

I did count it as a triumph, but only for the commentator—in the last analysis—not for the man, who had not the tradition of personal conquest. When I went back on the morrow the little maid-servant conducted me straight through the long sala—it opened there as before in large perspective and was lighter now, which I thought a good omen—into the apartment from which the recipient of my former visit had emerged on that occasion. It was a spacious shabby parlour with a fine old painted ceiling under which a strange figure sat alone at one of the windows. They come back to me now almost with the palpitation they caused, the successive states marking my consciousness that as the door of the room closed behind me I was really face to face with the Juliana of some of Aspern's most exquisite and most renowned lyrics. I grew used to her afterwards, though never completely; but as she sat there before me my heart beat as fast as if the miracle of resurrection had taken place for my benefit. Her presence seemed somehow to contain and express his own, and I felt nearer to him at that first moment of seeing her than I ever had been before or ever have been since. Yes, I remember my emotions in their order, even including a curious little tremor that took me when I saw the niece not to be there. With her, the day before, I had become sufficiently familiar, but it almost exceeded my courage—much as I had longed for the event—to be left alone with so terrible a relic as the aunt. She was too strange, too literally resurgent. Then came a check from the perception that we weren't really face to face, inasmuch as she had over her eyes a horrible green shade which served for her almost as a mask. I believed for the instant that she had put it on expressly, so that from underneath it she might take me all in without my getting at herself. At the same time it created a presumption of some ghastly death's-head lurking behind it. The divine Juliana as a grinning skull—the vision hung there until it passed. Then it came to me that she *was* tremendously old—so old that death might take her at any moment, before I should have time to compass my end. The next thought was a correction to that; it lighted up the situation. She would die next week, she would die tomorrow—then I could pounce on her possessions and ransack her drawers. Meanwhile she sat there neither moving nor speaking. She was very small and shrunken, bent forward with her hands in her lap. She was dressed in black and her head was wrapped in a piece of old black lace which showed no hair.

My emotion keeping me silent she spoke first, and the remark she made was exactly the most unexpected.

❧ 3 ❧

"Our house is very far from the centre, but the little canal is very *comme il faut.*"

"It's the sweetest corner of Venice and I can imagine nothing more charming," I hastened to reply. The old lady's voice was very thin and weak, but it had an agreeable, cultivated murmur and there was wonder in the thought that that individual note had been in Jeffrey Aspern's ear.

"Please to sit down there. I hear very well," she said quietly, as if perhaps I had been shouting; and the chair she pointed to was at a certain distance. I took possession of it, assuring her I was perfectly aware of my intrusion and of my not having been properly introduced, and that I could but throw myself on her indulgence. Perhaps the other lady, the one I had had the honour of seeing the day before, would have explained to her about the garden. That was literally what had given me courage to take a step so unconventional. 1 had fallen in love at sight with the whole place—she herself was probably so used to it that she didn't know the impression it was capable of making on a stranger—and I had felt it really a case to risk something. Was her own kindness in receiving me a sign that I was not wholly out in my calculation? It would make me extremely happy to think so. I could give her my word of honour that I was a most respectable inoffensive person and that as a co-tenant of the palace, so to speak, they would be barely conscious of my existence. I would conform to any regulations, any restrictions, if they would only let me enjoy the garden. Moreover I should be delighted to give her references, guarantees; they would be of the very best, both in Venice and in England, as well as in America.

She listened to me in perfect stillness and I felt her look at me with great penetration, though I could see only the lower part of her bleached and shrivelled face. Independently of the refining process of old age it had a delicacy which once must have been great. She had been very fair, she had had a wonderful complexion. She was silent a little after I had ceased speaking; then she began: "If you're so fond of a garden why don't you go to *terra firma,* where there are so many far better than this?"

"Oh it's the combination!" I answered, smiling; and then with rather a flight of fancy: "It's the idea of a garden in the middle of the sea."

"This isn't the middle of the sea; you can't so much as see the water."

I stared a moment, wondering if she wished to convict me of fraud. "Can't see the water? Why, dear madam, I can come up to the very gate in my boat."

She appeared inconsequent, for she said vaguely in reply to this: "Yes, if you've got a boat. I haven't any; it's many years since I've been in one of the *gondole.*" She uttered these words as if they designed a curious far-away craft known to her only by hearsay.

"Let me assure you of the pleasure with which I would put mine at your service!" I returned. I had scarcely said this however before I became aware that the speech was in questionable taste and might also do me the injury of making me appear too eager, too possessed of a hidden motive. But the old woman remained impenetrable and her attitude worried me by suggesting that she had a fuller vision of me than I had of her. She gave me no thanks for my somewhat extravagant offer, but remarked that the lady I had seen the day before was her niece; she would presently come in. She had asked her to stay away a little on purpose—had had her reasons for seeing me first alone. She relapsed into silence and I turned over the fact of these unmentioned reasons and the question of what might come yet; also that of whether I might venture on some judicious remark in praise of her companion. I went so far as to say I should be delighted to see our absent friend again: she had been so very patient with me, considering how odd she must have thought me—a declaration which drew from Miss Bordereau another of her whimsical speeches.

"She has very good manners; I bred her up myself!" I was on the point of saying that that accounted for the easy grace of the niece, but I arrested myself in time, and the next moment the old woman went on: "I don't care who you may be—I don't want to know: it signifies very little to-day." This had all the air of being a formula of dismissal, as if her next words would be that I might take myself off now that she had had the amusement of looking on the face of such a monster of indiscretion. Therefore I was all the more surprised when she added in her soft venerable quaver: "You may have as many rooms as you like—if you'll pay me a good deal of money."

I hesitated but an instant, long enough to measure what she meant in particular by this condition. First it struck me that she must have really a large sum in her mind; then I reasoned quickly that her idea of a large sum would probably not correspond to my own. My deliberation, I think, was not so visible as to diminish the promptitude with which I replied: "I will pay with pleasure and of course in advance whatever you may think it proper to ask me."

"Well then, a thousand francs a month," she said instantly, while her baffling green shade continued to cover her attitude.

The figure, as they say, was startling and my logic had been at fault. The sum she had mentioned was, by the Venetian measure of such matters, exceedingly large; there was many an old palace in an out-of-the-way corner that I might on such terms have enjoyed the whole of by the year. But so far as my resources allowed I was prepared to spend money, and my decision was quickly taken. I would pay her with a smiling face what she asked, but in that case I would make it up by getting hold of my "spoils" for nothing. Moreover if she had asked five times as much I should have risen to the occasion, so odious would it have seemed to me to stand chaffering with Aspern's Juliana. It was queer enough to have a question of money with her at all. I assured her that her views perfectly met my own and that on the morrow I should have the pleasure of putting three months' rent into her hand. She received this announcement with apparent complacency and with no discoverable sense that after all it would become her to say that I ought to see the rooms first. This didn't occur to her, and indeed her serenity was mainly what I wanted. Our little agreement was just concluded when the door opened and the younger lady appeared on the threshold. As soon as Miss Bordereau saw her niece she cried out almost gaily: "He'll give three thousand—three thousand to-morrow!"

Miss Tina stood still, her patient eyes turning from one of us to the other; then she brought out, scarcely above her breath: "Do you mean francs?"

"Did you mean francs or dollars?" the old woman asked of me at this.

"I think francs were what you said," I sturdily smiled.

"That's very good," said Miss Tina, as if she had felt how overreaching her own question might have looked.

"What do *you* know? You're ignorant," Miss Bordereau remarked; not with acerbity but with a strange soft coldness.

"Yes, of money—certainly of money!" Miss Tina hastened to concede.

"I'm sure you've your own fine branches of knowledge," I took the liberty of saying genially. There was something painful to me, somehow, in the turn the conversation had taken, in the discussion of dollars and francs.

"She had a very good education when she was young. I looked into that myself," said Miss Bordereau. Then she added: "But she has learned nothing since."

"I've always been with *you*," Miss Tina rejoined very mildly, and of a certainty with no intention of an epigram.

"Yes, but for that—!" her aunt declared with more satirical force. She evidently meant that but for this her niece would never have got on at all; the point of the observation however being lost on Miss Tina, though she blushed at hearing her history revealed to a stranger. Miss Bordereau went on, addressing herself to me: "And what time will you come to-morrow with the money?"

"The sooner the better. If it suits you I'll come at noon."

"I'm always here, but I have my hours," said the old woman as if her convenience were not to be taken for granted.

"You mean the times when you receive?"

"I never receive. But I'll see you at noon, when you come with the money."

"Very good, I shall be punctual." To which I added: "May I shake hands with you on our contract?" I thought there ought to be some little form; it would make me really feel easier, for I was sure there would be no other. Besides, though Miss Bordereau couldn't to-day be called personally attractive and there was something even in her wasted antiquity that bade one stand at one's distance, I felt an irresistible desire to hold in my own for a moment the hand Jeffrey Aspern had pressed.

For a minute she made no answer, and I saw that my proposal failed to meet with her approbation. She indulged in no movement of withdrawal, which I half-expected; she only said coldly: "I belong to a time when that was not the custom."

I felt rather snubbed but I exclaimed good-humouredly to Miss Tina "Oh you'll do as well!" I shook hands with her while she assented with a small flutter. "Yes, yes, to show it's all arranged!"

"Shall you bring the money in gold?" Miss Bordereau demanded as I was turning to the door.

I looked at her a moment. "Aren't you a little afraid, after all, of keeping such a sum as that in the house?" It was not that I was annoyed at her avidity, but was truly struck with the disparity between such a treasure and such scanty means of guarding it.

"Whom should I be afraid of if I'm not afraid of you?" she asked with her shrunken grimness.

"Ah well," I laughed, "I shall be in point of fact a protector and I'll bring gold if you prefer."

"Thank you," the old woman returned with dignity and with an inclination of her head which evidently signified my dismissal. I passed out of the room, thinking how hard it would be to circumvent her. As I stood in the sala again I saw that Miss Tina had followed me, and I supposed that as her aunt had neglected to suggest I should take a look at my quarters it was her purpose to repair the omission. But she made no such overture; she only stood there with a dim, though not a languid smile, and with an effect of irresponsible incompetent youth almost comically at variance with the faded facts of her person. She was not infirm, like her aunt, but she struck me as more deeply futile, because her inefficiency was inward, which was not the case with Miss Bordereau's. I waited to see if she would offer to show me the rest of the house, but I didn't precipitate the question, inasmuch as my plan was from this moment to spend as much of my time as possible in her society. A minute indeed elapsed before I committed myself.

"I've had better fortune than I hoped. It was very kind of her to see me. Perhaps you said a good word for me."

"It was the idea of the money," said Miss Tina.

"And did you suggest that?"

"I told her you'd perhaps pay largely."

"What made you think that?"

"I told her I thought you were rich."

"And what put that into your head?"

"I don't know; the way you talked."

"Dear me, I must talk differently now," I returned. "I'm sorry to say it's not the case."

"Well," said Miss Tina, "I think that in Venice the *forestieri* in general often give a great deal for something that after all isn't much." She appeared to make this remark with a comforting intention, to wish to remind me that if I had been extravagant I wasn't foolishly singular. We walked together along the sala, and as I took its magnificent measure I observed that I was afraid it wouldn't form a part of my *quartiere*. Were my rooms by chance to be among those that opened into it? "Not if you go above—to the second floor," she answered as if she had rather taken for granted I would know my proper place.

"And I infer that that's where your aunt would like me to be."

"She said your apartments ought to be very distinct."

"That certainly would be best." And I listened with respect while she told me that above I should be free to take whatever I might like; that there was another staircase, but only from the floor on which we stood, and that to pass from it to the garden-level or to come up to my lodging I should have in effect to cross the great hall. This was an immense point gained; I foresaw that it would constitute my whole leverage in my relations with the two ladies. When I asked Miss Tina how I was to manage at present to find my way up she replied with an access of that sociable shyness which constantly marked her manner:

"Perhaps you can't. I don't see—unless I should go with you." She evidently hadn't thought of this before.

We ascended to the upper floor and visited a long succession of empty rooms. The best of them looked over the garden; some of the others had above the opposite rough-tiled house-tops a view of the blue lagoon. They were all dusty and even a little disfigured with long neglect, but I saw that by spending a few hundred francs I should be able to make three or four of them habitable enough. My experiment was turning out costly, yet now that I had all but taken possession I ceased to allow this to trouble me. I mentioned to my companion a few of the things I should put in, but she replied rather more precipitately than usual that I might do exactly what I liked: she seemed to wish to notify me that the Misses Bordereau would take none but the most veiled interest in my proceedings. I guessed that her aunt had instructed her to adopt this tone, and I may as well say now that I came afterwards to distinguish perfectly (as I believed) between the speeches she made on her own responsibility and those the old woman imposed upon her. She took no notice of the unswept condition of the rooms and indulged neither in explanations nor in apologies. I said to myself that this was a sign Juliana and her niece—disenchanting idea!—were untidy persons with a low Italian standard; but I afterwards recognised that a lodger who had forced an entrance had no *locus standi* as a critic. We looked out of a good many windows, for there was nothing within the rooms to look at, and still I wanted to linger. I asked her what several different objects in the prospect might be, but in no case did she appear to know. She was evidently not familiar with the view—it was as if she had not looked at it for years—and I presently saw that she was too preoccupied with something else to pretend to care for it. Suddenly she said—the remark was not suggested:

"I don't know whether it will make any difference to you, but the money is for me."

"The money—?"

"The money you're going to bring."

"Why you'll make me wish to stay here two or three years!" I spoke as benevolently as possible, though it had begun to act on my nerves that these women so associated with Aspern should so constantly bring the pecuniary question back.

"That would be very good for me," she answered almost gaily.

"You put me on my honour!"

She looked as if she failed to understand this, but went on: "She wants me to have more. She thinks she's going to die."

"Ah not soon I hope!" I cried with genuine feeling. I had perfectly considered the possibility of her destroying her documents on the day she should feel her end at hand. I believed that she would cling to them till then, and I was as convinced of her reading Aspern's letters over every night or at least pressing them to her withered lips. I would have given a good deal for some view of those solemnities. I asked Miss Tina if her venerable relative were seriously ill, and she replied that she was only very tired—she had lived so extraordinarily long. That was what she said herself—she wanted to die for a change. Besides, all her friends had been dead for ages; either they ought to have remained or she ought to have gone. That was another thing her aunt often said: she was not at all resigned—resigned, that is, to life.

"But people don't die when they like, do they?" Miss Tina enquired. I took the liberty of asking why, if there was actually enough money to maintain both of them, there would not be more than enough in case of her being left alone. She considered this difficult problem a moment and then said: "Oh well, you know, she takes care of me. She thinks that when I'm alone I shall be a great fool and shan't know how to manage."

"I should have supposed rather that you took care of *her*. I'm afraid she's very proud."

"Why, have you discovered that already?" Miss Tina cried with a dimness of glad surprise.

"I was shut up with her there for a considerable time and she struck me, she interested me extremely. It didn't take me long to make my discovery. She won't have much to say to me while I'm here."

"No, I don't think she will," my companion averred.

"Do you suppose she has some suspicion of me?"

Miss Tina's honest eyes gave me no sign I had touched a mark. "I shouldn't think so—letting you in after all so easily."

"You call it easily? She has covered her risk," I said. "But where is it one could take an advantage of her?"

"I oughtn't to tell you if I knew, ought I?" And Miss Tina added, before I had time to reply to this, smiling dolefully: "Do you think we've any weak points?"

"That's exactly what I'm asking. You'd only have to mention them for me to respect them religiously."

She looked at me hereupon with that air of timid but candid and even gratified curiosity with which she had confronted me from the first; after which she said: "There's nothing to tell. We're terribly quiet. I don't know how the days pass. We've no life."

"I wish I might think I should bring you a little."

"Oh we know what we want," she went on. "It's all right."

There were twenty things I desired to ask her: how in the world they did live; whether they had any friends or visitors, any relations in America or in other countries. But I judged such probings premature; I must leave it to a later chance. "Well, don't *you* be proud," I contented myself with saying. "Don't hide from me altogether."

"Oh I must stay with my aunt," she returned without looking at me. And at the same moment, abruptly, without any ceremony of parting, she quitted me and disappeared, leaving me to make my own way downstairs. I stayed a while longer, wandering about the bright desert—the sun was pouring in—of the old house, thinking the situation over on the spot. Not even the pattering little *serva* came to look after me, and I reflected that after all this treatment showed confidence.

✻ 4 ✻

PERHAPS it did, but all the same, six weeks later, towards the middle of June, the moment when Mrs. Prest undertook her annual migration, I had made no measurable advance. I was obliged to confess to her that I had no results to speak of. My first step had been unexpectedly rapid, but there was no appearance it would be followed by a second. I was a thousand miles from taking tea with my hostesses—that privilege of which, as I reminded my good friend, we both had had a vision. She reproached me with lacking boldness and I answered that even to be bold you must have an opportunity: you may push on through a breach, but you can't batter down a dead wall. She returned that the breach I had already made was big enough to admit an army and accused me of wasting precious hours in whimpering in her salon when I ought to have been carrying on the struggle in the field. It is true that I went to see her very often—all on the theory that it would console me (I freely expressed my discouragement) for my want of success on my own premises. But I began to feel that it didn't console me to be perpetually chaffed for my scruples, especially since I was really so vigilant; and I was rather glad when my ironic friend closed her house for the summer. She had expected to draw amusement from the drama of my intercourse with the Misses Bordereau, and was disappointed that the intercourse, and consequently the drama, had not come off. "They'll lead you on to your ruin," she said before she left Venice. "They'll get all your money without showing you a scrap." I think I settled down to my business with more concentration after her departure.

It was a fact that up to that time I had not, save on a single brief occasion, had even a moment's contact with my queer hostesses. The exception had occurred when I carried them according to my promise the terrible three thousand francs. Then I found Miss Tina awaiting me in the hall, and she took the money from my hand with a promptitude that prevented my seeing her aunt. The old lady had promised to receive me, yet apparently thought nothing of breaking that vow. The money was contained in a bag of chamois leather, of respectable dimensions, which my banker had given me, and Miss Tina had to make a big fist to receive it. This she did with extreme solemnity, though I tried to treat the affair a little as a joke. It was in no jocular strain, yet it was with a clearness akin to a brightness that she enquired, weighing the money in her two palms: "Don't you think it's too much?" To which I replied that this would depend on the amount of pleasure I should get for it. Hereupon she turned away from me quickly, as she had done the day before, murmuring in a tone different from any she had used hitherto: "Oh pleasure, pleasure—there's no pleasure in this house!"

After that, for a long time, I never saw her, and I wondered the common chances of the day shouldn't have helped us to meet. It could only be evident that she was immensely on her guard against them; and in addition to this the house was so big that for each other we were lost in it. I used to look out for her hopefully as I crossed the sala in my comings and goings, but I was not rewarded with a glimpse of the tail of her dress. It was as if she never peeped out of her aunt's apartment. I used to wonder what she did there week after week and year after year. I had never met so stiff a policy of seclusion; it was more than keeping quiet—it was like hunted creatures feigning death. The two ladies appeared to have no visitors whatever and no sort of contact with the world. I judged at least that people couldn't have come to the house and that Miss Tina couldn't have gone out without my catching some view of it. I did what I disliked myself for doing—considering it but as once in a way: I questioned my servant about their habits and let him infer that I should be interested in any information he might glean. But he gleaned amazingly little for a knowing Venetian: it must be added that where there is a perpetual fast there are very few crumbs on the floor. His ability in other ways was sufficient, if not quite all I had attributed to him on the occasion of my first interview with Miss Tina. He had helped my gondolier to bring me round a boat-load of furniture; and when these articles had been carried to the top of the palace and distributed according to our associated wisdom he organised my household with such dignity as answered to its being composed exclusively of himself. He made me in short as comfortable as I could be with my indifferent prospects. I should have been glad if he had fallen in love with Miss Bordereau's maid or, failing this, had taken her in aversion: either event might have brought about some catastrophe, and a catastrophe might have led to some parley. It was my idea that she would have been sociable, and I myself on various occasions saw her flit to and fro on domestic errands, so that I was sure she was accessible. But I tasted of no gossip from that fountain, and I afterwards learned that Pasquale's affections were fixed upon an object that made him heedless of other women. This was a young lady with a powdered face, a yellow cotton gown and much leisure, who used often to come to see him. She practised, at her convenience, the art of a stringer of beads—these ornaments are made in Venice to profusion; she had her pocket full of them and I used to find them on the floor of my apartment—and kept an eye on the possible rival in the house. It was not for me of course to make the domestics tattle, and I never said a word to Miss Bordereau's cook.

It struck me as a proof of the old woman's resolve to have nothing to do with me that she should never have sent me a receipt for my three months' rent. For some days I looked out for it and then, when I had given it up, wasted a good deal of time in wondering what her reason had been for neglecting so indispensable and familiar a form. At first I was tempted to send her a reminder; after which I put by the idea—against my judgement as to what was right in the particular case—on the general ground of wishing to keep quiet. If Miss Bordereau suspected me of ulterior aims she would suspect me less if I should be businesslike, and yet I consented not to be. It was possible she intended her omission as an impertinence, a visible irony, to show how she could overreach people who attempted to overreach her. On that hypothesis it was well to let her see that one didn't notice her little tricks. The real reading of the matter, afterwards gathered, was simply the poor lady's desire to emphasise the fact that I was in the enjoyment of a favour as rigidly limited as it had been liberally bestowed. She had given me part of her house, but she wouldn't add to that so much as a morsel of paper with her name on it. Let me say that even at first this didn't make me too miserable, for the whole situation had the charm of its oddity. I foresaw that I should have a summer after my own literary heart, and the sense of playing with my opportunity was much greater after all than any sense of being played with. There could be no Venetian business without patience, and since I adored the place I was much more in the spirit of it for having laid in a large provision. That spirit kept me perpetual company and seemed to look out at me from the revived immortal face—in which all his genius shone—of the great poet who was my prompter. I had invoked him and he had come; he hovered before me half the time; it was as if his bright ghost had returned to earth to assure me he regarded the affair as his own no less than as mine and that we should see it fraternally and fondly to a conclusion. It was as if he had said: "Poor dear, be easy with her; she has some natural prejudices; only give her time. Strange as it may appear to you she was very attractive in 1820. Meanwhile aren't we in Venice together, and what better place is there for the meeting of dear friends? See how it glows with the advancing summer; how the sky and the sea and the rosy air and the marble of the palaces all shimmer and melt together." My eccentric private errand became a part of the general romance and the general glory—I felt even a mystic companionship, a moral fraternity with all those who in the past had been in the service of art. They had worked for beauty, for a devotion; and what else was I doing? That element was in everything that Jeffrey Aspern had written, and I was only bringing it to light.

I lingered in the sala when I went to and fro; I used to watch—as long as I thought decent—the door that led to Miss Bordereau's part of the house. A person observing me might have supposed I was trying to cast a spell on it or attempting some odd experiment in hypnotism. But I was only praying it might open or thinking what treasure probably lurked behind it. I hold it singular, as I look back, that I should never have doubted for a moment that the sacred relics were there; never have failed to know the joy of being beneath the same roof with them. After all they were under my hand—they had not escaped me yet; and they made my life continuous, in a fashion, with the illustrious life they had touched at the other end. I lost myself in this satisfaction to the point of assuming—in my quiet extravagance—that poor Miss Tina also went back, and still went back, as I used to phrase it. She did indeed, the gentle spinster, but not quite so far as Jeffrey Aspern, who was simple hearsay to her quite as he was to me. Only she had lived for years with Juliana, she had seen and handled all mementoes and—even though she was stupid—some esoteric knowledge had rubbed off on her. That was what the old woman represented—esoteric knowledge; and this was the idea with which my critical heart used to thrill. It literally beat faster often, of an evening when I had been out, as I stopped with my candle in the re-echoing hall on my way up to bed. It was as if at such a moment as that, in the stillness and after the long contradiction of the day, Miss Bordereau's secrets were in the air, the wonder of her survival more vivid. These were the acute impressions. I had them in another form, with more of a certain shade of reciprocity, during the hours I sat in the garden looking up over the top of my book at the closed windows of my hostess. In these windows no sign of life ever appeared; it was as if, for fear of my catching a glimpse of them, the two ladies passed their days in the dark. But this only emphasised their having matters to conceal; which was what I had wished to prove. Their motionless shutters became as expressive as eyes consciously closed, and I took comfort in the probability that, though invisible themselves, they kept me in view between the lashes.

I made a point of spending as much time as possible in the garden, to justify the picture I had originally given of my horticultural passion. And I not only spent time, but (hang it! as I said) spent precious money. As soon as I had got my rooms arranged and could give the question proper thought I surveyed the place with a clever expert and made terms for having it put in order. I was sorry to do this, for personally I liked it better as it was, with its weeds and its wild rich tangle, its sweet characteristic Venetian shabbiness. I had to be consistent, to keep my promise that I would smother the house in flowers. Moreover I clung to the fond fancy that by flowers I should make my way—I should succeed by big nosegays. I would batter the old women with lilies—I would bombard their citadel with roses. Their door would have to yield to the pressure when a mound of fragrance should be heaped against it. The place in truth had been brutally neglected. The Venetian capacity for dawdling is of the largest, and for a good many days unlimited litter was all my gardener had to show for his ministrations. There was a great digging of holes and carting about of earth, and after a while I grew so impatient that I had thoughts of sending for my "results" to the nearest stand. But I felt sure my friends would see through the chinks of their shutters where such tribute *couldn't* have been gathered, and might so make up their minds against my veracity. I possessed my soul and finally, though the delay was long, perceived some appearances of bloom. This encouraged me and I waited serenely enough till they multiplied. Meanwhile the real summer days arrived and began to pass, and as I look back upon them they seem to me almost the happiest of my life. I took more and more care to be in the garden whenever it was not too hot. I had an arbour arranged and a low table and an arm-chair put into it; and I carried out books and portfolios—I had always some business of writing in hand—and worked and waited and mused and hoped, while the golden hours elapsed and the plants drank in the light and the inscrutable old palace turned pale and then, as the day waned, began to recover and flush and my papers rustled in the wandering breeze of the Adriatic.

Considering how little satisfaction I got from it at first it is wonderful I shouldn't have grown more tired of trying to guess what mystic rites of ennui the Misses Bordereau celebrated in their darkened rooms; whether this had always been the tenor of their life and how in previous years they had escaped elbowing their neighbours. It was supposable they had then had other habits, forms and resources; that they must once have been young or at least middleaged. There was no end to the questions it was possible to ask about them and no end to the answers it was not possible to frame. I had known many of my country-people in Europe and was familiar with the strange ways they were liable to take up there; but the Misses Bordereau formed altogether a new type of the American absentee. Indeed it was clear the American name had ceased to have any application to them—I had seen this in the ten minutes I spent in the old woman's room. You could never have said whence they came from the appearance of either of them; wherever it was they had long ago shed and unlearned all native marks and notes. There was nothing in them one recognised or fitted, and, putting the question of speech aside, they might have been Norwegians or Spaniards. Miss Bordereau, after all, had been in Europe nearly three quarters of a century; it appeared by some verses addressed to her by Aspern on the occasion of his own second absence from America—verses of which Cumnor and I had after infinite conjecture established solidly enough the date—that she was even then, as a girl of twenty, on the foreign side of the sea. There was a profession in the poem—I hope not just for the phrase—that he had come back for her sake. We had no real light on her circumstances at that moment, any more than we had upon her origin, which we believed to be of the sort usually spoken of as modest. Cumnor had a theory that she had been a governess in some family in which the poet visited and that, in consequence of her position, there was from the first something unavowed, or rather something quite clandestine, in their relations. I on the other hand had hatched a little romance according to which she was the daughter of an artist, a painter or a sculptor, who had left the Western world, when the century was fresh, to study in the ancient schools. It was essential to my hypothesis that this amiable man should have lost his wife, should have been poor and unsuccessful and should have had a second daughter of a disposition quite different from Juliana's. It was also indispensable that he should have been accompanied to Europe by these young ladies and should have established himself there for the remainder of a struggling saddened life. There was a further implication that Miss Bordereau had had in her youth a perverse and reckless, albeit a generous and fascinating character, and that she had braved some wondrous chances. By what passions had she been ravaged, by what adventures and sufferings had she been blanched, what store of memories had she laid away for the monotonous future?

I asked myself these things as I sat spinning theories about her in my arbour and the bees droned in the flowers. It was incontestable that, whether for right or for wrong, most readers of certain of Aspern's poems (poems not as ambiguous as the sonnets—scarcely more divine, I think—of Shakespeare) had taken for granted that Juliana had not always adhered to the steep footway of renunciation. There hovered about her name a perfume of impenitent passion, an intimation that she had not been exactly as the respectable young person in general. Was this a sign that her singer had betrayed her, had given her away, as we say nowadays, to posterity? Certain it is that it would have been difficult to put one's finger on the passage in which her fair fame suffered injury. Moreover was not any fame fair enough that was so sure of duration and was associated with works immortal through their beauty? It was a part of my idea that the young lady had had a foreign lover—and say an unedifying tragical rupture—before her meeting with Jeffrey Aspern. She had lived with her father and sister in a queer old-fashioned expatriated artistic Bohemia of the days when the æsthetic was only the academic and the painters who knew the best models for *contadina* and *pifferaro* wore peaked hats and long hair. It was a society less awake than the coteries of to-day—in its ignorance of the wonderful chances, the opportunities of the early bird, with which its path was strewn—to tatters of old stuff and fragments of old crockery; so that Miss Bordereau appeared not to have picked up or have inherited many objects of importance. There was no enviable *bric-à-brac,* with its provoking legend of cheapness, in the room in which I had seen her. Such a fact as that suggested bareness, but none the less it worked happily into the sentimental interest I had always taken in the early movements of my countrymen as visitors to Europe. When Americans went abroad in 1820 there was something romantic, almost heroic in it, as compared with the perpetual ferryings of the present hour, the hour at which photography and other conveniences have annihilated surprise. Miss Bordereau had sailed with her family on a tossing brig in the days of long voyages and sharp differences; she had had her emotions on the top of yellow diligences, passed the night at inns where she dreamed of travellers' tales, and was most struck, on reaching the Eternal City, with the elegance of Roman pearls and scarfs and mosaic brooches. There was something touching to me in all that, and my imagination frequently went back to the period. If Miss Bordereau carried it there of course Jeffrey Aspern had at other times done so with greater force. It was a much more important fact, if one was looking at his genius critically, that he had lived in the days before the general transfusion. It had happened to me to regret that he had known Europe at all; I should have liked to see what he would have written without that experience, by which he had incontestably been enriched. But as his fate had ruled otherwise I went with him—I tried to judge how the general old order would have struck him. It was not only there, however, I watched him; the relations he had entertained with the special new had even a livelier interest. His own country after all had had most of his life, and his muse, as they said at that time, was essentially American. That was originally what I had prized him for: that at a period when our native land was nude and crude and provincial, when the famous "atmosphere" it is supposed to lack was not even missed, when literature was lonely there and art and form almost impossible, he had found means to live and write like one of the first; to be free and general and not at all afraid; to feel, understand and express everything.

5

I WAS seldom at home in the evening, for when I attempted to occupy myself in my apartments the lamplight brought in a swarm of noxious insects, and it was too hot for closed windows. Accordingly I spent the late hours either on the water—the moonlights of Venice are famous—or in the splendid square which serves as a vast forecourt to the strange old church of Saint Mark. I sat in front of Florian's café eating ices, listening to music, talking with acquaintances: the traveller will remember how the immense cluster of tables and little chairs stretches like a promontory into the smooth lake of the Piazza. The whole place, of a summer's evening, under the stars and with all the lamps, all the voices and light footsteps on marble—the only sounds of the immense arcade that encloses it—is an open-air saloon dedicated to cooling drinks and to a still finer degustation, that of the splendid impressions received during the day. When I didn't prefer to keep mine to myself there was always a stray tourist, disencumbered of his Bädeker, to discuss them with, or some domesticated painter rejoicing in the return of the season of strong effects. The great basilica, with its low domes and bristling embroideries, the mystery of its mosaic and sculpture, looked ghostly in the tempered gloom, and the sea-breeze passed between the twin columns of the Piazzetta, the lintels of a door no longer guarded, as gently as if a rich curtain swayed there. I used sometimes on these occasions to think of the Misses Bordereau and of the pity of their being shut up in apartments which in the Venetian July even Venetian vastness couldn't relieve of some stuffiness. Their life seemed miles away from the life of the Piazza, and no doubt it was really too late to make the austere Juliana change her habits. But poor Miss Tina would have enjoyed one of Florian's ices, I was sure; sometimes I even had thoughts of carrying one home to her. Fortunately my patience bore fruit and I was not obliged to do anything so ridiculous.

One evening about the middle of July I came in earlier than usual—I forget what chance had led to this—and instead of going up to my quarters made my way into the garden. The temperature was very high; it was such a night as one would gladly have spent in the open air, and I was in no hurry to go to bed. I had floated home in my gondola, listening to the slow splash of the oar in the dark narrow canals, and now the only thought that occupied me was that it would be good to recline at one's length in the fragrant darkness on a garden-bench. The odour of the canal was doubtless at the bottom of that aspiration, and the breath of the garden, as I entered it, gave consistency to my purpose. It was delicious—just such an air as must have trembled with Romeo's vows when he stood among the thick flowers and raised his arms to his mistress's balcony. I looked at the windows of the palace to see if by chance the example of Verona—Verona being not far off—had been followed; but everything was dim, as usual, and everything was still. Juliana might on the summer nights of her youth have murmured down from open windows at Jeffrey Aspern, but Miss Tina was not a poet's mistress any more than I was a poet. This however didn't prevent my gratification from being great as I became aware on reaching the end of the garden that my younger padrona was seated in one of the bowers. At first I made out but an indistinct figure, not in the least counting on such an overture from one of my hostesses; it even occurred to me that some enamoured maid-servant had stolen in to keep a tryst with her sweetheart. I was going to turn away, not to frighten her, when the figure rose to its height and I recognised Miss Bordereau's niece. I must do myself the justice that I didn't wish to frighten her either, and much as I had longed for some such accident I should have been capable of retreating. It was as if I had laid a trap for her by coming home earlier than usual and by adding to that oddity my invasion of the garden. As she rose she spoke to me, and then I guessed that perhaps, secure in my almost inveterate absence, it was her nightly practice to take a lonely airing. There was no trap in truth, because I had had no suspicion. At first I took the words she uttered for an impatience of my arrival; but as she repeated them—I hadn't caught them clearly—I had the surprise of hearing her say: "Oh dear, I'm so glad you've come!" She and her aunt had in common the property of unexpected speeches. She came out of the arbour almost as if to throw herself in my arms.

I hasten to add that I escaped this ordeal and that she didn't even then shake hands with me. It was an ease to her to see me and presently she told me why—because she was nervous when out of doors at night alone. The plants and shrubs looked so strange in the dark, and there were all sorts of queer sounds—she couldn't tell what they were—like the noises of animals. She stood close to me, looking about her with an air of greater security but without any demonstration of interest in me as an individual. Then I felt how little nocturnal prowlings could have been her habit, and I was also reminded—I had been afflicted by the same in talking with her before I took possession—that it was impossible to allow too much for her simplicity.

"You speak as if you were lost in the backwoods," I cheeringly laughed. "How you manage to keep out of this charming place when you've only three steps to take to get into it is more than I've yet been able to discover. You hide away amazingly so long as I'm on the premises, I know; but I had a hope you peeped out a little at other times. You and your poor aunt are worse off than Carmelite nuns in their cells. Should you mind telling me how you exist without air, without exercise, without any sort of human contact? I don't see how you carry on the common business of life."

She looked at me as if I had spoken a strange tongue, and her answer was so little of one that I felt it make for irritation. "We go to bed very early—earlier than you'd believe." I was on the point of saying that this only deepened the mystery, but she gave me some relief by adding: "Before you came we weren't so private. But I've never been out at night."

"Never in these fragrant alleys, blooming here under your nose?"

"Ah," said Miss Tina, "they were never nice till now!" There was a finer sense in this and a flattering comparison, so that it seemed to me I had gained some advantage. As I might follow that further by establishing a good grievance I asked her why, since she thought my garden nice, she had never thanked me in any way for the flowers I had been sending up in such quantities for the previous three weeks. I had not been discouraged—there had been, as she would have observed, a daily armful; but I had been brought up in the common forms and a word of recognition now and then would have touched me in the right place.

"Why I didn't know they were for me!"

"They were for both of you. Why should I make a difference?"

Miss Tina reflected as if she might be thinking of a reason for that, but she failed to produce one. Instead of this she asked abruptly: "Why in the world do you want so much to know us?"

"I ought after all to make a difference," I replied. "That question's your aunt's; it isn't yours. You wouldn't ask it if you hadn't been put up to it."

"She didn't tell me to ask you," Miss Tina replied without confusion. She was indeed the oddest mixture of shyness and straightness.

"Well, she has often wondered about it herself and expressed her wonder to you. She has insisted on it, so that she has put the idea into your head that I'm insufferably pushing. Upon my word I think I've been very discreet. And how completely your aunt must have lost every tradition of sociability, to see anything out of the way in the idea that respectable intelligent people, living as we do under the same roof, should occasionally exchange a remark! What could be more natural? We're of the same country and have at least some of the same tastes, since, like you, I'm intensely fond of Venice."

My friend seemed incapable of grasping more than one clause in any proposition, and she now spoke quickly, eagerly, as if she were answering my whole speech. "I'm not in the least fond of Venice. I should like to go far away!"

"Has she always kept you back so?" I went on, to show her I could be as irrelevant as herself.

"She told me to come out to-night; she has told me very often," said Miss Tina. "It is I who wouldn't come. I don't like to leave her."

"Is she too weak, is she really failing?" I demanded, with more emotion, I think, than I meant to betray. I measured this by the way her eyes rested on me in the darkness. It embarrassed me a little, and to turn the matter off I continued genially: "Do let us sit down together comfortably somewhere—while you tell me all about her."

Miss Tina made no resistance to this. We found a bench less secluded, less confidential, as it were, than the one in the arbour; and we were still sitting there when I heard midnight ring out from those clear bells of Venice which vibrate with a solemnity of their own over the lagoon and hold the air so much more than the chimes of other places. We were together more than an hour, and our interview gave, as it struck me, a great lift to my undertaking. Miss Tina accepted the situation without a protest; she had avoided me for three months, yet now she treated me almost as if these three months had made me an old friend. If I had chosen I might have gathered from this that though she had avoided me she had given a good deal of consideration to doing so. She paid no attention to the flight of time—never worried at my keeping her so long away from her aunt. She talked freely, answering questions and asking them and not even taking advantage of certain longish pauses by which they were naturally broken to say she thought she had better go in. It was almost as if she were waiting for something—something I might say to her—and intended to give me my opportunity. I was the more struck by this as she told me how much less well her aunt had been for a good many days, and in a way that was rather new. She was markedly weaker; at moments she showed no strength at all; yet more than ever before she wished to be left alone. That was why she had told her to come out—not even to remain in her own room, which was alongside; she pronounced poor Miss Tina "a worry, a bore and a source of aggravation." She sat still for hours together, as if for long sleep; she had always done that, musing and dozing; but at such times formerly she gave, in breaks, some small sign of life, of interest, liking her companion to be near her with her work. This sad personage confided to me that at present her aunt was so motionless as to create the fear she was dead; moreover she scarce ate or drank—one couldn't see what she lived on. The great thing was that she still on most days got up; the serious job was to dress her, to wheel her out of her bedroom. She clung to as many of her old habits as possible and had always, little company as they had received for years, made a point of sitting in the great parlour.

I scarce knew what to think of all this—of Miss Tina's sudden conversion to sociability and of the strange fact that the more the old woman appeared to decline to her end the less she should desire to be looked after. The story hung indifferently together, and I even asked myself if it mightn't be a trap laid for me, the result of a design to make me show my hand. I couldn't have told why my companions (as they could only by courtesy be called) should have this purpose—why they should try to trip up so lucrative a lodger. But at any hazard I kept on my guard, so that Miss Tina shouldn't have occasion again to ask me what I might really be "up to." Poor woman, before we parted for the night my mind was at rest as to what *she* might be. She was up to nothing at all.

She told me more about their affairs than I had hoped; there was no need to be prying, for it evidently drew her out simply to feel me listen and care. She ceased wondering why I *should,* and at last, while describing the brilliant life they had led years before, she almost chattered. It was Miss Tina who judged it brilliant; she said that when they first came to live in Venice, years and years back—I found her essentially vague about dates and the order in which events had occurred—there was never a week they hadn't some visitor or didn't make some pleasant *passeggio* in the town. They had seen all the curiosities; they had even been to the Lido in a boat—she spoke as if I might think there was a way on foot; they had had a collation there, brought in three baskets and spread out on the grass. I asked her what people they had known and she said Oh very nice ones—the Cavaliere Bombicci and the Contessa Altemura, with whom they had had a great friendship! Also English people—the Churtons and the Goldies and Mrs. Stock-Stock, whom they had loved dearly; she was dead and gone, poor dear. That was the case with most of their kind circle—this expression was Miss Tina's own; though a few were left, which was a wonder considering how they had neglected them. She mentioned the names of two or three Venetian old women; of a certain doctor, very clever, who was so attentive—he came as a friend, he had really given up practice; of the *avvocato* Pochintesta, who wrote beautiful poems and had addressed one to her aunt. These people came to see them without fail every year, usually at the *capo d'anno,* and of old her aunt used to make them some little present—her aunt and she together: small things that she, Miss Tina, turned out with her own hand, paper lamp-shades, or mats for the decanters of wine at dinner, or those woollen things that in cold weather are worn on the wrists. The last few years there hadn't been many presents; she couldn't think what to make and her aunt had lost interest and never suggested. But the people came all the same; if the good Venetians liked you once they liked you for ever.

There was affecting matter enough in the good faith of this sketch of former social glories; the picnic at the Lido had remained vivid through the ages and poor Miss Tina evidently was of the impression that she had had a dashing youth. She had in fact had a glimpse of the Venetian world in its gossiping home-keeping parsimonious professional walks; for I noted for the first time how nearly she had acquired by contact the trick of the familiar soft-sounding almost infantile prattle of the place. I judged her to have imbibed this invertebrate dialect from the natural way the names of things and people—mostly purely local—rose to her lips. If she knew little of what they represented she knew still less of anything else. Her aunt had drawn in—the failure of interest in the table-mats and lamp-shades was a sign of that—and she hadn't been able to mingle in society or to entertain it alone; so that her range of reminiscence struck one as an old world altogether. Her tone, hadn't it been so decent, would have seemed to carry one back to the queer rococo Venice of Goldoni and Casanova. I found myself mistakenly thinking of her too as one of Jeffrey Aspern's contemporaries; this came from her having so little in common with my own. It was possible, I indeed reasoned, that she hadn't even heard of him; it might very well be that Juliana had forborne to lift for innocent eyes the veil that covered the temple of her glory. In this case she perhaps wouldn't know of the existence of the papers, and I welcomed that presumption—it made me feel more safe with her—till I remembered we had believed the letter of disavowal received by Cumnor to be in the handwriting of the niece. If it had been dictated to her she had of course to know what it was about; though the effect of it withal was to repudiate the idea of any connexion with the poet. I held it probable at all events that Miss Tina hadn't read a word of his poetry. Moreover if, with her companion, she had always escaped invasion and research, there was little occasion for her having got it into her head that people were "after" the letters. People had not been after them, for people hadn't heard of them. Cumnor's fruitless feeler would have been a solitary accident.

When midnight sounded Miss Tina got up; but she stopped at the door of the house only after she had wandered two or three times with me round the garden. "When shall I see you again?" I asked before she went in; to which she replied with promptness that she should like to come out the next night. She added however that she shouldn't come—she was so far from doing everything she liked.

"You might do a few things *I* like," I quite sincerely sighed.

"Oh you—I don't believe you!" she murmured at this, facing me with her simple solemnity.

"Why don't you believe me?"

"Because I don't understand you."

"That's just the sort of occasion to have faith." I couldn't say more, though I should have liked to, as I saw I only mystified her; for I had no wish to have it on my conscience that I might pass for having made love to her. Nothing less should I have seemed to do had I continued to beg a lady to "believe in me" in an Italian garden on a midsummer night. There was some merit in my scruples, for Miss Tina lingered and lingered: I made out in her the conviction that she shouldn't really soon come down again and the wish therefore to protract the present. She insisted too on making the talk between us personal to ourselves; and altogether her behaviour was such as would have been possible only to a perfectly artless and a considerably witless woman.

"I shall like the flowers better now that I know them also meant for me."

"How could you have doubted it? If you'll tell me the kind you like best I'll send a double lot."

"Oh I like them all best!" Then she went on familiarly: "Shall you study—shall you read and write—when you go up to your rooms?"

"I don't do that at night—at this season. The lamplight brings in the animals."

"You might have known that when you came."

"I did know it!"

"And in winter do you work at night?"

"I read a good deal, but I don't often write." She listened as if these details had a rare interest, and suddenly a temptation quite at odds with all the prudence I had been teaching myself glimmered at me in her plain mild face. Ah yes, she was safe and I could make her safer! It seemed to me from one moment to another that I couldn't wait longer—that I really must take a sounding. So I went on: "In general before I go to sleep (very often in bed; it's a bad habit, but I confess to it) I read some great poet. In nine cases out of ten it's a volume of Jeffrey Aspern."

I watched her well as I pronounced that name, but I saw nothing wonderful. Why should I indeed? Wasn't Jeffrey Aspern the property of the human race?

"Oh *we* read him—we *have* read him," she quietly replied.

"He's my poet of poets—I know him almost by heart."

For an instant Miss Tina hesitated; then her sociability was too much for her. "Oh by heart—that's nothing"; and, though dimly, she quite lighted. "My aunt used to know him, to know him"—she paused an instant and I wondered what she was going to say—"to know him as a visitor."

"As a visitor?" I guarded my tone.

"He used to call on her and take her out."

I continued to stare. "My dear lady, he died a hundred years ago!"

"Well," she said amusingly, "my aunt's a hundred and fifty."

"Mercy on us!" I cried; "why didn't you tell me before? I should like so to ask her about him."

"She wouldn't care for that—she wouldn't tell you," Miss Tina returned.

"I don't care what she cares for! She *must* tell me—it's not a chance to be lost."

"Oh you should have come twenty years ago. Then she still talked about him."

"And what did she say?" I eagerly asked.

"I don't know—that he liked her immensely."

"And she—didn't she like *him?*"

"She said he was a god." Miss Tina gave me this information flatly, without expression; her tone might have made it a piece of trivial gossip. But it stirred me deeply as she dropped the words into the summer night; their sound might have been the light rustle of an old unfolded love-letter.

"Fancy, fancy!" I murmured. And then: "Tell me this, please—has she got a portrait of him? They're distressingly rare."

"A portrait? I don't know," said Miss Tina; and now there was discomfiture in her face. "Well, good-night!" she added; and she turned into the house.

I accompanied her into the wide dusky stone-paved passage that corresponded on the ground floor with our great sala. It opened at one end into the garden, at the other upon the canal, and was lighted now only by the small lamp always left for me to take up as I went to bed. An extinguished candle which Miss Tina apparently had brought down with her stood on the same table with it. "Good-night, good-night!" I replied, keeping beside her as she went to get her light. "Surely you'd know, shouldn't you, if she had one?"

"If she had what?" the poor lady asked, looking at me queerly over the flame of her candle.

"A portrait of the god. I don't know what I wouldn't give to see it."

"I don't know what she has got. She keeps her things locked up." And Miss Tina went away toward the staircase with the sense evidently of having said too much.

I let her go—I wished not to frighten her—and I contented myself with remarking that Miss Bordereau wouldn't have locked up such a glorious possession as that: a thing a person would be proud of and hang up in a prominent place on the parlour-wall. Therefore of course she hadn't any portrait. Miss Tina made no direct answer to this and, candle in hand, with her back to me, mounted two or three degrees. Then she stopped short and turned round, looking at me across the dusky space.

"Do you write—do you write?" There was a shake in her voice—she could scarcely bring it out.

"Do I write? Oh don't speak of my writing on the same day with Aspern's!"

"Do you write about *him*—do you pry into his life?"

"Ah, that's your aunt's question; it can't be yours!" I said in a tone of slightly wounded sensibility.

"All the more reason then that you should answer it. Do you, please?"

I thought I had allowed for the falsehoods I should have to tell, but I found that in fact when it came to the point I hadn't. Besides, now that I had an opening there was a kind of relief in being frank. Lastly—it was perhaps fanciful, even fatuous—I guessed that Miss Tina personally wouldn't in the last resort be less my friend. So after a moment's hesitation I answered: "Yes, I've written about him and I'm looking for more material. In heaven's name have you got any?"

"*Santo Dio!*" she exclaimed without heeding my question; and she hurried upstairs and out of sight. I might count upon her in the last resort, but for the present she was visibly alarmed. The proof of it was that she began to hide again, so that for a fortnight I kept missing her. I found my patience ebbing and after four or five days of this I told the gardener to stop the "floral tributes."

6

ONE afternoon, at last, however, as I came down from my quarters to go out, I found her in the sala: it was our first encounter on that ground since I had come to the house. She put on no air of being there by accident; there was an ignorance of such arts in her honest angular diffidence. That I might be quite sure she was waiting for me she mentioned it at once, but telling me with it that Miss Bordereau wished to see me: she would take me into the room at that moment if I had time. If I had been late for a love-tryst I would have stayed for this, and I quickly signified that I should be delighted to wait on my benefactress. "She wants to talk with you—to know you," Miss Tina said, smiling as if she herself appreciated that idea; and she led me to the door of her aunt's apartment. I stopped her a moment before she had opened it, looking at her with some curiosity. I told her that this was a great satisfaction to me and a great honour; but all the same I should like to ask what had made Miss Bordereau so markedly and suddenly change. It had been only the other day that she wouldn't suffer me near her. Miss Tina was not embarrassed by my question; she had as many little unexpected serenities, plausibilities almost, as if she told fibs, but the odd part of them was that they had on the contrary their source in her truthfulness. "Oh my aunt varies," she answered; "it's so terribly dull—I suppose she's tired."

"But you told me she wanted more and more to be alone."

Poor Miss Tina coloured as if she found me too pushing. "Well, if you don't believe she wants to see you, I haven't invented it! I think people often are capricious when they're very old."

"That's perfectly true. I only wanted to be clear as to whether you've repeated to her what I told you the other night."

"What you told me?"

"About Jeffrey Aspern—that I'm looking for materials."

"If I had told her do you think she'd have sent for you?"

"That's exactly what I want to know. If she wants to keep him to herself she might have sent for me to tell me so."

"She won't speak of him," said Miss Tina. Then as she opened the door she added in a lower tone: "I told her nothing."

The old woman was sitting in the same place in which I had seen her last, in the same position, with the same mystifying bandage over her eyes. Her welcome was to turn her almost invisible face to me and show me that while she sat silent she saw me clearly. I made no motion to shake hands with her; I now felt too well that this was out of place for ever. It had been sufficiently enjoined on me that she was too sacred for trivial modernisms—too venerable to touch. There was something so grim in her aspect—it was partly the accident of her green shade—as I stood there to be measured, that I ceased on the spot to doubt her suspecting me, though I didn't in the least myself suspect that Miss Tina hadn't just spoken the truth. She hadn't betrayed me, but the old woman's brooding instinct had served her; she had turned me over and over in the long still hours and had guessed. The worst of it was that she looked terribly like an old woman who at a pinch would, even like Sardanapalus, burn her treasure. Miss Tina pushed a chair forward, saying to me "This will be a good place for you to sit." As I took possession of it I asked after Miss Bordereau's health; expressed the hope that in spite of the very hot weather it was satisfactory. She answered that it was good enough—good enough; that it was a great thing to be alive.

"Oh as to that, it depends upon what you compare it with!" I returned with a laugh.

"I don't compare—I don't compare. If I did that I should have given everything up long ago."

I liked to take this for a subtle allusion to the rapture she had known in the society of Jeffrey Aspern—though it was true that such an allusion would have accorded ill with the wish I imputed to her to keep him buried in her soul. What it accorded with was my constant conviction that no human being had ever had a happier social gift than his, and what it seemed to convey was that nothing in the world was worth speaking of if one pretended to speak of that. But one didn't pretend! Miss Tina sat down beside her aunt, looking as if she had reason to believe some wonderful talk would come off between us.

"It's about the beautiful flowers," said the old lady; "you sent us so many—I ought to have thanked you for them before. But I don't write letters and I receive company but at long intervals."

She hadn't thanked me while the flowers continued to come, but she departed from her custom so far as to send for me as soon as she began to fear they wouldn't come any more. I noted this; I remembered what an acquisitive propensity she had shown when it was a question of extracting gold from me, and I privately rejoiced at the happy thought I had had in suspending my tribute. She had missed it and was willing to make a concession to bring it back. At the first sign of this concession I could only go to meet her. "I'm afraid you haven't had many, of late, but they shall begin again immediately—to-morrow, to-night."

"Oh do send us some to-night!" Miss Tina cried as if it were a great affair.

"What else should you do with them? It isn't a manly taste to make a bower of your room," the old woman remarked.

"I don't make a bower of my room, but I'm exceedingly fond of growing flowers, of watching their ways. There's nothing unmanly in that; it has been the amusement of philosophers, of statesmen in retirement; even I think of great captains."

"I suppose you know you can sell them—those you don't use," Miss Bordereau went on. "I dare say they wouldn't give you much for them; still, you could make a bargain."

"Oh I've never in my life made a bargain, as you ought pretty well to have gathered. My gardener disposes of them and I ask no questions."

"I'd ask a few, I can promise you!" said Miss Bordereau; and it was so I first heard the strange sound of her laugh, which was as if the faint "walking" ghost of her old-time tone had suddenly cut a caper. I couldn't get used to the idea that this vision of pecuniary profit was most what drew out the divine Juliana.

"Come into the garden yourself and pick them; come as often as you like; come every day. The flowers are all for you," I pursued, addressing Miss Tina and carrying off this veracious statement by treating it as an innocent joke. "I can't imagine why she doesn't come down," I added for Miss Bordereau's benefit.

"You must make her come; you must come up and fetch her," the old woman said to my stupefaction. "That odd thing you've made in the corner will do very well for her to sit in."

The allusion to the most elaborate of my shady coverts, a sketchy "summer-house," was irreverent; it confirmed the impression I had already received that there was a flicker of impertinence in Miss Bordereau's talk, a vague echo of the boldness or the archness of her adventurous youth and which had somehow automatically outlived passions and faculties. None the less I asked: "Wouldn't it be possible for you to come down there yourself? Wouldn't it do you good to sit there in the shade and the sweet air?"

"Oh sir, when I move out of this it won't be to sit in the air, and I'm afraid that any that may be stirring around me won't be particularly sweet! It will be a very dark shade indeed. But that won't be just yet," Miss Bordereau continued cannily, as if to correct any hopes this free glance at the last receptacle of her mortality might lead me to entertain. "I've sat here many a day and have had enough of arbours in my time. But I'm not afraid to wait till I'm called."

Miss Tina had expected, as I felt, rare conversation, but perhaps she found it less gracious on her aunt's side—considering I had been sent for with a civil intention—than she had hoped. As to give the position a turn that would put our companion in a light more favourable she said to me: "Didn't I tell you the other night that she had sent me out? You see I can do what I like!"

"Do you pity her—do you teach her to pity herself?" Miss Bordereau demanded, before I had time to answer this appeal. "She has a much easier life than I had at her age."

"You must remember it has been quite open to me," I said, "to think you rather inhuman."

"Inhuman? That's what the poets used to call the women a hundred years ago. Don't try that; you won't do as well as they!" Juliana went on. "There's no more poetry in the world—that *I* know of at least. But I won't bandy words with you," she said, and I well remember the old-fashioned artificial sound she gave the speech. "You make me talk, talk, talk! It isn't good for me at all." I got up at this and told her I would take no more of her time; but she detained me to put a question. "Do you remember, the day I saw you about the rooms, that you offered us the use of your gondola?" And when I assented promptly, struck again with her disposition to make a "good thing" of my being there and wondering what she now had in her eye, she produced: "Why don't you take that girl out in it and show her the place?"

"Oh dear aunt, what do you want to do with me?" cried the "girl" with a piteous quaver. "I know all about the place!"

"Well then go with him and explain!" said Miss Bordereau, who gave an effect of cruelty to her implacable power of retort. This showed her as a sarcastic profane cynical old woman. "Haven't we heard that there have been all sorts of changes in all these years? You ought to see them, and at your age—I don't mean because you're so young—you ought to take the chances that come. You're old enough, my dear, and this gentleman won't hurt you. He'll show you the famous sunsets, if they still go on—*do* they go on? The sun set for me so long ago. But that's not a reason. Besides, I shall never miss you; you think you're too important. Take her to the Piazza; it used to be very pretty," Miss Bordereau continued, addressing herself to me. "What have they done with the funny old church? I hope it hasn't tumbled down. Let her look at the shops; she may take some money, she may buy what she likes."

Poor Miss Tina had got up, discountenanced and helpless, and as we stood there before her aunt it would certainly have struck a spectator of the scene that our venerable friend was making rare sport of us. Miss Tina protested in a confusion of exclamations and murmurs; but I lost no time in saying that if she would do me the honour to accept the hospitality of my boat I would engage she really shouldn't be bored. Or if she didn't want so much of my company the boat itself, with the gondolier, was at her service; he was a capital oar and she might have every confidence. Miss Tina, without definitely answering this speech, looked away from me and out of the window, quite as if about to weep, and I remarked that once we had Miss Bordereau's approval we could easily come to an understanding. We would take an hour, whichever she liked, one of the very next days. As I made my obeisance to the old lady I asked her if she would kindly permit me to see her again.

For a moment she kept me; then she said: "Is it very necessary to your happiness?"

"It diverts me more than I can say."

"You're wonderfully civil. Don't you know it almost kills *me?*"

"How can I believe that when I see you more animated, more brilliant than when I came in?"

"That's very true, aunt," said Miss Tina. "I think it does you good."

"Isn't it touching, the solicitude we each have that the other shall enjoy herself?" sneered Miss Bordereau. "If you think me brilliant to-day you don't know what you're talking about; you've never seen an agreeable woman. What do you people know about good society?" she cried; but before I could tell her, "Don't try to pay me a compliment; I've been spoiled," she went on. "My door's shut, but you may sometimes knock."

With this she dismissed me and I left the room. The latch closed behind me, but Miss Tina, contrary to my hope, had remained within. I passed slowly across the hall and before taking my way downstairs waited a little. My hope was answered; after a minute my conductress followed me. "That's a delightful idea about the Piazza," I said. "When will you go—to-night, to-morrow?"

She had been disconcerted, as I have mentioned, but I had already perceived, and I was to observe again, that when Miss Tina was embarrassed she didn't—as most women would have in like case—turn away, floundering and hedging, but came closer, as it were, with a deprecating, a clinging appeal to be spared, to be protected. Her attitude was a constant prayer for aid and explanation, and yet no woman in the world could have been less of a comedian. From the moment you were kind to her she depended on you absolutely; her self-consciousness dropped and she took the greatest intimacy, the innocent intimacy that was all she could conceive, for granted. She didn't know, she now declared, what possessed her aunt, who had changed so quickly, who had got some idea. I replied that she must catch the idea and let me have it: we would go and take an ice together at Florian's and she should report while we listened to the band.

"Oh it will take me a long time to be able to 'report'!" she said rather ruefully; and she could promise me this satisfaction neither for that night nor for the next. I was patient now, however, for I felt I had only to wait; and in fact at the end of the week, one lovely evening after dinner, she stepped into my gondola, to which in honour of the occasion I had attached a second oar.

We swept in the course of five minutes into the Grand Canal; whereupon she uttered a murmur of ecstasy as fresh as if she had been a tourist just arrived. She had forgotten the splendour of the great water-way on a clear summer evening, and how the sense of floating between marble palaces and reflected lights disposed the mind to freedom and ease. We floated long and far, and though my friend gave no high-pitched voice to her glee I was sure of her full surrender. She was more than pleased, she was transported; the whole thing was an immense liberation. The gondola moved with slow strokes, to give her time to enjoy it, and she listened to the plash of the oars, which grew louder and more musically liquid as we passed into narrow canals, as if it were a revelation of Venice. When I asked her how long it was since she had thus floated she answered: "Oh I don't know; a long time—not since my aunt began to be ill." This was not the only show of her extreme vagueness about the previous years and the line marking off the period of Miss Bordereau's eminence. I was not at liberty to keep her out long, but we took a considerable *giro* before going to the Piazza. I asked her no questions, holding off by design from her life at home and the things I wanted to know; I poured, rather, treasures of information about the objects before and around us into her ears, describing also Florence and Rome, discoursing on the charms and advantages of travel. She reclined, receptive, on the deep leather cushions, turned her eyes conscientiously to everything I noted and never mentioned to me till some time afterwards that she might be supposed to know Florence better than I, as she had lived there for years with her kinswoman. At last she said with the shy impatience of a child: "Are we not really going to the Piazza? That's what I want to see!" I immediately gave the order that we should go straight, after which we sat silent with the expectation of arrival. As some time still passed, however, she broke out of her own movement: "I've found out what's the matter with my aunt: she's afraid you'll go!"

I quite gasped. "What has put that into her head?"

"She has had an idea you've not been happy. That's why she's different now."

"You mean she wants to make me happier?"

"Well, she wants you not to go. She wants you to stay."

"I suppose you mean on account of the rent," I remarked candidly.

Miss Tina's candour but profited. "Yes, you know; so that I shall have more."

"How much does she want you to have?" I asked with all the gaiety I now felt. "She ought to fix the sum, so that I may stay till it's made up."

"Oh that wouldn't please me," said Miss Tina. "It would be unheard of, your taking that trouble."

"But suppose I should have my own reasons for staying in Venice?"

"Then it would be better for you to stay in some other house."

"And what would your aunt say to that?"

"She wouldn't like it at all. But I should think you'd do well to give up your reasons and go away altogether."

"Dear Miss Tina," I said, "it's not so easy to give up my reasons!"

She made no immediate answer to this, but after a moment broke out afresh: "I think I know what your reasons are!"

"I dare say, because the other night I almost told you how I wished you'd help me to make them good."

"I can't do that without being false to my aunt."

"What do you mean by being false to her?"

"Why she would never consent to what you want. She has been asked, she has been written to. It makes her fearfully angry."

"Then she *has* papers of value?" I precipitately cried.

"Oh she has everything!" sighed Miss Tina with a curious weariness, a sudden lapse into gloom.

These words caused all my pulses to throb, for I regarded them as
precious evidence. I felt them too deeply to speak, and in the
interval the gondola approached the Piazzetta. After we had disembarked I asked my companion if she would rather walk round the
square or go and sit before the great café; to which she replied that
she would do whichever I liked best—I must only remember again
how little time she had. I assured her there was plenty to do both,
and we made the circuit of the long arcades. Her spirits revived at
the sight of the bright shop-windows, and she lingered and stopped,
admiring or disapproving of their contents, asking me what I
thought of things, theorising about prices. My attention wandered
from her; her words of a while before "Oh she has everything!"
echoed so in my consciousness. We sat down at last in the crowded
circle at Florian's, finding an unoccupied table among those that
were ranged in the square. It was a splendid night and all the world
out-of-doors; Miss Tina couldn't have wished the elements more
auspicious for her return to society. I saw she felt it all even more
than she told, but her impressions were well-nigh too many for her.
She had forgotten the attraction of the world and was learning that
she had for the best years of her life been rather mercilessly cheated
of it. This didn't make her angry; but as she took in the charming
scene her face had, in spite of its smile of appreciation, the flush of a
wounded surprise. She didn't speak, sunk in the sense of opportunities, for ever lost, that ought to have been easy; and this gave me a
chance to say to her: "Did you mean a while ago that your aunt has a
plan of keeping me on by admitting me occasionally to her presence?"

"She thinks it will make a difference with you if you sometimes see
her. She wants you so much to stay that she's willing to make that
concession."

"And what good does she consider I think it will do me to see
her?"

"I don't know; it must be interesting," said Miss Tina simply.
"You told her you found it so."

"So I did; but every one doesn't think that."

"No, of course not, or more people would try."

"Well, if she's capable of making that reflexion she's capable also of making this further one," I went on: "that I must have a particular reason for not doing as others do, in spite of the interest she offers—for not leaving her alone." Miss Tina looked as if she failed to grasp this rather complicated proposition; so I continued: "If you've not told her what I said to you the other night may she not at least have guessed it?"

"I don't know—she's very suspicious."

"But she hasn't been made so by indiscreet curiosity, by persecution?"

"No, no; it isn't that," said Miss Tina, turning on me a troubled face. "I don't know how to say it: it's on account of something—ages ago, before I was born—in her life."

"Something? What sort of thing?"—and I asked it as if I could have no idea.

"Oh she has never told me." And I was sure my friend spoke the truth.

Her extreme limpidity was almost provoking, and I felt for the moment that she would have been more satisfactory if she had been less ingenuous. "Do you suppose it's something to which Jeffrey Aspern's letters and papers—I mean the things in her possession—have reference?"

"I dare say it is!" my companion exclaimed as if this were a very happy suggestion. "I've never looked at any of those things."

"None of them? Then how do you know what they are?"

"I don't," said Miss Tina placidly. "I've never had them in my hands. But I've seen them when she has had them out."

"Does she have them out often?"

"Not now, but she used to. She's very fond of them."

"In spite of their being compromising?"

"Compromising?" Miss Tina repeated as if vague as to what that meant. I felt almost as one who corrupts the innocence of youth.

"I allude to their containing painful memories."

"Oh I don't think anything's painful."

"You mean there's nothing to affect her reputation?"

An odder look even than usual came at this into the face of Miss Bordereau's niece—a confession, it seemed, of helplessness, an appeal to me to deal fairly, generously with her. I had brought her to the Piazza, placed her among charming influences, paid her an attention she appreciated, and now I appeared to show it all as a bribe

—a bribe to make her turn in some way against her aunt. She was of a yielding nature and capable of doing almost anything to please a person markedly kind to her; but the greatest kindness of all would be not to presume too much on this. It was strange enough, as I afterwards thought, that she had not the least air of resenting my want of consideration for her aunt's character, which would have been in the worst possible taste if anything less vital—from my point of view—had been at stake. I don't think she really measured it. "Do you mean she ever did something bad?" she asked in a moment.

"Heaven forbid I should say so, and it's none of my business. Besides, if she did," I agreeably put it, "that was in other ages, in another world. But why shouldn't she destroy her papers?"

"Oh she loves them too much."

"Even now, when she may be near her end?"

"Perhaps when she's sure of that she will."

"Well, Miss Tina," I said, "that's just what I should like you to prevent."

"How can I prevent it?"

"Couldn't you get them away from her?"

"And give them to you?"

This put the case, superficially, with sharp irony, but I was sure of her not intending that. "Oh I mean that you might let me see them and look them over. It isn't for myself, or that I should want them at any cost to any one else. It's simply that they would be of such immense interest to the public, such immeasurable importance as a contribution to Jeffrey Aspern's history."

She listened to me in her usual way, as if I abounded in matters she had never heard of, and I felt almost as base as the reporter of a newspaper who forces his way into a house of mourning. This was marked when she presently said: "There was a gentleman who some time ago wrote to her in very much those words. He also wanted her papers."

"And did she answer him?" I asked, rather ashamed of not having my friend's rectitude.

"Only when he had written two or three times. He made her very angry."

"And what did she say?"

"She said he was a devil," Miss Tina replied categorically.

"She used that expression in her letter?"

"Oh no; she said it to me. She made me write to him."

"And what did you say?"

"I told him there were no papers at all."

"Ah poor gentleman!" I groaned.

"I knew there were, but I wrote what she bade me."

"Of course you had to do that. But I hope I shan't pass for a devil."

"It will depend upon what you ask me to do for you," my companion smiled.

"Oh if there's a chance of *your* thinking so my affair's in a bad way! I shan't ask you to steal for me, nor even to fib—for you *can't* fib, unless on paper. But the principal thing is this—to prevent her destroying the papers."

"Why I've no control of her," said Miss Tina. "It's she who controls me."

"But she doesn't control her own arms and legs, does she? The way she would naturally destroy her letters would be to burn them. Now she can't burn them without fire, and she can't get fire unless you give it her."

"I've always done everything she has asked," my poor friend pleaded. "Besides, there's Olimpia."

I was on the point of saying that Olimpia was probably corruptible, but I thought it best not to sound that note. So I simply put it that this frail creature might perhaps be managed.

"Every one can be managed by my aunt," said Miss Tina. And then she remembered that her holiday was over; she must go home.

I laid my hand on her arm, across the table, to stay her a moment. "What I want of you is a general promise to help me."

"Oh how *can* I, how *can* I?" she asked, wondering and troubled. She was half-surprised, half-frightened at my attaching that importance to her, at my calling on her for action.

"This is the main thing: to watch our friend carefully and warn me in time, before she commits that dreadful sacrilege."

"I can't watch her when she makes me go out."

"That's very true."

"And when you do too."

"Mercy on us—do you think she'll have done anything to-night?"

"I don't know. She's very cunning."

"Are you trying to frighten me?" I asked.

I felt this question sufficiently answered when my companion murmured in a musing, almost envious way: "Oh but she loves them—she loves them!"

This reflexion, repeated with such emphasis, gave me great comfort; but to obtain more of that balm I said: "If she shouldn't intend to destroy the objects we speak of before her death she'll probably have made some disposition by will."

"By will?"

"Hasn't she made a will for your benefit?"

"Ah she has so little to leave. That's why she likes money," said Miss Tina.

"Might I ask, since we're really talking things over, what you and she live on?"

"On some money that comes from America, from a gentleman—I think a lawyer—in New York. He sends it every quarter. It isn't much!"

"And won't she have disposed of that?"

My companion hesitated—I saw she was blushing. "I believe it's mine," she said; and the look and tone which accompanied these words betrayed so the absence of the habit of thinking of herself that I almost thought her charming. The next instant she added: "But she had in an *avvocato* here once, ever so long ago. And some people came and signed something."

"They were probably witnesses. And you weren't asked to sign? Well then," I argued, rapidly and hopefully, "it's because you're the legatee. She must have left all her documents to you!"

"If she has it's with very strict conditions," Miss Tina responded, rising quickly, while the movement gave the words a small character of decision. They seemed to imply that the bequest would be accompanied with a proviso that the articles bequeathed should remain concealed from every inquisitive eye, and that I was very much mistaken if I thought her the person to depart from an injunction so absolute.

"Oh of course you'll have to abide by the terms," I said; and she uttered nothing to mitigate the rigour of this conclusion. None the less, later on, just before we disembarked at her own door after a return which had taken place almost in silence, she said to me abruptly: "I'll do what I can to help you." I was grateful for this—it was very well so far as it went; but it didn't keep me from remembering that night in a worried waking hour that I now had her word for it to re-enforce my own impression that the old woman was full of craft.

❖ 7 ❖

THE fear of what this side of her character might have led her to do made me nervous for days afterwards. I waited for an intimation from Miss Tina; I almost read it as her duty to keep me informed, to let me know definitely whether or no Miss Bordereau had sacrificed her treasures. But as she gave no sign I lost patience and determined to put the case to the very touch of my own senses. I sent late one afternoon to ask if I might pay the ladies a visit, and my servant came back with surprising news. Miss Bordereau could be approached without the least difficulty; she had been moved out into the sala and was sitting by the window that overlooked the garden. I descended and found this picture correct; the old lady had been wheeled forth into the world and had a certain air, which came mainly perhaps from some brighter element in her dress, of being prepared again to have converse with it. It had not yet, however, begun to flock about her; she was perfectly alone and, though the door leading to her own quarters stood open, I had at first no glimpse of Miss Tina. The window at which she sat had the afternoon shade and, one of the shutters having been pushed back, she could see the pleasant garden, where the summer sun had by this time dried up too many of the plants—she could see the yellow light and the long shadows.

"Have you come to tell me you'll take the rooms for six months more?" she asked as I approached her, startling me by something coarse in her cupidity almost as much as if she hadn't already given me a specimen of it. Juliana's desire to make our acquaintance lucrative had been, as I have sufficiently indicated, a false note in my image of the woman who had inspired a great poet with immortal lines; but I may say here definitely that I after all recognised large allowance to be made for her. It was I who had kindled the unholy flame; it was I who had put into her head that she had the means of making money. She appeared never to have thought of that; she had been living wastefully for years, in a house five times too big for her, on a footing that I could explain only by the presumption that, excessive as it was, the space she enjoyed cost her next to nothing and that, small as were her revenues, they left her, for Venice, an appreciable margin. I had descended on her one day and taught her to calculate, and my almost extravagant comedy on the subject of the garden had presented me irresistibly in the light of a victim. Like all persons who achieve the miracle of changing their point of view late in life, she had been intensely converted: she had seized my hint with a desperate tremulous clutch.

I invited myself to go and get one of the chairs that stood, at a distance, against the wall—she had given herself no concern as to whether I should sit or stand; and while I placed it near her I began gaily: "Oh dear madam, what an imagination you have, what an intellectual sweep! I'm a poor devil of a man of letters who lives from day to day. How can I take palaces by the year? My existence is precarious. I don't know whether six months hence I shall have bread to put in my mouth. I've treated myself for once; it has been an immense luxury. But when it comes to going on—!"

"Are your rooms too dear? if they are you can have more for the same money," Juliana responded. "We can arrange, we can *combinare*, as they say here."

"Well yes, since you ask me, they're too dear, much too dear," I said. "Evidently you suppose me richer than I am."

She looked at me as from the mouth of her cave. "If you write books don't you sell them?"

"Do you mean don't people buy them? A little, a very little—not so much as I could wish. Writing books, unless one be a great genius—and even then!—is the last road to fortune. I think there's no more money to be made by good letters."

"Perhaps you don't choose nice subjects. What do you write about?" Miss Bordereau implacably pursued.

"About the books of other people. I'm a critic, a commentator, an historian, in a small way." I wondered what she was coming to.

"And what other people now?"

"Oh better ones than myself: the great writers mainly—the great

philosophers and poets of the past; those who are dead and gone and
can't, poor darlings, speak for themselves."

"And what do you say about them?"

"I say they sometimes attached themselves to very clever women!"
I replied as for pleasantness. I had measured, as I thought, my risk,
but as my words fell upon the air they were to strike me as imprudent. However, I had launched them and I wasn't sorry, for perhaps
after all the old woman would be willing to treat. It seemed tolerably
obvious that she knew my secret: why therefore drag the process out?
But she didn't take what I had said as a confession; she only asked:

"Do you think it's right to rake up the past?"

"I don't feel that I know what you mean by raking it up. How can
we get at it unless we dig a little? The present has such a rough way
of treading it down."

"Oh I like the past, but I don't like critics," my hostess declared
with her hard complacency.

"Neither do I, but I like their discoveries."

"Aren't they mostly lies?"

"The lies are what they sometimes discover," I said, smiling at the
quiet impertinence of this. "They often lay bare the truth."

"The truth is God's, it isn't man's: we had better leave it alone.
Who can judge of it?—who can say?"

"We're terribly in the dark, I know," I admitted; "but if we give
up trying what becomes of all the fine things? What becomes of the
work I just mentioned, that of the great philosophers and poets? It's
all vain words if there's nothing to measure it by."

"You talk as if you were a tailor," said Miss Bordereau whimsically; and then she added quickly and in a different manner: "This
house is very fine; the proportions are magnificent. To-day I wanted
to look at this part again. I made them bring me out here. When
your man came just now to learn if I would see you I was on the
point of sending for you to ask if you didn't mean to go on. I wanted
to judge what I'm letting you have. This sala is very grand," she
pursued like an auctioneer, moving a little, as I guessed, her invisible
eyes. "I don't believe you often have lived in such a house, eh?"

"I can't often afford to!" I said.

"Well then how much will you give me for six months?"

I was on the point of exclaiming—and the air of excruciation in my face would have denoted a moral fact—"Don't, Juliana; for *his* sake, don't!" But I controlled myself and asked less passionately: "Why should I remain so long as that?"

"I thought you liked it," said Miss Bordereau with her shrivelled dignity.

"So I thought I should."

For a moment she said nothing more, and I left my own words to suggest to her what they might. I half-expected her to say, coldly enough, that if I had been disappointed we needn't continue the discussion, and this in spite of the fact that I believed her now to have in her mind—however it had come there—what would have told her that my disappointment was natural. But to my extreme surprise she ended by observing: "If you don't think we've treated you well enough perhaps we can discover some way of treating you better." This speech was somehow so incongruous that it made me laugh again, and I excused myself by saying that she talked as if I were a sulky boy pouting in the corner and having to be "brought round." I hadn't a grain of complaint to make; and could anything have exceeded Miss Tina's graciousness in accompanying me a few nights before to the Piazza? At this the old woman went on: "Well, you brought it on yourself!" And then in a different tone: "She's a very fine girl." I assented cordially to this proposition, and she expressed the hope that I did so not merely to be obliging, but that I really liked her. Meanwhile I wondered still more what Miss Bordereau was coming to. "Except for me, to-day," she said, "she hasn't a relation in the world." Did she by describing her niece as amiable and unencumbered wish to represent her as a *parti?*

It was perfectly true that I couldn't afford to go on with my rooms at a fancy price and that I had already devoted to my undertaking almost all the hard cash I had set apart for it. My patience and my time were by no means exhausted, but I should be able to draw upon them only on a more usual Venetian basis. I was willing to pay the precious personage with whom my pecuniary dealings were such a discord twice as much as any other *padrona di casa* would have asked, but I wasn't willing to pay her twenty times as much. I told her so plainly, and my plainness appeared to have some success, for she exclaimed: "Very good; you've done what I asked—you've made an offer!"

"Yes, but not for half a year. Only by the month."

"Oh I must think of that then." She seemed disappointed that I wouldn't tie myself to a period, and I guessed that she wished both to secure me and to discourage me; to say severely: "Do you dream that you can get off with less than six months? Do you dream that even by the end of that time you'll be appreciably nearer your victory?" What was most in my mind was that she had a fancy to play me the trick of making me engage myself when in fact she had sacrificed her treasure. There was a moment when my suspense on this point was so acute that I all but broke out with the question, and what kept it back was but an instinctive recoil—lest it should be a mistake—from the last violence of self-exposure. She was such a subtle old witch that one could never tell where one stood with her. You may imagine whether it cleared up the puzzle when, just after she had said she would think of my proposal and without any formal transition, she drew out of her pocket with an embarrassed hand a small object wrapped in crumpled white paper. She held it there a moment and then resumed: "Do you know much about curiosities?"

"About curiosities?"

"About antiquities, the old gimcracks that people pay so much for to-day. Do you know the kind of price they bring?"

I thought I saw what was coming, but I said ingenuously: "Do you want to buy something?"

"No, I want to sell. What would an amateur give me for that?" She unfolded the white paper and made a motion for me to take from her a small oval portrait. I possessed myself of it with fingers of which I could only hope that they didn't betray the intensity of their clutch, and she added: "I would part with it only for a good price."

At the first glance I recognised Jeffrey Aspern, and was well aware that I flushed with the act. As she was watching me however I had the consistency to exclaim: "What a striking face! Do tell me who he is."

"He's an old friend of mine, a very distinguished man in his day. He gave it me himself, but I'm afraid to mention his name, lest you never should have heard of him, critic and historian as you are. I know the world goes fast and one generation forgets another. He was all the fashion when I was young."

She was perhaps amazed at my assurance, but I was surprised at hers; at her having the energy, in her state of health and at her time of life, to wish to sport with me to that tune simply for her private entertainment—the humour to test me and practise on me and befool me. This at least was the interpretation that I put upon her production of the relic, for I couldn't believe she really desired to sell it or cared for any information I might give her. What she wished was to dangle it before my eyes and put a prohibitive price on it. "The face comes back to me, it torments me," I said, turning the object this way and that and looking at it very critically. It was a careful but not a supreme work of art, larger than the ordinary miniature and representing a young man with a remarkably handsome face, in a high-collared green coat and a buff waistcoat. I felt in the little work a virtue of likeness and judged it to have been painted when the model was about twenty-five. There are, as all the world knows, three other portraits of the poet in existence, but none of so early a date as this elegant image. "I've never seen the original, clearly a man of a past age, but I've seen other reproductions of this face," I went on. "You expressed doubt of this generation's having heard of the gentleman, but he strikes me for all the world as a celebrity. Now who is he? I can't put my finger on him—I can't give him a label. Wasn't he a writer? Surely he's a poet." I was determined that it should be she, not I, who should first pronounce Jeffrey Aspern's name.

My resolution was taken in ignorance of Miss Bordereau's extremely resolute character, and her lips never formed in my hearing the syllables that meant so much for her. She neglected to answer my question, but raised her hand to take back the picture, using a gesture which though impotent was in a high degree peremptory. "It's only a person who should know for himself that would give me my price," she said with a certain dryness.

"Oh then you have a price?" I didn't restore the charming thing; not from any vindictive purpose, but because I instinctively clung to it. We looked at each other hard while I retained it.

"I know the least I would take. What it occurred to me to ask you about is the most I shall be able to get."

She made a movement, drawing herself together as if, in a spasm of dread at having lost her prize, she had been impelled to the immense effort of rising to snatch it from me. I instantly placed it in her hand again, saying as I did so: "I should like to have it myself, but with your ideas it would be quite beyond my mark."

She turned the small oval plate over in her lap, with its face down, and I heard her catch her breath as after a strain or an escape. This however did not prevent her saying in a moment: "You'd buy a likeness of a person you don't know by an artist who has no reputation?"

"The artist may have no reputation, but that thing's wonderfully well painted," I replied, to give myself a reason.

"It's lucky you thought of saying that, because the painter was my father."

"That makes the picture indeed precious!" I returned with gaiety; and I may add that a part of my cheer came from this proof I had been right in my theory of Miss Bordereau's origin. Aspern had of course met the young lady on his going to her father's studio as a sitter. I observed to Miss Bordereau that if she would entrust me with her property for twenty-four hours I should be happy to take advice on it; but she made no other reply than to slip it in silence into her pocket. This convinced me still more that she had no sincere intention of selling it during her lifetime, though she may have desired to satisfy herself as to the sum her niece, should she leave it to her, might expect eventually to obtain for it. "Well, at any rate, I hope you won't offer it without giving me notice," I said as she remained irresponsive. "Remember me as a possible purchaser."

"I should want your money first!" she returned with unexpected rudeness; and then, as if she bethought herself that I might well complain of such a tone and wished to turn the matter off, asked abruptly what I talked about with her niece when I went out with her that way of an evening.

"You speak as if we had set up the habit," I replied. "Certainly I should be very glad if it were to become our pleasant custom. But in that case I should feel a still greater scruple at betraying a lady's confidence."

"Her confidence? Has my niece confidence?"

"Here she is—she can tell you herself," I said; for Miss Tina now appeared on the threshold of the old woman's parlour. "Have you confidence, Miss Tina? Your aunt wants very much to know."

"Not in her, not in her!" the younger lady declared, shaking her head with a dolefulness that was neither jocular nor affected. "I don't know what to do with her; she has fits of horrid imprudence. She's so easily tired—and yet she has begun to roam, to drag herself about the house." And she looked down at her yoke-fellow of long years with a vacancy of wonder, as if all their contact and custom hadn't made her perversities, on occasion, any more easy to follow.

"I know what I'm about. I'm not losing my mind. I dare say you'd like to think so," said Miss Bordereau with a crudity of cynicism.

"I don't suppose you came out here yourself. Miss Tina must have had to lend you a hand," I interposed for conciliation.

"Oh she insisted we should push her; and when she insists!" said Miss Tina, in the same tone of apprehension: as if there were no knowing what service she disapproved of her aunt might force her next to render.

"I've always got most things done I wanted, thank God! The people I've lived with have humoured me," the old woman continued, speaking out of the white ashes of her vanity.

I took it pleasantly up. "I suppose you mean they've obeyed you."

"Well, whatever it is—when they like one."

"It's just because I like you that I want to resist," said Miss Tina with a nervous laugh.

"Oh I suspect you'll bring Miss Bordereau upstairs next to pay me a visit," I went on; to which the old lady replied:

"Oh no; I can keep an eye on you from here!"

"You're very tired; you'll certainly be ill tonight!" cried Miss Tina.

"Nonsense, dear; I feel better at this moment than I've done for a month. To-morrow I shall come out again. I want to be where I can see this clever gentleman."

"Shouldn't you perhaps see me better in your sitting-room?" I asked.

"Don't you mean shouldn't you have a better chance at *me?*" she returned, fixing me a moment with her green shade.

"Ah I haven't that anywhere! I look at you but don't see you."

"You agitate her dreadfully—and that's not good," said Miss Tina, giving me a reproachful deterrent headshake.

"I want to watch you—I want to watch you!" Miss Bordereau went on.

"Well then let us spend as much of our time together as possible—I don't care where. That will give you every facility."

"Oh I've seen you enough for to-day. I'm satisfied. Now I'll go home," Juliana said. Miss Tina laid her hands on the back of the wheeled chair and began to push, but I begged her to let me take her place. "Oh yes, you may move me this way—you shan't in any other!" the old woman cried as she felt herself propelled firmly and easily over the smooth hard floor. Before we reached the door of her own apartment she bade me stop, and she took a long last look up and down the noble sala. "Oh it's a prodigious house!" she murmured; after which I pushed her forward. When we had entered the parlour Miss Tina let me know she should now be able to manage, and at the same moment the little red-haired *donna* came to meet her mistress. Miss Tina's idea was evidently to get her aunt immediately back to bed. I confess that in spite of this urgency I was guilty of the indiscretion of lingering; it held me there to feel myself so close to the objects I coveted—which would be probably put away somewhere in the faded unsociable room. The place had indeed a bareness that suggested no hidden values; there were neither dusky nooks nor curtained corners, neither massive cabinets nor chests with iron bands. Moreover it was possible, it was perhaps even likely, that the old lady had consigned her relics to her bedroom, to some battered box that was shoved under the bed, to the drawer of some lame dressing-table, where they would be in the range of vision by the dim night-lamp. None the less I turned an eye on every article of furniture, on every conceivable cover for a hoard, and noticed that there were half a dozen things with drawers, and in particular a tall old secretary with brass ornaments of the style of the Empire— a receptacle somewhat infirm but still capable of keeping rare secrets. I don't know why this article so engaged me, small purpose as I had of breaking into it; but I stared at it so hard that Miss Tina noticed me and changed colour. Her doing this made me think I was right and that, wherever they might have been before, the Aspern papers at that moment languished behind the peevish little lock of the secretary. It was hard to turn my attention from the dull mahogany front when I reflected that a plain panel divided me from the goal of my hopes; but I gathered up my slightly scattered prudence and with an effort took leave of my hostess. To make the effort graceful I said to her that I should certainly bring her an opinion about the little picture.

"The little picture?" Miss Tina asked in surprise.

"What do *you* know about it, my dear?" the old woman demanded. "You needn't mind. I've fixed my price."

"And what may that be?"

"A thousand pounds."

"Oh Lord!" cried poor Miss Tina irrepressibly.

"Is that what she talks to you about?" said Miss Bordereau.

"Imagine your aunt's wanting to know!" I had to separate from my younger friend with only those words, though I should have liked immensely to add: "For heaven's sake meet me to-night in the garden!"

⧓ 8 ⧓

As it turned out the precaution had not been needed, for three hours later, just as I had finished my dinner, Miss Tina appeared, unannounced, in the open doorway of the room in which my simple repasts were served. I remember well that I felt no surprise at seeing her; which is not a proof of my not believing in her timidity. It was immense, but in a case in which there was a particular reason for boldness it never would have prevented her from running up to my floor. I saw that she was now quite full of a particular reason; it threw her forward—made her seize me, as I rose to meet her, by the arm.

"My aunt's very ill; I think she's dying!"

"Never in the world," I answered bitterly. "Don't you be afraid!"

"Do go for a doctor—do, do! Olimpia's gone for the one we always have, but she doesn't come back; I don't know what has happened to her. I told her that if he wasn't at home she was to follow him where he had gone; but apparently she's following him all over Venice. I don't know what to do—she looks so as if she were sinking."

"May I see her, may I judge?" I asked. "Of course I shall be delighted to bring some one; but hadn't we better send my man instead, so that I may stay with you?"

Miss Tina assented to this and I dispatched my servant for the best doctor in the neighbourhood. I hurried downstairs with her, and on the way she told me that an hour after I quitted them in the afternoon Miss Bordereau had had an attack of "oppression," a terrible difficulty in breathing. This had subsided, but had left her so exhausted that she didn't come up; she seemed all spent and gone. I repeated that she wasn't gone, that she wouldn't go yet; whereupon Miss Tina gave me a sharper sidelong glance than she had ever favoured me withal and said: "Really, what do you mean? I suppose you don't accuse her of making-believe!" I forget what reply I made to this, but I fear that in my heart I thought the old woman capable of any weird manœuvre. Miss Tina wanted to know what I had done to her; her aunt had told her I had made her so angry. I declared I had done nothing whatever—I had been exceedingly careful; to which my companion rejoined that our friend had assured her she had had a scene with me—a scene that had upset her. I answered with some resentment that the scene had been of *her* making—that I couldn't think what she was angry with me for unless for not seeing my way to give a thousand pounds for the portrait of Jeffrey Aspern. "And did she show you that? Oh gracious—oh deary me!" groaned Miss Tina, who seemed to feel the situation pass out of her control and the elements of her fate thicken round her. I answered her I'd give anything to possess it, yet that I had no thousand pounds; but I stopped when we came to the door of Miss Bordereau's room. I had an immense curiosity to pass it, but I thought it my duty to represent to Miss Tina that if I made the invalid angry she ought perhaps to be spared the sight of me. "The sight of you? Do you think she can *see?*" my companion demanded almost with indignation. I did think so but forbore to say it, and I softly followed my conductress.

I remember that what I said to her as I stood for a moment beside the old woman's bed was: "Does she never show you her eyes then? Have you never seen them?" Miss Bordereau had been divested of her green shade, but—it was not my fortune to behold Juliana in her nightcap—the upper half of her face was covered by the fall of a piece of dingy lacelike muslin, a sort of extemporised hood which, wound round her head, descended to the end of her nose, leaving nothing visible but her white withered cheeks and puckered mouth, closed tightly and, as it were, consciously. Miss Tina gave me a glance of surprise, evidently not seeing a reason for my impatience. "You mean she always wears something? She does it to preserve them."

"Because they're so fine?"

"Oh to-day, to-day!" And Miss Tina shook her head speaking very low. "But they used to be magnificent!"

"Yes indeed,—we've Aspern's word for that." And as I looked

again at the old woman's wrappings I could imagine her not having wished to allow any supposition that the great poet had overdone it. But I didn't waste my time in considering Juliana, in whom the appearance of respiration was so slight as to suggest that no human attention could ever help her more. I turned my eyes once more all over the room, rummaging with them the closets, the chests of drawers, the tables. Miss Tina at once noted their direction and read, I think, what was in them; but she didn't answer it, turning away restlessly, anxiously, so that I felt rebuked, with reason, for an appetite well-nigh indecent in the presence of our dying companion. All the same I took another view, endeavouring to pick out mentally the receptacle to try first, for a person who should wish to put his hand on Miss Bordereau's papers directly after her death. The place was a dire confusion; it looked like the dressing-room of an old actress. There were clothes hanging over chairs, odd-looking shabby bundles here and there, and various pasteboard boxes piled together, battered, bulging and discoloured, which might have been fifty years old. Miss Tina after a moment noticed the direction of my eyes again, and, as if she guessed how I judged such appearances—forgetting I had no business to judge them at all—said, perhaps to defend herself from the imputation of complicity in the disorder:

"She likes it this way; we can't move things. There are old bandboxes she has had most of her life." Then she added, half-taking pity on my real thought: "Those things were *there*." And she pointed to a small low trunk which stood under a sofa that just allowed room for it. It struck me as a queer superannuated coffer, of painted wood, with elaborate handles and shrivelled straps and with the colour—it had last been endued with a coat of light green—much rubbed off. It evidently had travelled with Juliana in the olden time—in the days of her adventures, which it had shared. It would have made a strange figure arriving at a modern hotel.

"*Were* there—they aren't now?" I asked, startled by Miss Tina's implication.

She was going to answer, but at that moment the doctor came in—the doctor whom the little maid had been sent to fetch and whom she had at last overtaken. My servant, going on his own errand, had met her with her companion in tow, and in the sociable Venetian spirit, retracing his steps with them, had also come up to the threshold of the padrona's room, where I saw him peep over the doctor's shoulder. I motioned him away the more instantly that the sight of his prying face reminded me how little I myself had to do there—an admonition confirmed by the sharp way the little doctor eyed me, his air of taking me for a rival who had the field before him. He was a short fat brisk gentleman who wore the tall hat of his profession and seemed to look at everything but his patient. He kept me still in range, as if it struck him I too should be better for a dose, so that I bowed to him and left him with the women, going down to smoke a cigar in the garden. I was nervous; I couldn't go further; I couldn't leave the place. I don't know exactly what I thought might happen, but I felt it important to be there. I wandered about the alleys—the warm night had come on—smoking cigar after cigar and studying the light in Miss Bordereau's windows. They were open now, I could see; the situation was different. Sometimes the light moved, but not quickly; it didn't suggest the hurry of a crisis. Was the old woman dying or was she already dead? Had the doctor said that there was nothing to be done at her tremendous age but to let her quietly pass away? or had he simply announced with a look a little more conventional that the end of the end had come? Were the other two women just going and coming over the offices that follow in such a case? It made me uneasy not to be nearer, as if I thought the doctor himself might carry away the papers with him. I bit my cigar hard while it assailed me again that perhaps there were now no papers to carry!

I wandered about an hour and more. I looked out for Miss Tina at one of the windows, having a vague idea that she might come there to give me some sign. Wouldn't she see the red tip of my cigar in the dark and feel sure I was hanging on to know what the doctor had said? I'm afraid it's a proof of the grossness of my anxieties that I should have taken in some degree for granted at such an hour, in the midst of the greatest change that could fall on her, poor Miss Tina's having also a free mind for them. My servant came down and spoke to me; he knew nothing save that the doctor had gone after a visit of half an hour. If he had stayed half an hour then Miss Bordereau was still alive: it couldn't have taken so long to attest her decease. I sent the man out of the house; there were moments when the sense of his curiosity annoyed me, and this was one of them. *He* had been watching my cigar-tip from an upper window, if Miss Tina hadn't; he couldn't know what I was after and I couldn't tell him, though I suspected in him fantastic private theories about me which he thought fine and which, had I more exactly known them, I should have thought offensive.

I went upstairs at last, but I mounted no higher than the sala. The door of Miss Bordereau's apartment was open, showing from the parlour the dimness of a poor candle. I went toward it with a light tread, and at the same moment Miss Tina appeared and stood looking at me as I approached. "She's better, she's better," she said even before I had asked. "The doctor has given her something; she woke up, came back to life while he was there. He says there's no immediate danger."

"No immediate danger? Surely he thinks her condition serious."

"Yes, because she had been excited. That affects her dreadfully."

"It will do so again then, because she works herself up. She did so this afternoon."

"Yes, she mustn't come out any more," said Miss Tina with one of her lapses into a deeper detachment.

"What's the use of making such a remark as that," I permitted myself to ask, "if you begin to rattle her about again the first time she bids you?"

"I won't—I won't do it any more."

"You must learn to resist her," I went on.

"Oh yes, I shall; I shall do so better if you tell me it's right."

"You mustn't do it for me—you must do it for yourself. It all comes back to you, if you're scared and upset."

"Well, I'm not upset now," said Miss Tina placidly enough. "She's very quiet."

"Is she conscious again—does she speak?"

"No, she doesn't speak, but she takes my hand. She holds it fast."

"Yes," I returned, "I can see what force she still has by the way she grabbed that picture this afternoon. But if she holds you fast how comes it that you're here?"

Miss Tina waited a little; though her face was in deep shadow—she had her back to the light in the parlour and I had put down my own candle far off, near the door of the sala—I thought I saw her smile ingenuously. "I came on purpose—I had heard your step."

"Why I came on tiptoe, as soundlessly as possible."

"Well, I had heard you," said Miss Tina.

"And is your aunt alone now?"

"Oh no—Olimpia sits there."

On my side I debated. "Shall we then pass in there?" And I nodded at the parlour; I wanted more and more to be on the spot.

"We can't talk there—she'll hear us."

I was on the point of replying that in that case we'd sit silent, but I felt too much this wouldn't do, there was something I desired so immensely to ask her. Thus I hinted we might walk a little in the sala, keeping more at the other end, where we shouldn't disturb our friend. Miss Tina assented unconditionally; the doctor was coming again, she said, and she would be there to meet him at the door. We strolled through the fine superfluous hall, where on the marble floor—particularly as at first we said nothing—our footsteps were more audible than I had expected. When we reached the other end—the wide window, inveterately closed, connecting with the balcony that overhung the canal—I submitted that we had best remain there, as she would see the doctor arrive the sooner. I opened the window and we passed out on the balcony. The air of the canal seemed even heavier, hotter than that of the sala. The place was hushed and void; the quiet neighbourhood had gone to sleep. A lamp, here and there, over the narrow black water, glimmered in double; the voice of a man going homeward singing, his jacket on his shoulder and his hat on his ear, came to us from a distance. This didn't prevent the scene from being very *comme il faut,* as Miss Bordereau had called it the first time I saw her. Presently a gondola passed along the canal with its slow rhythmical plash, and as we listened we watched it in silence. It didn't stop, it didn't carry the doctor; and after it had gone on I said to Miss Tina:

"And where are they now—the things that were in the trunk?"

"In the trunk?"

"That green box you pointed out to me in her room. You said her papers had been there; you seemed to mean she had transferred them."

"Oh yes; they're not in the trunk," said Miss Tina.

"May I ask if you've looked?"

"Yes, I've looked—for you."

"How for me, dear Miss Tina? Do you mean you'd have given them to me if you had found them?"—and I fairly trembled with the question.

She delayed to reply and I waited. Suddenly she broke out: "I don't know what I'd do—what I wouldn't!"

"Would you look again—somewhere else?"

She had spoken with a strange unexpected emotion, and she went on in the same tone: "I can't—I can't—while she lies there. It isn't decent."

"No, it isn't decent," I replied gravely. "Let the poor lady rest in peace." And the words, on my lips, were not hypocritical, for I felt reprimanded and shamed.

Miss Tina added in a moment, as if she had guessed this and were sorry for me, but at the same time wished to explain that I did push her, or at least harp on the chord, too much: "I can't deceive her that way. I can't deceive her—perhaps on her deathbed."

"Heaven forbid I should ask you, though I've been guilty myself!"

"You've been guilty?"

"I've sailed under false colours." I felt now I must make a clean breast of it, must tell her I had given her an invented name on account of my fear her aunt would have heard of me and so refuse to take me in. I explained this as well as that I had really been a party to the letter addressed them by John Cumnor months before.

She listened with great attention, almost in fact gaping for wonder, and when I had made my confession she said: "Then your real name—what is it?" She repeated it over twice when I had told her, accompanying it with the exclamation "Gracious, gracious!" Then she added: "I like your own best."

"So do I"—and I felt my laugh rueful. "Ouf! it's a relief to get rid of the other."

"So it was a regular plot—a kind of conspiracy?"

"Oh a conspiracy—we were only two," I replied, leaving out of course Mrs. Prest.

She considered; I thought she was perhaps going to pronounce us very base. But this was not her way, and she remarked after a moment, as in candid impartial contemplation: "How much you must want them!"

"Oh I do, passionately!" I grinned, I fear, to admit. And this chance made me go on, forgetting my compunction of a moment before. "How can she possibly have changed their place herself? How can she walk? How can she arrive at that sort of muscular exertion? How can she lift and carry things?"

"Oh when one wants and when one has so much will!" said Miss Tina as if she had thought over my question already herself and had simply had no choice but that answer—the idea that in the dead of night, or at some moment when the coast was clear, the old woman had been capable of a miraculous effort.

"Have you questioned Olimpia? Hasn't she helped her—hasn't she done it for her?" I asked; to which my friend replied promptly and positively that their servant had had nothing to do with the matter, though without admitting definitely that she had spoken to her. It was as if she were a little shy, a little ashamed now, of letting me see how much she had entered into my uneasiness and had me on her mind. Suddenly she said to me without any immediate relevance:

"I rather feel you a new person, you know, now that you've a new name."

"It isn't a new one; it's a very good old one, thank fortune!"

She looked at me a moment. "Well, I do like it better."

"Oh if you didn't I would almost go on with the other!"

"Would you really?"

I laughed again, but I returned for all answer: "Of course if she can rummage about that way she can perfectly have burnt them."

"You must wait—you must wait," Miss Tina mournfully moralised; and her tone ministered little to my patience, for it seemed after all to accept that wretched possibility. I would teach myself to wait, I declared nevertheless; because in the first place I couldn't do otherwise and in the second I had her promise, given me the other night, that she would help me.

"Of course if the papers are gone that's no use," she said; not as if she wished to recede, but only to be conscientious.

"Naturally. But if you could only find out!" I groaned, quivering again.

"I thought you promised you'd wait."

"Oh you mean wait even for that?"

"For what then?"

"Ah nothing," I answered rather foolishly, being ashamed to tell her what had been implied in my acceptance of delay—the idea that she would perhaps do more for me than merely find out.

I know not if she guessed this; at all events she seemed to bethink herself of some propriety of showing me more rigour. "I didn't promise to deceive, did I? I don't think I did."

"It doesn't much matter whether you did or not, for you couldn't!"

Nothing is more possible than that she wouldn't have contested this even hadn't she been diverted by our seeing the doctor's gondola shoot into the little canal and approach the house. I noted that he came as fast as if he believed our proprietress still in danger. We looked down at him while he disembarked and then went back into the sala to meet him. When he came up, however, I naturally left Miss Tina to go off with him alone, only asking her leave to come back later for news.

I went out of the house and walked far, as far as the Piazza, where my restlessness declined to quit me. I was unable to sit down; it was very late now though there were people still at the little tables in front of the cafés: I could but uneasily revolve, and I did so half a dozen times. The only comfort, none the less, was in my having told Miss Tina who I really was. At last I took my way home again, getting gradually and all but inextricably lost, as I did whenever I went out in Venice: so that it was considerably past midnight when I reached my door. The sala, upstairs, was as dark as usual and my lamp as I crossed it found nothing satisfactory to show me. I was disappointed, for I had notified Miss Tina that I would come back for a report, and I thought she might have left a light there as a sign. The door of the ladies' apartment was closed; which seemed a hint that my faltering friend had gone to bed in impatience of waiting for me. I stood in the middle of the place, considering, hoping she would hear me and perhaps peep out, saying to myself too that she would never go to bed with her aunt in a state so critical; she would sit up and watch—she would be in a chair, in her dressing-gown. I went nearer the door; I stopped there and listened. I heard nothing at all and at last I tapped gently. No answer came and after another minute I turned the handle. There was no light in the room; this ought to have prevented my entrance, but it had no such effect. If I have frankly stated the importunities, the indelicacies, of which my desire to possess myself of Jeffrey Aspern's papers had made me capable I needn't shrink, it seems to me, from confessing this last indiscretion. I regard it as the worst thing I did, yet there were extenuating circumstances. I was deeply though doubtless not disinterestedly anxious for more news of Juliana, and Miss Tina had accepted from me, as it were, a rendezvous which it might have been a point of honour with me to keep. It may be objected that her leaving the place dark was a positive sign that she released me, and to this I can only reply that I wished not to be released.

The door of Miss Bordereau's room was open and I could see beyond it the faintness of a taper. There was no sound—my footstep caused no one to stir. I came further into the room; I lingered there lamp in hand. I wanted to give Miss Tina a chance to come to me if, as I couldn't doubt, she were still with her aunt. I made no noise to call her; I only waited to see if she wouldn't notice my light. She didn't, and I explained this—I found afterwards I was right—by the idea that she had fallen asleep. If she had fallen asleep her aunt was not on her mind, and my explanation ought to have led me to go out as I had come. I must repeat again that it didn't, for I found myself at the same moment given up to something else. I had no definite purpose, no bad intention, but felt myself held to the spot by an acute, though absurd, sense of opportunity. Opportunity for what I couldn't have said, inasmuch as it wasn't in my mind that I might proceed to thievery. Even had this tempted me I was confronted with the evident fact that Miss Bordereau didn't leave her secretary, her cupboard and the drawers of her tables gaping. I had no keys, no tools and no ambition to smash her furniture. None the less it came to me that I was now, perhaps alone, unmolested, at the hour of freedom and safety, nearer to the source of my hopes than I had ever been. I held up my lamp, let the light play on the different objects as if it could tell me something. Still there came no movement from the other room. If Miss Tina was sleeping she was sleeping sound. Was she doing so—generous creature—on purpose to leave me the field? Did she know I was there and was she just keeping quiet to see what I would do—what I *could* do? Yet might I, when it came to that? She herself knew even better than I how little.

I stopped in front of the secretary, gaping at it vainly and no doubt grotesquely; for what had it to say to me after all? In the first place it was locked, and in the second it almost surely contained nothing in which I was interested. Ten to one the papers had been destroyed, and even if they hadn't the keen old woman wouldn't have put them in such a place as that after removing them from the green trunk—wouldn't have transferred them, with the idea of their safety on her brain, from the better hiding-place to the worse. The secretary was more conspicuous, more exposed in a room in which she could no longer mount guard. It opened with a key, but there was a small brass handle, like a button, as well: I saw this as I played my lamp over it. I did something more, for the climax of my crisis; I caught a glimpse of the possibility that Miss Tina wished me really to understand. If she didn't so wish me, if she wished me to keep away, why hadn't she locked the door of communication between the sitting-room and the sala? That would have been a definite sign that I was to leave them alone. If I didn't leave them alone she meant me to come for a purpose—a purpose now represented by the super-subtle inference that to oblige me she had unlocked the secretary. She hadn't left the key, but the lid would probably move if I touched the button. This possibility pressed me hard and I bent very close to judge. I didn't propose to do anything; not even—not in the least—to let down the lid; I only wanted to test my theory, to see if the cover *would* move. I touched the button with my hand—a mere touch would tell me; and as I did so—it is embarrassing for me to relate it—I looked over my shoulder. It was a chance, an instinct, for I had really heard nothing. I almost let my luminary drop and certainly I stepped back, straightening myself up at what I saw. Juliana stood there in her night-dress, by the doorway of her room, watching me; her hands were raised, she had lifted the everlasting curtain that covered half her face, and for the first, the last, the only time I beheld her extraordinary eyes. They glared at me; they were like the sudden drench, for a caught burglar, of a flood of gaslight; they made me horribly ashamed. I never shall forget her strange little bent white tottering figure, with its lifted head, her attitude, her expression; neither shall I forget the tone in which as I turned, looking at her, she hissed out passionately, furiously:

"Ah you publishing scoundrel!"

I can't now say what I stammered to excuse myself, to explain; but I went toward her to tell her I meant no harm. She waved me off with her old hands, retreating before me in horror; and the next thing I knew she had fallen back with a quick spasm, as if death had descended on her, into Miss Tina's arms.

�֎ 9 ֍

I LEFT Venice the next morning, directly on learning that my hostess had not succumbed, as I feared at the moment, to the shock I had given her—the shock I may also say she had given me. How in the world could I have supposed her capable of getting out of bed by herself? I failed to see Miss Tina before going; I only saw the *donna,* whom I entrusted with a note for her younger mistress. In this note I mentioned that I should be absent but a few days. I went to Treviso, to Bassano, to Castelfranco; I took walks and drives and looked at musty old churches with ill-lighted pictures; I spent hours seated smoking at the doors of cafés, where there were flies and yellow curtains, on the shady side of sleepy little squares. In spite of these pastimes, which were mechanical and perfunctory, I scantly enjoyed my travels: I had had to gulp down a bitter draught and couldn't get rid of the taste. It had been devilish awkward, as the young men say, to be found by Juliana in the dead of night examining the attach-ment of her bureau; and it had not been less so to have to believe for a good many hours after that it was highly probable I had killed her. My humiliation galled me, but I had to make the best of it, had, in writing to Miss Tina, to minimise it, as well as account for the posture in which I had been discovered. As she gave me no word of answer I couldn't know what impression I made on her. It rankled for me that I had been called a publishing scoundrel, since certainly I did publish and no less certainly hadn't been very delicate. There was a moment when I stood convinced that the only way to purge my dishonour was to take myself straight away on the instant; to sacrifice my hopes and relieve the two poor women for ever of the oppression of my intercourse. Then I reflected that I had better try a short absence first, for I must already have had a sense (unexpressed and dim) that in disappearing completely it wouldn't be merely my own hopes I should condemn to extinction. It would perhaps answer if I kept dark long enough to give the elder lady time to believe herself rid of me. That she would wish to be rid of me after this—if I wasn't rid of her—was now not to be doubted: that midnight monstrosity would have cured her of the disposition to put up with my company for the sake of my dollars. I said to myself that after all I couldn't abandon Miss Tina, and I continued to say this even while I noted that she quite ignored my earnest request—I had given her two or three addresses, at little towns, *poste restante*—for some sign of her actual state. I would have made my servant write me news but that he was unable to manage a pen. Couldn't I measure the scorn of Miss Tina's silence—little disdainful as she had ever been? Really the soreness pressed; yet if I had scruples about going back I had others about not doing so, and I wanted to put myself on a better footing. The end of it was that I did return to Venice on the twelfth day; and as my gondola gently bumped against our palace steps a fine palpitation of suspense showed me the violence my absence had done me.

I had faced about so abruptly that I hadn't even telegraphed to my servant. He was therefore not at the station to meet me, but he poked out his head from an upper window when I reached the house. "They have put her into earth, *quella vecchia*," he said to me in the lower hall while he shouldered my valise; and he grinned and almost winked as if he knew I should be pleased with his news.

"She's dead!" I cried, giving him a very different look.

"So it appears, since they've buried her."

"It's all over then? When was the funeral?"

"The other yesterday. But a funeral you could scarcely call it, signore: *roba da niente—un piccolo passeggio brutto* of two gondolas. Poveretta!" the man continued, referring apparently to Miss Tina. His conception of funerals was that they were mainly to amuse the living.

I wanted to know about Miss Tina, how she might be and generally where; but I asked him no more questions till we had got upstairs. Now that the fact had met me I took a bad view of it, especially of the idea that poor Miss Tina had had to manage by herself after the end. What did she know about arrangements, about the steps to take in such a case? Poveretta indeed! I could only hope the doctor had given her support and that she hadn't been neglected by the old friends of whom she had told me, the little band of the faithful whose fidelity consisted in coming to the house once a year. I elicited from my servant that two old ladies and an old gentleman had in fact rallied round Miss Tina and had supported her—they had come for her in a gondola of their own—during the journey to the cemetery, the little red-walled island of tombs which lies to the north of the town and on the way to Murano. It appeared from these signs that the Misses Bordereau were Catholics, a discovery I had never made, as the old woman couldn't go to church and her niece, so far as I perceived, either didn't, or went only to early mass in the parish before I was stirring. Certainly even the priests respected their seclusion; I had never caught the whisk of the curato's skirt. That evening, an hour later, I sent my servant down with five words on a card to ask if Miss Tina would see me a few moments. She was not in the house, where he had sought her, he told me when he came back, but in the garden walking about to refresh herself and picking the flowers quite as if they belonged to her. He had found her there and she would be happy to see me.

I went down and passed half an hour with poor Miss Tina. She had always had a look of musty mourning, as if she were wearing out old robes of sorrow that wouldn't come to an end; and in this particular she made no different show. But she clearly had been crying, crying a great deal—simply, satisfyingly, refreshingly, with a primitive retarded sense of solitude and violence. But she had none of the airs or graces of grief, and I was almost surprised to see her stand there in the first dusk with her hands full of admirable roses and smile at me with reddened eyes. Her white face, in the frame of her mantilla, looked longer, leaner than usual. I hadn't doubted her being irreconcileably disgusted with me, her considering I ought to have been on the spot to advise her, to help her; and, though I believed there was no rancour in her composition and no great conviction of the importance of her affairs, I had prepared myself for a change in her manner, for some air of injury and estrangement, which should say to my conscience: "Well, you're a nice person to have professed things!" But historic truth compels me to declare that this poor lady's dull face ceased to be dull, almost ceased to be plain, as she turned it gladly to her late aunt's lodger. That touched him extremely and he thought it simplified his situation until he found it didn't. I was as kind to her that evening as I knew how to be, and I walked about the garden with her as long as seemed good. There was no explanation of any sort between us; I didn't ask her why she hadn't answered my letter. Still less did I repeat what I had said to her in that communication; if she chose to let me suppose she had forgotten the position in which Miss Bordereau had surprised me and the effect of the discovery on the old woman, I was quite willing to take it that way: I was grateful to her for not treating me as if I had killed her aunt.

We strolled and strolled, though really not much passed between us save the recognition of her bereavement, conveyed in my manner and in the expression she had of depending on me now, since I let her see I still took an interest in her. Miss Tina's was no breast for the pride or the pretence of independence; she didn't in the least suggest that she knew at present what would become of her. I forbore to press on that question, however, for I certainly was not prepared to say that I would take charge of her. I was cautious; not ignobly, I think, for I felt her knowledge of life to be so small that in her unsophisticated vision there would be no reason why—since I seemed to pity her—I shouldn't somehow look after her. She told me how her aunt had died, very peacefully at the last, and how everything had been done afterwards by the care of her good friends—fortunately, thanks to me, she said, smiling, there was money in the house. She repeated that when once the "nice" Italians like you they are your friends for life, and when we had gone into this she asked me about my *giro,* my impressions, my adventures, the places I had seen. I told her what I could, making it up partly, I'm afraid, as in my disconcerted state I had taken little in; and after she had heard me she exclaimed, quite as if she had forgotten her aunt and her sorrow, "Dear, dear, how much I should like to do such things—to take an amusing little journey!" It came over me for the moment that I ought to propose some enterprise, say I would accompany her anywhere she liked; and I remarked at any rate that a pleasant excursion—to give her a change—might be managed: we would think of it, talk it over. I spoke never a word of the Aspern documents, asked no question as to what she had ascertained or what had otherwise happened with regard to them before Juliana's death. It wasn't that I wasn't on pins and needles to know, but that I thought it more decent not to show greed again so soon after the catastrophe. I hoped she herself would say something, but she never glanced that way, and I thought this natural at the time. Later on, however, that night, it occurred to me that her silence was matter for suspicion; since if she had talked of my movements, of anything so detached as the Giorgione at Castelfranco, she might have alluded to what she could easily remember was in my mind. It was not to be supposed the emotion produced by her aunt's death had blotted out the recollection that I was interested in that lady's relics, and I fidgeted afterwards as it came to me that her reticence might very possibly just mean that no relics survived. We separated in the garden—it was she who said she must go in; now that she was alone on the *piano nobile* I felt that (judged at any rate by Venetian ideas) I was on rather a different footing in regard to the invasion of it. As I shook hands with her for good-night I asked if she had some general plan, had thought over what she had best do. "Oh yes, oh yes, but I haven't settled anything yet," she replied quite cheerfully. Was her cheerfulness explained by the impression that I would settle for her?

I was glad the next morning that we had neglected practical questions, as this gave me a pretext for seeing her again immediately. There was a practical enough question now to be touched on. I owed it to her to let her know formally that of course I didn't expect her to keep me on as a lodger, as also to show some interest in her own tenure, what she might have on her hands in the way of a lease. But I was not destined, as befell, to converse with her for more than an instant on either of these points. I sent her no message; I simply went down to the sala and walked to and fro there. I knew she would come out; she would promptly see me accessible. Somehow I preferred not be shut up with her; gardens and big halls seemed better places to talk. It was a splendid morning, with something in the air that told of the waning of the long Venetian summer; a freshness from the sea that stirred the flowers in the garden and made a pleasant draught in the house, less shuttered and darkened now than when the old woman was alive. It was the beginning of autumn, of the end of the golden months. With this it was the end of my experiment—or would be in the course of half an hour, when I should really have learned that my dream had been reduced to ashes. After that there would be nothing left for me but to go to the station; for seriously—and as it struck me in the morning light—I couldn't linger there to act as guardian to a piece of middle-aged female helplessness. If she hadn't saved the papers wherein should I be indebted to her? I think I winced a little as I asked myself how much, if she *had* saved them, I should have to recognise and, as it were, reward such a courtesy. Mightn't that service after all saddle me with a guardianship? If this idea didn't make me more uncomfortable as I walked up and down it was because I was convinced I had nothing to look to. If the old woman hadn't destroyed everything before she pounced on me in the parlour she had done so the next day.

It took Miss Tina rather longer than I had expected to act on my calculation; but when at last she came out she looked at me without surprise. I mentioned I had been waiting for her and she asked why I hadn't let her know. I was glad a few hours later on that I had checked myself before remarking that a friendly intuition might have told her: it turned to comfort for me that I hadn't played even to that mild extent on her sensibility. What I did say was virtually the truth—that I was too nervous, since I expected her now to settle my fate.

"Your fate?" said Miss Tina, giving me a queer look; and as she spoke I noticed a rare change in her. Yes, she was other than she had been the evening before—less natural and less easy. She had been crying the day before and was not crying now, yet she struck me as less confident. It was as if something had happened to her during the night, or at least as if she had thought of something that troubled her—something in particular that affected her relations with me, made them more embarrassing and more complicated. Had she simply begun to feel that her aunt's not being there now altered my position?

"I mean about our papers. *Are* there any? You must know now."

"Yes, there are a great many; more than I supposed." I was struck with the way her voice trembled as she told me this.

"Do you mean you've got them in there—and that I may see them?"

"I don't think you can see them," said Miss Tina with an extraordinary expression of entreaty in her eyes, as if the dearest hope she had in the world now was that I wouldn't take them from her. But how could she expect me to make such a sacrifice as that after all that had passed between us? What had I come back to Venice for but to see them, to take them? My joy at learning they were still in existence was such that if the poor woman had gone down on her knees to beseech me never to mention them again I would have treated the proceeding as a bad joke. "I've got them but I can't show them," she lamentably added.

"Not even to me? Ah Miss Tina!" I broke into a tone of infinite remonstrance and reproach.

She coloured and the tears came back to her eyes; I measured the anguish it cost her to take such a stand, which a dreadful sense of duty had imposed on her. It made me quite sick to find myself confronted with that particular obstacle; all the more that it seemed to me I had been distinctly encouraged to leave it out of account. I quite held Miss Tina to have assured me that if she had no greater hindrance than that—! "You don't mean to say you made her a deathbed promise? It was precisely against your doing anything of that sort that I thought I was safe. Oh I would rather she had burnt the papers outright than have to reckon with such a treachery as that."

"No, it isn't a promise," said Miss Tina.

"Pray what is it then?"

She hung fire, but finally said: "She tried to burn them, but I prevented it. She had hid them in her bed."

"In her bed—?"

"Between the mattresses. That's where she put them when she took them out of the trunk. I can't understand how she did it, because Olimpia didn't help her. She tells me so and I believe her. My aunt only told her afterwards, so that she shouldn't undo the bed—anything but the sheets. So it was very badly made," added Miss Tina simply.

"I should think so! And how did she try to burn them?"

"She didn't try much; she was too weak those last days. But she told me—she charged me. Oh it was terrible! She couldn't speak after that night. She could only make signs."

"And what did you do?"

"I took them away. I locked them up."

"In the secretary?"

"Yes, in the secretary," said Miss Tina, reddening again.

"Did you tell her you'd burn them?"

"No, I didn't—on purpose."

"On purpose to gratify me?"

"Yes, only for that."

"And what good will you have done me if after all you won't show them?"

"Oh none. I know that—I know that," she dismally sounded.

"And did she believe you had destroyed them?"

"I don't know what she believed at the last. I couldn't tell—she was too far gone."

"Then if there was no promise and no assurance I can't see what ties you."

"Oh she hated it so—she hated it so! She was so jealous. But here's the portrait—you may have that," the poor woman announced, taking the little picture, wrapped up in the same manner in which her aunt had wrapped it, out of her pocket.

"I may have it—do you mean you give it to me?" I gasped as it passed into my hand.

"Oh yes."

"But it's worth money—a large sum."

"Well!" said Miss Tina, still with her strange look.

I didn't know what to make of it, for it could scarcely mean that she wanted to bargain like her aunt. She spoke as for making me a present. "I can't take it from you as a gift," I said, "and yet I can't afford to pay you for it according to the idea Miss Bordereau had of its value. She rated it at a thousand pounds."

"Couldn't we sell it?" my friend threw off.

"God forbid! I prefer the picture to the money."

"Well then keep it."

"You're very generous."

"So are you."

"I don't know why you should think so," I returned; and this was true enough, for the good creature appeared to have in her mind some rich reference that I didn't in the least seize.

"Well, you've made a great difference for me," she said.

I looked at Jeffrey Aspern's face in the little picture, partly in order not to look at that of my companion, which had begun to trouble me, even to frighten me a little—it had taken so very odd, so strained and unnatural a cast. I made no answer to this last declaration; I but privately consulted Jeffrey Aspern's delightful eyes with my own—they were so young and brilliant and yet so wise and so deep: I asked him what on earth was the matter with Miss Tina. He seemed to smile at me with mild mockery; he might have been amused at my case. I had got into a pickle for him—as if he needed it! He was unsatisfactory for the only moment since I had known him. Nevertheless, now that I held the little picture in my hand I felt it would be a precious possession. "Is this a bribe to make me give up the papers?" I presently and all perversely asked. "Much as I value this, you know, if I were to be obliged to choose the papers are what I should prefer. Ah but ever so much!"

"How can you choose—how can you choose?" Miss Tina returned slowly and woefully.

"I see! Of course there's nothing to be said if you regard the interdiction that rests on you as quite insurmountable. In this case it must seem to you that to part with them would be an impiety of the worst kind, a simple sacrilege!"

She shook her head, only lost in the queerness of her case. "You'd

understand if you had known her. I'm afraid," she quavered
suddenly—"I'm afraid! She was terrible when she was angry."

"Yes, I saw something of that, that night. She was terrible. Then I
saw her eyes. Lord, they were fine!"

"I see them—they stare at me in the dark!" said Miss Tina.

"You've grown nervous with all you've been through."

"Oh yes, very—very!"

"You mustn't mind; that will pass away," I said kindly. Then I
added resignedly, for it really seemed to me that I must accept the
situation: "Well, so it is, and it can't be helped. I must renounce."
My friend, at this, with her eyes on me, gave a low soft moan, and I
went on: "I only wish to goodness she had destroyed them: then
there would be nothing more to say. And I can't understand why,
with her ideas, she didn't."

"Oh she lived on them!" said Miss Tina.

"You can imagine whether that makes me want less to see them," I
returned not quite so desperately. "But don't let me stand here as if I
had it in my soul to tempt you to anything base. Naturally, you
understand, I give up my rooms. I leave Venice immediately." And I
took up my hat, which I had placed on a chair. We were still rather
awkwardly on our feet in the middle of the sala. She had left the
door of the apartments open behind her, but had not led me that
way.

A strange spasm came into her face as she saw me take my hat.
"Immediately—do you mean to-day?" The tone of the words was
tragic—they were a cry of desolation.

"Oh no; not so long as I can be of the least service to you."

"Well, just a day or two more—just two or three days," she
panted. Then controlling herself she added in another manner: "She
wanted to say something to me—the last day—something very particular. But she couldn't."

"Something very particular?"

"Something more about the papers."

"And did you guess—have you any idea?"

"No, I've tried to think—but I don't know. I've thought all kinds
of things."

"As for instance?"

"Well, that if you were a relation it would be different."

I wondered. "If I were a relation—?"

"If you weren't a stranger. Then it would be the same for you as for me. Anything that's mine would be yours, and you could do what you like. I shouldn't be able to prevent you—and you'd have no responsibility."

She brought out this droll explanation with a nervous rush and as if speaking words got by heart. They gave me the impression of a subtlety which at first I failed to follow. But after a moment her face helped me to see further, and then the queerest of lights came to me. It was embarrassing, and I bent my head over Jeffrey Aspern's portrait. What an odd expression was in his face! "Get out of it as you can, my dear fellow!" I put the picture into the pocket of my coat and said to Miss Tina: "Yes, I'll sell it for you. I shan't get a thousand pounds by any means, but I shall get something good."

She looked at me through pitiful tears, but seemed to try to smile as she returned: "We can divide the money."

"No, no, it shall be all yours." Then I went on: "I think I know what your poor aunt wanted to say. She wanted to give directions that her papers should be buried with her."

Miss Tina appeared to weigh this suggestion; after which she answered with striking decision, "Oh no, she wouldn't have thought that safe!"

"It seems to me nothing could be safer."

"She had an idea that when people want to publish they're capable—!" And she paused, very red.

"Of violating a tomb? Mercy on us, what must she have thought of me!"

"She wasn't just, she wasn't generous!" my companion cried with sudden passion.

The light that had come into my mind a moment before spread further. "Ah don't say that, for we *are* a dreadful race." Then I pursued: "If she left a will, that may give you some idea."

"I've found nothing of the sort—she destroyed it. She was very fond of me," Miss Tina added with an effect of extreme inconsequence. "She wanted me to be happy. And if any person should be kind to me—she wanted to speak of that."

I was almost awestricken by the astuteness with which the good lady found herself inspired, transparent astuteness as it was and stitching, as the phrase is, with white thread. "Depend upon it she didn't want to make any provision that would be agreeable to *me*."

"No, not to you, but quite to me. She knew I should like it if you could carry out your idea. Not because she cared for you, but because she did think of me," Miss Tina went on with her unexpected persuasive volubility. "You could see the things—you could use them." She stopped, seeing I grasped the sense of her conditional—stopped long enough for me to give some sign that I didn't give. She must have been conscious, however, that though my face showed the greatest embarrassment ever painted on a human countenance it was not set as a stone, it was also full of compassion. It was a comfort to me a long time afterwards to consider that she couldn't have seen in me the smallest symptom of disrespect. "I don't know what to do; I'm too tormented, I'm too ashamed!" she continued with vehemence. Then turning away from me and burying her face in her hands she burst into a flood of tears. If she didn't know what to do it may be imagined whether I knew better. I stood there dumb, watching her while her sobs resounded in the great empty hall. In a moment she was up at me again with her streaming eyes. "I'd give you everything, and she'd understand, where she is—she'd forgive me!"

"Ah Miss Tina—ah Miss Tina," I stammered for all reply. I didn't know what to do, as I say, but at a venture I made a wild vague movement in consequence of which I found myself at the door. I remember standing there and saying "It wouldn't do, it wouldn't do!"—saying it pensively, awkwardly, grotesquely, while I looked away to the opposite end of the sala as at something very interesting. The next thing I remember is that I was downstairs and out of the house. My gondola was there and my gondolier, reclining on the cushions, sprang up as soon as he saw me. I jumped in and to his usual *"Dove commanda?"* replied, in a tone that made him stare: "Anywhere, anywhere; out into the lagoon!"

He rowed me away and I sat there prostrate, groaning softly to myself, my hat pulled over my brow. What in the name of the preposterous did she mean if she didn't mean to offer me her hand? That was the price—that was the price! And did she think I wanted it, poor deluded infatuated extravagant lady? My gondolier, behind me, must have seen my ears red as I wondered, motionless there under the fluttering *tenda* with my hidden face, noticing nothing as we passed—wondered whether her delusion, her infatuation had been my own reckless work. Did she think I had made love to her even to get the papers? I hadn't, I hadn't; I repeated that over to myself for an hour, for two hours, till I was wearied if not convinced. I don't know where, on the lagoon, my gondolier took me; we floated aimlessly and with slow rare strokes. At last I became conscious that we were near the Lido, far up, on the right hand, as you turn your back to Venice, and I made him put me ashore. I wanted to walk, to move, to shed some of my bewilderment. I crossed the narrow strip and got to the sea-beach—I took my way toward Malamocco. But presently I flung myself down again on the warm sand, in the breeze, on the coarse dry grass. It took it out of me to think I had been so much at fault, that I had unwittingly but none the less deplorably trifled. But I hadn't given her cause—distinctly I hadn't. I had said to Mrs. Prest that I would make love to her; but it had been a joke without consequences and I had never said it to my victim. I had been as kind as possible because I really liked her; but since when had that become a crime where a woman of such an age and such an appearance was concerned? I am far from remembering clearly the succession of events and feelings during this long day of confusion, which I spent entirely in wandering about, without going home, until late at night: it only comes back to me that there were moments when I pacified my conscience and others when I lashed it into pain. I didn't laugh all day—that I do recollect; the case, however it might have struck others, seemed to me so little amusing. I should have been better employed perhaps in taking in the comic side of it. At any rate, whether I had given cause or not, there was no doubt whatever that I couldn't pay the price. I couldn't accept the proposal. I couldn't, for a bundle of tattered papers, marry a ridiculous pathetic provincial old woman. It was a proof of how little she supposed the idea would come to me that she should have decided to suggest it herself in that practical argumentative heroic way—with the timidity, however, so much more striking than the boldness, that her reasons appeared to come first and her feelings afterward.

As the day went on I grew to wish I had never heard of Aspern's relics, and I cursed the extravagant curiosity that had put John Cumnor on the scent of them. We had more than enough material without them, and my predicament was the just punishment of that most fatal of human follies, our not having known when to stop. It was very well to say it was no predicament, that the way out was simple, that I had only to leave Venice by the first train in the morning, after addressing Miss Tina a note which should be placed.

in her hand as soon as I got clear of the house; for it was strong proof
of my quandary that when I tried to make up the note to my taste in
advance—I would put it on paper as soon as I got home, before
going to bed—I couldn't think of anything but "How can I thank
you for the rare confidence you've placed in me?" That would never
do; it sounded exactly as if an acceptance were to follow. Of course I
might get off without writing at all, but that would be brutal, and
my idea was still to exclude brutal solutions. As my confusion cooled
I lost myself in wonder at the importance I had attached to
Juliana's crumpled scraps; the thought of them became odious to me
and I was as vexed with the old witch for the superstition that had
prevented her from destroying them as I was with myself for having
already spent more money than I could afford in attempting to
control their fate. I forget what I did, where I went after leaving the
Lido and at what hour or with what recovery of composure I made
my way back to my boat. I only know that in the afternoon, when
the air was aglow with the sunset, I was standing before the church
of Saints John and Paul and looking up at the small square-jawed
face of Bartolommeo Colleoni, the terrible *condottiere* who sits so
sturdily astride of his huge bronze horse on the high pedestal on
which Venetian gratitude maintains him. The statue is imcompa-
rable, the finest of all mounted figures, unless that of Marcus Aure-
lius, who rides benignant before the Roman Capitol, be finer: but I
was not thinking of that; I only found myself staring at the triumphant captain as if he had had an oracle on his lips. The western
light shines into all his grimness at that hour and makes it wonderfully personal. But he continued to look far over my head, at the red
immersion of another day—he had seen so many go down into the
lagoon through the centuries—and if he were thinking of battles and
stratagems they were of a different quality from any I had to tell him
of. He couldn't direct me what to do, gaze up at him as I might. Was
it before this or after that I wandered about for an hour in the small
canals, to the continued stupefaction of my gondolier, who had
never seen me so restless and yet so void of a purpose and could
extract from me no order but "Go anywhere—everywhere—all over
the place"? He reminded me that I had not lunched and expressed
therefore respectfully the hope that I would dine earlier. He had had
long periods of leisure during the day, when I had left the boat and
rambled, so that I was not obliged to consider him, and I told him

that till the morrow, for reasons, I should touch no meat. It was an effect of poor Miss Tina's proposal, not altogether auspicious, that I had quite lost my appetite. I don't know why it happened that on this occasion I was more than ever struck with that queer air of sociability, of cousinship and family life, which makes up half the expression of Venice. Without streets and vehicles, the uproar of wheels, the brutality of horses, and with its little winding ways where people crowd together, where voices sound as in the corridors of a house, where the human step circulates as if it skirted the angles of furniture and shoes never wear out, the place has the character of an immense collective apartment, in which Piazza San Marco is the most ornamented corner and palaces and churches, for the rest, play the part of great divans of repose, tables of entertainment, expanses of decoration. And somehow the splendid common domicile, familiar domestic and resonant, also resembles a theatre with its actors clicking over bridges and, in straggling processions, tripping along fondamentas. As you sit in your gondola the footways that in certain parts edge the canals assume to the eye the importance of a stage, meeting it at the same angle, and the Venetian figures, moving to and fro against the battered scenery of their little houses of comedy, strike you as members of an endless dramatic troupe.

I went to bed that night very tired and without being able to compose an address to Miss Tina. Was this failure the reason why I became conscious the next morning as soon as I awoke of a determination to see the poor lady again the first moment she would receive me? That had something to do with it, but what had still more was the fact that during my sleep the oddest revulsion had taken place in my spirit. I found myself aware of this almost as soon as I opened my eyes: it made me jump out of my bed with the movement of a man who remembers that he has left the house-door ajar or a candle burning under a shelf. Was I still in time to save my goods? That question was in my heart; for what had now come to pass was that in the unconscious cerebration of sleep I had swung back to a passionate appreciation of Juliana's treasure. The pieces composing it were now more precious than ever and a positive ferocity had come into my need to acquire them. The condition Miss Tina had attached to that act no longer appeared an obstacle worth thinking of, and for an hour this morning my repentant imagination brushed it aside. It was absurd I should be able to invent nothing; absurd to renounce so easily and turn away helpless from the idea that the only way to become possessed was to unite myself to her for life. I mightn't unite myself, yet I might still have what she had. I must add that by the time I sent down to ask if she would see me I had invented no alternative, though in fact I drew out my dressing in the interest of my wit. This failure was humiliating, yet what could the alternative be? Miss Tina sent back word I might come; and as I descended the stairs and crossed the sala to her door—this time she received me in her aunt's forlorn parlour—I hoped she wouldn't think my announcement was to be "favourable." She certainly would have understood my recoil of the day before.

As soon as I came into the room I saw that she had done so, but I also saw something which had not been in my forecast. Poor Miss Tina's sense of her failure had produced a rare alteration in her, but I had been too full of stratagems and spoils to think of that. Now I took it in; I can scarcely tell how it startled me. She stood in the middle of the room with a face of mildness bent upon me, and her look of forgiveness, of absolution, made her angelic. It beautified her; she was younger; she was not a ridiculous old woman. This trick of her expression, this magic of her spirit, transfigured her, and while I still noted it I heard a whisper somewhere in the depths of my conscience: "Why not, after all—why not?" It seemed to me I *could* pay the price. Still more distinctly however than the whisper I heard Miss Tina's own voice. I was so struck with the different effect she made on me that at first I wasn't clearly aware of what she was saying; then I recognised she had bade me good-bye—she said something about hoping I should be very happy.

"Good-bye—good-bye?" I repeated with an inflexion interrogative and probably foolish.

I saw she didn't feel the interrogation, she only heard the words: she had strung herself up to accepting our separation and they fell upon her ear as a proof. "Are you going to-day?" she asked. "But it doesn't matter, for whenever you go I shall not see you again. I don't want to." And she smiled strangely, with an infinite gentleness. She had never doubted my having left her the day before in horror. How *could* she, since I hadn't come back before night to contradict, even as a simple form, even as an act of common humanity, such an idea? And now she had the force of soul—Miss Tina with force of soul was a new conception—to smile at me in her abjection.

"What shall you do—where shall you go?" I asked.

"Oh I don't know. I've done the great thing. I've destroyed the papers."

"Destroyed them?" I wailed.

"Yes; what was I to keep them for? I burnt them last night, one by one, in the kitchen."

"One by one?" I coldly echoed it.

"It took a long time—there were so many." The room seemed to go round me as she said this and a real darkness for a moment descended on my eyes. When it passed Miss Tina was there still, but the transfiguration was over and she had changed back to a plain dingy elderly person. It was in this character she spoke as she said "I can't stay with you longer, I can't"; and it was in this character she turned her back upon me, as I had turned mine upon her twenty-four hours before, and moved to the door of her room. Here she did what I hadn't done when I quitted her—she paused long enough to give me one look. I have never forgotten it and I sometimes still suffer from it, though it was not resentful. No, there was no resentment, nothing hard or vindictive in poor Miss Tina; for when, later, I sent her, as the price of the portrait of Jeffrey Aspern, a larger sum of money than I had hoped to be able to gather for her, writing to her that I had sold the picture, she kept it with thanks; she never sent it back. I wrote her that I had sold the picture, but I admitted to Mrs. Prest at the time—I met this other friend in London that autumn—that it hangs above my writing-table. When I look at it I can scarcely bear my loss—I mean of the precious papers.

The Turn of the Screw

"The Turn of the Screw" has been called the greatest ghost story ever written. This may be because it involves both ghosts and children; because the innocence of childhood, surrounded by an atmosphere of sinister evil, is terrifying to adults, childhood being the time traditionally associated with freedom and the greatest measure of human happiness. That not all childhoods are carefree we know only too well, but it is the picture of childhood suffering that is the true horror of the tale. And in this story we have before us a particular "turn of the screw"; there is a governess, herself in late adolescence, who is haunted and frightened and who insists on telling us how calm she is, in the face of the danger to the children in her custody.

Dozens of speculative articles have been written about this tale: every reader—and certainly every critic—has his own theory about it. The best introduction to the story is the one that offers no theories. Ghostly tales lose their ghostliness if they are explained. We can only invite the reader to suspend disbelief; to take the ghosts as they are, together with the old house, the governess, the tower, the twilight—and to enter into the closely woven mysteries Henry James evokes for us. He worked hard to obtain his eerie effects. He held that daylight ghosts are the best kind of ghosts; he favored "the strange and the sinister" occurring in the midst of the usual, or as he put it "embroidered on the very type of the normal and the easy." He knew, moreover, that no matter how brave man is when he fights wars and climbs mountains—or, as in our time, journeys into space—he is capable of being terribly frightened in his own bed by his own nightmares. James sought to capture a nightmare quality in his ghostly tales. In "The Turn of the Screw" he wants the reader to experience an extraordinary "sense of evil." He accordingly does not name the evil: he allows the reader to imagine it. Every reader supplies his own feelings and his own terror. This explains the highly personal interpretations we have had of "The Turn of the Screw."

L. E.

THE story had held us, round the fire, sufficiently breathless, but except the obvious remark that it was gruesome, as on Christmas Eve in an old house a strange tale should essentially be, I remember no comment uttered till somebody happened to note it as the only case he had met in which such a visitation had fallen on a child. The case, I may mention, was that of an apparition in just such an old house as had gathered us for the occasion—an appearance, of a dreadful kind, to a little boy sleeping in the room with his mother and waking her up in the terror of it; waking her not to dissipate his dread and soothe him to sleep again, but to encounter also herself, before she had succeeded in doing so, the same sight that had shocked him. It was this observation that drew from Douglas—not immediately, but later in the evening—a reply that had the interesting consequence to which I call attention. Some one else told a story not particularly effective, which I saw he was not following. This I took for a sign that he had himself something to produce and that we should only have to wait. We waited in fact till two nights later; but that same evening, before we scattered, he brought out what was in his mind.

"I quite agree—in regard to Griffin's ghost, or whatever it was—that its appearing first to the little boy, at so tender an age, adds a particular touch. But it's not the first occurrence of its charming kind that I know to have been concerned with a child. If the child gives the effect another turn of the screw, what do you say to *two* children—?"

"We say of course," somebody exclaimed, "that two children give two turns! Also that we want to hear about them."

I can see Douglas there before the fire, to which he had got up to present his back, looking down at this converser with his hands in his pockets. "Nobody but me, till now, has ever heard. It's quite too horrible." This was naturally declared by several voices to give the thing the utmost price, and our friend, with quiet art, prepared his triumph by turning his eyes over the rest of us and going on: "It's beyond everything. Nothing at all that I know touches it."

"For sheer terror?" I remember asking.

He seemed to say it wasn't so simple as that; to be really at a loss how to qualify it. He passed his hand over his eyes, made a little wincing grimace. "For dreadful—dreadfulness!"

"Oh how delicious!" cried one of the women.

He took no notice of her; he looked at me, but as if, instead of me, he saw what he spoke of. "For general uncanny ugliness and horror and pain."

"Well then," I said, "just sit right down and begin."

He turned round to the fire, gave a kick to a log, watched it an instant. Then as he faced us again: "I can't begin. I shall have to send to town." There was a unanimous groan at this, and much reproach; after which, in his preoccupied way, he explained. "The story's written. It's in a locked drawer—it has not been out for years. I could write to my man and enclose the key; he could send down the packet as he finds it." It was to me in particular that he appeared to propound this—appeared almost to appeal for aid not to hesitate. He had broken a thickness of ice, the formation of many a winter; had had his reasons for a long silence. The others resented postponement, but it was just his scruples that charmed me. I adjured him to write by the first post and to agree with us for an early hearing; then I asked him if the experience in question had been his own. To this his answer was prompt. "Oh thank God, no!"

"And is the record yours? You took the thing down?"

"Nothing but the impression. I took that *here*"—he tapped his heart. "I've never lost it."

"Then your manuscript—?"

"Is in old faded ink and in the most beautiful hand." He hung fire again. "A woman's. She has been dead these twenty years. She sent me the pages in question before she died." They were all listening now, and of course there was somebody to be arch, or at any rate to draw the inference. But if he put the inference by without a smile it was also without irritation. "She was a most charming person, but she was ten years older than I. She was my sister's governess," he quietly said. "She was the most agreeable woman I've ever known in her position; she'd have been worthy of any whatever. It was long ago, and this episode was long before. I was at Trinity, and I found her at home on my coming down the second summer. I was much there that year—it was a beautiful one; and we had, in her off-hours, some strolls and talks in the garden—talks in which she struck me as awfully clever and nice. Oh yes; don't grin: I liked her extremely and am glad to this day to think she liked me too. If she hadn't she wouldn't have told me. She had never told any one. It wasn't simply that she said so, but that I knew she hadn't. I was sure; I could see. You'll easily judge why when you hear."

"Because the thing had been such a scare?"

He continued to fix me. "You'll easily judge," he repeated: "*you* will."

I fixed him too. "I see. She was in love."

He laughed for the first time. "You *are* acute. Yes, she was in love. That is she *had* been. That came out—she couldn't tell her story without its coming out. I saw it, and she saw I saw it; but neither of us spoke of it. I remember the time and the place—the corner of the lawn, the shade of the great beeches and the long hot summer afternoon. It wasn't a scene for a shudder; but oh—!" He quitted the fire and dropped back into his chair.

"You'll receive the packet Thursday morning?" I said.

"Probably not till the second post."

"Well then; after dinner—"

"You'll all meet me here?" He looked us round again. "Isn't anybody going?" It was almost the tone of hope.

"Everybody will stay!"

"*I* will—and *I* will!" cried the ladies whose departure had been fixed. Mrs. Griffin, however, expressed the need for a little more light. "Who was it she was in love with?"

"The story will tell," I took upon myself to reply.

"Oh I can't wait for the story!"

"The story *won't* tell," said Douglas; "not in any literal vulgar way."

"More's the pity then. That's the only way I ever understand."

"Won't *you* tell, Douglas?" somebody else enquired.

He sprang to his feet again. "Yes—to-morrow. Now I must go to bed. Good-night." And, quickly catching up a candlestick, he left us slightly bewildered. From our end of the great brown hall we heard his step on the stair; whereupon Mrs. Griffin spoke. "Well, if I don't know who she was in love with I know who *he* was."

"She was ten years older," said her husband.

"*Raison de plus*—at that age! But it's rather nice, his long reticence."

"Forty years!" Griffin put in.

"With this outbreak at last."

"The outbreak," I returned, "will make a tremendous occasion of Thursday night"; and every one so agreed with me that in the light of it we lost all attention for everything else. The last story, however incomplete and like the mere opening of a serial, had been told; we handshook and "candlestuck," as somebody said, and went to bed.

I knew the next day that a letter containing the key had, by the first post, gone off to his London apartments; but in spite of—or perhaps just on account of—the eventual diffusion of this knowledge we quite let him alone till after dinner, till such an hour of the evening in fact as might best accord with the kind of emotion on which our hopes were fixed. Then he became as communicative as we could desire, and indeed gave us his best reason for being so. We had it from him again before the fire in the hall, as we had had our mild wonders of the previous night. It appeared that the narrative he had promised to read us really required for a proper intelligence a few words of prologue. Let me say here distinctly, to have done with it, that this narrative, from an exact transcript of my own made much later, is what I shall presently give. Poor Douglas, before his death—when it was in sight—committed to me the manuscript that reached him on the third of these days and that, on the same spot, with immense effect, he began to read to our hushed little circle on the night of the fourth. The departing ladies who had said they would stay didn't, of course, thank heaven, stay: they departed, in consequence of arrangements made, in a rage of curiosity, as they professed, produced by the touches with which he had already worked us up. But that only made his little final auditory more compact and select, kept it, round the hearth, subject to a common thrill.

The first of these touches conveyed that the written statement took up the tale at a point after it had, in a manner, begun. The fact to be in possession of was therefore that his old friend, the youngest of several daughters of a poor country parson, had at the age of twenty, on taking service for the first time in the schoolroom, come up to London, in trepidation, to answer in person an advertisement that had already placed her in brief correspondence with the advertiser. This person proved, on her presenting herself for judgement at a house in Harley Street that impressed her as vast and imposing—this prospective patron proved a gentleman, a bachelor in the prime of life, such a figure as had never risen, save in a dream or an old novel, before a fluttered anxious girl out of a Hampshire vicarage. One could easily fix his type; it never, happily, dies out. He was handsome and bold and pleasant, off-hand and gay and kind. He struck her, inevitably, as gallant and splendid, but what took her most of all and gave her the courage she afterwards showed was that he put the whole thing to her as a favour, an obligation he should gratefully incur. She figured him as rich, but as fearfully extravagant—saw him all in a glow of high fashion, of good looks, of expensive habits, of charming ways with women. He had for his town residence a big house filled with the spoils of travel and the trophies of the chase; but it was to his country home, an old family place in Essex, that he wished her immediately to proceed.

He had been left, by the death of his parents in India, guardian to a small nephew and a small niece, children of a younger, a military brother whom he had lost two years before. These children were, by the strangest of chances for a man in his position—a lone man without the right sort of experience or a grain of patience—very heavy on his hands. It had all been a great worry, and, on his own part doubtless, a series of blunders, but he immensely pitied the poor chicks and had done all he could; had in particular sent them down to his other house, the proper place for them being of course the country, and kept them there from the first with the best people he could find to look after them, parting even with his own servants to wait on them and going down himself, whenever he might, to see how they were doing. The awkward thing was that they had practically no other relations and that his own affairs took up all his time. He had put them in possession of Bly, which was healthy and secure, and had placed at the head of their little establishment—but below-stairs only—an excellent woman, Mrs. Grose, whom he was sure his visitor would like and who had formerly been maid to his mother. She was now housekeeper and was also acting for the time as superintendent to the little girl, of whom, without children of her own, she was by good luck extremely fond. There were plenty of people to help, but of course the young lady who should go down as governess would be in supreme authority. She would also have, in holidays, to look after the small boy, who had been for a term at school—young as he was to be sent, but what else could be done?—and who, as the holidays were about to begin, would be back from one day to the other. There had been for the two children at first a young lady whom they had had the misfortune to lose. She had done for them quite beautifully—she was a most respectable person—till her death, the great awkwardness of which had, precisely, left no alternative but the school for little Miles. Mrs. Grose, since then, in the way of manners and things, had done as she could for Flora; and there were, further, a cook, a housemaid, a dairywoman, an old pony, an old groom and an old gardener, all likewise thoroughly respectable.

So far had Douglas presented his picture when some one put a question. "And what did the former governess die of? Of so much respectability?"

Our friend's answer was prompt. "That will come out. I don't anticipate."

"Pardon me—I thought that was just what you *are* doing."

"In her successor's place," I suggested, "I should have wished to learn if the office brought with it—"

"Necessary danger to life?" Douglas completed my thought. "She did wish to learn, and she did learn. You shall hear to-morrow what she learnt. Meanwhile of course the prospect struck her as slightly grim. She was young, untried, nervous: it was a vision of serious duties and little company, of really great loneliness. She hesitated—took a couple of days to consult and consider. But the salary offered much exceeded her modest measure, and on a second interview she faced the music, she engaged." And Douglas, with this, made a pause that, for the benefit of the company, moved me to throw in—

"The moral of which was of course the seduction exercised by the splendid young man. She succumbed to it."

He got up and, as he had done the night before, went to the fire, gave a stir to a log with his foot, then stood a moment with his back to us. "She saw him only twice."

"Yes, but that's just the beauty of her passion."

A little to my surprise, on this, Douglas turned round to me. "It *was* the beauty of it. There were others," he went on, "who hadn't succumbed. He told her frankly all his difficulty—that for several applicants the conditions had been prohibitive. They were somehow simply afraid. It sounded dull—it sounded strange; and all the more so because of his main condition."

"Which was—?"

"That she should never trouble him—but never, never: neither appeal nor complain nor write about anything; only meet all questions herself, receive all moneys from his solicitor, take the whole thing over and let him alone. She promised to do this, and she mentioned to me that when, for a moment, disburdened, delighted, he held her hand, thanking her for the sacrifice, she already felt rewarded."

"But was that all her reward?" one of the ladies asked.

"She never saw him again."

"Oh!" said the lady; which, as our friend immediately again left us, was the only other word of importance contributed to the subject till, the next night, by the corner of the hearth, in the best chair, he opened the faded red cover of a thin old-fashioned gilt-edged album. The whole thing took indeed more nights than one, but on the first occasion the same lady put another question. "What's your title?"

"I haven't one."

"Oh *I* have!" I said. But Douglas, without heeding me, had begun to read with a fine clearness that was like a rendering to the ear of the beauty of his author's hand.

⟫⟪ 1 ⟫⟪

I REMEMBER the whole beginning as a succession of flights and drops, a little see-saw of the right throbs and the wrong. After rising, in town, to meet his appeal I had at all events a couple of very bad days—found all my doubts bristle again, felt indeed sure I had made a mistake. In this state of mind I spent the long hours of bumping swinging coach that carried me to the stopping-place at which I was to be met by a vehicle from the house. This convenience, I was told, had been ordered, and I found, toward the close of the June afternoon, a commodious fly in waiting for me. Driving at that hour, on a lovely day, through a country the summer sweetness of which served as a friendly welcome, my fortitude revived and, as we turned into the avenue, took a flight that was probably but a proof of the point to which it had sunk. I suppose I had expected, or had dreaded, something so dreary that what greeted me was a good surprise. I remember as a thoroughly pleasant impression the broad clear front, its open windows and fresh curtains and the pair of maids looking out; I remember the lawn and the bright flowers and the crunch of my wheels on the gravel and the clustered tree-tops over which the rooks circled and cawed in the golden sky. The scene had a greatness that made it a different affair from my own scant home, and there immediately appeared at the door, with a little girl in her hand, a civil person who dropped me as decent a curtsey as if I had been the mistress or a distinguished visitor. I had received in Harley Street a narrower notion of the place, and that, as I recalled it, made me think the proprietor still more of a gentleman, suggested that what I was to enjoy might be a matter beyond his promise.

I had no drop again till the next day, for I was carried triumphantly through the following hours by my introduction to the younger of my pupils. The little girl who accompanied Mrs. Grose affected me on the spot as a creature too charming not to make it a great fortune to have to do with her. She was the most beautiful child I had ever seen, and I afterwards wondered why my employer hadn't made more of a point to me of this. I slept little that night—I was too much excited; and this astonished me too, I recollect, remained with me, adding to my sense of the liberality with which I was treated. The large impressive room, one of the best in the house, the great state bed, as I almost felt it, the figured full draperies, the long glasses in which, for the first time, I could see myself from head to foot, all struck me—like the wonderful appeal of my small charge—as so many things thrown in. It was thrown in as well, from the first moment, that I should get on with Mrs. Grose in a relation over which, on my way, in the coach, I fear I had rather brooded. The one appearance indeed that in this early outlook might have made me shrink again was that of her being so inordinately glad to see me. I felt within half an hour that she was so glad—stout simple plain clean wholesome woman—as to be positively on her guard against showing it too much. I wondered even then a little why she should wish *not* to show it, and that, with reflexion, with suspicion, might of course have made me uneasy.

But it was a comfort that there could be no uneasiness in a connexion with anything so beatific as the radiant image of my little girl, the vision of whose angelic beauty had probably more than anything else to do with the restlessness that, before morning, made me several times rise and wander about my room to take in the whole

picture and prospect; to watch from my open window the faint
summer dawn, to look at such stretches of the rest of the house as I
could catch, and to listen, while in the fading dusk the first birds
began to twitter, for the possible recurrence of a sound or two, less
natural and not without but within, that I had fancied I heard.
There had been a moment when I believed I recognised, faint and
far, the cry of a child; there had been another when I found myself
just consciously starting as at the passage, before my door, of a light
footstep. But these fancies were not marked enough not to be thrown
off, and it is only in the light, or the gloom, I should rather say, of
other and subsequent matters that they now come back to me. To
watch, teach, "form" little Flora would too evidently be the making
of a happy and useful life. It had been agreed between us downstairs
that after this first occasion I should have her as a matter of course at
night, her small white bed being already arranged, to that end, in my
room. What I had undertaken was the whole care of her, and she had
remained just this last time with Mrs. Grose only as an effect of our
consideration for my inevitable strangeness and her natural timidity.
In spite of this timidity—which the child herself, in the oddest way
in the world, had been perfectly frank and brave about, allowing it,
without a sign of uncomfortable consciousness, with the deep sweet
serenity indeed of one of Raphael's holy infants, to be discussed, to
be imputed to her and to determine us—I felt quite sure she would
presently like me. It was part of what I already liked Mrs. Grose
herself for, the pleasure I could see her feel in my admiration and
wonder as I sat at supper with four tall candles and with my pupil, in
a high chair and a bib, brightly facing me between them over bread
and milk. There were naturally things that in Flora's presence could
pass between us only as prodigious and gratified looks, obscure and
roundabout allusions.

"And the little boy—does he look like her? Is he too so very
remarkable?"

One wouldn't, it was already conveyed between us, too grossly
flatter a child. "Oh Miss, *most* remarkable. If you think well of this
one!"—and she stood there with a plate in her hand, beaming at our
companion, who looked from one of us to the other with placid
heavenly eyes that contained nothing to check us.

"Yes; if I do—?"

"You *will* be carried away by the little gentleman!"

"Well, that, I think, is what I came for—to be carried away. I'm afraid, however," I remember feeling the impulse to add, "I'm rather easily carried away. I was carried away in London!"

I can still see Mrs. Grose's broad face as she took this in. "In Harley Street?"

"In Harley Street."

"Well, Miss, you're not the first—and you won't be the last."

"Oh I've no pretensions," I could laugh, "to being the only one. My other pupil, at any rate, as I understand, comes back to-morrow?"

"Not to-morrow—Friday, Miss. He arrives, as you did, by the coach, under care of the guard, and is to be met by the same carriage."

I forthwith wanted to know if the proper as well as the pleasant and friendly thing wouldn't therefore be that on the arrival of the public conveyance I should await him with his little sister; a proposition to which Mrs. Grose assented so heartily that I somehow took her manner as a kind of comforting pledge—never falsified, thank heaven!—that we should on every question be quite at one. Oh she was glad I was there!

What I felt the next day was, I suppose, nothing that could be fairly called a reaction from the cheer of my arrival; it was probably at the most only a slight oppression produced by a fuller measure of the scale, as I walked round them, gazed up at them, took them in, of my new circumstances. They had, as it were, an extent and mass for which I had not been prepared and in the presence of which I found myself, freshly, a little scared not less than a little proud. Regular lessons, in this agitation, certainly suffered some wrong; I reflected that my first duty was, by the gentlest arts I could contrive, to win the child into the sense of knowing me. I spent the day with her out of doors; I arranged with her, to her great satisfaction, that it should be she, she only, who might show me the place. She showed it step by step and room by room and secret by secret, with droll delightful childish talk about it and with the result, in half an hour, of our becoming tremendous friends. Young as she was I was struck, throughout our little tour, with her confidence and courage, with the way, in empty chambers and dull corridors, on crooked staircases that made me pause and even on the summit of an old machicolated square tower that made me dizzy, her morning music, her disposition to tell me so many more things than she asked, rang out and led me on. I have not seen Bly since the day I left it, and I dare say that to my present older and more informed eyes it would show a very reduced importance. But as my little conductress, with her hair of gold and her frock of blue, danced before me round corners and pattered down passages, I had the view of a castle of romance inhabited by a rosy sprite, such a place as would somehow, for diversion of the young idea, take all colour out of story-books and fairy-tales. Wasn't it just a story-book over which I had fallen a-doze and a-dream? No; it was a big ugly antique but convenient house, embodying a few features of a building still older, half-displaced and half-utilised, in which I had the fancy of our being almost as lost as a handful of passengers in a great drifting ship. Well, I was strangely at the helm!

2

This came home to me when, two days later, I drove over with Flora to meet, as Mrs. Grose said, the little gentleman; and all the more for an incident that, presenting itself the second evening, had deeply disconcerted me. The first day had been, on the whole, as I have expressed, reassuring; but I was to see it wind up to a change of note. The postbag that evening—it came late—contained a letter for me which, however, in the hand of my employer, I found to be composed but of a few words enclosing another, addressed to himself, with a seal still unbroken. "This, I recognise, is from the head-master, and the head-master's an awful bore. Read him, please; deal with him; but mind you don't report. Not a word. I'm off!" I broke the seal with a great effort—so great a one that I was a long time coming to it; took the unopened missive at last up to my room and only attacked it just before going to bed. I had better have let it wait till morning, for it gave me a second sleepless night. With no counsel to take, the next day, I was full of distress; and it finally got so the better of me that I determined to open myself at least to Mrs. Grose.

"What does it mean? The child's dismissed his school."

She gave me a look that I remarked at the moment; then, visibly, with a quick blankness, seemed to try to take it back. "But aren't they all—?"

"Sent home—yes. But only for the holidays. Miles may never go back at all."

Consciously, under my attention, she reddened. "They won't take him?"

"They absolutely decline."

At this she raised her eyes, which she had turned from me; I saw them fill with good tears. "What has he done?"

I cast about; then I judged best simply to hand her my document—which, however, had the effect of making her, without taking it, simply put her hands behind her. She shook her head sadly. "Such things are not for me, Miss."

My counsellor couldn't read! I winced at my mistake, which I attenuated as I could, and opened the letter again to repeat it to her; then, faltering in the act and folding it up once more, I put it back in my pocket. "Is he really *bad?*"

The tears were still in her eyes. "Do the gentlemen say so?"

"They go into no particulars. They simply express their regret that it should be impossible to keep him. That can have but one meaning." Mrs. Grose listened with dumb emotion; she forbore to ask me what this meaning might be; so that, presently, to put the thing with some coherence and with the mere aid of her presence to my own mind, I went on: "That he's an injury to the others."

At this, with one of the quick turns of simple folk, she suddenly flamed up. "Master Miles!—*him* an injury?"

There was such a flood of good faith in it that, though I had not yet seen the child, my very fears made me jump to the absurdity of the idea. I found myself, to meet my friend the better, offering it, on the spot, sarcastically. "To his poor little innocent mates!"

"It's too dreadful," cried Mrs. Grose, "to say such cruel things! Why he's scarce ten years old."

"Yes, yes; it would be incredible."

She was evidently grateful for such a profession. "See him, Miss, first. *Then* believe it!" I felt forthwith a new impatience to see him; it was the beginning of a curiosity that, all the next hours, was to deepen almost to pain. Mrs. Grose was aware, I could judge, of what she had produced in me, and she followed it up with assurance. "You might as well believe it of the little lady. Bless her," she added the next moment—"*look* at her!"

I turned and saw that Flora, whom, ten minutes before, I had established in the schoolroom with a sheet of white paper, a pencil and a copy of nice "round O's," now presented herself to view at the open door. She expressed in her little way an extraordinary detachment from disagreeable duties, looking at me, however, with a great childish light that seemed to offer it as a mere result of the affection she had conceived for my person, which had rendered necessary that she should follow me. I needed nothing more than this to feel the full force of Mrs. Grose's comparison, and, catching my pupil in my arms, covered her with kisses in which there was a sob of atonement.

None the less, the rest of the day, I watched for further occasion to approach my colleague, especially as, toward evening, I began to fancy she rather sought to avoid me. I overtook her, I remember, on the staircase; we went down together and at the bottom I detained her, holding her there with a hand on her arm. "I take what you said to me at noon as a declaration that *you've* never known him to be bad."

She threw back her head; she had clearly by this time, and very honestly, adopted an attitude. "Oh never known him—I don't pretend *that!*"

I was upset again. "Then you *have* known him—?"

"Yes indeed, Miss, thank God!"

On reflexion I accepted this. "You mean that a boy who never is—?"

"Is no boy for *me!*"

I held her tighter. "You like them with the spirit to be naughty?" Then, keeping pace with her answer, "So do I!" I eagerly brought out. "But not to the degree to contaminate—"

"To contaminate?"—my big word left her at a loss.

I explained it. "To corrupt."

She stared, taking my meaning in; but it produced in her an odd laugh. "Are you afraid he'll corrupt *you?*" She put the question with such a fine bold humour that with a laugh, a little silly doubtless, to match her own, I gave way for the time to the apprehension of ridicule.

But the next day, as the hour for my drive approached, I cropped up in another place. "What was the lady who was here before?"

"The last governess? She was also young and pretty—almost as young and almost as pretty, Miss, even as you."

"Ah then I hope her youth and her beauty helped her!" I recollect throwing off. "He seems to like us young and pretty!"

"Oh he *did*," Mrs. Grose assented: "it was the way he liked every one!" She had no sooner spoken indeed than she caught herself up. "I mean that's *his* way—the master's."

I was struck. "But of whom did you speak first?"

She looked blank, but she coloured. "Why of *him*."

"Of the master?"

"Of who else?"

There was so obviously no one else that the next moment I had lost my impression of her having accidentally said more than she meant; and I merely asked what I wanted to know. "Did *she* see anything in the boy—?"

"That wasn't right? She never told me."

I had a scruple, but I overcame it. "Was she careful—particular?"

Mrs. Grose appeared to try to be conscientious. "About some things—yes."

"But not about all?"

Again she considered. "Well, Miss—she's gone. I won't tell tales."

"I quite understand your feeling," I hastened to reply; but I thought it after an instant not opposed to this concession to pursue: "Did she die here?"

"No—she went off."

I don't know what there was in this brevity of Mrs. Grose's that struck me as ambiguous. "Went off to die?" Mrs. Grose looked straight out of the window, but I felt that, hypothetically, I had a right to know what young persons engaged for Bly were expected to do. "She was taken ill, you mean, and went home?"

"She was not taken ill, so far as appeared, in this house. She left it, at the end of the year, to go home, as she said, for a short holiday, to which the time she had put in had certainly given her a right. We had then a young woman—a nursemaid who had stayed on and who was a good girl and clever; and *she* took the children altogether for the interval. But our young lady never came back, and at the very moment I was expecting her I heard from the master that she was dead."

I turned this over. "But of what?"

"He never told me! But please, Miss," said Mrs. Grose, "I must get to my work."

⚜ 3 ⚜

HER thus turning her back on me was fortunately not, for my just preoccupations, a snub that could check the growth of our mutual esteem. We met, after I had brought home little Miles, more intimately than ever on the ground of my stupefaction, my general emotion: so monstrous was I then ready to pronounce it that such a child as had now been revealed to me should be under an interdict. I was a little late on the scene of his arrival, and I felt, as he stood wistfully looking out for me before the door of the inn at which the coach had put him down, that I had seen him on the instant, without and within, in the great glow of freshness, the same positive fragrance of purity, in which I had from the first moment seen his little sister. He was incredibly beautiful, and Mrs. Grose had put her finger on it: everything but a sort of passion of tenderness for him was swept away by his presence. What I then and there took him to my heart for was something divine that I have never found to the same degree in any child—his indescribable little air of knowing nothing in the world but love. It would have been impossible to carry a bad name with a greater sweetness of innocence, and by the time I had got back to Bly with him I remained merely bewildered—so far, that is, as I was not outraged—by the sense of the horrible letter locked up in one of the drawers of my room. As soon as I could compass a private word with Mrs. Grose I declared to her that it was grotesque.

She promptly understood me "You mean the cruel charge—?"

"It doesn't live an instant. My dear woman, *look* at him!"

She smiled at my pretension to have discovered his charm. "I assure you, Miss, I do nothing else! What will you say then?" she immediately added.

"In answer to the letter?" I had made up my mind. "Nothing at all."

"And to his uncle?"

I was incisive. "Nothing at all."

"And to the boy himself?"

I was wonderful. "Nothing at all."

She gave with her apron a great wipe to her mouth. "Then I'll stand by you. We'll see it out."

"We'll see it out!" I ardently echoed, giving her my hand to make it a vow.

She held me there a moment, then whisked up her apron again with her detached hand. "Would you mind, Miss, if I used the freedom—"

"To kiss me? No!" I took the good creature in my arms and after we had embraced like sisters felt still more fortified and indignant.

This at all events was for the time: a time so full that as I recall the way it went it reminds me of all the art I now need to make it a little distinct. What I look back at with amazement is the situation I accepted. I had undertaken, with my companion, to see it out, and I was under a charm apparently that could smooth away the extent and the far and difficult connexions of such an effort. I was lifted aloft on a great wave of infatuation and pity. I found it simple, in my ignorance, my confusion and perhaps my conceit, to assume that I could deal with a boy whose education for the world was all on the point of beginning. I am unable even to remember at this day what proposal I framed for the end of his holidays and the resumption of his studies. Lessons with me indeed, that charming summer, we all had a theory that he was to have; but I now feel that for weeks the lessons must have been rather my own. I learnt something—at first certainly—that had not been one of the teachings of my small smothered life; learnt to be amused, and even amusing, and not to think for the morrow. It was the first time, in a manner, that I had known space and air and freedom, all the music of summer and all the mystery of nature. And then there was consideration—and consideration was sweet. Oh it was a trap—not designed but deep—to my imagination, to my delicacy, perhaps to my vanity; to whatever in me was most excitable. The best way to picture it all is to say that I was off my guard. They gave me so little trouble—they were of a gentleness so extraordinary. I used to speculate—but even this with a dim disconnectedness—as to how the rough future (for all futures are rough!) would handle them and might bruise them. They had the bloom of health and happiness; and yet, as if I had been in charge of a pair of little grandees, of princes of the blood, for whom everything, to be right, would have to be fenced about and ordered and arranged, the only form that in my fancy the after-years could take for them was that of a romantic, a really royal extension of the garden and the park. It may be of course above all that what suddenly broke into this gives the previous time a charm of stillness—that hush in which something gathers or crouches. The change was actually like the spring of a beast.

In the first weeks the days were long; they often, at their finest, gave me what I used to call my own hour, the hour when, for my pupils, tea-time and bed-time having come and gone, I had before my final retirement a small interval alone. Much as I liked my companions this hour was the thing in the day I liked most; and I liked it best of all when, as the light faded—or rather, I should say, the day lingered and the last calls of the last birds sounded, in a flushed sky, from the old trees—I could take a turn into the grounds and enjoy, almost with a sense of property that amused and flattered me, the beauty and dignity of the place. It was a pleasure at these moments to feel myself tranquil and justified; doubtless perhaps also to reflect that by my discretion, my quiet good sense and general high propriety, I was giving pleasure—if he ever thought of it!—to the person to whose pressure I had yielded. What I was doing was what he had earnestly hoped and directly asked of me, and that I *could,* after all, do it proved even a greater joy than I had expected. I dare say I fancied myself in short a remarkable young woman and took comfort in the faith that this would more publicly appear. Well, I needed to be remarkable to offer a front to the remarkable things that presently gave their first sign.

It was plump, one afternoon, in the middle of my very hour: the children were tucked away and I had come out for my stroll. One of the thoughts that, as I don't in the least shrink now from noting, used to be with me in these wanderings was that it would be as charming as a charming story suddenly to meet some one. Some one would appear there at the turn of a path and would stand before me and smile and approve. I didn't ask more than that—I only asked that he should *know;* and the only way to be sure he knew would be to see it, and the kind light of it, in his handsome face. That was exactly present to me—by which I mean the face was—when, on the first of these occasions, at the end of a long June day, I stopped short on emerging from one of the plantations and coming into view of the house. What arrested me on the spot—and with a shock much greater than any vision had allowed for—was the sense that my imagination had, in a flash, turned real. He did stand there!—but high up, beyond the lawn and at the very top of the tower to which, on that first morning, little Flora had conducted me. This tower was one of a pair—square incongruous crenellated structures—that were distinguished, for some reason, though I could see little difference, as the new and the old. They flanked opposite ends of the house and were probably architectural absurdities, redeemed in a measure indeed by not being wholly disengaged nor of a height too pretentious, dating, in their gingerbread antiquity, from a romantic revival that was already a respectable past. I admired them, had fancies about them, for we could all profit in a degree, especially when they loomed through the dusk, by the grandeur of their actual battlements; yet it was not at such an elevation that the figure I had so often invoked seemed most in place.

It produced in me, this figure, in the clear twilight, I remember, two distinct gasps of emotion, which were, sharply, the shock of my first and that of my second surprise. My second was a violent perception of the mistake of my first: the man who met my eyes was not the person I had precipitately supposed. There came to me thus a bewilderment of vision of which, after these years, there is no living view that I can hope to give. An unknown man in a lonely place is a permitted object of fear to a young woman privately bred; and the figure that faced me was—a few more seconds assured me—as little any one else I knew as it was the image that had been in my mind. I had not seen it in Harley Street—I had not seen it anywhere. The place moreover, in the strangest way in the world, had on the instant and by the very fact of its appearance become a solitude. To me at least, making my statement here with a deliberation with which I have never made it, the whole feeling of the moment returns. It was as if, while I took in, what I did take in, all the rest of the scene had been stricken with death. I can hear again, as I write, the intense hush in which the sounds of evening dropped. The rooks stopped cawing in the golden sky and the friendly hour lost for the unspeakable minute all its voice. But there was no other change in nature, unless indeed it were a change that I saw with a stranger sharpness. The gold was still in the sky, the clearness in the air, and the man who looked at me over the battlements was as definite as a picture in a frame. That's how I thought, with extraordinary quickness, of each person he might have been and that he wasn't. We were confronted across our distance quite long enough for me to ask myself with intensity who then he was and to feel, as an effect of my inability to say, a wonder that in a few seconds more became intense.

The great question, or one of these, is afterwards, I know, with regard to certain matters, the question of how long they have lasted. Well, this matter of mine, think what you will of it, lasted while I caught at a dozen possibilities, none of which made a difference for the better, that I could see, in there having been in the house—and for how long, above all?—a person of whom I was in ignorance. It lasted while I just bridled a little with the sense of how my office seemed to require that there should be no such ignorance and no such person. It lasted while this visitant, at all events—and there was a touch of the strange freedom, as I remember, in the sign of familiarity of his wearing no hat—seemed to fix me, from his posi-tion, with just the question, just the scrutiny through the fading light, that his own presence provoked. We were too far apart to call to each other, but there was a moment at which, at shorter range, some challenge between us, breaking the hush, would have been the right result of our straight mutual stare. He was in one of the angles, the one away from the house, very erect, as it struck me, and with both hands on the ledge. So I saw him as I see the letters I form on this page; then, exactly, after a minute, as if to add to the spectacle, he slowly changed his place—passed, looking at me hard all the while, to the opposite corner of the platform. Yes, it was intense to me that during this transit he never took his eyes from me, and I can see at this moment the way his hand, as he went, moved from one of the crenellations to the next. He stopped at the other corner, but less long, and even as he turned away still markedly fixed me. He turned away; that was all I knew.

✣ 4 ✣

It was not that I didn't wait, on this occasion, for more, since I was as deeply rooted as shaken. Was there a "secret" at Bly—a mystery of Udolpho or an insane, an unmentionable relative kept in unsus-pected confinement? I can't say how long I turned it over, or how long, in a confusion of curiosity and dread, I remained where I had

had my collision; I only recall that when I re-entered the house darkness had quite closed in. Agitation, in the interval, certainly had held me and driven me, for I must, in circling about the place, have walked three miles; but I was to be later on so much more overwhelmed that this mere dawn of alarm was a comparatively human chill. The most singular part of it in fact—singular as the rest had been—was the part I became, in the hall, aware of in meeting Mrs. Grose. This picture comes back to me in the general train—the impression, as I received it on my return, of the wide white panelled space, bright in the lamplight and with its portraits and red carpet, and of the good surprised look of my friend, which immediately told me she had missed me. It came to me straightway, under her contact, that, with plain heartiness, mere relieved anxiety at my appearance, she knew nothing whatever that could bear upon the incident I had there ready for her. I had not suspected in advance that her comfortable face would pull me up, and I somehow measured the importance of what I had seen by my thus finding myself hesitate to mention it. Scarce anything in the whole history seems to me so odd as this fact that my real beginning of fear was one, as I may say, with the instinct of sparing my companion. On the spot, accordingly, in the pleasant hall and with her eyes on me, I, for a reason that I couldn't then have phrased, achieved an inward revolution—offered a vague pretext for my lateness and, with the plea of the beauty of the night and of the heavy dew and wet feet, went as soon as possible to my room.

Here it was another affair; here, for many days after, it was a queer affair enough. There were hours, from day to day—or at least there were moments, snatched even from clear duties—when I had to shut myself up to think. It wasn't so much yet that I was more nervous than I could bear to be as that I was remarkably afraid of becoming so; for the truth I had now to turn over was simply and clearly the truth that I could arrive at no account whatever of the visitor with whom I had been so inexplicably and yet, as it seemed to me, so intimately concerned. It took me little time to see that I might easily sound, without forms of enquiry and without exciting remark, any domestic complication. The shock I had suffered must have sharpened all my senses; I felt sure, at the end of three days and as the result of mere closer attention, that I had not been practised upon by the servants nor made the object of any "game." Of whatever it was that I knew nothing was known around me. There was but one sane inference: some one had taken a liberty rather monstrous. That was what, repeatedly, I dipped into my room and locked the door to say to myself. We had been, collectively, subject to an intrusion; some unscrupulous traveller, curious in old houses, had made his way in unobserved, enjoyed the prospect from the best point of view and then stolen out as he came. If he had given me such a bold hard stare, that was but a part of his indiscretion. The good thing, after all, was that we should surely see no more of him.

This was not so good a thing, I admit, as not to leave me to judge that what, essentially, made nothing else much signify was simply my charming work. My charming work was just my life with Miles and Flora, and through nothing could I so like it as through feeling that to throw myself into it was to throw myself out of my trouble. The attraction of my small charges was a constant joy, leading me to wonder afresh at the vanity of my original fears, the distaste I had begun by entertaining for the probable grey prose of my office. There was to be no grey prose, it appeared, and no long grind; so how could work not be charming that presented itself as daily beauty? It was all the romance of the nursery and the poetry of the schoolroom. I don't mean by this of course that we studied only fiction and verse; I mean that I can express no otherwise the sort of interest my companions inspired. How can I describe that except by saying that instead of growing deadly used to them—and it's a marvel for a governess: I call the sisterhood to witness!—I made constant fresh discoveries. There was one direction, assuredly, in which these discoveries stopped: deep obscurity continued to cover the region of the boy's conduct at school. It had been promptly given me, I have noted, to face that mystery without a pang. Perhaps even it would be nearer the truth to say that—without a word—he himself had cleared it up. He had made the whole charge absurd. My conclusion bloomed there with the real rose-flush of his innocence: he was only too fine and fair for the little horrid unclean school-world, and he had paid a price for it. I reflected acutely that the sense of such individual differences, such superiorities of quality, always, on the part of the majority—which could include even stupid sordid head-masters—turns infallibly to the vindictive.

Both the children had a gentleness—it was their only fault, and it never made Miles a muff—that kept them (how shall I express it?)

almost impersonal and certainly quite unpunishable. They were like those cherubs of the anecdote who had—morally at any rate—nothing to whack! I remember feeling with Miles in especial as if he had had, as it were, nothing to call even an infinitesimal history. We expect of a small child scant enought "antecedents," but there was in this beautiful little boy something extraordinarily sensitive, yet extraordinarily happy, that, more than in any creature of his age I have seen, struck me as beginning anew each day. He had never for a second suffered. I took this as a direct disproof of his having really been chastised. If he had been wicked he would have "caught" it, and I should have caught it by the rebound—I should have found the trace, should have felt the wound and the dishonour. I could reconstitute nothing at all, and he was therefore an angel. He never spoke of his school, never mentioned a comrade or a master; and I, for my part, was quite too much disgusted to allude to them. Of course I was under the spell, and the wonderful part is that, even at the time, I perfectly knew I was. But I gave myself up to it; it was an antidote to any pain, and I had more pains than one. I was in receipt in these days of disturbing letters from home, where things were not going well. But with this joy of my children what things in the world mattered? That was the question I used to put to my scrappy retirements. I was dazzled by their loveliness.

There was a Sunday—to get on—when it rained with such force and for so many hours that there could be no procession to church; in consequence of which, as the day declined, I had arranged with Mrs. Grose that, should the evening show improvement, we would attend together the late service. The rain happily stopped, and I prepared for our walk, which, through the park and by the good road to the village, would be a matter of twenty minutes. Coming downstairs to meet my colleague in the hall, I remembered a pair of gloves that had required three stitches and that had received them—with a publicity perhaps not edifying—while I sat with the children at their tea, served on Sundays, by exception, in that cold clean temple of mahogany and brass, the "grown-up" dining-room. The gloves had been dropped there, and I turned in to recover them. The day was grey enough, but the afternoon light still lingered, and it enabled me, on crossing the threshold, not only to recognise, on a chair near the wide window, then closed, the articles I wanted, but to become aware of a person on the other side of the window and looking straight in. One step into the room had sufficed; my vision was instantaneous; it was all there. The person looking straight in was the person who had already appeared to me. He appeared thus again with I won't say greater distinctness, for that was impossible, but with a nearness that represented a forward stride in our intercourse and made me, as I met him, catch my breath and turn cold. He was the same—he was the same, and seen, this time, as he had been seen before, from the waist up, the window, though the dining-room was on the ground floor, not going down to the terrace on which he stood. His face was close to the glass, yet the effect of this better view was, strangely, just to show me how intense the former had been. He remained but a few seconds—long enough to convince me he also saw and recognised; but it was as if I had been looking at him for years and had known him always. Something, however, happened this time that had not happened before; his stare into my face, through the glass and across the room, was as deep and hard as then, but it quitted me for a moment during which I could still watch it, see it fix successively several other things. On the spot there came to me the added shock of a certitude that it was not for me he had come. He had come for some one else.

The flash of this knowledge—for it was knowledge in the midst of dread—produced in me the most extraordinary effect, starting, as I stood there, a sudden vibration of duty and courage. I say courage because I was beyond all doubt already far gone. I bounded straight out of the door again, reached that of the house, got in an instant upon the drive and, passing along the terrace as fast as I could rush, turned a corner and came full in sight. But it was in sight of nothing now—my visitor had vanished. I stopped, almost dropped, with the real relief of this; but I took in the whole scene—I gave him time to reappear. I call it time, but how long was it? I can't speak to the purpose to-day of the duration of these things. That kind of measure must have left me: they couldn't have lasted as they actually appeared to me to last. The terrace and the whole place, the lawn and the garden beyond it, all I could see of the park, were empty with a great emptiness. There were shrubberies and big trees, but I remember the clear assurance I felt that none of them concealed him. He was there or was not there: not there if I didn't see him. I got hold of this; then, instinctively, instead of returning as I had come, went to the window. It was confusedly present to me that I ought to place myself where he had stood. I did so; I applied my face to the pane and looked, as he had looked, into the room. As if, at this moment, to show me exactly what his range had been, Mrs. Grose, as I had done for himself just before, came in from the hall. With this I had the full image of a repetition of what had already occurred. She saw me as I had seen my own visitant; she pulled up short as I had done; I gave her something of the shock that I had received. She turned white, and this made me ask myself if I had blanched as much. She stared, in short, and retreated just on *my* lines, and I knew she had then passed out and come round to me and that I should presently meet her. I remained where I was, and while I waited I thought of more things than one. But there's only one I take space to mention. I wondered why *she* should be scared.

✦ 5 ✦

OH she let me know as soon as, round the corner of the house, she loomed again into view. "What in the name of goodness is the matter—?" She was now flushed and out of breath.

I said nothing till she came quite near. "With me?" I must have made a wonderful face. "Do I show it?"

"You're as white as a sheet. You look awful."

I considered; I could meet on this, without scruple, any degree of innocence. My need to respect the bloom of Mrs. Grose's had dropped, without a rustle, from my shoulders, and if I wavered for the instant it was not with what I kept back. I put out my hand to her and she took it; I held her hard a little, liking to feel her close to me. There was a kind of support in the shy heave of her surprise. "You came for me for church, of course, but I can't go."

"Has anything happened?"

"Yes. You must know now. Did I look very queer?"

"Through this window? Dreadful!"

"Well," I said, "I've been frightened." Mrs. Grose's eyes expressed plainly that *she* had no wish to be, yet also that she knew too well her place not to be ready to share with me any marked inconvenience. Oh it was quite settled that she *must* share! "Just what you saw from the dining-room a minute ago was the effect of that. What *I* saw—just before—was much worse."

Her hand tightened. "What was it?"

"An extraordinary man. Looking in."

"What extraordinary man?"

"I haven't the least idea."

Mrs. Grose gazed round us in vain. "Then where is he gone?"

"I know still less."

"Have you seen him before?"

"Yes—once. On the old tower."

She could only look at me harder. "Do you mean he's a stranger?"

"Oh very much!"

"Yet you didn't tell me?"

"No—for reasons. But now that you've guessed—"

Mrs. Grose's round eyes encountered this charge. "Ah I haven't guessed!" she said very simply. "How can I if *you* don't imagine?"

"I don't in the very least."

"You've seen him nowhere but on the tower?"

"And on this spot just now."

Mrs. Grose looked round again. "What was he doing on the tower?"

"Only standing there and looking down at me."

She thought a minute. "Was he a gentleman?"

I found I had no need to think. "No." She gazed in deeper wonder. "No."

"Then nobody about the place? Nobody from the village?"

"Nobody—nobody. I didn't tell you, but I made sure."

She breathed a vague relief: this was, oddly, so much to the good. It only went indeed a little way. "But if he isn't a gentleman—"

"What *is* he? He's a horror."

"A horror?"

"He's—God help me if I know *what* he is!"

Mrs. Grose looked round once more; she fixed her eyes on the duskier distance and then, pulling herself together, turned to me with full inconsequence. "It's time we should be at church."

"Oh I'm not fit for church!"

"Won't it do you good?"

"It won't do *them*—!" I nodded at the house.

"The children?"

"I can't leave them now."

"You're afraid—?"

I spoke boldly. "I'm afraid of *him*."

Mrs. Grose's large face showed me, at this, for the first time, the far-away faint glimmer of a consciousness more acute: I somehow made out in it the delayed dawn of an idea I myself had not given her and that was as yet quite obscure to me. It comes back to me that I thought instantly of this as something I could get from her; and I felt it to be connected with the desire she presently showed to know more. "When was it—on the tower?"

"About the middle of the month. At this same hour."

"Almost at dark," said Mrs. Grose.

"Oh no, not nearly. I saw him as I see you."

"Then how did he get in?"

"And how did he get out?" I laughed. "I had no opportunity to ask him! This evening, you see," I pursued, "he has not been able to get in."

"He only peeps?"

"I hope it will be confined to that!" She had now let go my hand; she turned away a little. I waited an instant; then I brought out: "Go to church. Good-bye. I must watch."

Slowly she faced me again. "Do you fear for them?"

We met in another long look. "Don't *you*?" Instead of answering she came nearer to the window and, for a minute, applied her face to the glass. "You see how he could see," I meanwhile went on.

She didn't move. "How long was he here?"

"Till I came out. I came to meet him."

Mrs. Grose at last turned round, and there was still more in her face. "*I* couldn't have come out."

"Neither could I!" I laughed again. "But I did come. I've my duty."

"So have I mine," she replied; after which she added: "What's he like?"

"I've been dying to tell you. But he's like nobody."

"Nobody?" she echoed.

"He has no hat." Then seeing in her face that she already, in this, with a deeper dismay, found a touch of picture, I quickly added stroke to stroke. "He has red hair, very red, close-curling, and a pale face, long in shape, with straight good features and little rather queer whiskers that are as red as his hair. His eyebrows are somehow darker; they look particularly arched and as if they might move a good deal. His eyes are sharp, strange—awfully; but I only know clearly that they're rather small and very fixed. His mouth's wide, and his lips are thin, and except for his little whiskers he's quite clean-shaven. He gives me a sort of sense of looking like an actor."

"An actor!" It was impossible to resemble one less, at least, than Mrs. Grose at that moment.

"I've never seen one, but so I suppose them. He's tall, active, erect," I continued, "but never—no, never!—a gentleman."

My companion's face had blanched as I went on; her round eyes started and her mild mouth gaped. "A gentleman?" she gasped, confounded, stupefied: "a gentleman *he?*"

"You know him then?"

She visibly tried to hold herself. "But he *is* handsome?"

I saw the way to help her. "Remarkably!"

"And dressed—?"

"In somebody's clothes. They're smart, but they're not his own."

She broke into a breathless affirmative groan. "They're the master's!"

I caught it up. "You *do* know him?"

She faltered but a second. "Quint!" she cried.

"Quint?"

"Peter Quint—his own man, his valet, when he was here!"

"When the master was?"

Gaping still, but meeting me, she pieced it all together. "He never wore his hat, but he did wear—well, there were waistcoats missed! They were both here—last year. Then the master went, and Quint was alone."

I followed, but halting a little. "Alone?"

"Alone with *us*." Then as from a deeper depth, "In charge," she added.

"And what became of him?"

She hung fire so long that I was still more mystified. "He went too," she brought out at last.

"Went where?"

Her expression, at this, became extraordinary. "God knows where! He died."

"Died?" I almost shrieked.

She seemed fairly to square herself, plant herself more firmly to express the wonder of it. "Yes. Mr. Quint's dead."

❧ 6 ❧

IT took of course more than that particular passage to place us together in presence of what we had now to live with as we could, my dreadful liability to impressions of the order so vividly exemplified, and my companion's knowledge henceforth—a knowledge half consternation and half compassion—of that liability. There had been this evening, after the revelation that left me for an hour so prostrate—there had been for either of us no attendance on any service but a little service of tears and vows, of prayers and promises, a climax to the series of mutual challenges and pledges that had straightway ensued on our retreating together to the schoolroom and shutting ourselves up there to have everything out. The result of our having everything out was simply to reduce our situation to the last rigour of its elements. She herself had seen nothing, not the shadow of a shadow, and nobody in the house but the governess was in the governess's plight; yet she accepted without directly impugning my sanity the truth as I gave it to her, and ended by showing me on this ground an awestricken tenderness, a deference to my more than questionable privilege, of which the very breath has remained with me as that of the sweetest of human charities.

What was settled between us accordingly that night was that we thought we might bear things together; and I was not even sure that in spite of her exemption it was she who had the best of the burden. I knew at this hour, I think, as well as I knew later, what I was capable of meeting to shelter my pupils; but it took me some time to be wholly sure of what my honest comrade was prepared for to keep terms with so stiff an agreement. I was queer company enough—quite as queer as the company I received; but as I trace over what we went through I see how much common ground we must have found in the one idea that, by good fortune, *could* steady us. It was the idea, the second movement, that led me straight out, as I may say, of the inner chamber of my dread. I could take the air in the court, at least, and there Mrs. Grose could join me. Perfectly can I recall now the particular way strength came to me before we separated for the night. We had gone over and over every feature of what I had seen.

"He was looking for some one else, you say—some one who was not you?"

"He was looking for little Miles." A portentous clearness now possessed me. "*That's* whom he was looking for."

"But how do you know?"

"I know, I know, I know!" My exaltation grew. "And *you* know, my dear!"

She didn't deny this, but I required, I felt, not even so much telling as that. She took it up again in a moment. "What if *he* should see him?"

"Little Miles? That's what he wants!"

She looked immensely scared again. "The child?"

"Heaven forbid! The man. He wants to appear to *them*." That he might was an awful conception, and yet somehow I could keep it at bay; which moreover, as we lingered there, was what I succeeded in practically proving. I had an absolute certainty that I should see again what I had already seen, but something within me said that by offering myself bravely as the sole subject of such experience, by accepting, by inviting, by surmounting it all, I should serve as an expiatory victim and guard the tranquillity of the rest of the household. The children in especial I should thus fence about and absolutely save. I recall one of the last things I said that night to Mrs. Grose.

"It does strike me that my pupils have never mentioned—!"

She looked at me hard as I musingly pulled up. "His having been here and the time they were with him?"

"The time they were with him, and his name, his presence, his history, in any way. They've never alluded to it."

"Oh the little lady doesn't remember. She never heard or knew."

"The circumstances of his death?" I thought with some intensity. "Perhaps not. But Miles would remember—Miles would know."

"Ah don't try him!" broke from Mrs. Grose.

I returned her the look she had given me. "Don't be afraid." I continued to think. "It *is* rather odd."

"That he has never spoken of him?"

"Never by the least reference. And you tell me they were 'great friends.'"

"Oh it wasn't *him!*" Mrs. Grose with emphasis declared. "It was Quint's own fancy. To play with him, I mean—to spoil him." She paused a moment; then she added: "Quint was much too free."

This gave me, straight from my vision of his face—*such* a face!—a sudden sickness of disgust. "Too free with *my* boy?"

"Too free with every one!"

I forbore for the moment to analyse this description further than by the reflexion that a part of it applied to several of the members of the household, of the half-dozen maids and men who were still of our small colony. But there was everything, for our apprehension, in the lucky fact that no discomfortable legend, no perturbation of scullions, had ever, within any one's memory, attached to the kind old place. It had neither bad name nor ill fame, and Mrs. Grose, most apparently, only desired to cling to me and to quake in silence. I even put her, the very last thing of all, to the test. It was when, at midnight, she had her hand on the schoolroom door to take leave. "I *have* it from you then—for it's of great importance—that he was definitely and admittedly bad?"

"Oh not admittedly. *I* knew it—but the master didn't."

"And you never told him?"

"Well, he didn't like tale-bearing—he hated complaints. He was terribly short with anything of that kind, and if people were all right to *him*—"

"He wouldn't be bothered with more?" This squared well enough with my impression of him: he was not a trouble-loving gentleman, nor so very particular perhaps about some of the company he himself kept. All the same, I pressed my informant. "I promise you *I* would have told!"

She felt my discrimination. "I dare say I was wrong. But really I was afraid."

"Afraid of what?"

"Of things that man could do. Quint was so clever—he was so deep."

I took this in still more than I probably showed. "You weren't afraid of anything else? Not of his effect—?"

"His effect?" she repeated with a face of anguish and waiting while I faltered.

"On innocent little precious lives. They were in your charge."

"No, they weren't in mine!" she roundly and distressfully returned. "The master believed in him and placed him here because he was supposed not to be quite in health and the country air so good for him. So he had everything to say. Yes"—she let me have it—"even about *them*."

"Them—that creature?" I had to smother a kind of howl. "And you could bear it?"

"No. I couldn't—and I can't now!" And the poor woman burst into tears.

A rigid control, from the next day, was, as I have said, to follow them; yet how often and how passionately, for a week, we came back together to the subject! Much as we had discussed it that Sunday night, I was, in the immediate later hours in especial—for it may be imagined whether I slept—still haunted with the shadow of something she had not told me. I myself had kept back nothing, but there was a word Mrs. Grose had kept back. I was sure moreover by morning that this was not from a failure of frankness, but because on every side there were fears. It seems to me indeed, in raking it all over, that by the time the morrow's sun was high I had restlessly read into the facts before us almost all the meaning they were to receive from subsequent and more cruel occurrences. What they gave me above all was just the sinister figure of the living man—the dead one would keep a while!—and of the months he had continuously passed at Bly, which, added up, made a formidable stretch. The limit of this evil time had arrived only when, on the dawn of a winter's morning, Peter Quint was found, by a labourer going to early work, stone dead on the road from the village: a catastrophe explained—superficially at least—by a visible wound to his head; such a wound as might have been produced (and as, on the final evidence, *had* been) by a fatal slip, in the dark and after leaving the public-house, on the steepish icy slope, a wrong path altogether, at the bottom of which he lay. The icy slope, the turn mistaken at night and in liquor, accounted for much—practically, in the end and after the inquest and boundless chatter, for everything; but there had been matters in his life, strange passages and perils, secret disorders, vices more than suspected, that would have accounted for a good deal more.

I scarce know how to put my story into words that shall be a credible picture of my state of mind; but I was in these days literally able to find a joy in the extraordinary flight of heroism the occasion demanded of me. I now saw that I had been asked for a service admirable and difficult; and there would be a greatness in letting it be seen—oh in the right quarter!—that I could succeed where many another girl might have failed. It was an immense help to me—I confess I rather applaud myself as I look back!—that I saw my response so strongly and so simply. I was there to protect and defend the little creatures in the world the most bereaved and the most loveable, the appeal of whose helplessness had suddenly become only too explicit, a deep constant ache of one's own engaged affection. We were cut off, really, together; we were united in our danger. They had nothing but me, and I—well, I had *them*. It was in short a magnificent chance. This chance presented itself to me in an image richly material. I was a screen—I was to stand before them. The more I saw the less they would. I began to watch them in a stifled suspense, a disguised tension, that might well, had it continued too long, have turned to something like madness. What saved me, as I now see, was that it turned to another matter altogether. It didn't last as suspense—it was superseded by horrible proofs. Proofs, I say, yes—from the moment I really took hold.

This moment dated from an afternoon hour that I happened to spend in the grounds with the younger of my pupils alone. We had left Miles indoors, on the red cushion of a deep window-seat; he had wished to finish a book, and I had been glad to encourage a purpose so laudable in a young man whose only defect was a certain ingenuity of restlessness. His sister, on the contrary, had been alert to come out, and I strolled with her half an hour, seeking the shade, for the sun was still high and the day exceptionally warm. I was aware afresh with her, as we went, of how, like her brother, she contrived—it was the charming thing in both children—to let me alone without appearing to drop me and to accompany me without appearing to oppress. They were never importunate and yet never listless. My attention to them all really went to seeing them amuse themselves immensely without me: this was a spectacle they seemed actively to prepare and that employed me as an active admirer. I walked in a world of their invention—they had no occasion whatever to draw upon mine; so that my time was taken only with being for them some remarkable person or thing that the game of the moment required and that was merely, thanks to my superior, my exalted stamp, a happy and highly distinguished sinecure. I forget what I was on the present occasion; I only remember that I was something very important and very quiet and that Flora was playing very hard. We were on the edge of the lake, and, as we had lately begun geography, the lake was the Sea of Azof.

Suddenly, amid these elements, I became aware that on the other side of the Sea of Azof we had an interested spectator. The way this knowledge gathered in me was the strangest thing in the world—the strangest, that is, except the very much stranger in which it quickly merged itself. I had sat down with a piece of work—for I was something or other that could sit—on the old stone bench which overlooked the pond; and in this position I began to take in with certitude and yet without direct vision the presence, a good way off, of a third person. The old trees, the thick shrubbery, made a great and pleasant shade, but it was all suffused with the brightness of the hot still hour. There was no ambiguity in anything; none whatever at least in the conviction I from one moment to another found myself forming as to what I should see straight before me and across the lake as a consequence of raising my eyes. They were attached at this juncture to the stitching in which I was engaged, and I can feel once more the spasm of my effort not to move them till I should so have steadied myself as to be able to make up my mind what to do. There was an alien object in view—a figure whose right of presence I instantly and passionately questioned. I recollect counting over perfectly the possibilities, reminding myself that nothing was more natural for instance than the appearance of one of the men about the place, or even of a messenger, a postman or a tradesman's boy, from the village. That reminder had as little effect on my practical certitude as I was conscious—still even without looking—of its having upon the character and attitude of our visitor. Nothing was more natural than that these things should be the other things they absolutely were not.

Of the positive identity of the apparition I would assure myself as soon as the small clock of my courage should have ticked out the right second; meanwhile, with an effort that was already sharp enough, I transferred my eyes straight to little Flora, who, at the moment, was about ten yards away. My heart had stood still for an instant with the wonder and terror of the question whether she too would see; and I held my breath while I waited for what a cry from her, what some sudden innocent sign either of interest or of alarm, would tell me. I waited, but nothing came; then in the first place—and there is something more dire in this, I feel, than in anything I have to relate—I was determined by a sense that within a minute all spontaneous sounds from her had dropped; and in the second by the circumstance that also within the minute she had, in her play, turned her back to the water. This was her attitude when I at last looked at her—looked with the confirmed conviction that we were still, together, under direct personal notice. She had picked up a small flat piece of wood which happened to have in it a little hole that had evidently suggested to her the idea of sticking in another fragment that might figure as a mast and make the thing a boat. This second morsel, as I watched her, she was very markedly and intently attempting to tighten in its place. My apprehension of what she was doing sustained me so that after some seconds I felt I was ready for more. Then I again shifted my eyes—I faced what I had to face.

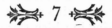

I GOT hold of Mrs. Grose as soon after this as I could; and I can give no intelligible account of how I fought out the interval. Yet I still hear myself cry as I fairly threw myself into her arms: "They *know*—it's too monstrous: they know, they know!"

"And what on earth—?" I felt her incredulity as she held me.

"Why all that *we* know—and heaven knows what more besides!" Then as she released me I made it out to her, made it out perhaps only now with full coherency even to myself. "Two hours ago, in the garden"—I could scarce articulate—"Flora *saw!*"

Mrs. Grose took it as she might have taken a blow in the stomach. "She has told you?" she panted.

"Not a word—that's the horror. She kept it to herself! The child of eight, *that* child!" Unutterable still for me was the stupefaction of it.

Mrs. Grose of course could only gape the wider. "Then how do you know?"

"I was there—I saw with my eyes: saw she was perfectly aware."

"Do you mean aware of *him?*"

"No—of *her*." I was conscious as I spoke that I looked prodigious things, for I got the slow reflexion of them in my companion's face. "Another person—this time; but a figure of quite as unmistakeable horror and evil: a woman in black, pale and dreadful—with such an air also, and such a face!—on the other side of the lake. I was there with the child—quiet for the hour; and in the midst of it she came."

"Came how—from where?"

"From where they come from! She just appeared and stood there—but not so near."

"And without coming nearer?"

"Oh for the effect and the feeling she might have been as close as you!"

My friend, with an odd impulse, fell back a step. "Was she some one you've never seen?"

"Never. But some one the child has. Some one *you* have." Then to show how I had thought it all out: "My predecessor—the one who died."

"Miss Jessel?"

"Miss Jessel. You don't believe me?" I pressed.

She turned right and left in her distress. "How can you be sure?"

This drew from me, in the state of my nerves, a flash of impatience. "Then ask Flora—*she's* sure!" But I had no sooner spoken than I caught myself up. "No, for God's sake *don't!* She'll say she isn't—she'll lie!"

Mrs. Grose was not too bewildered instinctively to protest. "Ah how *can* you?"

"Because I'm clear. Flora doesn't want me to know."

"It's only then to spare you."

"No, no—there are depths, depths! The more I go over it the more I see in it, and the more I see in it the more I fear. I don't know what I *don't* see, what I *don't* fear!"

Mrs. Grose tried to keep up with me. "You mean you're afraid of seeing her again?"

"Oh no; that's nothing—now!" Then I explained. "It's of *not* seeing her."

But my companion only looked wan. "I don't understand."

"Why, it's that the child may keep it up—and that the child assuredly *will*—without my knowing it."

At the image of this possibility Mrs. Grose for a moment collapsed, yet presently to pull herself together again as from the positive force of the sense of what, should we yield an inch, there would really be to give way to. "Dear, dear—we must keep our heads! And after all, if she doesn't mind it—!" She even tried a grim joke. "Perhaps she likes it!"

"Like *such* things—a scrap of an infant!"

"Isn't it just a proof of her blest innocence?" my friend bravely enquired.

She brought me, for the instant, almost round. "Oh we must clutch at *that*—we must cling to it! If it isn't a proof of what you say, it's a proof of—God knows what! For the woman's a horror of horrors."

Mrs. Grose, at this, fixed her eyes a minute on the ground; then at last raising them, "Tell me how you know," she said.

"Then you admit it's what she was?" I cried.

"Tell me how you know," my friend simply repeated.

"Know? By seeing her! By the way she looked."

"At you, do you mean—so wickedly?"

"Dear me, no—I could have borne that. She gave me never a glance. She only fixed the child."

Mrs. Grose tried to see it. "Fixed her?"

"Ah with such awful eyes!"

She stared at mine as if they might really have resembled them. "Do you mean of dislike?"

"God help us, no. Of something much worse."

"Worse than dislike?"—this left her indeed at a loss.

"With a determination—indescribable. With a kind of fury of intention."

I made her turn pale. "Intention?"

"To get hold of her." Mrs. Grose—her eyes just lingering on mine—gave a shudder and walked to the window; and while she stood there looking out I completed my statement. *"That's* what Flora knows."

After a little she turned round. "The person was in black, you say?"

"In mourning—rather poor, almost shabby. But—yes—with extraordinary beauty." I now recognised to what I had at last, stroke by stroke, brought the victim of my confidence, for she quite visibly weighed this. "Oh handsome—very, very," I insisted; "wonderfully handsome. But infamous."

She slowly came back to me. "Miss Jessel—*was* infamous." She once more took my hand in both her own, holding it as tight as if to fortify me against the increase of alarm I might draw from this disclosure. "They were both infamous," she finally said.

So for a little we faced it once more together; and I found

absolutely a degree of help in seeing it now so straight. "I appreciate," I said, "the great decency of your not having hitherto spoken; but the time has certainly come to give me the whole thing." She appeared to assent to this, but still only in silence; seeing which I went on: "I must have it now. Of what did she die? Come, there was something between them."

"There was everything."

"In spite of the difference—?"

"Oh of their rank, their condition"—she brought it woefully out. *"She* was a lady."

I turned it over; I again saw. "Yes—she was a lady."

"And he so dreadfully below," said Mrs. Grose.

I felt that I doubtless needn't press too hard, in such company, on the place of a servant in the scale; but there was nothing to prevent an acceptance of my companion's own measure of my predecessor's abasement. There was a way to deal with that, and I dealt; the more readily for my full vision—on the evidence—of our employer's late clever good-looking "own" man; impudent, assured, spoiled, depraved. "The fellow was a hound."

Mrs. Grose considered as if it were perhaps a little a case for a sense of shades. "I've never seen one like him. He did what he wished."

"With *her?*"

"With them all."

It was as if now in my friend's own eyes Miss Jessel had again appeared. I seemed at any rate for an instant to trace their evocation of her as distinctly as I had seen her by the pond; and I brought out with decision: "It must have been also what *she* wished!"

Mrs. Grose's face signified that it had been indeed, but she said at the same time: "Poor woman—she paid for it!"

"Then you do know what she died of?" I asked.

"No—I know nothing. I wanted not to know; I was glad enough I didn't; and I thanked heaven she was well out of this!"

"Yet you had then your idea—"

"Of her real reason for leaving? Oh yes—as to that. She couldn't have stayed. Fancy it here—for a governess! And afterwards I imagined—and I still imagine. And what I imagine is dreadful."

"Not so dreadful as what *I* do," I replied; on which I must have shown her—as I was indeed but too conscious—a front of miserable defeat. It brought out again all her compassion for me, and at the renewed touch of her kindness my power to resist broke down. I burst, as I had the other time made her burst, into tears; she took me to her motherly breast, where my lamentation overflowed. "I don't do it!" I sobbed in despair; "I don't save or shield them! It's far worse than I dreamed. They're lost!"

✥ 8 ✥

WHAT I had said to Mrs. Grose was true enough: there were in the matter I had put before her depths and possibilities that I lacked resolution to sound; so that when we met once more in the wonder of it we were of a common mind about the duty of resistance to extravagant fancies. We were to keep our heads if we should keep nothing else—difficult indeed as that might be in the face of all that, in our prodigious experience, seemed least to be questioned. Late that night, while the house slept, we had another talk in my room; when she went all the way with me as to its being beyond doubt that I had seen exactly what I had seen. I found that to keep her thoroughly in the grip of this I had only to ask her how, if I had "made it up," I came to be able to give, of each of the persons appearing to me, a picture disclosing, to the last detail, their special marks—a portrait on the exhibition of which she had instantly recognised and named them. She wished, of course—small blame to her!—to sink the whole subject; and I was quick to assure her that my own interest in it had now violently taken the form of a search for the way to escape from it. I closed with her cordially on the article of the likelihood that with recurrence—for recurrence we took for granted—I should get used to my danger; distinctly professing that my personal exposure had suddenly become the least of my discomforts. It was my new suspicion that was intolerable; and yet even to this complication the later hours of the day had brought a little ease.

On leaving her, after my first outbreak, I had of course returned to my pupils, associating the right remedy for my dismay with that sense of their charm which I had already recognised as a resource I could positively cultivate and which had never failed me yet. I had simply, in other words, plunged afresh into Flora's special society and there become aware—it was almost a luxury!—that she could put her little conscious hand straight upon the spot that ached. She had looked at me in sweet speculation and then had accused me to my face of having "cried." I had supposed the ugly signs of it brushed away; but I could literally—for the time at all events—rejoice, under this fathomless charity, that they had not entirely disappeared. To gaze into the depths of blue of the child's eyes and pronounce their loveliness a trick of premature cunning was to be guilty of a cynicism in preference to which I naturally preferred to abjure my judgement and, so far as might be, my agitation. I couldn't abjure for merely wanting to, but I could repeat to Mrs. Grose—as I did there, over and over, in the small hours—that with our small friends' voices in the air, their pressure on one's heart and their fragrant faces against one's cheek, everything fell to the ground but their incapacity and their beauty. It was a pity that, somehow, to settle this once for all, I had equally to re-enumerate the signs of subtlety that, in the afternoon, by the lake, had made a miracle of my show of self-possession. It was a pity to be obliged to re-investigate the certitude of the moment itself and repeat how it had come to me as a revelation that the inconceivable communion I then surprised must have been for both parties a matter of habit. It was a pity I should have had to quaver out again the reasons for my not having, in my delusion, so much as questioned that the little girl saw our visitant even as I actually saw Mrs. Grose herself, and that she wanted, by just so much as she did thus see, to make me suppose she didn't, and at the same time, without showing anything, arrive at a guess as to whether I myself did! It was a pity I needed to recapitulate the portentous little activities by which she sought to divert my attention—the perceptible increase of movement, the greater intensity of play, the singing, the gabbling of nonsense and the invitation to romp.

Yet if I had not indulged, to prove there was nothing in it, in this review, I should have missed the two or three dim elements of comfort that still remained to me. I shouldn't for instance have been able to asseverate to my friend that I was certain—which was so much to the good—that *I* at least had not betrayed myself. I shouldn't have been prompted, by stress of need, by desperation of mind—I scarce know what to call it—to invoke such further aid to intelligence as might spring from pushing my colleague fairly to the wall. She had told me, bit by bit, under pressure, a great deal; but a small shifty spot on the wrong side of it all still sometimes brushed my brow like the wing of a bat; and I remember how on this occasion—for the sleeping house and the concentration alike of our danger and our watch seemed to help—I felt the importance of giving the last jerk to the curtain. "I don't believe anything so horrible," I recollect saying; "no, let us put it definitely, my dear, that I don't. But if I did, you know, there's a thing I should require now, just without sparing you the least bit more—oh not a scrap, come!—to get out of you. What was it you had in mind when, in our distress, before Miles came back, over the letter from his school, you said, under my insistence, that you didn't pretend for him he hadn't literally *ever* been 'bad'? He has *not,* truly, 'ever,' in these weeks that I myself have lived with him and so closely watched him; he has been an imperturbable little prodigy of delightful loveable goodness. Therefore you might perfectly have made the claim for him if you had not, as it happened, seen an exception to take. What was your exception, and to what passage in your personal observation of him did you refer?"

It was a straight question enough, but levity was not our note, and in any case I had before the grey dawn admonished us to separate got my answer. What my friend had had in mind proved immensely to the purpose. It was neither more nor less than the particular fact that for a period of several months Quint and the boy had been perpetually together. It was indeed the very appropriate item of evidence of her having ventured to criticise the propriety, to hint at the incongruity, of so close an alliance, and even to go so far on the subject as a frank overture to Miss Jessel would take her. Miss Jessel had, with a very high manner about it, requested her to mind her business, and the good woman had on this directly approached little Miles. What she had said to him, since I pressed, was that *she* liked to see young gentlemen not forget their station.

I pressed again, of course, the closer for that. "You reminded him that Quint was only a base menial?"

"As you might say! And it was his answer, for one thing, that was bad."

"And for another thing?" I waited. "He repeated your words to Quint?"

"No, not that. It's just what he *wouldn't!*" she could still impress on me. "I was sure, at any rate," she added, "that he didn't. But he denied certain occasions."

"What occasions?"

"When they had been about together quite as if Quint were his tutor—and a very grand one—and Miss Jessel only for the little lady. When he had gone off with the fellow, I mean, and spent hours with him."

"He then prevaricated about it—he said he hadn't?" Her assent was clear enough to cause me to add in a moment: "I see. He lied."

"Oh!" Mrs. Grose mumbled. This was a suggestion that it didn't matter; which indeed she backed up by a further remark. "You see, after all, Miss Jessel didn't mind. She didn't forbid him."

I considered. "Did he put that to you as a justification?"

At this she dropped again. "No, he never spoke of it."

"Never mentioned her in connexion with Quint?"

She saw, visibly flushing, where I was coming out. "Well, he didn't show anything. He denied," she repeated; "he denied."

Lord, how I pressed her now! "So that you could see he knew what was between the two wretches?"

"I don't know—I don't know!" the poor woman wailed.

"You do know, you dear thing," I replied; "only you haven't my dreadful boldness of mind, and you keep back, out of timidity and modesty and delicacy, even the impression that in the past, when you had, without my aid, to flounder about in silence, most of all made you miserable. But I shall get it out of you yet! There was something in the boy that suggested to you," I continued, "his covering and concealing their relation."

"Oh he couldn't prevent—"

"Your learning the truth? I dare say! But, heavens," I fell, with vehemence, a-thinking, "what it shows that they must, to that extent, have succeeded in making of him!"

"Ah nothing that's not nice *now!*" Mrs. Grose lugubriously pleaded.

"I don't wonder you looked queer," I persisted, "when I mentioned to you the letter from his school!"

"I doubt if I looked as queer as you!" she retorted with homely force. "And if he was so bad then as that comes to, how is he such an angel now?"

"Yes indeed—and if he was a fiend at school! How, how, how? Well," I said in my torment, "you must put it to me again, though I

shall not be able to tell you for some days. Only put it to me again!"
I cried in a way that made my friend stare. "There are directions in
which I mustn't for the present let myself go." Meanwhile I returned
to her first example—the one to which she had just previously
referred—of the boy's happy capacity for an occasional slip. "If
Quint—on your remonstrance at the time you speak of—was a base
menial, one of the things Miles said to you, I find myself guessing,
was that you were another." Again her admission was so adequate
that I continued: "And you forgave him that?"

"Wouldn't *you?*"

"Oh yes!" And we exchanged there, in the stillness, a sound of the
oddest amusement. Then I went on: "At all events, while he was
with the man—"

"Miss Flora was with the woman. It suited them all!"

It suited me too, I felt, only too well; by which I mean that it
suited exactly the particular deadly view I was in the very act of
forbidding myself to entertain. But I so far succeeded in checking the
expression of this view that I will throw, just here, no further light
on it than may be offered by the mention of my final observation to
Mrs. Grose. "His having lied and been impudent are, I confess, less
engaging specimens than I had hoped to have from you of the
outbreak in him of the little natural man. Still," I mused, "they must
do, for they make me feel more than ever that I must watch."

It made me blush, the next minute, to see in my friend's face how
much more unreservedly she had forgiven him than her anecdote
struck me as pointing out to my own tenderness any way to do. This
was marked when, at the schoolroom door, she quitted me. "Surely
you don't accuse *him*—"

"Of carrying on an intercourse that he conceals from me? Ah
remember that, until further evidence, I now accuse nobody." Then
before shutting her out to go by another passage to her own place, "I
must just wait," I wound up.

✦ 9 ✦

I WAITED and waited, and the days took as they elapsed something
from my consternation. A very few of them, in fact, passing, in

constant sight of my pupils, without a fresh incident, sufficed to give to grievous fancies and even to odious memories a kind of brush of the sponge. I have spoken of the surrender to their extraordinary childish grace as a thing I could actively promote in myself, and it may be imagined if I neglected now to apply at this source for whatever balm it would yield. Stranger than I can express, certainly, was the effort to struggle against my new lights. It would doubtless have been a greater tension still, however, had it not been so frequently successful. I used to wonder how my little charges could help guessing that I thought strange things about them; and the circumstance that these things only made them more interesting was not by itself a direct aid to keeping them in the dark. I trembled lest they should see that they *were* so immensely more interesting. Putting things at the worst, at all events, as in meditation I so often did, any clouding of their innocence could only be—blameless and foredoomed as they were—a reason the more for taking risks. There were moments when I knew myself to catch them up by an irresistible impulse and press them to my heart. As soon as I had done so I used to wonder—"What will they think of that? Doesn't it betray too much?" It would have been easy to get into a sad wild tangle about how much I might betray; but the real account, I feel, of the hours of peace I could still enjoy was that the immediate charm of my companions was a beguilement still effective even under the shadow of the possibility that it was studied. For it if occurred to me that I might occasionally excite suspicion by the little outbreaks of my sharper passion for them, so too I remember asking if I mightn't see a queerness in the traceable increase of their own demonstrations.

They were at this period extravagantly and preternaturally fond of me; which, after all, I could reflect, was no more than a graceful response in children perpetually bowed down over and hugged. The homage of which they were so lavish succeeded in truth for my nerves quite as well as if I never appeared to myself, as I may say, literally to catch them at a purpose in it. They had never, I think, wanted to do so many things for their poor protectress; I mean—though they got their lessons better and better, which was naturally what would please her most—in the way of diverting, entertaining, surprising her; reading her passages, telling her stories, acting her charades, pouncing out at her, in disguises, as animals and historical characters, and above all astonishing her by the "pieces" they had secretly got by heart and could interminably recite. I should never get to the bottom—were I to let myself go even now—of the prodigious private commentary, all under still more private correction, with which I in these days overscored their full hours. They had shown me from the first a facility for everything, a general faculty which, taking a fresh start, achieved remarkable flights. They got their little tasks as if they loved them; they indulged, from the mere exuberance of the gift, in the most unimposed little miracles of memory. They not only popped out at me as tigers and as Romans, but as Shakespeareans, astronomers and navigators. This was so singularly the case that it had presumably much to do with the fact as to which, at the present day, I am at a loss for a different explanation: I allude to my unnatural composure on the subject of another school for Miles. What I remember is that I was content for the time not to open the question, and that contentment must have sprung from the sense of his perpetually striking show of cleverness. He was too clever for a bad governess, for a parson's daughter, to spoil; and the strangest if not the brightest thread in the pensive embroidery I just spoke of was the impression I might have got, if I had dared to work it out, that he was under some influence operating in his small intellectual life as a tremendous incitement.

If it was easy to reflect, however, that such a boy could postpone school, it was at least as marked that for such a boy to have been "kicked out" by a schoolmaster was a mystification without end. Let me add that in their company now—and I was careful almost never to be out of it—I could follow no scent very far. We lived in a cloud of music and affection and success and private theatricals. The musical sense in each of the children was of the quickest, but the elder in especial had a marvellous knack of catching and repeating. The schoolroom piano broke into all gruesome fancies; and when that failed there were confabulations in corners, with a sequel of one of them going out in the highest spirits in order to "come in" as something new. I had had brothers myself, and it was no revelation to me that little girls could be slavish idolaters of little boys. What surpassed everything was that there was a little boy in the world who could have for the inferior age, sex and intelligence so fine a consideration. They were extraordinarily at one, and to say that they never either quarrelled or complained is to make the note of praise coarse for their quality of sweetness. Sometimes perhaps indeed (when I

dropped into coarseness) I came across traces of little understand-
ings between them by which one of them should keep me occupied
while the other slipped away. There is a naïf side, I suppose, in all
diplomacy; but if my pupils practised upon me it was surely with the
minimum of grossness. It was all in the other quarter that, after a
lull, the grossness broke out.

I find that I really hang back; but I must take my horrid plunge.
In going on with the record of what was hideous at Bly I not only
challenge the most liberal faith—for which I little care; but (and
this is another matter) I renew what I myself suffered, I again push
my dreadful way through it to the end. There came suddenly an
hour after which, as I look back, the business seems to me to have
been all pure suffering; but I have at least reached the heart of it,
and the straightest road out is doubtless to advance. One
evening—with nothing to lead up or prepare it—I felt the cold
touch of the impression that had breathed on me the night of my
arrival and which, much lighter then as I have mentioned, I should
probably have made little of in memory had my subsequent sojourn
been less agitated. I had not gone to bed; I sat reading by a couple of
candles. There was a roomful of old books at Bly—last-century
fiction some of it, which, to the extent of a distinctly deprecated
renown, but never to so much as that of a stray specimen, had
reached the sequestered home and appealed to the unavowed curiosity of my youth. I remember that the book I had in my hand was
Fielding's "Amelia"; also that I was wholly awake. I recall further
both a general conviction that it was horribly late and a particular
objection to looking at my watch. I figure finally that the white
curtain draping, in the fashion of those days, the head of Flora's
little bed, shrouded, as I had assured myself long before, the perfection of childish rest. I recollect in short that though I was deeply
interested in my author I found myself, at the turn of a page and
with his spell all scattered, looking straight up from him and hard at
the door of my room. There was a moment during which I listened,
reminded of the faint sense I had had, the first night, of there being
something undefinably astir in the house, and noted the soft breath
of the open casement just move the half-drawn blind. Then, with all
the marks of a deliberation that must have seemed magnificent had
there been any one to admire it, I laid down my book, rose to my feet
and, taking a candle, went straight out of the room and, from the

passage, on which my light made little impression, noiselessly closed and locked the door.

I can say now neither what determined nor what guided me, but I went straight along the lobby, holding my candle high, till I came within sight of the tall window that presided over the great turn of the staircase. At this point I precipitately found myself aware of three things. They were practically simultaneous, yet they had flashes of succession. My candle, under a bold flourish, went out, and I perceived, by the uncovered window, that the yielding dusk of earliest morning rendered it unnecessary. Without it, the next instant, I knew that there was a figure on the stair. I speak of sequences, but I required no lapse of seconds to stiffen myself for a third encounter with Quint. The apparition had reached the landing halfway up and was therefore on the spot nearest the window, where, at sight of me, it stopped short and fixed me exactly as it had fixed me from the tower and from the garden. He knew me as well as I knew him; and so, in the cold faint twilight, with a glimmer in the high glass and another on the polish of the oak stair below, we faced each other in our common intensity. He was absolutely, on this occasion, a living detestable dangerous presence. But that was not the wonder of wonders; I reserve this distinction for quite another circumstance: the circumstance that dread had unmistakeably quitted me and that there was nothing in me unable to meet and measure him.

I had plenty of anguish after that extraordinary moment, but I had, thank God, no terror. And he knew I hadn't—I found myself at the end of an instant magnificently aware of this. I felt, in a fierce rigour of confidence, that if I stood my ground a minute I should cease—for the time at least—to have him to reckon with; and during the minute, accordingly, the thing was as human and hideous as a real interview: hideous just because it *was* human, as human as to have met alone, in the small hours, in a sleeping house, some enemy, some adventurer, some criminal. It was the dead silence of our long gaze at such close quarters that gave the whole horror, huge as it was, its only note of the unnatural. If I had met a murderer in such a place and at such an hour we still at least would have spoken. Something would have passed, in life, between us; if nothing had passed one of us would have moved. The moment was so prolonged that it would have taken but little more to make me doubt if even *I* were in life. I can't express what followed it save by saying that the silence itself—which was indeed in a manner an attestation of my strength—became the element into which I saw the figure disappear; in which I definitely saw it turn, as I might have seen the low wretch to which it had once belonged turn on receipt of an order, and pass, with my eyes on the villainous back that no hunch could have more disfigured, straight down the staircase and into the darkness in which the next bend was lost.

⁂ 10 ⁂

I REMAINED a while at the top of the stair, but with the effect presently of understanding that when my visitor had gone, he had gone; then I returned to my room. The foremost thing I saw there by the light of the candle I had left burning was that Flora's little bed was empty; and on this I caught my breath with all the terror that, five minutes before, I had been able to resist. I dashed at the place in which I had left her lying and over which—for the small silk counterpane and the sheets were disarranged—the white curtains had been deceivingly pulled forward; then my step, to my unutterable relief, produced an answering sound: I noticed an agitation of the window-blind, and the child, ducking down, emerged rosily from the other side of it. She stood there in so much of her candour and so little of her night-gown, with her pink bare feet and the golden glow of her curls. She looked intensely grave, and I had never had such a sense of losing an advantage acquired (the thrill of which had just been so prodigious) as on my consciousness that she addressed me with a reproach—"You naughty: where *have* you been?" Instead of challenging her own irregularity I found myself arraigned and explaining. She herself explained, for that matter, with the loveliest eagerest simplicity. She had known suddenly, as she lay there, that I was out of the room, and had jumped up to see what had become of me. I had dropped, with the joy of her reappearance, back into my chair—feeling then, and then only, a little faint; and she had pattered straight over to me, thrown herself upon my knee, given herself to be held with the flame of the candle full in the wonderful little face that was still flushed with sleep. I remember closing my eyes an instant, yieldingly, consciously, as before the excess of something beautiful that shone out of the blue of her own. "You were looking for me out of the window?" I said. "You thought I might be walking in the grounds?"

"Well, you know, I thought some one was"—she never blanched as she smiled out that at me.

Oh how I looked at her now! "And did you see any one?"

"Ah *no!*" she returned almost (with the full privilege of childish inconsequence) resentfully, though with a long sweetness in her little drawl of the negative.

At that moment, in the state of my nerves, I absolutely believed she lied; and if I once more closed my eyes it was before the dazzle of the three or four possible ways in which I might take this up. One of these for a moment tempted me with such singular force that, to resist it, I must have gripped my little girl with a spasm that, wonderfully, she submitted to without a cry or a sign of fright. Why not break out at her on the spot and have it all over?—give it to her straight in her lovely little lighted face? "You see, you see, you *know* that you do and that you already quite suspect I believe it; therefore why not frankly confess it to me, so that we may at least live with it together and learn perhaps, in the strangeness of our fate, where we are and what it means?" This solicitation dropped, alas, as it came: if I could immediately have succumbed to it I might have spared myself—well, you'll see what. Instead of succumbing I sprang again to my feet, looked at her bed and took a helpless middle way. "Why did you pull the curtain over the place to make me think you were still there?"

Flora luminously considered; after which, with her little divine smile: "Because I don't like to frighten you!"

"But if I had, by your idea, gone out—?"

She absolutely declined to be puzzled; she turned her eyes to the flame of the candle as if the question were as irrelevant, or at any rate as impersonal, as Mrs. Marcet or nine-times-nine. "Oh but you know," she quite adequately answered, "that you might come back, you dear, and that you *have!*" And after a little, when she had got into bed, I had, a long time, by almost sitting on her for the retention of her hand, to show how I recognised the pertinence of my return.

You may imagine the general complexion, from that moment, of my nights. I repeatedly sat up till I didn't know when; I selected moments when my room-mate unmistakeably slept, and, stealing out, took noiseless turns in the passage. I even pushed as far as to where I had last met Quint. But I never met him there again, and I may as well say at once that I on no other occasion saw him in the house. I just missed, on the staircase, nevertheless, a different adventure. Looking down it from the top I once recognised the presence of a woman seated on one of the lower steps with her back presented to me, her body half-bowed and her head, in an attitude of woe, in her hands. I had been there but an instant, however, when she vanished without looking round at me. I knew, for all that, exactly what dreadful face she had to show; and I wondered whether, if instead of being above I had been below, I should have had the same nerve for going up that I had lately shown Quint. Well, there continued to be plenty of call for nerve. On the eleventh night after my latest encounter with that gentleman—they were all numbered now—I had an alarm that perilously skirted it and that indeed, from the particular quality of its unexpectedness, proved quite my sharpest shock. It was precisely the first night during this series that, weary with vigils, I had conceived I might again without laxity lay myself down at my old hour. I slept immediately and, as I afterwards knew, till about one o'clock; but when I woke it was to sit straight up, as completely roused as if a hand had shaken me. I had left a light burning, but it was now out, and I felt an instant certainty that Flora had extinguished it. This brought me to my feet and straight, in the darkness, to her bed, which I found she had left. A glance at the window enlightened me further, and the striking of a match completed the picture.

The child had again got up—this time blowing out the taper, and had again, for some purpose of observation or response, squeezed in behind the blind and was peering out into the night. That she now saw—as she had not, I had satisfied myself, the previous time—was proved to me by the fact that she was disturbed neither by my re-illumination nor by the haste I made to get into slippers and into a wrap. Hidden, protected, absorbed, she evidently rested on the sill—the casement opened forward—and gave herself up. There was a great still moon to help her, and this fact had counted in my quick decision. She was face to face with the apparition we had met at the lake, and could now communicate with it as she had not then been able to do. What I, on my side, had to care for was, without disturbing her, to reach, from the corridor, some other window turned to the same quarter. I got to the door without her hearing me; I got out of it, closed it and listened, from the other side, for some sound from her. While I stood in the passage I had my eyes on her brother's door, which was but ten steps off and which, indescribably, produced in me a renewal of the strange impulse that I lately spoke of as my temptation. What if I should go straight in and march to *his* window?—what if, by risking to his boyish bewilderment a revelation of my motive, I should throw across the rest of the mystery the long halter of my boldness?

This thought held me sufficiently to make me cross to his threshold and pause again. I preternaturally listened; I figured to myself what might portentously be; I wondered if his bed were also empty and he also secretly at watch. It was a deep soundless minute, at the end of which my impulse failed. He was quiet; he might be innocent; the risk was hideous; I turned away. There was a figure in the grounds—a figure prowling for a sight, the visitor with whom Flora was engaged; but it wasn't the visitor most concerned with my boy. I hesitated afresh, but on other grounds and only a few seconds; then I had made my choice. There were empty rooms enough at Bly, and it was only a question of choosing the right one. The right one suddenly presented itself to me as the lower one—though high above the gardens—in the solid corner of the house that I have spoken of as the old tower. This was a large square chamber, arranged with some state as a bedroom, the extravagant size of which made it so inconvenient that it had not for years, though kept by Mrs. Grose in exemplary order, been occupied. I had often admired it and I knew my way about in it; I had only, after just faltering at the first chill gloom of its disuse, to pass across it and unbolt in all quietness one of the shutters. Achieving this transit I uncovered the glass without a sound and, applying my face to the pane, was able, the darkness without being much less than within, to see that I commanded the right direction. Then I saw something more. The moon made the night extraordinarily penetrable and showed me on the lawn a person, diminished by distance, who stood there motionless and as if fascinated, looking up to where I had appeared—looking, that is, not so much straight at me as at something that was apparently above me. There was clearly another person above me—there was a person on the tower; but the presence on the lawn was not in the least what I had conceived and had confidently hurried to meet. The presence on the lawn—I felt sick as I made it out—was poor little Miles himself.

11

IT was not till late next day that I spoke to Mrs. Grose; the rigour with which I kept my pupils in sight making it often difficult to meet her privately: the more as we each felt the importance of not provoking—on the part of the servants quite as much as on that of the children—any suspicion of a secret flurry or of a discussion of mysteries. I drew a great security in this particular from her mere smooth aspect. There was nothing in her fresh face to pass on to others the least of my horrible confidences. She believed me, I was sure, absolutely: if she hadn't I don't know what would have become of me, for I couldn't have borne the strain alone. But she was a magnificent monument to the blessing of a want of imagination, and if she could see in our little charges nothing but their beauty and amiability, their happiness and cleverness, she had no direct communication with the sources of my trouble. If they had been at all visibly blighted or battered she would doubtless have grown, on tracing it back, haggard enough to match them; as matters stood, however, I could feel her, when she surveyed them with her large white arms folded and the habit of serenity in all her look, thank the Lord's mercy that if they were ruined the pieces would still serve. Flights of fancy gave place, in her mind, to a steady fireside glow, and I had already begun to perceive how, with the development of the conviction that—as time went on without a public accident—our young things could, after all, look out for themselves, she addressed her greatest solicitude to the sad case presented by their deputy-guardian. That, for myself, was a sound simplification: I could engage that, to the world, my face should tell no tales, but it would have been, in the conditions, an immense added worry to find myself anxious about hers.

At the hour I now speak of she had joined me, under pressure, on the terrace, where, with the lapse of the season, the afternoon sun was now agreeable; and we sat there together while before us and at a distance, yet within call if we wished, the children strolled to and fro in one of their most manageable moods. They moved slowly, in unison, below us, over the lawn, the boy, as they went, reading aloud from a story-book and passing his arm round his sister to keep her quite in touch. Mrs. Grose watched them with positive placidity; then I caught the suppressed intellectual creak with which she conscientiously turned to take from me a view of the back of the tapestry. I had made her a receptacle of lurid things, but there was an odd recognition of my superiority—my accomplishments and my function—in her patience under my pain. She offered her mind to my disclosures as, had I wished to mix a witch's broth and proposed it with assurance, she would have held out a large clean saucepan. This had become thoroughly her attitude by the time that, in my recital of the events of the night, I reached the point of what Miles had said to me when, after seeing him, at such a monstrous hour, almost on the very spot where he happened now to be, I had gone down to bring him in; choosing then, at the window, with a concentrated need of not alarming the house, rather that method than any noisier process. I had left her meanwhile in little doubt of my small hope of representing with success even to her actual sympathy my sense of the real splendour of the little inspiration with which, after I had got him into the house, the boy met my final articulate challenge. As soon as I appeared in the moonlight on the terrace he had come to me as straight as possible; on which I had taken his hand without a word and led him, through the dark spaces, up the staircase where Quint had so hungrily hovered for him, along the lobby where I had listened and trembled, and so to his forsaken room.

Not a sound, on the way, had passed between us, and I had wondered—oh *how* I had wondered!—if he were groping about in his dreadful little mind for something plausible and not too grotesque. It would tax his invention certainly, and I felt, this time, over his real embarrassment, a curious thrill of triumph. It was a sharp trap for any game hitherto successful. He could play no longer at perfect propriety, nor could he pretend to it; so how the deuce would he get out of the scrape? There beat in me indeed, with the passionate throb of this question, an equal dumb appeal as to how the deuce *I* should. I was confronted at last, as never yet, with all the risk

attached even now to sounding my own horrid note. I remember in
fact that as we pushed into his little chamber, where the bed had not
been slept in at all and the window, uncovered to the moonlight,
made the place so clear that there was no need of striking a match—I
remember how I suddenly dropped, sank upon the edge of the bed
from the force of the idea that he must know how he really, as they
say, "had" me. He could do what he liked, with all his cleverness to
help him, so long as I should continue to defer to the old tradition of
the criminality of those caretakers of the young who minister to
superstitions and fears. He "had" me indeed, and in a cleft stick; for
who would ever absolve me, who would consent that I should go
unhung, if, by the faintest tremor of an overture, I were the first to
introduce into our perfect intercourse an element so dire? No, no: it
was useless to attempt to convey to Mrs. Grose, just as it is scarcely
less so to attempt to suggest here, how, during our short stiff brush
there in the dark, he fairly shook me with admiration. I was of course
thoroughly kind and merciful; never, never yet had I placed on his
small shoulders hands of such tenderness as those with which, while
I rested against the bed, I held him there well under fire. I had **no**
alternative but, in form at least, to put it to him.

"You must tell me now—and all the truth. What did you go out
for? What were you doing there?"

I can still see his wonderful smile, the whites of his beautiful eyes
and the uncovering of his clear teeth, shine to me in the dusk. "If I
tell you why, will you understand?" My heart, at this, leaped into my
mouth. *Would* he tell me why? I found no sound on my lips to press
it, and I was aware of answering only with a vague repeated grimac-
ing nod. He was gentleness itself, and while I wagged my head at him
he stood there more than ever a little fairy prince. It was his
brightness indeed that gave me a respite. Would it be so great if he
were really going to tell me? "Well," he said at last, "just exactly in
order that you should do this."

"Do what?"

"Think me—for a change—*bad!*" I shall never forget the sweetness and gaiety with which he brought out the word, nor how, on top
of it, he bent forward and kissed me. It was practically the end of
everything. I met his kiss and I had to make, while I folded him for a
minute in my arms, the most stupendous effort not to cry. He had
given exactly the account of himself that permitted least my going

behind it, and it was only with the effect of confirming my acceptance of it that, as I presently glanced about the room, I could say—

"Then you didn't undress at all?"

He fairly glittered in the gloom. "Not at all. I sat up and read."

"And when did you go down?"

"At midnight. When I'm bad I *am* bad!"

"I see, I see—it's charming. But how could you be sure I should
know it?"

"Oh I arranged that with Flora." His answers rang out with a
readiness! "She was to get up and look out."

"Which is what she did do." It was I who fell into the trap!

"So she disturbed you, and, to see what she was looking at, you also
looked—you saw."

"While you," I concurred, "caught your death in the night air!"

He literally bloomed so from this exploit that he could afford
radiantly to assent. "How otherwise should I have been bad
enough?" he asked. Then, after another embrace, the incident and
our interview closed on my recognition of all the reserves of goodness
that, for his joke, he had been able to draw upon.

⚜ 12 ⚜

THE particular impression I had received proved in the morning
light, I repeat, not quite successfully presentable to Mrs. Grose,
though I re-enforced it with the mention of still another remark that
he had made before we separated. "It all lies in half a dozen words,"
I said to her, "words that really settle the matter. 'Think, you know,
what I *might* do!' He threw that off to show me how good he is. He
knows down to the ground what he 'might do.' That's what he gave
them a taste of at school."

"Lord, you do change!" cried my friend.

"I don't change—I simply make it out. The four, depend upon it,
perpetually meet. If on either of these last nights you had been with
either child you'd clearly have understood. The more I've watched
and waited the more I've felt that if there were nothing else to make
it sure it would be made so by the systematic silence of each. *Never,*
by a slip of the tongue, have they so much as alluded to either of

their old friends, any more than Miles has alluded to his expulsion. Oh yes, we may sit here and look at them, and they may show off to us there to their fill; but even while they pretend to be lost in their fairy-tale they're steeped in their vision of the dead restored to them. He's not reading to her," I declared; "they're talking of *them*—they're talking horrors! I go on, I know, as if I were crazy; and it's a wonder I'm not. What I've seen would have made *you* so; but it has only made me more lucid, made me get hold of still other things."

My lucidity must have seemed awful, but the charming creatures who were victims of it, passing and repassing in their interlocked sweetness, gave my colleague something to hold on by; and I felt how tight she held as, without stirring in the breath of my passion, she covered them still with her eyes. "Of what other things have you got hold?"

"Why of the very things that have delighted, fascinated and yet, at bottom, as I now so strangely see, mystified and troubled me. Their more than earthly beauty, their absolutely unnatural goodness. It's a game," I went on; "it's a policy and a fraud!"

"On the part of little darlings—?"

"As yet mere lovely babies? Yes, mad as that seems!" The very act of bringing it out really helped me to trace it—follow it all up and piece it all together. "They haven't been good—they've only been absent. It has been easy to live with them because they're simply leading a life of their own. They're not mine—they're not ours. They're his and they're hers!"

"Quint's and that woman's?"

"Quint's and that woman's. They want to get to them."

Oh how, at this, poor Mrs. Grose appeared to study them! "But for what?"

"For the love of all the evil that, in those dreadful days, the pair put into them. And to ply them with that evil still, to keep up the work of demons, is what brings the others back."

"Laws!" said my friend under her breath. The exclamation was homely, but it revealed a real acceptance of my further proof of what, in the bad time—for there had been a worse even than this!—must have occurred. There could have been no such justification for me as the plain assent of her experience to whatever depth of depravity I found credible in our brace of scoundrels. It was in obvious submission of memory that she brought out after a moment: "They *were* rascals! But what can they now do?" she pursued.

"Do?" I echoed so loud that Miles and Flora, as they passed at their distance, paused an instant in their walk and looked at us. "Don't they do enough?" I demanded in a lower tone, while the children, having smiled and nodded and kissed hands to us, resumed their exhibition. We were held by it a minute; then I answered: "They can destroy them!" At this my companion did turn, but the appeal she launched was a silent one, the effect of which was to make me more explicit. "They don't know as yet quite how—but they're trying hard. They're seen only across, as it were, and beyond—in strange places and on high places, the top of towers, the roof of houses, the outside of windows, the further edge of pools; but there's a deep design, on either side, to shorten the distance and overcome the obstacle: so the success of the tempters is only a question of time. They've only to keep to their suggestions of danger."

"For the children to come?"

"And perish in the attempt!" Mrs. Grose slowly got up, and I scrupulously added: "Unless, of course, we can prevent!"

Standing there before me while I kept my seat she visibly turned things over. "Their uncle must do the preventing. He must take them away."

"And who's to make him?"

She had been scanning the distance, but she now dropped on me a foolish face. "You, Miss."

"By writing to him that his house is poisoned and his little nephew and niece mad?"

"But if they *are*, Miss?"

"And if I am myself, you mean? That's charming news to be sent him by a person enjoying his confidence and whose prime undertaking was to give him no worry."

Mrs. Grose considered, following the children again. "Yes, he do hate worry. That was the great reason—"

"Why those fiends took him in so long? No doubt, though his indifference must have been awful. As I'm not a fiend, at any rate, I shouldn't take him in."

My companion, after an instant and for all answer, sat down again and grasped my arm. "Make him at any rate come to you."

I stared. "To *me*?" I had a sudden fear of what she might do. " 'Him'?"

"He ought to *be* here—he ought to help."

I quickly rose and I think I must have shown her a queerer face than ever yet. "You see me asking him for a visit?" No, with her eyes on my face she evidently couldn't. Instead of it even—as a woman reads another—she could see what I myself saw: his derision, his amusement, his contempt for the breakdown of my resignation at being left alone and for the fine machinery I had set in motion to attract his attention to my slighted charms. She didn't know—no one knew—how proud I had been to serve him and to stick to our terms; yet she none the less took the measure, I think, of the warning I now gave her. "If you should so lose your head as to appeal to him for me—"

She was really frightened. "Yes, Miss?"

"I would leave, on the spot, both him and you."

❧ 13 ❧

It was all very well to join them, but speaking to them proved quite as much as ever an effort beyond my strength—offered, in close quarters, difficulties as insurmountable as before. This situation continued a month, and with new aggravations and particular notes, the note above all, sharper and sharper, of the small ironic consciousness on the part of my pupils. It was not, I am as sure to-day as I was sure then, my mere infernal imagination: it was absolutely traceable that they were aware of my predicament and that this strange relation made, in a manner, for a long time, the air in which we moved. I don't mean that they had their tongues in their cheeks or did anything vulgar, for that was not one of their dangers: I do mean, on the other hand, that the element of the unnamed and untouched became, between us, greater than any other, and that so much avoidance couldn't have been made successful without a great deal of tacit arrangement. It was as if, at moments, we were perpetually coming into sight of subjects before which we must stop short, turning suddenly out of alleys that we perceived to be blind, closing with a little bang that made us look at each other—for, like all bangs, it was something louder than we had intended—the doors we had indiscreetly opened. All roads lead to Rome, and there were times when it might have struck us that almost every branch of study or subject of conversation skirted forbidden ground. Forbidden ground was the question of the return of the dead in general and of whatever, in especial, might survive, for memory, of the friends little children had lost. There were days when I could have sworn that one of them had, with a small invisible nudge, said to the other: "She thinks she'll do it this time—but she *won't!*" To "do it" would have been to indulge for instance—and for once in a way—in some direct reference to the lady who had prepared them for my discipline. They had a delightful endless appetite for passages in my own history to which I had again and again treated them; they were in possession of everything that had ever happened to me, had had, with every circumstance, the story of my smallest adventures and of those of my brothers and sisters and of the cat and the dog at home, as well as many particulars of the whimsical bent of my father, of the furniture and arrangement of our house and of the conversation of the old women of our village. There were things enough, taking one with another, to chatter about, if one went very fast and knew by instinct when to go round. They pulled with an art of their own the strings of my invention and my memory; and nothing else perhaps, when I thought of such occasions afterwards, gave me so the suspicion of being watched from under cover. It was in any case over *my* life, *my* past and *my* friends alone that we could take anything like our ease; a state of affairs that led them sometimes without the least pertinence to break out into sociable reminders. I was invited—with no visible connexion—to repeat afresh Goody Gosling's celebrated *mot* or to confirm the details already supplied as to the cleverness of the vicarage pony.

It was partly at such junctures as these and partly at quite different ones that, with the turn my matters had now taken, my predicament, as I have called it, grew most sensible. The fact that the days passed for me without another encounter ought, it would have appeared, to have done something toward soothing my nerves. Since the light brush, that second night on the upper landing, of the presence of a woman at the foot of the stair, I had seen nothing, whether in or out of the house, that one had better not have seen. There was many a corner round which I expected to come upon Quint, and many a situation that, in a merely sinister way, would have favoured the appearance of Miss Jessel. The summer had turned, the summer had gone; the autumn had dropped upon Bly and had blown out half our lights. The place, with its grey sky and withered garlands, its bared spaces and scattered dead leaves, was like a theatre after the performance—all strewn with crumpled playbills. There were exactly states of the air, conditions of sound and of stillness, unspeakable impressions of the *kind* of ministering moment, that brought back to me, long enough to catch it, the feeling of the medium in which, that June evening out of doors, I had had my first sight of Quint, and in which too, at those other instants, I had, after seeing him through the window, looked for him in vain in the circle of shrubbery. I recognised the signs, the portents—I recognised the moment, the spot. But they remained unaccompanied and empty, and I continued unmolested; if unmolested one could call a young woman whose sensibility had, in the most extraordinary fashion, not declined but deepened. I had said in my talk with Mrs. Grose on that horrid scene of Flora's by the lake—and had perplexed her by so saying—that it would from that moment distress me much more to lose my power than to keep it. I had then expressed what was vividly in my mind: the truth that, whether the children really saw or not—since, that is, it was not yet definitely proved—I greatly preferred, as a safeguard, the fulness of my own exposure. I was ready to know the very worst that was to be known. What I had then had an ugly glimpse of was that my eyes might be sealed just while theirs were most opened. Well, my eyes *were* sealed, it appeared, at present—a consummation for which it seemed blasphemous not to thank God. There was, alas, a difficulty about that: I would have thanked him with all my soul had I not had in a proportionate measure this conviction of the secret of my pupils.

How can I retrace to-day the strange steps of my obsession? There were times of our being together when I would have been ready to swear that, literally, in my presence, but with my direct sense of it closed, they had visitors who were known and were welcome. Then it was that, had I not been deterred by the very chance that such an injury might prove greater than the injury to be averted, my exaltation would have broken out. "They're here, they're here, you little wretches," I would have cried, "and you can't deny it now!" The little wretches denied it with all the added volume of their sociability and their tenderness, just in the crystal depths of which—like the flash of a fish in a stream—the mockery of their advantage peeped up. The shock had in truth sunk into me still deeper than I knew on the night when, looking out either for Quint or for Miss Jessel under the stars, I had seen there the boy over whose rest I watched and who had immediately brought in with him—had straightway there turned on me—the lovely upward look with which, from the battlements above us, the hideous apparition of Quint had played. If it was a question of a scare my discovery on this occasion had scared me more than any other, and it was essentially in the scared state that I drew my actual conclusions. They harassed me so that sometimes, at odd moments, I shut myself up audibly to rehearse—it was at once a fantastic relief and a renewed despair—the manner in which I might come to the point. I approached it from one side and the other while, in my room, I flung myself about, but I always broke down in the monstrous utterance of names. As they died away on my lips I said to myself that I should indeed help them to represent something infamous if by pronouncing them I should violate as rare a little case of instinctive delicacy as any schoolroom probably had ever known. When I said to myself: "*They* have the manners to be silent, and you, trusted as you are, the baseness to speak!" I felt myself crimson and covered my face with my hands. After these secret scenes I chattered more than ever, going on volubly enough till one of our prodigious palpable hushes occurred—I can call them nothing else—the strange dizzy lift or swim (I try for terms!) into a stillness, a pause of all life, that had nothing to do with the more or less noise we at the moment might be engaged in making and that I could hear through any intensified mirth or quickened recitation or louder strum of the piano. Then it was that the others, the outsiders, were there. Though they were not angels they "passed," as the French say, causing me, while they stayed, to tremble with the fear of their addressing to their younger victims some yet more infernal message or more vivid image than they had thought good enough for myself.

What it was least possible to get rid of was the cruel idea that, whatever I had seen, Miles and Flora saw *more*—things terrible and unguessable and that sprang from dreadful passages of intercourse in the past. Such things naturally left on the surface, for the time, a chill that we vociferously denied we felt; and we had all three, with repetition, got into such splendid training that we went, each time, to mark the close of the incident, almost automatically through the very same movements. It was striking of the children at all events to kiss me inveterately with a wild irrelevance and never to fail—one or the other—of the precious question that had helped us through many a peril. "When do you think he *will* come? Don't you think we *ought* to write?"—there was nothing like that enquiry, we found by experience, for carrying off an awkwardness. "He" of course was their uncle in Harley Street; and we lived in much profusion of theory that he might at any moment arrive to mingle in our circle. It was impossible to have given less encouragement than he had administered to such a doctrine, but if we had not had the doctrine to fall back upon we should have deprived each other of some of our finest exhibitions. He never wrote to them—that may have been selfish, but it was a part of the flattery of his trust of myself; for the way in which a man pays his highest tribute to a woman is apt to be but by the more festal celebration of one of the sacred laws of his comfort. So I held that I carried out the spirit of the pledge given not to appeal to him when I let our young friends understand that their own letters were but charming literary exercises. They were too beautiful to be posted; I kept them myself; I have them all to this hour. This was a rule indeed which only added to the satiric effect of my being plied with the supposition that he might at any moment be among us. It was exactly as if our young friends knew how almost more awkward than anything else that might be for me. There appears to me moreover as I look back no note in all this more extraordinary than the mere fact that, in spite of my tension and of their triumph, I never lost patience with them. Adorable they must in truth have been, I now feel, since I didn't in these days hate them! Would exasperation, however, if relief had longer been postponed, finally have betrayed me? It little matters, for relief arrived. I call it relief though it was only the relief that a snap brings to a strain or the burst of a thunderstorm to a day of suffocation. It was at least change, and it came with a rush.

14

WALKING to church a certain Sunday morning, I had little Miles at my side and his sister, in advance of us and at Mrs. Grose's, well in sight. It was a crisp clear day, the first of its order for some time; the night had brought a touch of frost and the autumn air, bright and sharp, made the church-bells almost gay. It was an odd accident of thought that I should have happened at such a moment to be particularly and very gratefully struck with the obedience of my little charges. Why did they never resent my inexorable, my perpetual society? Something or other had brought nearer home to me that I had all but pinned the boy to my shawl, and that in the way our companions were marshalled before me I might have appeared to provide against some danger of rebellion. I was like a gaoler with an eye to possible surprises and escapes. But all this belonged—I mean their magnificent little surrender—just to the special array of the facts that were most abysmal. Turned out for Sunday by his uncle's tailor, who had had a free hand and a notion of pretty waistcoats and of his grand little air, Miles's whole title to independence, the rights of his sex and situation, were so stamped upon him that if he had suddenly struck for freedom I should have had nothing to say. I was by the strangest of chances wondering how I should meet him when the revolution unmistakeably occurred. I call it a revolution because I now see how, with the word he spoke, the curtain rose on the last act of my dreadful drama and the catastrophe was precipitated. "Look here, my dear, you know," he charmingly said, "when in the world, please, am I going back to school?"

Transcribed here the speech sounds harmless enough, particularly as uttered in the sweet, high, casual pipe with which, at all interlocutors, but above all at his eternal governess, he threw off intonations as if he were tossing roses. There was something in them that always made one "catch," and I caught at any rate now so effectually that I stopped as short as if one of the trees of the park had fallen across the road. There was something new, on the spot, between us, and he was perfectly aware I recognised it, though to enable me to do so he had no need to look a whit less candid and charming than usual. I could feel in him how he already, from my at first finding nothing to reply, perceived the advantage he had gained. I was so slow to find anything that he had plenty of time, after a minute, to continue with his suggestive but inconclusive smile: "You know, my dear, that for a fellow to be with a lady *always*—!" His "my dear" was constantly on his lips for me, and nothing could have expressed more the exact shade of the sentiment with which I desired to inspire my pupils than its fond familiarity. It was so respectfully easy.

But oh how I felt that at present I must pick my own phrases! I remember that, to gain time, I tried to laugh, and I seemed to see in the beautiful face with which he watched me how ugly and queer I looked. "And always with the same lady?" I returned.

He neither blenched nor winked. The whole thing was virtually out between us. "Ah of course she's a jolly 'perfect' lady; but after all I'm a fellow, don't you see? who's—well, getting on."

I lingered there with him an instant ever so kindly. "Yes, you're getting on." Oh but I felt helpless!

I have kept to this day the heartbreaking little idea of how he seemed to know that and to play with it. "And you can't say I've not been awfully good, can you?"

I laid my hand on his shoulder, for though I felt how much better it would have been to walk on I was not yet quite able. "No, I can't say that, Miles."

"Except just that one night, you know—!"

"That one night?" I couldn't look as straight as he.

"Why when I went down—went out of the house."

"Oh yes. But I forget what you did it for."

"You forget?"—he spoke with the sweet extravagance of childish reproach. "Why it was just to show you I could!"

"Oh yes—you could."

"And I can again."

I felt I might perhaps after all succeed in keeping my wits about me. "Certainly. But you won't."

"No, not *that* again. It was nothing."

"It was nothing," I said. "But we must go on."

He resumed our walk with me, passing his hand into my arm. "Then when *am* I going back?"

I wore, in turning it over, my most responsible air. "Were you very happy at school?"

He just considered. "Oh I'm happy enough anywhere!"

"Well then," I quavered, "if you're just as happy here—!"

"Ah but that isn't everything! Of course *you* know a lot—"

"But you hint that you know almost as much?" I risked as he paused.

"Not half I want to!" Miles honestly professed. "But it isn't so much that."

"What is it then?"

"Well—I want to see more life."

"I see; I see." We had arrived within sight of the church and of various persons, including several of the household of Bly, on their way to it and clustered about the door to see us go in. I quickened our step; I wanted to get there before the question between us opened up much further; I reflected hungrily that he would have for more than an hour to be silent; and I thought with envy of the comparative dusk of the pew and of the almost spiritual help of the hassock on which I might bend my knees. I seemed literally to be running a race with some confusion to which he was about to reduce me, but I felt he had got in first when, before we had even entered the churchyard, he threw out—

"I want my own sort!"

It literally made me bound forward. "There aren't many of your own sort, Miles!" I laughed. "Unless perhaps dear little Flora!"

"You really compare me to a baby girl?"

This found me singularly weak. "Don't you then *love* our sweet Flora?"

"If I didn't—and you too; if I didn't—!" he repeated as if retreating for a jump, yet leaving his thought so unfinished that, after we had come into the gate, another stop, which he imposed on me by the pressure of his arm, had become inevitable. Mrs. Grose and Flora had passed into the church, the other worshippers had followed and we were, for the minute, alone among the old thick graves. We had paused, on the path from the gate, by a low oblong table-like tomb.

"Yes, if you didn't—?"

He looked, while I waited, about at the graves. "Well, you know what!" But he didn't move, and he presently produced something that made me drop straight down on the stone slab as if suddenly to rest. "Does my uncle think what *you* think?"

I markedly rested. "How do you know what I think?"

"Ah well, of course I don't; for it strikes me you never tell me. But I mean does *he* know?"

"Know what, Miles?"

"Why the way I'm going on."

I recognised quickly enough that I could make, to this enquiry, no answer that wouldn't involve something of a sacrifice of my employer. Yet it struck me that we were all, at Bly, sufficiently sacrificed to make that venial. "I don't think your uncle much cares."

Miles, on this, stood looking at me. "Then don't you think he can be made to?"

"In what way?"

"Why by his coming down."

"But who'll get him to come down?"

"*I* will!" the boy said with extraordinary brightness and emphasis. He gave me another look charged with that expression and then marched off alone into church.

�֍ 15 ֍

THE business was practically settled from the moment I never followed him. It was a pitiful surrender to agitation, but my being aware of this had somehow no power to restore me. I only sat there on my tomb and read into what our young friend had said to me the fulness of its meaning; by the time I had grasped the whole of which I had also embraced, for absence, the pretext that I was ashamed to offer my pupils and the rest of the congregation such an example of delay. What I said to myself above all was that Miles had got something out of me and that the gage of it for him would be just this awkward collapse. He had got out of me that there was something I was much afraid of, and that he should probably be able to make use of my fear to gain, for his own purpose, more freedom. My fear was of having to deal with the intolerable question of the grounds of his dismissal from school, since that was really but the question of the horrors gathered behind. That his uncle should arrive to treat with me of these things was a solution that, strictly speaking, I ought now to have desired to bring on; but I could so little face the ugliness and the pain of it that I simply procrastinated and lived from hand to mouth. The boy, to my deep discomposure, was immensely in the right, was in a position to say to me: "Either you clear up with my guardian the mystery of this interruption of my studies, or you cease to expect me to lead with you a life that's so unnatural for a boy." What was so unnatural for the particular boy I was concerned with was this sudden revelation of a consciousness and a plan.

That was what really overcame me, what prevented my going in. I walked round the church, hesitating, hovering; I reflected that I had already, with him, hurt myself beyond repair. Therefore I could patch up nothing and it was too extreme an effort to squeeze beside him into the pew: he would be so much more sure than ever to pass his arm into mine and make me sit there for an hour in close mute contact with his commentary on our talk. For the first minute since his arrival I wanted to get away from him. As I paused beneath the high east window and listened to the sounds of worship I was taken with an impulse that might master me, I felt, and completely, should I give it the least encouragement. I might easily put an end to my ordeal by getting away altogether. Here was my chance; there was no one to stop me; I could give the whole thing up—turn my back and bolt. It was only a question of hurrying again, for a few preparations, to the house which the attendance at church of so many of the servants would practically have left unoccupied. No one, in short, could blame me if I should just drive desperately off. What was it to get away if I should get away only till dinner? That would be in a couple of hours, at the end of which—I had the acute prevision—my little pupils would play at innocent wonder about my non-appearance in their train.

"What *did* you do, you naughty bad thing? Why in the world, to worry us so—and take our thoughts off too, don't you know?—did you desert us at the very door?" I couldn't meet such questions nor, as they asked them, their false little lovely eyes; yet it was all so exactly what I should have to meet that, as the prospect grew sharp to me, I at last let myself go.

I got, so far as the immediate moment was concerned, away; I came straight out of the churchyard and, thinking hard, retraced my steps through the park. It seemed to me that by the time I reached the house I had made up my mind to cynical flight. The Sunday stillness both of the approaches and of the interior, in which I met no one, fairly stirred me with a sense of opportunity. Were I to get off quickly this way I should get off without a scene, without a word. My quickness would have to be remarkable, however, and the question of a conveyance was the great one to settle. Tormented, in the hall, with difficulties and obstacles, I remember sinking down at the foot of the staircase—suddenly collapsing there on the lowest step and then, with a revulsion, recalling that it was exactly where, more than a month before, in the darkness of night and just so bowed with evil things, I had seen the spectre of the most horrible of women. At this I was able to straighten myself; I went the rest of the way up; I made, in my turmoil, for the schoolroom, where there were objects belonging to me that I should have to take. But I opened the door to find again, in a flash, my eyes unsealed. In the presence of what I saw I reeled straight back upon resistance.

Seated at my own table in the clear noonday light I saw a person whom, without my previous experience, I should have taken at the first blush for some housemaid who might have stayed at home to look after the place and who, availing herself of rare relief from observation and of the schoolroom table and my pens, ink and paper, had applied herself to the considerable effort of a letter to her sweetheart. There was an effort in the way that, while her arms rested on the table, her hands, with evident weariness, supported her head; but at the moment I took this in I had already become aware that, in spite of my entrance, her attitude strangely persisted. Then it was—with the very act of its announcing itself—that her identity flared up in a change of posture. She rose, not as if she had heard me, but with an indescribable grand melancholy of indifference and detachment, and, within a dozen feet of me, stood there as my vile predecessor. Dishonoured and tragic, she was all before me; but even as I fixed and, for memory, secured it, the awful image passed away. Dark as midnight in her black dress, her haggard beauty and her unutterable woe, she had looked at me long enough to appear to say that her right to sit at my table was as good as mine to sit at hers. While these instants lasted indeed I had the extraordinary chill of a feeling that it was I who was the intruder. It was as a wild protest against it that, actually addressing her—"You terrible miserable woman!"—I heard myself break into a sound that, by the open door, rang through the long passage and the empty house. She looked at me as if she heard me, but I had recovered myself and cleared the air. There was nothing in the room the next minute but the sunshine and the sense that I must stay.

16

I HAD so perfectly expected the return of the others to be marked by a demonstration that I was freshly upset at having to find them merely dumb and discreet about my desertion. Instead of gaily denouncing and caressing me they made no allusion to my having failed them, and I was left, for the time, on perceiving that she too said nothing, to study Mrs. Grose's odd face. I did this to such purpose that I made sure they had in some way bribed her to silence; a silence that, however, I would engage to break down on the first private opportunity. This opportunity came before tea: I secured five minutes with her in the housekeeper's room, where, in the twilight, amid a smell of lately-baked bread, but with the place all swept and garnished, I found her sitting in pained placidity before the fire. So I see her still, so I see her best: facing the flame from her straight chair in the dusky shining room, a large clean picture of the "put away"—of drawers closed and locked and rest without a remedy.

"Oh yes, they asked me to say nothing; and to please them—so long as they were there—of course I promised. But what had happened to you?"

"I only went with you for the walk," I said. "I had then to come back to meet a friend."

She showed her surprise. "A friend—*you*?"

"Oh yes, I've a couple!" I laughed. "But did the children give you a reason?"

"For not alluding to your leaving us? Yes; they said you'd like it better. *Do* you like it better?"

My face had made her rueful. "No, I like it worse!" But after an instant I added: "Did they say why I should like it better?"

"No; Master Miles only said 'We must do nothing but what she likes!'"

"I wish indeed he would! And what did Flora say?"

"Miss Flora was too sweet. She said 'Oh of course, of course!'—and I said the same."

I thought a moment. "You were too sweet too—I can hear you all. But none the less, between Miles and me, it's now all out."

"All out?" My companion stared. "But what, Miss?"

"Everything. It doesn't matter. I've made up my mind. I came home, my dear," I went on, "for a talk with Miss Jessel."

I had by this time formed the habit of having Mrs. Grose literally well in hand in advance of my sounding that note; so that even now, as she bravely blinked under the signal of my word, I could keep her comparatively firm. "A talk! Do you mean she spoke?"

"It came to that. I found her, on my return, in the schoolroom."

"And what did she say?" I can hear the good woman still, and the candour of her stupefaction.

"That she suffers the torments—!"

It was this, of a truth, that made her, as she filled out my picture, gape. "Do you mean," she faltered "—of the lost?"

"Of the lost. Of the damned. And that's why, to share them—" I faltered myself with the horror of it.

But my companion, with less imagination, kept me up. "To share them—?"

"She wants Flora." Mrs. Grose might, as I gave it to her, fairly have fallen away from me had I not been prepared. I still held her there, to show I was. "As I've told you, however, it doesn't matter."

"Because you've made up your mind? But to what?"

"To everything."

"And what do you call 'everything'?"

"Why to sending for their uncle."

"Oh Miss, in pity do," my friend broke out.

"Ah but I will, I *will!* I see it's the only way. What's 'out,' as I told you, with Miles is that if he thinks I'm afraid to—and has ideas of what he gains by that—he shall see he's mistaken. Yes, yes; his uncle shall have it here from me on the spot (and before the boy himself if necessary) that if I'm to be reproached with having done nothing again about more school—"

"Yes, Miss—" my companion pressed me.

"Well, there's that awful reason."

There were now clearly so many of these for my poor colleague that she was excusable for being vague. "But—a—which?"

"Why the letter from his old place."

"You'll show it to the master?"

"I ought to have done so on the instant."

"Oh no!" said Mrs. Grose with decision.

"I'll put it before him," I went on inexorably, "that I can't undertake to work the question on behalf of a child who has been expelled—"

"For we've never in the least known what!" Mrs. Grose declared.

"For wickedness. For what else—when he's so clever and beautiful and perfect? Is he stupid? Is he untidy? Is he infirm? Is he ill-natured? He's exquisite—so it can be only *that;* and that would open up the whole thing. After all," I said, "it's their uncle's fault. If he left here such people—!"

"He didn't really in the least know them. The fault's mine." She had turned quite pale.

"Well, you shan't suffer," I answered.

"The children shan't!" she emphatically returned.

I was silent a while; we looked at each other. "Then what am I to tell him?"

"You needn't tell him anything. *I'll* tell him."

I measured this. "Do you mean you'll write—?" Remembering she couldn't, I caught myself up. "How do you communicate?"

"I tell the bailiff. *He* writes."

"And should you like him to write our story?"

My question had a sarcastic force that I had not fully intended, and it made her after a moment inconsequently break down. The tears were again in her eyes. "Ah Miss, *you* write!"

"Well—to-night," I at last returned; and on this we separated.

✦ 17 ✦

I WENT so far, in the evening, as to make a beginning. The weather had changed back, a great wind was abroad, and beneath the lamp, in my room, with Flora at peace beside me, I sat for a long time before a blank sheet of paper and listened to the lash of the rain and the batter of the gusts. Finally I went out, taking a candle; I crossed the passage and listened a minute at Miles's door. What, under my endless obsession, I had been impelled to listen for was some betrayal of his not being at rest, and I presently caught one, but not in the form I had expected. His voice tinkled out. "I say, you there—come in." It was gaiety in the gloom!

I went in with my light and found him in bed, very wide awake but very much at his ease. "Well, what are *you* up to?" he asked with a grace of sociability in which it occurred to me that Mrs. Grose, had she been present, might have looked in vain for proof that anything was "out."

I stood over him with my candle. "How did you know I was there?"

"Why of course I heard you. Did you fancy you made no noise? You're like a troop of cavalry!" he beautifully laughed.

"Then you weren't asleep?"

"Not much! I lie awake and think."

I had put my candle, designedly, a short way off, and then, as he held out his friendly old hand to me, had sat down on the edge of his bed. "What is it," I asked, "that you think of?"

"What in the world, my dear, but *you?*"

"Ah the pride I take in your appreciation doesn't insist on that! I had so far rather you slept."

"Well, I think also, you know, of this queer business of ours."

I marked the coolness of his firm little hand. "Of what queer business, Miles?"

"Why the way you bring me up. And all the rest!"

I fairly held my breath a minute, and even from my glimmering taper there was light enough to show how he smiled up at me from his pillow. "What do you mean by all the rest?"

"Oh you know, you know!"

I could say nothing for a minute, though I felt as I held his hand and our eyes continued to meet that my silence had all the air of admitting his charge and that nothing in the whole world of reality was perhaps at that moment so fabulous as our actual relation. "Certainly you shall go back to school," I said, "if it be that that troubles you. But not to the old place—we must find another, a better. How could I know it did trouble you, this question, when you never told me so, never spoke of it at all?" His clear listening face, framed in its smooth whiteness, made him for the minute as appealing as some wistful patient in a children's hospital; and I would have given, as the resemblance came to me, all I possessed on earth really to be the nurse or the sister of charity who might have helped to cure him. Well, even as it was I perhaps might help! "Do you know you've never said a word to me about your school—I mean the old one; never mentioned it in any way?"

He seemed to wonder; he smiled with the same loveliness. But he clearly gained time; he waited, he called for guidance. "Haven't I?" It wasn't for *me* to help him—it was for the thing I had met!

Something in his tone and the expression of his face, as I got this from him, set my heart aching with such a pang as it had never yet known; so unutterably touching was it to see his little brain puzzled and his little resources taxed to play, under the spell laid on him, a part of innocence and consistency. "No, never—from the hour you came back. You've never mentioned to me one of your masters, one of your comrades, nor the least little thing that ever happened to you at school. Never, little Miles—no never—have you given me an inkling of anything that *may* have happened there. Therefore you can fancy how much I'm in the dark. Until you came out, that way, this morning, you had since the first hour I saw you scarce even made a reference to anything in your previous life. You seemed so perfectly to accept the present." It was extraordinary how my absolute conviction of his secret precocity—or whatever I might call the poison of an influence that I dared but half-phrase—made him, in spite of the faint breath of his inward trouble, appear as accessible as an older person, forced me to treat him as an intelligent equal. "I thought you wanted to go on as you are."

It struck me that at this he just faintly coloured. He gave, at any rate, like a convalescent slightly fatigued, a languid shake of his head. "I don't—I don't. I want to get away."

"You're tired of Bly?"

"Oh no, I like Bly."

"Well then—?"

"Oh *you* know what a boy wants!"

I felt I didn't know so well as Miles, and I took temporary refuge. "You want to go to your uncle?"

Again, at this, with his sweet ironic face, he made a movement on the pillow. "Ah you can't get off with that!"

I was silent a little, and it was I now, I think, who changed colour. "My dear, I don't want to get off!"

"You can't even if you do. You can't, you can't!"—he lay beautifully staring. "My uncle must come down and you must completely settle things."

"If we do," I returned with some spirit, "you may be sure it will be to take you quite away."

"Well, don't you understand that that's exactly what I'm working for? You'll have to *tell* him—about the way you've let it all drop: you'll have to tell him a tremendous lot!"

The exultation with which he uttered this helped me somehow for the instant to meet him rather more. "And how much will *you*, Miles, have to tell him? There are things he'll ask you!"

He turned it over. "Very likely. But what things?"

"The things you've never told me. To make up his mind what to do with you. He can't send you back—"

"I don't want to go back!" he broke in. "I want a new field."

He said it with admirable serenity, with positive unimpeachable gaiety; and doubtless it was that very note that most evoked for me the poignancy, the unnatural childish tragedy, of his probable reappearance at the end of three months with all this bravado and still more dishonour. It overwhelmed me now that I should never be able to bear that, and it made me let myself go. I threw myself upon him and in the tenderness of my pity I embraced him. "Dear little Miles, dear little Miles—!"

My face was close to his, and he let me kiss him, simply taking it with indulgent good humour. "Well, old lady?"

"Is there nothing—nothing at all that you want to tell me?"

He turned off a little, facing round toward the wall and holding up his hand to look at as one had seen sick children look. "I've told you—I told you this morning."

Oh I was sorry for him! "That you just want me not to worry you?"

He looked round at me now as if in recognition of my understanding him; then ever so gently, "To let me alone," he replied.

There was even a strange little dignity in it, something that made me release him, yet, when I had slowly risen, linger beside him. God knows *I* never wished to harass him, but I felt that merely, at this, to turn my back on him was to abandon or, to put it more truly, lose him. "I've just begun a letter to your uncle," I said.

"Well then, finish it!"

I waited a minute. "What happened before?"

He gazed up at me again. "Before what?"

"Before you came back. And before you went away."

For some time he was silent, but he continued to meet my eyes. "What happened?"

It made me, the sound of the words, in which it seemed to me I caught for the very first time a small faint quaver of consenting consciousness—it made me drop on my knees beside the bed and seize once more the chance of possessing him. "Dear little Miles, dear little Miles, if you *knew* how I want to help you! It's only that, it's nothing but that, and I'd rather die than give you a pain or do you a wrong—I'd rather die than hurt a hair of you. Dear little Miles"—oh I brought it out now even if I *should* go too far—"I just want you to help me to save you!" But I knew in a moment after this that I had gone too far. The answer to my appeal was instantaneous, but it came in the form of an extraordinary blast and chill, a gust of frozen air and a shake of the room as great as if, in the wild wind, the casement had crashed in. The boy gave a loud high shriek which, lost in the rest of the shock of sound, might have seemed, indistinctly, though I was so close to him, a note either of jubilation or of terror. I jumped to my feet again and was conscious of darkness. So for a moment we remained, while I stared about me and saw the drawn curtains unstirred and the window still tight. "Why the candle's out!" I then cried.

"It was I who blew it, dear!" said Miles.

❧ 18 ❧

THE next day, after lessons, Mrs. Grose found a moment to say to me quietly: "Have you written, Miss?"

"Yes—I've written." But I didn't add—for the hour—that my letter, sealed and directed, was still in my pocket. There would be time enough to send it before the messenger should go to the village. Meanwhile there had been on the part of my pupils no more brilliant, more exemplary morning. It was exactly as if they had both had at heart to gloss over any recent little friction. They performed the dizziest feats of arithmetic, soaring quite out of *my* feeble range, and perpetrated, in higher spirits than ever, geographical and historical jokes. It was conspicuous of course in Miles in particular that he appeared to wish to show how easily he could let me down. This child, to my memory, really lives in a setting of beauty and misery that no words can translate; there was a distinction all his own in every impulse he revealed; never was a small natural creature, to the uninformed eye all frankness and freedom, a more ingenious, a more extraordinary little gentleman. I had perpetually to guard against the wonder of contemplation into which my initiated view betrayed me; to check the irrelevant gaze and discouraged sigh in which I constantly both attacked and renounced the enigma of what such a little gentleman could have done that deserved a penalty. Say that, by the dark prodigy I knew, the imagination of all evil *had* been opened up to him: all the justice within me ached for the proof that it could ever have flowered into an act.

He had never at any rate been such a little gentleman as when, after our early dinner on this dreadful day, he came round to me and asked if I shouldn't like him for half an hour to play to me. David playing to Saul could never have shown a finer sense of the occasion. It was literally a charming exhibition of tact, of magnanimity, and quite tantamount to his saying outright: "The true knights we love to read about never push an advantage too far. I know what you mean now: you mean that—to be let alone yourself and not followed up—you'll cease to worry and spy upon me, won't keep me so close to you, will let me go and come. Well, I 'come,' you see—but I don't go! There'll be plenty of time for that. I do really delight in your society and I only want to show you that I contended for a principle." It may be imagined whether I resisted this appeal or failed to accompany him again, hand in hand, to the schoolroom. He sat down at the old piano and played as he had never played; and if there are those who think he had better have been kicking a football I can only say that I wholly agree with them. For at the end of a time that under his influence I had quite ceased to measure I started up with a strange sense of having literally slept at my post. It was after luncheon, and by the schoolroom fire, and yet I hadn't really in the least slept; I had only done something much worse—I had forgotten. Where all this time was Flora? When I put the question to Miles he played on a minute before answering, and then could only say: "Why, my dear, how do *I* know?"—breaking moreover into a happy laugh which immediately after, as if it were a vocal accompaniment, he prolonged into incoherent extravagant song.

I went straight to my room, but his sister was not there; then, before going downstairs, I looked into several others. As she was nowhere about she would surely be with Mrs. Grose, whom in the comfort of that theory I accordingly proceeded in quest of. I found her where I had found her the evening before, but she met my quick challenge with blank scared ignorance. She had only supposed that, after the repast, I had carried off both the children; as to which she was quite in her right, for it was the very first time I had allowed the little girl out of my sight without some special provision. Of course now indeed she might be with the maids, so that the immediate thing was to look for her without an air of alarm. This we promptly arranged between us; but when, ten minutes later and in pursuance of our arrangement, we met in the hall, it was only to report on either side that after guarded enquiries we had altogether failed to trace her. For a minute there, apart from observation, we exchanged mute alarms, and I could feel with what high interest my friend returned me all those I had from the first given her.

"She'll be above," she presently said—"in one of the rooms you haven't searched."

"No; she's at a distance." I had made up my mind. "She has gone out."

Mrs. Grose stared. "Without a hat?"

I naturally also looked volumes. "Isn't that woman always without one?"

"She's with *her?*"

"She's with *her!*" I declared. "We must find them."

My hand was on my friend's arm, but she failed for the moment, confronted with such an account of the matter, to respond to my pressure. She communed, on the contrary, where she stood, with her uneasiness. "And where's Master Miles?"

"Oh *he's* with Quint. They'll be in the schoolroom."

"Lord, Miss!" My view, I was myself aware—and therefore I suppose my tone—had never yet reached so calm an assurance.

"The trick's played," I went on; "they've successfully worked their plan. He found the most divine little way to keep me quiet while she went off."

" 'Divine'?" Mrs. Grose bewilderedly echoed.

"Infernal then!" I almost cheerfully rejoined. "He has provided for himself as well. But come!"

She had helplessly gloomed at the upper regions. "You leave him—?"

"So long with Quint? Yes—I don't mind that now."

She always ended at these moments by getting possession of my hand, and in this manner she could at present still stay me. But after gasping an instant at my sudden resignation, "Because of your letter?" she eagerly brought out.

I quickly, by way of answer, felt for my letter, drew it forth, held it up, and then, freeing myself, went and laid it on the great hall-table. "Luke will take it," I said as I came back. I reached the house-door and opened it; I was already on the steps.

My companion still demurred: the storm of the night and the early morning had dropped, but the afternoon was damp and grey. I came down to the drive while she stood in the doorway. "You go with nothing on?"

"What do I care when the child has nothing? I can't wait to dress," I cried, "and if you must do so I leave you. Try meanwhile yourself upstairs."

"With *them?*" Oh on this the poor woman promptly joined me!

✺ 19 ✺

WE went straight to the lake, as it was called at Bly, and I dare say rightly called, though it may have been a sheet of water less remarkable than my untravelled eyes supposed it. My acquaintance with sheets of water was small, and the pool of Bly, at all events on the few occasions of my consenting, under the protection of my pupils, to affront its surface in the old flat-bottomed boat moored there for our use, had impressed me both with its extent and its agitation. The usual place of embarkation was half a mile from the house, but I had an intimate conviction that, wherever Flora might be, she was not near home. She had not given me the slip for any small adventure, and, since the day of the very great one that I had shared with her by the pond, I had been aware, in our walks, of the quarter to which she most inclined. This was why I had now given to Mrs. Grose's steps so marked a direction—a direction making her, when she perceived it, oppose a resistance that showed me she was freshly mystified. "You're going to the water, Miss?—you think she's *in*—?"

"She may be, though the depth is, I believe, nowhere very great. But what I judge most likely is that she's on the spot from which, the other day, we saw together what I told you."

"When she pretended not to see—?"

"With that astounding self-possession! I've always been sure she wanted to go back alone. And now her brother has managed it for her."

Mrs. Grose still stood where she had stopped. "You suppose they really *talk* of them?"

I could meet this with an assurance! "They say things that, if we heard them, would simply appal us."

"And if she *is* there—?"

"Yes?"

"Then Miss Jessel is?"

"Beyond a doubt. You shall see."

"Oh thank you!" my friend cried, planted so firm that, taking it in, I went straight on without her. By the time I reached the pool, however, she was close behind me, and I knew that, whatever, to her apprehension, might befall me, the exposure of sticking to me struck her as her least danger. She exhaled a moan of relief as we at last came in sight of the greater part of the water without a sight of the child. There was no trace of Flora on that nearer side of the bank where my observation of her had been most startling, and none on the opposite edge, where, save for a margin of some twenty yards, a thick copse came down to the pond. This expanse, oblong in shape, was so narrow compared to its length that, with its ends out of view, it might have been taken for a scant river. We looked at the empty stretch, and then I felt the suggestion in my friend's eyes. I knew what she meant and I replied with a negative headshake.

"No, no; wait! She has taken the boat."

My companion stared at the vacant mooring-place and then again across the lake. "Then where is it?"

"Our not seeing it is the strongest of proofs. She has used it to go over, and then has managed to hide it."

"All alone—that child?"

"She's not alone, and at such times she's not a child: she's an old, old woman." I scanned all the visible shore while Mrs. Grose took again, into the queer element I offered her, one of her plunges of submission; then I pointed out that the boat might perfectly be in a small refuge formed by one of the recesses of the pool, an indentation masked, for the hither side, by a projection of the bank and by a clump of trees growing close to the water.

"But if the boat's there, where on earth's *she?*" my colleague anxiously asked.

"That's exactly what we must learn." And I started to walk further.

"By going all the way round?"

"Certainly, far as it is. It will take us but ten minutes, yet it's far enough to have made the child prefer not to walk. She went straight over."

"Laws!" cried my friend again: the chain of my logic was ever too strong for her. It dragged her at my heels even now, and when we had got halfway round—a devious tiresome process, on ground much broken and by a path choked with overgrowth—I paused to give her breath. I sustained her with a grateful arm, assuring her that she might hugely help me; and this started us afresh, so that in the course of but few minutes more we reached a point from which we found the boat to be where I had supposed it. It had been intentionally left as much as possible out of sight and was tied to one of the stakes of a fence that came, just there, down to the brink and that had been an assistance to disembarking. I recognised, as I looked at the pair of short thick oars, quite safely drawn up, the prodigious character of the feat for a little girl; but I had by this time lived too long among wonders and had panted to too many livelier measures. There was a gate in the fence, through which we passed, and that brought us after a trifling interval more into the open. Then "There she is!" we both exclaimed at once.

Flora, a short way off, stood before us on the grass and smiled as if her performance had now become complete. The next thing she did, however, was to stoop straight down and pluck—quite as if it were all she was there for—a big ugly spray of withered fern. I at once felt sure she had just come out of the copse. She waited for us, not herself taking a step, and I was conscious of the rare solemnity with which we presently approached her. She smiled and smiled, and we met; but it was all done in a silence by this time flagrantly ominous. Mrs. Grose was the first to break the spell: she threw herself on her knees and, drawing the child to her breast, clasped in a long embrace the little tender yielding body. While this dumb convulsion lasted I could only watch it—which I did the more intently when I saw Flora's face peep at me over our companion's shoulder. It was serious now—the flicker had left it; but it strengthened the pang with which I at that moment envied Mrs. Grose the simplicity of *her* relation. Still, all this while, nothing more passed between us save that Flora had let her foolish fern again drop to the ground. What she and I had virtually said to each other was that pretexts were useless now. When Mrs. Grose finally got up she kept the child's hand, so that the two were still before me; and the singular reticence of our communion was even more marked in the frank look she addressed me. "I'll be hanged," it said, "if *I'll* speak!"

It was Flora who, gazing all over me in candid wonder, was the first. She was struck with our bareheaded aspect. "Why where are your things?"

"Where yours are, my dear!" I promptly returned.

She had already got back her gaiety and appeared to take this as an answer quite sufficient. "And where's Miles?" she went on.

There was something in the small valour of it that quite finished me: these three words from her were in a flash like the glitter of a drawn blade the jostle of the cup that my hand for weeks and weeks had held high and full to the brim and that now, even before speaking, I felt overflow in a deluge. "I'll tell you if you'll tell *me*—" I heard myself say, then heard the tremor in which it broke.

"Well, what?"

Mrs. Grose's suspense blazed at me, but it was too late now, and I brought the thing out handsomely. "Where, my pet, is Miss Jessel?"

 20

Just as in the churchyard with Miles, the whole thing was upon us. Much as I had made of the fact that this name had never once, between us, been sounded, the quick smitten glare with which the child's face now received it fairly likened my breach of the silence to the smash of a pane of glass. It added to the interposing cry, as if to stay the blow, that Mrs. Grose at the same instant uttered over my violence—the shriek of a creature scared, or rather wounded, which, in turn, within a few seconds, was completed by a gasp of my own. I seized my colleague's arm. "She's there, she's there!"

Miss Jessel stood before us on the opposite bank exactly as she had stood the other time, and I remember, strangely, as the first feeling now produced in me, my thrill of joy at having brought on a proof. She was there, so I was justified; she was there, so I was neither cruel nor mad. She was there for poor scared Mrs. Grose, but she was there most for Flora; and no moment of my monstrous time was perhaps so extraordinary as that in which I consciously threw out to her—with the sense that, pale and ravenous demon as she was, she would catch and understand it—an inarticulate message of gratitude. She rose erect on the spot my friend and I had lately quitted, and there wasn't in all the long reach of her desire an inch of her evil that fell short. This first vividness of vision and emotion were things of a few seconds, during which Mrs. Grose's dazed blink across to where I pointed struck me as showing that she too at last saw, just as it carried my own eyes precipitately to the child. The revelation then of the manner in which Flora was affected startled me in truth far more than it would have done to find her also merely agitated, for direct dismay was of course not what I had expected. Prepared and on her guard as our pursuit had actually made her, she would repress every betrayal; and I was therefore at once shaken by my first glimpse of the particular one for which I had not allowed. To see her, without a convulsion of her small pink face, not even feign to glance in the direction of the prodigy I announced, but only, instead of that, turn at *me* an expression of hard still gravity, an expression absolutely new and unprecedented and that appeared to read and accuse and judge me—this was a stroke that somehow converted the little girl herself into a figure portentous. I gasped at her coolness even though my certitude of her thoroughly seeing was never greater than at that instant, and then, in the immediate need to defend myself, I called her passionately to witness. "She's there, you little unhappy thing—there, there, *there,* and you know it as well as you know me!" I had said shortly before to Mrs. Grose that she was not at these times a child, but an old, old woman, and my description of her couldn't have been more strikingly confirmed than in the way in which, for all notice of this, she simply showed me, without an expressional concession or admission, a countenance of deeper and deeper, of indeed suddenly quite fixed reprobation. I was by this time—if I can put the whole thing at all together—more appalled at what I may properly call her manner than at anything else, though it was quite simultaneously that I became aware of having Mrs. Grose also, and very formidably, to reckon with. My elder companion, the next moment, at any rate, blotted out everything but her own flushed face and her loud shocked protest, a burst of high disapproval. "What a dreadful turn, to be sure, Miss! Where on earth do you see anything?"

I could only grasp her more quickly yet, for even while she spoke the hideous plain presence stood undimmed and undaunted. It had already lasted a minute, and it lasted while I continued, seizing my colleague, quite thrusting her at it and presenting her to it, to insist with my pointing hand. "You don't see her exactly as *we* see?—you mean to say you don't now—*now?* She's as big as a blazing fire! Only look, dearest woman, *look*—!" She looked, just as I did, and gave me, with her deep groan of negation, repulsion, compassion—the mixture with her pity of her relief at her exemption—a sense, touching to me even then, that she would have backed me up if she had been able. I might well have needed that, for with this hard blow of the proof that her eyes were hopelessly sealed I felt my own situation horribly crumble, I felt—I *saw*—my livid predecessor press, from her position, on my defeat, and I took the measure, more than all, of what I should have from this instant to deal with in the astounding little attitude of Flora. Into this attitude Mrs. Grose immediately and violently entered, breaking, even while there pierced through my sense of ruin a prodigious private triumph, into breathless reassurance.

"She isn't there, little lady, and nobody's there—and you never see nothing, my sweet! How can poor Miss Jessel—when poor Miss Jessel's dead and buried? *We* know, don't we, love?"—and she appealed, blundering in, to the child. "It's all a mere mistake and a worry and a joke—and we'll go home as fast as we can!"

Our companion, on this, had responded with a strange quick primness of propriety, and they were again, with Mrs. Grose on her feet, united, as it were, in shocked opposition to me. Flora continued to fix me with her small mask of disaffection, and even at that minute I prayed God to forgive me for seeming to see that, as she stood there holding tight to our friend's dress, her incomparable childish beauty had suddenly failed, had quite vanished. I've said it already—she was literally, she was hideously hard; she had turned common and almost ugly. "I don't know what you mean. I see nobody. I see nothing. I never *have*. I think you're cruel. I don't like you!" Then, after this deliverance, which might have been that of a vulgarly pert little girl in the street, she hugged Mrs. Grose more closely and buried in her skirts the dreadful little face. In this position she launched an almost furious wail. "Take me away, take me away—oh take me away from *her!*"

"From *me?*" I panted.

"From you—from you!" she cried.

Even Mrs. Grose looked across at me dismayed; while I had nothing to do but communicate again with the figure that, on the opposite bank, without a movement, as rigidly still as if catching, beyond the interval, our voices, was as vividly there for my disaster as it was not there for my service. The wretched child had spoken exactly as if she had got from some outside source each of her stabbing little words, and I could therefore, in the full despair of all I had to accept, but sadly shake my head at her. "If I had ever doubted all my doubt would at present have gone. I've been living with the miserable truth, and now it has only too much closed round me. Of course I've lost you: I've interfered, and you've seen, under *her* dictation"—with which I faced, over the pool again, our infernal witness—"the easy and perfect way to meet it. I've done my best, but I've lost you. Good-bye." For Mrs. Grose I had an imperative, an almost frantic "Go, go!" before which, in infinite distress, but mutely possessed of the little girl and clearly convinced, in spite of her blindness, that something awful had occurred and some collapse engulfed us, she retreated, by the way we had come, as fast as she could move.

Of what first happened when I was left alone I had no subsequent memory. I only knew that at the end of, I suppose, a quarter of an hour, an odorous dampness and roughness, chilling and piercing my trouble, had made me understand that I must have thrown myself, on my face, to the ground and given way to a wildness of grief. I must have lain there long and cried and wailed, for when I raised my head the day was almost done. I got up and looked a moment, through the twilight, at the grey pool and its blank haunted edge, and then I took, back to the house, my dreary and difficult course. When I reached the gate in the fence the boat, to my surprise, was gone, so that I had a fresh reflexion to make on Flora's extraordinary command of the situation. She passed that night, by the most tacit and, I should add, were not the word so grotesque a false note, the happiest of arrangements, with Mrs. Grose. I saw neither of them on my return, but on the other hand I saw, as by an ambiguous compensation, a great deal of Miles. I saw—I can use no other phrase—so much of him that it fairly measured more than it had ever measured. No evening I had passed at Bly was to have had the portentous quality of this one; in spite of which—and in spite also of the deeper depths of consternation that had opened beneath my feet—there was literally, in the ebbing actual, an extraordinarily sweet sadness. On reaching the house I had never so much as looked for the boy: I had simply gone straight to my room to change what I was wearing and to take in, at a glance, much material testimony to Flora's rupture. Her little belongings had all been removed. When later, by the schoolroom fire, I was served with tea by the usual maid, I indulged, on the article of my other pupil, in no enquiry whatever. He had his freedom now—he might have it to the end! Well, he did have it; and it consisted—in part at least—of his coming in at about eight o'clock and sitting down with me in silence. On the removal of the tea-things I had blown out the candles and drawn my chair closer: I was conscious of a mortal coldness and felt as if I should never again be warm. So when he appeared I was sitting in the glow with my thoughts. He paused a moment by the door as if to look at me; then—as if to share them—came to the other side of the hearth and sank into a chair. We sat there in absolute stillness; yet he wanted, I felt, to be with me.

✠ 21 ✠

BEFORE a new day, in my room, had fully broken, my eyes opened to Mrs. Grose, who had come to my bedside with worse news. Flora was so markedly feverish that an illness was perhaps at hand; she had passed a night of extreme unrest, a night agitated above all by fears that had for their subject not in the least her former but wholly her present governess. It was not against the possible re-entrance of Miss Jessel on the scene that she protested—it was conspicuously and passionately against mine. I was at once on my feet, and with an immense deal to ask; the more that my friend had discernibly now girded her loins to meet me afresh. This I felt as soon as I had put to her the question of her sense of the child's sincerity as against my own. "She persists in denying to you that she saw, or has ever seen, anything?"

My visitor's trouble truly was great. "Ah Miss, it isn't a matter on which I can push her! Yet it isn't either, I must say, as if I much needed to. It has made her, every inch of her, quite old."

"Oh I see her perfectly from here. She resents, for all the world like some high little personage, the imputation on her truthfulness and, as it were, her respectability. 'Miss Jessel indeed—*she!*' Ah she's 'respectable,' the chit! The impression she gave me there yesterday was, I assure you, the very strangest of all: it was quite beyond any of the others. I *did* put my foot in it! She'll never speak to me again."

Hideous and obscure as it all was, it held Mrs. Grose briefly silent; then she granted my point with a frankness which, I made sure, had more behind it. "I think indeed, Miss, she never will. She do have a grand manner about it!"

"And that manner"—I summed it up—"is practically what's the matter with her now."

Oh that manner, I could see in my visitor's face, and not a little else besides! "She asks me every three minutes if I think you're coming in."

"I see—I see." I too, on my side, had so much more than worked it out. "Has she said to you since yesterday—except to repudiate her familiarity with anything so dreadful—a single other word about Miss Jessel?"

"Not one, Miss. And of course, you know," my friend added, "I took it from her by the lake that just then and there at least there *was* nobody."

"Rather! And naturally you take it from her still."

"I don't contradict her. What else can I do?"

"Nothing in the world! You've the cleverest little person to deal with. They're made them—their two friends, I mean—still cleverer even than nature did; for it was wondrous material to play on! Flora has now her grievance, and she'll work it to the end."

"Yes, Miss; but to *what* end?"

"Why that of dealing with me to her uncle. She'll make me out to him the lowest creature—!"

I winced at the fair show of the scene in Mrs. Grose's face; she looked for a minute as if she sharply saw them together. "And him who thinks so well of you!"

"He has an odd way—it comes over me now," I laughed, "—of proving it! But that doesn't matter. What Flora wants of course is to get rid of me."

My companion bravely concurred. "Never again to so much as look at you."

"So that what you've come to me now for," I asked, "is to speed me on my way?" Before she had time to reply, however, I had her in check. "I've a better idea—the result of my reflexions. My going *would* seem the right thing, and on Sunday I was terribly near it. Yet that won't do. It's *you* who must go. You must take Flora."

My visitor, at this, did speculate. "But where in the world—?"

"Away from here. Away from *them*. Away, even most of all, now, from me. Straight to her uncle."

"Only to tell on you—?"

"No, not 'only'! To leave me, in addition, with my remedy."

She was still vague. "And what *is* your remedy?"

"Your loyalty, to begin with. And then Miles's."

She looked at me hard. "Do you think he—?"

"Won't, if he has the chance, turn on me? Yes, I venture still to think it. At all events I want to try. Get off with his sister as soon as possible and leave me with him alone." I was amazed, myself, at the spirit I had still in reserve, and therefore perhaps a trifle the more disconcerted at the way in which, in spite of this fine example of it, she hesitated. "There's one thing, of course," I went on: "they mustn't, before she goes, see each other for three seconds." Then it came over me that, in spite of Flora's presumable sequestration from the instant of her return from the pool, it might already be too late. "Do you mean," I anxiously asked, "that they *have* met?"

At this she quite flushed. "Ah, Miss, I'm not such a fool as that! If I've been obliged to leave her three or four times, it has been each time with one of the maids, and at present, though she's alone, she's locked in safe. And yet—and yet!" There were too many things.

"And yet what?"

"Well, are you so sure of the little gentleman?"

"I'm not sure of anything but *you*. But I have, since last evening, a new hope. I think he wants to give me an opening. I do believe that—poor little exquisite wretch!—he wants to speak. Last evening, in the firelight and the silence, he sat with me for two hours as if it were just coming."

Mrs. Grose looked hard through the window at the grey gathering day. "And did it come?"

"No, though I waited and waited I confess it didn't, and it was without a breach of the silence, or so much as a faint allusion to his sister's condition and absence, that we at last kissed for good-night. All the same," I continued, "I can't, if her uncle sees her, consent to his seeing her brother without my having given the boy—and most of all because things have got so bad—a little more time."

My friend appeared on this ground more reluctant than I could quite understand. "What do you mean by more time?"

"Well, a day or two—really to bring it out. He'll then be on *my* side—of which you see the importance. If nothing comes I shall only fail, and you at the worst have helped me by doing on your arrival in town whatever you may have found possible." So I put it before her, but she continued for a little so lost in other reasons that I came again to her aid. "Unless indeed," I wound up, "you really want *not* to go."

I could see it, in her face, at last clear itself: she put out her hand to me as a pledge. "I'll go—I'll go. I'll go this morning."

I wanted to be very just. "If you *should* wish still to wait I'd engage she shouldn't see me."

"No, no: it's the place itself. She must leave it." She held me a moment with heavy eyes, then brought out the rest. "Your idea's the right one. I myself, Miss—"

"Well?"

"I can't stay."

The look she gave me with it made me jump at possibilities. "You mean that, since yesterday, you *have* seen—?"

She shook her head with dignity. "I've *heard*—!"

"Heard?"

"From that child—horrors! There!" she sighed with tragic relief. "On my honour, Miss, she says things—!" But at this evocation she broke down; she dropped with a sudden cry upon my sofa and, as I had seen her do before, gave way to all the anguish of it.

It was quite in another manner that I for my part let myself go. "Oh thank God!"

She sprang up again at this, drying her eyes with a groan. " 'Thank God'?"

"It so justifies me!"

"It does that, Miss!"

I couldn't have desired more emphasis, but I just waited. "She's so horrible?"

I saw my colleague scarce knew how to put it. "Really shocking."

"And about me?"

"About you, Miss—since you must have it. It's beyond everything, for a young lady; and I can't think wherever she must have picked up—"

"The appalling language she applies to me? I can then!" I broke in with a laugh that was doubtless significant enough.

It only in truth left my friend still more grave. "Well, perhaps I ought to also—since I've heard some of it before! Yet I can't bear it," the poor woman went on while with the same movement she glanced, on my dressing-table, at the face of my watch. "But I must go back."

I kept her, however. "Ah if you can't bear it—!"

"How can I stop with her, you mean? Why just *for* that: to get her away. Far from this," she pursued, "far from *them*—"

"She may be different? she may be free?" I seized her almost with joy. "Then in spite of yesterday you *believe*—"

"In such doings?" Her simple description of them required, in the light of her expression, to be carried no further, and she gave me the whole thing as she had never done. "I believe."

Yes, it was a joy, and we were still shoulder to shoulder: if I might continue sure of that I should care but little what else happened. My support in the presence of disaster would be the same as it had been in my early need of confidence, and if my friend would answer for my honesty I would answer for all the rest. On the point of taking leave of her, none the less, I was to some extent embarrassed. "There's one thing of course—it occurs to me—to remember. My letter giving the alarm will have reached town before you."

I now felt still more how she had been beating about the bush and how weary at last it had made her. "Your letter won't have got there. Your letter never went."

"What then became of it?"

"Goodness knows! Master Miles—"

"Do you mean *he* took it?" I gasped.

She hung fire, but she overcame her reluctance. "I mean that I saw yesterday, when I came back with Miss Flora, that it wasn't where you had put it. Later in the evening I had the chance to question Luke, and he declared that he had neither noticed nor touched it." We could only exchange, on this, one of our deeper mutual soundings, and it was Mrs. Grose who first brought up the plumb with an almost elate "You see!"

"Yes, I see that if Miles took it instead he probably will have read it and destroyed it.

"And don't you see anything else?"

I faced her a moment with a sad smile. "It strikes me that by this time your eyes are open even wider than mine."

They proved to be so indeed, but she could still almost blush to show it. "I make out now what he must have done at school." And she gave, in her simple sharpness, an almost droll disillusioned nod. "He stole!"

I turned it over—I tried to be more judicial. "Well—perhaps."

She looked as if she found me unexpectedly calm. "He stole *letters!*"

She couldn't know my reasons for a calmness after all pretty shallow; so I showed them off as I might. "I hope then it was to more purpose than in this case! The note, at all events, that I put on the table yesterday," I pursued, "will have given him so scant an advantage—for it contained only the bare demand for an interview—that he's already much ashamed of having gone so far for so little, and that what he had on his mind last evening was precisely the need of confession." I seemed to myself for the instant to have mastered it, to see it all. "Leave us, leave us"—I was already, at the door, hurrying her off. "I'll get it out of him. He'll meet me. He'll confess. If he confesses he's saved. And if he's saved—"

"Then *you* are?" The dear woman kissed me on this, and I took her farewell. "I'll save you without him!" she cried as she went.

⚜ 22 ⚜

YET it was when she had got off—and I missed her on the spot—that the great pinch really came. If I had counted on what it would give me to find myself alone with Miles I quickly recognised that it would give me at least a measure. No hour of my stay in fact was so assailed with apprehensions as that of my coming down to learn that the carriage containing Mrs. Grose and my younger pupil had already rolled out of the gates. Now I *was,* I said to myself, face to face with the elements, and for much of the rest of the day, while I fought my weakness, I could consider that I had been supremely rash. It was a tighter place still than I had yet turned round in; all the more that, for the first time, I could see in the aspect of others a confused reflexion of the crisis. What had happened naturally caused them all to stare; there was too little of the explained, throw out whatever we might, in the suddenness of my colleague's act. The maids and the men looked blank; the effect of which on my nerves was an aggravation until I saw the necessity of making it a positive aid. It was in short by just clutching the helm that I avoided total wreck; and I dare say that, to bear up at all, I became that morning very grand and very dry. I welcomed the consciousness that I was charged with much to do, and I caused it to be known as well that, left thus to myself, I was quite remarkably firm. I wandered with that manner, for the next hour or two, all over the place and looked, I have no doubt, as if I were ready for any onset. So, for the benefit of whom it might concern, I paraded with a sick heart.

The person it appeared least to concern proved to be, till dinner, little Miles himself. My perambulations had given me meanwhile no glimpse of him, but they had tended to make more public the change taking place in our relation as a consequence of his having at the piano, the day before, kept me, in Flora's interest, so beguiled and befooled. The stamp of publicity had of course been fully given by her confinement and departure, and the change itself was now ushered in by our non-observance of the regular custom of the schoolroom. He had already disappeared when, on my way down, I pushed open his door, and I learned below that he had break-fasted—in the presence of a couple of the maids—with Mrs. Grose and his sister. He had then gone out, as he said, for a stroll; than which nothing, I reflected, could better have expressed his frank view of the abrupt transformation of my office. What he would now permit this office to consist of was yet to be settled: there was at least a queer relief—I mean for myself in especial—in the re-nouncement of one pretension. If so much had sprung to the sur-face I scarce put it too strongly in saying that what had perhaps sprung highest was the absurdity of our prolonging the fiction that I had anything more to teach him. It sufficiently stuck out that, by tacit little tricks in which even more than myself he car-ried out the care for my dignity, I had had to appeal to him to let me off straining to meet him on the ground of his true capacity. He had at any rate his freedom now; I was never to touch it again: as I had amply shown, moreover, when, on his joining me in the school-room the previous night, I uttered, in reference to the interval just concluded, neither challenge nor hint. I had too much, from this moment, my other ideas. Yet when he at last arrived the difficulty of applying them, the accumulations of my problem, were brought straight home to me by the beautiful little presence on which what had occurred had as yet, for the eye, dropped neither stain nor shadow.

To mark, for the house, the high state I cultivated I decreed that my meals with the boy should be served, as we called it, downstairs; so that I had been awaiting him in the ponderous pomp of the room outside the window of which I had had from Mrs. Grose, that first scared Sunday, my flash of something it would scarce have done to call light. Here at present I felt afresh—for I had felt it again and again—how my equilibrium depended on the success of my rigid will, the will to shut my eyes as tight as possible to the truth that what I had to deal with was, revoltingly, against nature. I could only get on at all by taking "nature" into my confidence and my account, by treating my monstrous ordeal as a push in a direction unusual, of course, and unpleasant, but demanding after all, for a fair front, only another turn of the screw of ordinary human virtue. No attempt, none the less, could well require more tact than just this attempt to supply, one's self, *all* the nature. How could I put even a little of that article into a suppression of reference to what had occurred? How on the other hand could I make a reference without a new plunge into the hideous obscure? Well, a sort of answer, after a time, had come to me, and it was so far confirmed as that I was met, incontestably, by the quickened vision of what was rare in my little companion. It was indeed as if he had found even now—as he had so often found at lessons—still some other delicate way to ease me off. Wasn't there light in the fact which, as we shared our solitude, broke out with a specious glitter it had never yet quite worn?—the fact that (opportunity aiding, precious opportunity which had now come) it would be preposterous, with a child so endowed, to forego the help one might wrest from absolute intelligence? What had his intelligence been given him for but to save him? Mightn't one, to reach his mind, risk the stretch of a stiff arm across his character? It was as if, when we were face to face in the dining-room, he had literally shown me the way. The roast mutton was on the table and I had dispensed with attendance. Miles, before he sat down, stood a moment with his hands in his pockets and looked at the joint, on which he seemed on the point of passing some humorous judgement. But what he presently produced was : "I say, my dear, is she really very awfully ill?"

"Little Flora? Not so bad but that she'll presently be better. London will set her up. Bly had ceased to agree with her. Come here and take your mutton."

He alertly obeyed me, carried the plate carefully to his seat and, when he was established, went on. "Did Bly disagree with her so terribly all at once?"

"Not so suddenly as you might think. One had seen it coming on."

"Then why didn't you get her off before?"

"Before what?"

"Before she became too ill to travel."

I found myself prompt. "She's *not* too ill to travel; she only might have become so if she had stayed. This was just the moment to seize. The journey will dissipate the influence"—oh I was grand!—"and carry it off."

"I see, I see"—Miles, for that matter, was grand too. He settled to his repast with the charming little "table manner" that, from the day of his arrival, had relieved me of all grossness of admonition. Whatever he had been expelled from school for, it wasn't for ugly feeding. He was irreproachable, as always, to-day; but was unmistakeably more conscious. He was discernibly trying to take for granted more things than he found, without assistance, quite easy; and he dropped into peaceful silence while he felt his situation. Our meal was of the briefest—mine a vain pretence, and I had the things immediately removed. While this was done Miles stood again with his hands in his little pockets and his back to me—stood and looked out of the wide window through which, that other day, I had seen what pulled me up. We continued silent while the maid was with us—as silent, it whimsically occurred to me, as some young couple who, on their wedding-journey, at the inn, feel shy in the presence of the waiter. He turned round only when the waiter had left us. "Well—so we're alone!"

❈ 23 ❈

"Oh more or less." I imagine my smile was pale. "Not absolutely. We shouldn't like that!" I went on.

"No—I suppose we shouldn't. Of course we've the others."

"We've the others—we've indeed the others," I concurred.

"Yet even though we have them," he returned, still with his hands in his pockets and planted there in front of me, "they don't much count, do they?"

I made the best of it, but I felt wan. "It depends on what you call 'much'!"

"Yes"—with all accommodation—"everything depends!" On this, however, he faced to the window again and presently reached it with his vague restless cogitating step. He remained there a while with his forehead against the glass, in contemplation of the stupid shrubs I knew and the dull things of November. I had always my hypocrisy of "work," behind which I now gained the sofa. Steadying myself with it there as I had repeatedly done at those moments of torment that I have described as the moments of my knowing the children to be given to something from which I was barred, I sufficiently obeyed my habit of being prepared for the worst. But an extraordinary impression dropped on me as I extracted a meaning from the boy's embarrassed back—none other than the impression that I was not barred now. This inference grew in a few minutes to sharp intensity and seemed bound up with the direct perception that it was positively *he* who was. The frames and squares of the great window were a kind of image, for him, of a kind of failure. I felt that I saw him, in any case, shut in or shut out. He was admirable but not comfortable: I took it in with a throb of hope. Wasn't he looking through the haunted pane for something he couldn't see?—and wasn't it the first time in the whole business that he had known such a lapse? The first, the very first: I found it a splendid portent. It made him anxious, though he watched himself; he had been anxious all day and, even while in his usual sweet little manner he sat at table, had needed all his small strange genius to give it a gloss. When he at last turned round to meet me it was almost as if this genius had succumbed. "Well, I think I'm glad Bly agrees with *me!*"

"You'd certainly seem to have seen, these twenty-four hours, a good deal more of it than for some time before. I hope," I went on bravely, "that you've been enjoying yourself."

"Oh yes, I've been ever so far; all round about—miles and miles away. I've never been so free."

He had really a manner of his own, and I could only try to keep up with him. "Well, do you like it?"

He stood there smiling; then at last he put into two words—"Do *you?*"—more discrimination than I had ever heard two words contain. Before I had time to deal with that, however, he continued as if with the sense that this was an impertinence to be softened. "Nothing could be more charming than the way you take it, for of course if we're alone together now it's you that are alone most. But I hope," he threw in, "you don't particularly mind!"

"Having to do with you?" I asked. "My dear child, how can I help minding? Though I've renounced all claim to your company—you're so beyond me—I at least greatly enjoy it. What else should I stay on for?"

He looked at me more directly, and the expression of his face, graver now, struck me as the most beautiful I had ever found in it. "You stay on just for *that?*"

"Certainly. I stay on as your friend and from the tremendous interest I take in you till something can be done for you that may be more worth your while. That needn't surprise you." My voice trembled so that I felt it impossible to suppress the shake. "Don't you remember how I told you, when I came and sat on your bed the night of the storm, that there was nothing in the world I wouldn't do for you?"

"Yes, yes!" He, on his side, more and more visibly nervous, had a tone to master; but he was so much more successful than I that, laughing out through his gravity, he could pretend we were pleasantly jesting. "Only that, I think, was to get me to do something for *you!*"

"It was partly to get you to do something," I conceded. "But, you know, you didn't do it."

"Oh yes," he said with the brightest superficial eagerness, "you wanted me to tell you something."

"That's it. Out, straight out. What you have on your mind, you know."

"Ah then is *that* what you've stayed over for?"

He spoke with a gaiety through which I could still catch the finest little quiver of resentful passion; but I can't begin to express the effect upon me of an implication of surrender even so faint. It was as if what I had yearned for had come at last only to astonish me.

"Well, yes—I may as well make a clean breast of it. It was precisely for that."

He waited so long that I supposed it for the purpose of repudiating the assumption on which my action had been founded; but what he finally said was: "Do you mean now—here?"

"There couldn't be a better place or time." He looked round him uneasily, and I had the rare—oh the queer!—impression of the very first symptom I had seen in him of the approach of immediate fear. It was as if he were suddenly afraid of me—which struck me indeed as perhaps the best thing to make him. Yet in the very pang of the effort I felt it vain to try sternness, and I heard myself the next instant so gentle as to be almost grotesque. "You want so to go out again?"

"Awfully!" He smiled at me heroically, and the touching little bravery of it was enhanced by his actually flushing with pain. He had picked up his hat, which he had brought in, and stood twirling it in a way that gave me, even as I was just nearly reaching port, a perverse horror of what I was doing. To do it in *any* way was an act of violence, for what did it consist of but the obtrusion of the idea of grossness and guilt on a small helpless creature who had been for me a revelation of the possibilities of beautiful intercourse? Wasn't it base to create for a being so exquisite a mere alien awkwardness? I suppose I now read into our situation a clearness it couldn't have had at the time, for I seem to see our poor eyes already lighted with some spark of a prevision of the anguish that was to come. So we circled about with terrors and scruples, fighters not daring to close. But it was for each other we feared! That kept us a little longer suspended and unbruised. "I'll tell you everything," Miles said—"I mean I'll tell you anything you like. You'll stay on with me, and we shall both be all right, and I *will* tell you—I *will*. But not now."

"Why not now?"

My insistence turned him from me and kept him once more at his window in a silence during which, between us, you might have heard a pin drop. Then he was before me again with the air of a person for whom, outside, some one who had frankly to be reckoned with was waiting. "I have to see Luke."

I had not yet reduced him to quite so vulgar a lie, and I felt proportionately ashamed. But, horrible as it was, his lies made up my truth. I achieved thoughtfully a few loops of my knitting. "Well then go to Luke, and I'll wait for what you promise. Only in return for that satisfy, before you leave me, one very much smaller request."

He looked as if he felt he had succeeded enough to be able still a little to bargain. "Very much smaller—?"

"Yes, a mere fraction of the whole. Tell me"—oh my work preoccupied me, and I was off-hand!—"if, yesterday afternoon, from the table in the hall, you took, you know, my letter."

✼ 24 ✼

My grasp of how he received this suffered for a minute from something that I can describe only as a fierce split of my attention—a stroke that at first, as I sprang straight up, reduced me to the mere blind movement of getting hold of him, drawing him close and, while I just fell for support against the nearest piece of furniture, instinctively keeping him with his back to the window. The appearance was full upon us that I had already had to deal with here: Peter Quint had come into view like a sentinel before a prison. The next thing I saw was that, from outside, he had reached the window, and then I knew that, close to the glass and glaring in through it, he offered once more to the room his white face of damnation. It represents but grossly what took place within me at the sight to say that on the second my decision was made; yet I believe that no woman so overwhelmed ever in so short a time recovered her command of the *act*. It came to me in the very horror of the immediate presence that the act would be, seeing and facing what I saw and faced, to keep the boy himself unaware. The inspiration—I can call it by no other name—was that I felt how voluntarily, how transcendently, I *might*. It was like fighting with a demon for a human soul, and when I had fairly so appraised it I saw how the human soul—held out, in the tremor of my hands, at arm's length—had a perfect dew of sweat on a lovely childish forehead. The face that was close to mine was as white as the face against the glass, and out of it presently came a sound, not low nor weak, but as if from much further away, that I drank like a waft of fragrance.

"Yes—I took it."

At this, with a moan of joy, I enfolded, I drew him close; and while I held him to my breast, where I could feel in the sudden fever of his little body the tremendous pulse of his little heart, I kept my eyes on the thing at the window and saw it move and shift its posture. I have likened it to a sentinel, but its slow wheel, for a moment, was rather the prowl of a baffled beast. My present quickened courage, however, was such that, not too much to let it through, I had to shade, as it were, my flame. Meanwhile the glare of the face was again at the window, the scoundrel fixed as if to watch and wait. It was the very confidence that I might now defy him, as well as the positive certitude, by this time, of the child's unconsciousness, that made me go on. "What did you take it for?"

"To see what you said about me."

"You opened the letter?"

"I opened it."

My eyes were now, as I held him off a little again, on Miles's own face, in which the collapse of mockery showed me how complete was the ravage of uneasiness. What was prodigious was that at last, by my success, his sense was sealed and his communication stopped: he knew that he was in presence, but knew not of what, and knew still less that I also was and that I did know. And what did this strain of trouble matter when my eyes went back to the window only to see that the air was clear again and—by my personal triumph—the influence quenched? There was nothing there. I felt that the cause was mine and that I should surely get *all*. "And you found nothing!"—I let my elation out.

He gave the most mournful, thoughtful little headshake. "Nothing."

"Nothing, nothing!" I almost shouted in my joy.

"Nothing, nothing," he sadly repeated.

I kissed his forehead; it was drenched. "So what have you done with it?"

"I've burnt it."

"Burnt it?" It was now or never. "Is that what you did at school?"

Oh what this brought up! "At school?"

"Did you take letters?—or other things?"

"Other things?" He appeared now to be thinking of something far off and that reached him only through the pressure of his anxiety. Yet it did reach him. "Did I *steal?*"

I felt myself redden to the roots of my hair as well as wonder if it

were more strange to put to a gentleman such a question or to see
him take it with allowances that gave the very distance of his fall in
the world. "Was it for that you mightn't go back?"

The only thing he felt was rather a dreary little surprise. "Did you
know I mightn't go back?"

"I know everything."

He gave me at this the longest and strangest look. "Everything?"

"Everything. Therefore *did* you—?" But I couldn't say it again.

Miles could, very simply. "No. I didn't steal."

My face must have shown him I believed him utterly; yet my
hands—but it was for pure tenderness—shook him as if to ask him
why, if it was all for nothing, he had condemned me to months of
torment. "What then did you do?"

He looked in vague pain all round the top of the room and drew
his breath, two or three times over, as if with difficulty. He might
have been standing at the bottom of the sea and raising his eyes to
some faint green twilight. "Well—I said things."

"Only that?"

"They thought it was enough!"

"To turn you out for?"

Never, truly, had a person "turned out" shown so little to explain
it as this little person! He appeared to weigh my question, but in a
manner quite detached and almost helpless. "Well, I suppose I
oughtn't."

"But to whom did you say them?"

He evidently tried to remember, but it dropped—he had lost it. "I
don't know!"

He almost smiled at me in the desolation of his surrender, which
was indeed practically, by this time, so complete that I ought to have
left it there. But I was infatuated—I was blind with victory, though
even then the very effect that was to have brought him so much
nearer was already that of added separation. "Was it to every one?" I
asked.

"No; it was only to—" But he gave a sick little headshake. "I don't
remember their names."

"Were they then so many?"

"No—only a few. Those I liked."

Those he liked? I seemed to float not into clearness, but into a
darker obscure, and within a minute there had come to me out of my

very pity the appalling alarm of his being perhaps innocent. It was for the instant confounding and bottomless, for if he *were* innocent what then on earth was I? Paralysed, while it lasted, by the mere brush of the question, I let him go a little, so that, with a deep-drawn sigh, he turned away from me again; which, as he faced toward the clear window, I suffered, feeling that I had nothing now there to keep him from. "And did they repeat what you said?" I went on after a moment.

He was soon at some distance from me, still breathing hard and again with the air, though now without anger for it, of being confined against his will. Once more, as he had done before, he looked up at the dim day as if, of what had hitherto sustained him, nothing was left but an unspeakable anxiety. "Oh yes," he nevertheless replied—"they must have repeated them. To those *they* liked," he added.

There was somehow less of it than I had expected; but I turned it over. "And these things came round—?"

"To the masters? Oh yes!" he answered very simply. "But I didn't know they'd tell."

"The masters? They didn't—they've never told. That's why I ask you."

He turned to me again his little beautiful fevered face. "Yes, it was too bad."

"Too bad?"

"What I suppose I sometimes said. To write home."

I can't name the exquisite pathos of the contradiction given to such a speech by such a speaker; I only know that the next instant I heard myself throw off with homely force: "Stuff and nonsense!" But the next after that I must have sounded stern enough. "What *were* these things?"

My sternness was all for his judge, his executioner; yet it made him avert himself again, and that movement made *me,* with a single bound and an irrepressible cry, spring straight upon him. For there again, against the glass, as if to blight his confession and stay his answer, was the hideous author of our woe—the white face of damnation. I felt a sick swim at the drop of my victory and all the return of my battle, so that the wildness of my veritable leap only served as a great betrayal. I saw him, from the midst of my act, meet it with a divination, and on the perception that even now he only

356 THE HENRY JAMES READER

guessed, and that the window was still to his own eyes free, I let the impulse flame up to convert the climax of his dismay into the very proof of his liberation. "No more, no more, no more!" I shrieked to my visitant as I tried to press him against me.

"Is she *here?*" Miles panted as he caught with his sealed eyes the direction of my words. Then as his strange "she" staggered me and, with a gasp, I echoed it, "Miss Jessel, Miss Jessel!" he with sudden fury gave me back.

I seized, stupefied, his supposition—some sequel to what we had done to Flora, but this made me only want to show him that it was better still than that. "It's not Miss Jessel! But it's at the window—straight before us. It's *there*—the coward horror, there for the last time!"

At this, after a second in which his head made the movement of a baffled dog's on a scent and then gave a frantic little shake for air and light, he was at me in a white rage, bewildered, glaring vainly over the place and missing wholly, though it now, to my sense, filled the room like the taste of poison, the wide overwhelming presence. "It's *he?*"

I was so determined to have all my proof that I flashed into ice to challenge him. "Whom do you mean by 'he'?"

"Peter Quint—you devil!" His face gave again, round the room, its convulsed supplication. "*Where?*"

They are in my ears still, his supreme surrender of the name and his tribute to my devotion. "What does he matter now, my own?—what will he *ever* matter? *I* have you," I launched at the beast, "but he has lost you for ever!" Then for the demonstration of my work, "There, *there!*" I said to Miles.

But he had already jerked straight round, stared, glared again, and seen but the quiet day. With the stroke of the loss I was so proud of he uttered the cry of a creature hurled over an abyss, and the grasp with which I recovered him might have been that of catching him in his fall. I caught him, yes, I held him—it may be imagined with what a passion; but at the end of a minute I began to feel what it truly was that I held. We were alone with the quiet day, and his little heart, dispossessed, had stopped.

The Beast in the Jungle

Written when James reached his sixtieth year, "The Beast in the Jungle" is perhaps the novelist's greatest tale. He coupled it, in his own mind, with his ghostly tales: he seems to have thought of it as a picture of a haunted state, a man obsessed by the strange notion that something extraordinary would happen to him, that some beast in the jungle of his life was waiting for him and would spring at an unexpected moment. The idea which prompted James to write the story was that this strange hero's adventure should turn out to be a "negative" adventure. Nothing really happens to him. There is no beast. He is haunted only by his own fears.

Out of this fancy James created a picture of two beings, in a city that is but a murmuring background to their meetings and their curious dissociated conversations. Step by step, in a few scenes, a whole lifetime is revealed to us in all its dreary mental self-indulgence and intellectual egotism. The story unfolds the power of an obsession, and an individual's inability to see that which is closest to him. In a way the tale also seems to speak of another theme that haunted James in these late years—the theme of "too late." The beast springs within John Marcher when May Bartram is no longer upon the scene; it is as if her departure were needed to show him how blind he has been. A story of mood and atmosphere and melancholy, it places James among the moderns, those who have sought to read the existential riddle of man and to recognize the tragedy of the individual alienated from the world and from love.

L. E.

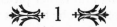

1

WHAT determined the speech that startled him in the course of their encounter scarcely matters, being probably but some words spoken by himself quite without intention—spoken as they lingered and slowly moved together after their renewal of acquaintance. He had been conveyed by friends an hour or two before to the house at which she was staying; the party of visitors at the other house, of whom he was one, and thanks to whom it was his theory, as always, that he was lost in the crowd, had been invited over to luncheon. There had been after luncheon much dispersal, all in the interest of the original motive, a view of Weatherend itself and the fine things, intrinsic features, pictures, heirlooms, treasures of all the arts, that made the place almost famous; and the great rooms were so numerous that guests could wander at their will, hang back from the principal group and in cases where they took such matters with the last seriousness give themselves up to mysterious appreciations and measurements. There were persons to be observed, singly or in couples, bending toward objects in out-of-the-way corners with their hands on their knees and their heads nodding quite as with the emphasis of an excited sense of smell. When they were two they either mingled their sounds of ecstasy or melted into silences of even deeper import, so that there were aspects of the occasion that gave it for Marcher much the air of the "look round," previous to a sale highly advertised, that excites or quenches, as may be, the dream of acquisition. The dream of acquisition at Weatherend would have had to be wild indeed, and John Marcher found himself, among such suggestions, disconcerted almost equally by the presence of those who knew too much and by that of those who knew nothing. The great rooms caused so much poetry and history to press upon him that he needed some straying apart to feel in a proper relation with them, though this impulse was not, as happened, like the gloating of some of his companions, to be compared to the movements of a dog sniffing a cupboard. It had an issue promptly enough in a direction that was not to have been calculated.

It led, briefly, in the course of the October afternoon, to his closer meeting with May Bartram, whose face, a reminder, yet not quite a remembrance, as they sat much separated at a very long table, had begun merely by troubling him rather pleasantly. It affected him as the sequel of something of which he had lost the beginning. He knew it, and for the time quite welcomed it, as a continuation, but didn't know what it continued, which was an interest or an amusement the greater as he was also somehow aware—yet without a direct sign from her—that the young woman herself hadn't lost the thread. She hadn't lost it, but she wouldn't give it back to him, he saw, without some putting forth of his hand for it; and he not only saw that, but saw several things more, things odd enough in the light of the fact that at the moment some accident of grouping brought them face to face he was still merely fumbling with the idea that any contact between them in the past would have had no importance. If it had had no importance he scarcely knew why his actual impression of her should so seem to have so much; the answer to which, however, was that in such a life as they all appeared to be leading for the moment one could but take things as they came. He was satisfied, without in the least being able to say why, that this young lady might roughly have ranked in the house as a poor relation; satisfied also that she was not there on a brief visit, but was more or less a part of the establishment—almost a working, a remunerated part. Didn't she enjoy at periods a protection that she paid for by helping, among other services, to show the place and explain it, deal with the tiresome people, answer questions about the dates of the building, the styles of the furniture, the authorship of the pictures, the favourite haunts of the ghost? It wasn't that she looked as if you could have given her shillings—it was impossible to look less so. Yet when she finally drifted toward him, distinctly handsome, though ever so much older—older than when he had seen her before—it might have been as an effect of her guessing that he had, within the couple of hours, devoted more imagination to her than to all the others put together, and had thereby penetrated to a kind of truth that the others were too stupid for. She *was* there on harder terms than any one; she was there as a consequence of things suffered, one way and another, in the interval of years; and she remembered him very much as she was remembered—only a good deal better.

By the time they at last thus came to speech they were alone in one of the rooms—remarkable for a fine portrait over the chimney-place—out of which their friends had passed, and the charm of it was that even before they had spoken they had practically arranged with each other to stay behind for talk. The charm, happily, was in other things too—partly in there being scarce a spot at Weatherend without something to stay behind for. It was in the way the autumn day looked into the high windows as it waned; the way the red light, breaking at the close from under a low sombre sky, reached out in a long shaft and played over old wainscots, old tapestry, old gold, old colour. It was most of all perhaps in the way she came to him as if, since she had been turned on to deal with the simpler sort, he might, should he choose to keep the whole thing down, just take her mild attention for a part of her general business. As soon as he heard her voice, however, the gap was filled up and the missing link supplied; the slight irony he divined in her attitude lost its advantage. He almost jumped at it to get there before her. "I met you years and years ago in Rome. I remember all about it." She confessed to disappointment—she had been so sure he didn't; and to prove how well he did he began to pour forth the particular recollections that popped up as he called for them. Her face and her voice, all at his service now, worked the miracle—the impression operating like the torch of a lamplighter who touches into flame, one by one, a long row of gas-jets. Marcher flattered himself the illumination was brilliant, yet he was really still more pleased on her showing him, with amusement, that in his haste to make everything right he had got most things rather wrong. It hadn't been at Rome—it had been at Naples; and it hadn't been eight years before—it had been more nearly ten. She hadn't been, either, with her uncle and aunt, but with her mother and her brother; in addition to which it was not with the Pembles *he* had been, but with the Boyers, coming down in their company from Rome—a point on which she insisted, a little to his confusion, and as to which she had her evidence in hand. The Boyers she had known, but didn't know the Pembles, though she had heard of them, and it was the people he was with who had made them acquainted. The incident of the thunderstorm that had raged round them with such violence as to drive them for refuge into an excavation—this incident had not occurred at the Palace of the Cæsars, but at Pompeii, on an occasion when they had been present there at an important find.

He accepted her amendments, he enjoyed her corrections, though the moral of them was, she pointed out, that he *really* didn't remember the least thing about her; and he only felt it as a drawback that when all was made strictly historic there didn't appear much of anything left. They lingered together still, she neglecting her office—for from the moment he was so clever she had no proper right to him—and both neglecting the house, just waiting as to see if a memory or two more wouldn't again breathe on them. It hadn't taken them many minutes, after all, to put down on the table, like the cards of a pack, those that constituted their respective hands; only what came out was that the pack was unfortunately not perfect—that the past, invoked, invited, encouraged, could give them, naturally, no more than it had. It had made them anciently meet—her at twenty, him at twenty-five; but nothing was so strange, they seemed to say to each other, as that, while so occupied, it hadn't done a little more for them. They looked at each other as with the feeling of an occasion missed; the present would have been so much better if the other, in the far distance, in the foreign land, hadn't been so stupidly meagre. There weren't apparently, all counted, more than a dozen little old things that had succeeded in coming to pass between them; trivialities of youth, simplicities of freshness, stupidities of ignorance, small possible germs, but too deeply buried—too deeply (didn't it seem?) to sprout after so many years. Marcher could only feel he ought to have rendered her some service—saved her from a capsized boat in the bay or at least recovered her dressing-bag, filched from her cab in the streets of Naples by a lazzarone with a stiletto. Or it would have been nice if he could have been taken with fever all alone at his hotel, and she could have come to look after him, to write to his people, to drive him out in convalescence. *Then* they would be in possession of the something or other that their actual show seemed to lack. It yet somehow presented itself, this show, as too good to be spoiled; so that they were reduced for a few minutes more to wondering a little helplessly why—since they seemed to know a certain number of the same people—their reunion had been so long averted. They didn't use that name for it, but their delay from minute to minute to join the others was a kind of confession that they didn't quite want it to be a failure. Their attempted supposition of reasons for their not having met but showed how little they knew of each other. There came in fact a moment when Marcher felt a positive pang. It was vain to pretend she was an old friend, for all the communities were wanting, in spite of which it was as an old friend that he saw she would have suited him. He had new ones enough—was surrounded with them for instance on the stage of the other house; as a new one he probably wouldn't have so much as noticed her. He would have liked to invent something, get her to make-believe with him that some passage of a romantic or critical kind *had* originally occurred. He was really almost reaching out in imagination—as against time—for something that would do, and saying to himself that if it didn't come this sketch of a fresh start would show for quite awkwardly bungled. They would separate, and now for no second or no third chance. They would have tried and not succeeded. Then it was, just at the turn, as he afterwards made it out to himself, that, everything else failing, she herself decided to take up the case and, as it were, save the situation. He felt as soon as she spoke that she had been consciously keeping back what she said and hoping to get on without it; a scruple in her that immensely touched him when, by the end of three or four minutes more, he was able to measure it. What she brought out, at any rate, quite cleared the air and supplied the link—the link it was so odd he should frivolously have managed to lose.

"You know you told me something I've never forgotten and that again and again has made me think of you since; it was that tremendously hot day when we went to Sorrento, across the bay, for the breeze. What I allude to was what you said to me, on the way back, as we sat under the awning of the boat enjoying the cool. Have you forgotten?"

He had forgotten and was even more surprised than ashamed. But the great thing was that he saw in this no vulgar reminder of any "sweet" speech. The vanity of women had long memories, but she was making no claim on him of a compliment or a mistake. With another woman, a totally different one, he might have feared the recall possibly even some imbecile "offer." So, in having to say that he had indeed forgotten, he was conscious rather of a loss than of a gain; he already saw an interest in the matter of her mention. "I try to think—but I give it up. Yet I remember the Sorrento day."

"I'm not very sure you do," May Bartram after a moment said; "and I'm not very sure I ought to want you to. It's dreadful to bring a person back at any time to what he was ten years before. If you've lived away from it," she smiled, "so much the better."

"Ah if *you* haven't why should I?" he asked.

"Lived away, you mean, from what I myself was?"

"From what *I* was. I was of course an ass," Marcher went on; "but I would rather know from you just the sort of ass I was than—from the moment you have something in your mind—not know anything."

Still, however, she hesitated. "But if you've completely ceased to be that sort—?"

"Why I can then all the more bear to know. Besides, perhaps I haven't."

"Perhaps. Yet if you haven't," she added, "I should suppose you'd remember. Not indeed that *I* in the least connect with my impression the invidious name you use. If I had only thought you foolish," she explained, "the thing I speak of wouldn't so have remained with me. It was about yourself." She waited as if it might come to him; but as, only meeting her eyes in wonder, he gave no sign, she burnt her ships. "Has it ever happened?"

Then it was that, while he continued to stare, a light broke for him and the blood slowly came to his face, which began to burn with recognition. "Do you mean I told you—?" But he faltered, lest what came to him shouldn't be right, lest he should only give himself away.

"It was something about yourself that it was natural one shouldn't forget—that is if one remembered you at all. That's why I ask you," she smiled, "if the thing you then spoke of has ever come to pass?"

Oh then he saw, but he was lost in wonder and found himself embarrassed. This, he also saw, made her sorry for him, as if her allusion had been a mistake. It took him but a moment, however, to feel it hadn't been, much as it had been a surprise. After the first little shock of it her knowledge on the contrary began, even if rather strangely, to taste sweet to him. She was the only other person in the world then who would have it, and she had had it all these years, while the fact of his having so breathed his secret had unaccountably faded from him. No wonder they couldn't have met as if nothing had happened. "I judge," he finally said, "that I know what you mean. Only I had strangely enough lost any sense of having taken you so far into my confidence."

"Is it because you've taken so many others as well?"

"I've taken nobody. Not a creature since then."

"So that I'm the only person who knows?"

"The only person in the world."

"Well," she quickly replied, "I myself have never spoken. I've never, never repeated of you what you told me." She looked at him so that he perfectly believed her. Their eyes met over it in such a way that he was without a doubt. "And I never will."

She spoke with an earnestness that, as if almost excessive, put him at ease about her possible derision. Somehow the whole question was a new luxury to him—that is from the moment she was in possession. If she didn't take the sarcastic view she clearly took the sympathetic, and that was what he had had, in all the long time, from no one whomsoever. What he felt was that he couldn't at present have begun to tell her, and yet could profit perhaps exquisitely by the accident of having done so of old. "Please don't then. We're just right as it is."

"Oh I am," she laughed, "if you are!" To which she added: "Then you do still feel in the same way?"

It was impossible he shouldn't take to himself that she was really interested, though it all kept coming as perfect surprise. He had thought of himself so long as abominably alone, and lo he wasn't alone a bit. He hadn't been, it appeared, for an hour—since those moments on the Sorrento boat. It was *she* who had been, he seemed to see as he looked at her—she who had been made so by the graceless fact of his lapse of fidelity. To tell her what he had told her—what had it been but to ask something of her? something that she had given, in her charity, without his having, by a remembrance, by a return of the spirit, failing another encounter, so much as thanked her. What he had asked of her had been simply at first not to laugh at him. She had beautifully not done so for ten years, and she was not doing so now. So he had endless gratitude to make up. Only for that he must see just how he had figured to her. "What, exactly, was the account I gave—?"

"Of the way you did feel? Well, it was very simple. You said you had had from your earliest time, as the deepest thing within you, the sense of being kept for something rare and strange, possibly prodigious and terrible, that was sooner or later to happen to you, that you had in your bones the foreboding and the conviction of, and that would perhaps overwhelm you."

"Do you call that very simple?" John Marcher asked.

She thought a moment. "It was perhaps because I seemed, as you spoke, to understand it."

"You do understand it?" he eagerly asked.

Again she kept her kind eyes on him. "You still have the belief?"

"Oh!" he exclaimed helplessly. There was too much to say.

"Whatever it's to be," she clearly made out, "it hasn't yet come."

He shook his head in complete surrender now. "It hasn't yet come. Only, you know, it isn't anything I'm to *do,* to achieve in the world, to be distinguished or admired for. I'm not such an ass as *that.* It would be much better, no doubt, if I were."

"It's to be something you're merely to suffer?"

"Well, say to wait for—to have to meet, to face, to see suddenly break out in my life; possibly destroying all further consciousness, possibly annihilating me; possibly, on the other hand, only altering everything, striking at the root of all my world and leaving me to the consequences, however they shape themselves."

She took this in, but the light in her eyes continued for him not to be that of mockery. "Isn't what you describe perhaps but the expectation—or at any rate the sense of danger, familiar to so many people—of falling in love?"

John Marcher wondered. "Did you ask me that before?"

"No—I wasn't so free-and-easy then. But it's what strikes me now."

"Of course," he said after a moment, "it strikes you. Of course it strikes *me.* Of course what's in store for me may be no more than that. The only thing is," he went on, "that I think if it had been that I should by this time know."

"Do you mean because you've *been* in love?" And then as he but looked at her in silence: "You've been in love, and it hasn't meant such a cataclysm, hasn't proved the great affair?"

"Here I am, you see. It hasn't been overwhelming."

"Then it hasn't been love," said May Bartram.

"Well, I at least thought it was. I took it for that—I've taken it till now. It was agreeable, it was delightful, it was miserable," he explained. "But it wasn't strange. It wasn't what *my* affair's to be."

"You want something all to yourself—something that nobody else knows or *has* known?"

"It isn't a question of what I 'want'—God knows I don't want anything. It's only a question of the apprehension that haunts me—that I live with day by day."

He said this so lucidly and consistently that he could see it further impose itself. If she hadn't been interested before she'd have been interested now. "Is it a sense of coming violence?"

Evidently now too again he liked to talk of it. "I don't think of it as—when it does come—necessarily violent. I only think of it as natural and as of course above all unmistakeable. I think of it simply as *the* thing. *The* thing will of itself appear natural."

"Then how will it appear strange?"

Marcher bethought himself. "It won't—to *me*."

"To whom then?"

"Well," he replied, smiling at last, "say to you."

"Oh then I'm to be present?"

"Why you *are* present—since you know."

"I see." She turned it over. "But I mean at the catastrophe."

At this, for a minute, their lightness gave way to their gravity; it was as if the long look they exchanged held them together. "It will only depend on yourself—if you'll watch with me."

"Are you afraid?" she asked.

"Don't leave me *now*," he went on.

"Are you afraid?" she repeated.

"Do you think me simply out of my mind?" he pursued instead of answering. "Do I merely strike you as a harmless lunatic?"

"No," said May Bartram. "I understand you. I believe you."

"You mean you feel how my obsession—poor old thing!—may correspond to some possible reality?"

"To some possible reality."

"Then you *will* watch with me?"

She hesitated, then for the third time put her question. "Are you afraid?"

"Did I tell you I was—at Naples?"

"No, you said nothing about it."

"Then I don't know. And I should *like* to know," said John Marcher. "You'll tell me yourself whether you think so. If you'll watch with me you'll see."

"Very good then." They had been moving by this time across the room, and at the door, before passing out, they paused as for the full wind-up of their understanding. "I'll watch with you," said May Bartram.

❧ 2 ❧

THE fact that she "knew"—knew and yet neither chaffed him nor betrayed him—had in a short time begun to constitute between them a goodly bond, which became more marked when, within the year that followed their afternoon at Weatherend, the opportunities for meeting multiplied. The event that thus promoted these occasions was the death of the ancient lady her great-aunt, under whose wing, since losing her mother, she had to such an extent found shelter, and who, though but the widowed mother of the new successor to the property, had succeeded—thanks to a high tone and a high temper—in not forfeiting the supreme position at the great house. The deposition of this personage arrived but with her death, which, followed by many changes, made in particular a difference for the young woman in whom Marcher's expert attention had recognised from the first a dependent with a pride that might ache though it didn't bristle. Nothing for a long time had made him easier than the thought that the aching must have been much soothed by Miss Bartram's now finding herself able to set up a small home in London. She had acquired property, to an amount that made that luxury just possible, under her aunt's extremely complicated will, and when the whole matter began to be straightened out, which indeed took time, she let him know that the happy issue was at last in view. He had seen her again before that day, both because she had more than once accompanied the ancient lady to town and because he had paid another visit to the friends who so conveniently made of Weatherend one of the charms of their own hospitality. These friends had taken him back there; he had achieved there again with Miss Bartram some quiet detachment; and he had in London succeeded in persuading her to more than one brief absence from her aunt. They went together, on these latter occasions, to the National Gallery and the South Kensington Museum, where, among vivid reminders, they talked of Italy at large—not now attempting to recover, as at first, the taste of their youth and their ignorance. That recovery, the first day at Weatherend, had served its purpose well, had given them quite enough; so that they were, to Marcher's sense, no longer hovering about the headwaters of their stream, but had felt their boat pushed sharply off and down the current.

They were literally afloat together; for our gentleman this was marked, quite as marked as that the fortunate cause of it was just the buried treasure of her knowledge. He had with his own hands dug up this little hoard, brought to light—that is to within reach of the dim day constituted by their discretions and privacies—the object of value the hiding-place of which he had, after putting it into the ground himself, so strangely, so long forgotten. The rare luck of his having again just stumbled on the spot made him indifferent to any other question; he would doubtless have devoted more time to the odd accident of his lapse of memory if he hadn't been moved to devote so much to the sweetness, the comfort, as he felt, for the future, that this accident itself had helped to keep fresh. It had never entered into his plan that any one should "know," and mainly for the reason that it wasn't in him to tell any one. That would have been impossible, for nothing but the amusement of a cold world would have waited on it. Since, however, a mysterious fate had opened his mouth betimes, in spite of him, he would count that a compensation and profit by it to the utmost. That the right person *should* know tempered the asperity of his secret more even than his shyness had permitted him to imagine; and May Bartram was clearly right, because—well, because there she was. Her knowledge simply settled it; he would have been sure enough by this time had she been wrong. There was that in his situation, no doubt, that disposed him too much to see her as a mere confidant, taking all her light for him from the fact—the fact only—of her interest in his predicament; from her mercy, sympathy, seriousness, her consent not to regard him as the funniest of the funny. Aware, in fine, that her price for him was just in her giving him this constant sense of his being admirably spared, he was careful to remember that she had also a life of her own, with things that might happen to *her*, things that in friendship one should likewise take account of. Something fairly remarkable came to pass with him, for that matter, in this connexion—something represented by a certain passage of his consciousness, in the suddenest way, from one extreme to the other.

He had thought himself, so long as nobody knew, the most disinterested person in the world, carrying his concentrated burden, his perpetual suspense, ever so quietly, holding his tongue about it, giving others no glimpse of it nor of its effect upon his life, asking of them no allowance and only making on his side all those that were asked. He hadn't disturbed people with the queerness of their having to know a haunted man, though he had had moments of rather special temptation on hearing them say they were forsooth "unsettled." If they were as unsettled as he was—he who had never been settled for an hour in his life—they would know what it meant. Yet it wasn't, all the same, for him to make them, and he listened to them civilly enough. This was why he had such good—though possibly such rather colourless—manners; this was why, above all, he could regard himself, in a greedy world, as decently—as in fact perhaps even a little sublimely—unselfish. Our point is accordingly that he valued this character quite sufficiently to measure his present danger of letting it lapse, against which he promised himself to be much on his guard. He was quite ready, none the less, to be selfish just a little, since surely no more charming occasion for it had come to him. "Just a little," in a word, was just as much as Miss Bartram, taking one day with another, would let him. He never would be in the least coercive, and would keep well before him the lines on which consideration for her—the very highest—ought to proceed. He would thoroughly establish the heads under which her affairs, her requirements, her peculiarities—he went so far as to give them the latitude of that name—would come into their intercourse. All this naturally was a sign of how much he took the intercourse itself for granted. There was nothing more to be done about *that*. It simply existed; had sprung into being with her first penetrating question to him in the autumn light there at Weatherend. The real form it should have taken on the basis that stood out large was the form of their marrying. But the devil in this was that the very basis itself put marrying out of the question. His conviction, his apprehension, his obsession, in short, wasn't a privilege he could invite a woman to share; and that consequence of it was precisely what was the matter with him. Something or other lay in wait for him, amid the twists and the turns of the months and the years, like a crouching beast in the jungle. It signified little whether the crouching beast were destined to slay him or to be slain. The definite point was the inevitable spring of the creature; and the definite lesson from that was that a man of feeling didn't cause himself to be accompanied by a lady on a tiger-hunt. Such was the image under which he had ended by figuring his life.

They had at first, none the less, in the scattered hours spent together, made no allusion to that view of it; which was a sign he was handsomely alert to give that he didn't expect, that he in fact didn't care, always to be talking about it. Such a feature in one's outlook was really like a hump on one's back. The difference it made every minute of the day existed quite independently of discussion. One discussed of course *like* a hunchback, for there was always, if nothing else, the hunchback face. That remained, and she was watching him; but people watched best, as a general thing, in silence, so that such would be predominantly the manner of their vigil. Yet he didn't want, at the same time, to be tense and solemn; tense and solemn was what he imagined he too much showed for with other people. The thing to be, with the one person who knew, was easy and natural—to make the reference rather than be seeming to avoid it, to avoid it rather than be seeming to make it, and to keep it, in any case, familiar, facetious even, rather than pedantic and portentous. Some such consideration as the latter was doubtless in his mind for instance when he wrote pleasantly to Miss Bartram that perhaps the great thing he had so long felt as in the lap of the gods was no more than this circumstance, which touched him so nearly, of her acquiring a house in London. It was the first allusion they had yet again made, needing any other hitherto so little; but when she replied, after having given him the news, that she was by no means satisfied with such a trifle as the climax to so special a suspense, she almost set him wondering if she hadn't even a larger conception of singularity for him than he had for himself. He was at all events destined to become aware little by little, as time went by, that she was all the while looking at his life, judging it, measuring it, in the light of the thing she knew, which grew to be at last, with the consecration of the years, never mentioned between them save as "the real truth" about him. That had always been his own form of reference to it, but she adopted the form so quietly that, looking back at the end of a period, he knew there was no moment at which it was traceable that she had, as he might say, got inside his idea, or exchanged the attitude of beautifully indulging for that of still more beautifully believing him.

It was always open to him to accuse her of seeing him but as the most harmless of maniacs, and this, in the long run—since it covered so much ground—was his easiest description of their friendship. He had a screw loose for her, but she liked him in spite of it and was practically, against the rest of the world, his kind wise keeper, unremunerated but fairly amused and, in the absence of other near ties, not disreputably occupied. The rest of the world of course thought him queer, but she, she only, knew how, and above all why, queer; which was precisely what enabled her to dispose the concealing veil in the right folds. She took his gaiety from him—since it had to pass with them for gaiety—as she took everything else; but she certainly so far justified by her unerring touch his finer sense of the degree to which he had ended by convincing her. *She* at least never spoke of the secret of his life except as "the real truth about you," and she had in fact a wonderful way of making it seem, as such, the secret of her own life too. That was in fine how he so constantly felt her as allowing for him; he couldn't on the whole call it anything else. He allowed for himself, but she, exactly, allowed still more; partly because, better placed for a sight of the matter, she traced his unhappy perversion through reaches of its course into which he could scarce follow it. He knew how he felt, but, besides knowing that, she knew how he *looked* as well; he knew each of the things of importance he was insidiously kept from doing, but she could add up the amount they made, understand how much, with a lighter weight on his spirit, he might have done, and thereby establish how, clever as he was, he fell short. Above all she was in the secret of the difference between the forms he went through—those of his little office under Government, those of caring for his modest patrimony, for his library, for his garden in the country, for the people in London whose invitations he accepted and repaid—and the detachment that reigned beneath them and that made of all behaviour, all that could in the least be called behaviour, a long act of dissimulation. What it had come to was that he wore a mask painted with the social simper, out of the eye-holes of which there looked eyes of an expression not in the least matching the other features. This the stupid world, even after years, had never more than half-discovered. It was only May Bartram who had, and she achieved, by an art indescribable, the feat of at once—or perhaps it was only alternately—meeting the eyes from in front and mingling her own vision, as from over his shoulder, with their peep through the apertures.

So while they grew older together she did watch with him, and so she let this association give shape and colour to her own existence.

Beneath *her* forms as well detachment had learned to sit, and behaviour had become for her, in the social sense, a false account of herself. There was but one account of her that would have been true all the while and that she could give straight to nobody, least of all to John Marcher. Her whole attitude was a virtual statement, but the perception of that only seemed called to take its place for him as one of the many things necessarily crowded out of his consciousness. If she had moreover, like himself, to make sacrifices to their real truth, it was to be granted that her compensation might have affected her as more prompt and more natural. They had long periods, in this London time, during which, when they were together, a stranger might have listened to them without in the least pricking up his ears; on the other hand the real truth was equally liable at any moment to rise to the surface, and the auditor would then have wondered indeed what they were talking about. They had from an early hour made up their mind that society was, luckily, unintelligent, and the margin allowed them by this had fairly become one of their commonplaces. Yet there were still moments when the situation turned almost fresh—usually under the effect of some expression drawn from herself. Her expressions doubtless repeated themselves, but her intervals were generous. "What saves us, you know, is that we answer so completely to so usual an appearance: that of the man and woman whose friendship has become such a daily habit—or almost—as to be at last indispensable." That for instance was a remark she had frequently enough had occasion to make, though she had given it at different times different developments. What we are especially concerned with is the turn it happened to take from her one afternoon when he had come to see her in honour of her birthday. This anniversary had fallen on a Sunday, at a season of thick fog and general outward gloom; but he had brought her his customary offering, having known her now long enough to have established a hundred small traditions. It was one of his proofs to himself, the present he made her on her birthday, that he hadn't sunk into real selfishness. It was mostly nothing more than a small trinket, but it was always fine of its kind, and he was regularly careful to pay for it more than he thought he could afford. "Our habit saves you at least, don't you see? because it makes you, after all, for the vulgar, indistinguishable from other men. What's the most inveterate mark of men in general? Why the capacity to spend endless time with dull women—to spend it I won't say without being bored, but without minding that they are, without being driven off at a tangent by it; which comes to the same thing. I'm your dull woman, a part of the daily bread for which you pray at church. That covers your tracks more than anything."

"And what covers yours?" asked Marcher, whom his dull woman could mostly to this extent amuse. "I see of course what you mean by your saving me, in this way and that, so far as other people are concerned—I've seen it all along. Only what is it that saves *you?* I often think, you know, of that."

She looked as if she sometimes thought of that too, but rather in a different way. "Where other people, you mean, are concerned?"

"Well, you're really so in with me, you know—as a sort of result of my being so in with yourself. I mean of my having such an immense regard for you, being so tremendously mindful of all you've done for me. I sometimes ask myself if it's quite fair. Fair I mean to have so involved and—since one may say it—interested you. I almost feel as if you hadn't really had time to do anything else."

"Anything else but be interested?" she asked. "Ah what else does one ever want to be? If I've been 'watching' with you, as we long ago agreed I was to do, watching's always in itself an absorption."

"Oh certainly," John Marcher said, "if you hadn't had your curiosity—! Only doesn't it sometimes come to you as time goes on that your curiosity isn't being particularly repaid?"

May Bartram had a pause. "Do you ask that, by any chance, because you feel at all that yours isn't? I mean because you have to wait so long."

Oh he understood what she meant! "For the thing to happen that never does happen? For the beast to jump out? No, I'm just where I was about it. It isn't a matter as to which I can *choose,* I can decide for a change. It isn't one as to which there *can* be a change. It's in the lap of the gods. One's in the hands of one's law—there one is. As to the form the law will take, the way it will operate, that's its own affair."

"Yes," Miss Bartram replied; "of course one's fate's coming, of course it *has* come in its own form and its own way, all the while. Only, you know, the form and the way in your case were to have been—well, something so exceptional and, as one may say, so particularly *your* own."

Something in this made him look at her with suspicion. "You say 'were to *have* been,' as if in your heart you had begun to doubt."

"Oh!" she vaguely protested.

"As if you believed," he went on, "that nothing will now take place."

She shook her head slowly but rather inscrutably. "You're far from my thought."

He continued to look at her. "What then is the matter with you?"

"Well," she said after another wait, "the matter with me is simply that I'm more sure than ever my curiosity, as you call it, will be but too well repaid."

They were frankly grave now; he had got up from his seat, had turned once more about the little drawing-room to which, year after year, he brought his inevitable topic; in which he had, as he might have said, tasted their intimate community with every sauce, where every object was as familiar to him as the things of his own house and the very carpets were worn with his fitful walk very much as the desks in old counting-houses are worn by the elbows of generations of clerks. The generations of his nervous moods had been at work there, and the place was the written history of his whole middle life. Under the impression of what his friend had just said he knew himself, for some reason, more aware of these things; which made him, after a moment, stop again before her. "Is it possibly that you've grown afraid?"

"Afraid?" He thought, as she repeated the word, that his question had made her, a little, change colour; so that, lest he should have touched on a truth, he explained very kindly: "You remember that that was what you asked *me* long ago—that first day at Weather-end."

"Oh yes, and you told me you didn't know—that I was to see for myself. We've said little about it since, even in so long a time."

"Precisely," Marcher interposed—"quite as if it were too delicate a matter for us to make free with. Quite as if we might find, on pressure, that I *am* afraid. For then," he said, "we shouldn't, should we? quite know what to do."

She had for the time no answer to this question. "There have been days when I thought you were. Only, of course," she added, "there have been days when we have thought almost anything."

"Everything. Oh!" Marcher softly groaned as with a gasp, half-spent, at the face, more uncovered just then than it had been for a long while, of the imagination always with them. It had always had its incalculable moments of glaring out, quite as with the very eyes of the very Beast, and, used as he was to them, they could still draw from him the tribute of a sigh that rose from the depths of his being. All they had thought, first and last, rolled over him; the past seemed to have been reduced to mere barren speculation. This in fact was what the place had just struck him as so full of—the simplification of everything but the state of suspense. That remained only by seeming to hang in the void surrounding it. Even his original fear, if fear it had been, had lost itself in the desert. "I judge, however," he continued, "that you see I'm not afraid now."

"What I see, as I make it out, is that you've achieved something almost unprecedented in the way of getting used to danger. Living with it so long and so closely you've lost your sense of it; you know it's there, but you're indifferent, and you cease even, as of old, to have to whistle in the dark. Considering what the danger is," May Bartram wound up, "I'm bound to say I don't think your attitude could well be surpassed."

John Marcher faintly smiled. "It's heroic?"

"Certainly—call it that."

It was what he would have liked indeed to call it. "I *am* then a man of courage?"

"That's what you were to show me."

He still, however, wondered. "But doesn't the man of courage know what he's afraid of—or *not* afraid of? I don't know *that,* you see. I don't focus it. I can't name it. I only know I'm exposed."

"Yes, but exposed—how shall I say?—so directly. So intimately. That's surely enough."

"Enough to make you feel then—as what we may call the end and the upshot of our watch—that I'm not afraid?"

"You're not afraid. But it isn't," she said, "the end of our watch. That is it isn't the end of yours. You've everything still to see."

"Then why haven't *you?*" he asked. He had had, all along, to-day, the sense of her keeping something back, and he still had it. As this was his first impression of that it quite made a date. The case was the more marked as she didn't at first answer; which in turn made him go on. "You know something I don't." Then his voice, for that of a

man of courage, trembled a little. "You know what's to happen."
Her silence, with the face she showed, was almost a confession—it
made him sure. "You know, and you're afraid to tell me. It's so bad
that you're afraid I'll find out."

All this might be true, for she did look as if, unexpectedly to her,
he had crossed some mystic line that she had secretly drawn round
her. Yet she might, after all, not have worried; and the real climax
was that he himself, at all events, needn't. "You'll never find out."

✦ 3 ✦

IT was all to have made, none the less, as I have said, a date; which
came out in the fact that again and again, even after long intervals,
other things that passed between them wore in relation to this hour
but the character of recalls and results. Its immediate effect had been
indeed rather to lighten insistence—almost to provoke a reaction; as
if their topic had dropped by its own weight and as if moreover, for
that matter, Marcher had been visited by one of his occasional
warnings against egotism. He had kept up, he felt, and very decently
on the whole, his consciousness of the importance of not being
selfish, and it was true that he had never sinned in that direction
without promptly enough trying to press the scales the other way. He
often repaired his fault, the season permitting, by inviting his friend
to accompany him to the opera; and it not infrequently thus happened that, to show he didn't wish her to have but one sort of food
for her mind, he was the cause of her appearing there with him a
dozen nights in the month. It even happened that, seeing her home
at such times, he occasionally went in with her to finish, as he called
it, the evening, and, the better to make his point, sat down to the
frugal but always careful little supper that awaited his pleasure. His
point was made, he thought, by his not eternally insisting with her
on himself; made for instance, at such hours, when it befell that, her
piano at hand and each of them familiar with it, they went over
passages of the opera together. It chanced to be on one of these
occasions, however, that he reminded her of her not having answered
a certain question he had put to her during the talk that had taken
place between them on her last birthday. "What is it that saves

you?"—saved her, he meant, from that appearance of variation from the usual human type. If he had practically escaped remark, as she pretended, by doing, in the most important particular, what most men do—find the answer to life in patching up an alliance of a sort with a woman no better than himself—how had she escaped it, and how could the alliance, such as it was, since they must suppose it had been more or less noticed, have failed to make her rather positively talked about?

"I never said," May Bartram replied, "that it hadn't made me a good deal talked about."

"Ah well then you're not 'saved.' "

"It hasn't been a question for me. If you've had your woman I've had," she said, "my man."

"And you mean that makes you all right?"

Oh it was always as if there were so much to say! "I don't know why it shouldn't make me—humanly, which is what we're speaking of—as right as it makes you."

"I see," Marcher returned. " 'Humanly,' no doubt, as showing that you're living for something. Not, that is, just for me and my se-cret."

May Bartram smiled. "I don't pretend it exactly shows that I'm not living for you. It's my intimacy with you that's in question."

He laughed as he saw what she meant. "Yes, but since, as you say, I'm only, so far as people make out, ordinary, you're—aren't you?—no more than ordinary either. You help me to pass for a man like another. So if I *am*, as I understand you, you're not compro-mised. Is that it?"

She had another of her waits, but she spoke clearly enough. "That's it. It's all that concerns me—to help you to pass for a man like another."

He was careful to acknowledge the remark handsomely. "How kind, how beautiful, you are to me! How shall I ever repay you?"

She had her last grave pause, as if there might be a choice of ways. But she chose. "By going on as you are."

It was into this going on as he was that they relapsed, and really for so long a time that the day inevitably came for a further sound-ing of their depths. These depths, constantly bridged over by a structure firm enough in spite of its lightness and of its occasional oscillation in the somewhat vertiginous air, invited on occasion, in the interest of their nerves, a dropping of the plummet and a measurement of the abyss. A difference had been made moreover, once for all, by the fact that she had all the while not appeared to feel the need of rebutting his charge of an idea within her that she didn't dare to express—a charge uttered just before one of the fullest of their later discussions ended. It had come up for him then that she "knew" something and that what she knew was bad—too bad to tell him. When he had spoken of it as visibly so bad that she was afraid he might find it out, her reply had left the matter too equivocal to be let alone and yet, for Marcher's special sensibility, almost too formidable again to touch. He circled about it at a distance that alternately narrowed and widened and that still wasn't much affected by the consciousness in him that there was nothing she could "know," after all, any better than he did. She had no source of knowledge he hadn't equally—except of course that she might have finer nerves. That was what women had where they were interested; they made out things, where people were concerned, that the people often couldn't have made out for themselves. Their nerves, their sensibility, their imagination, were conductors and revealers, and the beauty of May Bartram was in particular that she had given herself so to his case. He felt in these days what, oddly enough, he had never felt before, the growth of a dread of losing her by some catastrophe—some catastrophe that yet wouldn't at all be *the* catastrophe: partly because she had almost of a sudden begun to strike him as more useful to him than ever yet, and partly by reason of an appearance of uncertainty in her health, coincident and equally new. It was characteristic of the inner detachment he had hitherto so successfully cultivated and to which our whole account of him is a reference, it was characteristic that his complications, such as they were, had never yet seemed so as at this crisis to thicken about him, even to the point of making him ask himself if he were, by any chance, of a truth, within sight or sound, within touch or reach, within the immediate jurisdiction, of the thing that waited.

When the day came, as come it had to, that his friend confessed to him her fear of a deep disorder in her blood, he felt somehow the shadow of a change and the chill of a shock. He immediately began to imagine aggravations and disasters, and above all to think of her peril as the direct menace for himself of personal privation. This indeed gave him one of those partial recoveries of equanimity that were agreeable to him—it showed him that what was still first in his mind was the loss she herself might suffer. "What if she should have to die before knowing, before seeing—?" It would have been brutal, in the early stages of her trouble, to put that question to her; but it had immediately sounded for him to his own concern, and the possibility was what most made him sorry for her. If she did "know," moreover, in the sense of her having had some—what should he think?—mystical irresistible light, this would make the matter not better, but worse, inasmuch as her original adoption of his own curiosity had quite become the basis of her life. She had been living to see what would *be* to be seen, and it would quite lacerate her to have to give up before the accomplishment of the vision. These reflexions, as I say, quickened his generosity; yet, make them as he might, he saw himself, with the lapse of the period, more and more disconcerted. It lapsed for him with a strange steady sweep, and the oddest oddity was that it gave him, independently of the threat of much inconvenience, almost the only positive surprise his career, if career it could be called, had yet offered him. She kept the house as she had never done; he had to go to her to see her—she could meet him nowhere now, though there was scarce a corner of their loved old London in which she hadn't in the past, at one time or another, done so; and he found her always seated by her fire in the deep old-fashioned chair she was less and less able to leave. He had been struck one day, after an absence exceeding his usual measure, with her suddenly looking much older to him than he had ever thought of her being; then he recognised that the suddenness was all on his side—he had just simply and suddenly noticed. She looked older because inevitably, after so many years, she *was* old, or almost; which was of course true in still greater measure of her companion. If she was old, or almost, John Marcher assuredly was, and yet it was her showing of the lesson, not his own, that brought the truth home to him. His surprises began here; when once they had begun they multiplied; they came rather with a rush: it was as if, in the oddest way in the world, they had all been kept back, sown in a thick cluster, for the late afternoon of life, the time at which for people in general the unexpected has died out.

One of them was that he should have caught himself—for he *had* so done—*really* wondering if the great accident would take form now as nothing more than his being condemned to see this charming woman, this admirable friend, pass away from him. He had never so unreservedly qualified her as while confronted in thought with such a possibility; in spite of which there was small doubt for him that as an answer to his long riddle the mere effacement of even so fine a feature of his situation would be an abject anticlimax. It would represent, as connected with his past attitude, a drop of dignity under the shadow of which his existence could only become the most grotesque of failures. He had been far from holding it a failure—long as he had waited for the appearance that was to make it a success. He had waited for quite another thing, not for such a thing as that. The breath of his good faith came short, however, as he recognised how long he had waited, or how long at least his companion had. That she, at all events, might be recorded as having waited in vain—this affected him sharply, and all the more because of his at first having done little more than amuse himself with the idea. It grew more grave as the gravity of her condition grew, and the state of mind it produced in him, which he himself ended by watching as if it had been some definite disfigurement of his outer person, may pass for another of his surprises. This conjoined itself still with another, the really stupefying consciousness of a question that he would have allowed to shape itself had he dared. What did everything mean—what, that is, did *she* mean, she and her vain waiting and her probable death and the soundless admonition of it all—unless that, at this time of day, it was simply, it was overwhelmingly too late? He had never at any stage of his queer consciousness admitted the whisper of such a correction; he had never till within these last few months been so false to his conviction as not to hold that what was to come to him had time, whether *he* struck himself as having it or not. That at last, at last, he certainly hadn't it, to speak of, or had it but in the scantiest measure—such, soon enough, as things went with him, became the inference with which his old obsession had to reckon: and this it was not helped to do by the more and more confirmed appearance that the great vagueness casting the long shadow in which he had lived had, to attest itself, almost no margin left. Since it was in Time that he was to have met his fate, so it was in Time that his fate was to have acted; and as he waked up to the sense of no longer being young, which was exactly the sense of being stale, just as that, in turn, was the sense of being weak, he waked up to another matter beside. It all hung together; they were subject, he and the great vagueness, to an equal and indivisible law. When the possibilities themselves had accordingly turned stale, when the secret of the gods had grown faint, had perhaps even quite evaporated, that, and that only, was failure. It wouldn't have been failure to be bankrupt, dishonoured, pilloried, hanged; it was failure not to be anything. And so, in the dark valley into which his path had taken its unlooked-for twist, he wondered not a little as he groped. He didn't care what awful crash might overtake him, with what ignominy or what monstrosity he might yet be associated—since he wasn't after all too utterly old to suffer—if it would only be decently proportionate to the posture he had kept, all his life, in the threatened presence of it. He had but one desire left—that he shouldn't have been "sold."

4

THEN it was that, one afternoon, while the spring of the year was young and new she met all in her own way his frankest betrayal of these alarms. He had gone in late to see her, but evening hadn't settled and she was presented to him in that long fresh light of waning April days which affects us often with a sadness sharper than the greyest hours of autumn. The week had been warm, the spring was supposed to have begun early, and May Bartram sat, for the first time in the year, without a fire; a fact that, to Marcher's sense, gave the scene of which she formed part a smooth and ultimate look, an air of knowing, in its immaculate order and cold meaningless cheer, that it would never see a fire again. Her own aspect—he could scarce have said why—intensified this note. Almost as white as wax, with the marks and signs in her face as numerous and as fine as if they had been etched by a needle, with soft white draperies relieved by a faded green scarf on the delicate tone of which the years had further refined, she was the picture of a serene and exquisite but impenetrable sphinx, whose head, or indeed all whose person, might have been powdered with silver. She was a sphinx, yet with her white petals and green fronds she might have been a lily too—only an artificial lily, wonderfully imitated and constantly kept, without dust or stain, though not exempt from a slight droop and a complexity of faint creases, under some clear glass bell. The perfection of household care, of high polish and finish, always reigned in her rooms, but they now looked most as if everything had been wound up, tucked in, put away, so that she might sit with folded hands and with nothing more to do. She was "out of it," to Marcher's vision; her work was over; she communicated with him as across some gulf or from some island of rest that she had already reached, and it made him feel strangely abandoned. Was it—or rather wasn't it—that if for so long she had been watching with him the answer to their question must have swum into her ken and taken on its name, so that her occupation was verily gone? He had as much as charged her with this in saying to her, many months before, that she even then knew something she was keeping from him. It was a point he had never since ventured to press, vaguely fearing as he did that it might become a difference, perhaps a disagreement, between them. He had in this later time turned nervous, which was what he in all the other years had never been; and the oddity was that his nervousness should have waited till he had begun to doubt, should have held off so long as he was sure. There was something, it seemed to him, that the wrong word would bring down on his head, something that would so at least ease off his tension. But he wanted not to speak the wrong word; that would make everything ugly. He wanted the knowledge he lacked to drop on him, if drop it could, by its own august weight. If she was to forsake him it was surely for her to take leave. This was why he didn't directly ask her again what she knew; but it was also why, approaching the matter from another side, he said to her in the course of his visit: "What do you regard as the very worst that at this time of day *can* happen to me?"

He had asked her that in the past often enough; they had, with the odd irregular rhythm of their intensities and avoidances, exchanged ideas about it and then had seen the ideas washed away by cool intervals, washed like figures traced in sea-sand. It had ever been the mark of their talk that the oldest allusions in it required but a little dismissal and reaction to come out again, sounding for the hour as new. She could thus at present meet his enquiry quite freshly and patiently. "Oh yes, I've repeatedly thought, only it always seemed to me of old that I couldn't quite make up my mind. I thought of dreadful things, between which it was difficult to choose; and so must you have done."

"Rather! I feel now as if I had scarce done anything else. I appear to myself to have spent my life in thinking of nothing *but* dreadful things. A great many of them I've at different times named to you, but there were others I couldn't name."

"They were too, too dreadful?"

"Too, too dreadful—some of them."

She looked at him a minute, and there came to him as he met it an inconsequent sense that her eyes, when one got their full clearness, were still as beautiful as they had been in youth, only beautiful with a strange cold light—a light that somehow was a part of the effect, if it wasn't rather a part of the cause, of the pale hard sweetness of the season and the hour. "And yet," she said at last, "there are horrors we've mentioned."

It deepened the strangeness to see her, as such a figure in such a picture, talk of "horrors," but she was to do in a few minutes something stranger yet—though even of this he was to take the full measure but afterwards—and the note of it already trembled. It was, for the matter of that, one of the signs that her eyes were having again the high flicker of their prime. He had to admit, however, what she said. "Oh yes, there were times when we did go far." He caught himself in the act of speaking as if it all were over. Well, he wished it were; and the consummation depended for him clearly more and more on his friend.

But she had now a soft smile. "Oh far—!"

It was oddly ironic. "Do you mean you're prepared to go further?"

She was frail and ancient and charming as she continued to look at him, yet it was rather as if she had lost the thread. "Do you consider that we went far?"

"Why I thought it the point you were just making—that we *had* looked most things in the face."

"Including each other?" She still smiled. "But you're quite right. We've had together great imaginations, often great fears; but some of them have been unspoken."

"Then the worst—we haven't faced that. I *could* face it, I believe, if I knew what you think it. I feel," he explained, "as if I had lost my power to conceive such things." And he wondered if he looked as blank as he sounded. "It's spent."

"Then why do you assume," she asked, "that mine isn't?"

"Because you've given me signs to the contrary. It isn't a question for you of conceiving, imagining, comparing. It isn't a question now of choosing." At last he came out with it. "You know something I don't. You've shown me that before."

These last words had affected her, he made out in a moment, exceedingly, and she spoke with firmness. "I've shown you, my dear, nothing."

He shook his head. "You can't hide it."

"Oh, oh!" May Bartram sounded over what she couldn't hide. It was almost a smothered groan.

"You admitted it months ago, when I spoke of it to you as of something you were afraid I should find out. Your answer was that I couldn't, that I wouldn't, and I don't pretend I have. But you had something therefore in mind, and I now see how it must have been, how it still is, the possibility that, of all possibilities, has settled itself for you as the worst. This," he went on, "is why I appeal to you. I'm only afraid of ignorance to-day—I'm not afraid of knowledge." And then as for a while she said nothing: "What makes me sure is that I see in your face and feel here, in this air and amid these appearances, that you're out of it. You've done. You've had your experience. You leave me to my fate."

Well, she listened, motionless and white in her chair, as on a decision to be made, so that her manner was fairly an avowal, though still, with a small fine inner stiffness, an imperfect surrender. "It *would* be the worst," she finally let herself say. "I mean the thing I've never said."

It hushed him a moment. "More monstrous than all the monstrosities we've named?"

"More monstrous. Isn't that what you sufficiently express," she asked, "in calling it the worst?"

Marcher thought. "Assuredly—if you mean, as I do, something that includes all the loss and all the shame that are thinkable."

"It would if it *should* happen," said May Bartram. "What we're speaking of, remember, is only my idea."

"It's your belief," Marcher returned. "That's enough for me. I feel your beliefs are right. Therefore if, having this one, you give me no more light on it, you abandon me."

"No, no!" she repeated. "I'm with you—don't you see?—still." And as to make it more vivid to him she rose from her chair—a movement she seldom risked in these days—and showed herself, all draped and all soft, in her fairness and slimness. "I haven't forsaken you."

It was really, in its effort against weakness, a generous assurance, and had the success of the impulse not, happily, been great, it would have touched him to pain more than to pleasure. But the cold charm in her eyes had spread, as she hovered before him, to all the rest of her person, so that it was for the minute almost a recovery of youth. He couldn't pity her for that; he could only take her as she showed—as capable even yet of helping him. It was as if, at the same time, her light might at any instant go out; wherefore he must make the most of it. There passed before him with intensity the three or four things he wanted most to know; but the question that came of itself to his lips really covered the others. "Then tell me if I shall consciously suffer."

She promptly shook her head. "Never!"

It confirmed the authority he imputed to her, and it produced on him an extraordinary effect. "Well, what's better than that? Do you call that the worst?"

"You think nothing is better?" she asked.

She seemed to mean something so special that he again sharply wondered, though still with the dawn of a prospect of relief. "Why not, if one doesn't *know?*" After which, as their eyes, over his question, met in a silence, the dawn deepened and something to his purpose came prodigiously out of her very face. His own, as he took it in, suddenly flushed to the forehead, and he gasped with the force of a perception to which, on the instant, everything fitted. The sound of his gasp filled the air; then he became articulate. "I see—if I don't suffer!"

In her own look, however, was doubt. "You see what?"

"Why what you mean—what you've always meant."

She again shook her head. "What I mean isn't what I've always meant. It's different."

"It's something new?"

She hung back from it a little. "Something new. It's not what you think. I see what you think."

His divination drew breath then; only her correction might be wrong. "It isn't that I *am* a blockhead?" he asked between faintness and grimness. "It isn't that it's all a mistake?"

"A mistake?" she pityingly echoed. *That* possibility, for her, he saw, would be monstrous; and if she guaranteed him the immunity from pain it would accordingly not be what she had in mind. "Oh no," she declared; "it's nothing of that sort. You've been right."

Yet he couldn't help asking himself if she weren't, thus pressed, speaking but to save him. It seemed to him he should be most in a hole if his history should prove all a platitude. "Are you telling me the truth, so that I shan't have been a bigger idiot than I can bear to know? I *haven't* lived with a vain imagination, in the most besotted illusion? I haven't waited but to see the door shut in my face?"

She shook her head again. "However the case stands *that* isn't the truth. Whatever the reality, it *is* a reality. The door isn't shut. The door's open," said May Bartram.

"Then something's to come?"

She waited once again, always with her cold sweet eyes on him. "It's never too late." She had, with her gliding step, diminished the distance between them, and she stood nearer to him, close to him, a minute, as if still charged with the unspoken. Her movement might have been for some finer emphasis of what she was at once hesitating and deciding to say. He had been standing by the chimney-piece, fireless and sparely adorned, a small perfect old French clock and two morsels of rosy Dresden constituting all its furniture; and her hand grasped the shelf while she kept him waiting, grasped it a little as for support and encouragement. She only kept him waiting, however; that is he only waited. It had become suddenly, from her movement and attitude, beautiful and vivid to him that she had something more to give him; her wasted face delicately shone with it—it glittered almost as with the white lustre of silver in her expression. She was right, incontestably, for what he saw in her face was the truth, and strangely, without consequence, while their talk of it as dreadful was still in the air, she appeared to present it as inordinately soft. This, prompting bewilderment, made him but gape the more gratefully for her revelation, so that they continued for some minutes silent, her face shining at him, her contact imponderably pressing, and his stare all kind but all expectant. The end, none the less, was that what he had expected failed to come to him. Something else took place instead, which seemed to consist at first in the mere closing of her eyes. She gave way at the same instant to a slow fine shudder, and though he remained staring—though he stared in fact but the harder—turned off and regained her chair. It was the end of what she had been intending, but it left him thinking only of that.

"Well, you don't say—?"

She had touched in her passage a bell near the chimney and had sunk back strangely pale. "I'm afraid I'm too ill."

"Too ill to tell me?" It sprang up sharp to him, and almost to his lips, the fear she might die without giving him light. He checked himself in time from so expressing his question, but she answered as if she had heard the words.

"Don't you know—now?"

" 'Now'—?" She had spoken as if some difference had been made within the moment. But her maid, quickly obedient to her bell, was already with them. "I know nothing." And he was afterwards to say to himself that he must have spoken with odious impatience, such an impatience as to show that, supremely disconcerted, he washed his hands of the whole question.

"Oh!" said May Bartram.

"Are you in pain?" he asked as the woman went to her.

"No," said May Bartram.

Her maid, who had put an arm round her as if to take her to her room, fixed on him eyes that appealingly contradicted her; in spite of which, however, he showed once more his mystification. "What then has happened?"

She was once more, with her companion's help, on her feet, and, feeling withdrawal imposed on him, he had blankly found his hat and gloves and had reached the door. Yet he waited for her answer. "What *was* to," she said.

✖ 5 ✖

HE came back the next day, but she was then unable to see him, and as it was literally the first time this had occurred in the long stretch of their acquaintance he turned away, defeated and sore, almost angry—or feeling at least that such a break in their custom was really the beginning of the end—and wandered alone with his thoughts, especially with the one he was least able to keep down. She was dying and he would lose her; she was dying and his life would end. He stopped in the Park, into which he had passed, and stared before him at his recurrent doubt. Away from her the doubt pressed again; in her presence he had believed her, but as he felt his forlornness he threw himself into the explanation that, nearest at hand, had most of a miserable warmth for him and least of a cold torment. She had deceived him to save him—to put him off with something in which he should be able to rest. What could the thing that was to happen to him be, after all, but just this thing that had begun to happen? Her dying, her death, his consequent solitude—*that* was what he had figured as the Beast in the Jungle, that was what had been in the lap of the gods. He had had her word for it as he left her—what else on earth could she have meant? It wasn't a thing of a monstrous order; not a fate rare and distinguished; not a stroke of fortune that overwhelmed and immortalised; it had only the stamp of the common doom. But poor Marcher at this hour judged the common doom sufficient. It would serve his turn, and even as the consummation of infinite waiting he would bend his pride to accept it. He sat down on a bench in the twilight. He hadn't been a fool. Something had *been*, as she had said, to come. Before he rose indeed it had quite struck him that the final fact really matched with the long avenue through which he had had to reach it. As sharing his suspense and as giving herself all, giving her life, to bring it to an end, she had come with him every step of the way. He had lived by her aid, and to leave her behind would be cruelly, damnably to miss her. What could be more overwhelming than that?

Well, he was to know within the week, for though she kept him a while at bay, left him restless and wretched during a series of days on each of which he asked about her only again to have to turn away, she ended his trial by receiving him where she had always received him. Yet she had been brought out at some hazard into the presence of so many of the things that were, consciously, vainly, half their past, and there was scant service left in the gentleness of her mere desire, all too visible, to check his obsession and wind up his long trouble. That was clearly what she wanted, the one thing more for her own peace while she could still put out her hand. He was so affected by her state that, once seated by her chair, he was moved to let everything go; it was she herself therefore who brought him back, took up again, before she dismissed him, her last word of the other time. She showed how she wished to leave their business in order. "I'm not sure you understood. You've nothing to wait for more. It *has* come."

Oh how he looked at her! "Really?"

"Really."

"The thing that, as you said, *was* to?"

"The thing that we began in our youth to watch for."

Face to face with her once more he believed her; it was a claim to which he had so abjectly little to oppose. "You mean that it has come as a positive definite occurrence, with a name and a date?"

"Positive. Definite. I don't know about the 'name,' but oh with a date!"

He found himself again too helplessly at sea. "But come in the night—come and passed me by?"

May Bartram had her strange faint smile. "Oh no, it hasn't passed you by!"

"But if I haven't been aware of it and it hasn't touched me—?"

"Ah your not being aware of it"—and she seemed to hesitate an instant to deal with this—"your not being aware of it is the strangeness *in* the strangeness. It's the wonder *of* the wonder." She spoke as with the softness almost of a sick child, yet now at last, at the end of all, with the perfect straightness of a sibyl. She visibly knew that she knew, and the effect on him was of something co-ordinate, in its high character, with the law that had ruled him. It was the true voice of the law; so on her lips would the law itself have sounded. "It *has* touched you," she went on. "It has done its office. It has made you all its own."

"So utterly without my knowing it?"

"So utterly without your knowing it." His hand, as he leaned to her, was on the arm of her chair, and, dimly smiling always now, she placed her own on it. "It's enough if *I* know it."

"Oh!" he confusedly breathed, as she herself of late so often had done.

"What I long ago said is true. You'll never know now, and I think you ought to be content. You've *had* it," said May Bartram.

"But had what?"

"Why what was to have marked you out. The proof of your law. It has acted. I'm too glad," she then bravely added, "to have been able to see what it's *not*."

He continued to attach his eyes to her, and with the sense that it was all beyond him, and that *she* was too, he would still have sharply challenged her hadn't he so felt it an abuse of her weakness to do more than take devoutly what she gave him, take it hushed as to a revelation. If he did speak, it was out of the foreknowledge of his loneliness to come. "If you're glad of what it's 'not' it might then have been worse?"

She turned her eyes away, she looked straight before her; with which after a moment: "Well, you know our fears."

He wondered. "It's something then we never feared?"

On this slowly she turned to him. "Did we ever dream, with all our dreams, that we should sit and talk of it thus?"

He tried for a little to make out that they had; but it was as if their dreams, numberless enough, were in solution in some thick cold mist through which thought lost itself. "It might have been that we couldn't talk?"

"Well"—she did her best for him—"not from this side. This, you see," she said, "is the *other* side."

"I think," poor Marcher returned, "that all sides are the same to me." Then, however, as she gently shook her head in correction: "We mightn't, as it were, have got across—?"

"To where we are—no. We're *here*"—she made her weak emphasis.

"And much good does it do us!" was her friend's frank comment.

"It does us the good it can. It does us the good that *it* isn't here. It's past. It's behind," said May Bartram. "Before—" but her voice dropped.

He had got up, not to tire her, but it was hard to combat his yearning. She after all told him nothing but that his light had failed—which he knew well enough without her. "Before—?" he blankly echoed.

"Before, you see, it was always to *come*. That kept it present."

"Oh I don't care what comes now! Besides," Marcher added, "it seems to me I liked it better present, as you say, than I can like it absent with *your* absence."

"Oh mine!"—and her pale hands made light of it.

"With the absence of everything." He had a dreadful sense of standing there before her for—so far as anything but this proved.

this bottomless drop was concerned—the last time of their life. It rested on him with a weight he felt he could scarce bear, and this weight it apparently was that still pressed out what remained in him of speakable protest. "I believe you; but I can't begin to pretend I understand. *Nothing*, for me, is past; nothing *will* pass till I pass myself, which I pray my stars may be as soon as possible. Say, however," he added, "that I've eaten my cake, as you contend, to the last crumb—how can the thing I've never felt at all be the thing I was marked out to feel?"

She met him perhaps less directly, but she met him unperturbed. "You take your 'feelings' for granted. You were to suffer your fate. That was not necessarily to know it."

"How in the world—when what is such knowledge but suffering?"

She looked up at him a while in silence. "No—you don't understand."

"I suffer," said John Marcher.

"Don't, don't!"

"How can I help at least *that?*"

"*Don't!*" May Bartram repeated.

She spoke it in a tone so special, in spite of her weakness, that he stared an instant—stared as if some light, hitherto hidden, had shimmered across his vision. Darkness again closed over it, but the gleam had already become for him an idea. "Because I haven't the right—?"

"Don't *know*—when you needn't," she mercifully urged. "You needn't—for we shouldn't."

"Shouldn't?" If he could but know what she meant!

"No—it's too much."

"Too much?" he still asked but, with a mystification that was the next moment of a sudden to give way. Her words, if they meant something, affected him in this light—the light also of her wasted face—as meaning *all*, and the sense of what knowledge had been for herself came over him with a rush which broke through into a question. "Is it of that then you're dying?"

She but watched him, gravely at first, as to see, with this, where he was, and she might have seen something or feared something that moved her sympathy. "I would live for you still—if I could." Her eyes closed for a little, as if, withdrawn into herself, she were for a last time trying. "But I can't!" she said as she raised them again to take leave of him.

She couldn't indeed, as but too promptly and sharply appeared, and he had no vision of her after this that was anything but darkness and doom. They had parted for ever in that strange talk; access to her chamber of pain, rigidly guarded, was almost wholly forbidden him; he was feeling now moreover, in the face of doctors, nurses, the two or three relatives attracted doubtless by the presumption of what she had to "leave," how few were the rights, as they were called in such cases, that he had to put forward, and how odd it might even seem that their intimacy shouldn't have given him more of them. The stupidest fourth cousin had more, even though she had been nothing in such a person's life. She had been a feature of features in *his,* for what else was it to have been so indispensable? Strange beyond saying were the ways of existence, baffling for him the anomaly of his lack, as he felt it to be, of producible claim. A woman might have been, as it were, everything to him, and it might yet present him in no connexion that any one seemed held to recognise. If this was the case in these closing weeks it was the case more sharply on the occasion of the last offices rendered, in the great grey London cemetery, to what had been mortal, to what had been precious, in his friend. The concourse at her grave was not numerous, but he saw himself treated as scarce more nearly concerned with it than if there had been a thousand others. He was in short from this moment face to face with the fact that he was to profit extraordinarily little by the interest May Bartram had taken in him. He couldn't quite have said what he expected, but he hadn't surely expected this approach to a double privation. Not only had her interest failed him, but he seemed to feel himself unattended—and for a reason he couldn't seize—by the distinction, the dignity, the propriety, if nothing else, of the man markedly bereaved. It was as if in the view of society he had not *been* markedly bereaved, as if there still failed some sign or proof of it, and as if none the less his character could never be affirmed nor the deficiency ever made up. There were moments as the weeks went by when he would have liked, by some almost aggressive act, to take his stand on the intimacy of his loss, in order that it *might* be questioned and his retort, to the relief of his spirit, so recorded; but the moments of an irritation more helpless followed fast on these, the moments during which, turning things over with a good conscience but with a bare horizon, he found himself wondering if he oughtn't to have begun, so to speak, further back. He found himself wondering indeed at many things, and this last speculation had others to keep it company. What could he have done, after all, in her lifetime, without giving them both, as it were, away? He couldn't have made known she was watching him, for that would have published the superstition of the Beast. This was what closed his mouth now—now that the Jungle had been threshed to vacancy and that the Beast had stolen away. It sounded too foolish and too flat; the difference for him in this particular, the extinction in his life of the element of suspense, was such as in fact to surprise him. He could scarce have said what the effect resembled; the abrupt cessation, the positive prohibition, of music perhaps, more than anything else, in some place all adjusted and all accustomed to sonority and to attention. If he could at any rate have conceived lifting the veil from his image at some moment of the past (what had he done, after all, if not lift it to *her?*) so to do this to-day, to talk to people at large of the Jungle cleared and confide to them that he now felt it as safe, would have been not only to see them listen as to a goodwife's tale, but really to hear himself tell one. What it presently came to in truth was that poor Marcher waded through his beaten grass, where no life stirred, where no breath sounded, where no evil eye seemed to gleam from a possible lair, very much as if vaguely looking for the Beast, and still more as if acutely missing it. He walked about in an existence that had grown strangely more spacious, and, stopping fitfully in places where the undergrowth of life struck him as closer, asked himself yearningly, wondered secretly and sorely, if it would have lurked here or there. It would have at all events *sprung;* what was at least complete was his belief in the truth itself of the assurance given him. The change from his old sense to his new was absolute and final: what was to happen *had* so absolutely and finally happened that he was as little able to know a fear for his future as to know a hope; so absent in short was any question of anything still to come. He was to live entirely with the other question, that of his unidentified past, that of his having to see his fortune impenetrably muffled and masked.

The torment of this vision became then his occupation; he couldn't perhaps have consented to live but for the possibility of guessing. She had told him, his friend, not to guess; she had forbidden him, so far as he might, to know, and she had even in a sort denied the power in him to learn: which were so many things, precisely, to deprive him of rest. It wasn't that he wanted, he argued for fairness, that anything past and done should repeat itself; it was only that he shouldn't, as an anticlimax, have been taken sleeping so sound as not to be able to win back by an effort of thought the lost stuff of consciousness. He declared to himself at moments that he would either win it back or have done with consciousness for ever; he made this idea his one motive in fine, made it so much his passion that none other, to compare with it, seemed ever to have touched him. The lost stuff of consciousness became thus for him as a strayed or stolen child to an unappeasable father; he hunted it up and down very much as if he were knocking at doors and enquiring of the police. This was the spirit in which, inevitably, he set himself to travel; he started on a journey that was to be as long as he could make it; it danced before him that, as the other side of the globe couldn't possibly have less to say to him, it might, by a possibility of suggestion, have more. Before he quitted London, however, he made a pilgrimage to May Bartram's grave, took his way to it through the endless avenues of the grim suburban metropolis, sought it out in the wilderness of tombs, and, though he had come but for the renewal of the act of farewell, found himself, when he had at last stood by it, beguiled into long intensities. He stood for an hour, powerless to turn away and yet powerless to penetrate the darkness of death; fixing with his eyes her inscribed name and date, beating his forehead against the fact of the secret they kept, drawing his breath, while he waited, as if some sense would in pity of him rise from the stones. He kneeled on the stones, however, in vain; they kept what they concealed; and if the face of the tomb did become a face for him it was because her two names became a pair of eyes that didn't know him. He gave them a last long look, but no palest light broke.

6

HE stayed away, after this, for a year; he visited the depths of Asia, spending himself on scenes of romantic interest, of superlative sanctity; but what was present to him everywhere was that for a man who had known what *he* had known the world was vulgar and vain. The state of mind in which he had lived for so many years shone out to him, in reflexion, as a light that coloured and refined, a light beside which the glow of the East was garish cheap and thin. The terrible truth was that he had lost—with everything else—a distinction as well; the things he saw couldn't help being common when he had become common to look at them. He was simply now one of them himself—he was in the dust, without a peg for the sense of difference; and there were hours when, before the temples of gods and the sepulchres of kings, his spirit turned for nobleness of association to the barely discriminated slab in the London suburb. That had become for him, and more intensely with time and distance, his one witness of a past glory. It was all that was left to him for proof or pride, yet the past glories of Pharaohs were nothing to him as he thought of it. Small wonder then that he came back to it on the morrow of his return. He was drawn there this time as irresistibly as the other, yet with a confidence, almost, that was doubtless the effect of the many months that had elapsed. He had lived, in spite of himself, into his change of feeling, and in wandering over the earth had wandered, as might be said, from the circumference to the centre of his desert. He had settled to his safety and accepted perforce his extinction; figuring to himself, with some colour, in the likeness of certain little old men he remembered to have seen, of whom, all meagre and wizened as they might look, it was related that they had in their time fought twenty duels or been loved by ten princesses. They indeed had been wondrous for others while he was but wondrous for himself; which, however, was exactly the cause of his haste to renew the wonder by getting back, as he might put it, into his own presence. That had quickened his steps and checked his delay. If his visit was prompt it was because he had been separated so long from the part of himself that alone he now valued.

It's accordingly not false to say that he reached his goal with a certain elation and stood there again with a certain assurance. The creature beneath the sod *knew* of his rare experience, so that, strangely now, the place had lost for him its mere blankness of expression. It met him in mildness—not, as before, in mockery; it wore for him the air of conscious greeting that we find, after absence, in things that have closely belonged to us and which seem to confess of themselves to the connexion. The plot of ground, the graven tablet, the tended flowers affected him so as belonging to him that he resembled for the hour a contented landlord reviewing a piece of property. Whatever had happened—well, had happened. He had not come back this time with the vanity of that question, his former worrying "What, *what?*" now practically so spent. Yet he would none the less never again so cut himself off from the spot; he would come back to it every month, for if he did nothing else by its aid he at least held up his head. It thus grew for him, in the oddest way, a positive resource; he carried out his idea of periodical returns, which took their place at last among the most inveterate of his habits. What it all amounted to, oddly enough, was that in his finally so simplified world this garden of death gave him the few square feet of earth on which he could still most live. It was as if, being nothing anywhere else for any one, nothing even for himself, he were just everything here, and if not for a crowd of witnesses or indeed for any witness but John Marcher, then by clear right of the register that he could scan like an open page. The open page was the tomb of his friend, and *there* were the facts of the past, there the truth of his life, there the backward reaches in which he could lose himself. He did this from time to time with such effect that he seemed to wander through the old years with his hand in the arm of a companion who was, in the most extraordinary manner, his other, his younger self; and to wander, which was more extraordinary yet, round and round a third presence—not wandering she, but stationary, still, whose eyes, turning with his revolution, never ceased to follow him, and whose seat was his point, so to speak, of orientation. Thus in short he settled to live—feeding all on the sense that he once *had* lived, and dependent on it not alone for a support but for an identity.

It sufficed him in its way for months and the year elapsed; it would doubtless even have carried him further but for an accident, superficially slight, which moved him, quite in another direction, with a force beyond any of his impressions of Egypt or of India. It was a thing of the merest chance—the turn, as he afterwards felt, of a hair, though he was indeed to live to believe that if light hadn't come to him in this particular fashion it would still have come in another. He was to live to believe this, I say, though he was not to live, I may not less definitely mention, to do much else. We allow him at any rate the benefit of the conviction, struggling up for him at the end, that, whatever might have happened or not happened, he would have come round of himself to the light. The incident of an autumn day had put the match to the train laid from of old by his misery.

With the light before him he knew that even of late his ache had only been smothered. It was strangely drugged, but it throbbed; at the touch it began to bleed. And the touch, in the event, was the face of a fellow mortal. This face, one grey afternoon when the leaves were thick in the alleys, looked into Marcher's own, at the cemetery, with an expression like the cut of a blade. He felt it, that is, so deep down that he winced at the steady thrust. The person who so mutely assaulted him was a figure he had noticed, on reaching his own goal, absorbed by a grave a short distance away, a grave apparently fresh, so that the emotion of the visitor would probably match it for frankness. This fact alone forbade further attention, though during the time he stayed he remained vaguely conscious of his neighbour, a middle-aged man apparently, in mourning, whose bowed back, among the clustered monuments and mortuary yews, was constantly presented. Marcher's theory that these were elements in contact with which he himself revived, had suffered, on this occasion, it may be granted, a marked, an excessive check. The autumn day was dire for him as none had recently been, and he rested with a heaviness he had not yet known on the low stone table that bore May Bartram's name. He rested without power to move, as if some spring in him, some spell vouchsafed, had suddenly been broken for ever. If he could have done that moment as he wanted he would simply have stretched himself on the slab that was ready to take him, treating it as a place prepared to receive his last sleep. What in all the wide world had he now to keep awake for? He stared before him with the question, and it was then that, as one of the cemetery walks passed near him, he caught the shock of the face.

His neighbour at the other grave had withdrawn, as he himself, with force enough in him, would have done by now, and was advancing along the path on his way to one of the gates. This brought him close, and his pace was slow, so that—and all the more as there was a kind of hunger in his look—the two men were for a minute directly confronted. Marcher knew him at once for one of the deeply stricken—a perception so sharp that nothing else in the picture comparatively lived, neither his dress, his age, nor his presumable character and class; nothing lived but the deep ravage of the features he showed. He *showed* them—that was the point; he was moved, as he passed, by some impulse that was either a signal for sympathy or, more possibly, a challenge to an opposed sorrow. He might already have been aware of our friend, might at some previous hour have noticed in him the smooth habit of the scene, with which the state of his own senses so scantly consorted, and might thereby have been stirred as by an overt discord. What Marcher was at all events conscious of was in the first place that the image of scarred passion presented to him was conscious too—of something that profaned the air; and in the second that, roused, startled, shocked, he was yet the next moment looking after it, as it went, with envy. The most extraordinary thing that had happened to him—though he had given that name to other matters as well—took place, after his immediate vague stare, as a consequence of this impression. The stranger passed, but the raw glare of his grief remained, making our friend wonder in pity what wrong, what wound it expressed, what injury not to be healed. What had the man *had,* to make him by the loss of it so bleed and yet live?

Something—and this reached him with a pang—that *he,* John Marcher, hadn't; the proof of which was precisely John Marcher's arid end. No passion had ever touched him, for this was what passion meant; he had survived and maundered and pined, but where had been *his* deep ravage? The extraordinary thing we speak of was the sudden rush of the result of this question. The sight that had just met his eyes named to him, as in letters of quick flame, something he had utterly, insanely missed, and what he had missed made these things a train of fire, made them mark themselves in an anguish of inward throbs. He had seen *outside* of his life, not learned it within, the way a woman was mourned when she had been loved for herself: such was the force of his conviction of the meaning of the stranger's face, which still flared for him as a smoky torch. It hadn't come to him, the knowledge, on the wings of experience; it had brushed him, jostled him, upset him, with the disrespect of chance, the insolence of accident. Now that the illumination had begun, however, it blazed to the zenith, and what he presently stood there gazing at was the sounded void of his life. He gazed, he drew breath, in pain; he turned in his dismay, and, turning, he had before him in sharper incision than ever the open page of his story. The name on the table smote him as the passage of his neighbour had done, and what it said to him, full in the face, was that *she* was what he had missed. This was the awful thought, the answer to all the past, the vision at the dread clearness of which he grew as cold as the stone beneath him. Everything fell together, confessed, explained, overwhelmed; leaving him most of all stupefied at the blindness he had cherished. The fate he had been marked for he had met with a vengeance—he had emptied the cup to the lees; he had been the man of his time, *the* man, to whom nothing on earth was to have happened. That was the rare stroke—that was his visitation. So he saw it, as we say, in pale horror, while the pieces fitted and fitted. So *she* had seen it while he didn't, and so she served at this hour to drive the truth home. It was the truth, vivid and monstrous, that all the while he had waited the wait was itself his portion. This the companion of his vigil had at a given moment made out, and she had then offered him the chance to baffle his doom. One's doom, however, was never baffled, and on the day she told him his own had come down she had seen him but stupidly stare at the escape she offered him.

The escape would have been to love her; then, *then* he would have lived. *She* had lived—who could say now with what passion?—since she had loved him for himself; whereas he had never thought of her (ah how it hugely glared at him!) but in the chill of his egotism and the light of her use. Her spoken words came back to him—the chain stretched and stretched. The Beast had lurked indeed, and the Beast, at its hour, had sprung; it had sprung in that twilight of the cold April when, pale, ill, wasted, but all beautiful, and perhaps even then recoverable, she had risen from her chair to stand before him and let him imaginably guess. It had sprung as he didn't guess; it had sprung as she hopelessly turned from him, and the mark, by the time he left her, had fallen where it *was* to fall. He had justified his fear and achieved his fate; he had failed, with the last exactitude, of all he was to fail of; and a moan now rose to his lips as he remembered she had prayed he mightn't know. This horror of waking—*this* was knowledge, knowledge under the breath of which the very tears in his eyes seemed to freeze. Through them, none the less, he tried to fix it and hold it; he kept it there before him so that he might feel the pain. That at least, belated and bitter, had something of the taste of life. But the bitterness suddenly sickened him, and it was as if, horribly, he saw, in the truth, in the cruelty of his image, what had been appointed and done. He saw the Jungle of his life and saw the lurking Beast; then, while he looked, perceived it, as by a stir of the air, rise, huge and hideous, for the leap that was to settle him. His eyes darkened—it was close; and, instinctively turning, in his hallucination, to avoid it, he flung himself, face down, on the tomb.

The American Girl

During his early years, Henry James acquired a considerable reputation as the "historian" of the American girl. She was emerging in the middle class for the first time as a national figure and as a "type"— independent, forthright, unconventional by European standards, innocent, but also, in that era, ignorant and often brash. Her European sisters were not as free as she was; they were chaperoned, disciplined, limited both by conventions and by the extent of their parental purse. Their marriages were still arranged, whereas the American girl was free to choose, and to carry on flirtations. James had from the first, even in that time, noted the consequences of an excessive "permissiveness," and the abandoning by parents of all responsibility in the formation and education of their children. The sharply etched picture of Daisy's mother and her brat of a brother and the daughter-dominated family of Pandora Day place in an ironic light these social observations.

"Daisy" was James's first story to be published in an English magazine, and it brought him instant fame in 1878. His heroine became the toast of two continents in her vivacity and insouciance, her curious innocence and her gay and spirited belief that what was good for girls in Schenectady was good for them in Rome. Her American indifference to European customs and her defiance of European manners amused the Europeans and delighted the Americans. "Daisy Miller" thus was one of James's rare tales which pleased his audiences on both sides of the Atlantic. The comedy concealed the essential pathos of Daisy, a girl bright and shimmering, yet ill-prepared for life: she was, in her comedy version, the first of those American "heiresses of the ages" James was to document in his later works.

In the wake of the success of this tale he wrote other stories about American girls. His tale of "Pandora," set on a liner and later in Washington, was an attempt to "do" the self-made girl—"self-made" in the sense that her family has done nothing for her; it is she who arranges her life and her future. She knows what she wants and she makes the most of every opportunity—even to soliciting, and obtaining, a job for her friend from the President of the United States.

These two tales show James's treatment of the American girl as a figure of comedy. He was to treat her in larger and more serious works—as a dramatic figure in *The Portrait of a Lady* and as a tragic figure in *The Wings of the Dove*. But his own generation knew best these flighty young things, as James painted them in their descent from the trans-Atlantic liners, dressed in all their finery, bent on dazzling—but succeeding only in puzzling—the cynical and time-hardened Europeans.

L. E.

Daisy Miller

1

AT the little town of Vevey, in Switzerland, there is a particularly comfortable hotel; there are indeed many hotels, since the entertainment of tourists is the business of the place, which, as many travellers will remember, is seated upon the edge of a remarkably blue lake—a lake that it behoves every tourist to visit. The shore of the lake presents an unbroken array of establishments of this order, of every category, from the "grand hotel" of the newest fashion, with a chalk-white front, a hundred balconies, and a dozen flags flying from its roof, to the small Swiss pension of an elder day, with its name inscribed in German-looking lettering upon a pink or yellow wall and an awkward summer-house in the angle of the garden. One of the hotels at Vevey, however, is famous, even classical, being distinguished from many of its upstart neighbours by an air both of luxury and of maturity. In this region, through the month of June, American travellers are extremely numerous; it may be said indeed that Vevey assumes at that time some of the characteristics of an American watering-place. There are sights and sounds that evoke a vision, an echo, of Newport and Saratoga. There is a flitting hither and thither of "stylish" young girls, a rustling of muslin flounces, a rattle of dance-music in the morning hours, a sound of high-pitched voices at all times. You receive an impression of these things at the excellent inn of the "Trois Couronnes," and are transported in fancy to the Ocean House or to Congress Hall. But at the "Trois Couronnes," it must be added, there are other features much at variance with these suggestions: neat German waiters who look like secretaries of legation; Russian princesses sitting in the garden; little Polish boys walking about, held by the hand, with their governors; a view of the snowy crest of the Dent du Midi and the picturesque towers of the Castle of Chillon.

I hardly know whether it was the analogies or the differences that were uppermost in the mind of a young American, who, two or three years ago, sat in the garden of the "Trois Couronnes," looking about him rather idly at some of the graceful objects I have mentioned. It was a beautiful summer morning, and in whatever fashion the young American looked at things they must have seemed to him charming. He had come from Geneva the day before, by the little steamer, to see his aunt, who was staying at the hotel—Geneva having been for a long time his place of residence. But his aunt had a headache—his aunt had almost always a headache—and she was now shut up in her room smelling camphor, so that he was at liberty to wander about. He was some seven-and-twenty years of age; when his friends spoke of him they usually said that he was at Geneva "studying." When his enemies spoke of him they said—but after all he had no enemies: he was extremely amiable and generally liked. What I should say is simply that when certain persons spoke of him they conveyed that the reason of his spending so much time at Geneva was that he was extremely devoted to a lady who lived there—a foreign lady, a person older than himself. Very few Americans—truly I think none—had ever seen this lady, about whom there were some singular stories. But Winterbourne had an old attachment for the little capital of Calvinism; he had been put to school there as a boy and had afterwards even gone, on trial—trial of the grey old "Academy" on the steep and stony hillside—to college there; circumstances which had led to his forming a great many youthful friendships. Many of these he had kept, and they were a source of great satisfaction to him.

After knocking at his aunt's door and learning that she was indisposed he had taken a walk about the town and then he had come in to his breakfast. He had now finished that repast, but was enjoying a small cup of coffee which had been served him on a little table in the garden by one of the waiters who looked like *attachés*. At last he finished his coffee and lit a cigarette. Presently a small boy came walking along the path—an urchin of nine or ten. The child, who was diminutive for his years, had an aged expression of countenance, a pale complexion and sharp little features. He was dressed in knickerbockers and had red stockings that displayed his poor little spindle-shanks; he also wore a brilliant red cravat. He carried in his hand a long alpenstock, the sharp point of which he thrust into everything he approached—the flower-beds, the garden-benches, the trains of the ladies' dresses. In front of Winterbourne he paused, looking at him with a pair of bright and penetrating little eyes.

"Will you give me a lump of sugar?" he asked in a small sharp hard voice—a voice immature and yet somehow not young.

Winterbourne glanced at the light table near him, on which his coffee-service rested, and saw that several morsels of sugar remained. "Yes, you may take one," he answered; "but I don't think too much sugar good for little boys."

This little boy stepped forward and carefully selected three of the coveted fragments, two of which he buried in the pocket of his knickerbockers, depositing the other as promptly in another place. He poked his alpenstock, lance-fashion, into Winterbourne's bench and tried to crack the lump of sugar with his teeth.

"Oh blazes; it's har-r-d!" he exclaimed, divesting vowel and consonants, pertinently enough, of any taint of softness.

Winterbourne had immediately gathered that he might have the honour of claiming him as a countryman. "Take care you don't hurt your teeth," he said paternally.

"I haven't got any teeth to hurt. They've all come out. I've only got seven teeth. Mother counted them last night, and one came out right afterwards. She said she'd slap me if any more came out. I can't help it. It's this old Europe. It's the climate that makes them come out. In America they didn't come out. It's these hotels."

Winterbourne was much amused. "If you eat three lumps of sugar your mother will certainly slap you," he ventured.

"She's got to give me some candy then," rejoined his young interlocutor. "I can't get any candy here—any American candy. American candy's the best candy."

"And are American little boys the best little boys?" Winterbourne asked.

"I don't know. *I'm* an American boy," said the child.

"I see you're one of the best!" the young man laughed.

"Are you an American man?" pursued this vivacious infant. And then on his friend's affirmative reply, "American men are the best," he declared with assurance.

His companion thanked him for the compliment, and the child, who had now got astride of his alpenstock, stood looking about him while he attacked another lump of sugar. Winterbourne wondered if he himself had been like this in his infancy, for he had been brought to Europe at about the same age.

"Here comes my sister!" cried his young compatriot. "She's an American girl, you bet!"

Winterbourne looked along the path and saw a beautiful young lady advancing. "American girls are the best girls," he thereupon cheerfully remarked to his visitor.

"My sister ain't the best!" the child promptly returned. "She's always blowing at me."

"I imagine that's your fault, not hers," said Winterbourne. The young lady meanwhile had drawn near. She was dressed in white muslin, with a hundred frills and flounces and knots of pale-coloured ribbon. Bareheaded, she balanced in her hand a large parasol with a deep border of embroidery; and she was strikingly, admirably pretty. "How pretty they are!" thought our friend, who straightened himself in his seat as if he were ready to rise.

The young lady paused in front of his bench, near the parapet of the garden, which overlooked the lake. The small boy had now converted his alpenstock into a vaulting-pole, by the aid of which he was springing about in the gravel and kicking it up not a little. "Why Randolph," she freely began, "what *are* you doing?"

"I'm going up the Alps!" cried Randolph. "This is the way!" And he gave another extravagant jump, scattering the pebbles about Winterbourne's ears.

"That's the way they come down," said Winterbourne.

"He's an American man!" proclaimed Randolph in his harsh little voice.

The young lady gave no heed to this circumstance, but looked straight at her brother. "Well, I guess you'd better be quiet," she simply observed.

It seemed to Winterbourne that he had been in a manner presented. He got up and stepped slowly toward the charming creature, throwing away his cigarette. "This little boy and I have made acquaintance," he said with great civility. In Geneva, as he had been perfectly aware, a young man wasn't at liberty to speak to a young unmarried lady save under certain rarely-occurring conditions; but here at Vevey what conditions could be better than these?—a pretty American girl coming to stand in front of you in a garden with all the confidence in life. This pretty American girl, whatever that

might prove, on hearing Winterbourne's observation simply glanced
at him; she then turned her head and looked over the parapet, at the
lake and the opposite mountains. He wondered whether he had gone
too far, but decided that he must gallantly advance rather than
retreat. While he was thinking of something else to say the young
lady turned again to the little boy, whom she addressed quite as if
they were alone together. "I should like to know where you got that
pole."

"I bought it!" Randolph shouted.

"You don't mean to say you're going to take it to Italy!"

"Yes, I'm going to take it t' Italy!" the child rang out.

She glanced over the front of her dress and smoothed out a knot
or two of ribbon. Then she gave her sweet eyes to the prospect again.
"Well, I guess you'd better leave it somewhere," she dropped after a
moment.

"Are you going to Italy?" Winterbourne now decided very respectfully to enquire.

She glanced at him with lovely remoteness. "Yes, sir," she then
replied. And she said nothing more.

"And are you—a—thinking of the Simplon?" he pursued with a
slight drop of assurance.

"I don't know," she said. "I suppose it's some mountain. Randolph, what mountain are we thinking of?"

"Thinking of?"—the boy stared.

"Why going right over."

"Going to where?" he demanded.

"Why right down to Italy"—Winterbourne felt vague emula-
tions.

"I don't know," said Randolph. "I don't want to go t' Italy. I want
to go to America."

"Oh Italy's a beautiful place!" the young man laughed.

"Can you get candy there?" Randolph asked of all the echoes.

"I hope not," said his sister. "I guess you've had enough candy,
and mother thinks so too."

"I haven't had any for ever so long—for a hundred weeks!" cried
the boy, still jumping about.

The young lady inspected her flounces and smoothed her ribbons
again; and Winterbourne presently risked an observation on the
beauty of the view. He was ceasing to be in doubt, for he had begun

to perceive that she was really not in the least embarrassed. She might be cold, she might be austere, she might even be prim; for that was apparently—he had already so generalised—what the most "distant" American girls did: they came and planted themselves straight in front of you to show how rigidly unapproachable they were. There hadn't been the slightest flush in her fresh fairness however; so that she was clearly neither offended nor fluttered. Only she was composed—he had seen that before too—of charming little parts that didn't match and that made no *ensemble;* and if she looked another way when he spoke to her, and seemed not particularly to hear him, this was simply her habit, her manner, the result of her having no idea whatever of "form" (with such a tell-tale appendage as Randolph where in the world would she have got it?) in any such connexion. As he talked a little more and pointed out some of the objects of interest in the view, with which she appeared wholly unacquainted, she gradually, none the less, gave him more of the benefit of her attention; and then he saw that act unqualified by the faintest shadow of reserve. It wasn't however what would have been called a "bold" front that she presented, for her expression was as decently limpid as the very cleanest water. Her eyes were the very prettiest conceivable, and indeed Winterbourne hadn't for a long time seen anything prettier than his fair country-woman's various features—her complexion, her nose, her ears, her teeth. He took a great interest generally in that range of effects and was addicted to noting and, as it were, recording them; so that in regard to this young lady's face he made several observations. It wasn't at all insipid, yet at the same time wasn't pointedly—what point, on earth, could she ever make?—expressive; and though it offered such a collection of small finenesses and neatnesses he mentally accused it— very forgivingly—of a want of finish. He thought nothing more likely than that its wearer would have had her own experience of the action of her charms, as she would certainly have acquired a resulting confidence; but even should she depend on this for her main amusement her bright sweet superficial little visage gave out neither mockery nor irony. Before long it became clear that, however these things might be, she was much disposed to conversation. She remarked to Winterbourne that they were going to Rome for the winter—she and her mother and Randolph. She asked him if he was a "real American"; she wouldn't have taken him for one; he seemed more like a

German—this flower was gathered as from a large field of comparison—especially when he spoke. Winterbourne, laughing, answered that he had met Germans who spoke like Americans, but not, so far as he remembered, any American with the resemblance she noted. Then he asked her if she mightn't be more at ease should she occupy the bench he had just quitted. She answered that she liked hanging round, but she none the less resignedly, after a little, dropped to the bench. She told him she was from New York State—"if you know where that is"; but our friend really quickened this current by catching hold of her small slippery brother and making him stand a few minutes by his side.

"Tell me your honest name, my boy." So he artfully proceeded.

In response to which the child was indeed unvarnished truth. "Randolph C. Miller. And I'll tell you hers." With which he levelled his alpenstock at his sister.

"You had better wait till you're asked!" said this young lady quite at her leisure.

"I should like very much to know *your* name," Winterbourne made free to reply.

"Her name's Daisy Miller!" cried the urchin. "But that ain't her real name; that ain't her name on her cards."

"It's a pity you haven't got one of my cards!" Miss Miller quite as naturally remarked.

"Her real name's Annie P. Miller," the boy went on.

It seemed, all amazingly, to do her good. "Ask him *his* now"—and she indicated their friend.

But to this point Randolph seemed perfectly indifferent; he continued to supply information with regard to his own family. "My father's name is Ezra B. Miller. My father ain't in Europe—he's in a better place than Europe." Winterbourne for a moment supposed this the manner in which the child had been taught to intimate that Mr. Miller had been removed to the sphere of celestial rewards. But Randolph immediately added: "My father's in Schenectady. He's got a big business. My father's rich, you bet."

"Well!" ejaculated Miss Miller, lowering her parasol and looking at the embroidered border. Winterbourne presently released the child, who departed, dragging his alpenstock along the path. "He don't like Europe," said the girl as with an artless instinct for historic truth. "He wants to go back."

"To Schenectady, you mean?"

"Yes, he wants to go right home. He hasn't got any boys here. There's one boy here, but he always goes round with a teacher. They won't let him play."

"And your brother hasn't any teacher?" Winterbourne enquired.

It tapped, at a touch, the spring of confidence. "Mother thought of getting him one—to travel round with us. There was a lady told her of a very good teacher; an American lady—perhaps you know her—Mrs. Sanders. I think she came from Boston. She told her of this teacher, and we thought of getting him to travel round with us. But Randolph said he didn't want a teacher travelling round with us. He said he wouldn't have lessons when he was in the cars. And we *are* in the cars about half the time. There was an English lady we met in the cars—I think her name was Miss Featherstone; perhaps you know her. She wanted to know why I didn't give Randolph lessons—give him 'instruction,' she called it. I guess he could give me more instruction than I could give him. He's very smart."

"Yes," said Winterbourne; "he seems very smart."

"Mother's going to get a teacher for him as soon as we get t' Italy. Can you get good teachers in Italy?"

"Very good, I should think," Winterbourne hastened to reply.

"Or else she's going to find some school. He ought to learn some more. He's only nine. He's going to college." And in this way Miss Miller continued to converse upon the affairs of her family and upon other topics. She sat there with her extremely pretty hands, ornamented with very brilliant rings, folded in her lap, and with her pretty eyes now resting upon those of Winterbourne, now wandering over the garden, the people who passed before her and the beautiful view. She addressed her new acquaintance as if she had known him a long time. He found it very pleasant. It was many years since he had heard a young girl talk so much. It might have been said of this wandering maiden who had come and sat down beside him upon a bench that she chattered. She was very quiet, she sat in a charming tranquil attitude; but her lips and her eyes were constantly moving. She had a soft slender agreeable voice, and her tone was distinctly sociable. She gave Winterbourne a report of her movements and intentions, and those of her mother and brother, in Europe, and enumerated in particular the various hotels at which they had stopped. "That English lady in the cars," she said—"Miss Featherstone—asked me if we didn't all live in hotels in America. I told her I had never been in so many hotels in my life as since I came to Europe. I've never seen so many—it's nothing but hotels." But Miss Miller made this remark with no querulous accent; she appeared to be in the best humour with everything. She declared that the hotels were very good when once you got used to their ways and that Europe was perfectly entrancing. She wasn't disappointed—not a bit. Perhaps it was because she had heard so much about it before. She had ever so many intimate friends who had been there ever so many times, and that way she had got thoroughly posted. And then she had had ever so many dresses and things from Paris. Whenever she put on a Paris dress she felt as if she were in Europe.

"It was a kind of a wishing-cap," Winterbourne smiled.

"Yes," said Miss Miller at once and without examining this analogy; "it always made me wish I was here. But I needn't have done that for dresses. I'm sure they send all the pretty ones to America; you see the most frightful things here. The only thing I don't like," she proceeded, "is the society. There ain't any society—or if there is I don't know where it keeps itself. Do you? I suppose there's some society somewhere, but I haven't seen anything of it. I'm very fond of society and I've always had plenty of it. I don't mean only in Schenectady, but in New York. I used to go to New York every winter. In New York I had lots of society. Last winter I had seventeen dinners given me, and three of them were by gentlemen," added Daisy Miller. "I've more friends in New York than in Schenectady—more gentlemen friends; and more young lady friends too," she resumed in a moment. She paused again for an instant; she was looking at Winterbourne with all her prettiness in her frank gay eyes and in her clear rather uniform smile. "I've always had," she said, "a great deal of gentlemen's society."

Poor Winterbourne was amused and perplexed—above all he was charmed. He had never yet heard a young girl express herself in just this fashion; never at least save in cases where to say such things was to have at the same time some rather complicated consciousness about them. And yet was he to accuse Miss Daisy Miller of an actual or a potential *arrière-pensée*, as they said at Geneva? He felt he had lived at Geneva so long as to have got morally muddled; he had lost the right sense for the young American tone. Never indeed since he had grown old enough to appreciate things had he encountered a young compatriot of so "strong" a type as this. Certainly she was very charming, but how extraordinarily communicative and how tremendously easy! Was she simply a pretty girl from New York State—were they all like that, the pretty girls who had had a good deal of gentlemen's society? Or was she also a designing, an audacious, in short an expert young person? Yes, his instinct for such a question had ceased to serve him, and his reason could but mislead. Miss Daisy Miller looked extremely innocent. Some people had told him that after all American girls *were* exceedingly innocent, and others had told him that after all they weren't. He must on the whole take Miss Daisy Miller for a flirt—a pretty American flirt. He had never as yet had relations with representatives of that class. He had known here in Europe two or three women—persons older than Miss Daisy Miller and provided, for respectability's sake, with husbands—who were great coquettes; dangerous terrible women with whom one's light commerce might indeed take a serious turn. But this charming apparition wasn't a coquette in that sense; she was very unsophisticated; she was only a pretty American flirt. Winterbourne was almost grateful for having found the formula that applied to Miss Daisy Miller. He leaned back in his seat; he remarked to himself that she had the finest little nose he had ever seen; he wondered what were the regular conditions and limitations of one's intercourse with a pretty American flirt. It presently became apparent that he was on the way to learn.

"Have you been to that old castle?" the girl soon asked, pointing with her parasol to the far-shining walls of the Château de Chillon.

"Yes, formerly, more than once," said Winterbourne. "You too, I suppose, have seen it?"

"No, we haven't been there. I want to go there dreadfully. Of course I mean to go there. I wouldn't go away from here without having seen that old castle."

"It's a very pretty excursion," the young man returned, "and very easy to make. You can drive, you know, or you can go by the little steamer."

"You can go in the cars," said Miss Miller.

"Yes, you can go in the cars," Winterbourne assented.

"Our courier says they take you right up to the castle," she continued. "We were going last week, but mother gave out. She suffers dreadfully from dyspepsia. She said she couldn't any more go—!" But this sketch of Mrs. Miller's plea remained unfinished. "Randolph wouldn't go either; he says he don't think much of old castles. But I guess we'll go this week if we can get Randolph."

"Your brother isn't interested in ancient monuments?" Winterbourne indulgently asked.

He now drew her, as he guessed she would herself have said, every time. "Why no, he says he don't care much about old castles. He's only nine. He wants to stay at the hotel. Mother's afraid to leave him alone, and the courier won't stay with him; so we haven't been to many places. But it will be too bad if we don't go up there." And Miss Miller pointed again at the Château de Chillon.

"I should think it might be arranged," Winterbourne was thus emboldened to reply. "Couldn't you get some one to stay—for the afternoon—with Randolph?"

Miss Miller looked at him a moment, and then with all serenity, "I wish *you'd* stay with him!" she said.

He pretended to consider it. "I'd much rather go to Chillon with you."

"With me?" she asked without a shadow of emotion.

She didn't rise blushing, as a young person at Geneva would have done; and yet, conscious that he had gone very far, he thought it possible she had drawn back. "And with your mother," he answered very respectfully.

But it seemed that both his audacity and his respect were lost on Miss Daisy Miller. "I guess mother wouldn't go—for *you*," she smiled. "And she ain't much *bent* on going, anyway. She don't like to ride round in the afternoon." After which she familiarly proceeded: "But did you really mean what you said just now—that you'd like to go up there?"

"Most earnestly I meant it," Winterbourne declared.

"Then we may arrange it. If mother will stay with Randolph I guess Eugenio will."

"Eugenio?" the young man echoed.

"Eugenio's our courier. He doesn't like to stay with Randolph—he's the most fastidious man I ever saw. But he's a splendid courier. I guess he'll stay at home with Randolph if mother does, and then we can go to the castle."

Winterbourne reflected for an instant as lucidly as possible: "we" could only mean Miss Miller and himself. This prospect seemed almost too good to believe; he felt as if he ought to kiss the young lady's hand. Possibly he would have done so,—and quite spoiled his chance; but at this moment another person—presumably Eugenio— appeared. A tall handsome man, with superb whiskers and wearing a velvet morning-coat and a voluminous watch-guard, approached the young lady, looking sharply at her companion. "Oh Eugenio!" she said with the friendliest accent.

Eugenio had eyed Winterbourne from head to foot; he now bowed gravely to Miss Miller. "I have the honour to inform Mademoiselle that luncheon's on table."

Mademoiselle slowly rose. "See here, Eugenio, I'm going to that old castle anyway."

"To the Château de Chillon, Mademoiselle?" the courier enquired. "Mademoiselle has made arrangements?" he added in a tone that struck Winterbourne as impertinent.

Eugenio's tone apparently threw, even to Miss Miller's own apprehension, a slightly ironical light on her position. She turned to Winterbourne with the slightest blush. "You won't back out?"

"I shall not be happy till we go!" he protested.

"And you're staying in this hotel?" she went on. "And you're really American?"

The courier still stood there with an effect of offence for the young man so far as the latter saw in it a tacit reflexion on Miss Miller's behaviour and an insinuation that she "picked up" acquaintances. "I shall have the honour of presenting to you a person who'll tell you all about me," he said, smiling, and referring to his aunt.

"Oh well, we'll go some day," she beautifully answered; with which she gave him a smile and turned away. She put up her parasol and walked back to the inn beside Eugenio. Winterbourne stood watching her, and as she moved away, drawing her muslin furbelows over the walk, he spoke to himself of her natural elegance.

❧ 2 ❧

HE had, however, engaged to do more than proved feasible in promising to present his aunt, Mrs. Costello, to Miss Daisy Miller. As soon as that lady had got better of her headache he waited on her in her apartment and, after a show of the proper solicitude about her health, asked if she had noticed in the hotel an American family—a mamma, a daughter and an obstreperous little boy.

"An obstreperous little boy and a preposterous big courier?" said Mrs. Costello. "Oh yes, I've noticed them. Seen them, heard them and kept out of their way." Mrs. Costello was a widow of fortune, a person of much distinction and who frequently intimated that if she hadn't been so dreadfully liable to sick-headaches she would probably have left a deeper impress on her time. She had a long pale face, a high nose and a great deal of very striking white hair, which she wore in large puffs and over the top of her head. She had two sons married in New York and another who was now in Europe. This young man was amusing himself at Homburg and, though guided by his taste, was rarely observed to visit any particular city at the moment selected by his mother for her appearance there. Her nephew, who had come to Vevey expressly to see her, was therefore more attentive than, as she said, her very own. He had imbibed at Geneva the idea that one must be irreproachable in all such forms. Mrs. Costello hadn't seen him for many years and was now greatly pleased with him, manifesting her approbation by initiating him into many of the secrets of that social sway which, as he could see she would like him to think, she exerted from her stronghold in Forty-Second Street. She admitted that she was very exclusive, but if he had been better acquainted with New York he would see that one had to be. And her picture of the minutely hierarchical constitution of the society of that city, which she presented to him in many different lights, was, to Winterbourne's imagination, almost oppressively striking.

He at once recognised from her tone that Miss Daisy Miller's place in the social scale was low. "I'm afraid you don't approve of them," he pursued in reference to his new friends.

"They're horribly common"—it was perfectly simple. "They're the sort of Americans that one does one's duty by just ignoring."

"Ah you just ignore them?"—the young man took it in.

"I can't *not,* my dear Frederick. I wouldn't if I hadn't to, but I have to."

"The little girl's very pretty," he went on in a moment.

"Of course she's very pretty. But she's of the last crudity."

"I see what you mean of course," he allowed after another pause.

"She has that charming look they all have," his aunt resumed. "I can't think where they pick it up; and she dresses in perfection—no, you don't know how well she dresses. I can't think where they get their taste."

"But, my dear aunt, she's not, after all, a Comanche savage."

"She is a young lady," said Mrs. Costello, "who has an intimacy with her mamma's courier."

"An 'intimacy' with him?" Ah there it was!

"There's no other name for such a relation. But the skinny little mother's just as bad! They treat the courier as a familiar friend—as a gentleman and a scholar. I shouldn't wonder if he dines with them. Very likely they've never seen a man with such good manners, such fine clothes, so *like* a gentleman—or a scholar. He probably corresponds to the young lady's idea of a count. He sits with them in the garden of an evening. I think he smokes in their faces."

Winterbourne listened with interest to these disclosures; they helped him to make up his mind about Miss Daisy. Evidently she was rather wild. "Well," he said, "I'm not a courier and I didn't smoke in her face, and yet she was very charming to me."

"You had better have mentioned at first," Mrs. Costello returned with dignity, "that you had made her valuable acquaintance."

"We simply met in the garden and talked a bit."

"By appointment—no? Ah that's still to come! Pray what did you say?"

"I said I should take the liberty of introducing her to my admirable aunt."

"Your admirable aunt's a thousand times obliged to you."

"It was to guarantee my respectability."

"And pray who's to guarantee hers?"

"Ah you're cruel!" said the young man. "She's a very innocent girl."

"You don't say that as if you believed it," Mrs. Costello returned.

"She's completely uneducated," Winterbourne acknowledged, "but she's wonderfully pretty, and in short she's very nice. To prove I believe it I'm going to take her to the Château de Chillon."

Mrs. Costello made a wondrous face. "You two are going off there together? I should say it proved just the contrary. How long had you known her, may I ask, when this interesting project was formed? You haven't been twenty-four hours in the house."

"I had known her half an hour!" Winterbourne smiled.

"Then she's just what I supposed."

"And what do you suppose?"

"Why that she's a horror."

Our youth was silent for some moments. "You really think then," he presently began, and with a desire for trustworthy information, "you really think that—" But he paused again while his aunt waited.

"Think what, sir?"

"That she's the sort of young lady who expects a man sooner or later to—well, we'll call it carry her off?"

"I haven't the least idea what such young ladies expect a man to do. But I really consider you had better not meddle with little American girls who are uneducated, as you mildly put it. You've lived too long out of the country. You'll be sure to make some great mistake. You're too innocent."

"My dear aunt, not so much as that comes to!" he protested with a laugh and a curl of his moustache.

"You're too guilty then!"

He continued all thoughtfully to finger the ornament in question. "You won't let the poor girl know you then?" he asked at last.

"Is it literally true that she's going to the Château de Chillon with you?"

"I've no doubt she fully intends it."

"Then, my dear Frederick," said Mrs. Costello, "I must decline the honour of her acquaintance. I'm an old woman, but I'm not too old—thank heaven—to be honestly shocked!"

"But don't they all do these things—the little American girls at home?" Winterbourne enquired.

Mrs. Costello stared a moment. "I should like to see my granddaughters do them!" she then grimly returned.

This seemed to throw some light on the matter, for Winterbourne remembered to have heard his pretty cousins in New York, the daughters of this lady's two daughters, called "tremendous flirts." If therefore Miss Daisy Miller exceeded the liberal licence allowed to these young women it was probable she did go even by the American allowance rather far. Winterbourne was impatient to see her again, and it vexed, it even a little humiliated him, that he shouldn't by instinct appreciate her justly.

Though so impatient to see her again he hardly knew what

ground he should give for his aunt's refusal to become acquainted with her; but he discovered promptly enough that with Miss Daisy Miller there was no great need of walking on tiptoe. He found her that evening in the garden, wandering about in the warm starlight after the manner of an indolent sylph and swinging to and fro the largest fan he had ever beheld. It was ten o'clock. He had dined with his aunt, had been sitting with her since dinner, and had just taken leave of her till the morrow. His young friend frankly rejoiced to renew their intercourse; she pronounced it the stupidest evening she had ever passed.

"Have you been all alone?" he asked with no intention of an epigram and no effect of her perceiving one.

"I've been walking round with mother. But mother gets tired walking round," Miss Miller explained.

"Has she gone to bed?"

"No, she doesn't like to go to bed. She doesn't sleep scarcely any—not three hours. She says she doesn't know how she lives. She's dreadfully nervous. I guess she sleeps more than she thinks. She's gone somewhere after Randolph; she wants to try to get him to go to bed. He doesn't like to go to bed."

The soft impartiality of her *constatations,* as Winterbourne would have termed them, was a thing by itself—exquisite little fatalist as they seemed to make her. "Let us hope she'll persuade him," he encouragingly said.

"Well, she'll talk to him all she can—but he doesn't like her to talk to him": with which Miss Daisy opened and closed her fan. "She's going to try to get Eugenio to talk to him. But Randolph ain't afraid of Eugenio. Eugenio's a splendid courier, but he can't make much impression on Randolph! I don't believe he'll go to bed before eleven." Her detachment from any invidious judgement of this was, to her companion's sense, inimitable; and it appeared that Randolph's vigil was in fact triumphantly prolonged, for Winterbourne attended her in her stroll for some time without meeting her mother. "I've been looking round for that lady you want to introduce me to," she resumed—"I guess she's your aunt." Then on his admitting the fact and expressing some curiosity as to how she had learned it, she said she had heard all about Mrs. Costello from the chambermaid. She was very quiet and very *comme il faut;* she wore white puffs; she spoke to no one and she never dined at the common table. Every two days she had a headache. "I think that's a lovely description, head-ache and all!" said Miss Daisy, chattering along in her thin gay voice. "I want to know her ever so much. I know just what *your* aunt would be; I know I'd like her. She'd be very exclusive. I like a lady to be exclusive; I'm dying to be exclusive myself. Well, I guess we *are* exclusive, mother and I. We don't speak to any one—or they don't speak to us. I suppose it's about the same thing. Anyway, I shall be ever so glad to meet your aunt."

Winterbourne was embarrassed—he could but trump up some evasion. "She'd be most happy, but I'm afraid those tiresome head-aches are always to be reckoned with."

The girl looked at him through the fine dusk. "Well, I suppose she doesn't have a headache every day."

He had to make the best of it. "She tells me she wonderfully does." He didn't know what else to say.

Miss Miller stopped and stood looking at him. Her prettiness was still visible in the darkness; she kept flapping to and fro her enor-mous fan. "She doesn't want to know me!" she then lightly broke out. "Why don't you say so? You needn't be afraid. *I'm* not afraid!" And she quite crowed for the fun of it.

Winterbourne distinguished however a wee false note in this: he was touched, shocked, mortified by it. "My dear young lady, she knows no one. She goes through life immured. It's her wretched health."

The young girl walked on a few steps in the glee of the thing. "You needn't be afraid," she repeated. "Why should she want to know me?" Then she paused again; she was close to the parapet of the garden, and in front of her was the starlit lake. There was a vague sheen on its surface, and in the distance were dimly-seen mountain forms. Daisy Miller looked out at these great lights and shades and again proclaimed a gay indifference—"Gracious! she *is* exclusive!" Winterbourne wondered if she were seriously wounded and for a moment almost wished her sense of injury might be such as to make it becoming in him to reassure and comfort her. He had a pleasant sense that she would be all accessible to a respectful tenderness at that moment. He felt quite ready to sacrifice his aunt—conversation-ally; to acknowledge she was a proud rude woman and to make the point that they needn't mind her. But before he had time to commit himself to this questionable mixture of gallantry and impiety, the young lady, resuming her walk, gave an exclamation in quite another tone. "Well, here's mother! I guess she *hasn't* got Randolph to go to bed." The figure of a lady appeared, at a distance, very indistinct in the darkness; it advanced with a slow and wavering step and then suddenly seemed to pause.

"Are you sure it's your mother? Can you make her out in this thick dusk?" Winterbourne asked.

"Well," the girl laughed, "I guess I know my own mother! And when she has got on my shawl too. She's always wearing my things."

The lady in question, ceasing now to approach, hovered vaguely about the spot at which she had checked her steps.

"I'm afraid your mother doesn't see you," said Winterbourne. "Or perhaps," he added—thinking, with Miss Miller, the joke permissible—"perhaps she feels guilty about your shawl."

"Oh it's a fearful old thing!" his companion placidly answered. "I told her she could wear it if she didn't mind looking like a fright. She won't come here because she sees you."

"Ah then," said Winterbourne, "I had better leave you."

"Oh no—come on!" the girl insisted.

"I'm afraid your mother doesn't approve of my walking with you."

She gave him, he thought, the oddest glance. "It isn't for me; it's for you—that is it's for *her*. Well, I don't know who it's for! But mother doesn't like any of my gentlemen friends. She's right down timid. She always makes a fuss if I introduce a gentleman. But I *do* introduce them—almost always. If I didn't introduce my gentlemen friends to mother," Miss Miller added, in her small flat monotone, "I shouldn't think I was natural."

"Well, to introduce me," Winterbourne remarked, "you must know my name." And he proceeded to pronounce it.

"Oh my—I can't say all that!" cried his companion, much amused. But by this time they had come up to Mrs. Miller, who, as they drew near, walked to the parapet of the garden and leaned on it, looking intently at the lake and presenting her back to them. "Mother!" said the girl in a tone of decision—upon which the elder lady turned round. "Mr. Frederick Forsyth Winterbourne," said the latter's young friend, repeating his lesson of a moment before and introducing him very frankly and prettily. "Common" she might be, as Mrs. Costello had pronounced her; yet what provision was made by that epithet for her queer little native grace?

Her mother was a small spare light person, with a wandering eye, a scarce perceptible nose, and, as to make up for it, an unmistakeable forehead, decorated—but too far back, as Winterbourne mentally described it—with thin much-frizzled hair. Like her daughter Mrs. Miller was dressed with extreme elegance; she had enormous diamonds in her ears. So far as the young man could observe, she gave him no greeting—she certainly wasn't looking at him. Daisy was near her, pulling her shawl straight. "What are you doing, poking round here?" this young lady enquired—yet by no means with the harshness of accent her choice of words might have implied.

"Well, I don't know"—and the new-comer turned to the lake again.

"I shouldn't think you'd want that shawl!" Daisy familiarly proceeded.

"Well—I do!" her mother answered with a sound that partook for Winterbourne of an odd strain between mirth and woe.

"Did you get Randolph to go to bed?" Daisy asked.

"No, I couldn't induce him"—and Mrs. Miller seemed to confess to the same mild fatalism as her daughter. "He wants to talk to the waiter. He *likes* to talk to that waiter."

"I was just telling Mr. Winterbourne," the girl went on; and to the young man's ear her tone might have indicated that she had been uttering his name all her life.

"Oh yes!" he concurred—"I've the pleasure of knowing your son."

Randolph's mamma was silent; she kept her attention on the lake. But at last a sigh broke from her. "Well, I don't see how he lives!"

"Anyhow, it isn't so bad as it was at Dover," Daisy at least opined.

"And what occurred at Dover?" Winterbourne desired to know.

"He wouldn't go to bed at all. I guess he sat up all night—in the public parlour. He wasn't in bed at twelve o'clock: it seemed as if he couldn't budge."

"It was half-past twelve when *I* gave up," Mrs. Miller recorded with passionless accuracy.

It was of great interest to Winterbourne. "Does he sleep much during the day?"

"I guess he doesn't sleep *very* much," Daisy rejoined.

"I wish he just *would!*" said her mother. "It seems as if he *must* make it up somehow."

"Well, I guess it's we that make it up. I think he's real tiresome," Daisy pursued.

After which, for some moments, there was silence. "Well, Daisy Miller," the elder lady then unexpectedly broke out, "I shouldn't think you'd want to talk against your own brother!"

"Well, he *is* tiresome, mother," said the girl, but with no sharpness of insistence.

"Well, he's only nine," Mrs. Miller lucidly urged.

"Well, he wouldn't go up to that castle, anyway," her daughter replied as for accommodation. "I'm going up there with Mr. Winterbourne."

To this announcement, very placidly made, Daisy's parent offered no response. Winterbourne took for granted on this that she opposed such a course; but he said to himself at the same time that she was a simple easily-managed person and that a few deferential protestations would modify her attitude. "Yes," he therefore interposed, "your daughter has kindly allowed me the honour of being her guide."

Mrs. Miller's wandering eyes attached themselves with an appealing air to her other companion, who, however, strolled a few steps further, gently humming to herself. "I presume you'll go in the cars," she then quite colourlessly remarked.

"Yes, or in the boat," said Winterbourne.

"Well, of course I don't know," Mrs. Miller returned. "I've never been up to that castle."

"It is a pity you shouldn't go," he observed, beginning to feel reassured as to her opposition. And yet he was quite prepared to find that as a matter of course she meant to accompany her daughter.

It was on this view accordingly that light was projected for him. "We've been thinking ever so much about going, but it seems as if we couldn't. Of course Daisy—she wants to go round everywhere. But there's a lady here—I don't know her name—she says she shouldn't think we'd want to go to see castles *here;* she should think we'd want to wait till we got t' Italy. It seems as if there would be so many there," continued Mrs. Miller with an air of increasing confidence. "Of course we only want to see the principal ones. We visited several in England," she presently added.

"Ah yes, in England there are beautiful castles," said Winterbourne. "But Chillon here is very well worth seeing."

"Well, if Daisy feels up to it—" said Mrs. Miller in a tone that seemed to break under the burden of such conceptions. "It seems as if there's nothing she won't undertake."

"Oh I'm pretty sure she'll enjoy it!" Winterbourne declared. And he desired more and more to make it a certainty that he was to have the privilege of a *tête-à-tête* with the young lady who was still strolling along in front of them and softly vocalising. "You're not disposed, Madam," he enquired, "to make the so interesting excursion yourself?"

So addressed Daisy's mother looked at him an instant with a certain scared obliquity and then walked forward in silence. Then, "I guess she had better go alone," she said simply.

It gave him occasion to note that this was a very different type of maternity from that of the vigilant matrons who massed themselves in the forefront of social intercourse in the dark old city at the other end of the lake. But his meditations were interrupted by hearing his name very distinctly pronounced by Mrs. Miller's unprotected daughter. "Mr. Winterbourne!" she piped from a considerable distance.

"Mademoiselle!" said the young man.

"Don't you want to take me out in a boat?"

"At present?" he asked.

"Why of course!" she gaily returned.

"Well, Annie Miller!" exclaimed her mother.

"I beg you, Madam, to let her go," he hereupon eagerly pleaded; so instantly had he been struck with the romantic side of this chance to guide through the summer starlight a skiff freighted with a fresh and beautiful young girl.

"I shouldn't think she'd want to," said her mother. "I should think she'd rather go indoors."

"I'm sure Mr. Winterbourne wants to *take* me," Daisy declared. "He's so awfully devoted!"

"I'll row you over to Chillon under the stars."

"I don't believe it!" Daisy laughed.

"Well!" the elder lady again gasped, as in rebuke of this freedom.

"You haven't spoken to me for half an hour," her daughter went on.

"I've been having some very pleasant conversation with your mother," Winterbourne replied.

"Oh pshaw! I want you to take me out in a boat!" Daisy went on as if nothing else had been said. They had all stopped and she had turned round and was looking at her friend. Her face wore a charming smile, her pretty eyes gleamed in the darkness, she swung her great fan about. No, he felt, it was impossible to be prettier than that.

"There are half a dozen boats moored at that landing-place," and he pointed to a range of steps that descended from the garden to the lake. "If you'll do me the honour to accept my arm we'll go and select one of them."

She stood there smiling; she threw back her head; she laughed as for the drollery of this. "I like a gentleman to be formal!"

"I assure you it's a formal offer."

"I was bound I'd make you say something," Daisy agreeably mocked.

"You see it's not very difficult," said Winterbourne. "But I'm afraid you're chaffing me."

"I think not, sir," Mrs. Miller shyly pleaded.

"Do then let me give you a row," he persisted to Daisy.

"It's quite lovely, the way you say that!" she cried in reward.

"It will be still more lovely to do it."

"Yes, it would be lovely!" But she made no movement to accompany him; she only remained an elegant image of free light irony.

"I guess you'd better find out what time it is," her mother impartially contributed.

"It's eleven o'clock, Madam," said a voice with a foreign accent out of the neighbouring darkness; and Winterbourne, turning, recognised the florid personage he had already seen in attendance. He had apparently just approached.

"Oh Eugenio," said Daisy, "I'm going out with Mr. Winterbourne in a boat!"

Eugenio bowed. "At this hour of the night, Mademoiselle?"

"I'm going with Mr. Winterbourne," she repeated with her shining smile. "I'm going this very minute."

"Do tell her she can't, Eugenio," Mrs. Miller said to the courier.

"I think you had better not go out in a boat, Mademoiselle," the man declared.

Winterbourne wished to goodness this pretty girl were not on such familiar terms with her courier; but he said nothing, and she meanwhile added to his ground. "I suppose you don't think it's proper! My!" she wailed; "Eugenio doesn't think anything's proper."

"I'm nevertheless quite at your service," Winterbourne hastened to remark.

"Does Mademoiselle propose to go alone?" Eugenio asked of Mrs. Miller.

"Oh no, with this gentleman!" cried Daisy's mamma for reassurance.

"I *meant* alone with the gentleman." The courier looked for a moment at Winterbourne—the latter seemed to make out in his face a vague presumptuous intelligence as at the expense of their companions—and then solemnly and with a bow, "As Mademoiselle pleases!" he said.

But Daisy broke off at this. "Oh I hoped you'd make a fuss! I don't care to go now."

"Ah but I myself shall make a fuss if you don't go," Winterbourne declared with spirit.

"That's all I want—a little fuss!" With which she began to laugh again.

"Mr. Randolph has retired for the night!" the courier hereupon importantly announced.

"Oh Daisy, now we can go then!" cried Mrs. Miller.

Her daughter turned away from their friend, all lighted with her odd perversity. "Good-night—I hope you're disappointed or disgusted or something!"

He looked at her gravely, taking her by the hand she offered. "I'm puzzled, if you want to know!" he answered.

"Well, I hope it won't keep you awake!" she said very smartly; and, under the escort of the privileged Eugenio, the two ladies passed toward the house.

Winterbourne's eyes followed them; he was indeed quite mystified. He lingered beside the lake a quarter of an hour, baffled by the question of the girl's sudden familiarities and caprices. But the only very definite conclusion he came to was that he should enjoy deucedly "going off" with her somewhere.

Two days later he went off with her to the Castle of Chillon. He waited for her in the large hall of the hotel, where the couriers, the servants, the foreign tourists were lounging about and staring. It wasn't the place he would have chosen for a tryst, but she had placidly appointed it. She came tripping downstairs, buttoning her long gloves, squeezing her folded parasol against her pretty figure, dressed exactly in the way that consorted best, to his fancy, with their adventure. He was a man of imagination and, as our ancestors used to say, of sensibility; as he took in her charming air and caught from the great staircase her impatient confiding step the note of some small sweet strain of romance, not intense but clear and sweet, seemed to sound for their start. He could have believed he was *really* "going off" with her. He led her out through all the idle people assembled—they all looked at her straight and hard: she had begun to chatter as soon as she joined him. His preference had been that they should be conveyed to Chillon in a carriage, but she expressed a lively wish to go in the little steamer—there would be such a lovely breeze upon the water and they should see such lots of people. The sail wasn't long, but Winterbourne's companion found time for many characteristic remarks and other demonstrations, not a few of which were, from the extremity of their candour, slightly disconcerting. To the young man himself their small excursion showed so for delightfully irregular and incongruously intimate that, even allowing for her habitual sense of freedom, he had some expectation of seeing her appear to find in it the same savour. But it must be confessed that he was in this particular rather disappointed. Miss Miller was highly animated, she was in the brightest spirits; but she was clearly not at all in a nervous flutter—as she should have been to match *his* tension; she avoided neither his eyes nor those of any one else; she neither coloured from an awkward consciousness when she looked at him nor when she saw that people were looking at herself. People continued to look at her a great deal, and Winterbourne could at least take pleasure in his pretty companion's distinguished air. He had been privately afraid she would talk loud, laugh overmuch, and even perhaps desire to move extravagantly about the boat. But he quite forgot his fears; he sat smiling with his eyes on her face while, without stirring from her place, she delivered herself of a great number of original reflexions. It was the most charming innocent prattle he had ever heard, for, by his own experience hitherto, when young persons were so ingenuous they were less articulate and when they were so confident were more sophisticated. If he had assented to the idea that she was "common," at any rate, *was* she proving so, after all, or was he simply getting used to her commonness? Her discourse was for the most part of what immediately and superficially surrounded them, but there were moments when it threw out a longer look or took a sudden straight plunge.

"What on *earth* are you so solemn about?" she suddenly demanded, fixing her agreeable eyes on her friend's.

"*Am* I solemn?" he asked. "I had an idea I was grinning from ear to ear."

"You look as if you were taking me to a prayer-meeting or a funeral. If that's a grin your ears are very near together."

"Should you like me to dance a hornpipe on the deck?"

"Pray do, and I'll carry round your hat. It will pay the expenses of our journey."

"I never was better pleased in my life," Winterbourne returned.

She looked at him a moment, then let it renew her amusement. "I like to make you say those things. You're a queer mixture!"

In the castle, after they had landed, nothing could exceed the light independence of her humour. She tripped about the vaulted chambers, rustled her skirts in the corkscrew staircases, flirted back with a pretty little cry and a shudder from the edge of the oubliettes and turned a singularly well-shaped ear to everything Winterbourne told her about the place. But he saw she cared little for mediæval history and that the grim ghosts of Chillon loomed but faintly before her. They had the good fortune to have been able to wander without other society than that of their guide; and Winterbourne arranged with this companion that they shouldn't be hurried—that they should linger and pause wherever they chose. He interpreted the bargain generously—Winterbourne on his side had been generous— and ended by leaving them quite to themselves. Miss Miller's observations were marked by no logical consistency; for anything she wanted to say she was sure to find a pretext. She found a great many, in the tortuous passages and rugged embrasures of the place, for asking her young man sudden questions about himself, his family, his previous history, his tastes, his habits, his designs, and for supplying information on corresponding points in her own situation. Of her own tastes, habits and designs the charming creature was prepared to give the most definite and indeed the most favourable account.

"Well, I hope you know enough!" she exclaimed after Winterbourne had sketched for her something of the story of the unhappy

Bonnivard. "I never saw a man that knew so much!" The history of Bonnivard had evidently, as they say, gone into one ear and out of the other. But this easy erudition struck her none the less as wonderful, and she was soon quite sure she wished Winterbourne would travel with them and "go round" with them: they too in that case might learn something about something. "Don't you want to come and teach Randolph?" she asked; "I guess he'd improve with a gentleman teacher." Winterbourne was certain that nothing could possibly please him so much, but that he had unfortunately other occupations. "Other occupations? I don't believe a speck of it!" she protested. "What do you mean now? You're not in business." The young man allowed that he was not in business, but he had engagements which even within a day or two would necessitate his return to Geneva. "Oh bother!" she panted, "I don't believe it!" and she began to talk about something else. But a few moments later, when he was pointing out to her the interesting design of an antique fireplace, she broke out irrelevantly: "You don't mean to say you're going back to Geneva?"

"It is a melancholy fact that I shall have to report myself there tomorrow."

She met it with a vivacity that could only flatter him. "Well, Mr. Winterbourne, I think you're horrid!"

"Oh don't say such dreadful things!" he quite sincerely pleaded—"just at the last."

"The last?" the girl cried; "I call it the very first! I've half a mind to leave you here and go straight back to the hotel alone." And for the next ten minutes she did nothing but call him horrid. Poor Winterbourne was fairly bewildered; no young lady had as yet done him the honour to be so agitated by the mention of his personal plans. His companion, after this, ceased to pay any attention to the curiosities of Chillon or the beauties of the lake; she opened fire on the special charmer in Geneva whom she appeared to have instantly taken it for granted that he was hurrying back to see. How did Miss Daisy Miller know of that agent of his fate in Geneva? Winterbourne, who denied the existence of such a person, was quite unable to discover; and he was divided between amazement at the rapidity of her induction and amusement at the directness of her criticism. She struck him afresh, in all this, as an extraordinary mixture of innocence and crudity. "Does she never allow you more than three days at a time?" Miss Miller wished ironically to know. "Doesn't she give you a vacation in summer? there's no one so hard-worked but they can get leave to go off somewhere at this season. I suppose if you stay another day she'll come right after you in the boat. Do wait over till Friday and I'll go down to the landing to see her arrive!" He began at last even to feel he had been wrong to be disappointed in the temper in which his young lady had embarked. If he had missed the personal accent, the personal accent was now making its appearance. It sounded very distinctly, toward the end, in her telling him she'd stop "teasing" him if he'd promise her solemnly to come down to Rome that winter.

"That's not a difficult promise to make," he hastened to acknowledge. "My aunt has taken an apartment in Rome from January and has already asked me to come and see her."

"I don't want you to come for your aunt," said Daisy; "I want you just to come for me." And this was the only allusion he was ever to hear her make again to his invidious kinswoman. He promised her that at any rate he would certainly come, and after this she forbore from teasing. Winterbourne took a carriage and they drove back to Vevey in the dusk; the girl at his side, her animation a little spent, was now quite distractingly passive.

In the evening he mentioned to Mrs. Costello that he had spent the afternoon at Chillon with Miss Daisy Miller.

"The Americans—of the courier?" asked this lady.

"Ah happily the courier stayed at home."

"She went with you all alone?"

"All alone."

Mrs. Costello sniffed a little at her smelling-bottle. "And that," she exclaimed, "is the little abomination you wanted me to know!"

✻✤ 3 ✤✻

Winterbourne, who had returned to Geneva the day after his excursion to Chillon, went to Rome toward the end of January. His aunt had been established there a considerable time and he had received from her a couple of characteristic letters. "Those people you were so devoted to last summer at Vevey have turned up here, courier and all," she wrote. "They seem to have made several acquaintances, but the courier continues to be the most *intime*. The young lady, however, is also very intimate with various third-rate Italians, with whom she rackets about in a way that makes much talk. Bring me that pretty novel of Cherbuliez's—'Paule Méré'—and don't come later than the 23d."

Our friend would in the natural course of events, on arriving in Rome, have presently ascertained Mrs. Miller's address at the American banker's and gone to pay his compliments to Miss Daisy. "After what happened at Vevey I certainly think I may call upon them," he said to Mrs. Costello.

"If after what happens—at Vevey and everywhere—you desire to keep up the acquaintance, you're very welcome. Of course you're not squeamish—a man may know every one. Men are welcome to the privilege!"

"Pray what is it then that 'happens'—here for instance?" Winterbourne asked.

"Well, the girl tears about alone with her unmistakeably low foreigners. As to what happens further you must apply elsewhere for information. She has picked up half a dozen of the regular Roman fortune-hunters of the inferior sort and she takes them about to such houses as she may put *her* nose into. When she comes to a party—such a party as she can come to—she brings with her a gentleman with a good deal of manner and a wonderful moustache."

"And where's the mother?"

"I haven't the least idea. They're very dreadful people."

Winterbourne thought them over in these new lights. "They're very ignorant—very innocent only, and utterly uncivilised. Depend on it they're not 'bad.'"

"They're hopelessly vulgar," said Mrs. Costello. "Whether or no being hopelessly vulgar is being 'bad' is a question for the metaphysicians. They're bad enough to blush for, at any rate; and for this short life that's quite enough."

The news that his little friend the child of nature of the Swiss lakeside was now surrounded by half a dozen wonderful moustaches checked Winterbourne's impulse to go straightway to see her. He had perhaps not definitely flattered himself that he had made an ineffaceable impression upon her heart, but he was annoyed at hearing of a state of affairs so little in harmony with an image that had lately flitted in and out of his own meditations; the image of a very pretty girl looking out of an old Roman window and asking herself urgently when Mr. Winterbourne would arrive. If, however, he determined to wait a little before reminding this young lady of his claim to her faithful remembrance, he called with more promptitude on two or three other friends. One of these friends was an American lady who had spent several winters at Geneva, where she had placed her children at school. She was a very accomplished woman and she lived in Via Gregoriana. Winterbourne found her in a little crimson drawing-room on a third floor; the room was filled with southern sunshine. He hadn't been there ten minutes when the servant, appearing in the doorway, announced complacently "Madame Mila!" This announcement was presently followed by the entrance of little Randolph Miller, who stopped in the middle of the room and stood staring at Winterbourne. An instant later his pretty sister crossed the threshold; and then, after a considerable interval, the parent of the pair slowly advanced.

"I guess I know you!" Randolph broke ground without delay.

"I'm sure you know a great many things"—and his old friend clutched him all interestedly by the arm. "How's your education coming on?"

Daisy was engaged in some pretty babble with her hostess, but when she heard Winterbourne's voice she quickly turned her head with a "Well, I declare!" which he met smiling. "I told you I should come, you know."

"Well, I didn't believe it," she answered.

"I'm much obliged to you for that," laughed the young man.

"You might have come to see me then," Daisy went on as if they had parted the week before.

"I arrived only yesterday."

"I don't believe any such thing!" the girl declared afresh.

Winterbourne turned with a protesting smile to her mother, but this lady evaded his glance and, seating herself, fixed her eyes on her son. "We've got a bigger place than this," Randolph hereupon broke out. "It's all gold on the walls."

Mrs. Miller, more of a fatalist apparently than ever, turned uneasily in her chair. "I told you if I was to bring you you'd say something!" she stated as for the benefit of such of the company as might hear it.

"I told *you!*" Randolph retorted. "I tell *you*, sir!" he added jocosely, giving Winterbourne a thump on the knee. "It *is* bigger too!"

As Daisy's conversation with her hostess still occupied her Winterbourne judged it becoming to address a few words to her mother—such as "I hope you've been well since we parted at Vevey."

Mrs. Miller now certainly looked at him—at his chin. "Not very well, sir," she answered.

"She's got the dyspepsia," said Randolph. "I've got it too. Father's got it bad. But I've got it worst!"

This proclamation, instead of embarrassing Mrs. Miller, seemed to soothe her by reconstituting the environment to which she was most accustomed. "I suffer from the liver," she amiably whined to Winterbourne. "I think it's this climate; it's less bracing than Schenectady, especially in the winter season. I don't know whether you know we reside at Schenectady. I was saying to Daisy that I certainly hadn't found any one like Dr. Davis and I didn't believe I *would*. Oh up in Schenectady, he stands first; they think everything of Dr. Davis. He has so much to do, and yet there was nothing he wouldn't do for *me*. He said he never saw anything like my dyspepsia, but he was bound to get at it. I'm sure there was nothing he wouldn't try, and I didn't care what he did to me if he only brought me relief. He was just going to try something new, and I just longed for it, when we came right off. Mr. Miller felt as if he wanted Daisy to see Europe for herself. But I couldn't help writing the other day that I supposed it was all right for Daisy, but that I didn't know as I *could* get on much longer without Dr. Davis. At Schenectady he stands at the very top; and there's a great deal of sickness there too. It affects my sleep."

Winterbourne had a good deal of pathological gossip with Dr. Davis's patient, during which Daisy chattered unremittingly to her own companion. The young man asked Mrs. Miller how she was pleased with Rome. "Well, I must say I'm disappointed," she confessed. "We had heard so much about it—I supposed we had heard too much. But we couldn't help that. We had been led to expect something different."

Winterbourne, however, abounded in reassurance. "Ah wait a little, and you'll grow very fond of it."

"I hate it worse and worse every day!" cried Randolph.

"You're like the infant Hannibal," his friend laughed.

"No I ain't—like any infant!" Randolph declared at a venture.

"Well, that's so—and you never *were!*" his mother concurred. "But we've seen places," she resumed, "that I'd put a long way ahead of Rome." And in reply to Winterbourne's interrogation, "There's Zürich—up there in the mountains," she instanced; "I think Zürich's real lovely, and we hadn't heard half so much about it."

"The best place we've seen's the *City of Richmond!*" said Randolph.

"He means the ship," Mrs. Miller explained. "We crossed in that ship. Randolph had a good time on the *City of Richmond.*"

"It's the best place *I've* struck," the child repeated. "Only it was turned the wrong way."

"Well, we've got to turn the right way some time," said Mrs. Miller with strained but weak optimism. Winterbourne expressed the hope that her daughter at last appreciated the so various interest of Rome, and she declared with some spirit that Daisy was quite carried away. "It's on account of the society—the society's splendid. She goes round everywhere; she has made a great number of acquaintances. Of course she goes round more than I do. I must say they've all been very sweet—they've taken her right in. And then she knows a great many gentlemen. Oh she thinks there's nothing like Rome. Of course it's a great deal pleasanter for a young lady if she knows plenty of gentlemen."

By this time Daisy had turned her attention again to Winterbourne, but in quite the same free form. "I've been telling Mrs. Walker how mean you were!"

"And what's the evidence you've offered?" he asked, a trifle disconcerted, for all his superior gallantry, by her inadequate measure of the zeal of an admirer who on his way down to Rome had stopped neither at Bologna nor at Florence, simply because of a certain sweet appeal to his fond fancy, not to say to his finest curiosity. He remembered how a cynical compatriot had once told him that American women—the pretty ones, and this gave a largeness to the axiom—were at once the most exacting in the world and the least endowed with a sense of indebtedness.

"Why you were awfuly mean up at Vevey," Daisy said. "You wouldn't do most anything. You wouldn't stay there when I asked you."

"Dearest young lady," cried Winterbourne, with generous passion, "have I come all the way to Rome only to be riddled by your silver shafts?"

"Just hear him say that!"—and she gave an affectionate twist to a bow on her hostess's dress. "Did you ever hear anything so quaint?"

"So 'quaint,' my dear?" echoed Mrs. Walker more critically—quite in the tone of a partisan of Winterbourne.

"Well, I don't know"—and the girl continued to finger her ribbons. "Mrs. Walker, I want to tell you something."

"Say, mother-r," broke in Randolph with his rough ends to his words, "I tell you you've got to go. Eugenio'll raise something!"

"I'm not afraid of Eugenio," said Daisy with a toss of her head. "Look here, Mrs. Walker," she went on, "you know I'm coming to your party."

"I'm delighted to hear it."

"I've got a lovely dress."

"I'm very sure of that."

"But I want to ask a favour—permission to bring a friend."

"I shall be happy to see any of your friends," said Mrs. Walker, who turned with a smile to Mrs. Miller.

"Oh they're not my friends," cried that lady, squirming in shy repudiation. "It seems as if they didn't take to *me*—I never spoke to one of them!"

"It's an intimate friend of mine, Mr. Giovanelli," Daisy pursued without a tremor in her young clearness or a shadow on her shining bloom.

Mrs. Walker had a pause and gave a rapid glance at Winterbourne. "I shall be glad to see Mr. Giovanelli," she then returned.

"He's just the finest kind of Italian," Daisy pursued with the prettiest serenity. "He's a great friend of mine and the handsomest man in the world—except Mr. Winterbourne! He knows plenty of Italians, but he wants to know some Americans. It seems as if he was crazy about Americans. He's tremendously bright. He's perfectly lovely!"

It was settled that this paragon should be brought to Mrs. Walker's party, and then Mrs. Miller prepared to take her leave. "I guess we'll go right back to the hotel," she remarked with a confessed failure of the larger imagination.

"You may go back to the hotel, mother," Daisy replied, "but I'm just going to walk round."

"She's going to go it with Mr. Giovanelli," Randolph unscrupulously commented.

"I'm going to go it on the Pincio," Daisy peaceably smiled, while the way that she "condoned" these things almost melted Winterbourne's heart.

"Alone, my dear—at this hour?" Mrs. Walker asked. The afternoon was drawing to a close—it was the hour for the throng of carriages and of contemplative pedestrians. "I don't consider it's safe, Daisy," her hostess firmly asserted.

"Neither do I then," Mrs. Miller thus borrowed confidence to add. "You'll catch the fever as sure as you live. Remember what Dr. Davis told you!"

"Give her some of that medicine before she starts in," Randolph suggested.

The company had risen to its feet; Daisy, still showing her pretty teeth, bent over and kissed her hostess. "Mrs. Walker, you're too perfect," she simply said. "I'm not going alone; I'm going to meet a friend."

"Your friend won't keep you from catching the fever even if it *is* his own second nature," Mrs. Miller observed.

"Is it Mr. Giovanelli that's the dangerous attraction?" Mrs. Walker asked without mercy.

Winterbourne was watching the challenged girl; at this question his attention quickened. She stood there smiling and smoothing her bonnet-ribbons; she glanced at Winterbourne. Then, while she glanced and smiled, she brought out all affirmatively and without a shade of hesitation: "Mr. Giovanelli—the beautiful Giovanelli."

"My dear young friend"—and, taking her hand, Mrs. Walker turned to pleading—"don't prowl off to the Pincio at this hour to meet a beautiful Italian."

"Well, he speaks first-rate English," Mrs. Miller incoherently mentioned.

"Gracious me," Daisy piped up, "I don't want to do anything that's going to affect my health—or my character either! There's an easy way to settle it." Her eyes continued to play over Winterbourne.

"The Pincio's only a hundred yards off, and if Mr. Winterbourne were as polite as he pretends he'd offer to walk right in with me!"

Winterbourne's politeness hastened to proclaim itself, and the girl gave him gracious leave to accompany her. They passed downstairs before her mother, and at the door he saw Mrs. Miller's carriage drawn up, with the ornamental courier whose acquaintance he had made at Vevey seated within. "Good-bye, Eugenio," cried Daisy; "I'm going to take a walk!" The distance from Via Gregoriana to the beautiful garden at the other end of the Pincian Hill is in fact rapidly traversed. As the day was splendid, however, and the concourse of vehicles, walkers and loungers numerous, the young Americans found their progress much delayed. This fact was highly agreeable to Winterbourne, in spite of his consciousness of his singular situation. The slow-moving, idly-gazing Roman crowd bestowed much attention on the extremely pretty young woman of English race who passed through it, with some difficulty, on his arm; and he wondered what on earth had been in Daisy's mind when she proposed to exhibit herself unattended to its appreciation. His own mission, to her sense, was apparently to consign her to the hands of Mr. Giovanelli; but, at once annoyed and gratified, he resolved that he would do no such thing.

"Why haven't you been to see me?" she meanwhile asked. "You can't get out of that."

"I've had the honour of telling you that I've only just stepped out of the train."

"You must have stayed in the train a good while after it stopped!" she derisively cried. "I suppose you were asleep. You've had time to go to see Mrs. Walker."

"I knew Mrs. Walker—" Winterbourne began to explain.

"I know where you knew her. You knew her at Geneva. She told me so. Well, you knew me at Vevey. That's just as good. So you ought to have come." She asked him no other question than this; she began to prattle about her own affairs. "We've got splendid rooms at the hotel; Eugenio says they're the best rooms in Rome. We're going to stay all winter—if we don't die of the fever; and I guess we'll stay then! It's a great deal nicer than I thought; I thought it would be fearfully quiet—in fact I was sure it would be deadly pokey. I foresaw we should be going round all the time with one of those dreadful old men who explain about the pictures and things. But we only had about a week of that, and now I'm enjoying myself. I know ever so many people, and they're all so charming. The society's extremely select. There are all kinds—English and Germans and Italians. I think I like the English best. I like their style of conversation. But there are some lovely Americans. I never saw anything so hospitable. There's something or other every day. There's not much dancing—but I must say I never thought dancing was everything. I was always fond of conversation. I guess I'll have plenty at Mrs. Walker's—her rooms are so small." When they had passed the gate of the Pincian Gardens Miss Miller began to wonder where Mr. Giovanelli might be. "We had better go straight to that place in front, where you look at the view."

Winterbourne at this took a stand. "I certainly shan't help you to find him."

"Then I shall find him without you," Daisy said with spirit.

"You certainly won't leave me!" he protested.

She burst into her familiar little laugh. "Are you afraid you'll get lost—or run over? But there's Giovanelli leaning against that tree. He's staring at the women in the carriages: did you ever see anything so cool?"

Winterbourne descried hereupon at some distance a little figure that stood with folded arms and nursing its cane. It had a handsome face, a hat artfully poised, a glass in one eye and a nosegay in its buttonhole. Daisy's friend looked at it a moment and then said: "Do you mean to speak to that thing?"

"Do I mean to speak to him? Why you don't suppose I mean to communicate by signs!"

"Pray understand then," the young man returned, "that I intend to remain with you."

Daisy stopped and looked at him without a sign of troubled consciousness, with nothing in her face but her charming eyes, her charming teeth and her happy dimples. "Well, she's a cool one!" he thought.

"I don't like the way you say that," she declared. "It's too imperious."

"I beg your pardon if I say it wrong. The main point's to give you an idea of my meaning."

The girl looked at him more gravely, but with eyes that were prettier than ever. "I've never allowed a gentleman to dictate to me or to interfere with anything I do."

"I think that's just where your mistake has come in," he retorted. "You should sometimes listen to a gentleman—the right one."

At this she began to laugh again. "I do nothing but listen to gentlemen! Tell me if Mr. Giovanelli is the right one."

The gentleman with the nosegay in his bosom had now made out our two friends and was approaching Miss Miller with obsequious rapidity. He bowed to Winterbourne as well as to the latter's compatriot; he seemed to shine, in his coxcombical way, with the desire to please and the fact of his own intelligent joy, though Winterbourne thought him not a bad-looking fellow. But he nevertheless said to Daisy: "No, he's not the right one."

She had clearly a natural turn for free introductions; she mentioned with the easiest grace the name of each of her companions to the other. She strolled forward with one of them on either hand; Mr. Giovanelli, who spoke English very cleverly—Winterbourne afterwards learned that he had practised the idiom upon a great many American heiresses—addressed her a great deal of very polite nonsense. He had the best possible manners, and the young American, who said nothing, reflected on that depth of Italian subtlety, so strangely opposed to Anglo-Saxon simplicity, which enables people to show a smoother surface in proportion as they're more acutely displeased. Giovanelli of course had counted upon something more intimate—he had not bargained for a party of three; but he kept his temper in a manner that suggested far-stretching intentions. Winterbourne flattered himself he had taken his measure. "He's anything but a gentleman," said the young American; "he isn't even a very plausible imitation of one. He's a music-master or a penny-a-liner or a third-rate artist. He's awfully on his good behaviour, but damn his fine eyes!" Mr. Giovanelli had indeed great advantages; but it was deeply disgusting to Daisy's other friend that something in her shouldn't have instinctively discriminated against such a type. Giovanelli chattered and jested and made himself agreeable according to his honest Roman lights. It was true that if he was an imitation the imitation was studied. "Nevertheless," Winterbourne said to himself, "a nice girl ought to know!" And then he came back to the dreadful question of whether this *was* in fact a nice girl. Would a nice girl—even allowing for her being a little American flirt—make a rendezvous with a presumably low-lived foreigner? The rendezvous in this case indeed had been in broad daylight and in the most crowded corner of Rome; but wasn't it possible to regard the choice of these very circumstances as a proof more of vulgarity than of anything else? Singular though it may seem, Winterbourne was vexed that the girl, in joining her *amoroso,* shouldn't appear more impatient of his own company, and he was vexed precisely because of his inclination. It was impossible to regard her as a wholly unspotted flower—she lacked a certain indispensable fineness; and it would therefore much simplify the situation to be able to treat her as the subject of one of the visitations known to romancers as "lawless passions." That she should seem to wish to get rid of him would have helped him to think more lightly of her, just as to be able to think more lightly of her would have made her less perplexing. Daisy at any rate continued on this occasion to present herself as an inscrutable combination of audacity and innocence.

She had been walking some quarter of an hour, attended by her two cavaliers and responding in a tone of very childish gaiety, as it after all struck one of them, to the pretty speeches of the other, when a carriage that had detached itself from the revolving train drew up beside the path. At the same moment Winterbourne noticed that his friend Mrs. Walker—the lady whose house he had lately left—was seated in the vehicle and was beckoning to him. Leaving Miss Miller's side, he hastened to obey her summons—and all to find her flushed, excited, scandalised. "It's really too dreadful"—she earnestly appealed to him. "That crazy girl mustn't do this sort of thing. She mustn't walk here with you two men. Fifty people have remarked her."

Winterbourne—suddenly and rather oddly rubbed the wrong way by this—raised his grave eyebrows. "I think it's a pity to make too much fuss about it."

"It's a pity to let the girl ruin herself!"

"She's very innocent," he reasoned in his own troubled interest.

"She's very reckless," cried Mrs. Walker, "and goodness knows how far—left to itself—it may go. Did you ever," she proceeded to enquire, "see anything so blatantly imbecile as the mother? After you had all left me just now I couldn't sit still for thinking of it. It seemed too pitiful not even to attempt to save them. I ordered the carriage and put on my bonnet and came here as quickly as possible. Thank heaven I've found you!"

"What do you propose to do with us?" Winterbourne uncomfortably smiled.

"To ask her to get in, to drive her about here for half an hour—so that the world may see she's not running absolutely wild—and then take her safely home."

"I don't think it's a very happy thought," he said after reflexion, "but you're at liberty to try."

Mrs. Walker accordingly tried. The young man went in pursuit of their young lady who had simply nodded and smiled, from her distance, at her recent patroness in the carriage and then had gone her way with her own companion. On learning, in the event, that Mrs. Walker had followed her, she retraced her steps, however, with a perfect good grace and with Mr. Giovanelli at her side. She professed herself "enchanted" to have a chance to present this gentleman to her good friend, and immediately achieved the introduction; declaring with it, and as if it were of as little importance, that she had never in her life seen anything so lovely as that lady's carriage-rug.

"I'm glad you admire it," said her poor pursuer, smiling sweetly. "Will you get in and let me put it over you?"

"Oh no, thank you!"—Daisy knew her mind. "I'll admire it ever so much more as I see you driving round with it."

"Do get in and drive round *with* me," Mrs. Walker pleaded.

"That would be charming, but it's so fascinating just as I am!"—with which the girl radiantly took in the gentlemen on either side of her.

"It may be fascinating, dear child, but it's not the custom here," urged the lady of the victoria, leaning forward in this vehicle with her hands devoutly clasped.

"Well, it ought to be then!" Daisy imperturbably laughed. "If I didn't walk I'd expire."

"You should walk with your mother, dear," cried Mrs. Walker with a loss of patience.

"With my mother dear?" the girl amusedly echoed. Winterbourne saw she scented interference. "My mother never walked ten steps in hei life. And then, you know," she blandly added, "I'm more than five years old."

"You're old enough to be more reasonable. You're old enough, dear Miss Miller, to be talked about."

Daisy wondered to extravagance. "Talked about? What do you mean?"

"Come into my carriage and I'll tell you."

Daisy turned shining eyes again from one of the gentlemen beside her to the other. Mr. Giovanelli was bowing to and fro, rubbing down his gloves and laughing irresponsibly; Winterbourne thought the scene the most unpleasant possible. "I don't think I want to know what you mean," the girl presently said. "I don't think I should like it."

Winterbourne only wished Mrs. Walker would tuck up her carriage-rug and drive away; but this lady, as she afterwards told him, didn't feel she could "rest there." "Should you prefer being thought a very reckless girl?" she accordingly asked.

"Gracious me!" exclaimed Daisy. She looked again at Mr. Giovanelli, then she turned to her other companion. There was a small pink flush in her cheek; she was tremendously pretty. "Does Mr. Winterbourne think," she put to him with a wonderful bright intensity of appeal, "that—to save my reputation—I ought to get into the carriage?"

It really embarrassed him; for an instant he cast about—so strange was it to hear her speak that way of her "reputation." But he himself in fact had to speak in accordance with gallantry. The finest gallantry here was surely just to tell her the truth; and the truth, for our young man, as the few indications I have been able to give have made him known to the reader, was that his charming friend should listen to the voice of civilised society. He took in again her exquisite prettiness and then said the more distinctly: "I think you should get into the carriage."

Daisy gave the rein to her amusement. "I never heard anything so stiff! If this is improper, Mrs. Walker," she pursued, "then I'm *all* improper, and you had better give me right up. Good-bye; I hope you'll have a lovely ride!"—and with Mr. Giovanelli, who made a triumphantly obsequious salute, she turned away.

Mrs. Walker sat looking after her, and there were tears in Mrs. Walker's eyes. "Get in here, sir," she said to Winterbourne, indicating the place beside her. The young man answered that he felt bound to accompany Miss Miller; whereupon the lady of the victoria declared that if he refused her this favour she would never speak to him again. She was evidently wound up. He accordingly hastened to overtake Daisy and her more faithful ally, and, offering her his hand, told her that Mrs. Walker had made a stringent claim on his presence. He had expected her to answer with something rather free, something still more significant of the perversity from which the voice of society, through the lips of their distressed friend, had so earnestly endeavoured to dissuade her. But she only let her hand slip, as she scarce looked at him, through his slightly awkward grasp; while Mr. Giovanelli, to make it worse, bade him farewell with too emphatic a flourish of the hat.

Winterbourne was not in the best possible humour as he took his seat beside the author of his sacrifice. "That was not clever of you," he said candidly, as the vehicle mingled again with the throng of carriages.

"In such a case," his companion answered, "I don't want to be clever—I only want to be *true!*"

"Well, your truth has only offended the strange little creature—it has only put her off."

"It has happened very well"—Mrs. Walker accepted her work. "If she's so perfectly determined to compromise herself the sooner one knows it the better—one can act accordingly."

"I suspect she meant no great harm, you know," Winterbourne maturely opined.

"So I thought a month ago. But she has been going too far."

"What has she been doing?"

"Everything that's not done here. Flirting with any man she can pick up; sitting in corners with mysterious Italians; dancing all the evening with the same partners; receiving visits at eleven o'clock at night. Her mother melts away when the visitors come."

"But her brother," laughed Winterbourne, "sits up till two in the morning."

"He must be edified by what he sees. I'm told that at their hotel every one's talking about her and that a smile goes round among the servants when a gentleman comes and asks for Miss Miller."

"Ah we needn't mind the servants!" Winterbourne compassionately signified. "The poor girl's only fault," he presently added, "is her complete lack of education."

"She's naturally indelicate," Mrs. Walker, on her side, reasoned.

"Take that example this morning. How long had you known her at Vevey?"

"A couple of days."

"Imagine then the taste of her making it a personal matter that you should have left the place!"

He agreed that taste wasn't the strong point of the Millers—after which he was silent for some moments; but only at last to add: "I suspect, Mrs. Walker, that you and I have lived too long at Geneva!" And he further noted that he should be glad to learn with what particular design she had made him enter her carriage.

"I wanted to enjoin on you the importance of your ceasing your relations with Miss Miller; that of your not appearing to flirt with her; that of your giving her no further opportunity to expose herself; that of your in short letting her alone."

"I'm afraid I can't do anything quite so enlightened as *that*," he returned. "I like her awfully, you know."

"All the more reason you shouldn't help her to make a scandal."

"Well, there shall be nothing scandalous in my attentions to her," he was willing to promise.

"There certainly will be in the way she takes them. But I've said what I had on my conscience," Mrs. Walker pursued. "If you wish to rejoin the young lady I'll put you down. Here, by the way, you have a chance."

The carriage was engaged in that part of the Pincian drive which overhangs the wall of Rome and overlooks the beautiful Villa Borghese. It is bordered by a large parapet, near which are several seats. One of these, at a distance, was occupied by a gentleman and a lady, toward whom Mrs. Walker gave a toss of her head. At the same moment these persons rose and walked to the parapet. Winterbourne had asked the coachman to stop; he now descended from the carriage. His companion looked at him a moment in silence and then, while he raised his hat, drove majestically away. He stood where he had alighted; he had turned his eyes toward Daisy and her cavalier. They evidently saw no one; they were too deeply occupied with each other. When they reached the low garden-wall they remained a little looking off at the great flat-topped pine-clusters of Villa Borghese; then the girl's attendant admirer seated himself familiarly on the broad ledge of the wall. The western sun in the opposite sky sent out a brilliant shaft through a couple of cloud-bars;

whereupon the gallant Giovanelli took her parasol out of her hands and opened it. She came a little nearer and he held the parasol over her; then, still holding it, he let it so rest on her shoulder that both of their heads were hidden from Winterbourne. This young man stayed but a moment longer; then he began to walk. But he walked—not toward the couple united beneath the parasol, rather toward the residence of his aunt Mrs. Costello.

❄ 4 ❄

HE FLATTERED himself on the following day that there was no smiling among the servants when he at least asked for Mrs. Miller at her hotel. This lady and her daughter, however, were not at home; and on the next day after, repeating his visit, Winterbourne again was met by a denial. Mrs. Walker's party took place on the evening of the third day, and in spite of the final reserves that had marked his last interview with that social critic our young man was among the guests. Mrs. Walker was one of those pilgrims from the younger world who, while in contact with the elder, make a point, in their own phrase, of studying European society; and she had on this occasion collected several specimens of diversely-born humanity to serve, as might be, for text-books. When Winterbourne arrived the little person he desired most to find wasn't there; but in a few moments he saw Mrs. Miller come in alone, very shyly and ruefully. This lady's hair, above the dead waste of her temples, was more frizzled than ever. As she approached their hostess Winterbourne also drew near.

"You see I've come all alone," said Daisy's unsupported parent. "I'm so frightened I don't know what to do; it's the first time I've ever been to a party alone—especially in this country. I wanted to bring Randolph or Eugenio or some one, but Daisy just pushed me off by myself. I ain't used to going round alone."

"And doesn't your daughter intend to favour us with her society?" Mrs. Walker impressively enquired.

"Well, Daisy's all dressed," Mrs. Miller testified with that accent of the dispassionate, if not of the philosophic, historian with which she always recorded the current incidents of her daughter's career. "She got dressed on purpose before dinner. But she has a friend of hers there; that gentleman—the handsomest of the Italians—that she wanted to bring. They've got going at the piano—it seems as if they couldn't leave off. Mr. Giovanelli does sing splendidly. But I guess they'll come before very long," Mrs. Miller hopefully concluded.

"I'm sorry she should come—in that particular way," Mrs. Walker permitted herself to observe.

"Well, I told her there was no use in her getting dressed before dinner if she was going to wait three hours," returned Daisy's mamma. "I didn't see the use of her putting on such a dress as that to sit round with Mr. Giovanelli."

"This is most horrible!" said Mrs. Walker, turning away and addressing herself to Winterbourne. *"Elle s'affiche, la malheureuse.* It's her revenge for my having ventured to remonstrate with her. When she comes I shan't speak to her."

Daisy came after eleven o'clock, but she wasn't, on such an occasion, a young lady to wait to be spoken to. She rustled forward in radiant loveliness, smiling and chattering, carrying a large bouquet and attended by Mr. Giovanelli. Every one stopped talking and turned and looked at her while she floated up to Mrs. Walker. "I'm afraid you thought I never was coming, so I sent mother off to tell you. I wanted to make Mr. Giovanelli practise some things before he came; you know he sings beautifully, and I want you to ask him to sing. This is Mr. Giovanelli; you know I introduced him to you; he's got the most lovely voice and he knows the most charming set of songs. I made him go over them this evening on purpose; we had the greatest time at the hotel." Of all this Daisy delivered herself with the sweetest brightest loudest confidence, looking now at her hostess and now at all the room, while she gave a series of little pats, round her very white shoulders, to the edges of her dress. "Is there any one I know?" she as undiscourageably asked.

"I think every one knows you!" said Mrs. Walker as with a grand intention; and she gave a very cursory greeting to Mr. Giovanelli. This gentleman bore himself gallantly; he smiled and bowed and showed his white teeth, he curled his moustaches and rolled his eyes and performed all the proper functions of a handsome Italian at an evening party. He sang, very prettily, half a dozen songs, though Mrs. Walker afterwards declared that she had been quite unable to find out who asked him. It was apparently not Daisy who had set him in motion—this young lady being seated a distance from the piano and though she had publicly, as it were, professed herself his musical patroness or guarantor, giving herself to gay and audible discourse while he warbled.

"It's a pity these rooms are so small; we can't dance," she remarked to Winterbourne as if she had seen him five minutes before.

"I'm not sorry we can't dance," he candidly returned. "I'm incapable of a step."

"Of course you're incapable of a step," the girl assented. "I should think your legs *would* be stiff cooped in there so much of the time in that victoria."

"Well, they were very restless there three days ago," he amicably laughed; "all they really wanted was to dance attendance on you."

"Oh my other friend—my friend in need—stuck to me; he seems more at one with his limbs than you are—I'll say that for him. But did you ever hear anything so cool," Daisy demanded, "as Mrs. Walker's wanting me to get into her carriage and drop poor Mr. Giovanelli, and under the pretext that it was proper? People have different ideas! It would have been most unkind; he had been talking about that walk for ten days."

"He shouldn't have talked about it at all," Winterbourne decided to make answer on this: "he would never have proposed to a young lady of this country to walk about the streets of Rome with him."

"About the streets?" she cried with her pretty stare. "Where then would he have proposed to her to walk? The Pincio ain't the streets either, I guess; and I besides, thank goodness, am not a young lady of this country. The young ladies of this country have a dreadfully pokey time of it, by what I can discover; I don't see why I should change my habits for *such* stupids."

"I'm afraid your habits are those of a ruthless flirt," said Winterbourne with studied severity.

"Of course they are!"—and she hoped, evidently, by the manner of it, to take his breath away. "I'm a fearful frightful flirt! Did you ever hear of a nice girl that wasn't? But I suppose you'll tell me now I'm not a nice girl."

He remained grave indeed under the shock of her cynical profession. "You're a very nice girl, but I wish you'd flirt with me, and me only."

"Ah thank you, thank you very much: you're the last man I should think of flirting with. As I've had the pleasure of informing you, you're too stiff."

"You say that too often," he resentfully remarked.

Daisy gave a delighted laugh. "If I could have the sweet hope of making you angry I'd say it again."

"Don't do that—when I'm angry I'm stiffer than ever. But if you won't flirt with me do cease at least to flirt with your friend at the piano. They don't," he declared as in full sympathy with "them," "understand that sort of thing here."

"I thought they understood nothing else!" Daisy cried with startling world-knowledge.

"Not in young unmarried women."

"It seems to me much more proper in young unmarried than in old married ones," she retorted.

"Well," said Winterbourne, "when you deal with natives you must go by the custom of the country. American flirting is a purely American silliness; it has—in its ineptitude of innocence—no place in *this* system. So when you show yourself in public with Mr. Giovanelli and without your mother—"

"Gracious, poor mother!"—and she made it beautifully unspeakable.

Winterbourne had a touched sense for this, but it didn't alter his attitude. "Though *you* may be flirting Mr. Giovanelli isn't—he means something else."

"He isn't preaching at any rate," she returned. "And if you want very much to know, we're neither of us flirting—not a little speck. We're too good friends for that. We're real intimate friends."

He was to continue to find her thus at moments inimitable. "Ah," he then judged, "if you're in love with each other it's another affair altogether!"

She had allowed him up to this point to speak so frankly that he had no thought of shocking her by the force of his logic; yet she now none the less immediately rose, blushing visibly and leaving him mentally to exclaim that the name of little American flirts was incoherence. "Mr. Giovanelli at least," she answered, sparing but a single small queer glance for it, a queerer small glance, he felt, than he had ever yet had from her—"Mr. Giovanelli never says to me such very disagreeable things."

It had an effect on him—he stood staring. The subject of their contention had finished singing; he left the piano, and his recognition of what—a little awkwardly—didn't take place in celebration of this might nevertheless have been an acclaimed operatic tenor's series of repeated ducks before the curtain. So he bowed himself over to Daisy. "Won't you come to the other room and have some tea?" he asked—offering Mrs. Walker's slightly thin refreshment as he might have done all the kingdoms of the earth.

Daisy at last turned on Winterbourne a more natural and calculable light. He was but the more muddled by it, however, since so inconsequent a smile made nothing clear—it seemed at the most to prove in her a sweetness and softness that reverted instinctively to the pardon of offences. "It has never occurred to Mr. Winterbourne to offer me any tea," she said with her finest little intention of torment and triumph.

"I've offered you excellent advice," the young man permitted himself to growl.

"I prefer weak tea!" cried Daisy, and she went off with the brilliant Giovanelli. She sat with him in the adjoining room, in the embrasure of the window, for the rest of the evening. There was an interesting performance at the piano, but neither of these conversers gave heed to it. When Daisy came to take leave of Mrs. Walker this lady conscientiously repaired the weakness of which she had been guilty at the moment of the girl's arrival—she turned her back straight on Miss Miller and left her to depart with what grace she might. Winterbourne happened to be near the door; he saw it all. Daisy turned very pale and looked at her mother, but Mrs. Miller was humbly unconscious of any rupture of any law or of any deviation from any custom. She appeared indeed to have felt an incongruous impulse to draw attention to her own striking conformity. "Good-night, Mrs. Walker," she said; "we've had a beautiful evening. You see if I let Daisy come to parties without me I don't want her to go away without me." Daisy turned away, looking with a small white prettiness, a blighted grace, at the circle near the door: Winterbourne saw that for the first moment she was too much shocked and puzzled even for indignation. He on his side was greatly touched.

"That was very cruel," he promptly remarked to Mrs. Walker.

But this lady's face was also as a stone. "She never enters my drawing-room again."

Since Winterbourne then, hereupon, was not to meet her in Mrs. Walker's drawing-room he went as often as possible to Mrs. Miller's hotel. The ladies were rarely at home, but when he found them the devoted Giovanelli was always present. Very often the glossy little Roman, serene in success, but not unduly presumptuous, occupied with Daisy alone the florid salon enjoyed by Eugenio's care, Mrs. Miller being apparently ever of the opinion that discretion is the better part of solicitude. Winterbourne noted, at first with surprise, that Daisy on these occasions was neither embarrassed nor annoyed by his own entrance; but he presently began to feel that she had no more surprises for him and that he really liked, after all, not making out what she was "up to." She showed no displeasure for the interruption of her *tête-à-tête* with Giovanelli; she could chatter as freshly and freely with two gentlemen as with one, and this easy flow had ever the same anomaly for her earlier friend that it was so free without availing itself of its freedom. Winterbourne reflected that if she was seriously interested in the Italian it was odd she shouldn't take more trouble to preserve the sanctity of their interviews, and he liked her the better for her innocent-looking indifference and her inexhaustible gaiety. He could hardly have said why, but she struck him as a young person not formed for a troublesome jealousy. Smile at such a betrayal though the reader may, it was a fact with regard to the women who had hitherto interested him that, given certain contingencies, Winterbourne could see himself afraid—literally afraid—of these ladies. It pleased him to believe that even were twenty other things different and Daisy should love him and he should know it and like it, he would still never be afraid of Daisy. It must be added that this conviction was not altogether flattering to her: it represented that she was nothing every way if not light.

But she was evidently very much interested in Giovanelli. She looked at him whenever he spoke; she was perpetually telling him to do this and to do that; she was constantly chaffing and abusing him. She appeared completely to have forgotten that her other friend had said anything to displease her at Mrs. Walker's entertainment. One Sunday afternoon, having gone to Saint Peter's with his aunt, Winterbourne became aware that the young woman held in horror by that lady was strolling about the great church under escort of her coxcomb of the Corso. It amused him, after a debate, to point out the exemplary pair—even at the cost, as it proved, of Mrs. Costello's saying when she had taken them in through her eye-glass: "That's what makes you so pensive in these days, eh?"

"I hadn't the least idea I was pensive," he pleaded.

"You're very much preoccupied; you're always thinking of something."

"And what is it," he asked, "that you accuse me of thinking of?"

"Of that young lady's, Miss Baker's, Miss Chandler's—what's her name?—Miss Miller's intrigue with that little barber's block."

"Do you call it an intrigue," he asked—"an affair that goes on with such peculiar publicity?"

"That's their folly," said Mrs. Costello, "it's not their merit."

"No," he insisted with a hint perhaps of the preoccupation to which his aunt had alluded—"I don't believe there's anything to be called an intrigue."

"Well"—and Mrs. Costello dropped her glass—"I've heard a dozen people speak of it: they say she's quite carried away by him."

"They're certainly as thick as thieves," our embarrassed young man allowed.

Mrs. Costello came back to them, however, after a little; and Winterbourne recognised in this a further illustration—than that supplied by his own condition—of the spell projected by the case. "He's certainly very handsome. One easily sees how it is. She thinks him the most elegant man in the world, the finest gentleman possible. She has never seen anything like him—he's better even than the courier. It was the courier probably who introduced him, and if he succeeds in marrying the young lady the courier will come in for a magnificent commission."

"I don't believe she thinks of marrying him," Winterbourne reasoned, "and I don't believe he hopes to marry her."

"You may be very sure she thinks of nothing at all. She romps on from day to day, from hour to hour, as they did in the Golden Age. I can imagine nothing more vulgar," said Mrs. Costello, whose figure of speech scarcely went on all fours. "And at the same time," she added, "depend upon it she may tell you any moment that she is 'engaged.' "

"I think that's more than Giovanelli really expects," said Winterbourne.

"And who is Giovanelli?"

"The shiny—but, to do him justice, not greasy—little Roman. I've asked questions about him and learned something. He's apparently a perfectly respectable little man. I believe he's in a small way a *cavaliere avvocato*. But he doesn't move in what are called the first

circles. I think it really not absolutely impossible the courier introduced him. He's evidently immensely charmed with Miss Miller. If
she thinks him the finest gentleman in the world, he, on his side, has
never found himself in personal contact with such splendour, such
opulence, such personal daintiness, as this young lady's. And then
she must seem to him wonderfully pretty and interesting. Yes, he
can't really hope to pull it off. That must appear to him too
impossible a piece of luck. He has nothing but his handsome face to
offer, and there's a substantial, a possibly explosive Mr. Miller in
that mysterious land of dollars and six-shooters. Giovanelli's but too
conscious that he hasn't a title to offer. If he were only a count or a
marchese! What on earth can he make of the way they've taken him
up?"

"He accounts for it by his handsome face and thinks Miss Miller a
young lady *qui se passe ses fantaisies!*"

"It's very true," Winterbourne pursued, "that Daisy and her
mamma haven't yet risen to that stage of—what shall I call it?—of
culture, at which the idea of catching a count or a *marchese* begins. I
believe them intellectually incapable of that conception."

"Ah but the *cavaliere avvocato* doesn't believe them!" cried Mrs.
Costello.

Of the observation excited by Daisy's "intrigue" Winterbourne
gathered that day at Saint Peter's sufficient evidence. A dozen of the
American colonists in Rome came to talk with his relative, who sat
on a small portable stool at the base of one of the great pilasters. The
vesper-service was going forward in splendid chants and organ-tones
in the adjacent choir, and meanwhile, between Mrs. Costello and her
friends, much was said about poor little Miss Miller's going really
"too far." Winterbourne was not pleased with what he heard; but
when, coming out upon the great steps of the church, he saw Daisy,
who had emerged before him, get into an open cab with her accom-
plice and roll away through the cynical streets of Rome, the measure
of her course struck him as simply there to take. He felt very sorry for
her—not exactly that he believed she had completely lost her wits,
but because it was painful to see so much that was pretty and
undefended and natural sink so low in human estimation. He made
an attempt after this to give a hint to Mrs. Miller. He met one day in
the Corso a friend—a tourist like himself—who had just come out of
the Doria Palace, where he had been walking through the beautiful

gallery. His friend "went on" for some moments about the great portrait of Innocent X, by Velasquez, suspended in one of the cabinets of the palace, and then said: "And in the same cabinet, by the way, I enjoyed sight of an image of a different kind; that little American who's so much more a work of nature than of art and whom you pointed out to me last week." In answer to Winterbourne's enquiries his friend narrated that the little American—prettier now than ever—was seated with a companion in the secluded nook in which the papal presence is enshrined.

"All alone?" the young man heard himself disingenuously ask.

"Alone with a little Italian who sports in his button-hole a stack of flowers. The girl's a charming beauty, but I thought I understood from you the other day that she's a young lady *du meilleur monde.*"

"So she is!" said Winterbourne; and having assured himself that his informant had seen the interesting pair but ten minutes before, he jumped into a cab and went to call on Mrs. Miller. She was at home, but she apologised for receiving him in Daisy's absence.

"She's gone out somewhere with Mr. Giovanelli. She's always going round with Mr. Giovanelli."

"I've noticed they're intimate indeed," Winterbourne concurred.

"Oh it seems as if they couldn't live without each other!" said Mrs. Miller. "Well, he's a real gentleman anyhow. I guess I have the joke on Daisy—that she *must* be engaged!"

"And how does your daughter *take* the joke?"

"Oh she just says she ain't. But she might as *well* be!" this philosophic parent resumed. "She goes on as if she was. But I've made Mr. Giovanelli promise to tell me if Daisy don't. I'd want to write to Mr. Miller about it—wouldn't you?"

Winterbourne replied that he certainly should; and the state of mind of Daisy's mamma struck him as so unprecedented in the annals of parental vigilance that he recoiled before the attempt to educate at a single interview either her conscience or her wit.

After this Daisy was never at home and he ceased to meet her at the houses of their common acquaintance, because, as he perceived, these shrewd people had quite made up their minds as to the length she must have gone. They ceased to invite her, intimating that they wished to make, and make strongly, for the benefit of observant

Europeans, the point that though Miss Daisy Miller was a pretty American girl all right, her behaviour wasn't pretty at all—was in fact regarded by her compatriots as quite monstrous. Winterbourne wondered how she felt about all the cold shoulders that were turned upon her, and sometimes found himself suspecting with impatience that she simply didn't feel and didn't know. He set her down as hopelessly childish and shallow, as such mere giddiness and ignorance incarnate as was powerless either to heed or to suffer. Then at other moments he couldn't doubt that she carried about in her elegant and irresponsible little organism a defiant, passionate, perfectly observant consciousness of the impression she produced. He asked himself whether the defiance would come from the consciousness of innocence or from her being essentially a young person of the reckless class. Then it had to be admitted, he felt, that holding fast to a belief in her "innocence" was more and more but a matter of gallantry too fine-spun for use. As I have already had occasion to relate, he was reduced without pleasure to this chopping of logic and vexed at his poor fallibility, his want of instinctive certitude as to how far her extravagance was generic and national and how far it was crudely personal. Whatever it was he had helplessly missed her, and now it was too late. She was "carried away" by Mr. Giovanelli.

A few days after his brief interview with her mother he came across her at that supreme seat of flowering desolation known as the Palace of the Cæsars. The early Roman spring had filled the air with bloom and perfume, and the rugged surface of the Palatine was muffled with tender verdure. Daisy moved at her ease over the great mounds of ruin that are embanked with mossy marble and paved with monumental inscriptions. It seemed to him he had never known Rome so lovely as just then. He looked off at the enchanting harmony of line and colour that remotely encircles the city—he inhaled the softly humid odours and felt the freshness of the year and the antiquity of the place reaffirm themselves in deep interfusion. It struck him also that Daisy had never showed to the eye for so utterly charming; but this had been his conviction on every occasion of their meeting. Giovanelli was of course at her side, and Giovanelli too glowed as never before with something of the glory of his race.

"Well," she broke out upon the friend it would have been such mockery to designate as the latter's rival, "I should think you'd be quite lonesome!"

"Lonesome?" Winterbourne resignedly echoed.

"You're always going round by yourself. Can't you get any one to walk with you?"

"I'm not so fortunate," he answered, "as your gallant companion."

Giovanelli had from the first treated him with distinguished politeness; he listened with a deferential air to his remarks; he laughed punctiliously at his pleasantries; he attached such importance as he could find terms for to Miss Miller's cold compatriot. He carried himself in no degree like a jealous wooer; he had obviously a great deal of tact; he had no objection to any one's expecting a little humility of him. It even struck Winterbourne that he almost yearned at times for some private communication in the interest of his character for common sense; a chance to remark to him as another intelligent man that, bless him, *he* knew how extraordinary was their young lady and didn't flatter himself with confident—at least *too* confident and too delusive—hopes of matrimony and dollars. On this occasion he strolled away from his charming charge to pluck a sprig of almond-blossom which he carefully arranged in his button-hole.

"I know why you say that," Daisy meanwhile observed. "Because you think I go round too much with *him!*" And she nodded at her discreet attendant.

"Every one thinks so—if you care to know," was all Winterbourne found to reply.

"Of course I care to know!"—she made this point with much expression. "But I don't believe a word of it. They're only pretending to be shocked. They don't really care a straw what I do. Besides, I don't go round so much."

"I think you'll find they do care. They'll show it—disagreeably," he took on himself to state.

Daisy weighed the importance of that idea. "How—disagreeably?"

"Haven't you noticed anything?" he compassionately asked.

"I've noticed *you*. But I noticed you've no more 'give' than a ramrod the first time ever I saw you."

"You'll find at least that I've more 'give' than several others," he patiently smiled.

"How shall I find it?"

"By going to see the others."

"What will they do to me?"

"They'll show you the cold shoulder. Do you know what that means?"

Daisy was looking at him intently; she began to colour. "Do you mean as Mrs. Walker did the other night?"

"Exactly as Mrs. Walker did the other night."

She looked away at Giovanelli, still titivating with his almond-blossom. Then with her attention again on the important subject: "I shouldn't think you'd let people be so unkind!"

"How can I help it?"

"I should think you'd want to say something."

"I do want to say something"—and Winterbourne paused a moment. "I want to say that your mother tells me she believes you engaged."

"Well, I guess she does," said Daisy very simply.

The young man began to laugh. "And does Randolph believe it?"

"I guess Randolph doesn't believe anything." This testimony to Randolph's scepticism excited Winterbourne to further mirth, and he noticed that Giovanelli was coming back to them. Daisy, observing it as well, addressed herself again to her countryman. "Since you've mentioned it," she said, "I *am* engaged." He looked at her hard—he had stopped laughing. "You don't believe it!" she added.

He asked himself, and it was for a moment like testing a heart-beat; after which, "Yes, I believe it!" he said.

"Oh no, you don't," she answered. "But *if* you possibly do," she still more perversely pursued—"well, I ain't!"

Miss Miller and her constant guide were on their way to the gate of the enclosure, so that Winterbourne, who had but lately entered, presently took leave of them. A week later on he went to dine at a beautiful villa on the Cælian Hill, and, on arriving, dismissed his hired vehicle. The evening was perfect and he promised himself the satisfaction of walking home beneath the Arch of Constantine and past the vaguely-lighted monuments of the Forum. Above was a moon half-developed, whose radiance was not brilliant but veiled in a thin cloud-curtain that seemed to diffuse and equalise it. When on his return from the villa at eleven o'clock he approached the dusky circle of the Colosseum the sense of the romantic in him easily suggested that the interior, in such an atmosphere, would well repay a glance. He turned aside and walked to one of the empty arches, near which, as he observed, an open carriage—one of the little Roman street-cabs—was stationed. Then he passed in among the cavernous shadows of the great structure and emerged upon the clear and silent arena. The place had never seemed to him more impressive. One half of the gigantic circus was in deep shade while the other slept in the luminous dusk. As he stood there he began to murmur Byron's famous lines out of "Manfred"; but before he had finished his quotation he remembered that if nocturnal meditation thereabouts was the fruit of a rich literary culture it was none the less deprecated by medical science. The air of other ages surrounded one; but the air of other ages, coldly analysed, was no better than a villainous miasma. Winterbourne sought, however, toward the middle of the arena, a further reach of vision, intending the next moment a hasty retreat. The great cross in the centre was almost obscured; only as he drew near did he make it out distinctly. He thus also distinguished two persons stationed on the low steps that formed its base. One of these was a woman seated; her companion hovered before her.

Presently the sound of the woman's voice came to him distinctly in the warm night-air. "Well, he looks at us as one of the old lions or tigers may have looked at the Christian martyrs!" These words were winged with their accent, so that they fluttered and settled about him in the darkness like vague white doves. It was Miss Daisy Miller who had released them for flight.

"Let us hope he's not very hungry"—the bland Giovanelli fell in with her humour. "He'll have to take *me* first; you'll serve for dessert."

Winterbourne felt himself pulled up with final horror now—and, it must be added, with final relief. It was as if a sudden clearance had taken place in the ambiguity of the poor girl's appearances and the whole riddle of her contradictions had grown easy to read. She was a young lady about the *shades* of whose perversity a foolish puzzled gentleman need no longer trouble his head or his heart. That once questionable quantity *had* no shades—it was a mere black little blot. He stood there looking at her, looking at her companion too, and not reflecting that though he saw them vaguely he himself must have been more brightly presented. He felt angry at all his shiftings of view—he felt ashamed of all his tender little scruples and all his witless little mercies. He was about to advance again, and then again checked himself; not from the fear of doing her injustice, but from a sense of the danger of showing undue exhilaration for this disburdenment of cautious criticism. He turned away toward the entrance of the place; but as he did so he heard Daisy speak again.

"Why it was Mr. Winterbourne! He saw me and he cuts me dead!"

What a clever little reprobate she was, he was amply able to reflect at this, and how smartly she feigned, how promptly she sought to play off on him, a surprised and injured innocence! But nothing would induce him to cut her either "dead" or to within any measurable distance even of the famous "inch" of her life. He came forward again and went toward the great cross. Daisy had got up and Giovanelli lifted his hat. Winterbourne had now begun to think simply of the madness, on the ground of exposure and infection, of a frail young creature's lounging away such hours in a nest of malaria. What if she *were* the most plausible of little reprobates? That was no reason for her dying of the *perniciosa.* "How long have you been 'fooling round' here?" he asked with conscious roughness.

Daisy, lovely in the sinister silver radiance, appraised him a moment, roughness and all. "Well, I guess all the evening." She answered with spirit and, he could see even then, with exaggeration. "I never saw anything so quaint."

"I'm afraid," he returned, "you'll not think a bad attack of Roman fever very quaint. This is the way people catch it. I wonder," he added to Giovanelli, "that you, a native Roman, should countenance such extraordinary rashness."

"Ah," said this seasoned subject, "for myself I have no fear."

"Neither have I—for you!" Winterbourne retorted in French. "I'm speaking for this young lady."

Giovanelli raised his well-shaped eyebrows and showed his shining teeth, but took his critic's rebuke with docility. "I assured Mademoiselle it was a grave indiscretion, but when was Mademoiselle ever prudent?"

"I never was sick, and I don't mean to be!" Mademoiselle declared. "I don't look like much, but I'm healthy! I was bound to see the Colosseum by moonlight—I wouldn't have wanted to go home without *that;* and we've had the most beautiful time, haven't we, Mr. Giovanelli? If there has been any danger Eugenio can give me some pills. Eugenio has got some splendid pills."

"*I* should advise you then," said Winterbourne, "to drive home as fast as possible and take one!"

Giovanelli smiled as for the striking happy thought. "What you say is very wise. I'll go and make sure the carriage is at hand." And he went forward rapidly.

Daisy followed with Winterbourne. He tried to deny himself the small fine anguish of looking at her, but his eyes themselves refused to spare him, and she seemed moreover not in the least embarrassed. He spoke no word; Daisy chattered over the beauty of the place: "Well, I *have* seen the Colosseum by moonlight—that's one thing I can rave about!" Then noticing her companion's silence she asked him why he was so stiff—it had always been her great word. He made no answer, but he felt his laugh an immense negation of stiffness. They passed under one of the dark archways; Giovanelli was in front with the carriage. Here Daisy stopped a moment, looking at her compatriot. "*Did* you believe I was engaged the other day?"

"It doesn't matter now what I believed the other day!" he replied with infinite point.

It was a wonder how she didn't wince for it. "Well, what do you believe now?"

"I believe it makes very little difference whether you're engaged or not!"

He felt her lighted eyes fairly penetrate the thick gloom of the vaulted passage—as if to seek some access to him she hadn't yet compassed. But Giovanelli, with a graceful inconsequence, was at present all for retreat. "Quick, quick; if we get in by midnight we're quite safe!"

Daisy took her seat in the carriage and the fortunate Italian placed himself beside her. "Don't forget Eugenio's pills!" said Winterbourne as he lifted his hat.

"I don't care," she unexpectedly cried out for this, "whether I have Roman fever or not!" On which the cab-driver cracked his whip and they rolled across the desultory patches of antique pavement.

Winterbourne—to do him justice, as it were—mentioned to no one that he had encountered Miss Miller at midnight in the Colosseum with a gentleman; in spite of which deep discretion, however, the fact of the scandalous adventure was known a couple of days later, with a dozen vivid details, to every member of the little American circle, and was commented accordingly. Winterbourne judged thus that the people about the hotel had been thoroughly empowered to testify, and that after Daisy's return there would have been an exchange of jokes between the porter and the cab-driver. But the young man became aware at the same moment of how thoroughly it had ceased to ruffle him that the little American flirt should be "talked about" by low-minded menials. These sources of current criticism a day or two later abounded still further: the little American flirt was alarmingly ill and the doctors now in possession of the scene. Winterbourne, when the rumour came to him, immediately went to the hotel for more news. He found that two or three charitable friends had preceded him and that they were being entertained in Mrs. Miller's salon by the all-efficient Randolph.

"It's going round at night that way, you bet—that's what has made her so sick. She's always going round at night. I shouldn't think she'd want to—it's so plaguey dark over here. You can't see anything over here without the moon's right up. In America they don't go round by the moon!" Mrs. Miller meanwhile wholly surrendered to her genius for unapparent uses; her salon knew her less than ever, and she was presumably now at least giving her daughter the advantage of her society. It was clear that Daisy was dangerously ill.

Winterbourne constantly attended for news from the sick-room, which reached him, however, but with worrying indirectness, though he once had speech, for a moment, of the poor girl's physician and once saw Mrs. Miller, who, sharply alarmed, struck him as thereby more happily inspired than he could have conceived and indeed as the most noiseless and light-handed of nurses. She invoked a good deal the remote shade of Dr. Davis, but Winterbourne paid her the compliment of taking her after all for less monstrous a goose. To this indulgence indeed something she further said perhaps even more insidiously disposed him. "Daisy spoke of you the other day quite pleasantly. Half the time she doesn't know what she's saying, but that time I think she did. She gave me a message—she told me to tell you. She wanted you to know she never was engaged to that handsome Italian who was always round. I'm sure I'm very glad; Mr. Giovanelli hasn't been near us since she was taken ill. I thought he was so much of a gentleman, but I don't call that very polite! A lady told me he was afraid I hadn't approved of his being round with her so much evenings. Of course it ain't as if their evenings were as pleasant as ours—since *we* don't seem to feel that way about the poison. I guess I *don't* see the point now; but I suppose he knows I'm a lady and I'd scorn to raise a fuss. Anyway, she wants you to realise she ain't engaged. I don't know why she makes so much of it, but she said to me three times 'Mind you tell Mr. Winterbourne.' And then she told me to ask if you remembered the time you went up to that castle in Switzerland. But I said I wouldn't give any such messages as *that*. Only if she ain't engaged I guess I'm glad to realise it too."

But, as Winterbourne had originally judged, the truth on this question had small actual relevance. A week after this the poor girl died; it had been indeed a terrible case of the *perniciosa*. A grave was found for her in the little Protestant cemetery, by an angle of the wall of imperial Rome, beneath the cypresses and the thick spring-flowers. Winterbourne stood there beside it with a number of other mourners; a number larger than the scandal excited by the young lady's career might have made probable. Near him stood Giovanelli, who came nearer still before Winterbourne turned away. Giovanelli, in decorous mourning, showed but a whiter face; his button-hole lacked its nosegay and he had visibly something urgent—and even to distress—to say, which he scarce knew how to "place." He decided at last to confide it with a pale convulsion to Winterbourne. "She was the most beautiful young lady I ever saw, and the most amiable." To which he added in a moment: "Also—naturally!—the most innocent."

Winterbourne sounded him with hard dry eyes, but presently repeated his words, "The most innocent?"

"The most innocent!"

It came somehow so much too late that our friend could only glare at its having come at all. "Why the devil," he asked, "did you take her to that fatal place?"

Giovanelli raised his neat shoulders and eyebrows to within suspicion of a shrug. "For myself I had no fear; and *she*—she did what she liked."

Winterbourne's eyes attached themselves to the ground. "She did what she liked!"

It determined on the part of poor Giovanelli a further pious, a further candid, confidence. "If she had lived I should have got nothing. She never would have married me."

It had been spoken as if to attest, in all sincerity, his disinterestedness, but Winterbourne scarce knew what welcome to give it. He said, however, with a grace inferior to his friend's: "I dare say not."

The latter was even by this not discouraged. "For a moment I hoped so. But no. I'm convinced."

Winterbourne took it in; he stood staring at the raw protuberance among the April daisies. When he turned round again his fellow mourner had stepped back.

He almost immediately left Rome, but the following summer he again met his aunt Mrs. Costello at Vevey. Mrs. Costello extracted from the charming old hotel there a value that the Miller family hadn't mastered the secret of. In the interval Winterbourne had often thought of the most interesting member of that trio—of her mystifying manners and her queer adventure. One day he spoke of her to his aunt—said it was on his conscience he had done her injustice.

"I'm sure I don't know"—that lady showed caution. "How did your injustice affect her?"

"She sent me a message before her death which I didn't understand at the time. But I've understood it since. She would have appreciated one's esteem."

"She took an odd way to gain it! But do you mean by what you say," Mrs. Costello asked, "that she would have reciprocated one's affection?"

As he made no answer to this she after a little looked round at him—he hadn't been directly within sight; but the effect of that wasn't to make her repeat her question. He spoke, however, after a while. "You were right in that remark that you made last summer. I was booked to make a mistake. I've lived too long in foreign parts." And this time she herself said nothing.

Nevertheless he soon went back to live at Geneva, whence there continue to come the most contradictory accounts of his motives of sojourn: a report that he's "studying" hard—an intimation that he's much interested in a very clever foreign lady.

Pandora

❧ 1 ❧

IT has long been the custom of the North German Lloyd steamers, which convey passengers from Bremen to New York, to anchor for several hours in the pleasant port of Southampton, where their human cargo receives many additions. An intelligent young German, Count Otto Vogelstein, hardly knew a few years ago whether to condemn this custom or approve it. He leaned over the bulwarks of the *Donau* as the American passengers crossed the plank—the travellers who embark at Southampton are mainly of that nationality—and curiously, indifferently, vaguely, through the smoke of his cigar, saw them absorbed in the huge capacity of the ship, where he had the agreeable consciousness that his own nest was comfortably made. To watch from such a point of vantage the struggles of those less fortunate than ourselves—of the uninformed, the unprovided, the belated, the bewildered—is an occupation not devoid of sweetness, and there was nothing to mitigate the complacency with which our young friend gave himself up to it; nothing, that is, save a natural benevolence which had not yet been extinguished by the consciousness of official greatness. For Count Vogelstein was official, as I think you would have seen from the straightness of his back, the lustre of his light elegant spectacles, and something discreet and diplomatic in the curve of his moustache, which looked as if it might well contribute to the principal function, as cynics say, of the lips—the active concealment of thought. He had been appointed to the secretaryship of the German legation at Washington and in these first days of the autumn was about to take possession of his post. He was a model character for such a purpose—serious civil ceremonious curious stiff, stuffed with knowledge and convinced that, as lately rearranged, the German Empire places in the most striking light the highest of all the possibilities of the greatest of all the peoples. He was quite aware, however, of the claims to economic and other consideration of the United States, and that this quarter of the globe offered a vast field for study.

The process of enquiry had already begun for him, in spite of his having as yet spoken to none of his fellow passengers; the case being that Vogelstein enquired not only with his tongue, but with his eyes—that is with his spectacles—with his ears, with his nose, with his palate, with all his senses and organs. He was a highly upright young man, whose only fault was that his sense of comedy, or of the humour of things, had never been specifically disengaged from his several other senses. He vaguely felt that something should be done about this, and in a general manner proposed to do it, for he was on his way to explore a society abounding in comic aspects. This consciousness of a missing measure gave him a certain mistrust of what might be said of him; and if circumspection is the essence of diplomacy our young aspirant promised well. His mind contained several millions of facts, packed too closely together for the light breeze of the imagination to draw through the mass. He was impatient to report himself to his superior in Washington, and the loss of time in an English port could only incommode him, inasmuch as the study of English institutions was no part of his mission. On the other hand the day was charming; the blue sea, in Southampton Water, pricked all over with light, had no movement but that of its infinite shimmer. Moreover he was by no means sure that he should be happy in the United States, where doubtless he should find himself soon enough disembarked. He knew that this was not an important question and that happiness was an unscientific term, such as a man of his education should be ashamed to use even in the silence of his thoughts. Lost none the less in the inconsiderate crowd and feeling himself neither in his own country nor in that to which he was in a manner accredited, he was reduced to his mere personality; so that during the hour, to save his importance, he cultivated such ground as lay in sight for a judgement of this delay to which the German steamer was subjected in English waters. Mightn't it be proved, facts, figures and documents—or at least watch—in hand, considerably greater than the occasion demanded?

Count Vogelstein was still young enough in diplomacy to think it necessary to have opinions. He had a good many indeed which had been formed without difficulty; they had been received ready-made from a line of ancestors who knew what they liked. This was of course—and under pressure, being candid, he would have admitted it—an unscientific way of furnishing one's mind. Our young man was a stiff conservative, a Junker of Junkers; he thought modern democracy a temporary phase and expected to find many arguments against it in the great Republic. In regard to these things it was a pleasure to him to feel that, with his complete training, he had been taught thoroughly to appreciate the nature of evidence. The ship was heavily laden with German emigrants, whose mission in the United States differed considerably from Count Otto's. They hung over the bulwarks, densely grouped; they leaned forward on their elbows for hours, their shoulders kept on a level with their ears; the men in furred caps, smoking long-bowled pipes, the women with babies hidden in remarkably ugly shawls. Some were yellow Germans and some were black, and all looked greasy and matted with the sea-damp. They were destined to swell still further the huge current of the Western democracy; and Count Vogelstein doubtless said to himself that they wouldn't improve its quality. Their numbers, however, were striking, and I know not what he thought of the nature of this particular evidence.

The passengers who came on board at Southampton were not of the greasy class; they were for the most part American families who had been spending the summer, or a longer period, in Europe. They had a great deal of luggage, innumerable bags and rugs and hampers and sea-chairs, and were composed largely of ladies of various ages, a little pale with anticipation, wrapped also in striped shawls, though in prettier ones than the nursing mothers of the steerage, and crowned with very high hats and feathers. They darted to and fro across the gangway, looking for each other and for their scattered parcels; they separated and reunited, they exclaimed and declared, they eyed with dismay the occupants of the forward quarter, who seemed numerous enough to sink the vessel, and their voices sounded faint and far as they rose to Vogelstein's ear over the latter's great tarred sides. He noticed that in the new contingent there were many young girls, and he remembered what a lady in Dresden had once said to him—that America was the country of the Mädchen. He wondered whether he should like that, and reflected that it would be an aspect to study, like everything else. He had known in Dresden an American family in which there were three daughters who used to skate with the officers, and some of the ladies now coming on board struck him as of that same habit, except that in the Dresden days feathers weren't worn quite so high.

At last the ship began to creak and slowly budge, and the delay at

Southampton came to an end. The gangway was removed and the vessel indulged in the awkward evolutions that were to detach her from the land. Count Vogelstein had finished his cigar, and he spent a long time in walking up and down the upper deck. The charming English coast passed before him, and he felt this to be the last of the old world. The American coast also might be pretty—he hardly knew what one would expect of an American coast; but he was sure it would be different. Differences, however, were notoriously half the charm of travel, and perhaps even most when they couldn't be expressed in figures, numbers, diagrams or the other merely useful symbols. As yet indeed there were very few among the objects presented to sight on the steamer. Most of his fellow passengers appeared of one and the same persuasion, and that persuasion the least to be mistaken. They were Jews and commercial to a man. And by this time they had lighted their cigars and put on all manner of seafaring caps, some of them with big ear-lappets which somehow had the effect of bringing out their peculiar facial type. At last the new voyagers began to emerge from below and to look about them, vaguely, with that suspicious expression of face always to be noted in the newly embarked and which, as directed to the receding land, resembles that of a person who begins to perceive himself the victim of a trick. Earth and ocean, in such glances, are made the subject of a sweeping objection, and many travellers, in the general plight, have an air at once duped and superior, which seems to say that they could easily go ashore if they would.

It still wanted two hours of dinner, and by the time Vogelstein's long legs had measured three or four miles on the deck he was ready to settle himself in his sea-chair and draw from his pocket a Tauchnitz novel by an American author whose pages, he had been assured, would help to prepare him for some of the oddities. On the back of his chair his name was painted in rather large letters, this being a precaution taken at the recommendation of a friend who had told him that on the American steamers the passengers—especially the ladies—thought nothing of pilfering one's little comforts. His friend had even hinted at the correct reproduction of his coronet. This marked man of the world had added that the Americans are greatly impressed by a coronet. I know not whether it was scepticism or modesty, but Count Vogelstein had omitted every pictured plea for his rank; there were others of which he might have made use. The precious piece of furniture which on the Atlantic voyage is trusted never to flinch among universal concussions was emblazoned simply with his title and name. It happened, however, that the blazonry was huge; the back of the chair was covered with enormous German characters. This time there can be no doubt: it was modesty that caused the secretary of legation, in placing himself, to turn this portion of his seat outward, away from the eyes of his companions—to present it to the balustrade of the deck. The ship was passing the Needles—the beautiful uttermost point of the Isle of Wight. Certain tall white cones of rock rose out of the purple sea; they flushed in the afternoon light and their vague rosiness gave them a human expression in face of the cold expanse toward which the prow was turned; they seemed to say farewell, to be the last note of a peopled world. Vogelstein saw them very comfortably from his place and after a while turned his eyes to the other quarter, where the elements of air and water managed to make between them so comparatively poor an opposition. Even his American novelist was more amusing than that, and he prepared to return to this author. In the great curve which it described, however, his glance was arrested by the figure of a young lady who had just ascended to the deck and who paused at the mouth of the companionway.

This was not in itself an extraordinary phenomenon; but what attracted Vogelstein's attention was the fact that the young person appeared to have fixed her eyes on him. She was slim, brightly dressed, rather pretty; Vogelstein remembered in a moment that he had noticed her among the people on the wharf at Southampton. She was soon aware he had observed her; whereupon she began to move along the deck with a step that seemed to indicate a purpose of approaching him. Vogelstein had time to wonder whether she could be one of the girls he had known at Dresden; but he presently reflected that they would now be much older than that. It was true they were apt to advance, like this one, straight upon their victim. Yet the present specimen was no longer looking at him, and though she passed near him it was now tolerably clear she had come above but to take a general survey. She was a quick handsome competent girl, and she simply wanted to see what one could think of the ship, of the weather, of the appearance of England, from such a position as that; possibly even of one's fellow passengers. She satisfied herself promptly on these points, and then she looked about, while she walked, as if in keen search of a missing object; so that Vogelstein finally arrived at a conviction of her real motive. She passed near him again and this time almost stopped, her eyes bent upon him attentively. He thought her conduct remarkable even after he had gathered that it was not at his face, with its yellow moustache, she was looking, but at the chair on which he was seated. Then those words of his friend came back to him—the speech about the tendency of the people, especially of the ladies, on the American steamers to take to themselves one's little belongings. Especially the ladies, he might well say; for here was one who apparently wished to pull from under him the very chair he was sitting on. He was afraid she would ask him for it, so he pretended to read, systematically avoiding her eye. He was conscious she hovered near him, and was moreover curious to see what she would do. It seemed to him strange that such a nice-looking girl—for her appearance was really charming— should endeavour by arts so flagrant to work upon the quiet dignity of a secretary of legation. At last it stood out that she was trying to look round a corner, as it were—trying to see what was written on the back of his chair. "She wants to find out my name; she wants to see who I am!" This reflexion passed through his mind and caused him to raise his eyes. They rested on her own—which for an appreciable moment she didn't withdraw. The latter were brilliant and expressive, and surmounted a delicate aquiline nose, which, though pretty, was perhaps just a trifle too hawk-like. It was the oddest coincidence in the world; the story Vogelstein had taken up treated of a flighty forward little American girl who plants herself in front of a young man in the garden of an hotel. Wasn't the conduct of this young lady a testimony to the truthfulness of the tale, and wasn't Vogelstein himself in the position of the young man in the garden? That young man—though with more, in such connexions in general, to go upon—ended by addressing himself to his aggressor, as she might be called, and after a very short hesitation Vogelstein followed his example. "If she wants to know who I am she's welcome," he said to himself; and he got out of the chair, seized it by the back and, turning it round, exhibited the superscription to the girl. She coloured slightly, but smiled and read his name, while Vogelstein raised his hat.

"I'm much obliged to you. That's all right," she remarked as if the discovery had made her very happy.

It affected him indeed as all right that he should be Count Otto
Vogelstein; this appeared even rather a flippant mode of disposing of
the fact. By way of rejoinder he asked her if she desired of him the
surrender of his seat.

"I'm much obliged to you; of course not. I thought you had one of
our chairs, and I didn't like to ask you. It looks exactly like one of
ours; not so much now as when you sit in it. Please sit down again. I
don't want to trouble you. We've lost one of ours, and I've been
looking for it everywhere. They look so much alike; you can't tell till
you see the back. Of course I see there will be no mistake about
yours," the young lady went on with a smile of which the serenity
matched her other abundance. "But we've got such a small
name—you can scarcely see it," she added with the same friendly
intention. "Our name's just Day—you mightn't think it *was* a name,
might you? if we didn't make the most of it. If you see that on
anything, I'd be so obliged if you'd tell me. It isn't for myself, it's for
my mother; she's so dependent on her chair, and that one I'm
looking for pulls out so beautifully. Now that you sit down again
and hide the lower part it does look just like ours. Well, it must be
somewhere. You must excuse me; I wouldn't disturb you."

This was a long and even confidential speech for a young woman,
presumably unmarried, to make to a perfect stranger; but Miss Day
acquitted herself of it with perfect simplicity and self-possession. She
held up her head and stepped away, and Vogelstein could see that
the foot she pressed upon the clean smooth deck was slender and
shapely. He watched her disappear through the trap by which she
had ascended, and he felt more than ever like the young man in his
American tale. The girl in the present case was older and not so
pretty, as he could easily judge, for the image of her smiling eyes and
speaking lips still hovered before him. He went back to his book
with the feeling that it would give him some information about her.
This was rather illogical, but it indicated a certain amount of
curiosity on the part of Count Vogelstein. The girl in the book had a
mother, it appeared, and so had this young lady; the former had also
a brother, and he now remembered that he had noticed a young man
on the wharf—a young man in a high hat and a white
overcoat—who seemed united to Miss Day by this natural tie. And
there was some one else too, as he gradually recollected, an older
man, also in a high hat, but in a black overcoat—in black

altogether—who completed the group and who was presumably the head of the family. These reflexions would indicate that Count Vogelstein read his volume of Tauchnitz rather interruptedly. More-over they represented but the loosest economy of consciousness; for wasn't he to be afloat in an oblong box for ten days with such people, and could it be doubted he should see at least enough of them?

It may as well be written without delay that he saw a great deal of them. I have sketched in some detail the conditions in which he made the acquaintance of Miss Day, because the event had a certain importance for this fair square Teuton; but I must pass briefly over the incidents that immediately followed it. He wondered what it was open to him, after such an introduction, to do in relation to her, and he determined he would push through his American tale and dis-cover what the hero did. But he satisfied himself in a very short time that Miss Day had nothing in common with the heroine of that work save certain signs of habitat and climate—and save, further, the fact that the male sex wasn't terrible to her. The local stamp sharply, as he gathered, impressed upon her he estimated indeed rather in a borrowed than in a natural light, for if she was native to a small town in the interior of the American continent one of their fellow passengers, a lady from New York with whom he had a good deal of conversation, pronounced her "atrociously" provincial. How the lady arrived at this certitude didn't appear, for Vogelstein observed that she held no communication with the girl. It was true she gave it the support of her laying down that certain Americans could tell immediately who other Americans were, leaving him to judge whether or no she herself belonged to the critical or only to the criticised half of the nation. Mrs. Dangerfield was a handsome confidential insinuating woman, with whom Vogelstein felt his talk take a very wide range indeed. She convinced him rather effectually that even in a great democracy there are human differences, and that American life was full of social distinctions, of delicate shades, which foreigners often lack the intelligence to perceive. Did he suppose every one knew every one else in the biggest country in the world, and that one wasn't as free to choose one's company there as in the most monarchical and most exclusive societies? She laughed such delusions to scorn as Vogelstein tucked her beautiful furred coverlet—they reclined together a great deal in their elongated chairs—well over her feet. How free an American lady was to choose her company she abundantly proved by not knowing any one on the steamer but Count Otto.

He could see for himself that Mr. and Mrs. Day had not at all her grand air. They were fat plain serious people who sat side by side on the deck for hours and looked straight before them. Mrs. Day had a white face, large cheeks and small eyes; her forehead was surrounded with a multitude of little tight black curls; her lips moved as if she had always a lozenge in her mouth. She wore entwined about her head an article which Mrs. Dangerfield spoke of as a "nuby," a knitted pink scarf concealing her hair, encircling her neck and having among its convolutions a hole for her perfectly expressionless face. Her hands were folded on her stomach, and in her still, swathed figure her little bead-like eyes, which occasionally changed their direction, alone represented life. Her husband had a stiff grey beard on his chin and a bare spacious upper lip, to which constant shaving had imparted a hard glaze. His eyebrows were thick and his nostrils wide, and when he was uncovered, in the saloon, it was visible that his grizzled hair was dense and perpendicular. He might have looked rather grim and truculent hadn't it been for the mild familiar accommodating gaze with which his large light-coloured pupils—the leisurely eyes of a silent man—appeared to consider surrounding objects. He was evidently more friendly than fierce, but he was more diffident than friendly. He liked to have you in sight, but wouldn't have pretended to understand you much or to classify you, and would have been sorry it should put you under an obligation. He and his wife spoke sometimes, but seldom talked, and there was something vague and patient in them, as if they had become victims of a wrought spell. The spell however was of no sinister cast; it was the fascination of prosperity, the confidence of security, which sometimes makes people arrogant, but which had had such a different effect on this simple satisfied pair, in whom further development of every kind appeared to have been happily arrested.

Mrs. Dangerfield made it known to Count Otto that every morning after breakfast, the hour at which he wrote his journal in his cabin, the old couple were guided upstairs and installed in their customary corner by Pandora. This she had learned to be the name of their elder daughter, and she was immensely amused by her discovery. "Pandora"—that was in the highest degree typical; it placed them in the social scale if other evidence had been wanting; you could tell that a girl was from the interior, the mysterious

interior about which Vogelstein's imagination was now quite excited, when she had such a name as that. This young lady managed
the whole family, even a little the small beflounced sister, who, with
bold pretty innocent eyes, a torrent of fair silky hair, a crimson fez,
such as is worn by male Turks, very much askew on top of it, and a
way of galloping and straddling about the ship in any company she
could pick up—she had long thin legs, very short skirts and stockings
of every tint—was going home, in elegant French clothes, to resume
an interrupted education. Pandora overlooked and directed her
relatives; Vogelstein could see this for himself, could see she was very
active and decided, that she had in a high degree the sentiment of
responsibility, settling on the spot most of the questions that could
come up for a family from the interior.

The voyage was remarkably fine, and day after day it was possible
to sit there under the salt sky and feel one's self rounding the great
curves of the globe. The long deck made a white spot in the sharp
black circle of the ocean and in the intense sea-light, while the
shadow of the smoke-streamers trembled on the familiar floor, the
shoes of fellow passengers, distinctive now, and in some cases irritating, passed and repassed, accompanied, in the air so tremendously
"open," that rendered all voices weak and most remarks rather flat,
by fragments of opinion on the run of the ship. Vogelstein by this
time had finished his little American story and now definitely judged
that Pandora Day was not at all like the heroine. She was of quite
another type; much more serious and strenuous, and not at all keen,
as he had supposed, about making the acquaintance of gentlemen.
Her speaking to him that first afternoon had been, he was bound to
believe, an incident without importance for herself; in spite of her
having followed it up the next day by the remark, thrown at him as
she passed, with a smile that was almost fraternal: "It's all right, sir!
I've found that old chair." After this she hadn't spoken to him again
and had scarcely looked at him. She read a great deal, and almost
always French books, in fresh yellow paper; not the lighter forms of
that literature, but a volume of Sainte-Beuve, of Renan or at the
most, in the way of dissipation, of Alfred de Musset. She took
frequent exercise and almost always walked alone, apparently not
having made many friends on the ship and being without the
resource of her parents, who, as has been related, never budged out
of the cosy corner in which she planted them for the day.

Her brother was always in the smoking-room, where Vogelstein observed him, in very tight clothes, his neck encircled with a collar like a palisade. He had a sharp little face, which was not disagreeable; he smoked enormous cigars and began his drinking early in the day: but his appearance gave no sign of these excesses. As regards euchre and poker and the other distractions of the place he was guilty of none. He evidently understood such games in perfection, for he used to watch the players and even at moments impartially advise them; but Vogelstein never saw the cards in his hand. He was referred to as regards disputed points, and his opinion carried the day. He took little part in the conversation, usually much relaxed, that prevailed in the smoking-room, but from time to time he made, in his soft flat youthful voice, a remark which every one paused to listen to and which was greeted with roars of laughter. Vogelstein, well as he knew English, could rarely catch the joke; but he could see at least that these must be choice specimens of that American humour admired and practised by a whole continent and yet to be rendered accessible to a trained diplomatist, clearly, but by some special and incalculable revelation. The young man, in his way, was very remarkable, for, as Vogelstein heard some one say once after the laughter had subsided, he was only nineteen. If his sister didn't resemble the dreadful little girl in the tale already mentioned, there was for Vogelstein at least an analogy between young Mr. Day and a certain small brother—a candy-loving Madison, Hamilton or Jefferson—who was, in the Tauchnitz volume, attributed to that unfortunate maid. This was what the little Madison would have grown up to at nineteen, and the improvement was greater than might have been expected.

The days were long, but the voyage was short, and it had almost come to an end before Count Otto yielded to an attraction peculiar in its nature and finally irresistible and, in spite of Mrs. Dangerfield's emphatic warning, sought occasion for a little continuous talk with Miss Pandora. To mention that this impulse took effect without mentioning sundry other of his current impressions with which it had nothing to do is perhaps to violate proportion and give a false idea; but to pass it by would be still more unjust. The Germans, as we know, are a transcendental people, and there was at last an irresistible appeal for Vogelstein in this quick bright silent girl who could smile and turn vocal in an instant, who imparted a rare originality to the filial character and whose profile was delicate as she bent it over a volume which she cut as she read, or presented it in musing attitudes, at the side of the ship, to the horizon they had left behind. But he felt it to be a pity, as regards a possible acquaintance with her, that her parents should be heavy little burghers, that her brother should not correspond to his conception of a young man of the upper class and that her sister should be a Daisy Miller *en herbe*. Repeatedly admonished by Mrs. Dangerfield, the young diplomatist was doubly careful as to the relations he might form at the beginning of his sojourn in the United States. That lady reminded him, and he had himself made the observation in other capitals, that the first year, and even the second, is the time for prudence. One was ignorant of proportions and values; one was exposed to mistakes and thankful for attention, and one might give one's self away to people who would afterwards be as a millstone round one's neck: Mrs. Dangerfield struck and sustained that note, which resounded in the young man's imagination. She assured him that if he didn't "look out" he would be committing himself to some American girl with an impossible family. In America, when one committed one's self there was nothing to do but march to the altar, and what should he say for instance to finding himself a near relation of Mr. and Mrs. P. W. Day?—since such were the initials inscribed on the back of the two chairs of that couple. Count Otto felt the peril, for he could immediately think of a dozen men he knew who had married American girls. There appeared now to be a constant danger of marrying the American girl; it was something one had to reckon with, like the railway, the telegraph, the discovery of dynamite, the Chassepôt rifle, the Socialistic spirit: it was one of the complications of modern life.

It would doubtless be too much to say that he feared being carried away by a passion for a young woman who was not strikingly beautiful and with whom he had talked, in all, but ten minutes. But, as we recognise, he went so far as to wish that the human belongings of a person whose high spirit appeared to have no taint either of fastness, as they said in England, or of subversive opinion, and whose mouth had charming lines, should not be a little more distinguished. There was an effect of drollery in her behaviour to these subjects of her zeal, whom she seemed to regard as a care, but not as an interest; it was as if they had been entrusted to her honour and she had engaged to convey them safe to a certain point; she was detached and inadvertent, and then suddenly remembered, repented and came back to tuck them into their blankets, to alter the position of her mother's umbrella, to tell them something about the run of the ship. These little offices were usually performed deftly, rapidly, with the minimum of words, and when their daughter drew near them Mr. and Mrs. Day closed their eyes after the fashion of a pair of household dogs who expect to be scratched.

One morning she brought up the Captain of the ship to present to them; she appeared to have a private and independent acquaintance with this officer, and the introduction to her parents had the air of a sudden happy thought. It wasn't so much an introduction as an exhibition, as if she were saying to him: "This is what they look like; see how comfortable I make them. Aren't they rather queer and rather dear little people? But they leave me perfectly free. Oh I can assure you of that. Besides, you must see it for yourself." Mr. and Mrs. Day looked up at the high functionary who thus unbent to them with very little change of countenance; then looked at each other in the same way. He saluted, he inclined himself a moment; but Pandora shook her head, she seemed to be answering for them; she made little gestures as if in explanation to the good Captain of some of their peculiarities, as for instance that he needn't expect them to speak. They closed their eyes at last; she appeared to have a kind of mesmeric influence on them, and Miss Day walked away with the important friend, who treated her with evident consideration, bowing very low, for all his importance, when the two presently after separated. Vogelstein could see she was capable of making an impression; and the moral of our little matter is that in spite of Mrs. Dangerfield, in spite of the resolutions of his prudence, in spite of the limits of such acquaintance as he had momentarily made with her, in spite of Mr. and Mrs. Day and the young man in the smoking-room, she had fixed his attention.

It was in the course of the evening after the scene with the Captain that he joined her, awkwardly, abruptly, irresistibly, on the deck, where she was pacing to and fro alone, the hour being auspiciously mild and the stars remarkably fine. There were scattered talkers and smokers and couples, unrecogniseable, that moved quickly through the gloom. The vessel dipped with long regular pulsations; vague and spectral under the low stars, its swaying pinnacles spotted here and there with lights, it seemed to rush through the darkness faster than by day. Count Otto had come up to walk, and as the girl brushed past him he distinguished Pandora's face—with Mrs. Dangerfield he always spoke of her as Pandora—under the veil worn to protect it from the sea-damp. He stopped, turned, hurried after her, threw away his cigar—then asked her if she would do him the honour to accept his arm. She declined his arm but accepted his company, and he allowed her to enjoy it for an hour. They had a great deal of talk, and he was to remember afterwards some of the things she had said. There was now a certainty of the ship's getting into dock the next morning but one, and this prospect afforded an obvious topic. Some of Miss Day's expressions struck him as singular, but of course, as he was aware, his knowledge of English was not nice enough to give him a perfect measure.

"I'm not in a hurry to arrive; I'm very happy here," she said. "I'm afraid I shall have such a time putting my people through."

"Putting them through?"

"Through the Custom-House. We've made so many purchases. Well, I've written to a friend to come down, and perhaps he can help us. He's very well acquainted with the head. Once I'm chalked I don't care. I feel like a kind of blackboard by this time anyway. We found them awful in Germany."

Count Otto wondered if the friend she had written to were her lover and if they had plighted their troth, especially when she alluded to him again as "that gentleman who's coming down." He asked her about her travels, her impressions, whether she had been long in Europe and what she liked best, and she put it to him that they had gone abroad, she and her family, for a little fresh experience. Though he found her very intelligent he suspected she gave this as a reason because he was a German and she had heard the Germans were rich in culture. He wondered what form of culture Mr. and Mrs. Day had brought back from Italy, Greece and Palestine—they had travelled for two years and been everywhere—especially when their daughter said: "I wanted father and mother to see the best things. I kept them three hours on the Acropolis. I guess they won't forget that!" Perhaps it was of Phidias and Pericles they were thinking, Vogelstein reflected, as they sat ruminating in their rugs. Pandora remarked also that she wanted to show her little sister everything while she was comparatively unformed ("comparatively!" he mutely gasped) ; remarkable sights made so much more impression when the mind was fresh: she had read something of that sort somewhere in Goethe. She had wanted to come herself when she was her sister's age; but her father was in business then and they couldn't leave Utica. The young man thought of the little sister frisking over the Parthenon and the Mount of Olives and sharing for two years, the years of the schoolroom, this extraordinary pilgrimage of her parents; he wondered whether Goethe's dictum had been justified in this case. He asked Pandora if Utica were the seat of her family, if it were an important or typical place, if it would be an interesting city for him, as a stranger, to see. His companion replied frankly that this was a big question, but added that all the same she would ask him to "come and visit us at our home," if it weren't that they should probably soon leave it.

"Ah you're going to live elsewhere?" Vogelstein asked as if that fact too would be typical.

"Well, I'm working for New York. I flatter myself I've loosened them while we've been away," the girl went on. "They won't find in Utica the same charm; that was my idea. I want a big place, and of course Utica—!" She broke off as before a complex statement.

"I suppose Utica is inferior—?" Vogelstein seemed to see his way to suggest.

"Well no, I guess I can't have you call Utica inferior. It isn't supreme—that's what's the matter with it, and I hate anything middling," said Pandora Day. She gave a light dry laugh, tossing back her head a little as she made this declaration. And looking at her askance in the dusk, as she trod the deck that vaguely swayed, he recognised something in her air and port that matched such a pronouncement.

"What's her social position?" he enquired of Mrs. Dangerfield the next day. "I can't make it out at all—it's so contradictory. She strikes me as having much cultivation and much spirit. Her appearance, too, is very neat. Yet her parents are complete little burghers. That's easily seen."

"Oh social position," and Mrs. Dangerfield nodded two or three times portentously. "What big expressions you use! Do you think everybody in the world has a social position? That's reserved for an infinitely small majority of mankind. You can't have a social position at Utica any more than you can have an opera-box. Pandora hasn't got one; where, if you please, should she have got it? Poor girl, it isn't fair of you to make her the subject of such questions as that."

"Well," said Vogelstein, "if she's of the lower class it seems to me very—very—" And he paused a moment, as he often paused in speaking English, looking for his word.

"Very what, dear Count?"

"Very significant, very representative."

"Oh dear, she isn't of the lower class," Mrs. Dangerfield returned with an irritated sense of wasted wisdom. She liked to explain her country, but that somehow always required two persons.

"What is she then?"

"Well, I'm bound to admit that since I was at home last she's a novelty. A girl like that with such people—it *is* a new type."

"I like novelties"—and Count Otto smiled with an air of considerable resolution. He couldn't however be satisfied with a demonstration that only begged the question; and when they disembarked in New York he felt, even amid the confusion of the wharf and the heaps of disembowelled baggage, a certain acuteness of regret at the idea that Pandora and her family were about to vanish into the unknown. He had a consolation however: it was apparent that for some reason or other—illness or absence from town—the gentleman to whom she had written had not, as she said, come down. Vogelstein was glad—he couldn't have told you why—that this sympathetic person had failed her; even though without him Pandora had to engage single-handed with the United States Custom-House. Our young man's first impression of the Western world was received on the landing-place of the German steamers at Jersey City—a huge wooden shed covering a wooden wharf which resounded under the feet, an expanse palisaded with rough-hewn piles that leaned this way and that, and bestrewn with masses of heterogeneous luggage. At one end, toward the town, was a row of tall painted palings, behind which he could distinguish a press of hackney-coachmen, who brandished their whips and awaited their victims, while their voices rose, incessant, with a sharp strange sound, a challenge at once fierce and familiar. The whole place, behind the fence, appeared to bristle and resound. Out there was America, Count Otto said to himself, and he looked toward it with a sense that he should have to muster resolution. On the wharf people were rushing about amid their trunks, pulling their things together, trying to unite their scattered parcels. They were heated and angry, or else quite bewildered and discouraged. The few that had succeeded in collecting their battered boxes had an air of flushed indifference to the efforts of their neighbours, not even looking at people with whom they had been fondly intimate on the steamer. A detachment of the officers of the Customs was in attendance, and energetic passengers were engaged in attempts to drag them toward their luggage or to drag heavy pieces toward them. These functionaries were good-natured and taciturn, except when occasionally they remarked to a passenger whose open trunk stared up at them, eloquent, imploring, that they were afraid the voyage had been "rather glassy." They had a friendly leisurely speculative way of discharging their duty, and if they perceived a victim's name written on the portmanteau they addressed him by it in a tone of old acquaintance. Vogelstein found however that if they were familiar they weren't indiscreet. He had heard that in America all public functionaries were the same, that there wasn't a different *tenue*, as they said in France, for different positions, and he wondered whether at Washington the President and ministers, whom he expected to see—to *have* to see—a good deal of, would be like that.

He was diverted from these speculations by the sight of Mr. and Mrs. Day seated side by side upon a trunk and encompassed apparently by the accumulations of their tour. Their faces expressed more consciousness of surrounding objects than he had hitherto recognised, and there was an air of placid expansion in the mysterious couple which suggested that this consciousness was agreeable. Mr. and Mrs. Day were, as they would have said, real glad to get back. At a little distance, on the edge of the dock, our observer remarked their son, who had found a place where, between the sides of two big ships, he could see the ferry-boats pass; the large pyramidal low-laden ferry-boats of American waters. He stood there, patient and considering, with his small neat foot on a coil of rope, his back to everything that had been disembarked, his neck elongated in its polished cylinder, while the fragrance of his big cigar mingled with the odour of the rotting piles and his little sister, beside him, hugged a huge post and tried to see how far she could crane over the water without falling in. Vogelstein's servant was off in search of an examiner; Count Otto himself had got his things together and was waiting to be released, fully expecting that for a person of his importance the ceremony would be brief. Before it began he said a word to young Mr. Day, raising his hat at the same time to the little girl, whom he had not yet greeted and who dodged his salute by swinging herself boldly outward to the dangerous side of the pier. She was indeed still unformed, but was evidently as light as a feather.

"I see you're kept waiting like me. It's very tiresome," Count Otto said.

The young American answered without looking behind him. "As soon as we're started we'll go all right. My sister has written to a gentleman to come down."

"I've looked for Miss Day to bid her good-bye," Vogelstein went on; "but I don't see her."

"I guess she has gone to meet that gentleman; he's a great friend of hers."

"I guess he's her lover!" the little girl broke out. "She was always writing to him in Europe."

Her brother puffed his cigar in silence a moment. "That was only for this. I'll tell on you, sis," he presently added.

But the younger Miss Day gave no heed to his menace; she addressed herself only, though with all freedom, to Vogelstein. "This is New York; I like it better than Utica."

He had no time to reply, for his servant had arrived with one of the dispensers of fortune; but as he turned away he wondered, in the light of the child's preference, about the towns of the interior. He was naturally exempt from the common doom. The officer who took him in hand and who had a large straw hat and a diamond breastpin, was quite a man of the world and in reply to the Count's formal declarations only said "Well, I guess it's all right; I guess I'll just pass you"; distributing chalk-marks as if they had been so many love-pats. The servant had done some superfluous unlocking and unbuckling, and while he closed the pieces the officer stood there wiping his forehead and conversing with Vogelstein. "First visit to our country, sir?—quite alone—no ladies? Of course the ladies are what we're most after." It was in this manner he expressed himself while the young diplomatist wondered what he was waiting for and whether he ought to slip something into his palm. But this representative of order left our friend only a moment in suspense; he presently turned away with the remark, quite paternally uttered, that he hoped the

Count would make quite a stay; upon which the young man saw how wrong he should have been to offer a tip. It was simply the American manner, which had a finish of its own after all. Vogelstein's servant had secured a porter with a truck, and he was about to leave the place when he saw Pandora Day dart out of the crowd and address herself with much eagerness to the functionary who had just liberated him. She had an open letter in her hand which she gave him to read and over which he cast his eyes, thoughtfully stroking his beard. Then she led him away to where her parents sat on their luggage. Count Otto sent off his servant with the porter and followed Pandora, to whom he really wished to address a word of farewell. The last thing they had said to each other on the ship was that they should meet again on shore. It seemed improbable however that the meeting would occur anywhere but just here on the dock; inasmuch as Pandora was decidedly not in society, where Vogelstein would be of course, and as, if Utica—he had her sharp little sister's word for it—was worse than what was about him there, he'd be hanged if he'd go to Utica. He overtook Pandora quickly; she was in the act of introducing the representative of order to her parents, quite in the same manner in which she had introduced the Captain of the ship. Mr. and Mrs. Day got up and shook hands with him and they evidently all prepared to have a little talk. "I should like to introduce you to my brother and sister," he heard the girl say, and he saw her look about for these appendages. He caught her eye as she did so, and advanced with his hand outstretched, reflecting the while that evidently the Americans, whom he had always heard described as silent and practical, rejoiced to extravagance in the social graces. They dawdled and chattered like so many Neapolitans.

"Good-bye, Count Vogelstein," said Pandora, who was a little flushed with her various exertions but didn't look the worse for it. "I hope you'll have a splendid time and appreciate our country."

"I hope you'll get through all right," Vogelstein answered, smiling and feeling himself already more idiomatic.

"That gentleman's sick that I wrote to," she rejoined; "isn't it too bad? But he sent me down a letter to a friend of his—one of the examiners—and I guess we won't have any trouble. Mr. Lansing, let me make you acquainted with Count Vogelstein," she went on, presenting to her fellow passenger the wearer of the straw hat and the breastpin, who shook hands with the young German as if he had never seen him before. Vogelstein's heart rose for an instant to his throat; he thanked his stars he hadn't offered a tip to the friend of a gentleman who had often been mentioned to him and who had also been described by a member of Pandora's family as Pandora's lover.

"It's a case of ladies this time," Mr. Lansing remarked to him with a smile which seemed to confess surreptitiously, and as if neither party could be eager, to recognition.

"Well, Mr. Bellamy says you'll do anything for *him*," Pandora said, smiling very sweetly at Mr. Lansing. "We haven't got much; we've been gone only two years."

Mr. Lansing scratched his head a little behind, with a movement that sent his straw hat forward in the direction of his nose. "I don't know as I'd do anything for him that I wouldn't do for you," he responded with an equal geniality. "I guess you'd better open that one"—and he gave a little affectionate kick to one of the trunks.

"Oh mother, isn't he lovely? It's only your sea-things," Pandora cried, stooping over the coffer with the key in her hand.

"I don't know as I like showing them," Mrs. Day modestly murmured.

Vogelstein made his German salutation to the company in general, and to Pandora he offered an audible good-bye, which she returned in a bright friendly voice, but without looking round as she fumbled at the lock of her trunk.

"We'll try another, if you like," said Mr. Lansing good-humouredly.

"Oh no, it has got to be this one! Good-bye, Count Vogelstein. I hope you'll judge us correctly!"

The young man went his way and passed the barrier of the dock. Here he was met by his English valet with a face of consternation which led him to ask if a cab weren't forthcoming.

"They call 'em 'acks 'ere, sir," said the man, "and they're beyond everything. He wants thirty shillings to take you to the inn."

Vogelstein hesitated a moment. "Couldn't you find a German?"

"By the way he talks he *is* a German!" said the man; and in a moment Count Otto began his career in America by discussing the tariff of hackney-coaches in the language of the fatherland.

2

HE WENT wherever he was asked, on principle, partly to study American society and partly because in Washington pastimes seemed to him not so numerous that one could afford to neglect occasions. At the end of two winters he had naturally had a good many of various kinds—his study of American society had yielded considerable fruit. When, however, in April, during the second year of his residence, he presented himself at a large party given by Mrs. Bonnycastle and of which it was believed that it would be the last serious affair of the season, his being there (and still more his looking very fresh and talkative) was not the consequence of a rule of conduct. He went to Mrs. Bonnycastle's simply because he liked the lady, whose receptions were the pleasantest in Washington, and because if he didn't go there he didn't know what he should do; that absence of alternatives having become familiar to him by the waters of the Potomac. There were a great many things he did because if he didn't do them he didn't know what he should do. It must be added that in this case even if there had been an alternative he would still have decided to go to Mrs. Bonnycastle's. If her house wasn't the pleasantest there it was at least difficult to say which was pleasanter; and the complaint sometimes made of it that it was too limited, that it left out, on the whole, more people than it took in, applied with much less force when it was thrown open for a general party. Toward the end of the social year, in those soft scented days of the Washington spring when the air began to show a southern glow and the Squares and Circles (to which the wide empty avenues converged according to a plan so ingenious, yet so bewildering) to flush with pink blossom and to make one wish to sit on benches—under this magic of expansion and condonation Mrs. Bonnycastle, who during the winter had been a good deal on the defensive, relaxed her vigilance a little, became whimsically wilful, vernally reckless, as it were, and ceased to calculate the consequences of an hospitality which a reference to the back files or even to the morning's issue of the newspapers might easily prove a mistake. But Washington life, to Count Otto's apprehension, was paved with mistakes; he felt himself in a society founded on fundamental fallacies and triumphant blunders. Little addicted as he was to the sportive view of existence, he had said to himself at an early stage of his sojourn that the only way to enjoy the great Republic would be to burn one's standards and warm one's self at the blaze. Such were the reflexions of a theoretic Teuton who now walked for the most part amid the ashes of his prejudices.

Mrs. Bonnycastle had endeavoured more than once to explain to him the principles on which she received certain people and ignored certain others; but it was with difficulty that he entered into her discriminations. American promiscuity, goodness knew, had been strange to him, but it was nothing to the queerness of American criticism. This lady would discourse to him *à perte de vue* on differences where he only saw resemblances, and both the merits and the defects of a good many members of Washington society, as this society was interpreted to him by Mrs. Bonnycastle, he was often at a loss to understand. Fortunately she had a fund of good humour which, as I have intimated, was apt to come uppermost with the April blossoms and which made the people she didn't invite to her house almost as amusing to her as those she did. Her husband was not in politics, though politics were much in him; but the couple had taken upon themselves the responsibilities of an active patriotism; they thought it right to live in America, differing therein from many of their acquaintances who only, with some grimness, thought it inevitable. They had that burdensome heritage of foreign reminiscence with which so many Americans were saddled; but they carried it more easily than most of their country-people, and one knew they had lived in Europe only by their present exultation, never in the least by their regrets. Their regrets, that is, were only for their ever having lived there, as Mrs. Bonnycastle once told the wife of a foreign minister. They solved all their problems successfully, including those of knowing none of the people they didn't wish to, and of finding plenty of occupation in a society supposed to be meagrely provided with resources for that body which Vogelstein was to hear invoked, again and again, with the mixture of desire and of deprecation that might have attended the mention of a secret vice, under the name of a leisure-class. When as the warm weather approached they opened both the wings of their house-door, it was because they thought it would entertain them and not because they were conscious of a pressure. Alfred Bonnycastle all winter indeed chafed a little at the definiteness of some of his wife's reserves; it struck him that for Washington their society was really a little too good. Vogelstein still remembered the puzzled feeling—it had cleared up somewhat now—with which, more than a year before, he had heard Mr. Bonnycastle exclaim one evening, after a dinner in his own house, when every guest but the German secretary (who often sat late with the pair) had departed: "Hang it, there's only a month left; let us be vulgar and have some fun—let us invite the President."

This was Mrs. Bonnycastle's carnival, and on the occasion to which I began my chapter by referring the President had not only been invited but had signified his intention of being present. I hasten to add that this was not the same august ruler to whom Alfred Bonnycastle's irreverent allusion had been made. The White House had received a new tenant—the old one was then just leaving it—and Count Otto had had the advantage, during the first eighteen months of his stay in America, of seeing an electoral campaign, a presidential inauguration and a distribution of spoils. He had been bewildered during those first weeks by finding that at the national capital, in the houses he supposed to be the best, the head of the State was not a coveted guest; for this could be the only explanation of Mr. Bonnycastle's whimsical suggestion of their inviting him, as it were, in carnival. His successor went out a good deal for a President.

The legislative session was over, but this made little difference in the aspect of Mrs. Bonnycastle's rooms, which even at the height of the congressional season could scarce be said to overflow with the representatives of the people. They were garnished with an occasional Senator, whose movements and utterances often appeared to be regarded with a mixture of alarm and indulgence, as if they would be disappointing if they weren't rather odd and yet might be dangerous if not carefully watched. Our young man had come to entertain a kindness for these conscript fathers of invisible families, who had something of the toga in the voluminous folds of their conversation, but were otherwise rather bare and bald, with stony wrinkles in their faces, like busts and statues of ancient law-givers. There seemed to him something chill and exposed in their being at once so exalted and so naked; there were frequent lonesome glances in their eyes, as if in the social world their legislative consciousness longed for the warmth of a few comfortable laws ready-made. Members of the House were very rare, and when Washington was new to the enquiring secretary he used sometimes to mistake them, in the halls and on the staircases where he met them, for the functionaries engaged, under stress, to usher in guests and wait at supper. It was only a little later that he perceived these latter public characters almost always to be impressive and of that rich racial hue which of itself served as a livery. At present, however, such confounding figures were much less to be met than during the months of winter, and indeed they were never frequent at Mrs. Bonnycastle's. At present the social vistas of Washington, like the vast fresh flatness of the lettered and numbered streets, which at this season seemed to Vogelstein more spacious and vague than ever, suggested but a paucity of political phenomena. Count Otto that evening knew every one or almost every one. There were often enquiring strangers, expecting great things, from New York and Boston, and to them, in the friendly Washington way, the young German was promptly introduced. It was a society in which familiarity reigned and in which people were liable to meet three times a day, so that their ultimate essence really became a matter of importance.

"I've got three new girls," Mrs. Bonnycastle said. "You must talk to them all."

"All at once?" Vogelstein asked, reversing in fancy a position not at all unknown to him. He had so repeatedly heard himself addressed in even more than triple simultaneity.

"Oh no; you must have something different for each; you can't get off that way. Haven't you discovered that the American girl expects something especially adapted to herself? It's very well for Europe to have a few phrases that will do for any girl. The American girl isn't *any* girl; she's a remarkable specimen in a remarkable species. But you must keep the best this evening for Miss Day."

"For Miss Day!"—and Vogelstein had a stare of intelligence. "Do you mean for Pandora?"

Mrs. Bonnycastle broke on her side into free amusement. "One would think you had been looking for her over the globe! So you know her already—and you call her by her pet name?"

"Oh no, I don't know her; that is I haven't seen her or thought of her from that day to this. We came to America in the same ship."

"Isn't she an American then?"

"Oh yes; she lives at Utica—in the interior."

"In the interior of Utica? You can't mean my young woman then, who lives in New York, where she's a great beauty and a great belle and has been immensely admired this winter."

"After all," said Count Otto, considering and a little disappointed, "the name's not so uncommon; it's perhaps another. But has she rather strange eyes, a little yellow, but very pretty, and a nose a little arched?"

"I can't tell you all that; I haven't seen her. She's staying with Mrs. Steuben. She only came a day or two ago, and Mrs. Steuben's to bring her. When she wrote to me to ask leave she told me what I tell you. They haven't come yet."

Vogelstein felt a quick hope that the subject of this correspondence might indeed be the young lady he had parted from on the dock at New York, but the indications seemed to point another way, and he had no wish to cherish an illusion. It didn't seem to him probable that the energetic girl who had introduced him to Mr. Lansing would have the entrée of the best house in Washington; besides, Mrs. Bonnycastle's guest was described as a beauty and belonging to the brilliant city.

"What's the social position of Mrs. Steuben?" it occurred to him to ask while he meditated. He had an earnest artless literal way of putting such a question as that; you could see from it that he was very thorough.

Mrs. Bonnycastle met it, however, but with mocking laughter. "I'm sure I don't know! What's your own?"—and she left him to turn to her other guests, to several of whom she repeated his question. Could they tell her what was the social position of Mrs. Steuben? There was Count Vogelstein who wanted to know. He instantly became aware of course that he oughtn't so to have expressed himself. Wasn't the lady's place in the scale sufficiently indicated by Mrs. Bonnycastle's acquaintance with her? Still there were fine degrees, and he felt a little unduly snubbed. It was perfectly true, as he told his hostess, that with the quick wave of new impressions that had rolled over him after his arrival in America the image of Pandora was almost completely effaced; he had seen innumerable things that were quite as remarkable in their way as the heroine of the *Donau,* but at the touch of the idea that he might see her and hear her again at any moment she became as vivid in his mind as if they had parted the day before: he remembered the exact shade of the eyes he had described to Mrs. Bonnycastle as yellow, the tone of her voice when at the last she expressed the hope he might judge America correctly. *Had* he judged America correctly? If he were to meet her again she doubtless would try to ascertain. It would be going much too far to say that the idea of such an ordeal was terrible to Count Otto; but it may at least be said that the thought of meeting Pandora Day made him nervous. The fact is certainly singular, but I shall not take on myself to explain it; there are some things that even the most philosophic historian isn't bound to account for.

He wandered into another room, and there, at the end of five minutes, he was introduced by Mrs. Bonnycastle to one of the young ladies of whom she had spoken. This was a very intelligent girl who came from Boston and showed much acquaintance with Spielhagen's novels. "Do you like them?" Vogelstein asked rather vaguely, not taking much interest in the matter, as he read works of fiction only in case of a sea-voyage. The young lady from Boston looked pensive and concentrated; then she answered that she liked *some* of them *very* much, but that there were others she didn't like—and she enumerated the works that came under each of these heads. Spielhagen is a voluminous writer, and such a catalogue took some time; at the end of it moreover Vogelstein's question was not answered, for he couldn't have told us whether she liked Spielhagen or not.

On the next topic, however, there was no doubt about her feelings. They talked about Washington as people talk only in the place itself, revolving about the subject in widening and narrowing circles, perching successively on its many branches, considering it from every point of view. Our young man had been long enough in America to discover that after half a century of social neglect Washington had become the fashion and enjoyed the great advantage of being a new resource in conversation. This was especially the case in the months of spring, when the inhabitants of the commercial cities came so far southward to escape, after the long winter, that final affront. They were all agreed that Washington was fascinating, and none of them were better prepared to talk it over than the Bostonians. Vogelstein originally had been rather out of step with them; he hadn't seized their point of view, hadn't known with what they compared this object of their infatuation. But now he knew everything; he had settled down to the pace; there wasn't a possible phase of the discussion that could find him at a loss. There was a kind of Hegelian element in it; in the light of these considerations the American capital took on the semblance of a monstrous mystical infinite *Werden*. But they fatigued Vogelstein a little, and it was his preference, as a general thing, not to engage the same evening with more than one new-comer, one visitor in the freshness of initiation. This was why Mrs. Bonnycastle's expression of a wish to introduce him to three young ladies had startled him a little; he saw a certain process, in which he flattered himself that he had become proficient, but which was after all tolerably exhausting, repeated for each of the damsels. After separating from his judicious Bostonian he rather evaded Mrs. Bonnycastle, contenting himself with the conversation of old friends, pitched for the most part in a lower and easier key.

At last he heard it mentioned that the President had arrived, had been some half-hour in the house, and he went in search of the illustrious guest, whose whereabouts at Washington parties was never indicated by a cluster of courtiers. He made it a point, whenever he found himself in company with the President, to pay him his respects, and he had not been discouraged by the fact that there was no association of ideas in the eye of the great man as he put out his hand presidentially and said "Happy to meet you, sir." Count Otto felt himself taken for a mere loyal subject, possibly for an office-seeker; and he used to reflect at such moments that the monarchical form had its merits: it provided a line of heredity for the faculty of quick recognition. He had now some difficulty in finding the chief magistrate, and ended by learning that he was in the tea-room, a small apartment devoted to light refection near the entrance of the house. Here our young man presently perceived him seated on a sofa and in conversation with a lady. There were a number of people about the table, eating, drinking, talking; and the couple on the sofa, which was not near it but against the wall, in a shallow recess, looked a little withdrawn, as if they had sought seclusion and were disposed to profit by the diverted attention of the others. The President leaned back; his gloved hands, resting on either knee, made large white spots. He looked eminent, but he looked relaxed, and the lady beside him ministered freely and without scruple, it was clear, to this effect of his comfortably unbending. Vogelstein caught her voice as he approached. He heard her say "Well now, remember; I consider it a promise." She was beautifully dressed, in rose-colour;

her hands were clasped in her lap and her eyes attached to the presidential profile.

"Well, madam, in that case it's about the fiftieth promise I've given to-day."

It was just as he heard these words, uttered by her companion in reply, that Count Otto checked himself, turned away and pretended to be looking for a cup of tea. It wasn't usual to disturb the President, even simply to shake hands, when he was sitting on a sofa with a lady, and the young secretary felt it in this case less possible than ever to break the rule, for the lady on the sofa was none other than Pandora Day. He had recognised her without her appearing to see him, and even with half an eye, as they said, had taken in that she was now a person to be reckoned with. She had an air of elation, of success; she shone, to intensity, in her rose-coloured dress; she was extracting promises from the ruler of fifty millions of people. What an odd place to meet her, her old ship-mate thought, and how little one could tell, after all, in America, who people were! He didn't want to speak to her yet; he wanted to wait a little and learn more; but meanwhile there was something attractive in the fact that she was just behind him, a few yards off, that if he should turn he might see her again. It was she Mrs. Bonnycastle had meant, it was she who was so much admired in New York. Her face was the same, yet he had made out in a moment that she was vaguely prettier; he had recognised the arch of her nose, which suggested a fine ambition. He took some tea, which he hadn't desired, in order not to go away. He remembered her *entourage* on the steamer; her father and mother, the silent senseless burghers, so little "of the world," her infant sister, so much of it, her humorous brother with his tall hat and his influence in the smoking-room. He remembered Mrs. Dangerfield's warnings—yet her perplexities too—and the letter from Mr. Bellamy, and the introduction to Mr. Lansing, and the way Pandora had stooped down on the dirty dock, laughing and talking, mistress of the situation, to open her trunk for the Customs. He was pretty sure she had paid no duties that day; this would naturally have been the purpose of Mr. Bellamy's letter. Was she still in correspondence with that gentleman, and had he got over the sickness interfering with their reunion? These images and these questions coursed through Count Otto's mind, and he saw it must be quite in Pandora's line to be mistress of the situation, for there was evidently nothing on the present occasion that could call itself her master. He drank his tea and as he put down his cup heard the President, behind him, say: "Well, I guess my wife will wonder why I don't come home."

"Why didn't you bring her with you?" Pandora benevolently asked.

"Well, she doesn't go out much. Then she has got her sister staying with her—Mrs. Runkle, from Natchez. She's a good deal of an invalid, and my wife doesn't like to leave her."

"She must be a very kind woman"—and there was a high mature competence in the way the girl sounded the note of approval.

"Well, I guess she isn't spoiled—yet."

"I should like very much to come and see her," said Pandora.

"Do come round. Couldn't you come some night?" the great man responded.

"Well, I'll come some time. And I shall remind you of your promise."

"All right. There's nothing like keeping it up. Well," said the President, "I must bid good-bye to these bright folks."

Vogelstein heard him rise from the sofa with his companion; after which he gave the pair time to pass out of the room before him. They did it with a certain impressive deliberation, people making way for the ruler of fifty millions and looking with a certain curiosity at the striking pink person at his side. When a little later he followed them across the hall, into one of the other rooms, he saw the host and hostess accompany the President to the door and two foreign ministers and a judge of the Supreme Court address themselves to Pandora Day. He resisted the impulse to join this circle: if he should speak to her at all he would somehow wish it to be in more privacy. She continued nevertheless to occupy him, and when Mrs. Bonnycastle came back from the hall he immediately approached her with an appeal. "I wish you'd tell me something more about that girl—that one opposite and in pink."

"The lovely Day—that's what they call her, I believe? I wanted you to talk with her."

"I find she *is* the one I've met. But she seems to be so different here. I can't make it out," said Count Otto.

There was something in his expression that again moved Mrs. Bonnycastle to mirth. "How we do puzzle you Europeans! You look quite bewildered."

"I'm sorry I look so—I try to hide it. But of course we're very simple. Let me ask then a simple earnest childlike question. Are her parents also in society?"

"Parents in society? *D'où tombez-vous?* Did you ever hear of the parents of a triumphant girl in rose-colour, with a nose all her own, in society?"

"Is she then all alone?" he went on with a strain of melancholy in his voice.

Mrs. Bonnycastle launched at him all her laughter. "You're too pathetic. Don't you know what she is? I supposed of course you knew."

"It's exactly what I'm asking you."

"Why she's the new type. It has only come up lately. They have had articles about it in the papers. That's the reason I told Mrs. Steuben to bring her."

"The new type? *What* new type, Mrs. Bonnycastle?" he returned pleadingly—so conscious was he that all types in America were new.

Her laughter checked her reply a moment, and by the time she had recovered herself the young lady from Boston, with whom Vogelstein had been talking, stood there to take leave. This, for an American type, was an old one, he was sure; and the process of parting between the guest and her hostess had an ancient elaboration. Count Otto waited a little; then he turned away and walked up to Pandora Day, whose group of interlocutors had now been re-enforced by a gentleman who had held an important place in the cabinet of the late occupant of the presidential chair. He had asked Mrs. Bonnycastle if she were "all alone"; but there was nothing in her present situation to show her for solitary. She wasn't sufficiently alone for our friend's taste; but he was impatient and he hoped she'd give him a few words to himself. She recognised him without a moment's hesitation and with the sweetest smile, a smile matching to a shade the tone in which she said: "I was watching you. I wondered if you weren't going to speak to me."

"Miss Day was watching him!" one of the foreign ministers exclaimed; "and we flattered ourselves that her attention was all with us."

"I mean before," said the girl, "while I was talking with the President."

At which the gentlemen began to laugh, one of them remarking that this was the way the absent were sacrificed, even the great; while another put on record that he hoped Vogelstein was duly flattered.

"Oh I was watching the President too," said Pandora. "I've got to watch *him*. He has promised me something."

"It must be the mission to England," the judge of the Supreme Court suggested. "A good position for a lady; they've got a lady at the head over there."

"I wish they would send you to *my* country," one of the foreign ministers suggested. "I'd immediately get recalled."

"Why perhaps in your country I wouldn't speak to you! It's only because you're here," the ex-heroine of the *Donau* returned with a gay familiarity which evidently ranked with her but as one of the arts of defence. "You'll see what mission it is when it comes out. But I'll speak to Count Vogelstein anywhere," she went on. "He's an older friend than any right here. I've known him in difficult days."

"Oh yes, on the great ocean," the young man smiled. "On the watery waste, in the tempest!"

"Oh I don't mean that so much; we had a beautiful voyage and there wasn't any tempest. I mean when I was living in Utica. That's a watery waste if you like, and a tempest there would have been a pleasant variety."

"Your parents seemed to me so peaceful!" her associate in the other memories sighed with a vague wish to say something sympathetic.

"Oh you haven't seen them ashore! At Utica they were very lively. But that's no longer our natural home. Don't you remember I told you I was working for New York? Well, I worked—I had to work hard. But we've moved."

Count Otto clung to his interest. "And I hope they're happy."

"My father and mother? Oh they will be, in time. I must give them time. They're very young yet, they've years before them. And you've been always in Washington?" Pandora continued. "I suppose you've found out everything about everything."

"Oh no—there are some things I *can't* find out."

"Come and see me and perhaps I can help you. I'm very different from what I was in that phase. I've advanced a great deal since then."

"Oh how was Miss Day in that phase?" asked a cabinet minister of the last administration.

"She was delightful of course," Count Otto said.

"He's very flattering; I didn't open my mouth!" Pandora cried. "Here comes Mrs. Steuben to take me to some other place. I believe it's a literary party near the Capitol. Everything seems so separate in Washington. Mrs. Steuben's going to read a poem. I wish she'd read it here; wouldn't it do as well?"

This lady, arriving, signified to her young friend the necessity of their moving on. But Miss Day's companions had various things to say to her before giving her up. She had a vivid answer for each, and it was brought home to Vogelstein while he listened that this would be indeed, in her development, as she said, another phase. Daughter of small burghers as she might be she was really brilliant. He turned away a little and while Mrs. Steuben waited put her a question. He had made her half an hour before the subject of that enquiry to which Mrs. Bonnycastle returned so ambiguous an answer; but this wasn't because he failed of all direct acquaintance with the amiable woman or of any general idea of the esteem in which she was held. He had met her in various places and had been at her house. She was the widow of a commodore, was a handsome mild soft swaying person, whom every one liked, with glossy bands of black hair and a little ringlet depending behind each ear. Some one had said that she looked like the *vieux jeu* idea of the queen in "Hamlet." She had written verses which were admired in the South, wore a full-length portrait of the commodore on her bosom and spoke with the accent of Savannah. She had about her a positive strong odour of Washington. It had certainly been very superfluous in our young man to question Mrs. Bonnycastle about her social position.

"Do kindly tell me," he said, lowering his voice, "what's the type to which that young lady belongs? Mrs. Bonnycastle tells me it's a new one."

Mrs. Steuben for a moment fixed her liquid eyes on the secretary of legation. She always seemed to be translating the prose of your speech into the finer rhythms with which her own mind was familiar. "Do you think anything's really new?" she then began to flute. "I'm very fond of the old; you know that's a weakness of we Southerners." The poor lady, it will be observed, had another weakness as well. "What we often take to be the new is simply the old under some novel form. Were there not remarkable natures in the past? If you doubt it you should visit the South, where the past still lingers."

Vogelstein had been struck before this with Mrs. Steuben's pronunciation of the word by which her native latitudes were designated; transcribing it from her lips you would have written it (as the nearest approach) the Sooth. But at present he scarce heeded this peculiarity; he was wondering rather how a woman could be at once so copious and so uninforming. What did he care about the past or even about the Sooth? He was afraid of starting her again. He looked at her, discouraged and helpless, as bewildered almost as Mrs. Bonnycastle had found him half an hour before; looked also at the commodore, who, on her bosom, seemed to breathe again with his widow's respirations. "Call it an old type then if you like," he said in a moment. "All I want to know is what type it *is!* It seems impossible," he gasped, "to find out."

"You can find out in the newspapers. They've had articles about it. They write about everything now. But it isn't true about Miss Day. It's one of the first families. Her great-grandfather was in the Revolution." Pandora by this time had given her attention again to Mrs. Steuben. She seemed to signify that she was ready to move on. "Wasn't your great-grandfather in the Revolution?" the elder lady asked. "I'm telling Count Vogelstein about him."

"Why are you asking about my ancestors?" the girl demanded of the young German with untempered brightness. "Is that the thing you said just now that you can't find out? Well, if Mrs. Steuben will only be quiet you never will."

Mrs. Steuben shook her head rather dreamily. "Well, it's no trouble for we of the Sooth to be quiet. There's a kind of languor in our blood. Besides, we have to be to-day. But I've got to show some energy to-night. I've got to get you to the end of Pennsylvania Avenue."

Pandora gave her hand to Count Otto and asked him if he thought they should meet again. He answered that in Washington people were always meeting again and that at any rate he shouldn't fail to wait upon her. Hereupon, just as the two ladies were detaching themselves, Mrs. Steuben remarked that if the Count and Miss Day wished to meet again the picnic would be a good chance—the picnic she was getting up for the following Thursday. It was to consist of about twenty bright people, and they'd go down the Potomac to Mount Vernon. The Count answered that if Mrs. Steuben thought him bright enough he should be delighted to join the party; and he was told the hour for which the tryst was taken.

He remained at Mrs. Bonnycastle's after every one had gone, and then he informed this lady of his reason for waiting. Would she have mercy on him and let him know, in a single word, before he went to rest—for without it rest would be impossible—what was this famous type to which Pandora Day belonged?

"Gracious, you don't mean to say you've not found out that type yet!" Mrs. Bonnycastle exclaimed with a return of her hilarity. "What have you been doing all the evening? You Germans may be thorough, but you certainly are not quick!"

It was Alfred Bonnycastle who at last took pity on him. "My dear Vogelstein, she's the latest freshest fruit of our great American evolution. She's the self-made girl!"

Count Otto gazed a moment. "The fruit of the great American Revolution? Yes, Mrs. Steuben told me her great-grandfather—" but the rest of his sentence was lost in a renewed explosion of Mrs. Bonnycastle's sense of the ridiculous. He bravely pushed his advantage, such as it was, however, and, desiring his host's definition to be defined, enquired what the self-made girl might be.

"Sit down and we'll tell you all about it," Mrs. Bonnycastle said. "I like talking this way, after a party's over. You can smoke if you like, and Alfred will open another window. Well, to begin with, the self-made girl's a new feature. That, however, you know. In the second place she isn't self-made at all. We all help to make her—we take such an interest in her."

"That's only after she's made!" Alfred Bonnycastle broke in. "But it's Vogelstein that takes an interest. What on earth has started you up so on the subject of Miss Day?"

The visitor explained as well as he could that it was merely the accident of his having crossed the ocean in the steamer with her; but he felt the inadequacy of this account of the matter, felt it more than his hosts, who could know neither how little actual contact he had had with her on the ship, how much he had been affected by Mrs. Dangerfield's warnings, nor how much observation at the same time he had lavished on her. He sat there half an hour, and the warm dead stillness of the Washington night—nowhere are the nights so silent—came in at the open window, mingled with a soft sweet earthy smell, the smell of growing things and in particular, as he thought, of Mrs. Steuben's Sooth. Before he went away he had heard all about the self-made girl, and there was something in the picture that strongly impressed him. She was possible doubtless only in America; American life had smoothed the way for her. She was not fast, nor emancipated, nor crude, nor loud, and there wasn't in her, of necessity at least, a grain of the stuff of which the adventuress is made. She was simply very successful, and her success was entirely personal. She hadn't been born with the silver spoon of social opportunity; she had grasped it by honest exertion. You knew her by many different signs, but chiefly, infallibly, by the appearance of her parents. It was her parents who told her story; you always saw how little her parents could have made her. Her attitude with regard to them might vary in different ways. As the great fact on her own side was that she had lifted herself from a lower social plane, done it all herself, and done it by the simple lever of her personality, it was naturally to be expected that she would leave the authors of her mere material being in the shade. Sometimes she had them in her wake, lost in the bubbles and the foam that showed where she had passed; sometimes, as Alfred Bonnycastle said, she let them slide altogether; sometimes she kept them in close confinement, resorting to them under cover of night and with every precaution; sometimes she exhibited them to the public in discreet glimpses, in prearranged attitudes. But the general characteristic of the self-made girl was that, though it was frequently understood that she was privately devoted to her kindred, she never attempted to impose them on society, and it was striking that, though in some of her manifestations a bore, she was at her worst less of a bore than they. They were almost always solemn and portentous, and they were for the most part of a deathly respectability. She wasn't necessarily snobbish, unless it was snobbish to want the best. She didn't cringe, she didn't make herself smaller than she was; she took on the contrary a stand of her own and attracted things to herself. Naturally she was possible only in America—only in a country where whole ranges of competition and comparison were absent. The natural history of this interesting creature was at last completely laid bare to the earnest stranger, who, as he sat there in the animated stillness, with the fragrant breath of the Western world in his nostrils, was convinced of what he had already suspected, that conversation in the great

Republic was more yearningly, not to say gropingly, psychological than elsewhere. Another thing, as he learned, that you knew the self-made girl by was her culture, which was perhaps a little too restless and obvious. She had usually got into society more or less by reading, and her conversation was apt to be garnished with literary allusions, even with familiar quotations. Vogelstein hadn't time to observe this element as a developed form in Pandora Day; but Alfred Bonny-castle hinted that he wouldn't trust her to keep it under in a *tête-à-tête*. It was needless to say that these young persons had always been to Europe; that was usually the first place they got to. By such arts they sometimes entered society on the other side before they did so at home; it was to be added at the same time that this resource was less and less valuable, for Europe, in the American world, had less and less prestige and people in the Western hemisphere now kept a watch on that roundabout road. All of which quite applied to Pandora Day—the journey to Europe, the culture (as exemplified in the books she read on the ship), the relegation, the effacement, of the family. The only thing that was exceptional was the rapidity of her march; for the jump she had taken since he left her in the hands of Mr. Lansing struck Vogelstein, even after he had made all allowance for the abnormal homogeneity of the American mass, as really considerable. It took all her cleverness to account for such things. When she "moved" from Utica—mobilised her commissariat—the battle appeared virtually to have been gained.

Count Otto called the next day, and Mrs. Steuben's blackamoor informed him, in the communicative manner of his race, that the ladies had gone out to pay some visits and look at the Capitol. Pandora apparently had not hitherto examined this monument, and our young man wished he had known, the evening before, of her omission, so that he might have offered to be her initiator. There is too obvious a connexion for us to fail of catching it between his regret and the fact that in leaving Mrs. Steuben's door he reminded himself that he wanted a good walk, and that he thereupon took his way along Pennsylvania Avenue. His walk had become fairly good by the time he reached the great white edifice that unfolds its repeated colonnades and uplifts its isolated dome at the end of a long vista of saloons and tobacco-shops. He slowly climbed the great steps, hesitating a little, even wondering why he had come. The superficial reason was obvious enough, but there was a real one behind it that struck him as rather wanting in the solidity which should characterise the motives of an emissary of Prince Bismarck. The superficial reason was a belief that Mrs. Steuben would pay her visit first—it was probably only a question of leaving cards—and bring her young friend to the Capitol at the hour when the yellow afternoon light would give a tone to the blankness of its marble walls. The Capitol was a splendid building, but it was rather wanting in tone. Vogelstein's curiosity about Pandora Day had been much more quickened than checked by the revelations made to him in Mrs. Bonnycastle's drawing-room. It was a relief to have the creature classified; but he had a desire, of which he had not been conscious before, to see really to the end how well, in other words how completely and artistically, a girl could make herself. His calculations had been just, and he had wandered about the rotunda for only ten minutes, looking again at the paintings, commemorative of the national annals, which occupy its lower spaces, and at the simulated sculptures, so touchingly characteristic of early American taste, which adorn its upper reaches, when the charming women he had been counting on presented themselves in charge of a licensed guide. He went to meet them and didn't conceal from them that he had marked them for his very own. The encounter was happy on both sides, and he accompanied them through the queer and endless interior, through labyrinths of bleak bare development, into legislative and judicial halls. He thought it a hideous place; he had seen it all before and asked himself what senseless game he was playing. In the lower House were certain bedaubed walls, in the basest style of imitation, which made him feel faintly sick, not to speak of a lobby adorned with artless prints and photographs of eminent defunct Congressmen that was all too serious for a joke and too comic for a Valhalla. But Pandora was greatly interested; she thought the Capitol very fine; it was easy to criticise the details, but as a whole it was the most impressive building she had ever seen. She proved a charming fellow tourist; she had constantly something to say, but never said it too much; it was impossible to drag in the wake of a *cicerone* less of a lengthening or an irritating chain. Vogelstein could see too that she wished to improve her mind; she looked at the historical pictures, at the uncanny statues of local worthies, presented by the different States—they were of different sizes, as if they had been "numbered," in a shop—she asked questions of the guide and in the chamber of the Senate requested him to show her the chairs of the gentlemen from New York. She sat down in one of them, though Mrs. Steuben told her *that* Senator (she mistook the chair, dropping into another State) was a horrid old thing.

Throughout the hour he spent with her Vogelstein seemed to see how it was she had made herself. They walked about afterwards on the splendid terrace that surrounds the Capitol, the great marble floor on which it stands, and made vague remarks—Pandora's were the most definite—about the yellow sheen of the Potomac, the hazy hills of Virginia, the far-gleaming pediment of Arlington, the raw confused-looking country. Washington was beneath them, bristling and geometrical; the long lines of its avenues seemed to stretch into national futures. Pandora asked Count Otto if he had ever been to Athens and, on his admitting so much, sought to know whether the eminence on which they stood didn't give him an idea of the Acropolis in its prime. Vogelstein deferred the satisfaction of this appeal to their next meeting; he was glad—in spite of the appeal—to make pretexts for seeing her again. He did so on the morrow; Mrs. Steuben's picnic was still three days distant. He called on Pandora a second time, also met her each evening in the Washington world. It took very little of this to remind him that he was forgetting both Mrs. Dangerfield's warnings and the admonitions—long familiar to him—of his own conscience. Was he in peril of love? Was he to be sacrificed on the altar of the American girl, an altar at which those other poor fellows had poured out some of the bluest blood in Germany and he had himself taken oath he would never seriously worship? He decided that he wasn't in real danger, that he had rather clinched his precautions. It was true that a young person who had succeeded so well for herself might be a great help to her husband; but this diplomatic aspirant preferred on the whole that his success should be his own: it wouldn't please him to have the air of being pushed by his wife. Such a wife as that would wish to push him, and he could hardly admit to himself that this was what fate had in reserve for him—to be propelled in his career by a young lady who would perhaps attempt to talk to the Kaiser as he had heard her the other night talk to the President. Would she consent to discontinue relations with her family, or would she wish still to borrow plastic relief from that domestic background? That her family was so impossible was to a certain extent an advantage; for if they had been a little better the question of a rupture would be less easy. He turned over these questions in spite of his security, or perhaps indeed because of it. The security made them speculative and disinterested.

They haunted him during the excursion to Mount Vernon, which took place according to traditions long established. Mrs. Steuben's confederates assembled on the steamer and were set afloat on the big brown stream which had already seemed to our special traveller to have too much bosom and too little bank. Here and there, however, he became conscious of a shore where there was something to look at, even though conscious at the same time that he had of old lost great opportunities of an idyllic cast in not having managed to be more "thrown with" a certain young lady on the deck of the North German Lloyd. The two turned round together to hang over Alexandria, which for Pandora, as she declared, was a picture of Old Virginia. She told Vogelstein that she was always hearing about it during the Civil War, ages before. Little girl as she had been at the time she remembered all the names that were on people's lips during those years of reiteration. This historic spot had a touch of the romance of rich decay, a reference to older things, to a dramatic past. The past of Alexandria appeared in the vista of three or four short streets sloping up a hill and lined with poor brick warehouses erected for merchandise that had ceased to come or go. It looked hot and blank and sleepy, down to the shabby waterside where tattered darkies dangled their bare feet from the edge of rotting wharves. Pandora was even more interested in Mount Vernon—when at last its wooded bluff began to command the river—than she had been in the Capitol, and after they had disembarked and ascended to the celebrated mansion she insisted on going into every room it contained. She "claimed for it," as she said—some of her turns were so characteristic both of her nationality and her own style—the finest situation in the world, and was distinct as to the shame of their not giving it to the President for his country-seat. Most of her companions had seen the house often, and were now coupling themselves in the grounds according to their sympathies, so that it was easy for Vogelstein to offer the benefit of his own experience to the most inquisitive member of the party. They were not to lunch for another hour, and in the interval the young man roamed with his first and fairest acquaintance. The breath of the Potomac, on the boat, had been a little harsh, but on the softly-curving lawn, beneath the clustered trees, with the river relegated to a mere shining presence far below and in the distance, the day gave out nothing but its mildness, the whole scene became noble and genial.

Count Otto could joke a little on great occasions, and the present one was worthy of his humour. He maintained to his companion that the shallow painted mansion resembled a false house, a "wing" or structure of daubed canvas, on the stage; but she answered him so well with certain economical palaces she had seen in Germany, where, as she said, there was nothing but china stoves and stuffed birds, that he was obliged to allow the home of Washington to be after all really *gemüthlich*. What he found so in fact was the soft texture of the day, his personal situation, the sweetness of his suspense. For suspense had decidedly become his portion; he was under a charm that made him feel he was watching his own life and that his susceptibilities were beyond his control. It hung over him that things might take a turn, from one hour to the other, which would make them very different from what they had been yet; and his heart certainly beat a little faster as he wondered what that turn might be. Why did he come to picnics on fragrant April days with American girls who might lead him too far? Wouldn't such girls be glad to marry a Pomeranian count? And *would* they, after all, talk that way to the Kaiser? If he were to marry one of them he should have to give her several thorough lessons.

In their little tour of the house our young friend and his companion had had a great many fellow visitors, who had also arrived by the steamer and who had hitherto not left them an ideal privacy. But the others gradually dispersed; they circled about a kind of showman who was the authorised guide, a big slow genial vulgar heavily-bearded man, with a whimsical edifying patronising tone, a tone that had immense success when he stopped here and there to make his points—to pass his eyes over his listening flock, then fix them quite above it with a meditative look and bring out some ancient pleasantry as if it were a sudden inspiration. He made a cheerful thing, an echo of the platform before the booth of a country fair, even of a visit to the tomb of the *pater patriæ*. It is enshrined in a kind of grotto in the grounds, and Vogelstein remarked to Pandora that he was a good man for the place, but was too familiar. "Oh he'd have been familiar with Washington," said the girl with the bright dryness with which she often uttered amusing things. Vogelstein looked at her a moment, and it came over him, as he smiled, that she herself probably wouldn't have been abashed even by the hero with whom history has taken fewest liberties. "You look as if you could hardly believe that," Pandora went on. "You Germans are always in such awe of great people." And it occurred to her critic that perhaps after all Washington would have liked her manner, which was wonderfully fresh and natural. The man with the beard was an ideal minister to American shrines; he played on the curiosity of his little band with the touch of a master, drawing them at the right moment away to see the classic ice-house where the old lady had been found weeping in the belief it was Washington's grave. While this monument was under inspection our interesting couple had the house to themselves, and they spent some time on a pretty terrace where certain windows of the second floor opened—a little roofless verandah which overhung, in a manner, obliquely, all the magnificence of the view; the immense sweep of the river, the artistic plantations, the last-century garden with its big box hedges and remains of old espaliers. They lingered here for nearly half an hour, and it was in this retirement that Vogelstein enjoyed the only approach to intimate conversation appointed for him, as was to appear, with a young woman in whom he had been unable to persuade himself that he was not absorbed. It's not necessary, and it's not possible, that I should reproduce this colloquy; but I may mention that it began—as they leaned against the parapet of the terrace and heard the cheerful voice of the showman wafted up to them from a distance—with his saying to her rather abruptly that he couldn't make out why they hadn't had more talk together when they crossed the Atlantic.

"Well, I can if you can't," said Pandora. "I'd have talked quick enough if you had spoken to me. I spoke to you first."

"Yes, I remember that"—and it affected him awkwardly.

"You listened too much to Mrs. Dangerfield."

He feigned a vagueness. "To Mrs. Dangerfield?"

"That woman you were always sitting with; she told you not to speak to me. I've seen her in New York; she speaks to me now herself. She recommended you to have nothing to do with me."

"Oh how can you say such dreadful things?" Count Otto cried with a very becoming blush.

"You know you can't deny it. You weren't attracted by my family. They're charming people when you know them. I don't have a better time anywhere than I have at home," the girl went on loyally. "But what does it matter? My family are very happy. They're getting quite used to New York. Mrs. Dangerfield's a vulgar wretch—next winter she'll call on me."

"You are unlike any Mädchen I've ever seen—I don't understand you," said poor Vogelstein with the colour still in his face.

"Well, you never *will* understand me—probably; but what difference does it make?"

He attempted to tell her what difference, but I've no space to follow him here. It's known that when the German mind attempts to explain things it doesn't always reduce them to simplicity, and Pandora was first mystified, then amused, by some of the Count's revelations. At last I think she was a little frightened, for she remarked irrelevantly, with some decision, that luncheon would be ready and that they ought to join Mrs. Steuben. Her companion walked slowly, on purpose, as they left the house together, for he knew the pang of a vague sense that he was losing her.

"And shall you be in Washington many days yet?" he appealed as they went.

"It will all depend. I'm expecting important news. What I shall do will be influenced by that."

The way she talked about expecting news—and important!—made him feel somehow that she had a career, that she was active and independent, so that he could scarcely hope to stop her as she passed. It was certainly true that he had never seen any girl like her. It would have occurred to him that the news she was expecting might have reference to the favour she had begged of the President, if he hadn't already made up his mind—in the calm of meditation after that talk with the Bonnycastles—that this favour must be a pleasantry. What she had said to him had a discouraging, a somewhat chilling effect; nevertheless it was not without a certain ardour that he enquired of her whether, so long as she stayed in Washington, he mightn't pay her certain respectful attentions.

"As many as you like—and as respectful ones; but you won't keep them up for ever!"

"You try to torment me," said Count Otto.

She waited to explain. "I mean that I may have some of my family."

"I shall be delighted to see them again."

Again she just hung fire. "There are some you've never seen."

In the afternoon, returning to Washington on the steamer, Vogelstein received a warning. It came from Mrs. Bonnycastle and constituted, oddly enough, the second juncture at which an officious female friend had come while sociably afloat with him, advised him on the subject of Pandora Day.

"There's one thing we forgot to tell you the other night about the self-made girl," said the lady of infinite mirth. "It's not safe to fix your affections on her, because she has almost always an impediment somewhere in the background."

He looked at her askance, but smiled and said: "I should understand your information—for which I'm so much obliged—a little better if I knew what you mean by an impediment."

"Oh I mean she's always engaged to some young man who belongs to her earlier phase."

"Her earlier phase?"

"The time before she had made herself—when she lived unconscious of her powers. A young man from Utica, say. They usually have to wait; he's probably in a store. It's a long engagement."

Count Otto somehow preferred to understand as little as possible. "Do you mean a betrothal—to take effect?"

"I don't mean anything German and moonstruck. I mean that piece of peculiarly American enterprise—a premature engagement—to take effect, but too complacently, at the end of time."

Vogelstein very properly reflected that it was no use his having entered the diplomatic career if he weren't able to bear himself as if this interesting generalisation had no particular message for him. He did Mrs. Bonnycastle moreover the justice to believe that she wouldn't have approached the question with such levity if she had supposed she should make him wince. The whole thing was, like everything else, but for her to laugh at, and the betrayal moreover of a good intention. "I see, I see—the self-made girl has of course always had a past. Yes, and the young man in the store—from Utica—is part of her past."

"You express it perfectly," said Mrs. Bonnycastle. "I couldn't say it better myself."

"But with her present, with her future, when they change like this young lady's, I suppose everything else changes. How do you say it in America? She lets him slide."

"We don't say it at all!" Mrs. Bonnycastle cried. "She does nothing of the sort; for what do you take her? She sticks to him; that at least is what we *expect* her to do," she added with less assurance. "As I tell you, the type's new and the case under consideration. We haven't yet had time for complete study."

"Oh of course I hope she sticks to him," Vogelstein declared simply and with his German accent more audible, as it always was when he was slightly agitated.

For the rest of the trip he was rather restless. He wandered about the boat, talking little with the returning picnickers. Toward the last, as they drew near Washington and the white dome of the Capitol hung aloft before them, looking as simple as a suspended snowball, he found himself, on the deck, in proximity to Mrs. Steuben. He reproached himself with having rather neglected her during an entertainment for which he was indebted to her bounty, and he sought to repair his omission by a proper deference. But the only act of homage that occurred to him was to ask her as by chance whether Miss Day were, to her knowledge, engaged.

Mrs. Steuben turned her Southern eyes upon him with a look of almost romantic compassion. "To my knowledge? Why of course I'd know! I should think you'd know too. Didn't you know she was engaged? Why she has been engaged since she was sixteen."

Count Otto gazed at the dome of the Capitol. "To a gentleman from Utica?"

"Yes, a native of her place. She's expecting him soon."

"I'm so very glad to hear it," said Vogelstein, who decidedly, for his career, had promise. "And is she going to marry him?"

"Why what do people fall in love with each other *for?* I presume they'll marry when she gets round to it. Ah if she had only been from the Sooth—!"

At this he broke quickly in: "But why have they never brought it off, as you say, in so many years?"

"Well, at first she was too young, and then she thought her family ought to see Europe—of course they could see it better *with* her— and they spent some time there. And then Mr. Bellamy had some business difficulties that made him feel as if he didn't want to marry just then. But he has given up business and I presume feels more free. Of course it's rather long, but all the while they've been engaged. It's a true, true love," said Mrs. Steuben, whose sound of the adjective was that of a feeble flute.

"Is his name Mr. Bellamy?" the Count asked with his haunting reminiscence. "D. F. Bellamy, so? And has he been in a store?"

"I don't know what kind of business it was: it was some kind of business in Utica. I think he had a branch in New York. He's one of the leading gentlemen of Utica and very highly educated. He's a good deal older than Miss Day. He's a very fine man—I presume a college man. He stands very high in Utica. I don't know why you look as if you doubted it."

Vogelstein assured Mrs. Steuben that he doubted nothing, and indeed what she told him was probably the more credible for seeming to him eminently strange. Bellamy had been the name of the gentleman who, a year and a half before, was to have met Pandora on the arrival of the German steamer; it was in Bellamy's name that she had addressed herself with such effusion to Bellamy's friend, the man in the straw hat who was about to fumble in her mother's old clothes. This was a fact that seemed to Count Otto to finish the picture of her contradictions; it wanted at present no touch to be complete. Yet even as it hung there before him it continued to fascinate him, and he stared at it, detached from surrounding things and feeling a little as if he had been pitched out of an overturned vehicle, till the boat bumped against one of the outstanding piles of the wharf at which Mrs. Steuben's party was to disembark. There was some delay in getting the steamer adjusted to the dock, during which the passengers watched the process over its side and extracted what entertainment they might from the appearance of the various persons collected to receive it. There were darkies and loafers and hackmen, and also vague individuals, the loosest and blankest he had ever seen anywhere, with tufts on their chins, toothpicks in their mouths, hands in their pockets, rumination in their jaws and diamond pins in their shirt-fronts, who looked as if they had sauntered over from Pennsylvania Avenue to while away half an hour, forsaking for that interval their various slanting postures in the porticoes of the hotels and the doorways of the saloons.

"Oh I'm so glad! How sweet of you to come down!" It was a voice close to Count Otto's shoulder that spoke these words, and he had no need to turn to see from whom it proceeded. It had been in his ears the greater part of the day, though, as he now perceived, without the fullest richness of expression of which it was capable. Still less was he obliged to turn to discover to whom it was addressed, for the few simple words I have quoted had been flung across the narrowing interval of water, and a gentleman who had stepped to the edge of the dock without our young man's observing him tossed back an immediate reply.

"I got here by the three o'clock train. They told me in K Street where you were, and I thought I'd come down and meet you."

"Charming attention!" said Pandora Day with the laugh that seemed always to invite the whole of any company to partake in it; though for some moments after this she and her interlocutor appeared to continue the conversation only with their eyes. Meanwhile Vogelstein's also were not idle. He looked at her visitor from head to foot, and he was aware that she was quite unconscious of his own proximity. The gentleman before him was tall, good-looking, well-dressed; evidently he would stand well not only at Utica, but, judging from the way he had planted himself on the dock, in any position that circumstances might compel him to take up. He was about forty years old; he had a black moustache and he seemed to look at the world over some counter-like expanse on which he invited it all warily and pleasantly to put down first its idea of the terms of a transaction. He waved a gloved hand at Pandora as if, when she exclaimed "Gracious, ain't they long!" to urge her to be patient. She was patient several seconds and then asked him if he had any news. He looked at her briefly, in silence, smiling, after which he drew from his pocket a large letter with an official-looking seal and shook it jocosely above his head. This was discreetly, covertly done. No one but our young man appeared aware of how much was taking place—and poor Count Otto mainly felt it in the air. The boat was touching the wharf and the space between the pair inconsiderable.

"Department of State?" Pandora very prettily and soundlessly mouthed across at him.

"That's what they call it."

"Well, what country?"

"What's your opinion of the Dutch?" the gentleman asked for answer.

"Oh gracious!" cried Pandora.

"Well, are you going to wait for the return trip?" said the gentleman.

Our silent sufferer turned away, and presently Mrs. Steuben and her companion disembarked together. When this lady entered a carriage with Miss Day the gentleman who had spoken to the girl followed them; the others scattered, and Vogelstein, declining with thanks a "lift" from Mrs. Bonnycastle, walked home alone and in some intensity of meditation. Two days later he saw in a newspaper an announcement that the President had offered the post of Minister to Holland to Mr. D. F. Bellamy of Utica; and in the course of a month he heard from Mrs. Steuben that Pandora, a thousand other duties performed, had finally "got round" to the altar of her own nuptials. He communicated this news to Mrs. Bonnycastle, who had not heard it but who, shrieking at the queer face he showed her, met it with the remark that there was now ground for a new induction as to the self-made girl.

Four Tales

The four shorter tales grouped together here illustrate James's mastery of the highly condensed medium and his ability to treat large subjects within it. "The Author of Beltraffio" is a subtle little tale of a child-victim of a struggle between parents. Its Medea-subject—the mother's complicity in her child's death—makes it a horror story; but the terror is concealed behind the suavity of the narrator, his civilized air of describing a curious and semi-pathological "case." There is just enough "distance" in it to soften the horror. A secondary theme in the tale, and a frequent one in James, is that of the artist misunderstood by someone closest to him.

"Owen Wingrave" was regarded by James as a piece of hack-work. It was written for the Christmas issue of an illustrated magazine; yet it is unique among his stories. It demonstrates how, even in a manufactured tale, James could create an atmosphere. Moreover he effectively conveys the power of "family" in the life of the dedicated young man who loves poetry rather than the arts of war for which he is destined. The tale presents James in the unusual role of proclaiming the doctrines of pacifism; and later, when he made a one-act play of the story, Bernard Shaw tried unsuccessfully to convince him that he should change the ending. Instead of the ghost killing the young man, Shaw argued, the young man should kill the ghost. James, however, rejected this. He wanted to show that the young pacifist is, in spite of himself, a brave young soldier, capable of winning his grave (as his name suggests) on the field of honor.

"The Real Thing" is one of James's most reprinted tales; a fable of the reality of the imagination and the uselessness of the "real." The tale embodies the very heart of James's artistic credo. As with most of his stories of writers and artists, he shapes his parable in the form of a brief but telling anecdote.

The fourth tale in this group is one of James's late stories. It illustrates how the writer could handle the strong stuff of jealousy within the framework of a drawing-room. The rejected woman gets her chance to take her revenge; it is all a matter of dress and decorum and her position in society. But the final glimpse of the two faces—the triumphant jealous countenance and that of the victim—becomes a moment of deep and intense drama, one that has in it the rage and passion, the deep and powerful aggressions, that can lie beneath the quiet of social decorum.

L. E.

The Author of Beltraffio

✤ 1 ✤

MUCH as I wished to see him I had kept my letter of introduction three weeks in my pocket-book. I was nervous and timid about meeting him—conscious of youth and ignorance, convinced that he was tormented by strangers, and especially by my country-people, and not exempt from the suspicion that he had the irritability as well as the dignity of genius. Moreover, the pleasure, if it should occur— for I could scarcely believe it was near at hand—would be so great that I wished to think of it in advance, to feel it there against my breast, not to mix it with satisfactions more superficial and usual. In the little game of new sensations that I was playing with my ingenuous mind I wished to keep my visit to the author of "Beltraffio" as a trump-card. It was three years after the publication of that fascinating work, which I had read over five times and which now, with my riper judgement, I admire on the whole as much as ever. This will give you about the date of my first visit—of any duration—to England; for you will not have forgotten the commotion, I may even say the scandal, produced by Mark Ambient's masterpiece. It was the most complete presentation that had yet been made of the gospel of art; it was a kind of æsthetic war-cry. People had endeavoured to sail nearer to "truth" in the cut of their sleeves and the shape of their sideboards; but there had not as yet been, among English novels, such an example of beauty of execution and "intimate" importance of theme. Nothing had been done in that line from the point of view of art for art. That served me as a fond formula, I may mention, when I was twenty-five; how much it still serves I won't take upon myself to say—especially as the discerning reader will be able to judge for himself. I had been in England, briefly, a twelve-month before the time to which I began by alluding, and had then learned that Mr. Ambient was in distant lands—was making a considerable tour in the East; so that there was nothing to do but to keep my letter till I should be in London again. It was of little use to me to hear that his wife had not left England and was, with her little boy, their only child, spending the period of her husband's absence—a good many months—at a small place they had down in Surrey. They had a house in London, but actually in the occupation of other persons. All this I had picked up, and also that Mrs. Ambient was charming—my friend the American poet, from whom I had my introduction, had never seen her, his relations with the great man confined to the exchange of letters; but she wasn't, after all, though she had lived so near the rose, the author of "Beltraffio," and I didn't go down into Surrey to call on her. I went to the Continent, spent the following winter in Italy and returned to London in May. My visit to Italy had opened my eyes to a good many things, but to nothing more than the beauty of certain pages in the works of Mark Ambient. I carried his productions about in my trunk—they are not, as you know, very numerous, but he had preluded to "Beltraffio" by some exquisite things—and I used to read them over in the evening at the inn. I used profoundly to reason that the man who drew those characters and wrote that style understood what he saw and knew what he was doing. This is my sole ground for mentioning my winter in Italy. He had been there much in former years—he was saturated with what painters call the "feeling" of that classic land. He expressed the charm of the old hill-cities of Tuscany, the look of certain lonely grass-grown places which, in the past, had echoed with life; he understood the great artists, he understood the spirit of the Renaissance; he understood everything. The scene of one of his earlier novels was laid in Rome, the scene of another in Florence, and I had moved through these cities in company with the figures he set so firmly on their feet. This is why I was now so much happier even than before in the prospect of making his acquaintance.

At last, when I had dallied with my privilege long enough, I dispatched to him the missive of the American poet. He had already gone out of town; he shrank from the rigour of the London "season," and it was his habit to migrate on the first of June. Moreover I had heard he was this year hard at work on a new book, into which some of his impressions of the East were to be wrought, so that he desired nothing so much as quiet days. That knowledge, however, didn't prevent me—*cet âge est sans pitié*—from sending with my friend's letter a note of my own, in which I asked his leave to come down and see him for an hour or two on some day to be named by himself. My proposal was accompanied with a very frank expression of my sentiments, and the effect of the entire appeal was to elicit from the great man the kindest possible invitation. He would be delighted to see me, especially if I should turn up on the following Saturday and would remain till the Monday morning. We would take a walk over the Surrey commons, and I could tell him all about the other great man, the one in America. He indicated to me the best train, and it may be imagined whether on the Saturday afternoon I was punctual at Waterloo. He carried his benevolence to the point of coming to meet me at the little station at which I was to alight, and my heart beat very fast as I saw his handsome face, surmounted with a soft wide-awake and which I knew by a photograph long since enshrined on my mantel-shelf, scanning the carriage-windows as the train rolled up. He recognised me as infallibly as I had recognised himself; he appeared to know by instinct how a young American of critical pretensions, rash youth, would look when much divided between eagerness and modesty. He took me by the hand and smiled at me and said: "You must be—a—*you*, I think!" and asked if I should mind going on foot to his house, which would take but a few minutes. I remember feeling it a piece of extraordinary affability that he should give directions about the conveyance of my bag; I remember feeling altogether very happy and rosy, in fact quite transported, when he laid his hand on my shoulder as we came out of the station.

I surveyed him, askance, as we walked together; I had already, I had indeed instantly, seen him as all delightful. His face is so well known that I needn't describe it; he looked to me at once an English gentleman and a man of genius, and I thought that a happy combination. There was a brush of the Bohemian in his fineness; you would easily have guessed his belonging to the artist guild. He was addicted to velvet jackets, to cigarettes, to loose shirt-collars, to looking a little dishevelled. His features, which were firm but not perfectly regular, are fairly enough represented in his portraits; but no portrait I have seen gives any idea of his expression. There were innumerable things in it, and they chased each other in and out of his face. I have seen people who were grave and gay in quick alternation; but Mark Ambient was grave and gay at one and the same moment. There were other strange oppositions and contradictions in his slightly faded and fatigued countenance. He affected me somehow as at once fresh and stale, at once anxious and indifferent.

He had evidently had an active past, which inspired one with curiosity; yet what was that compared to his obvious future? He was just enough above middle height to be spoken of as tall, and rather lean and long in the flank. He had the friendliest frankest manner possible, and yet I could see it cost him something. It cost him small spasms of the self-consciousness that is an Englishman's last and dearest treasure—the thing he pays his way through life by sacrificing small pieces of even as the gallant but moneyless adventurer in "Quentin Durward" broke off links of his brave gold chain. He had been thirty-eight years old at the time "Beltraffio" was published. He asked me about his friend in America, about the length of my stay in England, about the last news in London and the people I had seen there; and I remember looking for the signs of genius in the very form of his questions and thinking I found it. I liked his voice as if I were somehow myself having the use of it.

There was genius in his house too I thought when we got there; there was imagination in the carpets and curtains, in the pictures and books, in the garden behind it, where certain old brown walls were muffled in creepers that appeared to me to have been copied from a masterpiece of one of the pre-Raphaelites. That was the way many things struck me at that time, in England—as reproductions of something that existed primarily in art or literature. It was not the picture, the poem, the fictive page, that seemed to me a copy; these things were the originals, and the life of happy and distinguished people was fashioned in their image. Mark Ambient called his house a cottage, and I saw afterwards he was right; for if it hadn't been a cottage it must have been a villa, and a villa, in England at least, was not a place in which one could fancy him at home. But it was, to my vision, a cottage glorified and translated; it was a palace of art, on a slightly reduced scale—and might besides have been the dearest haunt of the old English *genius loci*. It nestled under a cluster of magnificent beeches, it had little creaking lattices that opened out of, or into, pendent mats of ivy, and gables, and old red tiles, as well as a general aspect of being painted in water-colours and inhabited by people whose lives would go on in chapters and volumes. The lawn seemed to me of extraordinary extent, the garden-walls of incalculable height, the whole air of the place delightfully still, private, proper to itself. "My wife must be somewhere about," Mark Ambient said as we went in. "We shall find her perhaps—we've about an hour before dinner. She may be in the garden. I'll show you my little place."

We passed through the house and into the grounds, as I should have called them, which extended into the rear. They covered scarce three or four acres, but, like the house, were very old and crooked and full of traces of long habitation, with inequalities of level and little flights of steps—mossy and cracked were these—which connected the different parts with each other. The limits of the place, cleverly dissimulated, were muffled in the great verdurous screens. They formed, as I remember, a thick loose curtain at the further end, in one of the folds of which, as it were, we presently made out from afar a little group. "Ah there she is!" said Mark Ambient; "and she has got the boy." He noted that last fact in a slightly different tone from any in which he yet had spoken. I wasn't fully aware of this at the time, but it lingered in my ear and I afterwards understood it.

"Is it your son?" I enquired, feeling the question not to be brilliant.

"Yes, my only child. He's always in his mother's pocket. She coddles him too much." It came back to me afterwards too—the sound of these critical words. They weren't petulant; they expressed rather a sudden coldness, a mechanical submission. We went a few steps further, and then he stopped short and called the boy, beckoning to him repeatedly.

"Dolcino, come and see your daddy!" There was something in the way he stood still and waited that made me think he did it for a purpose. Mrs. Ambient had her arm round the child's waist, and he was leaning against her knee; but though he moved at his father's call she gave no sign of releasing him. A lady, apparently a neighbour, was seated near her, and before them was a garden-table on which a tea-service had been placed.

Mark Ambient called again, and Dolcino struggled in the maternal embrace; but, too tightly held, he after two or three fruitless efforts jerked about and buried his head deep in his mother's lap. There was a certain awkwardness in the scene; I thought it odd Mrs. Ambient should pay so little attention to her husband. But I wouldn't for the world have betrayed my thought and, to conceal it, I began loudly to rejoice in the prospect of our having tea in the garden. "Ah she won't let him come!" said my host with a sigh; and we went our way till we reached the two ladies. He mentioned my name to his wife, and I noticed that he addressed her as "My dear," very genially, without a trace of resentment at her detention of the child. The quickness of the transition made me vaguely ask myself if he were perchance henpecked—a shocking surmise which I instantly dismissed. Mrs. Ambient was quite such a wife as I should have expected him to have; slim and fair, with a long neck and pretty eyes and an air of good breeding. She shone with a certain coldness and practised in intercourse a certain bland detachment, but she was clothed in gentleness as in one of those vaporous redundant scarves that muffle the heroines of Gainsborough and Romney. She had also a vague air of race, justified by my afterwards learning that she was "connected with the aristocracy." I have seen poets married to women of whom it was difficult to conceive that they should gratify the poetic fancy—women with dull faces and glutinous minds, who were none the less, however, excellent wives. But there was no obvious disparity in Mark Ambient's union. My hostess—so far as she could be called so—delicate and quiet, in a white dress, with her beautiful child at her side, was worthy of the author of a work so distinguished as "Beltraffio." Round her neck she wore a black velvet ribbon, of which the long ends, tied behind, hung down her back, and to which, in front, was attached a miniature portrait of her little boy. Her smooth shining hair was confined in a net. She gave me an adequate greeting and Dolcino—I thought this small name of endearment delightful—took advantage of her getting up to slip away from her and go to his father, who seized him in silence and held him high for a long moment, kissing him several times.

I had lost no time in observing that the child, not more than seven years old, was extraordinarily beautiful. He had the face of an angel—the eyes, the hair, the smile of innocence, the more than mortal bloom. There was something that deeply touched, that almost alarmed, in his beauty, composed, one would have said, of elements too fine and pure for the breath of this world. When I spoke to him and he came and held out his hand and smiled at me I felt a sudden strange pity for him—quite as if he had been an orphan or a changeling or stamped with some social stigma. It was impossible to be in fact more exempt from these misfortunes, and yet, as one kissed him, it was hard to keep from murmuring all tenderly "Poor little devil!" though why one should have applied this epithet to a living cherub is more than I can say. Afterwards indeed I knew a trifle better; I grasped the truth of his being too fair to live, wondering at the same time that his parents shouldn't have guessed it and have been in proportionate grief and despair. For myself I had no doubt of his evanescence, having already more than once caught in the fact the particular infant charm that's as good as a death-warrant.

The lady who had been sitting with Mrs. Ambient was a jolly ruddy personage in velveteen and limp feathers, whom I guessed to be the vicar's wife—our hostess didn't introduce me—and who immediately began to talk to Ambient about chrysanthemums. This was a safe subject, and yet there was a certain surprise for me in seeing the author of "Beltraffio" even in such superficial communion with the Church of England. His writings implied so much detachment from that institution, expressed a view of life so profane, as it were, so independent and so little likely in general to be thought edifying, that I should have expected to find him an object of horror to vicars and their ladies—of horror repaid on his own part by any amount of effortless derision. This proved how little I knew as yet of the English people and their extraordinary talent for keeping up their forms, as well as of some of the mysteries of Mark Ambient's hearth and home. I found afterwards that he had, in his study, between nervous laughs and free cigar-puffs, some wonderful comparisons for his clerical neighbours; but meanwhile the chrysanthemums were a source of harmony, as he and the vicaress were equally attached to them, and I was surprised at the knowledge they exhibited of this interesting plant. The lady's visit, however, had presumably been long, and she presently rose for departure and kissed Mrs. Ambient. Mark started to walk with her to the gate of the grounds, holding Dolcino by the hand.

"Stay with me, darling," Mrs. Ambient said to the boy, who had surrendered himself to his father.

Mark paid no attention to the summons, but Dolcino turned and looked at her in shy appeal. "Can't I go with papa?"

"Not when I ask you to stay with me."

"But please don't ask me, mamma," said the child in his small clear new voice.

"I must ask you when I want you. Come to me, dearest." And Mrs. Ambient, who had seated herself again, held out her long slender slightly too osseous hands.

Her husband stopped, his back turned to her, but without releasing the child. He was still talking to the vicaress, but this good lady, I think, had lost the thread of her attention. She looked at Mrs. Ambient and at Dolcino, and then looked at me, smiling in a highly amused cheerful manner and almost to a grimace.

"Papa," said the child, "mamma wants me not to go with you."

"He's very tired—he has run about all day. He ought to be quiet till he goes to bed. Otherwise he won't sleep." These declarations fell successively and very distinctly from Mrs. Ambient's lips.

Her husband, still without turning round, bent over the boy and looked at him in silence. The vicaress gave a genial irrelevant laugh and observed that he was a precious little pet. "Let him choose," said Mark Ambient. "My dear little boy, will you go with me or will you stay with your mother?"

"Oh it's a shame!" cried the vicar's lady with increased hilarity.

"Papa, I don't think I can choose," the child answered, making his voice very low and confidential. "But I've been a great deal with mamma to-day," he then added.

"And very little with papa! My dear fellow, I think you *have* chosen!" On which Mark Ambient walked off with his son, accompanied by re-echoing but inarticulate comments from my fellow visitor.

His wife had seated herself again, and her fixed eyes, bent on the ground, expressed for a few moments so much mute agitation that anything I could think of to say would be but a false note. Yet she none the less quickly recovered herself, to express the sufficiently civil hope that I didn't mind having had to walk from the station. I reassured her on this point, and she went on: "We've got a thing that might have gone for you, but my husband wouldn't order it." After which and another longish pause, broken only by my plea that the pleasure of a walk with our friend would have been quite what I would have chosen, she found for reply: "I believe the Americans walk very little."

"Yes, we always run," I laughingly allowed.

She looked at me seriously, yet with an absence in her pretty eyes. "I suppose your distances are so great."

"Yes, but we break our marches! I can't tell you the pleasure to me of finding myself here," I added. "I've the greatest admiration for Mr. Ambient."

"He'll like that. He likes being admired."

"He must have a very happy life then. He has many worshippers."

"Oh yes, I've seen some of them," she dropped, looking away, very far from me, rather as if such a vision were before her at the moment. It seemed to indicate, her tone, that the sight was scarcely edifying, and I guessed her quickly enough to be in no great intellectual sympathy with the author of "Beltraffio." I thought the fact strange, but somehow, in the glow of my own enthusiasm, didn't think it important: it only made me wish rather to emphasise that homage.

"For me, you know," I returned—doubtless with a due *suffisance*—"he's quite the greatest of living writers."

"Of course I can't judge. Of course he's very clever," she said with a patient cheer.

"He's nothing less than supreme, Mrs. Ambient! There are pages in each of his books of a perfection classing them with the greatest things. Accordingly for me to see him in this familiar way, in his habit as he lives, and apparently to find the man as delightful as the artist—well, I can't tell you how much too good to be true it seems and how great a privilege I think it." I knew I was gushing, but I couldn't help it, and what I said was a good deal less than what I felt. I was by no means sure I should dare to say even so much as this to the master himself, and there was a kind of rapture in speaking it out to his wife which was not affected by the fact that, as a wife, she appeared peculiar. She listened to me with her face grave again and her lips a little compressed, listened as if in no doubt, of course, that her husband was remarkable, but as if at the same time she had heard it frequently enough and couldn't treat it as stirring news There was even in her manner a suggestion that I was so young as to expose myself to being called forward—an imputation and a word I had always loathed; as well as a hinted reminder that people usually got over their early extravagance. "I assure you that for me this is a red-letter day," I added.

She didn't take this up, but after a pause, looking round her, said abruptly and a trifle dryly: "We're very much afraid about the fruit this year."

My eyes wandered to the mossy mottled garden-walls, where plum-trees and pears, flattened and fastened upon the rusty bricks, looked like crucified figures with many arms. "Doesn't it promise well?"

"No, the trees look very dull. We had such late frosts."

Then there was another pause. She addressed her attention to the opposite end of the grounds, kept it for her husband's return with the child. "Is Mr. Ambient fond of gardening?" it occurred to me to ask, irresistibly impelled as I felt myself, moreover, to bring the conversation constantly back to him.

"He's very fond of plums," said his wife.

"Ah well then I hope your crop will be better than you fear. It's a lovely old place," I continued. "The whole impression's that of certain places he has described. Your house is like one of his pictures."

She seemed a bit frigidly amused at my glow. "It's a pleasant little place. There are hundreds like it."

"Oh it has his *tone*," I laughed, but sounding my epithet and insisting on my point the more sharply that my companion appeared to see in my appreciation of her simple establishment a mark of mean experience.

It was clear I insisted too much. "His tone?" she repeated with a harder look at me and a slightly heightened colour.

"Surely he has a tone, Mrs. Ambient."

"Oh yes, he has indeed! But I don't in the least consider that I'm living in one of his books at all. I shouldn't care for that in the least," she went on with a smile that had in some degree the effect of converting her really sharp protest into an insincere joke. "I'm afraid I'm not very literary. And I'm not artistic," she stated.

"I'm very sure you're not ignorant, not stupid," I ventured to reply, with the accompaniment of feeling immediately afterwards that I had been both familiar and patronising. My only consolation was in the sense that she had begun it, had fairly dragged me into it. She had thrust forward her limitations.

"Well, whatever I am I'm very different from my husband. If you like him you won't like me. You needn't say anything. Your liking me isn't in the least necessary!"

"Don't defy me!" I could but honourably make answer.

She looked as if she hadn't heard me, which was the best thing she could do; and we sat some time without further speech. Mrs. Ambient had evidently the enviable English quality of being able to be mute without unrest. But at last she spoke—she asked me if there seemed many people in town. I gave her what satisfaction I could on this point, and we talked a little of London and of some of its characteristics at that time of the year. At the end of this I came back irrepressibly to Mark.

"Doesn't he like to be there now? I suppose he doesn't find the proper quiet for his work. I should think his things had been written for the most part in a very still place. They suggest a great stillness following on a kind of tumult. Don't you think so?" I laboured on. "I suppose London's a tremendous place to collect impressions, but a refuge like this, in the country, must be better for working them up. Does he get many of his impressions in London, should you say?" I proceeded from point to point in this malign enquiry simply because my hostess, who probably thought me an odious chattering person, gave me time; for when I paused—I've not represented my pauses—she simply continued to let her eyes wander while her long fair fingers played with the medallion on her neck. When I stopped altogether, however, she was obliged to say something, and what she said was that she hadn't the least idea where her husband got his impressions. This made me think her, for a moment, positively disagreeable; delicate and proper and rather aristocratically fine as she sat there. But I must either have lost that view a moment later or been goaded by it to further aggression, for I remember asking her if our great man were in a good vein of work and when we might look for the appearance of the book on which he was engaged. I've every reason now to know that she found me insufferable.

She gave a strange small laugh as she said: "I'm afraid you think I know much more about my husband's work than I do. I haven't the least idea what he's doing," she then added in a slightly different, that is a more explanatory, tone and as if from a glimpse of the enormity of her confession. "I don't read what he writes."

She didn't succeed, and wouldn't even had she tried much harder, in making this seem to me anything less than monstrous. I stared at her and I think I blushed. "Don't you admire his genius? Don't you admire 'Beltraffio'?"

She waited, and I wondered what she could possibly say. She didn't speak, I could see, the first words that rose to her lips; she repeated what she had said a few minutes before. "Oh of course he's very clever!" And with this she got up; our two absentees had reappeared.

✣ 2 ✣

Mrs. Ambient left me and went to meet them; she stopped and had a few words with her husband that I didn't hear and that ended in her taking the child by the hand and returning with him to the house. Her husband joined me in a moment, looking, I thought, the least bit conscious and constrained, and said that if I would come in with him he would show me my room. In looking back upon these first moments of my visit I find it important to avoid the error of appearing to have at all fully measured his situation from the first or made out the signs of things mastered only afterwards. This later knowledge throws a backward light and makes me forget that, at least on the occasion of my present reference—I mean that first afternoon—Mark Ambient struck me as only enviable. Allowing for this he must yet have failed of much expression as we walked back to the house, though I remember well the answer he made to a remark of mine on his small son.

"That's an extraordinary little boy of yours. I've never seen such a child."

"Why," he asked while we went, "do you call him extraordinary?"

"He's so beautiful, so fascinating. He's like some perfect little work of art."

He turned quickly in the passage, grasping my arm. "Oh don't call him that, or you'll—you'll—!" But in his hesitation he broke off suddenly, laughing at my surprise. Immediately afterwards, however, he added: "You'll make his little future very difficult."

I declared that I wouldn't for the world take any liberties with his little future—it seemed to me to hang by threads of such delicacy. I should only be highly interested in watching it.

"You Americans are very keen," he commented on this. "You notice more things than we do."

"Ah if you want visitors who aren't struck with you," I cried, "you shouldn't have asked me down here!"

He showed me my room, a little bower of chintz, with open windows where the light was green, and before he left me said irrelevantly: "As for my small son, you know, we shall probably kill him between us before we've done with him!" And he made this assertion as if he really believed it, without any appearance of jest, his fine near-sighted expressive eyes looking straight into mine.

"Do you mean by spoiling him?"

"No, by fighting for him!"

"You had better give him to me to keep for you," I said. "Let me remove the apple of discord!"

It was my extravagance of course, but he had the air of being perfectly serious. "It would be quite the best thing we could do. I should be all ready to do it."

"I'm greatly obliged to you for your confidence."

But he lingered with his hands in his pockets. I felt as if within a few moments I had, morally speaking, taken several steps nearer to him. He looked weary, just as he faced me then, looked preoccupied and as if there were something one might do for him. I was terribly conscious of the limits of my young ability, but I wondered what such a service might be, feeling at bottom nevertheless that the only thing I could do for him was to like him. I suppose he guessed this and was grateful for what was in my mind, since he went on presently: "I haven't the advantage of being an American, but I also notice a little, and I've an idea that"—here he smiled and laid his hand on my shoulder—"even counting out your nationality you're not destitute of intelligence. I've only known you half an hour, but—!" For which again he pulled up. "You're very young after all."

"But you may treat me as if I could understand you!" I said; and before he left me to dress for dinner he had virtually given me a promise that he would.

When I went down into the drawing-room—I was very punctual—I found that neither my hostess nor my host had appeared. A lady rose from a sofa, however, and inclined her head as I rather surprisedly gazed at her. "I dare say you don't know me," she said with the modern laugh. "I'm Mark Ambient's sister." Whereupon I shook hands with her, saluting her very low. Her laugh was modern—by which I mean that it consisted of the vocal agitation serving between people who meet in drawing-rooms as the solvent of social disparities, the medium of transitions; but her appearance was—what shall I call it?—mediæval. She was pale and angular, her long thin face was inhabited by sad dark eyes and her black hair intertwined with golden fillets and curious clasps. She wore a faded velvet robe which clung to her when she moved and was "cut," as to the neck and sleeves, like the garments of old Italians. She suggested a symbolic picture, something akin even to Dürer's Melancholia, and was so perfect an image of a type which I, in my ignorance, supposed to be extinct, that while she rose before me I was almost as much startled as if I had seen a ghost. I afterwards concluded that Miss Ambient wasn't incapable of deriving pleasure from this weird effect, and I now believe that reflexion concerned in her having sunk again to her seat with her long lean but not ungraceful arms locked together in an archaic manner on her knees and her mournful eyes addressing me a message of intentness which foreshadowed what I was subsequently to suffer. She was a singular fatuous artificial creature, and I was never more than half to penetrate her motives and mysteries. Of one thing I'm sure at least: that they were considerably less insuperable than her appearance announced. Miss Ambient was a restless romantic disappointed spinster, consumed with the love of Michael-Angelesque attitudes and mystical robes; but I'm now convinced she hadn't in her nature those depths of unutterable thought which, when you first knew her, seemed to look out from her eyes and to prompt her complicated gestures. Those features in especial had a misleading eloquence; they lingered on you with a far-off dimness, an air of obstructed sympathy, which was certainly not always a key to the spirit of their owner; so that, of a truth, a young lady could scarce have been so dejected and disillusioned without having committed a crime for which she was consumed with remorse, or having parted with a hope that she couldn't sanely have entertained. She had, I believe, the usual allowance of rather vain motives: she wished to be looked at, she wished to be married, she wished to be thought original.

It costs me a pang to speak in this irreverent manner of one of Ambient's name, but I shall have still less gracious things to say before I've finished my anecdote, and moreover—I confess it—I owe the young lady a bit of a grudge. Putting aside the curious cast of her face she had no natural aptitude for an artistic development, had little real intelligence. But her affectations rubbed off on her brother's renown, and as there were plenty of people who darkly disapproved of him they could easily point to his sister as a person formed by his influence. It was quite possible to regard her as a warning, and she had almost compromised him with the world at large. He was the original and she the inevitable imitation. I suppose him scarce aware of the impression she mainly produced, beyond having a general idea that she made up very well as a Rossetti; he was used to her and was sorry for her, wishing she would marry and observing how she didn't. Doubtless I take her too seriously, for she did me no harm, though I'm bound to allow that I can only half-account for her. She wasn't so mystical as she looked, but was a strange indirect uncomfortable embarrassing woman. My story gives the reader at best so very small a knot to untie that I needn't hope to excite his curiosity by delaying to remark that Mrs. Ambient hated her sister-in-law. This I learned but later on, when other matters came to my knowledge. I mention it, however, at once, for I shall perhaps not seem to count too much on having beguiled him if I say he must promptly have guessed it. Mrs. Ambient, a person of conscience, put the best face on her kinswoman, who spent a month with her twice a year; but it took no great insight to recognise the very different personal paste of the two ladies, and that the usual feminine hypocrisies would cost them on either side much more than the usual effort. Mrs. Ambient, smooth-haired, thin-lipped, perpetually fresh, must have regarded her crumpled and dishevelled visitor as an equivocal joke; she herself so the opposite of a Rossetti, she herself a Reynolds or a Lawrence, with no more far-fetched note in her composition than a cold ladylike candour and a well-starched muslin dress.

It was in a garment and with an expression of this kind that she made her entrance after I had exchanged a few words with Miss Ambient. Her husband presently followed her and, there being no other company, we went to dinner. The impressions I received at that repast are present to me still. The elements of oddity in the air hovered, as it were, without descending—to any immediate check of my delight. This came mainly of course from Ambient's talk, the easiest and richest I had ever heard. I mayn't say to-day whether he laid himself out to dazzle a rather juvenile pilgrim from over the sea; but that matters little—it seemed so natural to him to shine. His spoken wit or wisdom, or whatever, had thus a charm almost beyond his written; that is if the high finish of his printed prose be really, as some people have maintained, a fault. There was such a kindness in him, however, that I've no doubt it gave him ideas for me, or about me, to see me sit as open-mouthed as I now figure myself. Not so the two ladies, who not only were very nearly dumb from beginning to end of the meal, but who hadn't even the air of being struck with such an exhibition of fancy and taste. Mrs. Ambient, detached, and inscrutable, met neither my eye nor her husband's: she attended to her dinner, watched her servants, arranged the puckers in her dress, exchanged at wide intervals a remark with her sister-in-law and, while she slowly rubbed her lean white hands between the courses, looked out of the window at the first signs of evening—the long June day allowing us to dine without candles. Miss Ambient appeared to give little direct heed to anything said by her brother; but on the other hand she was much engaged in watching its effect upon me. Her "die-away" pupils continued to attach themselves to my countenance, and it was only her air of belonging to another century that kept them from being importunate. She seemed to look at me across the ages, and the interval of time diminished for me the inconvenience. It was as if she knew in a general way that he must be talking very well, but she herself was so at home among such allusions that she had no need to pick them up and was at liberty to see what would become of the exposure of a candid young American to a high æsthetic temperature.

The temperature was æsthetic certainly, but it was less so than I could have desired, for I failed of any great success in making our friend abound about himself. I tried to put him on the ground of his own genius, but he slipped through my fingers every time and shifted the saddle to one or other of his contemporaries. He talked about Balzac and Browning, about what was being done in foreign countries, about his recent tour in the East and the extraordinary forms of life to be observed in that part of the world. I felt he had reasons for holding off from a direct profession of literary faith, a full consistency or sincerity, and therefore dealt instead with certain social topics, treating them with extraordinary humour and with a due play of that power of ironic evocation in which his books abound. He had a deal to say about London as London appears to the observer who has the courage of some of his conclusions during the high-pressure time—from April to July—of its gregarious life. He flashed his faculty of playing with the caught image and liberating the wistful idea over the whole scheme of manners or conception of intercourse of his compatriots, among whom there were evidently not a few types for which he had little love. London in short was grotesque to him, and he made capital sport of it; his only allusion that I can remember to his own work was his saying that he meant some day to do an immense and general, a kind of epic, social satire. Miss Ambient's perpetual gaze seemed to put to me: "Do you perceive how artistic, how very strange and interesting, we are? Frankly now is it possible to be *more* artistic, *more* strange and interesting, than this? You surely won't deny that we're remarkable." I was irritated by her use of the plural pronoun, for she had no right to pair herself with her brother; and moreover of course I couldn't see my way to—at all genially—include Mrs. Ambient. Yet there was no doubt they were, taken together, unprecedented enough, and, with all allowances, I had never been left, or condemned, to draw so many rich inferences.

After the ladies had retired my host took me into his study to smoke, where I appealingly brought him round, or so tried, to some disclosure of fond ideals. I was bent on proving I was worthy to listen to him, on repaying him for what he had said to me before dinner, by showing him how perfectly I understood. He liked to talk; he liked to defend his convictions and his honour (not that I attacked them) ; he liked a little perhaps—it was a pardonable weakness—to bewilder the youthful mind even while wishing to win it over. My ingenuous sympathy received at any rate a shock from three or four of his professions—he made me occasionally gasp and stare. He couldn't help forgetting, or rather couldn't know, how little, in another and dryer clime, I had ever sat in the school in which he was master; and he promoted me as at a jump to a sense of its penetralia. My trepidations, however, were delightful; they were just what I had hoped for, and their only fault was that they passed away too quickly; since I found that for the main points I was essentially, I was quite constitutionally, on Mark Ambient's "side." This was the taken stand of the artist to whom every manifestation of human energy was a thrilling spectacle and who felt for ever the desire to resolve his experience of life into a literary form. On that high head of the passion for form—the attempt at perfection, the quest for which was to his mind the real search for the holy grail—he said the most interesting, the most inspiring things. He mixed with them a thousand illustrations from his own life, from other lives he had known, from history and fiction, and above all from the annals of the time that was dear to him beyond all periods, the Italian cinque-cento. It came to me thus that in his books he had uttered but half his thought, and that what he had kept back—from motives I deplored when I made them out later—was the finer, and braver part. It was his fate to make a great many still more "prepared" people than me not inconsiderably wince; but there was no grain of bravado in his ripest things (I've always maintained it, though often contradicted), and at bottom the poor fellow, disinterested to his finger-tips and regarding imperfection not only as an æsthetic but quite also as a social crime, had an extreme dread of scandal. There are critics who regret that having gone so far he didn't go further; but I regret nothing—putting aside two or three of the motives I just mentioned—since he arrived at a noble rarity and I don't see how you can go beyond that. The hours I spent in his study—this first one and the few that followed it; they were not after all so numerous—seem to glow, as I look back on them, with a tone that is partly that of the brown old room, rich, under the shaded candle-light where we sat and smoked, with the dusky delicate bindings of valuable books; partly that of his voice, of which I still catch the echo, charged with the fancies and figures that came at his command. When we went back to the drawing-room we found Miss Ambient alone in possession and prompt to mention that her sister-in-law had a quarter of an hour before been called by the nurse to see the child, who appeared rather unwell—a little feverish.

"Feverish! how in the world comes he to be feverish?" Ambient asked. "He was perfectly right this afternoon."

"Beatrice says you walked him about too much—you almost killed him."

"Beatrice must be very happy—she has an opportunity to triumph!" said my friend with a bright bitterness which was all I could have wished it.

"Surely not if the child's ill," I ventured to remark by way of pleading for Mrs. Ambient.

"My dear fellow, you aren't married—you don't know the nature of wives!" my host returned with spirit.

I tried to match it. "Possibly not; but I know the nature of mothers."

"Beatrice is perfect as a mother," sighed Miss Ambient quite tremendously and with her fingers interlaced on her embroidered knees.

"I shall go up and see my boy," her brother went on. "Do you suppose he's asleep?"

"Beatrice won't let you see him, dear"—as to which our young lady looked at me, though addressing our companion.

"Do you call that being perfect as a mother?" Ambient asked.

"Yes, from her point of view."

"Damn her point of view!" cried the author of "Beltraffio." And he left the room; after which we heard him ascend the stairs.

I sat there for some ten minutes with Miss Ambient, and we naturally had some exchange of remarks, which began, I think, by my asking her what the point of view of her sister-in-law could be.

"Oh it's so very odd. But we're so very odd altogether. Don't you find us awfully unlike others of our class?—which indeed mostly, in England, is awful. We've lived so much abroad. I adore 'abroad.' Have you people like us in America?"

"You're not all alike, you interesting three—or, counting Dolcino, four—surely, surely; so that I don't think I understand your question. We've no one like your brother—I may go so far as that."

"You've probably more persons like his wife," Miss Ambient desolately smiled.

"I can tell you that better when you've told me about her point of view."

"Oh yes—oh yes. Well," said my entertainer, "she doesn't like his ideas. She doesn't like them for the child. She thinks them undesirable."

Being quite fresh from the contemplation of some of Mark Ambient's *arcana* I was particularly in a position to appreciate this announcement. But the effect of it was to make me, after staring a moment, burst into laughter which I instantly checked when I remembered the indisposed child above and the possibility of parents nervously or fussily anxious.

"What has that infant to do with ideas?" I asked. "Surely he can't tell one from another. Has he read his father's novels?"

"He's very precocious and very sensitive, and his mother thinks she can't begin to guard him too early." Miss Ambient's head drooped a little to one side and her eyes fixed themselves on futurity. Then of a sudden came a strange alteration; her face lighted to an effect more joyless than any gloom, to that indeed of a conscious insincere grimace, and she added: "When one has children what one writes becomes a great responsibility."

"Children are terrible critics," I prosaically answered. "I'm really glad I haven't any."

"Do you also write then? And in the same style as my brother? And do you like that style? And do people appreciate it in America? I don't write, but I think I feel." To these and various other enquiries and observations my young lady treated me till we heard her brother's step in the hall again and Mark Ambient reappeared. He was so flushed and grave that I supposed he had seen something symptomatic in the condition of his child. His sister apparently had another idea; she gazed at him from afar—as if he had been a burning ship on the horizon—and simply murmured "Poor old Mark!"

"I hope you're not anxious," I as promptly pronounced.

"No, but I'm disappointed. She won't let me in. She has locked the door, and I'm afraid to make a noise." I dare say there might have been a touch of the ridiculous in such a confession, but I liked my new friend so much that it took nothing for me from his dignity. "She tells me—from behind the door—that she'll let me know if he's worse."

"It's very good of her," said Miss Ambient with a hollow sound.

I had exchanged a glance with Mark in which it's possible he read that my pity for him was untinged with contempt, though I scarce know why he should have cared; and as his sister soon afterward got up and took her bedroom candlestick he proposed we should go back to his study. We sat there till after midnight; he put himself into his slippers and an old velvet jacket, he lighted an ancient pipe, but he talked considerably less than before. There were longish pauses in our communion, but they only made me feel we had advanced in intimacy. They helped me further to understand my friend's personal situation and to imagine it by no means the happiest possible. When his face was quiet it was vaguely troubled, showing, to my increase of interest—if that was all that was wanted!—that for him too life was the same struggle it had been for so many another man of genius. At last I prepared to leave him, and then, to my ineffable joy, he gave me some of the sheets of his forthcoming book—which, though unfinished, he had indulged in the luxury, so dear to writers of deliberation, of having "set up," from chapter to chapter, as he advanced. These early pages, the *prémices,* in the language of letters, of that new fruit of his imagination, I should take to my room and look over at my leisure. I was in the act of leaving him when the door of the study noiselessly opened and Mrs. Ambient stood before us. She observed us a moment, her candle in her hand, and then said to her husband that as she supposed he hadn't gone to bed she had come down to let him know Dolcino was more quiet and would probably be better in the morning. Mark Ambient made no reply; he simply slipped past her in the doorway, as if for fear she might seize him in his passage, and bounded upstairs to judge for himself of his child's condition. She looked so frankly discomfited that I for a moment believed her about to give him chase. But she resigned herself with a sigh and her eyes turned, ruefully and without a ray, to the lamplit room where various books at which I had been looking were pulled out of their places on the shelves and the fumes of tobacco hung in midair. I bade her good-night and then, without intention, by a kind of fatality, a perversity that had already made me address her overmuch on that question of her husband's powers, I alluded to the precious proof-sheets with which Ambient had entrusted me and which I nursed there under my arm. "They're the opening chapters of his new book," I said. "Fancy my satisfaction at being allowed to carry them to my room!"

She turned away, leaving me to take my candlestick from the table in the hall; but before we separated, thinking it apparently a good occasion to let me know once for all—since I was beginning, it would seem, to be quite "thick" with my host—that there was no fitness in my appealing to her for sympathy in such a case; before we separated, I say, she remarked to me with her quick fine well-bred inveterate curtness: "I dare say you attribute to me ideas I haven't got. I don't take that sort of interest in my husband's proof-sheets. I consider his writings most objectionable!"

✄ 3 ✄

I HAD an odd colloquy the next morning with Miss Ambient, whom I found strolling in the garden before breakfast. The whole place looked as fresh and trim, amid the twitter of the birds, as if, an hour before, the housemaids had been turned into it with their dust-pans and feather-brushes. I almost hesitated to light a cigarette and was doubly startled when, in the act of doing so, I suddenly saw the sister of my host, who had, at the best, something of the weirdness of an apparition, stand before me. She might have been posing for her photograph. Her sad-coloured robe arranged itself in serpentine folds at her feet; her hands locked themselves listlessly together in front; her chin rested on a cinque-cento ruff. The first thing I did after bidding her good-morning was to ask her for news of her little nephew—to express the hope she had heard he was better. She was able to gratify this trust—she spoke as if we might expect to see him during the day. We walked through the shrubberies together and she gave me further light on her brother's household, which offered me an opportunity to repeat to her what his wife had so startled and distressed me with the night before. *Was* it the sorry truth that she thought his productions objectionable?

"She doesn't usually come out with that so soon!" Miss Ambient returned in answer to my breathlessness.

"Poor lady," I pleaded, "she saw I'm a fanatic."

"Yes, she won't like you for that. But you mustn't mind, if the rest of us like you! Beatrice thinks a work of art ought to have a 'purpose.' But she's a charming woman—don't you think her charming? I find in her quite the grand air."

"She's very beautiful," I produced with an effort; while I reflected that though it was apparently true that Mark Ambient was mismated it was also perceptible that his sister was perfidious. She assured me her brother and his wife had no other difference but this one—that she thought his writings immoral and his influence pernicious. It was a fixed idea; she was afraid of these things for the child. I answered that it was in all conscience enough, the trifle of a woman's regarding her husband's mind as a well of corruption, and she seemed much struck with the novelty of my remark. "But there hasn't been any of the sort of trouble that there so often is among married people," she said. "I suppose you can judge for yourself that Beatrice isn't at all—well, whatever they call it when a woman kicks over! And poor Mark doesn't make love to other people either. You might think he would, but I assure you he doesn't. All the same of course, from her point of view, you know, she has a dread of my brother's influence on the child—on the formation of his character, his 'ideals,' poor little brat, his principles. It's as if it were a subtle poison or a contagion—something that would rub off on his tender sensibility when his father kisses him or holds him on his knee. If she could she'd prevent Mark from even so much as touching him. Every one knows it—visitors see it for themselves; so there's no harm in my telling you. Isn't it excessively odd? It comes from Beatrice's being so religious and so tremendously moral—so *à cheval* on fifty thousand *riguardi*. And then of course we mustn't forget," my companion added, a little unexpectedly, to this polyglot proposition, "that some of Mark's ideas are—well, really—rather impossible, don't you know?"

I reflected as we went into the house, where we found Ambient unfolding *The Observer* at the breakfast-table, that none of them were probably quite so "impossible, don't you know?" as his sister. Mrs. Ambient, a little "the worse," as was mentioned, for her ministrations, during the night to Dolcino, didn't appear at breakfast. Her husband described her however as hoping to go to church. I afterwards learnt that she did go, but nothing naturally was less on the cards than that we should accompany her. It was while the church-bell droned near at hand that the author of "Beltraffio" led me forth for the ramble he had spoken of in his note. I shall attempt here no record of where we went or of what we saw. We kept to the fields and copses and commons, and breathed the same sweet air as the nibbling donkeys and the browsing sheep, whose woolliness seemed to me, in those early days of acquaintance with English objects, but part of the general texture of the small dense landscape, which looked as if the harvest were gathered by the shears and with all nature bleating and braying for the violence. Everything was full of expression for Mark Ambient's visitor—from the big bandy-legged geese whose whiteness was a "note" amid all the tones of green as they wandered beside a neat little oval pool, the foreground of a thatched and whitewashed inn, with a grassy approach and a pictorial sign—from these humble wayside animals to the crests of high woods which let a gable or a pinnacle peep here and there and looked even at a distance like trees of good company, conscious of an individual profile. I admired the hedge-rows, I plucked the faint-hued heather, and I was for ever stopping to say how charming I thought the threadlike footpaths across the fields, which wandered in a diagonal of finer grain from one smooth stile to another. Mark Ambient was abundantly good-natured and was as much struck, dear man, with some of my observations as I was with the literary allusions of the landscape. We sat and smoked on stiles, broaching paradoxes in the decent English air; we took short cuts across a park or two where the bracken was deep and my companion nodded to the old woman at the gate; we skirted rank coverts which rustled here and there as we passed, and we stretched ourselves at last on a heathery hillside where if the sun wasn't too hot neither was the earth too cold, and where the country lay beneath us in a rich blue mist. Of course I had already told him what I thought of his new novel, having the previous night read every word of the opening chapters before I went to bed.

"I'm not without hope of being able to make it decent enough," he said as I went back to the subject while we turned up our heels to the sky. "At least the people who dislike my stuff—and there are plenty of them, I believe—will dislike this thing (if it does turn out well) most." This was the first time I had heard him allude to the people who couldn't read him—a class so generally conceived to sit heavy on the consciousness of the man of letters. A being organised for literature as Mark Ambient was must certainly have had the normal proportion of sensitiveness, of irritability; the artistic *ego,* capable in some cases of such monstrous development, must have been in his composition sufficiently erect and active. I won't therefore go so far as to say that he never thought of his detractors or that he had any illusions with regard to the number of his admirers—he could never so far have deceived himself as to believe he was popular, but I at least then judged (and had occasion to be sure later on) that stupidity ruffled him visibly but little, that he had an air of thinking it quite natural he should leave many simple folk, tasting of him, as simple as ever he found them, and that he very seldom talked about the newspapers, which, by the way, were always even abnormally vulgar about him. Of course he may have thought them over—the newspapers—night and day; the only point I make is that he didn't show it; while at the same time he didn't strike one as a man actively on his guard. I may add that, touching his hope of making the work on which he was then engaged the best of his books, it was only partly carried out. That place belongs incontestably to "Beltraffio," in spite of the beauty of certain parts of its successor. I quite believe, however, that he had at the moment of which I speak no sense of having declined; he was in love with his idea, which was indeed magnificent, and though for him, as I suppose for every sane

artist, the act of execution had in it as much torment as joy, he saw
his result grow like the crescent of the young moon and promise to
fill the disk. "I want to be truer than I've ever been," he said, settling
himself on his back with his hands clasped behind his head; "I want
to give the impression of life itself. No, you may say what you will,
I've always arranged things too much, always smoothed them down
and rounded them off and tucked them in—done everything to them
that life doesn't do. I've been a slave to the old superstitions."

"You a slave, my dear Mark Ambient? You've the freest imagination of our day!"

"All the more shame to me to have done some of the things I have!
The reconciliation of the two women in 'Natalina,' for instance,
which could never really have taken place. That sort of thing's
ignoble—I blush when I think of it! This new affair must be a
golden vessel, filled with the purest distillation of the actual; and oh
how it worries me, the shaping of the vase, the hammering of the
metal! I have to hammer it so fine, so smooth; I don't do more than
an inch or two a day. And all the while I have to be so careful not to
let a drop of the liquor escape! When I see the kind of things Life
herself, the brazen hussy, does, I despair of ever catching her peculiar
trick. She has an impudence, Life! If one risked a fiftieth part of the
effects she risks! It takes ever so long to believe it. You don't
know yet, my dear youth. It isn't till one has been watching her some
forty years that one finds out half of what she's up to! Therefore
one's earlier things must inevitably contain a mass of rot. And with
what one sees, on one side, with its tongue in its cheek, defying one
to be real enough, and on the other the *bonnes gens* rolling up their
eyes at one's cynicism, the situation has elements of the ludicrous
which the poor reproducer himself is doubtless in a position to
appreciate better than any one else. Of course one mustn't worry
about the *bonnes gens*," Mark Ambient went on while my thoughts
reverted to his ladylike wife as interpreted by his remarkable
sister.

"To sink your shaft deep and polish the plate through which
people look into it—that's what your work consists of," I remember
ingeniously observing.

"Ah polishing one's plate—that's the torment of execution!" he
exclaimed, jerking himself up and sitting forward. "The effort to
arrive at a surface, if you think anything of that decent sort

necessary—some people don't, happily for them! My dear fellow, if you could see the surface I dream of as compared with the one with which I've to content myself. Life's really too short for art—one hasn't time to make one's shell ideally hard. Firm and bright, firm and bright is very well to say—the devilish thing has a way sometimes of being bright, and even of being hard, as mere tough frozen pudding is hard, without being firm. When I rap it with my knuckles it doesn't give the right sound. There are horrible sandy stretches where I've taken the wrong turn because I couldn't for the life of me find the right. If you knew what a dunce I am sometimes! Such things figure to me now base pimples and ulcers on the brow of beauty!"

"They're very bad, very bad," I said as gravely as I could.

"Very bad? They're the highest social offence I know; it ought—it absolutely ought; I'm quite serious—to be capital. If I knew I should be publicly thrashed else I'd manage to find the true word. The people who can't—some of them don't so much as know it when they see it—would shut their inkstands, and we shouldn't be deluged by this flood of rubbish!"

I shall not attempt to repeat everything that passed between us, nor to explain just how it was that, every moment I spent in his company, Mark Ambient revealed to me more and more the consistency of his creative spirit, the spirit in him that felt all life as plastic material. I could but envy him the force of that passion, and it was at any rate through the receipt of this impression that by the time we returned I had gained the sense of intimacy with him that I have noted. Before we got up for the homeward stretch he alluded to his wife's having once—or perhaps more than once—asked him whether he should like Dolcino to read "Beltraffio." He must have been unaware at the moment of all that this conveyed to me—as well doubtless of my extreme curiosity to hear what he had replied. He had said how much he hoped Dolcino would read *all* his works—when he was twenty; he should like him to know what his father had done. Before twenty it would be useless; he wouldn't understand them.

"And meanwhile do you propose to hide them—to lock them up in a drawer?" Mrs. Ambient had proceeded.

"Oh no—we must simply tell him they're not intended for small boys. If you bring him up properly after that he won't touch them."

To this Mrs. Ambient had made answer that it might be very awkward when he was about fifteen, say; and I asked her husband if it were his opinion in general then that young people shouldn't read novels.

"Good ones—certainly not!" said my companion. I suppose I had had other views, for I remember saying that for myself I wasn't sure it was bad for them if the novels were "good" to the right intensity of goodness. "Bad for *them,* I don't say so much!" my companion returned. "But very bad, I'm afraid, for the poor dear old novel itself." That oblique accidental allusion to his wife's attitude was followed by a greater breadth of reference as we walked home. "The difference between us is simply the opposition between two distinct ways of looking at the world, which have never succeeded in getting on together, or in making any kind of common household, since the beginning of time. They've borne all sorts of names, and my wife would tell you it's the difference between Christian and pagan. I may be a pagan, but I don't like the name; it sounds sectarian. She thinks me at any rate no better than an ancient Greek. It's the difference between making the most of life and making the least, so that you'll get another better one in some other time and place. Will it be a sin to make the most of that one too, I wonder; and shall we have to be bribed off in the future state as well as in the present? Perhaps I care too much for beauty—I don't know, I doubt if a poor devil *can;* I delight in it, I adore it, I think of it continually, I try to produce it, to reproduce it. My wife holds that we shouldn't cultivate or enjoy it without extraordinary precautions and reserves. She's always afraid of it, always on her guard. I don't know what it can ever have done to her, what grudge it owes her or what resentment rides. And she's so pretty too herself! Don't you think she's lovely? She was at any rate when we married. At that time I wasn't aware of that difference I speak of—I thought it all came to the same thing: in the end, as they say. Well, perhaps it will in the end. I don't know what the end will be. Moreover I care for seeing things as they are; that's the way I try to show them in any professed picture. But you mustn't talk to Mrs. Ambient about things as they are. She has a mortal dread of things as they are."

"She's afraid of them for Dolcino," I said: surprised a moment afterwards at being in a position—thanks to Miss Ambient—to be so explanatory; and surprised even now that Mark shouldn't have shown visibly that he wondered what the deuce I knew about it. But he didn't; he simply declared with a tenderness that touched me: "Ah nothing shall ever hurt *him!*"

He told me more about his wife before we arrived at the gate of home, and if he be judged to have aired overmuch his grievance I'm afraid I must admit that he had some of the foibles as well as the gifts of the artistic temperament; adding, however, instantly that hitherto, to the best of my belief, he had rarely let this particular cat out of the bag. "She thinks me immoral—that's the long and short of it," he said as we paused outside a moment and his hand rested on one of the bars of his gate; while his conscious expressive perceptive eyes— the eyes of a foreigner, I had begun to account them, much more than of the usual Englishman—viewing me now evidently as quite a familiar friend, took part in the declaration. "It's very strange when one thinks it all over, and there's a grand comicality in it that I should like to bring out. She's a very nice woman, extraordinarily well-behaved, upright and clever and with a tremendous lot of good sense about a good many matters. Yet her conception of a novel— she has explained it to me once or twice, and she doesn't do it badly as exposition—is a thing so false that it makes me blush. It's a thing so hollow, so dishonest, so lying, in which life is so blinked and blinded, so dodged and disfigured, that it makes my ears burn. It's two different ways of looking at the whole affair," he repeated, pushing open the gate. "And they're irreconcileable!" he added with a sigh. We went forward to the house, but on the walk, halfway to the door, he stopped and said to me: "If you're going into this kind of thing there's a fact you should know beforehand; it may save you some disappointment. There's a hatred of art, there's a hatred of literature—I mean of the genuine kinds. Oh the shams—*those* they'll swallow by the bucket!" I looked up at the charming house, with its genial colour and crookedness, and I answered with a smile that those evil passions might exist, but that I should never have expected to find them there. "Ah it doesn't matter after all," he a bit nervously laughed; which I was glad to hear, for I was reproaching myself with having worked him up.

If I had it soon passed off, for at luncheon he was delightful; strangely delightful considering that the difference between himself and his wife was, as he had said, irreconcileable. He had the art, by his manner, by his smile, by his natural amenity, of reducing the importance of it in the common concerns of life; and Mrs. Ambient,

I must add, lent herself to this transaction with a very good grace. I watched her at table for further illustrations of that fixed idea of which Miss Ambient had spoken to me; for in the light of the united revelations of her sister-in-law and her husband she had come to seem to me almost a sinister personage. Yet the signs of a sombre fanaticism were not more immediately striking in her than before; it was only after a while that her air of incorruptible conformity, her tapering monosyllabic correctness, began to affect me as in themselves a cold thin flame. Certainly, at first, she resembled a woman with as few passions as possible; but if she had a passion at all it would indeed be that of Philistinism. She might have been (for there are guardian-spirits, I suppose, of all great principles) the very angel of the pink of propriety—putting the pink for a principle, though I'd rather put some dismal cold blue. Mark Ambient, apparently, ten years before, had simply and quite inevitably taken her for an angel, without asking himself of what. He had been right in calling my attention to her beauty. In looking for some explanation of his original surrender to her I saw more than before that she was, physically speaking, a wonderfully cultivated human plant—that he might well have owed her a brief poetic inspiration. It was impossible to be more propped and pencilled, more delicately tinted and petalled.

 If I had had it in my heart to think my host a little of a hypocrite for appearing to forget at table everything he had said to me in our walk, I should instantly have cancelled such a judgement on reflecting that the good news his wife was able to give him about their little boy was ground enough for any optimistic reaction. It may have come partly too from a certain compunction at having breathed to me at all harshly on the cool fair lady who sat there—a desire to prove himself not after all so mismated. Dolcino continued to be much better, and it had been promised him he should come downstairs after his dinner. As soon as we had risen from our own meal Mark slipped away, evidently for the purpose of going to his child; and no sooner had I observed this than I became aware his wife had simultaneously vanished. It happened that Miss Ambient and I, both at the same moment, saw the tail of her dress whisk out of a doorway; an incident that led the young lady to smile at me as if I now knew all the secrets of the Ambients. I passed with her into the garden and we sat down on a dear old bench that rested against the west wall of the house. It was a perfect spot for the middle period of a Sunday in June, and its felicity seemed to come partly from an antique sun-dial which, rising in front of us and forming the centre of a small intricate parterre, measured the moments ever so slowly and made them safe for leisure and talk. The garden bloomed in the suffused afternoon, the tall beeches stood still for an example, and, behind and above us, a rose-tree of many seasons, clinging to the faded grain of the brick, expressed the whole character of the scene in a familiar exquisite smell. It struck me as a place to offer genius every favour and sanction—not to bristle with challenges and checks. Miss Ambient asked me if I had enjoyed my walk with her brother and whether we had talked of many things.

"Well, of most things," I freely allowed, though I remembered we hadn't talked of Miss Ambient.

"And don't you think some of his theories are very peculiar?"

"Oh I guess I agree with them all." I was very particular, for Miss Ambient's entertainment, to guess.

"Do you think art's everything?" she put to me in a moment.

"In art, of course I do!"

"And do you think beauty's everything?"

"Everything's a big word, which I think we should use as little as possible. But how can we not want beauty?"

"Ah there you are!" she sighed, though I didn't quite know what she meant by it. "Of course it's difficult for a woman to judge how far to go," she went on. "I adore everything that gives a charm to life. I'm intensely sensitive to form. But sometimes I draw back—don't you see what I mean?—I don't quite see where I shall be landed. I only want to be quiet, after all," Miss Ambient continued as if she had long been baffled of this modest desire. "And one must be good, at any rate, must not one?" she pursued with a dubious quaver—an intimation apparently that what I might say one way or the other would settle it for her. It was difficult for me to be very original in reply, and I'm afraid I repaid her confidence with an unblushing platitude. I remember moreover attaching to it an enquiry, equally destitute of freshness and still more wanting perhaps in tact, as to whether she didn't mean to go to church, since that was an obvious way of being good. She made answer that she had performed this duty in the morning, and that for her, of Sunday afternoons, su-preme virtue consisted in answering the week's letters. Then suddenly and without transition she brought out: "It's quite a mistake about Dolcino's being better. I've seen him and he's not at all right."

I wondered, and somehow I think I scarcely believed. "Surely his mother would know, wouldn't she?"

She appeared for a moment to be counting the leaves on one of the great beeches. "As regards most matters one can easily say what, in a given situation, my sister-in-law will, or would, do. But in the present case there are strange elements at work."

"Strange elements? Do you mean in the constitution of the child?"

"No, I mean in my sister-in-law's feelings."

"Elements of affection of course; elements of anxiety," I concurred. "But why do you call them strange?"

She repeated my words. "Elements of affection, elements of anxiety. She's very anxious."

Miss Ambient put me indescribably ill at ease; she almost scared me, and I wished she would go and write her letters. "His father will have seen him now," I said, "and if he's not satisfied he will send for the doctor."

"The doctor ought to have been here this morning," she promptly returned. "He lives only two miles away."

I reflected that all this was very possibly but a part of the general tragedy of Miss Ambient's view of things; yet I asked her why she hadn't urged that view on her sister-in-law. She answered me with a smile of extraordinary significance and observed that I must have very little idea of her "peculiar" relations with Beatrice; but I must do her the justice that she re-enforced this a little by the plea that any distinguishable alarm of Mark's was ground enough for a difference of his wife's. He was always nervous about the child, and as they were predestined by nature to take opposite views, the only thing for the mother was to cultivate a false optimism. In Mark's absence and that of his betrayed fear she would have been less easy. I remembered what he had said to me about their dealings with their son—that between them they'd probably put an end to him; but I didn't repeat this to Miss Ambient: the less so that just then her brother emerged from the house, carrying the boy in his arms. Close behind him moved his wife, grave and pale; the little sick face was turned over Ambient's shoulder and toward the mother. We rose to receive the group, and as they came near us Dolcino twisted himself about. His enchanting eyes showed me a smile of recognition, in which, for the moment, I should have taken a due degree of comfort. Miss Ambient, however, received another impression, and I make haste to say that her quick sensibility, which visibly went out to the child, argues that in spite of her affectations she might have been of some human use. "It won't do at all—it won't do at all," she said to me under her breath. "I shall speak to Mark about the Doctor."

Her small nephew was rather white, but the main difference I saw in him was that he was even more beautiful than the day before. He had been dressed in his festal garments—a velvet suit and a crimson sash—and he looked like a little invalid prince too young to know condescension and smiling familiarly on his subjects.

"Put him down, Mark, he's not a bit at his ease," Mrs. Ambient said.

"Should you like to stand on your feet, my boy?" his father asked.

He made a motion that quickly responded. "Oh yes; I'm remarkably well."

Mark placed him on the ground; he had shining pointed shoes with enormous bows. "Are you happy now, Mr. Ambient?"

"Oh yes, I'm particularly happy," Dolcino replied. But the words were scarce out of his mouth when his mother caught him up and, in a moment, holding him on her knees, took her place on the bench where Miss Ambient and I had been sitting. This young lady said something to her brother, in consequence of which the two wandered away into the garden together.

4

I REMAINED with Mrs. Ambient, but as a servant had brought out a couple of chairs I wasn't obliged to seat myself beside her. Our conversation failed of ease, and I, for my part, felt there would be a shade of hypocrisy in my now trying to make myself agreeable to the partner of my friend's existence. I didn't dislike her—I rather admired her; but I was aware that I differed from her inexpressibly.

Then I suspected, what I afterwards definitely knew and have already intimated, that the poor lady felt small taste for her husband's so undisguised disciple; and this of course was not encouraging. She thought me an obtrusive and designing, even perhaps a depraved, young man whom a perverse Providence had dropped upon their quiet lawn to flatter his worst tendencies. She did me the honour to say to Miss Ambient, who repeated the speech, that she didn't know when she had seen their companion take such a fancy to a visitor; and she measured apparently my evil influence by Mark's appreciation of my society. I had a consciousness, not oppressive but quite sufficient, of all this; though I must say that if it chilled my flow of small-talk it yet didn't prevent my thinking the beautiful mother and beautiful child, interlaced there against their background of roses, a picture such as I doubtless shouldn't soon see again. I was free, I supposed, to go into the house and write letters, to sit in the drawing-room, to repair to my own apartment and take a nap; but the only use I made of my freedom was to linger still in my chair and say to myself that the light hand of Sir Joshua might have painted Mark Ambient's wife and son. I found myself looking perpetually at the latter small mortal, who looked constantly back at me, and that was enough to detain me. With these vaguely-amused eyes he smiled, and I felt it an absolute impossibility to abandon a child with such an expression. His attention never strayed; it attached itself to my face as if among all the small incipient things of his nature throbbed a desire to say something to me. If I could have taken him on my own knee he perhaps would have managed to say it; but it would have been a critical matter to ask his mother to give him up, and it has remained a constant regret for me that on that strange Sunday afternoon I didn't even for a moment hold Dolcino in my arms. He had said he felt remarkably well and was especially happy; but though peace may have been with him as he pillowed his charming head on his mother's breast, dropping his little crimson silk legs from her lap, I somehow didn't think security was. He made no attempt to walk about; he was content to swing his legs softly and strike one as languid and angelic.

Mark returned to us with his sister; and Miss Ambient, repeating her mention of the claims of her correspondence, passed into the house. Mark came and stood in front of his wife, looking down at the child, who immediately took hold of his hand and kept it while he stayed. "I think Mackintosh ought to see him," he said; "I think I'll walk over and fetch him."

"That's Gwendolen's idea, I suppose," Mrs. Ambient replied very sweetly.

"It's not such an out-of-the-way idea when one's child's ill," he returned.

"I'm not ill, papa; I'm much better now," sounded in the boy's silver pipe.

"Is that the truth, or are you only saying it to be agreeable? You've a great idea of being agreeable, you know."

The child seemed to meditate on this distinction, this imputation, for a moment; then his exaggerated eyes, which had wandered, caught my own as I watched him. "Do *you* think me agreeable?" he enquired with the candour of his age and with a look that made his father turn round to me laughing and ask, without saying it, "Isn't he adorable?"

"Then why don't you hop about, if you feel so lusty!" Ambient went on while his son swung his hand.

"Because mamma's holding me close!"

"Oh yes; I know how mamma holds you when I come near!" cried Mark with a grimace at his wife.

She turned her charming eyes up to him without deprecation or concession. "You can go for Mackintosh if you like. I think myself it would be better. You ought to drive."

"She says that to get me away," he put to me with a gaiety that I thought a little false; after which he started for the Doctor's.

I remained there with Mrs. Ambient, though even our exchange of twaddle had run very thin. The boy's little fixed white face seemed, as before, to plead with me to stay, and after a while it produced still another effect, a very curious one, which I shall find it difficult to express. Of course I expose myself to the charge of an attempt to justify by a strained logic after the fact a step which may have been on my part but the fruit of a native want of discretion; and indeed the traceable consequences of that perversity were too lamentable to leave me any desire to trifle with the question. All I can say is that I acted in perfect good faith and that Dolcino's friendly little gaze gradually kindled the spark of my inspiration. What helped it to glow were the other influences—the silent suggestive garden-nook, the perfect opportunity (if it was not an opportunity for that it was an opportunity for nothing) and the plea I speak of, which issued from the child's eyes and seemed to make him say: "The mother who bore me and who presses me here to her bosom—sympathetic little organism that I am—has really the kind of sensibility she has been represented to you as lacking, if you only look for it patiently and respectfully. How is it conceivable she shouldn't have it? How is it possible that *I* should have so much of it—for I'm quite full of it, dear strange gentleman—if it weren't also in some degree in her? I'm my great father's child, but I'm also my beautiful mother's, and I'm sorry for the difference between them!" So it shaped itself before me, the vision of reconciling Mrs. Ambient with her husband, of putting an end to their ugly difference. The project was absurd of course, for had I not had his word for it—spoken with all the bitterness of experience—that the gulf dividing them was well-nigh bottomless? Nevertheless, a quarter of an hour after Mark had left us, I observed to my hostess that I couldn't get over what she had told me the night before about her thinking her husband's compositions "objectionable." I had been so very sorry to hear it, had thought of it constantly and wondered whether it mightn't be possible to make her change her mind. She gave me a great cold stare, meant apparently as an admonition to me to mind my business. I wish I had taken this mute counsel, but I didn't take it. I went on to remark that it seemed an immense pity so much that was interesting should be lost on her.

"Nothing's lost upon me," she said in a tone that didn't make the contradiction less. "I know they're very interesting."

"Don't you like papa's books?" Dolcino asked, addressing his mother but still looking at me. Then he added to me: "Won't you read them to me, American gentleman?"

"I'd rather tell you some stories of my own," I said. "I know some that are awfully good."

"When will you tell them? To-morrow?"

"To-morrow with pleasure, if that suits you."

His mother took this in silence. Her husband, during our walk, had asked me to remain another day; my promise to her son was an implication that I had consented, and it wasn't possible the news could please her. This ought doubtless to have made me more careful as to what I said next, but all I can plead is that it didn't. I soon mentioned that just after leaving her the evening before, and after hearing her apply to her husband's writings the epithet already quoted, I had on going up to my room sat down to the perusal of those sheets of his new book that he had been so good as to lend me. I had sat entranced till nearly three in the morning—I had read them twice over. "You say you haven't looked at them. I think it's such a pity you shouldn't. Do let me beg you to take them up. They're so very remarkable. I'm sure they'll convert you. They place him in—really—such a dazzling light. All that's best in him is there. I've no doubt it's a great liberty, my saying all this; but pardon me, and *do* read them!"

"Do read them, mamma!" the boy again sweetly shrilled. "Do read them!"

She bent her head and closed his lips with a kiss. "Of course I know he has worked immensely over them," she said; after which she made no remark, but attached her eyes thoughtfully to the ground. The tone of these last words was such as to leave me no spirit for further pressure, and after hinting at a fear that her husband mightn't have caught the Doctor I got up and took a turn about the grounds. When I came back ten minutes later she was still in her place watching her boy, who had fallen asleep in her lap. As I drew near she put her finger to her lips and a short time afterwards rose, holding him; it being now best, she said, that she should take him upstairs. I offered to carry him and opened my arms for the purpose; but she thanked me and turned away with the child still in her embrace, his head on her shoulder. "I'm very strong," was her last word as she passed into the house, her slim flexible figure bent backward with the filial weight. So I never laid a longing hand on Dolcino.

I betook myself to Ambient's study, delighted to have a quiet hour to look over his books by myself. The windows were open to the garden; the sunny stillness, the mild light of the English summer, filled the room without quite chasing away the rich dusky tone that was a part of its charm and that abode in the serried shelves where old morocco exhaled the fragrance of curious learning, as well as in the brighter intervals where prints and medals and miniatures were suspended on a surface of faded stuff. The place had both colour and quiet; I thought it a perfect room for work and went so far as to say to myself that, if it were mine to sit and scribble in, there was no knowing but I might learn to write as well as the author of "Beltraffio." This distinguished man still didn't reappear, and I rummaged freely among his treasures. At last I took down a book that detained me a while and seated myself in a fine old leather chair by the window to turn it over. I had been occupied in this way for half an hour—a good part of the afternoon had waned—when I became conscious of another presence in the room and, looking up from my quarto, saw that Mrs. Ambient, having pushed open the door quite again in the same noiseless way marking or disguising her entrance the night before, had advanced across the threshold. On seeing me she stopped; she had not, I think, expected to find me. But her hesitation was only of a moment; she came straight to her husband's writing-table as if she were looking for something. I got up and asked her if I could help her. She glanced about an instant and then put her hand upon a roll of papers which I recognised, as I had placed it on that spot at the early hour of my descent from my room.

"Is this the new book?" she asked, holding it up.

"The very sheets," I smiled; "with precious annotations."

"I mean to take your advice"—and she tucked the little bundle under her arm. I congratulated her cordially and ventured to make of my triumph, as I presumed to call it, a subject of pleasantry. But she was perfectly grave and turned away from me, as she had presented herself, without relaxing her rigour; after which I settled down to my quarto again with the reflexion that Mrs. Ambient was truly an eccentric. My triumph too suddenly seemed to me rather vain. A woman who couldn't unbend at a moment exquisitely indicated would never understand Mark Ambient. He came back to us at last in person, having brought the Doctor with him. "He was away from home," Mark said, "and I went after him to where he was supposed to be. He had left the place, and I followed him to two or three others, which accounts for my delay." He was now with Mrs. Ambient, looking at the child, and was to see Mark again before leaving the house. My host noticed at the end of two minutes that the proof-sheets of his new book had been removed from the table; and when I told him, in reply to his question as to what I knew about them, that Mrs. Ambient had carried them off to read he turned almost pale with surprise. "What has suddenly made her so curious?" he cried; and I was obliged to tell him that I was at the bottom of the mystery. I had had it on my conscience to assure her that she really ought to know of what her husband was capable. "Of

what I'm capable? *Elle ne s'en doute que trop!"* said Ambient with a
laugh; but he took my meddling very good-naturedly and contented
himself with adding that he was really much afraid she would burn
up the sheets, his emendations and all, of which latter he had no
duplicate. The Doctor paid a long visit in the nursery, and before he
came down I retired to my own quarters, where I remained till
dinner-time. On entering the drawing-room at this hour I found
Miss Ambient in possession, as she had been the evening before.

"I was right about Dolcino," she said, as soon as she saw me, with
an air of triumph that struck me as the climax of perversity. "He's
really very ill."

"Very ill! Why when I last saw him, at four o'clock, he was in
fairly good form."

"There has been a change for the worse, very sudden and rapid,
and when the Doctor got here he found diphtheritic symptoms. He
ought to have been called, as I knew, in the morning, and the child
oughtn't to have been brought into the garden."

"My dear lady, he was very happy there," I protested with horror.

"He would be very happy anywhere. I've no doubt he's very happy
now, with his poor little temperature—!" She dropped her voice as
her brother came in, and Mark let us know that as a matter of course
Mrs. Ambient wouldn't appear. It was true the boy had developed
diphtheritic symptoms, but he was quiet for the present and his
mother earnestly watching him. She was a perfect nurse, Mark said,
and Mackintosh would come back at ten. Our dinner wasn't very
gay—with my host worried and absent; and his sister annoyed me by
her constant tacit assumption, conveyed in the very way she nibbled
her bread and sipped her wine, of having "told me so." I had had no
disposition to deny anything she might have told me, and I couldn't
see that her satisfaction in being justified by the event relieved her
little nephew's condition. The truth is that, as the sequel was to
prove, Miss Ambient had some of the qualities of the sibyl and had
therefore perhaps a right to the sibylline contortions. Her brother
was so preoccupied that I felt my presence an indiscretion and was
sorry I had promised to remain over the morrow. I put it to Mark
that clearly I had best leave them in the morning; to which he
replied that, on the contrary, if he was to pass the next days in the
fidgets my company would distract his attention. The fidgets had

already begun for him, poor fellow; and as we sat in his study with our cigars after dinner he wandered to the door whenever he heard the sound of the Doctor's wheels. Miss Ambient, who shared this apartment with us, gave me at such moments significant glances; she had before rejoining us gone upstairs to ask about the child. His mother and his nurse gave a fair report, but Miss Ambient found his fever high and his symptoms very grave. The Doctor came at ten o'clock, and I went to bed after hearing from Mark that he saw no present cause for alarm. He had made every provision for the night and was to return early in the morning.

I quitted my room as eight struck the next day and when I came downstairs saw, through the open door of the house, Mrs. Ambient standing at the front gate of the grounds in colloquy with Mackintosh. She wore a white dressing-gown, but her shining hair was carefully tucked away in its net, and in the morning freshness, after a night of watching, she looked as much "the type of the lady" as her sister-in-law had described her. Her appearance, I suppose, ought to have reassured me; but I was still nervous and uneasy, so that I shrank from meeting her with the necessary challenge. None the less, however, was I impatient to learn how the new day found him; and as Mrs. Ambient hadn't seen me I passed into the grounds by a roundabout way and, stopping at a further gate, hailed the Doctor just as he was driving off. Mrs. Ambient had returned to the house before he got into his cart.

"Pardon me, but as a friend of the family I should like very much to hear about the little boy."

The stout sharp circumspect man looked at me from head to foot and then said: "I'm sorry to say I haven't seen him."

"Haven't seen him?"

"Mrs. Ambient came down to meet me as I alighted, and told me he was sleeping so soundly, after a restless night, that she didn't wish him disturbed. I assured her I wouldn't disturb him, but she said he was quite safe now and she could look after him herself."

"Thank you very much. Are you coming back?"

"No sir; I'll be hanged if I come back!" cried the honest practitioner in high resentment. And the horse started as he settled beside his man.

I wandered back into the garden, and five minutes later Miss Ambient came forth from the house to greet me. She explained that breakfast wouldn't be served for some time and that she desired a moment herself with the Doctor. I let her know that the good vexed man had come and departed, and I repeated to her what he had told me about his dismissal. This made Miss Ambient very serious, very serious indeed, and she sank into a bench, with dilated eyes, hugging her elbows with crossed arms. She indulged in many strange signs, she confessed herself immensely distressed, and she finally told me what her own last news of her nephew had been. She had sat up very late—after me, after Mark—and before going to bed had knocked at the door of the child's room, opened to her by the nurse. This good woman had admitted her and she had found him quiet, but flushed and "unnatural," with his mother sitting by his bed. "She held his hand in one of hers," said Miss Ambient, "and in the other—what do you think?—the proof-sheets of Mark's new book! She was reading them there intently: did you ever hear of anything so extraordinary? Such a very odd time to be reading an author whom she never could abide!" In her agitation Miss Ambient was guilty of this vulgarism of speech, and I was so impressed by her narrative that only in recalling her words later did I notice the lapse. Mrs. Ambient had looked up from her reading with her finger on her lips—I recognised the gesture she had addressed me in the afternoon—and, though the nurse was about to go to rest, had not encouraged her sister-in-law to relieve her of any part of her vigil. But certainly at that time the boy's state was far from reassuring—his poor little breathing so painful; and what change could have taken place in him in those few hours that would justify Beatrice in denying Mackintosh access. This was the moral of Miss Ambient's anecdote, the moral for herself at least. The moral for me, rather, was that it *was* a very singular time for Mrs. Ambient to be going into a novelist she had never appreciated and who had simply happened to be recommended to her by a young American she disliked. I thought of her sitting there in the sick-chamber in the still hours of the night and after the nurse had left her, turning and turning those pages of genius and wrestling with their magical influence.

I must be sparing of the minor facts and the later emotions of this sojourn—it lasted but a few hours longer—and devote but three words to my subsequent relations with Ambient. They lasted five years—till his death—and were full of interest, of satisfaction and, I may add, of sadness. The main thing to be said of these years is that I had a secret from him which I guarded to the end. I believe he never suspected it, though of this I'm not absolutely sure. If he had so much as an inkling the line he had taken, the line of absolute negation of the matter to himself, shows an immense effort of the will. I may at last lay bare my secret, giving it for what it is worth; now that the main sufferer has gone, that he has begun to be alluded to as one of the famous early dead and that his wife has ceased to survive him; now too that Miss Ambient, whom I also saw at intervals during the time that followed, has, with her embroideries and her attitudes, her necromantic glances and strange intuitions, retired to a Sisterhood, where, as I am told, she is deeply immured and quite lost to the world.

Mark came in to breakfast after this lady and I had for some time been seated there. He shook hands with me in silence, kissed my companion, opened his letters and newspapers and pretended to drink his coffee. But I took these movements for mechanical and was little surprised when he suddenly pushed away everything that was before him and, with his head in his hands and his elbows on the table, sat staring strangely at the cloth.

"What's the matter, *caro fratello mio?*" Miss Ambient quavered, peeping from behind the urn.

He answered nothing, but got up with a certain violence and strode to the window. We rose to our feet, his relative and I, by a common impulse, exchanging a glance of some alarm; and he continued to stare into the garden. "In heaven's name what has got possession of Beatrice?" he cried at last, turning round on us a ravaged face. He looked from one of us to the other—the appeal was addressed to us alike.

Miss Ambient gave a shrug. "My poor Mark, Beatrice is always—Beatrice!"

"She has locked herself up with the boy—bolted and barred the door. She refuses to let me come near him!" he went on.

"She refused to let Mackintosh see him an hour ago!" Miss Ambient promptly returned.

"Refused to let Mackintosh see him? By heaven I'll smash in the door!" And Mark brought his fist down upon the sideboard, which he had now approached, so that all the breakfast-service rang.

I begged Miss Ambient to go up and try to have speech of her sister-in-law, and I drew Mark out into the garden. "You're exceed-

ingly nervous, and Mrs. Ambient's probably right," I there undertook to plead. "Women know; women should be supreme in such a
situation. Trust a mother—a devoted mother, my dear friend!" With
such words as these I tried to soothe and comfort him, and, marvellous to relate, I succeeded, with the help of many cigarettes, in
making him walk about the garden and talk, or suffer me at least to
do so for near an hour. When about that time had elapsed his sister
reappeared, reaching us rapidly and with a convulsed face while she
held her hand to her heart.

"Go for the Doctor, Mark—go for the Doctor this moment!"

"Is he dying? Has she killed him?" my poor friend cried, flinging
away his cigarette.

"I don't know what she has done! But she's frightened, and now
she wants the Doctor."

"He told me he'd be hanged if he came back!" I felt myself obliged
to mention.

"Precisely—therefore Mark himself must go for him, and not a
messenger. You must see him and tell him it's to save your child. The
trap has been ordered—it's ready."

"To save him? I'll save him, please God!" Ambient cried, bound-
ing with his great strides across the lawn.

As soon as he had gone I felt I ought to have volunteered in his
place, and I said as much to Miss Ambient; but she checked me by
grasping my arm while we heard the wheels of the dog-cart rattle
away from the gate. "He's off—he's off—and now I can think! To get
him away—while I think—while I think!"

"While you think of what, Miss Ambient?"

"Of the unspeakable thing that has happened under this roof!"

Her manner was habitually that of such a prophetess of ill that I at
first allowed for some great extravagance. But I looked at her hard,
and the next thing felt myself turn white. "Dolcino *is* dying
then—he's dead?"

"It's too late to save him. His mother has let him die! I tell you
that because you're sympathetic, because you've imagination," Miss
Ambient was good enough to add, interrupting my expression of
horror. "That's why you had the idea of making her read Mark's new
book!"

"What has that to do with it? I don't understand you. Your
accusation's monstrous."

"I see it all—I'm not stupid," she went on, heedless of my emphasis. "It was the book that finished her—it was that decided her!"

"Decided her? Do you mean she has murdered her child?" I demanded, trembling at my own words.

"She sacrificed him; she determined to do nothing to make him live. Why else did she lock herself in, why else did she turn away the Doctor? The book gave her a horror; she determined to rescue him—to prevent him from ever being touched. He had a crisis at two o'clock in the morning. I know that from the nurse, who had left her then, but whom, for a short time, she called back. The darling got much worse, but she insisted on the nurse's going back to bed, and after that she was alone with him for hours."

I listened with a dread that stayed my credence, while she stood there with her tearless glare. "Do you pretend then she has no pity, that she's cruel and insane?"

"She held him in her arms, she pressed him to her breast, not to see him; but she gave him no remedies; she did nothing the Doctor ordered. Everything's there untouched. She has had the honesty not even to throw the drugs away!"

I dropped upon the nearest bench, overcome with my dismay—quite as much at Miss Ambient's horrible insistence and distinctness as at the monstrous meaning of her words. Yet they came amazingly straight, and if they did have a sense I saw myself too woefully figure in it. Had I been then a proximate cause—? "You're a very strange woman and you say incredible things," I could only reply.

She had one of her tragic headshakes. "You think it necessary to protest, but you're really quite ready to believe me. You've received an impression of my sister-in-law—you've guessed of what she's capable."

I don't feel bound to say what concession on this score I made to Miss Ambient, who went on to relate to me that within the last half-hour Beatrice had had a revulsion, that she was tremendously frightened at what she had done; that her fright itself betrayed her; and that she would now give heaven and earth to save the child. "Let us hope she will!" I said, looking at my watch and trying to time poor Ambient; whereupon my companion repeated all portentously "Let us hope so!" When I asked her if she herself could do nothing, and whether she oughtn't to be with her sister-in-law, she replied: "You had better go and judge! She's like a wounded tigress!"

I never saw Mrs. Ambient till six months after this, and therefore can't pretend to have verified the comparison. At the latter period she was again the type of the perfect lady. "She'll treat him better after this," I remember her sister-in-law's saying in response to some quick outburst, on my part, of compassion for her brother. Though I had been in the house but thirty-six hours this young lady had treated me with extraordinary confidence, and there was therefore a certain demand I might, as such an intimate, make of her. I extracted from her a pledge that she'd never say to her brother what she had just said to me, that she'd let him form his own theory of his wife's conduct. She agreed with me that there was misery enough in the house without her contributing a new anguish, and that Mrs. Ambient's proceedings might be explained, to her husband's mind, by the extravagance of a jealous devotion. Poor Mark came back with the Doctor much sooner than we could have hoped, but we knew five minutes afterwards that it was all too late. His sole, his adored little son was more exquisitely beautiful in death than he had been in life. Mrs. Ambient's grief was frantic; she lost her head and said strange things. As for Mark's—but I won't speak of that. *Basta, basta,* as he used to say. Miss Ambient kept her secret—I've already had occasion to say that she had her good points—but it rankled in her conscience like a guilty participation and, I imagine, had something to do with her ultimately retiring from the world. And, apropos of consciences, the reader is now in a position to judge of my compunction for my effort to convert my cold hostess. I ought to mention that the death of her child in some degree converted her. When the new book came out (it was long delayed) she read it over as a whole, and her husband told me that during the few supreme weeks before her death—she failed rapidly after losing her son, sank into a consumption and faded away at Mentone—she even dipped into the black "Beltraffio."

Owen Wingrave

1

"UPON my honour you must be off your head!" cried Spencer Coyle as the young man, with a white face, stood there panting a little and repeating "Really I've quite decided," and "I assure you I've thought it all out." They were both pale, but Owen Wingrave smiled in a manner exasperating to his supervisor, who however still discriminated sufficiently to feel his grimace—it was like an irrelevant leer—the result of extreme and conceivable nervousness.

"It was certainly a mistake to have gone so far; but that's exactly why it strikes me I mustn't go further," poor Owen said, waiting mechanically, almost humbly—he wished not to swagger, and indeed had nothing to swagger about—and carrying through the window to the stupid opposite houses the dry glitter of his eyes.

"I'm unspeakably disgusted. You've made me dreadfully ill"—and Mr. Coyle looked in truth thoroughly upset.

"I'm very sorry. It was the fear of the effect on you that kept me from speaking sooner."

"You should have spoken three months ago. Don't you know your mind from one day to the other?" the elder of the pair demanded.

The young man for a moment held himself: then he quavered his plea. "You're very angry with me and I expected it. I'm awfully obliged to you for all you've done for me. I'll do anything else for you in return, but I can't do that. Every one else will let me have it of course. I'm prepared for that—I'm prepared for everything. It's what has taken the time: to be sure I was prepared. I think it's your displeasure I feel most and regret most. But little by little you'll get over it," Owen wound up.

"*You'll* get over it rather faster, I suppose!" the other satirically exclaimed. He was quite as agitated as his young friend, and they were evidently in no condition to prolong an encounter in which each drew blood. Mr. Coyle was a professional "coach"; he prepared aspirants for the army, taking only three or four at a time, to whom he applied the irresistible stimulus the possession of which was both his secret and his fortune. He hadn't a great establishment; he would have said himself that it was not a wholesale business. Neither his system, his health nor his temper could have concorded with numbers; so he weighed and measured his pupils and turned away more applicants than he passed. He was an artist in his line, caring only for picked subjects and capable of sacrifices almost passionate for the individual. He liked ardent young men—there were types of facility and kinds of capacity to which he was indifferent—and he had taken a particular fancy to Owen Wingrave. This young man's particular shade of ability, to say nothing of his whole personality, almost cast a spell and at any rate worked a charm. Mr. Coyle's candidates usually did wonders, and he might have sent up a multitude. He was a person exactly of the stature of the great Napoleon, with a certain flicker of genius in his light blue eye: it had been said of him that he looked like a concert-giving pianist. The tone of his favourite pupil now expressed, without intention indeed, a superior wisdom that irritated him. He hadn't at all suffered before from Wingrave's high opinion of himself, which had seemed justified by remarkable parts; but to-day, of a sudden, it struck him as intolerable. He cut short the discussion, declining absolutely to regard their relations as terminated, and remarked to his pupil that he had better go off somewhere—down to Eastbourne, say: the sea would bring him round—and take a few days to find his feet and come to his senses. He could afford the time, he was so well up: when Spencer Coyle remembered how well up he was he could have boxed his ears. The tall athletic young man wasn't physically a subject for simplified reasoning; but a troubled gentleness in his handsome face, the index of compunction mixed with resolution, virtually signified that if it could have done any good he would have turned both cheeks. He evidently didn't pretend that his wisdom was superior; he only presented it as his own. It was his own career after all that was in question. He couldn't refuse to go through the form of trying Eastbourne or at least of holding his tongue, though there was that in his manner which implied that if he should do so it would be really to give Mr. Coyle a chance to recuperate. He didn't feel a bit overworked, but there was nothing more natural than that, with their tremendous pressure, Mr. Coyle should be. Mr. Coyle's own intellect would derive an advantage from his pupil's holiday. Mr. Coyle saw what he meant, but controlled himself; he only demanded, as his right, a truce of three days. Owen granted it, though as fostering sad illusions this went visibly against his conscience; but before they separated the famous crammer remarked: "All the same I feel I ought to see some one. I think you mentioned to me that your aunt had come to town?"

"Oh yes—she's in Baker Street. Do go and see her," the boy said for comfort.

His tutor sharply eyed him. "Have you broached this folly to her?"

"Not yet—to no one. I thought it right to speak to you first."

"Oh what you 'think right'!" cried Spencer Coyle, outraged by his young friend's standards. He added that he would probably call on Miss Wingrave; after which the recreant youth got out of the house.

The latter didn't, none the less, start at once for Eastbourne; he only directed his steps to Kensington Gardens, from which Mr. Coyle's desirable residence—he was terribly expensive and had a big house—was not far removed. The famous coach "put up" his pupils, and Owen had mentioned to the butler that he would be back to dinner. The spring day was warm to his young blood, and he had a book in his pocket which, when he had passed into the Gardens and, after a short stroll, dropped into a chair, he took out with the slow soft sigh that finally ushers in a pleasure postponed. He stretched his long legs and began to read it; it was a volume of Goethe's poems. He had been for days in a state of the highest tension, and now that the cord had snapped the relief was proportionate; only it was characteristic of him that this deliverance should take the form of an intellectual pleasure. If he had thrown up the probability of a magnificent career it wasn't to dawdle along Bond Street nor parade his indifference in the window of a club. At any rate he had in a few moments forgotten everything—the tremendous pressure, Mr. Coyle's disappointment and even his formidable aunt in Baker Street. If these watchers had overtaken him there would surely have been some excuse for their exasperation. There was no doubt he was perverse, for his very choice of a pastime only showed how he had got up his German.

"What the devil's the matter with him, do *you* know?" Spencer Coyle asked that afternoon of young Lechmere, who had never

before observed the head of the establishment to set a fellow such an
example of bad language. Young Lechmere was not only Wingrave's
fellow pupil, he was supposed to be his intimate, indeed quite his
best friend, and had unconsciously performed for Mr. Coyle the
office of making the promise of his great gifts more vivid by contrast.
He was short and sturdy and as a general thing uninspired, and Mr.
Coyle, who found no amusement in believing in him, had never
thought him less exciting than as he stared now out of a face from
which you could no more guess whether he had caught an idea than
you could judge of your dinner by looking at a dish-cover. Young
Lechmere concealed such achievements as if they had been youthful
indiscretions. At any rate he could evidently conceive no reason why
it should be thought there was anything more than usual the matter
with the companion of his studies; so Mr. Coyle had to continue:
"He declines to go up. He chucks the whole shop!"

The first thing that struck young Lechmere in the case was the
freshness, as of a forgotten vernacular, it had imparted to the gover-
nor's vocabulary. "He doesn't want to go to Sandhurst?"

"He doesn't want to go anywhere. He gives up the army altogether. He objects," said Mr. Coyle in a tone that made young
Lechmere almost hold his breath, "to the military profession."

"Why it has been the profession of all his family!"

"Their profession? It has been their religion! Do you know Miss
Wingrave?"

"Oh yes. Isn't she awful?" young Lechmere candidly ejaculated.

His instructor demurred. "She's formidable, if you mean that, and
it's right she should be; because somehow in her very person, good
maiden lady as she is, she represents the might, she represents the
traditions and the exploits, of the British army. She represents the
expansive property of the English name. I think his family can be
trusted to come down on him, but every influence should be set in
motion. I want to know what yours is. Can *you* do anything in the
matter?"

"I can try a couple of rounds with him," said young Lechmere
reflectively. "But he knows a fearful lot. He has the most extraordinary ideas."

"Then he has told you some of them—he has taken you into his
confidence?"

"I've heard him jaw by the yard," smiled the honest youth. "He has told me he despises it."

"What *is* it he despises? I can't make out."

The most consecutive of Mr. Coyle's nurslings considered a moment, as if he were conscious of a responsibility. "Why I think just soldiering, don't you know? He says we take the wrong view of it."

"He oughtn't to talk to *you* that way. It's corrupting the youth of Athens. It's sowing sedition."

"Oh I'm all right!" said young Lechmere. "And he never told me he meant to chuck it. I always thought he meant to see it through, simply because he had to. He'll argue on any side you like. He can talk your head off—I will say *that* for him. But it's a tremendous pity—I'm sure he'd have a big career."

"Tell him so then; plead with him; struggle with him—for God's sake."

"I'll do what I can—I'll tell him it's a regular shame."

"Yes, strike *that* note—insist on the disgrace of it."

The young man gave Mr. Coyle a queer look. "I'm sure he wouldn't do anything dishonourable."

"Well—it won't look right. He must be made to feel *that*—work it up. Give him a comrade's point of view—that of a brother-in-arms."

"That's what I thought we were going to be!" young Lechmere mused romantically, much uplifted by the nature of the mission imposed on him. "He's an awfully good sort."

"No one will think so if he backs out!" said Spencer Coyle.

"Well, they mustn't say it to *me!*" his pupil rejoined with a flush.

Mr. Coyle debated, noting his tone and aware that in the perversity of things, though this young man was a born soldier, no excitement would ever attach to *his* alternatives save perhaps on the part of the nice girl to whom at an early day he was sure to be placidly united. "Do you like him very much—do you believe in him?"

Young Lechmere's life in these days was spent in answering terrible questions, but he had never been put through so straight a lot as these. "Believe in him? Rather!"

"Then *save* him!"

The poor boy was puzzled, as if it were forced upon him by this

intensity that there was more in such an appeal than could appear
on the surface; and he doubtless felt that he was but apprehending a
complex situation when after another moment, with his hands in his
pockets, he replied hopefully but not pompously: "I dare say I can
bring him round!"

2

BEFORE seeing young Lechmere Mr. Coyle had determined to telegraph an enquiry to Miss Wingrave. He had prepaid the answer,
which, being promptly put into his hand, brought the interview we
have just related to a close. He immediately drove off to Baker Street,
where the lady had said she awaited him, and five minutes after he
got there, as he sat with Owen Wingrave's remarkable aunt, he
repeated several times over, in his angry sadness and with the infalli-
bility of his experience: "He's so intelligent—he's so intelligent!" He
had declared it had been a luxury to put such a fellow through.

"Of course he's intelligent; what else could he be? We've never,
that I know of, had but *one* idiot in the family!" said Jane Wingrave.
This was an allusion that Mr. Coyle could understand, and it
brought home to him another of the reasons for the disappointment, the humiliation as it were, of the good people at Paramore, at the same time that it gave an example of the conscientious
coarseness he had on former occasions observed in his hostess. Poor
Philip Wingrave, her late brother's eldest son, was literally imbecile
and banished from view; deformed, unsocial, irretrievable, he had
been relegated to a private asylum and had become among the
friends of the family only a little hushed lugubrious legend. All the
hopes of the house, picturesque Paramore, now unintermittently old
Sir Philip's rather melancholy home—his infirmities would keep
him there to the last—were therefore gathered on the second boy's
head, which nature, as if in compunction for her previous botch,
had, in addition to making it strikingly handsome, filled with a
marked and general readiness. These two had been the only children
of the old man's only son, who, like so many of his ancestors, had
given up a gallant young life to the service of his country. Owen
Wingrave the elder had received his death-cut, in close quarters,

from an Afghan sabre; the blow had come crashing across his skull. His wife, at that time in India, was about to give birth to her third child; and when the event took place, in darkness and anguish, the baby came lifeless into the world and the mother sank under the multiplication of her woes. The second of the little boys in England, who was at Paramore with his grandfather, became the peculiar charge of his aunt, the only unmarried one, and during the interesting Sunday that, by urgent invitation, Spencer Coyle, busy as he was, had, after consenting to put Owen through, spent under that roof, the celebrated crammer received a vivid impression of the influence exerted at least in intention by Miss Wingrave. Indeed the picture of this short visit remained with the observant little man a curious one—the vision of an impoverished Jacobean house, shabby and remarkably "creepy," but full of character still and full of felicity as a setting for the distinguished figure of the peaceful old soldier. Sir Philip Wingrave, a relic rather than a celebrity, was a small brown erect octogenarian, with smouldering eyes and a studied courtesy. He liked to do the diminished honours of his house, but even when with a shaky hand he lighted a bedroom candle for a deprecating guest it was impossible not to feel him, beneath the surface, a merciless old man of blood. The eye of the imagination could glance back into his crowded Eastern past—back at episodes in which his scrupulous forms would only have made him more terrible. He had his legend—and oh there were stories about him!

Mr. Coyle remembered also two other figures—a faded inoffensive Mrs. Julian, domesticated there by a system of frequent visits as the widow of an officer and a particular friend of Miss Wingrave, and a remarkably clever little girl of eighteen, who was this lady's daughter and who struck the speculative visitor as already formed for other relations. She was very impertinent to Owen, and in the course of a long walk that he had taken with the young man and the effect of which, in much talk, had been to clinch his high opinion of him, he had learned—for Owen chattered confidentially—that Mrs. Julian was the sister of a very gallant gentleman, Captain Hume-Walker of the Artillery, who had fallen in the Indian Mutiny and between whom and Miss Wingrave (it had been that lady's one known concession) a passage of some delicacy, taking a tragic turn, was believed to have been enacted. They had been engaged to be married, but she had given way to the jealousy of her nature—had broken with him and sent him off to his fate, which had been horrible. A passionate sense of having wronged him, a hard eternal remorse had thereupon taken possession of her, and when his poor sister, linked also to a soldier, had by a still heavier blow been left almost without resources, she had devoted herself grimly to a long expiation. She had sought comfort in taking Mrs. Julian to live much of the time at Paramore, where she became an unremunerated though not uncriticised housekeeper, and Spencer Coyle rather fancied it a part of this comfort that she could at leisure trample on her. The impression of Jane Wingrave was not the faintest he had gathered on that intensifying Sunday—an occasion singularly tinged for him with the sense of bereavement and mourning and memory, of names never mentioned, of the far-away plaint of widows and the echoes of battles and bad news. It was all military indeed, and Mr. Coyle was made to shudder a little at the profession of which he helped to open the door to otherwise harmless young men. Miss Wingrave might moreover have made such a bad conscience worse—so cold and clear a good one looked at him out of her hard fine eyes and trumpeted in her sonorous voice.

She was a high distinguished person, angular but not awkward, with a large forehead and abundant black hair arranged like that of a woman conceiving perhaps excusably of her head as "noble," and to-day irregularly streaked with white. If however she represented for our troubled friend the genius of a military race it was not that she had the step of a grenadier or the vocabulary of a camp-follower; it was only that such sympathies were vividly implied in the general fact to which her very presence and each of her actions and glances and tones were a constant and direct allusion—the paramount valour of her family. If she was military it was because she sprang from a military house and because she wouldn't for the world have been anything but what the Wingraves had been. She was almost vulgar about her ancestors, and if one had been tempted to quarrel with her one would have found a fair pretext in her defective sense of proportion. This temptation however said nothing to Spencer Coyle, for whom, as a strong character revealing itself in colour and sound, she was almost a "treat" and who was glad to regard her as a force exerted on his own side. He wished her nephew had more of her narrowness instead of being almost cursed with the tendency to look at things in their relations. He wondered why when she came up to town she always resorted to Baker Street for lodgings. He had never known nor heard of Baker Street as a residence—he associated it only with bazaars and photographers. He divined in her a rigid indifference to everything that was not the passion of her life. Nothing really mattered to her but that, and she would have occupied apartments in Whitechapel if they had been an item in her tactics. She had received her visitor in a large cold faded room, furnished with slippery seats and decorated with alabaster vases and wax-flowers. The only little personal comfort for which she appeared to have looked out was a fat catalogue of the Army and Navy Stores, which reposed on a vast desolate table-cover of false blue. Her clear forehead—it was like a porcelain slate, a receptacle for addresses and sums—had flushed when her nephew's crammer told her the extraordinary news; but he saw she was fortunately more angry than frightened. She had essentially, she would always have, too little imagination for fear, and the healthy habit moreover of facing everything had taught her that the occasion usually found her a quantity to reckon with. He saw that her only present fear could have been that of the failure to prevent her nephew's showing publicly for an ass, or for worse, and that to such an apprehension as this she was in fact inaccessible. Practically too she was not troubled by surprise; she recognised none of the futile, none of the subtle sentiments. If Owen had for an hour made a fool of himself she was angry; disconcerted as she would have been on learning that he had confessed to debts or fallen in love with a low girl. But there remained in any annoyance the saving fact that no one could make a fool of *her*.

"I don't know when I've taken such an interest in a young man—I think I've never done it since I began to handle them," Mr. Coyle said. "I like him, I believe in him. It's been a delight to see how he was going."

"Oh I know how they go!" Miss Wingrave threw back her head with an air as acquainted as if a headlong array of the generations had flashed before her with a rattle of their scabbards and spurs. Spencer Coyle recognised the intimation that she had nothing to learn from anybody about the natural carriage of a Wingrave, and he even felt convicted by her next words of being, in her eyes, with the troubled story of his check, his weak complaint of his pupil, rather a poor creature. "If you like him," she exclaimed, "for mercy's sake keep him quiet!"

Mr. Coyle began to explain to her that this was less easy than she appeared to imagine; but it came home to him that she really grasped little of what he said. The more he insisted that the boy had a kind of intellectual independence, the more this struck her as a conclusive proof that her nephew was a Wingrave and a soldier. It was not till he mentioned to her that Owen had spoken of the profession of arms as of something that would be "beneath" him, it was not till her attention was arrested by this intenser light on the complexity of the problem, that she broke out after a moment's stupefied reflexion: "Send him to see me at once!"

"That's exactly what I wanted to ask your leave to do. But I've wanted also to prepare you for the worst, to make you understand that he strikes me as really obstinate, and to suggest to you that the most powerful arguments at your command—especially if you should be able to put your hand on some intensely practical one—will be none too effective."

"I think I've got a powerful argument"—and Miss Wingrave looked hard at her visitor. He didn't know in the least what this engine might be, but he begged her to drag it without delay into the field. He promised their young man should come to Baker Street that evening, mentioning however that he had already urged him to spend a couple of the very next days at Eastbourne. This led Jane Wingrave to enquire with surprise what virtue there might be in *that* expensive remedy, and to reply with decision when he had said "The virtue of a little rest, a little change, a little relief to over-wrought nerves," "Ah don't coddle him—he's costing us a great deal of money! I'll talk to him and I'll take him down to Paramore; he'll be dealt with there, and I'll send him back to you straightened out."

Spencer Coyle hailed this pledge superficially with satisfaction, but before he quitted the strenuous lady he knew he had really taken on a new anxiety—a restlessness that made him say to himself, groaning inwardly: "Oh she *is* a grenadier at bottom, and she'll have no tact. I don't know what her powerful argument is; I'm only afraid she'll be stupid and make him worse. The old man's better—*he's* capable of tact, though he's not quite an extinct volcano. Owen will probably put him in a rage. In short it's a difficulty that the boy's the best of them."

He felt afresh that evening at dinner that the boy was the best of them. Young Wingrave—who, he was pleased to observe, had not yet proceeded to the seaside—appeared at the repast as usual, looking inevitably a little self-conscious, but not too original for Bayswater. He talked very naturally to Mrs. Coyle, who had thought him from the first the most beautiful young man they had ever received; so that the person most ill at ease was poor Lechmere, who took great trouble, as if from the deepest delicacy, not to meet the eye of his misguided mate. Spencer Coyle however paid the price of his own profundity in feeling more and more worried; he could so easily see that there were all sorts of things in his young friend that the people of Paramore wouldn't understand. He began even already to react against the notion of his being harassed—to reflect that after all he had a right to his ideas—to remember that he was of a substance too fine to be handled with blunt fingers. It was in this way that the ardent little crammer, with his whimsical perceptions and complicated sympathies, was generally condemned not to settle down comfortably either to his displeasures or to his enthusiasms. His love of the real truth never gave him a chance to enjoy them. He mentioned to Wingrave after dinner the propriety of an immediate visit to Baker Street, and the young man, looking "queer," as he thought—that is smiling again with the perverse high spirit in a wrong cause that he had shown in their recent interview—went off to face the ordeal. Spencer Coyle was sure he was scared—he was afraid of his aunt; but somehow this didn't strike him as a sign of pusillanimity. *He* should have been scared, he was well aware, in the poor boy's place, and the sight of his pupil marching up to the battery in spite of his terrors was a positive suggestion of the temperament of the soldier. Many a plucky youth would have funked this special exposure.

"He *has* got ideas!" young Lechmere broke out to his instructor after his comrade had quitted the house. He was bewildered and rather rueful—he had an emotion to work off. He had before dinner gone straight at his friend, as Mr. Coyle had requested, and had elicited from him that his scruples were founded on an overwhelming conviction of the stupidity—the "crass barbarism" he called it—of war. His great complaint was that people hadn't invented anything cleverer, and he was determined to show, the only way he could, that *he* wasn't so dull a brute.

"And he thinks all the great generals ought to have been shot, and that Napoleon Bonaparte in particular, the greatest, was a scoundrel, a criminal, a monster for whom language has no adequate name!" Mr. Coyle rejoined, completing young Lechmere's picture. "He favoured you, I see, with exactly the same pearls of wisdom that he produced for me. But I want to know what *you* said."

"I said they were awful rot!" Young Lechmere spoke with emphasis and was slightly surprised to hear Mr. Coyle laugh, out of tune, at this just declaration, and then after a moment continue:

"It's all very curious—I dare say there's something in it. But it's a pity!"

"He told me when it was that the question began to strike him in that light. Four or five years ago, when he did a lot of reading about all the great swells and their campaigns—Hannibal and Julius Cæsar, Marlborough and Frederick and Bonaparte. He *has* done a lot of reading, and he says it opened his eyes. He says that a wave of disgust rolled over him. He talked about the 'immeasurable misery' of wars, and asked me why nations don't tear to pieces the governments, the rulers that go in for them. He hates poor old Bonaparte worst of all."

"Well, poor old Bonaparte *was* a scoundrel. He was a frightful ruffian," Mr. Coyle unexpectedly declared. "But I suppose you didn't admit that."

"Oh I dare say he was objectionable, and I'm very glad we laid him on his back. But the point I made to Wingrave was that his own behaviour would excite no end of remark." And young Lechmere hung back but an instant before adding: "I told him he must be prepared for the worst."

"Of course he asked you what you meant by the 'worst,' " said Spencer Coyle.

"Yes, he asked me that, and do you know what I said? I said people would call his conscientious scruples and his wave of disgust a mere pretext. Then he asked 'A pretext for what?' "

"Ah he rather had you there!" Mr. Coyle returned with a small laugh that was mystifying to his pupil.

"Not a bit—for I told him."

"What did you tell him?"

Once more, for a few seconds, with his conscious eyes in his instructor's, the young man delayed. "Why what we spoke of a few hours ago. The appearance he'd present of not having—" The honest youth faltered afresh, but brought it out: "The military

temperament, don't you know? But do you know how he cheeked us
on that?" young Lechmere went on.

"Damn the military temperament!" the crammer promptly replied.

Young Lechmere stared. Mr. Coyle's tone left him uncertain if he
were attributing the phrase to Wingrave or uttering his own opinion, but he exclaimed: "Those were exactly his words!"

"He doesn't care," said Mr. Coyle.

"Perhaps not. But it isn't fair for him to abuse *us* fellows. I told
him it's the finest temperament in the world, and that there's nothing so splendid as pluck and heroism."

"Ah there you had *him!*"

"I told him it was unworthy of him to abuse a gallant, a
magnificent profession. I told him there's no type so fine as that of
the soldier doing his duty."

"That's essentially *your* type, my dear boy." Young Lechmere
blushed; he couldn't make out—and the danger was naturally unexpected to him—whether at that moment he didn't exist mainly for
the recreation of his friend. But he was partly reassured by the genial
way this friend continued, laying a hand on his shoulder: "Keep *at*
him that way! We may do something. I'm in any case extremely
obliged to you."

Another doubt however remained unassuaged—a doubt which led
him to overflow yet again before they dropped the painful subject:
"He *doesn't* care! But it's awfully odd he shouldn't!"

"So it is, but remember what you said this afternoon—I mean
about your not advising people to make insinuations to *you.*"

"I believe I should knock the beggar down!" said young Lechmere. Mr. Coyle had got up; the conversation had taken place while
they sat together after Mrs. Coyle's withdrawal from the dinner-
table, and the head of the establishment administered to his candid
charge, on principles that were a part of his thoroughness, a glass of
excellent claret. The disciple in question, also on his feet, lingered
an instant, not for another "go," as he would have called it, at the
decanter, but to wipe his microscopic moustache with prolonged and
unusual care. His companion saw he had something to bring out
which required a final effort, and waited for him an instant with a
hand on the knob of the door. Then as young Lechmere drew nearer
Spencer Coyle grew conscious of an unwonted intensity in the round

and ingenuous face. The boy was nervous, but tried to behave like a man of the world. "Of course it's between ourselves," he stammered, "and I wouldn't breathe such a word to any one who wasn't interested in poor Wingrave as you are. But do you think he funks it?"

Mr. Coyle looked at him so hard an instant that he was visibly frightened at what he had said. "Funks it! Funks what?"

"Why what we're talking about—the service." Young Lechmere gave a little gulp and added with a want of active wit almost pathetic to Spencer Coyle: "The dangers, you know!"

"Do you mean he's thinking of his skin?"

Young Lechmere's eyes expanded appealingly, and what his instructor saw in his pink face—even thinking he saw a tear—was the dread of a disappointment shocking in the degree in which the loyalty of admiration had been great.

"Is he—is he beastly *afraid?*" repeated the honest lad with a quaver of suspense.

"Dear no!" said Spencer Coyle, turning his back.

On which young Lechmere felt a little snubbed and even a little ashamed. But still more he felt relieved.

🕸 3 🕸

LESS than a week after this the elder man received a note from Miss Wingrave, who had immediately quitted London with her nephew. She proposed he should come down to Paramore for the following Sunday—Owen was really so tiresome. On the spot, in that house of examples and memories and in combination with her poor dear father, who was "dreadfully annoyed," it might be worth their while to make a last stand. Mr. Coyle read between the lines of this letter that the party at Paramore had got over a good deal of ground since Miss Wingrave, in Baker Street, had treated his despair as superficial. She wasn't an insinuating woman, but she went so far as to put the question on the ground of his conferring a particular favour on an afflicted family; and she expressed the pleasure it would give them should he be accompanied by Mrs. Coyle, for whom she enclosed a separate invitation. She mentioned that she was also writing, subject to Mr. Coyle's approval, to young Lechmere. She thought such a nice manly boy might do her wretched nephew some good. The celebrated crammer decided to embrace this occasion; and now it was the case not so much that he was angry as that he was anxious. As he directed his answer to Miss Wingrave's letter he caught himself smiling at the thought that at bottom he was going to defend his ex-pupil rather than to give him away. He said to his wife, who was a fair fresh slow woman—a person of much more presence than himself—that she had better take Miss Wingrave at her word: it was such an extraordinary, such a fascinating specimen of an old English home. This last allusion was softly sarcastic—he had accused the good lady more than once of being in love with Owen Wingrave. She admitted that she was, she even gloried in her passion; which shows that the subject, between them, was treated in a liberal spirit. She carried out the joke by accepting the invitation with eagerness. Young Lechmere was delighted to do the same; his instructor had good-naturedly taken the view that the little break would freshen him up for his last spurt.

It was the fact that the occupants of Paramore did indeed take their trouble hard that struck our friend after he had been an hour or two in that fine old house. This very short second visit, beginning on the Saturday evening, was to constitute the strangest episode of his life. As soon as he found himself in private with his wife—they had retired to dress for dinner—they called each other's attention with effusion and almost with alarm to the sinister gloom diffused through the place. The house was admirable from its old grey front, which came forward in wings so as to form three sides of a square, but Mrs. Coyle made no scruple to declare that if she had known in advance the sort of impression she was going to receive she would never have put her foot in it. She characterised it as "uncanny" and as looking wicked and weird, and she accused her husband of not having warned her properly. He had named to her in advance some of the appearances she was to expect, but while she almost feverishly dressed she had innumerable questions to ask. He hadn't told her about the girl, the extraordinary girl, Miss Julian—that is, he hadn't told her that this young lady, who in plain terms was a mere dependent, would be in effect, and as a consequence of the way she carried herself, the most important person in the house. Mrs. Coyle was already prepared to announce that she hated Miss Julian's affectations. Her husband above all hadn't told her that they should find their young charge looking five years older.

"I couldn't imagine that," Spencer said, "nor that the character of the crisis here would be quite so perceptible. But I suggested to Miss Wingrave the other day that they should press her nephew in real earnest, and she has taken me at my word. They've cut off his supplies—they're trying to starve him out. That's not what I meant—but indeed I don't quite *know* to-day what I meant. Owen feels the pressure, but he won't yield." The strange thing was that, now he was there, the brooding little coach knew still better, even while half-closing his eyes to it, that his own spirit had been caught up by a wave of reaction. If he was there it was because he was on poor Owen's side. His whole impression, his whole apprehension, had on the spot become much deeper. There was something in the young fanatic's very resistance that began to charm him. When his wife, in the intimacy of the conference I have mentioned, threw off the mask and commended even with extravagance the stand his pupil had taken (he was too good to be a horrid soldier and it was noble of him to suffer for his convictions—wasn't he as upright as a young hero, even though as pale as a Christian martyr?) the good lady only expressed the sympathy which, under cover of regarding his late inmate as a rare exception, he had already recognised in his own soul.

For, half an hour ago, after they had had superficial tea in the brown old hall of the house, that searcher into the reasons of things had proposed to him, before going to dress, a short turn outside, and had even, on the terrace, as they walked together to one of the far ends, passed his hand entreatingly into his companion's arm, permitting himself thus a familiarity unusual between pupil and master and calculated to show he had guessed whom he could most depend on to be kind to him. Spencer Coyle had on his own side guessed something, so that he wasn't surprised at the boy's having a particular confidence to make. He had felt on arriving that each member of the party would want to get hold of him first, and he knew that at that moment Jane Wingrave was peering through the ancient blur of one of the windows—the house had been modernised so little that the thick dim panes were three centuries old—to see whether her nephew looked as if he were poisoning the visitor's mind. Mr. Coyle lost no time therefore in reminding the youth—though careful to turn it to a laugh as he did so—that he hadn't come down to Paramore to be corrupted. He had come down to make, face to face, a last appeal, which he hoped wouldn't be utterly vain. Owen smiled sadly as they went, asking him if he thought he had the general air of a fellow who was going to knock under.

"I think you look odd—I think you look ill," Spencer Coyle said very honestly. They had paused at the end of the terrace.

"I've had to exercise a great power of resistance, and it rather takes it out of one."

"Ah my dear boy, I wish your great power—for you evidently possess it—were exerted in a better cause!"

Owen Wingrave smiled down at his small but erect instructor. "I don't believe that!" Then he added, to explain why: Isn't what you want (if you're so good as to think well of my character) to see me exert *most* power, in whatever direction? Well, this is the way I exert most." He allowed he had had some terrible hours with his grandfather, who had denounced him in a way to make his hair stand up on his head. He had expected them not to like it, not a bit, but had had no idea they would make such a row. His aunt was different, but she was equally insulting. Oh they had made him feel they were ashamed of him; they accused him of putting a public dishonour on their name. He was the only one who had ever backed out—he was the first for three hundred years. Every one had known he was to go up, and now every one would know him for a young hypocrite who suddenly pretended to have scruples. They talked of his scruples as you wouldn't talk of a cannibal's god. His grandfather had called him outrageous names. "He called me—he called me—" Here Owen faltered and his voice failed him. He looked as haggard as was possible to a young man in such splendid health.

"I probably know!" said Spencer Coyle with a nervous laugh.

His companion's clouded eyes, as if following the last strange consequences of things, rested for an instant on a distant object. Then they met his own and for another moment sounded them deeply. "It isn't true. No, it isn't. It's not *that!*"

"I don't suppose it is! But what *do* you propose instead of it?"

"Instead of what?"

"Instead of the stupid solution of war. If you take that away you should suggest at least a substitute."

"That's for the people in charge, for governments and cabinets," said Owen. *"They'll* arrive soon enough at a substitute, in the particular case, if they're made to understand that they'll be hanged—and also drawn and quartered—if they don't find one.

Make it a capital crime; *that* will quicken the wits of ministers!" His eyes brightened as he spoke, and he looked assured and exalted. Mr. Coyle gave a sigh of sad surrender—it was really a stiff obsession. He saw the moment after this when Owen was on the point of asking if he too thought him a coward; but he was relieved to be able to judge that he either didn't suspect him of it or shrank uncomfortably from putting the question to the test. Spencer Coyle wished to show confidence, but somehow a direct assurance that he didn't doubt of his courage was too gross a compliment—it would be like saying he didn't doubt of his honesty. The difficulty was presently averted by Owen's continuing: "My grandfather can't break the entail, but I shall have nothing but this place, which, as you know, is small and, with the way rents are going, has quite ceased to yield an income. He has some money—not much, but such as it is he cuts me off. My aunt does the same—she has let me know her intentions. She was to have left me her six hundred a year. It was all settled, but now what's definite is that I don't get a penny of it if I give up the army. I must add in fairness that I have from my mother three hundred a year of my own. And I tell you the simple truth when I say I don't care a rap for the loss of the money." The young man drew the long slow breath of a creature in pain; then he added: *"That's* not what worries me!"

"What are you going to do instead then?" his friend asked without other comment.

"I don't know—perhaps nothing. Nothing great at all events. Only something peaceful!"

Owen gave a weary smile, as if, worried as he was, he could yet appreciate the humorous effect of such a declaration from a Wingrave; but what it suggested to his guest, who looked up at him with a sense that he was after all not a Wingrave for nothing and had a military steadiness under fire, was the exasperation that such a profession, made in such a way and striking them as the last word of the inglorious, might well have produced on the part of his grandfather and his aunt. "Perhaps nothing"—when he might carry on the great tradition! Yes, he wasn't weak, and he was interesting; but there was clearly a point of view from which he was provoking. "What *is* it then that worries you?" Mr. Coyle demanded.

"Oh the house—the very air and feeling of it. There are strange voices in it that seem to mutter at me—to say dreadful things as I pass. I mean the general consciousness and responsibility of what I'm doing. Of course it hasn't been easy for me—anything rather! I assure you I don't enjoy it." With a light in them that was like a longing for justice Owen again bent his eyes on those of the little coach; then he pursued: "I've started up all the old ghosts. The very portraits glower at me on the walls. There's one of my great-great-grandfather (the one the extraordinary story you know is about—the old fellow who hangs on the second landing of the big staircase) that fairly stirs on the canvas, just heaves a little, when I come near it. I have to go up and down stairs—it's rather awkward! It's what my aunt calls the family-circle, and they sit, ever so grimly, in judgement. The circle's all constituted here, it's a kind of awful encompassing presence, it stretches away into the past, and when I came back with her the other day Miss Wingrave told me I wouldn't have the impudence to stand in the midst of it and say such things. I *had* to say them to my grandfather; but now that I've said them it seems to me the question's ended. I want to go away—I don't care if I never come back again."

"Oh you *are* a soldier; you must fight it out!" Mr. Coyle laughed.

The young man seemed discouraged at his levity, but as they turned round, strolling back in the direction from which they had come, he himself smiled faintly after an instant and replied: "Ah we're tainted all!"

They walked in silence part of the way to the old portico; then the elder of the pair, stopping short after having assured himself he was at a sufficient distance from the house not to be heard, suddenly put the question: "What does Miss Julian say?"

"Miss Julian?" Owen had perceptibly coloured.

"I'm sure *she* hasn't concealed her opinion."

"Oh it's the opinion of the family-circle, for she's a member of it of course. And then she has her own as well."

"Her own opinion?"

"Her own family-circle."

"Do you mean her mother—that patient lady?"

"I mean more particularly her father, who fell in battle. And her grandfather, and *his* father, and her uncles and great-uncles—they all fell in battle."

Mr. Coyle, his face now rather oddly set, took it in. "Hasn't the sacrifice of so many lives been sufficient? Why should she sacrifice *you?*"

"Oh she *hates* me!" Owen declared as they resumed their walk.

"Ah the hatred of pretty girls for fine young men!" cried Spencer Coyle.

He didn't believe in it, but his wife did, it appeared perfectly, when he mentioned this conversation while, in the fashion that has been described, the visitors dressed for dinner. Mrs. Coyle had already discovered that nothing could have been nastier than Miss Julian's manner to the disgraced youth during the half-hour the party had spent in the hall; and it was this lady's judgement that one must have had no eyes in one's head not to see that she was already trying outrageously to flirt with young Lechmere. It was a pity they had brought that silly boy: he was down in the hall with the creature at that moment. Spencer Coyle's version was different—he believed finer elements involved. The girl's footing in the house was inexplicable on any ground save that of her being predestined to Miss Wingrave's nephew. As the niece of Miss Wingrave's own unhappy intended she had been devoted early by this lady to the office of healing by a union with the hope of the race the tragic breach that had separated their elders; and if in reply to this it was to be said that a girl of spirit couldn't enjoy in such a matter having her duty cut out for her, Owen's enlightened friend was ready with the argument that a young person in Miss Julian's position would never be such a fool as really to quarrel with a capital chance. She was familiar at Paramore and she felt safe; therefore she might treat herself to the amusement of pretending she had her option. It was all innocent tricks and airs. She had a curious charm, and it was vain to pretend that the heir of that house wouldn't seem good enough to a girl, clever as she might be, of eighteen. Mrs. Coyle reminded her husband that their late charge was precisely now *not* of that house: this question was among the articles that exercised their wits after the two men had taken the turn on the terrace. Spencer then mentioned to his wife that Owen was afraid of the portrait of his great-great-grandfather. He would show it to her, since she hadn't noticed it, on their way downstairs.

"Why of his great-great-grandfather more than of any of the others?"

"Oh because he's the most formidable. He's the one who's sometimes seen."

"Seen where?" Mrs. Coyle had turned round with a jerk.

"In the room he was found dead in—the White Room they've always called it."

"Do you mean to say the house has a proved *ghost?*" Mrs. Coyle almost shrieked. "You brought me here without telling me?"

"Didn't I mention it after my other visit?"

"Not a word. You only talked about Miss Wingrave."

"Oh I was full of the story—you've simply forgotten."

"Then you should have reminded me!"

"If I had thought of it I'd have held my peace—for you wouldn't have come."

"I wish indeed I hadn't!" cried Mrs. Coyle. "But what," she immediately asked, "*is* the story?"

"Oh a deed of violence that took place here ages ago. I think it was in George the Second's time that Colonel Wingrave, one of their ancestors, struck in a fit of passion one of his children, a lad just growing up, a blow on the head of which the unhappy child died. The matter was hushed up for the hour and some other explanation put about. The poor boy was laid out in one of those rooms on the other side of the house, and amid strange smothered rumours the funeral was hurried on. The next morning, when the household assembled, Colonel Wingrave was missing; he was looked for vainly, and at last it occurred to some one that he might perhaps be in the room from which his child had been carried to burial. The seeker knocked without an answer—then opened the door. The poor man lay dead on the floor, in his clothes, as if he had reeled and fallen back, without a wound, without a mark, without anything in his appearance to indicate that he had either struggled or suffered. He was a strong sound man—there was nothing to account for such a stroke. He's supposed to have gone to the room during the night, just before going to bed, in some fit of compunction or some fascination of dread. It was only after this that the truth about the boy came out. But no one ever sleeps in the room."

Mrs. Coyle had fairly turned pale. "I hope not indeed! Thank heaven they haven't put *us* there!"

"We're at a comfortable distance—I know the scene of the event."

"Do you mean you've been *in*—?"

"For a few moments. They're rather proud of the place and my young friend showed it me when I was here before."

Mrs. Coyle stared. "And what is it like?"

"Simply an empty dull old-fashioned bedroom, rather big and furnished with the things of the 'period.' It's panelled from floor to ceiling, and the panels evidently, years and years ago, were painted white. But the paint has darkened with time and there are three or four quaint little ancient 'samplers,' framed and glazed, hung on the walls."

Mrs. Coyle looked round with a shudder. "I'm glad there are no samplers here! I never heard anything so jumpy! Come down to dinner."

On the staircase as they went her husband showed her the portrait of Colonel Wingrave—a representation, with some force and style, for the place and period, of a gentleman with a hard handsome face, in a red coat and a peruke. Mrs. Coyle pronounced his descendant old Sir Philip wonderfully like him; and her husband could fancy, though he kept it to himself, that if one should have the courage to walk the old corridors of Paramore at night one might meet a figure that resembled him roaming, with the restlessness of a ghost, hand in hand with the figure of a tall boy. As he proceeded to the drawing-room with his wife he found himself suddenly wishing he had made more of a point of his pupil's going to Eastbourne. The evening however seemed to have taken upon itself to dissipate any such whimsical forebodings, for the grimness of the family-circle, as he had preconceived its composition, was mitigated by an infusion of the "neighbourhood." The company at dinner was recruited by two cheerful couples, one of them the vicar and his wife, and by a silent young man who had come down to fish. This was a relief to Mr. Coyle, who had begun to wonder what was after all expected of him and why he had been such a fool as to come, and who now felt that for the first hours at least the situation wouldn't have directly to be dealt with. Indeed he found, as he had found before, sufficient occupation for his ingenuity in reading the various symptoms of which the social scene that spread about him was an expression. He should probably have a trying day on the morrow: he foresaw the difficulty of the long decorous Sunday and how dry Jane Wingrave's ideas, elicited in strenuous conference, would taste. She and her father would make him feel they depended upon him for the impossible, and if they should try to associate him with too tactless a policy he might end by telling them what he thought of it—an accident not required to make his visit a depressed mistake. The old man's actual design was evidently to let their friends see in it a positive mark of their being all right. The presence of the great London coach was tantamount to a profession of faith in the results of the impending examination. It had clearly been obtained from Owen, rather to the principal visitor's surprise, that he would do nothing to interfere with the apparent concord. He let the allusions to his hard work pass and, holding his tongue about his affairs, talked to the ladies as amicably as if he hadn't been "cut off." When Mr. Coyle looked at him once or twice across the table, catching his eye, which showed an indefinable passion, he found a puzzling pathos in his laughing face: one couldn't resist a pang for a young lamb so visibly marked for sacrifice. "Hang him, what a pity he's such a fighter!" he privately sighed—and with a want of logic that was only superficial.

This idea however would have absorbed him more if so much of his attention hadn't been for Kate Julian, who now that he had her well before him struck him as a remarkable and even as a possibly interesting young woman. The interest resided not in any extraordinary prettiness, for if she was handsome, with her long Eastern eyes, her magnificent hair and her general unabashed originality, he had seen complexions rosier and features that pleased him more: it dwelt in a strange impression that she gave of being exactly the sort of person whom, in her position, common considerations, those of prudence and perhaps even a little those of decorum, would have enjoined on her not to be. She was what was vulgarly termed a dependent—penniless patronised tolerated; but something in all her air conveyed that if her situation was inferior her spirit, to make up for it, was above precautions or submissions. It wasn't in the least that she was aggressive—she was too indifferent for that; it was only as if, having nothing either to gain or to lose, she could afford to do as she liked. It occurred to Spencer Coyle that she might really have had more at stake than her imagination appeared to take account of; whatever this quantity might be, at any rate, he had never seen a young woman at less pains to keep the safe side. He wondered inevitably what terms prevailed between Jane Wingrave and such an inmate as this; but those questions of course were unfathomable deeps. Perhaps keen Kate lorded it even over her protectress. The other time he was at Paramore he had received an impression that, with Sir Philip beside her, the girl could fight with her back to the wall. She amused Sir Philip, she charmed him, and he liked people who weren't afraid; between him and his daughter moreover there was no doubt which was the higher in command. Miss Wingrave took many things for granted, and most of all the rigour of discipline and the fate of the vanquished and the captive.

But between their clever boy and so original a companion of his childhood what odd relation would have grown up? It couldn't be indifference, and yet on the part of happy handsome youthful creatures it was still less likely to be aversion. They weren't Paul and Virginia, but they must have had their common summer and their idyll: no nice girl could have disliked such a nice fellow for anything but not liking *her,* and no nice fellow could have resisted such propinquity. Mr. Coyle remembered indeed that Mrs. Julian had spoken to him as if the propinquity had been by no means constant, owing to her daughter's absences at school, to say nothing of Owen's; her visits to a few friends who were so kind as to "take" her from time to time; her sojourns in London—so difficult to manage, but still managed by God's help—for "advantages," for drawing and singing, especially drawing, or rather painting in oils, for which she had gained high credit. But the good lady had also mentioned that the young people were quite brother and sister, which *was* a little, after all, like Paul and Virginia. Mrs. Coyle had been right, and it was apparent that Virginia was doing her best to make the time pass agreeably for young Lechmere. There was no such whirl of conversation as to render it an effort for our critic to reflect on these things: the tone of the occasion, thanks principally to the other guests, was not disposed to stray—it tended to the repetition of anecdote and the discussion of rents, topics that huddled together like uneasy animals. He could judge how intensely his hosts wished the evening to pass off as if nothing had happened; and this gave him the measure of their private resentment. Before dinner was over he found himself fidgety about his second pupil. Young Lechmere, since he began to cram, had done all that might have been expected of him; but this couldn't blind his instructor to a present perception of his being in moments of relaxation as innocent as a babe. Mr. Coyle had considered that the amusements of Paramore would probably give him a fillip, and the poor youth's manner testified to the soundness of the forecast. The fillip had been unmistakeably administered; it had come in the form of a revelation. The light on young Lechmere's brow announced with a candour that was almost an appeal for compassion, or at least a deprecation of ridicule, that he had never seen anything like Miss Julian.

✦ 4 ✦

IN the drawing-room after dinner the girl found a chance to approach Owen's late preceptor. She stood before him a moment, smiling while she opened and shut her fan, and then said abruptly, raising her strange eyes: "I know what you've come for, but it isn't any use."

"I've come to look after *you* a little. Isn't *that* any use?"

"It's very kind. But I'm not the question of the hour. You won't do anything with Owen."

Spencer Coyle hesitated a moment. "What will *you* do with his young friend?"

She stared, looked round her. "Mr. Lechmere? Oh poor little lad! We've been talking about Owen. He admires him so."

"So do I. I should tell you that."

"So do we all. That's why we're in such despair."

"Personally then you'd *like* him to be a soldier?" the visitor asked.

"I've quite set my heart on it. I adore the army and I'm awfully fond of my old playmate," said Miss Julian.

Spencer recalled the young man's own different version of her attitude; but he judged it loyal not to challenge her. "It's not conceivable that your old playmate shouldn't be fond of you. He must therefore wish to please you; and I don't see why—between you, such clever young people as you are!—you don't set the matter right."

"Wish to please me!" Miss Julian echoed. "I'm sorry to say he shows no such desire. He thinks me an impudent wretch. I've told him what I think of *him,* and he simply hates me."

"But you think so highly! You just told me you admire him."

"His talents, his possibilities, yes; even his personal appearance, if I may allude to such a matter. But I don't admire his present behaviour."

"Have you had the question out with him?" Spencer asked.

"Oh yes, I've ventured to be frank—the occasion seemed to excuse it. He couldn't like what I said."

"What did you say?"

The girl, thinking a moment, opened and shut her fan again. "Why—as we're such good old friends—that such conduct doesn't begin to be that of a gentleman!"

After she had spoken her eyes met Mr. Coyle's, who looked into their ambiguous depths. "What then would you have said without that tie?"

"How odd for *you* to ask that—in such a way!" she returned with a laugh. "I don't understand your position: I thought your line was to *make* soldiers!"

"You should take my little joke. But, as regards Owen Wingrave, there's no 'making' needed," he declared. "To my sense"—and the little crammer paused as with a consciousness of responsibility for his paradox—"to my sense he *is,* in a high sense of the term, a fighting man."

"Ah let him prove it!" she cried with impatience and turning short off.

Spencer Coyle let her go; something in her tone annoyed and even not a little shocked him. There had evidently been a violent passage between these young persons, and the reflexion that such a matter was after all none of his business but troubled him the more. It was indeed a military house, and she was at any rate a damsel who placed her ideal of manhood—damsels doubtless always had their ideals of manhood—in the type of the belted warrior. It was a taste like another; but even a quarter of an hour later, finding himself near young Lechmere, in whom this type was embodied, Spencer Coyle was still so ruffled that he addressed the innocent lad with a certain magisterial dryness. "You're under no pressure to sit up late, you know. That's not what I brought you down for." The dinner-guests were taking leave and the bedroom candles twinkled in a monitory row. Young Lechmere however was too agreeably agitated to be accessible to a snub: he had a happy preoccupation which almost engendered a grin.

"I'm only too eager for bedtime. Do you know there's an awfully jolly room?"

Coyle debated a moment as to whether he should take the allusion—then spoke from his general tension. "Surely they haven't put you there?"

"No indeed: no one has passed a night in it for ages. But that's exactly what I want to do—it would be tremendous fun."

"And have you been trying to get Miss Julian's leave?"

"Oh *she* can't give it she says. But she believes in it, and she maintains that no man has ever dared."

"No man *shall* ever!" said Spencer with decision. "A fellow in your critical position in particular must have a quiet night."

Young Lechmere gave a disappointed but reasonable sigh. "Oh all right. But mayn't I sit up for a little go at Wingrave? I haven't had any yet."

Mr. Coyle looked at his watch. "You may smoke *one* cigarette."

He felt a hand on his shoulder and turned round to see his wife tilting candle-grease upon his coat. The ladies were going to bed and it was Sir Philip's inveterate hour; but Mrs. Coyle confided to her husband that after the dreadful things he had told her she positively declined to be left alone, for no matter how short an interval, in any part of the house. He promised to follow her within three minutes, and after the orthodox handshakes the ladies rustled away. The forms were kept up at Paramore as bravely as if the old house had no present intensity of heartache. The only one of which Coyle noticed the drop was some salutation to himself from Kate Julian. She gave him neither a word nor a glance, but he saw her look hard at Owen. Her mother, timid and pitying, was apparently the only person from whom this young man caught an inclination of the head. Miss Wingrave marshalled the three ladies—her little procession of twinkling tapers—up the wide oaken stairs and past the watching portrait of her ill-fated ancestor. Sir Philip's servant appeared and offered his arm to the old man, who turned a perpendicular back on poor Owen when the boy made a vague movement to anticipate this office. Mr. Coyle learned later that before Owen had forfeited favour it had always, when he was at home, been his privilege at bedtime to conduct his grandfather ceremoniously to rest. Sir Philip's habits were contemptuously different now. His apartments were on the lower floor and he shuffled stiffly off to them with his valet's help, after fixing for a moment significantly on the most responsible of his visitors the thick red ray, like the glow of stirred embers, that always made his eyes conflict oddly with his mild manners. They seemed to say to poor Spencer "We'll let the young scoundrel have it to-morrow!" One might have gathered from them that the young scoundrel, who had now strolled to the other end of the hall, had at least forged a cheque. His friend watched him an instant, saw him drop nervously into a chair and then with a restless movement get up. The same movement brought him back to where Mr. Coyle stood addressing a last injunction to young Lechmere.

"I'm going to bed and I should like you particularly to conform to what I said to you a short time ago. Smoke a single cigarette with our host here and then go to your room. You'll have me down on you if I hear of your having, during the night, tried any preposterous games." Young Lechmere, looking down with his hands in his pockets, said nothing—he only poked at the corner of a rug with his toe; so that his fellow visitor, dissatisfied with so tacit a pledge, presently went on to Owen: "I must request you, Wingrave, not to keep so sensitive a subject sitting up—and indeed to put him to bed and turn his key in the door." As Owen stared an instant, apparently not understanding the motive of so much solicitude, he added: "Lechmere has a morbid curiosity about one of your legends—of your historic rooms. Nip it in the bud."

"Oh the legend's rather good, but I'm afraid the room's an awful sell!" Owen laughed.

"You know you don't *believe* that, my boy!" young Lechmere returned.

"I don't think he does"—Mr. Coyle noticed Owen's mottled flush.

"He wouldn't try a night there himself!" their companion pursued.

"I know who told you that," said Owen, lighting a cigarette in an embarrassed way at the candle, without offering one to either of his friends.

"Well, what if she did?" asked the younger of these gentlemen, rather red. "Do you want them *all* yourself?" he continued facetiously, fumbling in the cigarette-box.

Owen Wingrave only smoked quietly; then he brought out: "Yes—what if she did? But she doesn't know," he added.

"She doesn't know what?"

"She doesn't know anything!—I'll tuck him in!" Owen went on gaily to Mr. Coyle, who saw that his presence, now a certain note had been struck, made the young men uncomfortable. He was curious, but there were discretions and delicacies, with his pupils, that he had always pretended to practise; scruples which however didn't prevent, as he took his way upstairs, his recommending them not to be donkeys.

At the top of the staircase, to his surprise, he met Miss Julian, who was apparently going down again. She hadn't begun to undress, nor was she perceptibly disconcerted at seeing him. She nevertheless, in a manner slightly at variance with the rigour with which she had overlooked him ten minutes before, dropped the words: "I'm going down to look for something. I've lost a jewel."

"A jewel?"

"A rather good turquoise, out of my locket. As it's the only *real* ornament I've the honour to possess—!" And she began to descend.

"Shall I go with you and help you?" asked Spencer Coyle.

She paused a few steps below him, looking back with her Oriental eyes. "Don't I hear our friends' voices in the hall?"

"Those remarkable young men are there."

"*They'll* help me." And Kate Julian passed down.

Spencer Coyle was tempted to follow her, but remembering his standard of tact he rejoined his wife in their apartment. He delayed nevertheless to go to bed and, though he looked into his dressing-room, couldn't bring himself even to take off his coat. He pretended for half an hour to read a novel; after which, quietly, or perhaps I should say agitatedly, he stepped from the dressing-room into the corridor. He followed this passage to the door of the room he knew to have been assigned to young Lechmere and was comforted to see it closed. Half an hour earlier he had noticed it stand open; therefore he could take for granted the bewildered boy had come to bed. It was of this he had wished to assure himself, and having done so he was on the point of retreating. But at the same instant he heard a sound in the room—the occupant was doing, at the window, something that showed him he might knock without the reproach of waking his pupil up. Young Lechmere came in fact to the door in his shirt and trousers. He admitted his visitor in some surprise, and when the door

was closed again the latter said: "I don't want to make your life a
burden, but I had it on my conscience to see for myself that you're
not exposed to undue excitement."

"Oh there's plenty of that!" said the ingenuous youth. "Miss
Julian came down again."

"To look for a turquoise?"

"So she said."

"Did she find it?"

"I don't know. I came up. I left her with poor Owen."

"Quite the right thing," said Spencer Coyle.

"I don't know," young Lechmere repeated uneasily. "I left them
quarrelling."

"What about?"

"I don't understand. They're a quaint pair!"

Spencer turned it over. He had, fundamentally, principles and
high decencies, but what he had in particular just now was a curiosity, or rather, to recognise it for what it was, a sympathy, which
brushed them away. "Does it strike you that *she's* down on him?" he
permitted himself to enquire.

"Rather!—when she tells him he lies!"

"What do you mean?"

"Why before *me*. It made me leave them; it was getting too hot. I
stupidly brought up the question of that bad room again, and said
how sorry I was I had had to promise you not to try my luck with
it."

"You can't pry about in that gross way in other people's
houses—you can't take such liberties, you know!" Mr. Coyle inter-
jected.

"I'm all right—see how good I am. I don't want to go *near* the
place!" said young Lechmere confidingly. "Miss Julian said to me
'Oh I dare say *you'd* risk it, but'—and she turned and laughed at
poor Owen—'that's more than we can expect of a gentleman who has
taken *his* extraordinary line.' I could see that something had already
passed between them on the subject—some teasing or challenging of
hers. It may have been only chaff, but his chucking the profession
had evidently brought up the question of the white feather—I mean
of his pluck."

"And what did Owen say?"

"Nothing at first; but presently he brought out very quietly: 'I spent all last night in the confounded place.' We both stared and cried out at this and I asked him what he had seen there. He said he had seen nothing, and Miss Julian replied that he ought to tell his story better than that—he ought to make something good of it. 'It's not a story—it's a simple fact,' said he; on which she jeered at him and wanted to know why, if he had done it, he hadn't told her in the morning, since he knew what she thought of him. 'I know, my dear, but I don't care,' the poor devil said. This made her angry, and she asked him quite seriously whether he'd care if he should know she believed him to be trying to deceive us."

"Ah what a brute!" cried Spencer Coyle.

"She's a most extraordinary girl—I don't know what she's up to," young Lechmere quite panted.

"Extraordinary indeed—to be romping and bandying words at that hour of the night with fast young men!"

But young Lechmere made his distinction. "I mean because I think she likes him."

Mr. Coyle was so struck with this unwonted symptom of subtlety that he flashed out: "And do you think he likes *her?*"

It produced on his pupil's part a drop and a plaintive sigh. "I don't know—I give it up!—But I'm sure he *did* see something or hear something," the youth added.

"In that ridiculous place? What makes you sure?"

"Well, because he looks as if he had. I've an idea you can tell—in such a case. He behaves as if he had."

"Why then shouldn't he name it?"

Young Lechmere wondered and found. "Perhaps it's too bad to mention."

Spencer Coyle gave a laugh. "Aren't you glad then *you're* not in it?"

"Uncommonly!"

"Go to bed, you goose," Spencer said with renewed nervous derision. "But before you go tell me how he met her charge that he was trying to deceive you."

" 'Take me there yourself then and lock me in!' "

"And *did* she take him?"

"I don't know—I came up."

He exchanged a long look with his pupil. "I don't think they're in the hall now. Where's Owen's own room?"

"I haven't the least idea."

Mr. Coyle was at a loss; he was in equal ignorance and he couldn't go about trying doors. He bade young Lechmere sink to slumber; after which he came out into the passage. He asked himself if he should be able to find his way to the room Owen had formerly shown him, remembering that in common with many of the others it had its ancient name painted on it. But the corridors of Paramore were intricate; moreover some of the servants would still be up, and he didn't wish to appear unduly to prowl. He went back to his own quarters, where Mrs. Coyle soon noted the continuance of his inability to rest. As she confessed for her own part, in the dreadful place, to an increased sense of "creepiness," they spent the early part of the night in conversation, so that a portion of their vigil was inevitably beguiled by her husband's account of his colloquy with little Lechmere and by their exchange of opinions upon it. Toward two o'clock Mrs. Coyle became so nervous about their persecuted young friend, and so possessed by the fear that that wicked girl had availed herself of his invitation to put him to an abominable test, that she begged her husband to go and look into the matter at whatever cost to his own tranquillity. But Spencer, perversely, had ended, as the perfect stillness of the night settled upon them, by charming himself into a pale acceptance of Owen's readiness to face God knew what unholy strain—an exposure the more trying to excited sensibilities as the poor boy had now learned by the ordeal of the previous night how resolute an effort he should have to make. "I hope he *is* there," he said to his wife: "it puts them all so hideously in the wrong!" At any rate he couldn't take on himself to explore a house he knew so little. He was inconsequent—he didn't prepare for bed. He sat in the dressing-room with his light and his novel—he waited to find himself nod. At last however Mrs. Coyle turned over and ceased to talk, and at last too he fell asleep in his chair. How long he slept he only knew afterwards by computation; what he knew to begin with was that he had started up in confusion and under the shock of an appalling sound. His consciousness cleared itself fast, helped doubtless by a confirmatory cry of horror from his wife's room. But he gave no heed to his wife; he had already bounded into the passage. There the sound was repeated—it was the "Help! help!" of a woman in agonised terror. It came from a distant quarter of the house, but the quarter was sufficiently indicated. He rushed straight before him, the sound of opening doors and alarmed voices in his ears and the faintness of the early dawn in his eyes. At a turn of one of the passages he came upon the white figure of a girl in a swoon on a bench, and in the vividness of the revelation he read as he went that Kate Julian, stricken in her pride too late with a chill of compunction for what she had mockingly done, had, after coming to release the victim of her derision, reeled away, overwhelmed, from the catastrophe that was her work—the catastrophe that the next moment he found himself aghast at on the threshold of an open door. Owen Wingrave, dressed as he had last seen him, lay dead on the spot on which his ancestor had been found. He was all the young soldier on the gained field.

The Real Thing

❧ 1 ❧

When the porter's wife, who used to answer the house-bell, announced "A gentleman and a lady, sir," I had, as I often had in those days—the wish being father to the thought—an immediate vision of sitters. Sitters my visitors in this case proved to be; but not in the sense I should have preferred. There was nothing at first however to indicate that they mightn't have come for a portrait. The gentleman, a man of fifty, very high and very straight, with a moustache slightly grizzled and a dark grey walking-coat admirably fitted, both of which I noted professionally—I don't mean as a barber or yet a tailor—would have struck me as a celebrity if celebrities often were striking. It was a truth of which I had for some time been conscious that a figure with a good deal of frontage was, as one might say, almost never a public institution. A glance at the lady helped to remind me of this paradoxical law: she also looked too distinguished to be a "personality." Moreover one would scarcely come across two variations together.

Neither of the pair immediately spoke—they only prolonged the preliminary gaze suggesting that each wished to give the other a chance. They were visibly shy; they stood there letting me take them in—which, as I afterwards perceived, was the most practical thing they could have done. In this way their embarrassment served their cause. I had seen people painfully reluctant to mention that they desired anything so gross as to be represented on canvas; but the scruples of my new friends appeared almost insurmountable. Yet the gentleman might have said "I should like a portrait of my wife," and the lady might have said "I should like a portrait of my husband." Perhaps they weren't husband and wife—this naturally would make the matter more delicate. Perhaps they wished to be done together—in which case they ought to have brought a third person to break the news.

"We come from Mr. Rivet," the lady finally said with a dim smile that had the effect of a moist sponge passed over a "sunk" piece of painting, as well as of a vague allusion to vanished beauty. She was as tall and straight, in her degree, as her companion, and with ten years less to carry. She looked as sad as a woman could look whose face was not charged with expression; that is her tinted oval mask showed waste as an exposed surface shows friction. The hand of time had played over her freely, but to an effect of elimination. She was slim and stiff, and so well-dressed, in dark blue cloth, with lappets and pockets and buttons, that it was clear she employed the same tailor as her husband. The couple had an indefinable air of prosperous thrift—they evidently got a good deal of luxury for their money. If I was to be one of their luxuries it would behove me to consider my terms.

"Ah Claude Rivet recommended me?" I echoed; and I added that it was very kind of him, though I could reflect that, as he only painted landscape, this wasn't a sacrifice.

The lady looked very hard at the gentleman, and the gentleman looked round the room. Then staring at the floor a moment and stroking his moustache, he rested his pleasant eyes on me with the remark: "He said you were the right one."

"I try to be, when people want to sit."

"Yes, we should like to," said the lady anxiously.

"Do you mean together?"

My visitors exchanged a glance. "If you could do anything with *me* I suppose it would be double," the gentleman stammered.

"Oh yes, there's naturally a higher charge for two figures than for one."

"We should like to make it pay," the husband confessed.

"That's very good of you," I returned, appreciating so unwonted a sympathy—for I supposed he meant pay the artist.

A sense of strangeness seemed to dawn on the lady. "We mean for the illustrations—Mr. Rivet said you might put one in."

"Put in—an illustration?" I was equally confused.

"Sketch her off, you know," said the gentleman, colouring.

It was only then that I understood the service Claude Rivet had rendered me; he had told them how I worked in black-and-white, for magazines, for story-books, for sketches of contemporary life, and consequently had copious employment for models. These things were true, but it was not less true—I may confess it now; whether because the aspiration was to lead to everything or to nothing I leave the reader to guess—that I couldn't get the honours, to say nothing of the emoluments, of a great painter of portraits out of my head. My "illustrations" were my pot-boilers; I looked to a different branch of art—far and away the most interesting it had always seemed to me—to perpetuate my fame. There was no shame in looking to it also to make my fortune; but that fortune was by so much further from being made from the moment my visitors wished to be "done" for nothing. I was disappointed; for in the pictorial sense I had immediately *seen* them. I had seized their type—I had already settled what I would do with it. Something that wouldn't absolutely have pleased them, I afterwards reflected.

"Ah you're—you're—a—?" I began as soon as I had mastered my surprise. I couldn't bring out the dingy word "models": it seemed so little to fit the case.

"We haven't had much practice," said the lady.

"We've got to *do* something, and we've thought that an artist in your line might perhaps make something of us," her husband threw off. He further mentioned that they didn't know many artists and that they had gone first, on the off-chance—he painted views of course, but sometimes put in figures; perhaps I remembered—to Mr. Rivet, whom they had met a few years before at a place in Norfolk where he was sketching.

"We used to sketch a little ourselves," the lady hinted.

"It's very awkward, but we absolutely *must* do something," her husband went on.

"Of course we're not so *very* young," she admitted with a wan smile.

With the remark that I might as well know something more about them the husband had handed me a card extracted from a neat new pocket-book—their appurtenances were all of the freshest—and inscribed with the words "Major Monarch." Impressive as these words were they didn't carry my knowledge much further; but my visitor presently added: "I've left the army and we've had the misfortune to lose our money. In fact our means are dreadfully small."

"It's awfully trying—a regular strain," said Mrs. Monarch.

They evidently wished to be discreet—to take care not to swagger because they were gentlefolk. I felt them willing to recognise this as something of a drawback, at the same time that I guessed at an underlying sense—their consolation in adversity—that they *had* their points. They certainly had; but these advantages struck me as preponderantly social; such for instance as would help to make a drawing-room look well. However, a drawing-room was always, or ought to be, a picture.

In consequence of his wife's allusion to their age Major Monarch observed: "Naturally it's more for the figure that we thought of going in. We can still hold ourselves up." On the instant I saw that the figure was indeed their strong point. His "naturally" didn't sound vain, but it lighted up the question. "*She* has the best one," he continued, nodding at his wife with a pleasant after-dinner absence of circumlocution. I could only reply, as if we were in fact sitting over our wine, that this didn't prevent his own from being very good; which led him in turn to make answer: "We thought that if you ever have to do people like us we might be something like it. *She* particularly—for a lady in a book, you know."

I was so amused by them that, to get more of it, I did my best to take their point of view; and though it was an embarrassment to find myself appraising physically, as if they were animals on hire or useful blacks, a pair whom I should have expected to meet only in one of the relations in which criticism is tacit, I looked at Mrs. Monarch judicially enough to be able to exclaim after a moment with conviction: "Oh yes, a lady in a book!" She was singularly like a bad illustration.

"We'll stand up, if you like," said the Major; and he raised himself before me with a really grand air.

I could take his measure at a glance—he was six feet two and a perfect gentleman. It would have paid any club in process of formation and in want of a stamp to engage him at a salary to stand in the principal window. What struck me at once was that in coming to me they had rather missed their vocation; they could surely have been turned to better account for advertising purposes. I couldn't of course see the thing in detail, but I could see them make somebody's fortune—I don't mean their own. There was something in them for a waistcoat-maker, an hotel-keeper or a soap-vendor. I could imagine "We always use it" pinned on their bosoms with the greatest effect; I had a vision of the brilliancy with which they would launch a table d'hôte.

Mrs. Monarch sat still, not from pride but from shyness, and presently her husband said to her: "Get up, my dear, and show how smart you are." She obeyed, but she had no need to get up to show it.

She walked to the end of the studio and then came back blushing, her fluttered eyes on the partner of her appeal. I was reminded of an incident I had accidentally had a glimpse of in Paris—being with a friend there, a dramatist about to produce a play, when an actress came to him to ask to be entrusted with a part. She went through her paces before him, walked up and down as Mrs. Monarch was doing. Mrs. Monarch did it quite as well, but I abstained from applauding. It was very odd to see such people apply for such poor pay. She looked as if she had ten thousand a year. Her husband had used the word that described her: she was in the London current jargon essentially and typically "smart." Her figure was, in the same order of ideas, conspicuously and irreproachably "good." For a woman of her age her waist was surprisingly small; her elbow moreover had the orthodox crook. She held her head at the conventional angle, but why did she come to *me?* She ought to have tried on jackets at a big shop. I feared my visitors were not only destitute but "artistic"—which would be a great complication. When she sat down again I thanked her, observing that what a draughtsman most valued in his model was the faculty of keeping quiet.

"Oh *she* can keep quiet," said Major Monarch. Then he added jocosely: "I've always kept her quiet."

"I'm not a nasty fidget, am I?" It was going to wring tears from me, I felt, the way she hid her head, ostrich-like, in the other broad bosom.

The owner of this expanse addressed his answer to me. "Perhaps it isn't out of place to mention—because we ought to be quite business-like, oughtn't we?—that when I married her she was known as the Beautiful Statue."

"Oh dear!" said Mrs. Monarch ruefully.

"Of course I should want a certain amount of expression," I rejoined.

"Of *course!*"—and I had never heard such unanimity.

"And then I suppose you know that you'll get awfully tired."

"Oh we *never* get tired!" they eagerly cried.

"Have you had any kind of practice?"

They hesitated—they looked at each other. "We've been photographed—*immensely*," said Mrs. Monarch.

"She means the fellows have asked us themselves," added the Major.

"I see—because you're so good-looking."

"I don't know what they thought, but they were always after us."

"We always got our photographs for nothing," smiled Mrs. Monarch.

"We might have brought some, my dear," her husband remarked.

"I'm not sure we have any left. We've given quantities away," she explained to me.

"With our autographs and that sort of thing," said the Major.

"Are they to be got in the shops?" I enquired as a harmless pleasantry.

"Oh yes, *hers*—they used to be."

"Not now," said Mrs. Monarch with her eyes on the floor.

❋ 2 ❋

I COULD fancy the "sort of thing" they put on the presentation copies of their photographs, and I was sure they wrote a beautiful hand. It was odd how quickly I was sure of everything that concerned them. If they were now so poor as to have to earn shillings and pence they could never have had much of a margin. Their good looks had been their capital, and they had good-humouredly made the most of the career that this resource marked out for them. It was in their faces, the blankness, the deep intellectual repose of the twenty years of country-house visiting that had given them pleasant intonations. I could see the sunny drawing-rooms, sprinkled with periodicals she didn't read, in which Mrs. Monarch had continuously sat; I could see the wet shrubberies in which she had walked, equipped to admiration for either exercise. I could see the rich covers the Major had helped to shoot and the wonderful garments in which, late at night, he repaired to the smoking-room to talk about them. I could imagine their leggings and waterproofs, their knowing tweeds and rugs, their rolls of sticks and cases of tackle and neat umbrellas; and I could evoke the exact appearance of their servants and the compact variety of their luggage on the platforms of country stations.

They gave small tips, but they were liked; they didn't do anything themselves, but they were welcome. They looked so well everywhere; they gratified the general relish for stature, complexion and "form." They knew it without fatuity or vulgarity, and they respected themselves in consequence. They weren't superficial; they were thorough and kept themselves up—it had been their line. People with such a taste for activity had to have some line. I could feel how even in a dull house they could have been counted on for the joy of life. At present something had happened—it didn't matter what, their little income had grown less, it had grown least—and they had to do something for pocket-money. Their friends could like them, I made out, without liking to support them. There was something about them that represented credit—their clothes, their manners, their type; but if credit is a large empty pocket in which an occasional chink reverberates, the chink at least must be audible. What they wanted of me was to help to make it so. Fortunately they had no children—I soon divined that. They would also perhaps wish our relations to be kept secret: this was why it was "for the figure"—the reproduction of the face would betray them.

I liked them—I felt, quite as their friends must have done—they were so simple; and I had no objection to them if they would suit. But somehow with all their perfections I didn't easily believe in them. After all they were amateurs, and the ruling passion of my life was the detestation of the amateur. Combined with this was another perversity—an innate preference for the represented subject over the real one: the defect of the real one was so apt to be a lack of representation. I liked things that appeared; then one was sure. Whether they *were* or not was a subordinate and almost always a profitless question. There were other considerations, the first of which was that I already had two or three recruits in use, notably a young person with big feet, in alpaca, from Kilburn, who for a couple of years had come to me regularly for my illustrations and with whom I was still—perhaps ignobly—satisfied. I frankly explained to my visitors how the case stood, but they had taken more precautions than I supposed. They had reasoned out their opportunity, for Claude Rivet had told them of the projected *édition de luxe* of one of the writers of our day—the rarest of the novelists—who, long neglected by the multitudinous vulgar and dearly prized by the attentive (need I mention Philip Vincent?), had had the happy fortune of seeing, late in life, the dawn and then the full light of a higher criticism; an estimate in which on the part of the public there was something really of expiation. The edition preparing, planned by a publisher of taste, was practically an act of high reparation; the wood-cuts with which it was to be enriched were the homage of English art to one of the most independent representatives of English letters. Major and Mrs. Monarch confessed to me they had hoped I might be able to work *them* into my branch of the enterprise. They knew I was to do the first of the books, "Rutland Ramsay," but I had to make clear to them that my participation in the rest of the affair—this first book was to be a test—must depend on the satisfaction I should give. If this should be limited my employers would drop me with scarce common forms. It was therefore a crisis for me, and naturally I was making special preparations, looking about for new people, should they be necessary, and securing the best types. I admitted however that I should like to settle down to two or three good models who would do for everything.

"Should we have often to—a—put on special clothes?" Mrs. Monarch timidly demanded.

"Dear yes—that's half the business."

"And should we be expected to supply our own costumes?"

"Oh no; I've got a lot of things. A painter's models put on—or put off—anything he likes."

"And you mean—a—the same?"

"The same?"

Mrs. Monarch looked at her husband again.

"Oh she was just wondering," he explained, "if the costumes are in *general* use." I had to confess that they were, and I mentioned further that some of them—I had a lot of genuine greasy last-century things—had served their time, a hundred years ago, on living world-stained men and women; on figures not perhaps so far removed, in that vanished world, from *their* type, the Monarchs', *quoi!* of a breeched and bewigged age. "We'll put on anything that *fits*," said the Major.

"Oh I arrange that—they fit in the pictures."

"I'm afraid I should do better for the modern books. I'd come as you like," said Mrs. Monarch.

"She has got a lot of clothes at home: they might do for contemporary life," her husband continued.

"Oh I can fancy scenes in which you'd be quite natural." And indeed I could see the slipshod rearrangements of stale properties—the stories I tried to produce pictures for without the exasperation of reading them—whose sandy tracts the good lady might help to people. But I had to return to the fact that for this sort of work—the daily mechanical grind—I was already equipped: the people I was working with were fully adequate.

"We only thought we might be more like *some* characters," said Mrs. Monarch mildly, getting up.

Her husband also rose; he stood looking at me with a dim wistfulness that was touching in so fine a man. "Wouldn't it be rather a pull sometimes to have—a—to have—?" He hung fire; he wanted me to help him by phrasing what he meant. But I couldn't—I didn't know. So he brought it out awkwardly: "The *real* thing; a gentleman, you know, or a lady." I was quite ready to give a general assent—I admitted that there was a great deal in that. This encouraged Major Monarch to say, following up his appeal with an unacted gulp: "It's awfully hard—we've tried everything." The gulp was communicative; it proved too much for his wife. Before I knew it Mrs. Monarch had dropped again upon a divan and burst into tears. Her husband sat down beside her, holding one of her hands; whereupon she quickly dried her eyes with the other, while I felt embarrassed as she looked up at me. "There isn't a confounded job I haven't applied for—waited for—prayed for. You can fancy we'd be pretty bad first. Secretaryships and that sort of thing? You might as well ask for a peerage. I'd be *anything*—I'm strong; a messenger or a coal-heaver. I'd put on a gold-laced cap and open carriage-doors in front of the haberdasher's; I'd hang about a station to carry portmanteaux; I'd be a postman. But they won't *look* at you; there are thousands as good as yourself already on the ground. *Gentlemen*, poor beggars, who've drunk their wine, who've kept their hunters!"

I was as reassuring as I knew how to be, and my visitors were presently on their feet again while, for the experiment, we agreed on an hour. We were discussing it when the door opened and Miss Churm came in with a wet umbrella. Miss Churm had to take the omnibus to Maida Vale and then walk half a mile. She looked a trifle blowsy and slightly splashed. I scarcely ever saw her come in without thinking afresh how odd it was that, being so little in herself, she should yet be so much in others. She was a meagre little Miss Churm, but was such an ample heroine of romance. She was only a freckled cockney, but she could represent everything, from a fine lady to a shepherdess; she had the faculty as she might have had a fine voice or long hair. She couldn't spell and she loved beer, but she had two or three "points," and practice, and a knack, and mother-wit, and a whimsical sensibility, and a love of the theatre, and seven sisters, and not an ounce of respect, especially for the "h." The first thing my visitors saw was that her umbrella was wet, and in their spotless perfection they visibly winced at it. The rain had come on since their arrival.

"I'm all in a soak; there *was* a mess of people in the 'bus. I wish you lived near a styion," said Miss Churm. I requested her to get ready as quickly as possible, and she passed into the room in which she always changed her dress. But before going out she asked me what she was to get into this time.

"It's the Russian princess, don't you know?" I answered; "the one with the 'golden eyes,' in black velvet, for the long thing in the *Cheapside*."

"Golden eyes? I *say!*" cried Miss Churm, while my companions watched her with intensity as she withdrew. She always arranged herself, when she was late, before I could turn round; and I kept my visitors a little on purpose, so that they might get an idea, from seeing her, what would be expected of themselves. I mentioned that she was quite my notion of an excellent model—she was really very clever.

"Do you think she looks like a Russian princess?" Major Monarch asked with lurking alarm.

"When I make her, yes."

"Oh if you have to *make* her—!" he reasoned, not without point.

"That's the most you can ask. There are so many who are not makeable."

"Well now, *here's* a lady"—and with a persuasive smile he passed his arm into his wife's—"who's already made!"

"Oh I'm not a Russian princess," Mrs. Monarch protested a little coldly. I could see she had known some and didn't like them. There at once was a complication of a kind I never had to fear with Miss Churm.

This young lady came back in black velvet—the gown was rather rusty and very low on her lean shoulders—and with a Japanese fan in her red hands. I reminded her that in the scene I was doing she had to look over some one's head. "I forget whose it is; but it doesn't matter. Just look over a head."

"I'd rather look over a stove," said Miss Churm; and she took her station near the fire. She fell into position, settled herself into a tall attitude, gave a certain backward inclination to her head and a certain forward droop to her fan, and looked, at least to my prejudiced sense, distinguished and charming, foreign and dangerous. We left her looking so while I went downstairs with Major and Mrs. Monarch.

"I believe I could come about as near it as that," said Mrs. Monarch.

"Oh you think she's shabby, but you must allow for the alchemy of art."

However, they went off with an evident increase of comfort founded on their demonstrable advantage in being the real thing. I could fancy them shuddering over Miss Churm. She was very droll about them when I went back, for I told her what they wanted.

"Well, if *she* can sit I'll tyke to bookkeeping," said my model.

"She's very ladylike," I replied as an innocent form of aggravation.

"So much the worse for *you*. That means she can't turn round."

"She'll do for the fashionable novels."

"Oh yes, she'll *do* for them!" my model humorously declared. "Ain't they bad enough without her?" I had often sociably denounced them to Miss Churm.

✦ 3 ✦

IT was for the elucidation of a mystery in one of these works that I first tried Mrs. Monarch. Her husband came with her, to be useful if necessary—it was sufficiently clear that as a general thing he would prefer to come with her. At first I wondered if this were for "propriety's" sake—if he were going to be jealous and meddling. The idea was too tiresome, and if it had been confirmed it would speedily have brought our acquaintance to a close. But I soon saw there was nothing in it and that if he accompanied Mrs. Monarch it was—in addition to the chance of being wanted—simply because he had nothing else to do. When they were separate his occupation was gone and they never *had* been separate. I judged rightly that in their awkward situation their close union was their main comfort and that this union had no weak spot. It was a real marriage, an encouragement to the hesitating, a nut for pessimists to crack. Their address was humble—I remember afterwards thinking it had been the only thing about them that was really professional—and I could fancy the lamentable lodgings in which the Major would have been left alone. He could sit there more or less grimly with his wife—he couldn't sit there anyhow without her.

He had too much tact to try and make himself agreeable when he couldn't be useful; so when I was too absorbed in my work to talk he simply sat and waited. But I liked to hear him talk—it made my work, when not interrupting it, less mechanical, less special. To listen to him was to combine the excitement of going out with the economy of staying at home. There was only one hindrance—that I seemed not to know any of the people this brilliant couple had known. I think he wondered extremely, during the term of our intercourse, whom the deuce I *did* know. He hadn't a stray sixpence of an idea to fumble for, so we didn't spin it very fine; we confined ourselves to questions of leather and even of liquor—saddlers and breeches-makers and how to get excellent claret cheap—and matters like "good trains" and the habits of small game. His lore on these last subjects was astonishing—he managed to interweave the station-master with the ornithologist. When he couldn't talk about greater things he could talk cheerfully about smaller, and since I couldn't accompany him into reminiscences of the fashionable world he could lower the conversation without a visible effort to my level.

So earnest a desire to please was touching in a man who could so easily have knocked one down. He looked after the fire and had an opinion on the draught of the stove without my asking him, and I could see that he thought many of my arrangements not half knowing. I remember telling him that if I were only rich I'd offer him a salary to come and teach me how to live. Sometimes he gave a random sigh of which the essence might have been: "Give me even such a bare old barrack as *this,* and I'd do something with it!" When

I wanted to use him he came alone; which was an illustration of the superior courage of women. His wife could bear her solitary second floor, and she was in general more discreet; showing by various small reserves that she was alive to the propriety of keeping our relations markedly professional—not letting them slide into sociability. She wished it to remain clear that she and the Major were employed, not cultivated, and if she approved of me as a superior, who could be kept in his place, she never thought me quite good enough for an equal.

She sat with great intensity, giving the whole of her mind to it, and was capable of remaining for an hour almost as motionless as before a photographer's lens. I could see she had been photographed often, but somehow the very habit that made her good for that purpose unfitted her for mine. At first I was extremely pleased with her ladylike air, and it was a satisfaction, on coming to follow her lines, to see how good they were and how far they could lead the pencil. But after a little skirmishing I began to find her too insurmountably stiff; do what I would with it my drawing looked like a photograph or a copy of a photograph. Her figure had no variety of expression—she herself had no sense of variety. You may say that this was my business and was only a question of placing her. Yet I placed her in every conceivable position and she managed to obliterate their differences. She was always a lady certainly, and into the bargain was always the same lady. She was the real thing, but always the same thing. There were moments when I rather writhed under the serenity of her confidence that she *was* the real thing. All her dealings with me and all her husband's were an implication that this was lucky for *me*. Meanwhile I found myself trying to invent types that approached her own, instead of making her own transform itself —in the clever way that was not impossible for instance to poor Miss Churm. Arrange as I would and take the precautions I would, she always came out, in my pictures, too tall—landing me in the dilemma of having represented a fascinating woman as seven feet high, which (out of respect perhaps to my own very much scantier inches) was far from my idea of such a personage.

The case was worse with the Major—nothing I could do would keep *him* down. so that he became useful only for the representation of brawny giants. I adored variety and range, I cherished human accidents, the illustrative note; I wanted to characterise closely, and the thing in the world I most hated was the danger of being ridden by a type. I had quarrelled with some of my friends about it; I had parted company with them for maintaining that one *had* to be, and that if the type was beautiful— witness Raphael and Leonardo—the servitude was only a gain. I was neither Leonardo nor Raphael—I might only be a presumptuous young modern searcher; but I held that everything was to be sacrificed sooner than character. When they claimed that the obsessional form could easily *be* character I retorted, perhaps superficially, "Whose?" It couldn't be everybody's —it might end in being nobody's.

After I had drawn Mrs. Monarch a dozen times I felt surer even than before that the value of such a model as Miss Churm resided precisely in the fact that she had no positive stamp, combined of course with the other fact that what she did have was a curious and inexplicable talent for imitation. Her usual appearance was like a curtain which she could draw up at request for a capital performance. This performance was simply suggestive; but it was a word to the wise—it was vivid and pretty. Sometimes even I thought it, though she was plain herself, too insipidly pretty; I made it a reproach to her that the figures drawn from her were monotonously (*bêtement,* as we used to say) graceful. Nothing made her more angry: it was so much her pride to feel she could sit for characters that had nothing in common with each other. She would accuse me at such moments of taking away her "reputytion."

It suffered a certain shrinkage, this queer quantity, from the repeated visits of my new friends. Miss Churm was greatly in demand, never in want of employment, so I had no scruple in putting her off occasionally, to try them more at my ease. It was certainly amusing at first to do the real thing—it was amusing to do Major Monarch's trousers. They *were* the real thing, even if he did come out colossal. It was amusing to do his wife's back hair—it was so mathematically neat—and the particular "smart" tension of her tight stays. She lent herself especially to positions in which the face was somewhat averted or blurred; she abounded in ladylike back views and *profils perdus.* When she stood erect she took naturally one of the attitudes in which court-painters represent queens and princesses; so that I found myself wondering whether, to draw out this accomplishment, I couldn't get the editor of the *Cheapside* to publish a really royal romance, "A Tale of Buckingham Palace." Sometimes however the

real thing and the make-believe came into contact; by which I mean
that Miss Churm, keeping an appointment or coming to make one
on days when I had much work in hand, encountered her invidious
rivals. The encounter was not on their part, for they noticed her no
more than if she had been the housemaid; not from intentional
loftiness, but simply because as yet, professionally, they didn't know
how to fraternise, as I could imagine they would have liked—or at
least that the Major would. They couldn't talk about the
omnibus—they always walked; and they didn't know what else to
try—she wasn't interested in good trains or cheap claret. Besides,
they must have felt—in the air—that she was amused at them,
secretly derisive of their ever knowing how. She wasn't a person to
conceal the limits of her faith if she had had a chance to show them.
On the other hand Mrs. Monarch didn't think her tidy; for why else
did she take pains to say to me—it was going out of the way, for Mrs.
Monarch—that she didn't like dirty women?

One day when my young lady happened to be present with my
other sitters—she even dropped in, when it was convenient, for a
chat—I asked her to be so good as to lend a hand in getting tea, a
service with which she was familiar and which was one of a class that,
living as I did in a small way, with slender domestic resources, I often
appealed to my models to render. They liked to lay hands on my
property, to break the sitting, and sometimes the china—it made
them feel Bohemian. The next time I saw Miss Churm after this
incident she surprised me greatly by making a scene about it—she
accused me of having wished to humiliate her. She hadn't resented
the outrage at the time, but had seemed obliging and amused,
enjoying the comedy of asking Mrs. Monarch, who sat vague and
silent, whether she would have cream and sugar, and putting an
exaggerated simper into the question. She had tried intonations—as
if she too wished to pass for the real thing—till I was afraid my other
visitors would take offence.

Oh they were determined not to do this, and their touching
patience was the measure of their great need. They would sit by the
hour, uncomplaining, till I was ready to use them; they would come
back on the chance of being wanted and would walk away cheerfully
if it failed. I used to go to the door with them to see in what
magnificent order they retreated. I tried to find other employment
for them—I introduced them to several artists. But they didn't

"take," for reasons I could appreciate, and I became rather anxiously aware that after such disappointments they fell back upon me with a heavier weight. They did me the honour to think me most *their* form. They weren't romantic enough for the painters, and in those days there were few serious workers in black-and-white. Besides, they had an eye to the great job I had mentioned to them—they had secretly set their hearts on supplying the right essence for my pictorial vindication of our fine novelist. They knew that for this undertaking I should want no costume-effects, none of the frippery of past ages—that it was a case in which everything would be contemporary and satirical and presumably genteel. If I could work them into it their future would be assured, for the labour would of course be long and the occupation steady.

One day Mrs. Monarch came without her husband—she explained his absence by his having had to go to the City. While she sat there in her usual relaxed majesty there came at the door a knock which I immediately recognised as the subdued appeal of a model out of work. It was followed by the entrance of a young man whom I at once saw to be a foreigner and who proved in fact an Italian acquainted with no English word but my name, which he uttered in a way that made it seem to include all others. I hadn't then visited his country, nor was I proficient in his tongue; but as he was not so meanly constituted—what Italian is?—as to depend only on that member for expression he conveyed to me, in familiar but graceful mimicry, that he was in search of exactly the employment in which the lady before me was engaged. I was not struck with him at first, and while I continued to draw I dropped few signs of interest or encouragement. He stood his ground however—not importunately, but with a dumb dog-like fidelity in his eyes that amounted to innocent impudence, the manner of a devoted servant—he might have been in the house for years—unjustly suspected. Suddenly it struck me that this very attitude and expression made a picture; whereupon I told him to sit down and wait till I should be free. There was another picture in the way he obeyed me, and I observed as I worked that there were others still in the way he looked wonderingly, with his head thrown back, about the high studio. He might have been crossing himself in Saint Peter's. Before I finished I said to myself "The fellow's a bankrupt orange-monger, but a treasure."

When Mrs. Monarch withdrew he passed across the room like a

flash to open the door for her, standing there with the rapt pure gaze of the young Dante spellbound by the young Beatrice. As I never insisted, in such situations, on the blankness of the British domestic, I reflected that he had the making of a servant—and I needed one, but couldn't pay him to be only that—as well as of a model; in short I resolved to adopt my bright adventurer if he would agree to officiate in the double capacity. He jumped at my offer, and in the event my rashness—for I had really known nothing about him—wasn't brought home to me. He proved a sympathetic though a desultory ministrant, and had in a wonderful degree the *sentiment de la pose*. It was uncultivated, instinctive, a part of the happy instinct that had guided him to my door and helped him to spell out my name on the card nailed to it. He had had no other introduction to me than a guess, from the shape of my high north window, seen outside, that my place was a studio and that as a studio it would contain an artist. He had wandered to England in search of fortune, like other itinerants, and had embarked, with a partner and a small green hand-cart, on the sale of penny ices. The ices had melted away and the partner had dissolved in their train. My young man wore tight yellow trousers with reddish stripes and his name was Oronte. He was sallow but fair, and when I put him into some old clothes of my own he looked like an Englishman. He was as good as Miss Churm, who could look, when requested, like an Italian.

✳ 4 ✳

I THOUGHT Mrs. Monarch's face slightly convulsed when, on her coming back with her husband, she found Oronte installed. It was strange to have to recognise in a scrap of a lazzarone a competitor to her magnificent Major. It was she who scented danger first, for the Major was anecdotically unconscious. But Oronte gave us tea, with a hundred eager confusions—he had never been concerned in so queer a process—and I think she thought better of me for having at last an "establishment." They saw a couple of drawings that I had made of the establishment, and Mrs. Monarch hinted that it never would have struck her he had sat for them. "Now the drawings you make from *us*, they look exactly like us," she reminded me, smiling in triumph; and I recognised that this was indeed just their defect. When I drew the Monarchs I couldn't anyhow get away from them—get into the character I wanted to represent; and I hadn't the least desire my model should be discoverable in my picture. Miss Churm never was, and Mrs. Monarch thought I hid her, very properly, because she was vulgar; whereas if she was lost it was only as the dead who go to heaven are lost—in the gain of an angel the more.

By this time I had got a certain start with "Rutland Ramsay," the first novel in the great projected series; that is I had produced a dozen drawings, several with the help of the Major and his wife, and I had sent them in for approval. My understanding with the publishers, as I have already hinted, had been that I was to be left to do my work, in this particular case, as I liked, with the whole book committed to me; but my connexion with the rest of the series was only contingent. There were moments when, frankly, it *was* a comfort to have the real thing under one's hand; for there were characters in "Rutland Ramsay" that were very much like it. There were people presumably as erect as the Major and women of as good a fashion as Mrs. Monarch. There was a great deal of country-house life—treated, it is true, in a fine fanciful ironical generalised way—and there was a considerable implication of knickerbockers and kilts. There were certain things I had to settle at the outset; such things for instance as the exact appearance of the hero and the particular bloom and figure of the heroine. The author of course gave me a lead, but there was a margin for interpretation. I took the Monarchs into my confidence, I told them frankly what I was about, I mentioned my embarrassments and alternatives. "Oh take *him!*" Mrs. Monarch murmured sweetly, looking at her husband; and "What could you want better than my wife?" the Major enquired with the comfortable candour that now prevailed between us.

I wasn't obliged to answer these remarks—I was only obliged to place my sitters. I wasn't easy in mind, and I postponed a little timidly perhaps the solving of my question. The book was a large canvas, the other figures were numerous, and I worked off at first some of the episodes in which the hero and the heroine were not concerned. When once I had set *them* up I should have to stick to them—I couldn't make my young man seven feet high in one place and five feet nine in another. I inclined on the whole to the latter measurement, though the Major more than once reminded me that *he* looked about as young as any one. It was indeed quite possible to arrange him, for the figure, so that it would have been difficult to detect his age. After the spontaneous Oronte had been with me a month, and after I had given him to understand several times over that his native exuberance would presently constitute an insurmountable barrier to our further intercourse, I waked to a sense of his heroic capacity. He was only five feet seven, but the remaining inches were latent. I tried him almost secretly at first, for I was really rather afraid of the judgement my other models would pass on such a choice. If they regarded Miss Churm as little better than a snare what would they think of the representation by a person so little the real thing as an Italian street-vendor of a protagonist formed by a public school?

If I went a little in fear of them it wasn't because they bullied me, because they had got an oppressive foothold, but because in their really pathetic decorum and mysteriously permanent newness they counted on me so intensely. I was therefore very glad when Jack Hawley came home: he was always of such good counsel. He painted badly himself, but there was no one like him for putting his finger on the place. He had been absent from England for a year; he had been somewhere—I don't remember where—to get a fresh eye. I was in a good deal of dread of any such organ, but we were old friends; he had been away for months and a sense of emptiness was creeping into my life. I hadn't dodged a missile for a year.

He came back with a fresh eye, but with the same old black velvet blouse, and the first evening he spent in my studio we smoked cigarettes till the small hours. He had done no work himself, he had only got the eye; so the field was clear for the production of my little things. He wanted to see what I had produced for the *Cheapside,* but he was disappointed in the exhibition. That at least seemed the meaning of two or three comprehensive groans which, as he lounged on my big divan, his leg folded under him, looking at my latest drawings, issued from his lips with the smoke of the cigarette.

"What's the matter with you?" I asked.

"What's the matter with *you?*"

"Nothing save that I'm mystified."

"You are indeed. You're quite off the hinge. What's the meaning of this new fad?" And he tossed me, with visible irreverence, a drawing in which I happened to have depicted both my elegant models. I asked if he didn't think it good, and he replied that it struck him as execrable, given the sort of thing I had always represented myself to him as wishing to arrive at; but I let that pass—I was so anxious to see exactly what he meant. The two figures in the picture looked colossal, but I supposed this was *not* what he meant, inasmuch as, for aught he knew to the contrary, I might have been trying for some such effect. I maintained that I was working exactly in the same way as when he last had done me the honour to tell me I might do something some day. "Well, there's a screw loose somewhere," he answered; "wait a bit and I'll discover it." I depended upon him to do so: where else was the fresh eye? But he produced at last nothing more luminous than "I don't know—I don't like your types." This was lame for a critic who had never consented to discuss with me anything but the question of execution, the direction of strokes and the mystery of values.

"In the drawings you've been looking at I think my types are very handsome."

"Oh they won't do!"

"I've been working with new models."

"I see you have. *They* won't do."

"Are you very sure of that?"

"Absolutely—they're stupid."

"You mean *I* am—for I ought to get round that."

"You *can't*—with such people. Who are they?"

I told him, so far as was necessary, and he concluded heartlessly: "*Ce sont des gens qu'il faut mettre à la porte.*"

"You've never seen them; they're awfully good"—I flew to their defence.

"Not seen them? Why all this recent work of yours drops to pieces with them. It's all I want to see of them."

"No one else has said anything against it—the *Cheapside* people are pleased."

"Every one else is an ass, and the *Cheapside* people the biggest asses of all. Come, don't pretend at this time of day to have pretty illusions about the public, especially about publishers and editors. It's not for *such* animals you work—it's for those who know, *coloro che sanno;* so keep straight for *me* if you can't keep straight for yourself. There was a certain sort of thing you used to try for—and a very good thing it was. But this twaddle isn't *in* it." When I talked

with Hawley later about "Rutland Ramsay" and its possible succes-
sors he declared that I must get back into my boat again or I should
go to the bottom. His voice in short was the voice of warning.

I noted the warning, but I didn't turn my friends out of doors.
They bored me a good deal; but the very fact that they bored me
admonished me not to sacrifice them—if there was anything to be
done with them—simply to irritation. As I looked back at this
phase they seem to me to have pervaded my life not a little. I
have a vision of them as most of the time in my studio, seated
against the wall on an old velvet bench to be out of the way, and
resembling the while a pair of patient courtiers in a royal ante-
chamber. I'm convinced that during the coldest weeks of the winter
they held their ground because it saved them fire. Their newness was
losing its gloss, and it was impossible not to feel them objects of
charity. Whenever Miss Churm arrived they went away, and after I
was fairly launched in "Rutland Ramsay" Miss Churm arrived
pretty often. They managed to express to me tacitly that they supposed I wanted her for the low life of the book, and I let them
suppose it, since they had attempted to study the work—it was lying
about the studio—without discovering that it dealt only with the
highest circles. They had dipped into the most brilliant of our
novelists without deciphering many passages. I still took an hour
from them, now and again, in spite of Jack Hawley's warning: it
would be time enough to dismiss them, if dismissal should be
necessary, when the rigour of the season was over. Hawley had
made their acquaintance—he had met them at my fireside—and
thought them a ridiculous pair. Learning that he was a painter they
tried to approach him, to show him too that they were the real thing;
but he looked at them, across the big room, as if they were miles
away: they were a compendium of everything he most objected to in
the social system of his country. Such people as that, all convention
and patent-leather, with ejaculations that stopped conversation, had
no business in a studio. A studio was a place to learn to see, and how
could you see through a pair of feather-beds?

The main inconvenience I suffered at their hands was that at first I
was shy of letting it break upon them that my artful little servant
had begun to sit to me for "Rutland Ramsay." They knew I had
been odd enough—they were prepared by this time to allow oddity
to artists—to pick a foreign vagabond out of the streets when I might

have had a person with whiskers and credentials; but it was some time before they learned how high I rated his accomplishments. They found him in an attitude more than once, but they never doubted I was doing him as an organ-grinder. There were several things they never guessed, and one of them was that for a striking scene in the novel, in which a footman briefly figured, it occurred to me to make use of Major Monarch as the menial. I kept putting this off, I didn't like to ask him to don the livery—besides the difficulty of finding a livery to fit him. At last, one day late in the winter, when I was at work on the despised Oronte, who caught one's idea on the wing, and was in the glow of feeling myself go very straight, they came in, the Major and his wife, with their society laugh about nothing (there was less and less to laugh at) ; came in like country-callers—they always reminded me of that—who have walked across the park after church and are presently persuaded to stay to luncheon. Luncheon was over, but they could stay to tea—I knew they wanted it. The fit was on me, however, and I couldn't let my ardour cool and my work wait, with the fading daylight, while my model prepared it. So I asked Mrs. Monarch if she would mind laying it out—a request which for an instant brought all the blood to her face. Her eyes were on her husband's for a second, and some mute telegraphy passed between them. Their folly was over the next instant; his cheerful shrewdness put an end to it. So far from pitying their wounded pride, I must add, I was moved to give it as complete a lesson as I could. They bustled about together and got out the cups and saucers and made the kettle boil. I know they felt as if they were waiting on my servant, and when the tea was prepared I said: "He'll have a cup, please—he's tired." Mrs. Monarch brought him one where he stood, and he took it from her as if he had been a gentleman at a party squeezing a crush-hat with an elbow.

Then it came over me that she had made a great effort for me—made it with a kind of nobleness—and that I owed her a compensation. Each time I saw her after this I wondered what the compensation could be. I couldn't go on doing the wrong thing to oblige them. Oh it *was* the wrong thing, the stamp of the work for which they sat—Hawley was not the only person to say it now. I sent in a large number of the drawings I had made for "Rutland Ramsey," and I received a warning that was more to the point than Hawley's. The artistic adviser of the house for which I was working was of opinion that many of my illustrations were not what had been looked for. Most of these illustrations were the subjects in which the Monarchs had figured. Without going into the question of what *had* been looked for, I had to face the fact that at this rate I shouldn't get the other books to do. I hurled myself in despair on Miss Churm—I put her through all her paces. I not only adopted Oronte publicly as my hero, but one morning when the Major looked in to see if I didn't require him to finish a *Cheapside* figure for which he had begun to sit the week before, I told him I had changed my mind—I'd do the drawing from my man. At this my visitor turned pale and stood looking at me. "Is *he* your idea of an English gentleman?" he asked.

I was disappointed, I was nervous, I wanted to get on with my work; so I replied with irritation: "Oh my dear Major—I can't be ruined for *you!*"

It was a horrid speech, but he stood another moment—after which, without a word, he quitted the studio. I drew a long breath, for I said to myself that I shouldn't see him again. I hadn't told him definitely that I was in danger of having my work rejected, but I was vexed at his not having felt the catastrophe in the air, read with me the moral of our fruitless collaboration, the lesson that in the deceptive atmosphere of art even the highest respectability may fail of being plastic.

I didn't owe my friends money, but I did see them again. They reappeared together three days later, and, given all the other facts, there was something tragic in that one. It was a clear proof they could find nothing else in life to do. They had threshed the matter out in a dismal conference—they had digested the bad news that they were not in for the series. If they weren't useful to me even for the *Cheapside* their function seemed difficult to determine, and I could only judge at first that they had come, forgivingly, decorously, to take a last leave. This made me rejoice in secret that I had little leisure for a scene; for I had placed both my other models in position together and I was pegging away at a drawing from which I hoped to derive glory. It had been suggested by the passage in which Rutland Ramsay, drawing up a chair to Artemisia's piano-stool, says extraordinary things to her while she ostensibly fingers out a difficult piece of music. I had done Miss Churm at the piano before—it was an attitude in which she knew how to take on an absolutely poetic grace. I wished the two figures to "compose" together with intensity, and my little Italian had entered perfectly into my conception. The pair were vividly before me, the piano had been pulled out; it was a charming show of blended youth and murmured love, which I had only to catch and keep. My visitors stood and looked at it, and I was friendly to them over my shoulder.

They made no response, but I was used to silent company and went on with my work, only a little disconcerted—even though exhilarated by the sense that *this* was at least the ideal thing—at not having got rid of them after all. Presently I heard Mrs. Monarch's sweet voice beside or rather above me: "I wish her hair were a little better done." I looked up and she was staring with a strange fixedness at Miss Churm, whose back was turned to her. "Do you mind my just touching it?" she went on—a question which made me spring up for an instant as with the instinctive fear that she might do the young lady a harm. But she quieted me with a glance I shall never forget—I confess I should like to have been able to paint *that*—and went for a moment to my model. She spoke to her softly, laying a hand on her shoulder and bending over her; and as the girl, understanding, gratefully assented, she disposed her rough curls, with a few quick passes, in such a way as to make Miss Churm's head twice as charming. It was one of the most heroic personal services I've ever seen rendered. Then Mrs. Monarch turned away with a low sigh and, looking about her as if for something to do, stooped to the floor with a noble humility and picked up a dirty rag that had dropped out of my paint-box.

The Major meanwhile had also been looking for something to do, and, wandering to the other end of the studio, saw before him my breakfast-things neglected, unremoved. "I say, can't I be useful *here?*" he called out to me with an irrepressible quaver. I assented with a laugh that I fear was awkward, and for the next ten minutes, while I worked, I heard the light clatter of china and the tinkle of spoons and glass. Mrs. Monarch assisted her husband—they washed up my crockery, they put it away. They wandered off into my little scullery, and I afterwards found that they had cleaned my knives and that my slender stock of plate had an unprecedented surface. When it came over me, the latent eloquence of what they were doing, I confess that my drawing was blurred for a moment—the picture swam. They had accepted their failure, but they couldn't accept their fate. They had bowed their heads in bewilderment to the perverse and cruel law in virtue of which the real thing could be so much less precious than the unreal; but they didn't want to starve. If my servants were my models, then my models might be my servants. They would reverse the parts—the others would sit for the ladies and gentlemen and *they* would do the work. They would still be in the studio—it was an intense dumb appeal to me not to turn them out. "Take us on," they wanted to say—"we'll do *anything*."

My pencil dropped from my hand; my sitting was spoiled and I got rid of my sitters, who were also evidently rather mystified and awestruck. Then, alone with the Major and his wife I had a most uncomfortable moment. He put their prayer into a single sentence: "I say, you know—just let *us* do for you, can't you?" I couldn't—it was dreadful to see them emptying my slops; but I pretended I could, to oblige them, for about a week. Then I gave them a sum of money to go away, and I never saw them again. I obtained the remaining books, but my friend Hawley repeats that Major and Mrs. Monarch did me a permanent harm, got me into false ways. If it be true I'm content to have paid the price—for the memory.

The Two Faces

1

THE servant, who, in spite of his sealed stamped look, appeared to have his reasons, stood there for instruction in a manner not quite usual after announcing the name. Mrs. Grantham, however, took it up—"Lord Gwyther?"—with a quick surprise that for an instant justified him even to the small scintilla in the glance she gave her companion, which might have had exactly the sense of the butler's hesitation. This companion, a shortish fairish youngish man, clean-shaven and keen-eyed, had, with a promptitude that would have struck an observer—which the butler indeed was—sprung to his feet and moved to the chimney-piece, though his hostess herself meanwhile managed not otherwise to stir. "Well?" she said as for the visitor to advance; which she immediately followed with a sharper "He's not there?"

"Shall I show him up, ma'am?"

"But of course!" The point of his doubt made her at last rise for impatience, and Bates, before leaving the room, might still have caught the achieved irony of her appeal to the gentleman into whose communion with her he had broken. "Why in the world not—? What a way—!" she exclaimed as Sutton felt beside his cheek the passage of her eyes to the glass behind him.

"He wasn't sure you'd see any one."

"I don't see 'any one,' but I see individuals."

"That's just it—and sometimes you don't see them."

"Do you mean ever because of you?" she asked as she touched into place a tendril of hair. "That's just his impertinence, as to which I shall speak to him."

"Don't," said Shirley Sutton. "Never notice anything."

"That's nice advice from you," she laughed, "who notice everything!"

"Ah but I speak of nothing."

She looked at him a moment. "You're still more impertinent than Bates. You'll please not budge," she went on.

"Really? I must sit him out?" he continued as, after a minute, she had not again spoken—only glancing about, while she changed her place, partly for another look at the glass and partly to see if she could improve her seat. What she felt was rather more than, clever and charming though she was, she could hide. "If you're wondering how you seem I can tell you. Awfully cool and easy."

She gave him another stare. She was beautiful and conscious. "And if you're wondering how *you* seem—"

"Oh I'm not!" he laughed from before the fire. "I always perfectly know."

"How you seem," she retorted, "is as if you didn't!"

Once more for a little he watched her. "You're looking lovely for him—extraordinarily lovely, within the marked limits of your range. But that's enough. Don't be clever."

"Then who *will* be?"

"There you are!" he sighed with amusement.

"Do you know him?" she asked as, through the door left open by Bates, they heard steps on the landing.

Sutton had to think an instant, and produced a "No" just as Lord Gwyther was again announced, which gave an unexpectedness to the greeting offered him a moment later by this personage—a young man, stout and smooth and fresh, but not at all shy, who, after the happiest rapid passage with Mrs. Grantham, put out a hand with a straight free "How d' ye do?"

"Mr. Shirley Sutton," Mrs. Grantham explained.

"Oh yes," said her second visitor quite as if he knew; which, as he couldn't have known, had for her first the interest of confirming a perception that his lordship would be—no, not at all, in general, embarrassed, only was now exceptionally and especially agitated. As it is, for that matter, with Sutton's total impression that we are particularly and almost exclusively concerned, it may be further mentioned that he was not less clear as to the really handsome way in which the young man kept himself together and little by little—though with all proper aid indeed—finally found his feet. All sorts of things, for the twenty minutes, occurred to Sutton, though one of them was certainly not that it would, after all, be better he should go. One of them was that their hostess was doing it in perfection—simply, easily, kindly, yet with something the least bit queer in her wonderful eyes; another was that if he had been recognised without the least ground it was through a tension of nerves on the part of his fellow guest that produced inconsequent motions; still another was that, even had departure been indicated, he would positively have felt dissuasion in the rare promise of the scene. This was in especial after Lord Gwyther not only had announced that he was now married, but had mentioned that he wished to bring his wife to Mrs. Grantham for the benefit so certain to be derived. It was the passage immediately produced by that speech that provoked in Sutton the intensity, as it were, of his arrest. He already knew of the marriage as well as Mrs. Grantham herself, and as well also as he knew of some other things; and this gave him doubtless the better measure of what took place before him and the keener consciousness of the quick look that, at a marked moment—though it was not absolutely meant for him any more than for his companion—Mrs. Grantham let him catch.

She smiled, but it had a gravity. "I think, you know, you ought to have told me before."

"Do you mean when I first got engaged? Well, it all took place so far away, and we really told, at home, so few people."

Oh there might have been reasons; but it had not been quite right. "You were married at Stuttgart? That wasn't too far for *my* interest, at least, to reach."

"Awfully kind of you—and of course one knew you *would* be kind. But it wasn't at Stuttgart; it was over there, but quite in the country. We should have managed it in England but that her mother naturally wished to be present, yet wasn't in health to come. So it was really, you see, a sort of little hole-and-corner German affair."

This didn't in the least check Mrs. Grantham's claim, but it started a slight anxiety. "Will she be—a—then German?"

Sutton knew her to know perfectly what Lady Gwyther would "be," but he had by this time, while their friend explained, his independent interest. "Oh dear no! My father-in-law has never parted with the proud birthright of a Briton. But his wife, you see, holds an estate in Würtemberg from *her* mother, Countess Kremnitz, on which, with the awful condition of his English property, you know, they've found it for years a tremendous saving to live. So that though Valda was luckily born at home she has practically spent her life over there."

"Oh I see." Then, after a slight pause, "Is Valda her pretty name?" Mrs. Grantham asked.

"Well," said the young man, only wishing, in his candour, it was clear, to be drawn out—"well, she has, in the manner of her mother's people, about thirteen; but that's the one we generally use."

Mrs. Grantham waited but an instant. "Then may *I* generally use it?"

"It would be too charming of you; and nothing would give her—as I assure you nothing would give *me*—greater pleasure." Lord Gwyther quite glowed with the thought.

"Then I think that instead of coming alone you might have brought her to see me."

"It's exactly what," he instantly replied, "I came to ask your leave to do." He explained that for the moment Lady Gwyther was not in town, having as soon as she arrived gone down to Torquay to put in a few days with one of her aunts, also her godmother, to whom she was an object of great interest. She had seen no one yet, and no one—not that *that* mattered—had seen her; she knew nothing whatever of London and was awfully frightened at facing it and at what (however little) might be expected of her. "She wants some one," he said, "some one who knows the whole thing, don't you see? and who's thoroughly kind and clever, as you would be, if I may say so, to take her by the hand." It was at this point and on these words that the eyes of Lord Gwyther's two auditors inevitably and wonderfully met. But there was nothing in the way he kept it up to show he caught the encounter. "She wants, if I may tell you so, a real friend for the great labyrinth; and asking myself what I could do to make things ready for her, and who would be absolutely the best woman in London—"

"You thought naturally of *me?*" Mrs. Grantham had listened with no sign but the faint flash just noted; now, however, she gave him the full light of her expressive face—which immediately brought Shirley Sutton, looking at his watch, once more to his feet.

"She *is* the best woman in London!" He addressed himself with a laugh to the other visitor, but offered his hand in farewell to their hostess.

"You're going?"

"I must," he said without scruple.

"Then we do meet at dinner?"

"I hope so." On which, to take leave, he returned with interest to

Lord Gwyther the friendly clutch he had a short time before received.

✥ 2 ✥

THEY did meet at dinner, and if they were not, as it happened, side by side, they made that up afterwards in the happiest angle of a drawing-room that offered both shine and shadow and that was positively much appreciated, in the circle in which they moved, for the favourable "corners" created by its shrewd mistress. Mrs. Grantham's face, charged with something produced in it by Lord Gwyther's visit, had been with him so constantly for the previous hours that, when she instantly challenged him on his "treatment" of her in the afternoon, he was on the point of naming it as his reason for not having remained with her. Something new had quickly come into her beauty; he couldn't as yet have said what, nor whether on the whole to its advantage or its loss. Till he should see this clearer, at any rate he would say nothing; so that he found with sufficient presence of mind a better excuse. If in short he had in defiance of her particular request left her alone with Lord Gwyther it was simply because the situation had suddenly turned so exciting that he had fairly feared the contagion of it—the temptation of its making him, most improperly, put in his word.

They could now talk of these things at their ease. Other couples, ensconced and scattered, enjoyed the same privilege, and Sutton had more and more the profit, such as it was, of feeling that his interest in Mrs. Grantham had become—what was the luxury of so high a social code—an acknowledged and protected relation. He knew his London well enough to know that he was on the way to be regarded as her main source of consolation for the trick Lord Gwyther had several months before publicly played her. Many persons had not held that, by the high social code in question, his lordship could have "reserved the right" to turn up that way, from one day to another, engaged to be married. For himself London took, with its short cuts and its cheap psychology, an immense deal for granted. To his own sense he was never—could in the nature of things never be—any man's "successor." Just what had constituted the predecessorship of other men was apparently that they had been able to make up their mind. He, worse luck, was at the mercy of her face, and more than ever at the mercy of it now, which meant moreover not that it made a slave of him, but that it made, disconcertingly, a sceptic. It was the absolute perfection of the handsome, but things had a way of coming into it. "I felt," he said, "that you were there together at a point at which you had a right to the ease the absence of a listener would give. I was sure that when you made me promise to stay you hadn't guessed—"

"That he could possibly have come to me on such an extraordinary errand? No, of course I hadn't guessed. Who *would?* But didn't you see how little I was upset by it?"

Sutton demurred. Then with a smile: "I think *he* saw how little."

"You yourself didn't then?"

He again held back, but not, after all, to answer. "He was wonderful, wasn't he?"

"I think he was," she returned after a moment. To which she added: "Why did he pretend that way he knew you?"

"He didn't pretend. He somehow felt on the spot that I was 'in it.' " Sutton had found this afterwards and found it to represent a reality. "It was an effusion of cheer and hope. He was so glad to see me there and to find you happy."

"Happy?"

"Happy. Aren't you?"

"Because of *you?*"

"Well—according to the impression he received as he came in."

"That was sudden then," she asked, "and unexpected?"

Her companion thought. "Prepared in some degree, but confirmed by the sight of us, there together, so awfully jolly and sociable over your fire."

Mrs. Grantham turned this round. "If he knew I was 'happy' then—which, by the way, is none of his business, nor of yours either—why in the world did he come?"

"Well, for good manners, and for his idea," said Sutton.

She took it in, appearing to have no hardness of rancour that could bar discussion. "Do you mean by his idea his proposal that I should grandmother his wife? And if you do is the proposal your reason for calling him wonderful?"

Sutton laughed. "Pray what's yours?" As this was a question, however, that she took her time to answer or not to answer—only appearing interested for a moment in a combination that had formed itself on the other side of the room—he presently went on. "What's *his?*—that would seem to be the point. His, I mean, for having decided on the extraordinary step of throwing his little wife, bound hands and feet, into your arms. Intelligent as you are, and with these three or four hours to have thought it over, I yet don't see how that can fail still to mystify you."

She continued to watch their opposite neighbours. "'Little,' you call her. Is she so very small?"

"Tiny, tiny—she *must* be; as different as possible in every way—of necessity—from you. They always *are* the opposite pole, you know," said Shirley Sutton.

She glanced at him now. "You strike me as of an impudence—!"

"No, no. I only like to make it out with you."

She looked away again and after a little went on. "I'm sure she's charming, and only hope one isn't to gather he's already tired of her."

"Not a bit! He's tremendously in love, and he'll remain so."

"So much the better. And if it's a question," said Mrs. Grantham, "of one's doing what one can for her, he has only, as I told him when you had gone, to give me the chance."

"Good! So he *is* to commit her to you?"

"You use extraordinary expressions, but it's settled that he brings her."

"And you'll really and truly help her?"

"Really and truly?" said Mrs. Grantham with her eyes again on him. "Why not? For what do you take me?"

"Ah isn't that just what I still have the discomfort, every day I live, of asking myself?"

She had made, as she spoke, a movement to rise, which, as if she was tired of his tone, his last words appeared to determine. But, also getting up, he held her, when they were on their feet, long enough to hear the rest of what he had to say. "If you do help her, you know, you'll show him you've understood."

"Understood what?"

"Why, his idea—the deep acute train of reasoning that has led him to take, as one may say, the bull by the horns; to reflect that as you might, as you probably *would,* in any case, get at her, he plays the wise game, as well as the bold one, by treating your generosity as a real thing and placing himself publicly under an obligation to you."

Mrs. Grantham showed not only that she had listened, but that she had for an instant considered. "What is it you elegantly describe as my getting 'at' her?"

"He takes his risk, but puts you, you see, on your honour."

She thought a moment more. "What profundities indeed then over the simplest of matters! And if your idea is," she went on, "that if I do help her I shall show him I've understood them, so it will be that if I don't—"

"You'll show him"—Sutton took her up—"that you haven't? Precisely. But in spite of not wanting to appear to have understood *too* much—"

"I may still be depended on to do what I can? Quite certainly. You'll see what I may still be depended on to do." And she moved away.

3

IT was not, doubtless, that there had been anything in their rather sharp separation at that moment to sustain or prolong the interruption; it definitely befell that, circumstances aiding, they practically failed to meet again before the great party at Burbeck. This occasion was to gather in some thirty persons from a certain Friday to the following Monday, and it was on the Friday that Sutton went down. He had known in advance that Mrs. Grantham was to be there, and this perhaps, during the interval of hindrance, had helped him a little to be patient. He had before him the certitude of a real full cup—two days brimming over with the sight of her. He found, however, on his arrival that she was not yet in the field, and presently learned that her place would be in a small contingent that was to join the party on the morrow. This knowledge he extracted from Miss Banker, who was always the first to present herself at any gathering that was to enjoy her, and whom moreover—partly on that very account—the wary not less than the speculative were apt to hold themselves well-advised to engage with at as early as possible a stage of the business. She was stout red rich mature universal—a massive much-fingered volume, alphabetical wonderful indexed, that opened of itself at the right place. She opened for Sutton instinctively at G——, which happened to be remarkably convenient. "What she's really waiting over for is to bring down Lady Gwyther."

"Ah the Gwythers are coming?"

"Yes; caught, through Mrs. Grantham, just in time. *She'll* be the feature—every one wants to see her."

Speculation and wariness met and combined at this moment in Shirley Sutton. "Do you mean—a—Mrs. Grantham?"

"Dear no! Poor little Lady Gwyther, who, but just arrived in England, appears now literally for the first time in her life in any society whatever, and whom (don't you know the extraordinary story? you ought to—*you!*) she, of all people, has so wonderfully taken up. It will be quite—here—as if she were 'presenting' her."

Sutton of course took in more things than even appeared. "I never know what I ought to know; I only know, inveterately, what I oughtn't. So what *is* the extraordinary story?"

"You really haven't heard—?"

"Really," he replied without winking.

"It happened indeed but the other day," said Miss Banker, "yet every one's already wondering. Gwyther has thrown his wife on her mercy—but I won't believe you if you pretend to me you don't know why he shouldn't."

Sutton asked himself then what he *could* pretend. "Do you mean because she's merciless?"

She hesitated. "If you don't know perhaps I oughtn't to tell you."

He liked Miss Banker and found just the right tone to plead. "*Do* tell me."

"Well," she sighed, "it will be your own fault—! They had been such friends that there could have been but one name for the crudity of his original *procédé*. When I was a girl we used to call it throwing over. They call it in French to *lâcher*. But I refer not so much to the act itself as to the manner of it, though you may say indeed of course that there's in such cases after all only one manner. Least said soonest mended."

Sutton seemed to wonder. "Oh he said too much?"

"He said nothing. That was it."

Sutton kept it up. "But was *what?*"

"Why, what she must, like any woman in her shoes, have felt to be his perfidy. He simply went and *did* it—took to himself this child, that is, without the preliminary of a scandal or a rupture—before she could turn round."

"I follow you. But it would appear from what you say that she *has* turned round now."

"Well," Miss Banker laughed, "we shall see for ourselves how far. It will be what every one will try to see."

"Oh then we've work cut out!" And Sutton certainly felt that he himself had—an impression that lost nothing from a further talk with Miss Banker in the course of a short stroll in the grounds with her the next day. He spoke as one who had now considered many things.

"Did I understand from you yesterday that Lady Gwyther's a 'child'?"

"Nobody knows. It's prodigious the way she has managed."

"The way Lady Gwyther has—?"

"No, the way May Grantham has kept her till this hour in her pocket."

He was quick at his watch. "Do you mean by 'this hour' that they're due now?"

"Not till tea. All the others arrive together in time for that." Miss Banker had clearly, since the previous day, filled in gaps and become, as it were, revised and enlarged. "She'll have kept a cat from seeing her, so as to produce her entirely herself."

"Well," Sutton mused, "that will have been a very noble sort of return—"

"For Gwyther's behaviour? Very. Yet I feel creepy."

"Creepy?"

"Because so much depends for the girl—in the way of the right start or the wrong start—on the signs and omens of this first appearance. It's a great house and a great occasion, and we're assembled here, it strikes me, very much as the Roman mob at the circus used to be to see the next Christian maiden brought out to the tigers."

"Oh if she *is* a Christian maiden—!" Sutton murmured. But he stopped at what his imagination called up.

It perhaps fed that faculty a little that Miss Banker had the effect of making out that Mrs. Grantham might individually be, in any case, something of a Roman matron. "She has kept her in the dark so that we may only take her from her hand. She'll have formed her for us."

"In so few days?"

"Well, she'll have prepared her—decked her for the sacrifice with ribbons and flowers."

"Ah if you only mean that she'll have taken her to her dressmaker—!" And it came to Sutton, at once as a new light and as a check, almost, to anxiety, that this was all poor Gwyther, mistrustful probably of a taste formed by Stuttgart, might have desired of their friend.

There were usually at Burbeck many things taking place at once; so that wherever else, on such occasions, tea might be served, it went forward with matchless pomp, weather permitting, on a shaded stretch of one of the terraces and in presence of one of the prospects. Shirley Sutton, moving, as the afternoon waned, more restlessly about and mingling in dispersed groups only to find they had nothing to keep him quiet, came upon it as he turned a corner of the house—saw it seated there in all its state. It might be said that at Burbeck it was, like everything else, made the most of. It constituted immediately, with multiplied tables and glittering plate, with rugs and cushions and ices and fruit and wonderful porcelain and beautiful women, a scene of splendour, almost an incident of grand opera. One of the beautiful women might quite have been expected to rise with a gold cup and a celebrated song.

One of them did rise, as happened, while Sutton drew near, and he found himself a moment later seeing nothing and nobody but Mrs. Grantham. They met on the terrace, just away from the others, and the movement in which he had the effect of arresting her might have been that of withdrawal. He quickly saw, however, that if she had been about to pass into the house it was only on some errand—to get something or to call some one—that would immediately have restored her to her public. It somehow struck him on the spot—and more than ever yet, though the impression was not wholly new to him—that she felt herself a figure for the forefront of the stage and indeed would have been recognised by any one at a glance as the *prima donna assoluta*. She caused, in fact, during the few minutes he stood talking to her, an extraordinary series of waves to roll extraordinarily fast over his sense, not the least mark of the matter being that the appearance with which it ended was again the one with which it had begun. "The face—the face," as he kept dumbly repeating; that was at last, as at first, all he could clearly see. She had a perfection resplendent, but what in the world had it done, this perfection, to her beauty? It was her beauty doubtless that looked out at him, but it was into something else that, as their eyes met, he strangely found himself looking.

It was as if something had happened in consequence of which she had changed, and there was that in this swift perception that made him glance eagerly about for Lady Gwyther. But as he took in the recruited group—identities of the hour added to those of the previous twenty-four—he saw, among his recognitions, one of which was the husband of the person missing, that Lady Gwyther was not there. Nothing in the whole business was more singular than his consciousness that, as he came back to his interlocutress after the nods and smiles and hand-waves he had launched, she knew what had been his thought. She knew for whom he had looked without success; but why should this knowledge visibly have hardened and sharpened her, and precisely at a moment when she was unprecedentedly magnificent? The indefinable apprehension that had somewhat sunk after his second talk with Miss Banker and then had perversely risen again—this nameless anxiety now produced on him, with a sudden sharper pinch, the effect of a great suspense. The action of that, in turn, was to show him that he hadn't yet fully known how much he had at stake on a final view. It was revealed to him for the first time that he "really cared" whether Mrs. Grantham were a safe nature. It was too ridiculous by what a thread it hung, but something was certainly in the air that would definitely tell him.

What was in the air descended the next moment to earth. He turned round as he caught the expression with which her eyes attached themselves to something that approached. A little person, very young and very much dressed, had come out of the house, and the expression in Mrs. Grantham's eyes was that of the artist confronted with her work and interested, even to impatience, in the judgement of others. The little person drew nearer, and though Sutton's companion, without looking at him now, gave it a name and met it, he had jumped for himself at certitude. He saw many things—too many, and they appeared to be feathers, frills, excrescences of silk and lace—massed together and conflicting, and after a moment also saw struggling out of them a small face that struck him as either scared or sick. Then, with his eyes again returning to Mrs. Grantham, he saw another.

He had no more talk with Miss Banker till late that evening—an evening during which he had felt himself too noticeably silent; but something had passed between this pair, across dinner-table and drawing-room, without speech, and when they at last found words it was in the needed ease of a quiet end of the long, lighted gallery, where she opened again at the very paragraph.

"You were right—that *was* it. She did the only thing that, at such short notice, she *could* do. She took her to her dressmaker."

Sutton, with his back to the reach of the gallery, had, as if to banish a vision, buried his eyes for a minute in his hands. "And oh the face—the face!"

"Which?" Miss Banker asked.

"Whichever one looks at."

"But May Grantham's glorious. She has turned herself out—"

"With a splendour of taste and a sense of effect, eh? Yes." Sutton showed he saw far.

"She *has* the sense of effect. The sense of effect as exhibited in Lady Gwyther's clothes—!" was something Miss Banker failed of words to express. "Everybody's overwhelmed. Here, you know, that sort of thing's grave. The poor creature's lost."

"Lost?"

"Since on the first impression, as we said, so much depends. The first impression's made—oh made! I defy her now ever to unmake it. Her husband, who's proud, won't like her the better for it. And I don't see," Miss Banker went on, "that her prettiness *was* enough—a mere little feverish frightened freshness; what *did* he see in her?—to be so blasted. It has been done with an atrocity of art—"

"That supposes the dressmaker then also a devil?"

"Oh your London women and their dressmakers!" Miss Banker laughed.

"But the face—the face!" Sutton woefully repeated.

"May's?"

"The little girl's. It's exquisite."

"Exquisite?"

"For unimaginable pathos."

"Oh!" Miss Banker dropped.

"She has at last begun to see." Sutton showed again how far *he* saw. "It glimmers upon her innocence, she makes it dimly out—what has been done with her. She's even worse this evening—the way, my eye, she looked at dinner!—than when she came. Yes"—he was confident—"it has dawned (how couldn't it, out of all of you?) and she knows."

"She ought to have known before!" Miss Banker intelligently sighed.

"No; she wouldn't in that case have been so beautiful."

"Beautiful?" cried Miss Banker; "overloaded like a monkey in a show!"

"The face, yes; which goes to the heart. It's that that makes it," said Shirley Sutton. "And it's that"—he thought it out—"that makes the other."

"I see. Conscious?"

"Horrible!"

"You take it hard," said Miss Banker.

Lord Gwyther, just before she spoke, had come in sight and now was near them. Sutton on this, appearing to wish to avoid him, reached, before answering his companion's observation, a door that opened close at hand. "So hard," he replied from that point, "that I shall be off to-morrow morning."

"And not see the rest?" she called after him.

But he had already gone, and Lord Gwyther, arriving, amiably took up her question. "The rest of what?"

Miss Banker looked him well in the eyes. "Of Mrs. Grantham's clothes."